Thomas Hardy was born in Hig
Dorchester, in 1840, the first of f
was a stone-mason and builder. At sixteen he trained as an architect and in 1862 went to work in London. He wrote poetry but failed to get it or his first novel, 'The Poor Man and the Lady' (1868), published before returning to Bockhampton in 1867.

In 1870 he worked on the restoration of the church at St Juliot in Cornwall where he met Emma Gifford. They married in 1874. Having financed his novel *Desperate Remedies* (1871) he then lost money on it. *Under the Greenwood Tree* (1872) and *A Pair of Blue Eyes* (1873) followed. *Far from the Madding Crowd*, his first real success, was published in 1874. He published *The Hand of Ethelberta* (1876), *The Return of the Native* (1878) and *The Trumpet-Major* (1880). Moving to London 1878–81, he fell seriously ill between 1880–81. *A Laodicean* (1881) and *Two on a Tower* (1882) were followed by *The Mayor of Casterbridge* (1886) and *The Woodlanders* (1887). In 1883 he settled in Dorchester and moved into the house he had designed, Max Gate, in 1885. His first collection of short stories, *Wessex Tales*, appeared in 1888; three further collections were published between 1891 and 1913. *Tess of the d'Urbervilles* (1891) brought him fame, although its advanced moral stance caused an outcry. After further controversy on the publication of *Jude the Obscure* (1896), he returned to poetry. A revised version of *The Well-Beloved*, serialised in 1892, appeared in 1897.

Wessex Poems, his first book of verse, was published in 1898, and was followed by seven further volumes. In 1904–8, *The Dynasts*, an epic drama, was published. Hardy was awarded the Order of Merit in 1910. His wife's death in 1912 inspired some of his greatest poems. He married Florence Dugdale in 1914, and died in 1928.

THOMAS HARDY

THE COMPLETE STORIES

Edited by

NORMAN PAGE

J. M. Dent London

A DENT PAPERBACK

This paperback edition first published in Great Britain in 1996
by J. M. Dent, a division of Orion Books Ltd,
Orion House, 5 Upper St Martin's Lane,
London WC2H 9EA

A CIP catalogue for this book is available
from the British Library

ISBN 1 85799 438 8

Typeset at The Spartan Press Ltd,
Lymington, Hants
Printed in Great Britain by
Clays Ltd, St Ives plc

The editor and publishers wish to thank James Gibson for
permission to use his biographical note on Thomas Hardy.

CONTENTS

Introduction vii

WESSEX TALES 1

Preface 3
The Three Strangers 7
A Tradition of Eighteen Hundred and Four 26
The Melancholy Hussar of the German Legion 32
The Withered Arm 48
Fellow-Townsmen 72
Interlopers at the Knap 114
The Distracted Preacher 140

A GROUP OF NOBLE DAMES 189

Preface 191
Part First: Before Dinner 193
Dame the First – The First Countess of Wessex. By the Local Historian 193
Dame the Second – Barbara of the House of Grebe. By the Old Surgeon 228
Dame the Third – The Marchioness of Stonehenge. By the Rural Dean 256
Dame the Fourth – Lady Mottisfont. By the Sentimental Member 268

Part Second: After Dinner 282
Dame the Fifth – The Lady Icenway. By the Churchwarden 282
Dame the Sixth – Squire Petrick's Lady. By the Crimson Maltster 292
Dame the Seventh – Anna, Lady Baxby. By the Colonel 301
Dame the Eighth – The Lady Penelope. By the Man of Family 307
Dame the Ninth – The Duchess of Hamptonshire. By the Quiet Gentleman 316
Dame the Tenth – The Honourable Laura. By the Spark 328

LIFE'S LITTLE IRONIES 349

Prefatory Note 351
An Imaginative Woman 353

The Son's Veto 374
For Conscience' Sake 387
A Tragedy of Two Ambitions 402
On the Western Circuit 423
To Please His Wife 444
The Fiddler of the Reels 459
A Few Crusted Characters 475
Introduction 475
Tony Kytes, the Arch-Deceiver 478
The History of the Hardcomes 486
The Superstitious Man's Story 494
Andrey Satchel and the Parson and Clerk 497
Old Andrey's Experience as a Musician 504
Absent-Mindedness in a Parish Choir 506
The Winters and the Palmleys 509
Incident in the Life of Mr George Crookhill 516
Netty Sargent's Copyhold 519

A CHANGED MAN AND OTHER TALES 527
Prefatory Note 529
A Changed Man 531
The Waiting Supper 547
Alicia's Diary 589
The Grave by the Handpost 617
Enter a Dragoon 627
A Tryst at an Ancient Earthwork 645
What the Shepherd Saw 655
A Committee-Man of 'the Terror' 673
Master John Horseleigh, Knight 685
The Duke's Reappearance 696
A Mere Interlude 703
The Romantic Adventures of a Milkmaid 731

UNCOLLECTED STORIES 805
Destiny and a Blue Cloak 807
The Thieves Who Couldn't Help Sneezing 827
Old Mrs Chundle 833
The Doctor's Legend 840

Sources 849

INTRODUCTION

In October 1989 a man was found hanged in a remote spot in the Derwent Valley in Derbyshire. There was nothing that made it possible for him to be identified – even the makers' labels had been removed from his clothing – but in one of his pockets was a paperback copy of Hardy's volume of short stories, *A Group of Noble Dames*. 'Perhaps,' speculated one Sunday newspaper, reporting this bizarre tragedy on its front page, 'the mysterious man was a victim of unrequited love.' Despite police inquiries, the mystery of his identity was never solved.

Hardy, who was a great reader of newspapers, whether national or local, current or yellowing with age, and who had a keen eye for odd happenings reported in the press, would surely have reached for his pen if he had come across this grim and inconclusive story. For it is exactly the kind of incident that he liked to jot down in his notebook with a view to its creative potential. Many of his stories begin from a very simple idea that may be, for instance, a matter of local report, history or legend. In others the source may be different but the starting-point equally simple: a woman's infatuation with a poet she has never met, for example, or a man's uneasy conscience concerning a lover he has wronged in the past. As Edgar Allan Poe pointed out, the essence of the short story is a unity of effect, a single-mindedness often derived from an idea that can be expressed in a single phrase or sentence but that is strong enough to convey something significant about human experience.

At the same time there is considerable variety to be found in the short stories that Hardy wrote over a period of about a quarter of a century. Some draw on history or pseudo-history and present famous figures or local worthies. In 'A Tradition of Eighteen Hundred and Four' he revives the legend that Napoleon paid a secret visit to the Dorset coast with a view to the possibility of an invasion. Another story of the Napoleonic Wars – the historical period with which Hardy had a lifelong love affair – is 'The Melancholy Hussar of the German Legion', and F. B. Pinion has pointed out in his useful *A Hardy Companion* that this may be an offshoot of his novel *The Trumpet-Major* and that he is likely to have come across some of the material used in the story while engaged in research for that novel in the British Museum and, specifically, while turning over the pages of the *Morning Chronicle* for 4 July 1801. Yet another Napoleonic story is 'A Committee Man of "the Terror"'. 'The Duke's Reappearance' refers to an earlier period and was, as Pinion notes, a traditional tale 'handed down in the Swetman family from which Hardy was descended on his mother's side'.

The stories collected in *A Group of Noble Dames*, held together by a simple framework reminiscent of Chaucer and Boccaccio, belong to this same category of historical tale, and here an important source is known to have been John Hutchins's *History and Antiquities of the County of Dorset*, a work Hardy was very fond of and a copy of which he possessed. Here, too, as so often with Hardy, the historical past is not presented through the actions of monarchs, generals, and other public figures, but mediated through local scenes, characters and events. Like Thackeray in *Vanity Fair*, he inverts the normal priorities of nineteenth-century historiography and foregrounds private experience.

Another group of stories with a strong local flavour is those which, like 'The Distracted Preacher', depict rural life with a mixture of affection, irony and detailed observation. The affinity here is with the early novel *Under the Greenwood Tree* and with the rustic elements in subsequent novels – as well as, ultimately, with the pastoral novels of George Eliot such as *Adam Bede* and *Silas Marner*. 'The Distracted Preacher' deals with smuggling, a part-time occupation popular with the people among whom Hardy had grown up. The linked stories titled 'A Few Crusted Characters' belong to this same group.

In complete contrast is a group of sombre and highly realistic stories of contemporary urban life, many of which are to be found in the volume *Life's Little Ironies*. With their emphasis on frustrated aspirations and unsuccessful marriages, they are much closer to the world of Hardy's later novels. 'On the Western Circuit', for instance, depicts a woman trapped within a loveless union who engages in a kind of spiritual affair with a young barrister who has seduced her servant: writing love-letters on behalf of the illiterate girl, she finds herself emotionally involved in a situation that rests on a deception. An interesting point is that when the story was published in a magazine Hardy found himself compelled to bowdlerize certain elements in order to make it acceptable to the editor: the heroine is made a widow, and references to the girl's pregnancy are removed. He was able to restore his original version when he published it in a collection of his tales, and this pattern of composition, bowdlerization and restoration is similar to that to which his great novels *Tess of the d'Urbervilles* and *Jude the Obscure* were subjected in the same decade.

Another powerful story of this type is 'An Imaginative Woman', written in 1893 between the two novels just mentioned. Again, a platonic and idealized relationship is presented: a woman, seeking escape through romantic fantasy from a marriage that has brought her no fulfilment, becomes infatuated with a poet who has lived in the lodgings in which she is spending a holiday. The tragic and ironic conclusion shows her widowed husband's rejection of his own child. In 'For Conscience' Sake', on the other hand, the sexual 'offence' has been actual rather than spiritualized, and this story, through the account of a man's failed attempt to ease a nagging conscience by undoing the past, casts an ironic light on prevailing notions of 'conscience' and 'making amends'. The world of these stories is urban and bourgeois: the families concerned are those of professional or business men committed to the preservation at all costs of outward propriety and respectability, and Hardy's self-imposed mission, not unlike that of his contemporary Ibsen (with whose work Hardy was familiar from about 1890), is to reveal the hypocrisy and sadness of lives lived on these terms.

Yet another group of stories uses elements of the supernatural or the uncanny. The rational and enlightened late Victorian world accommodated a strong, even passionate interest in the paranormal – it was the age of the English ghost story and the Society for Psychical Research as well as of scientific and technological advance – and Hardy was in a strong position to move easily between the two worlds. A self-trained intellectual, he was also able to draw on early memories of folklore and popular literature. Hence a story like 'The Withered Arm' turns on a grisly superstition concerning the healing of a physical affliction. Even more macabre is 'Barbara of the House of Grebe', one of Hardy's most powerful stories. Despite its historical setting, the theme – a woman powerless in a marriage that has become a mockery and at the mercy of a sadistic husband – is one of Hardy's most prominent. What the setting and the elements of Gothic fantasy enable Hardy to do, however, is to present the wife's infatuation with another man and the husband's jealousy and cruelty in much bolder terms than would have been possible in a story of contemporary life. Paradoxically, by being set in the past the story can be given a treatment that is startlingly 'modern'. The statue of the dead lover, so effectively 'tinted to the hues of life' that it becomes an object of erotic adoration, has echoes of classical myth, but its role as a symbol of ideal and unchanging love is again characteristic of a recurring preoccupation in Hardy's work and an important element in his sensibility. (His late novel *The Well-Beloved* explores these ideas more thoroughly.)

In a more light-hearted vein, 'The Romantic Adventures of a Milkmaid' attractively blends realistic and fairy-tale elements: the heroine is a kind of rustic Cinderella who passes from a recognizable rural world of milk-sheds and dewy meadows to a dream-like world presided over by a mysterious foreign aristocrat. It will have become evident already that many of these stories deal, in different ways, with the power of love, and this is also true of 'The Fiddler of the Reels', in which Mop's music-making becomes a metaphor for his sexual power. The starting-point is precisely historical: the opening lines place the action at the time of the Great Exhibition of 1851 in Hardy's childhood (the reference to 'World's Fairs' hints at the occasion on which the story first appeared, in a special number of an American magazine devoted to the Chicago World Fair of 1893). Quickly, however, we are transported to a very unVictorian world of a demon lover and a woman helpless in his power that recalls the traditional ballads.

The greatly expanded reading public in Britain and overseas during the second half of the nineteenth century led to a rapid increase in the number of magazines publishing short fiction, and – like many great writers of the time, as well as many other writers now forgotten – Hardy responded to the demands of this new market. For a professional author there were obvious attractions in the short story, which could be produced relatively quickly and for which prompt payment could be received. Although Hardy's short stories were at one time dismissed as potboilers, however, this is no longer a tenable view. His manuscripts show that he devoted great pains to their composition, and he cared enough about them to revise them scrupulously when they were later reprinted.

The best of them are of very high quality – comparable, say, to the best of Kipling or Conrad. They display an impressive range and variety of settings and moods, and for the reader of Hardy's novels they have an added interest in touching on many of the themes to be found there, and even offering parallel situations and character-types.

A final point that is surely significant is that Hardy was prepared to use the commercial medium of the magazine story to explore controversial and sensitive issues in terms so frank that his editors were sometimes horrified – and this even when he was apparently engaged in the harmless occupation of writing historical fiction. When *A Group of Noble Dames*, commissioned by the *Graphic*, was duly delivered in May 1890, the editor sent the famous author a letter of stern reproof that demanded

'Now, what do you propose to do? Will you write us an entirely fresh story, or will you take the "Noble Dames" and alter them to suit our taste . . . ' He went on to indicate that some of the stories Hardy had written could be rendered tolerable by 'chastening', but that two of them were wholly unacceptable. Hardy yielded, as he was soon to yield over *Tess*, but that he should in the first place have used the magazine story medium as a vehicle for his strongly-held convictions should surely leave us in no doubt that he took the short story seriously.

NORMAN PAGE

WESSEX TALES

PREFACE TO 'WESSEX TALES'

An apology is perhaps needed for the neglect of contrast which is shown by presenting two stories of hangmen and one of a military execution in such a small collection as the following. But as to the former, in the neighbourhood of county-towns hanging matters used to form a large proportion of the local tradition; and though never personally acquainted with any chief operator at such scenes, the writer of these pages had as a boy the privilege of being on speaking terms with a man who applied for the office, and who sank into an incurable melancholy because he failed to get it, some slight mitigation of his grief being to dwell upon striking episodes in the lives of those happier ones who had held it with success and renown. His tale of disappointment used to cause his listener some wonder why his ambition should have taken such an unfortunate form, by limiting itself to a profession of which there could be only one practitioner in England at one time, when it might have aimed at something more commonplace – that would have afforded him more chances – such as the office of a judge, a bishop, or even a member of Parliament – but its nobleness was never questioned. In those days, too, there was still living an old woman who, for the cure of some eating disease, had been taken in her youth to have her 'blood turned' by a convict's corpse, in the manner described in 'The Withered Arm'.

Since writing this story some years ago I have been reminded by an aged friend who knew 'Rhoda Brook' that, in relating her dream, my forgetfulness has weakened the facts out of which the tale grew. In reality it was while lying down on a hot afternoon that the incubus oppressed her and she flung it off, with the results upon the body of the original as described. To my mind the occurrence of such a vision in the daytime is more impressive than if it had happened in a midnight dream. Readers are therefore asked to correct the misrelation, which affords an instance of how our imperfect memories insensibly formalize the fresh originality of living fact – from whose shape they slowly depart, as machine-made castings depart by degrees from the sharp hand-work of the mould.

Among the many devices for concealing smuggled goods in caves and pits of the earth, that of planting an apple-tree in a tray or box which was placed over the mouth of the pit is, I believe, unique, and it is detailed in 'The Distracted Preacher' precisely as described by an old carrier of 'tubs' – a man who was afterwards in my father's employ for over thirty years. I never gathered from his reminiscences what means were adopted for lifting the tree, which, with its roots, earth, and receptacle, must have been of considerable weight. There is no doubt, however, that the thing was done through many years. My informant often spoke, too, of the horribly suffocating sensation produced by the pair of spirit-tubs slung upon the chest and back, after stumbling with the burden of them for several miles inland over a rough country and in darkness. He said that though years of his youth and young manhood were spent in this irregular business, his profits from the same, taken all together, did not average the wages he might have earned in a steady employment, whilst the fatigues and risks were excessive.

I may add that the action of this story is founded on certain smuggling exploits that occurred between 1825 and 1830, and were brought to a close in the latter year by the trial of the chief actors at the Assizes before Baron Bolland for their desperate armed resistance to the Custom-house officers during the landing of a cargo of spirits. This happened only a little time after the doings recorded in the narrative, in which some incidents that came out at the trial are also embodied.

In the culminating affray the character called Owlett was badly wounded, and several of the Preventive-men would have lost their lives through being overpowered by the far more numerous body of smugglers, but for the forbearance and manly conduct of the latter. This served them in good stead at their trial, in which the younger Erskine prosecuted, their defence being entrusted to Erle. Baron Bolland's summing up was strongly in their favour; they were merely ordered to enter into their own recognizances for good behaviour and discharged. (See also as to facts the note at the end of the tale.)

However, the stories are but dreams, and not records. They were first collected and published under their present title, in two volumes, in 1888.

APRIL 1896–MAY 1912

An experience of the writer in respect of the tale called 'A Tradition of Eighteen Hundred and Four' is curious enough to be mentioned here. The incident of Napoleon's visit to the English coast by night, with a view to discovering a convenient spot for landing his army of invasion, was an invention of the author's on which he had some doubts because of its improbability. This was in 1882, when it was first published. Great was his surprise several years later to be told that it was a real tradition. How far this is true he is unaware.

T.H.

JUNE 1919

THE THREE STRANGERS

Among the few features of agricultural England which retain an appearance but little modified by the lapse of centuries, may be reckoned the long, grassy and furzy downs, coombs, or ewe-leases, as they are called according to their kind, that fill a large area of certain counties in the south and south-west. If any mark of human occupation is met with hereon, it usually takes the form of the solitary cottage of some shepherd.

Fifty years ago such a lonely cottage stood on such a down, and may possibly be standing there now. In spite of its loneliness, however, the spot, by actual measurement, was not three miles from a county-town. Yet that affected it little. Three miles of irregular upland, during the long inimical seasons, with their sleets, snows, rains, and mists, afford withdrawing space enough to isolate a Timon or a Nebuchadnezzar; much less, in fair weather, to please that less repellent tribe, the poets, philosophers, artists, and others who 'conceive and meditate of pleasant things'.

Some old earthen camp or barrow, some clump of trees, at least some starved fragment of ancient hedge is usually taken advantage of in the erection of these forlorn dwellings. But, in the present case, such a kind of shelter had been disregarded. Higher Crowstairs, as the house was called, stood quite detached and undefended. The only reason for its precise situation seemed to be the crossing of two footpaths at right angles hard by, which may have crossed there and thus for a good five hundred years. Hence the house was exposed to the elements on all sides. But, though the wind up here blew unmistakably when it did blow, and the rain hit hard whenever it fell, the various weathers of the winter season were not quite so formidable on the down as they were imagined to be by dwellers on low ground. The raw rimes were not so pernicious as in the hollows, and the frosts were scarcely so severe. When the shepherd and his family who tenanted the house were pitied for their sufferings from the exposure, they said that upon the whole they were less inconvenienced by 'wuzzes and flames' (hoarses and phlegms) than when they had lived by the stream of a snug neighbouring valley.

The night of March 28, 182–, was precisely one of the nights that were wont to call forth these expressions of commiseration. The level rainstorm smote walls, slopes, and hedges like the clothyard shafts of Senlac and Crecy. Such sheep and outdoor animals as had no shelter stood with their buttocks to the winds; while the tails of little birds trying to roost on some scraggy thorn were blown inside-out like umbrellas. The gable-end of the cottage was stained with wet, and the eavesdroppings flapped against the wall. Yet never was commiseration for the shepherd more misplaced. For that cheerful rustic was entertaining a large party in glorification of the christening of his second girl.

The guests had arrived before the rain began to fall, and they were all now assembled in the chief or living-room of the dwelling. A glance into the apartment at eight o'clock on this eventful evening would have resulted in the opinion that it was as cosy and comfortable a nook as could be wished for in boisterous weather. The calling of its inhabitant was proclaimed by a number of highly-polished sheep-crooks without stems that were hung ornamentally over the fireplace, the curl of each shining crook varying from the antiquated type engraved in the patriarchal pictures of old family Bibles to the most approved fashion of the last local sheep-fair. The room was lighted by half-a-dozen candles, having wicks only a trifle smaller than the grease which enveloped them, in candlesticks that were never used but at high-days, holy-days, and family feasts. The lights were scattered about the room, two of them standing on the chimney-piece. This position of candles was in itself significant. Candles on the chimney-piece always meant a party.

On the hearth, in front of a back-brand to give substance, blazed a fire of thorns, that crackled 'like the laughter of the fool'.

Nineteen persons were gathered here. Of these, five women, wearing gowns of various bright hues, sat in chairs along the wall; girls shy and not shy filled the window-bench; four men, including Charley Jake the hedge-carpenter, Elijah New the parish-clerk, and John Pitcher, a neighbouring dairyman, the shepherd's father-in-law, lolled in the settle; a young man and maid, who were blushing over tentative *pourparlers* on a life-companionship, sat beneath the corner-cupboard; and an elderly engaged man of fifty or upward moved restlessly about from spots where his betrothed was not to the spot where she was. Enjoyment was pretty general, and so much the more prevailed in being unhampered by conventional restrictions. Absolute confidence in each other's good opinion begat perfect ease, while the finishing stroke of manner, amounting to a truly princely serenity, was lent to the majority by the absence of any expression or trait denoting that they wished to get on in the world, enlarge their minds, or do any eclipsing thing whatever – which nowadays so generally nips the bloom and *bonhomie* of all except the two extremes of the social scale.

Shepherd Fennel had married well, his wife being a dairyman's daughter from a vale at a distance, who brought fifty guineas in her pocket – and kept them there, till they should be required for ministering to the needs of a coming family. This frugal woman had been somewhat exercised as to the character that should be given to the gathering. A sit-still party had its advantages; but an undisturbed position of ease in chairs and settles was apt to lead on the men to such an unconscionable deal of toping that they would sometimes fairly drink the house dry. A dancing-party was the alternative; but this, while avoiding the foregoing objection on the score of good drink, had a counterbalancing disadvantage in the matter of good victuals, the ravenous appetites engendered by the exercise causing immense havoc in the buttery. Shepherdess Fennel fell back upon the intermediate plan of mingling short dances with short periods of talk and singing, so as to hinder any ungovernable rage in either. But this scheme was entirely confined to her own gentle mind: the shepherd himself was in the mood to exhibit the most reckless phases of hospitality.

The fiddler was a boy of those parts, about twelve years of age, who had a wonderful dexterity in jigs and reels, though his fingers were so small and short as to necessitate a constant shifting for the high notes, from which he scrambled back to the first position with sounds not of unmixed purity of tone. At seven the shrill tweedledee of this youngster had begun, accompanied by a booming ground-bass from Elijah New, the parish-clerk, who had thoughtfully brought with him his favourite musical instrument, the serpent. Dancing was instantaneous, Mrs Fennel privately enjoining the players on no account to let the dance exceed the length of a quarter of an hour.

But Elijah and the boy in the excitement of their position quite forgot the injunction. Moreover, Oliver Giles, a man of seventeen, one of the dancers, who was enamoured of his partner, a fair girl of thirty-three rolling years, had recklessly handed a new crown-piece to the musicians, as a bribe to keep going as long as they had muscle and wind. Mrs Fennel, seeing the steam begin to generate on the countenances of her guests, crossed over and touched the fiddler's elbow and put her hand on the serpent's mouth. But they took no notice, and fearing she might lose her character of genial hostess if she were to interfere too markedly, she retired and sat down helpless. And so the dance whizzed on with cumulative fury, the performers moving in their planet-like courses, direct and retrograde, from apogee to perigee, till the hand of the well-kicked clock at the bottom of the room had travelled over the circumference of an hour.

While these cheerful events were in course of enactment within Fennel's pastoral dwelling an incident having considerable bearing on the party had occurred in the gloomy night without. Mrs Fennel's concern about the growing fierceness of the dance corresponded in point of time with the ascent of a human figure to the solitary hill of Higher Crowstairs from the direction of the distant town. This personage strode on through the rain without a pause, following the little-worn path which, further on in its course, skirted the shepherd's cottage.

It was nearly the time of full moon, and on this account, though the sky was lined with a uniform sheet of dripping cloud, ordinary objects out of doors were readily visible. The sad wan light revealed the lonely pedestrian to be a man of supple frame; his gait suggested that he had somewhat passed the period of perfect and instinctive agility, though not so far as to be otherwise than rapid of motion when occasion required. At a rough guess, he might have been about forty years of age. He appeared tall, but a recruiting sergeant, or other person accustomed to the judging of men's heights by the eye, would have discerned that this was chiefly owing to his gauntness, and that he was not more than five-feet-eight or nine.

Notwithstanding the regularity of his tread there was caution in it, as in that of one who mentally feels his way; and despite the fact that it was not a black coat nor a dark garment of any sort that he wore, there was something about him which suggested that he naturally belonged to the black-coated tribes of men. His clothes were of fustian, and his boots hobnailed, yet in his progress he showed not the mud-accustomed bearing of hobnailed and fustianed peasantry.

By the time that he had arrived abreast of the shepherd's premises the rain came down, or rather came along, with yet more determined violence. The outskirts of the little settlement partially broke the force of wind and rain, and this induced him to stand still. The most salient of the shepherd's domestic erections was an empty sty at the forward corner of his hedgeless garden, for in these latitudes the principle of masking the homelier features of your establishment by a conventional frontage was unknown. The traveller's eye was attracted to this small building by the pallid shine of the wet slates that covered it. He turned aside, and, finding it empty, stood under the pent-roof for shelter.

While he stood, the boom of the serpent within the adjacent house, and the lesser strains of the fiddler, reached the spot as an accompaniment to the surging hiss of the flying rain on the sod, its louder beating on the cabbage-leaves of the garden, on the straw hackles of eight or ten beehives just discernible by the path, and its dripping from the eaves into a row of buckets and pans that had been placed under the walls of the cottage. For at Higher Crowstairs, as at all such elevated domiciles, the grand difficulty of housekeeping was an insufficiency of water; and a casual rainfall was utilized by turning out, as catchers, every utensil that the house contained. Some queer stories might be told of the contrivances for economy in suds and dish-waters that are absolutely necessitated in upland habitations during the droughts of summer. But at this season there were no such exigencies; a mere acceptance of what the skies bestowed was sufficient for an abundant store.

At last the notes of the serpent ceased and the house was silent. This cessation of activity aroused the solitary pedestrian from the reverie into which he had lapsed, and, emerging from the shed, with an apparently new intention, he walked up the path to the house-door. Arrived here, his first act was to kneel down on a large stone beside the row of vessels, and to drink a copious draught from one of them. Having quenched his thirst he rose and lifted his hand to knock, but paused with his eye upon the panel. Since the dark surface of the wood revealed absolutely nothing, it was evident that he must be mentally looking through the door, as if he wished to measure thereby all the possibilities that a house of this sort might include, and how they might bear upon the question of his entry.

In his indecision he turned and surveyed the scene around. Not a soul was anywhere visible. The garden-path stretched downward from his feet, gleaming like the track of a snail; the roof of the little well (mostly dry), the well-cover, the top rail of the garden gate, were varnished with the same dull liquid glaze; while, far away in the vale, a faint whiteness of more than usual extent showed that the rivers were high in the meads. Beyond all this winked a few bleared lamplights through the beating drops – lights that denoted the situation of the county-town from which he had appeared to come. The absence of all notes of life in that direction seemed to clinch his intentions, and he knocked at the door.

Within, a desultory chat had taken the place of movement and musical sound. The hedge-carpenter was suggesting a song to the company, which nobody just then was inclined to undertake, so that the knock afforded a not unwelcome diversion.

'Walk in!' said the shepherd promptly.

The latch clicked upward, and out of the night our pedestrian appeared upon the door-mat. The shepherd arose, snuffed two of the nearest candles, and turned to look at him.

Their light disclosed that the stranger was dark in complexion and not unprepossessing as to feature. His hat, which for a moment he did not remove, hung low over his eyes, without concealing that they were large, open, and determined, moving with a flash rather than a glance round the room. He seemed pleased with his survey, and, baring his shaggy head, said, in a rich deep voice, 'The rain is so heavy, friends, that I ask leave to come in and rest awhile.'

'To be sure, stranger,' said the shepherd. 'And faith, you've been lucky in choosing your time, for we are having a bit of a fling for a glad cause – though, to be sure, a man could hardly wish that glad cause to happen more than once a year.'

'Nor less,' spoke up a woman. 'For 'tis best to get your family over and done with, as soon as you can, so as to be all the earlier out of the fag o't.'

'And what may be this glad cause?' asked the stranger.

'A birth and christening,' said the shepherd.

The stranger hoped his host might not be made unhappy either by too many or too few of such episodes, and being invited by a gesture to a pull at the mug, he readily acquiesced. His manner, which, before entering, had been so dubious, was now altogether that of a careless and candid man.

'Late to be traipsing athwart this coomb – hey?' said the engaged man of fifty.

'Late it is, master, as you say. – I'll take a seat in the chimney-corner, if you have nothing to urge against it, ma'am; for I am a little moist on the side that was next the rain.'

Mrs Shepherd Fennel assented, and made room for the self-invited comer, who, having got completely inside the chimney-corner, stretched out his legs and his arms with the expansiveness of a person quite at home.

'Yes, I am rather cracked in the vamp,' he said freely, seeing that the eyes of the shepherd's wife fell upon his boots, 'and I am not well fitted either. I have had some rough times lately, and have been forced to pick up what I can get in the way of wearing, but I must find a suit better fit for working-days when I reach home.'

'One of hereabouts?' she inquired.

'Not quite that – further up the country.'

'I thought so. And so be I; and by your tongue you come from my neighbourhood.'

'But you would hardly have heard of me,' he said quickly. 'My time would be long before yours, ma'am, you see.'

This testimony to the youthfulness of his hostess had the effect of stopping her cross-examination.

'There is only one thing more wanted to make me happy,' continued the new-comer. 'And that is a little baccy, which I am sorry to say I am out of.'

'I'll fill your pipe,' said the shepherd.

'I must ask you to lend me a pipe likewise.'

'A smoker, and no pipe about 'ee?'

'I have dropped it somewhere on the road.'

The shepherd filled and handed him a new clay pipe, saying, as he did so, 'Hand me your baccy-box – I'll fill that too, now I am about it.'

The man went through the movement of searching his pockets.

'Lost that too?' said his entertainer, with some surprise.

'I am afraid so,' said the man with some confusion. 'Give it to me in a screw of paper.' Lighting his pipe at the candle with a suction that drew the whole flame into the bowl, he resettled himself in the corner and bent his looks upon the faint steam from his damp legs, as if he wished to say no more.

Meanwhile the general body of guests had been taking little notice of this visitor by reason of an absorbing discussion in which they were engaged with the band about a tune for the next dance. The matter being settled, they were about to stand up when an interruption came in the shape of another knock at the door.

At sound of the same the man in the chimney-corner took up the poker and began stirring the brands as if doing it thoroughly were the one aim of his existence; and a second time the shepherd said, 'Walk in!' In a moment another man stood upon the straw-woven door-mat. He too was a stranger.

This individual was one of a type radically different from the first. There was more of the commonplace in his manner, and a certain jovial cosmopolitanism sat upon his features. He was several years older than the first arrival, his hair being slightly frosted, his eyebrows bristly, and his whiskers cut back from his cheeks. His face was rather full and flabby, and yet it was not altogether a face without power. A few grogblossoms marked the neighbourhood of his nose. He flung back his long drab greatcoat, revealing that beneath it he wore a suit of cinder-gray shade throughout, large heavy seals, of some metal or other that would take a polish, dangling from his fob as his only personal ornament. Shaking the water-drops from his low-crowned glazed hat, he said, 'I must ask for a few minutes' shelter, comrades, or I shall be wetted to my skin before I get to Casterbridge.'

'Make yourself at home, master,' said the shepherd, perhaps a trifle less heartily than on the first occasion. Not that Fennel had the least tinge of niggardliness in his composition; but the room was far from large, spare chairs were not numerous, and damp companions were not altogether desirable at close quarters for the women and girls in their bright-coloured gowns.

However, the second comer, after taking off his greatcoat, and hanging his hat on a nail in one of the ceiling-beams as if he had been specially invited to put it there, advanced and sat down at the table. This had been pushed so closely into the chimney-corner, to give all available room to the dancers, that its inner edge grazed the elbow of the man who had ensconced himself by the fire; and thus the two strangers were brought into close companionship. They nodded to each other by way of breaking the ice of unacquaintance, and the first stranger handed his neighbour the family mug – a huge vessel of brown ware, having its upper edge worn away like a threshold by the rub of whole generations of thirsty lips that had gone the way of all flesh, and bearing the following inscription burnt upon its rotund side in yellow letters:

THERE IS NO FUN
UNTILL i CUM

The other man, nothing loth, raised the mug to his lips, and drank on, and on, and on – till a curious blueness overspread the countenance of the shepherd's wife, who had regarded with no little surprise the first stranger's free offer to the second of what did not belong to him to dispense.

'I knew it!' said the toper to the shepherd with much satisfaction. 'When I walked up your garden before coming in, and saw the hives all of a row, I said to myself, "Where there's bees there's honey, and where there's honey there's mead." But mead of such a truly comfortable sort as this I really didn't expect to meet in my older days.' He took yet another pull at the mug, till it assumed an ominous elevation.

'Glad you enjoy it!' said the shepherd warmly.

'It is goodish mead,' assented Mrs Fennel, with an absence of enthusiasm which seemed to say that it was possible to buy praise for one's cellar at too heavy a price. 'It is trouble enough to make – and really I hardly think we shall make any more. For honey sells well, and we ourselves can make shift with a drop o' small mead and metheglin for common use from the comb-washings.'

'O, but you'll never have the heart!' reproachfully cried the stranger in cinder-gray, after taking up the mug a third time and setting it down empty. 'I love mead, when 'tis old like this, as I love to go to church o' Sundays or to relieve the needy any day of the week.'

'Ha, ha, ha!' said the man in the chimney-corner, who, in spite of the taciturnity induced by the pipe of tobacco, could not or would not refrain from this slight testimony to his comrade's humour.

Now the old mead of those days, brewed of the purest first-year or maiden honey, four pounds to the gallon – with its due complement of white of eggs, cinnamon, ginger, cloves, mace, rosemary, yeast, and processes of working, bottling and cellaring – tasted remarkably strong; but it did not taste so strong as it actually was. Hence, presently, the stranger in cinder-gray at the table, moved by its creeping influence, unbuttoned his waistcoat, threw himself back in his chair, spread his legs, and made his presence felt in various ways.

'Well, well, as I say,' he resumed, 'I am going to Casterbridge, and to Casterbridge I must go. I should have been almost there by this time; but the rain drove me into your dwelling, and I'm not sorry for it.'

'You don't live in Casterbridge?' said the shepherd.

'Not as yet; though I shortly mean to move there.'

'Going to set up in trade, perhaps?'

'No, no,' said the shepherd's wife. 'It is easy to see that the gentleman is rich, and don't want to work at anything.'

The cinder-gray stranger paused, as if to consider whether he would accept that definition of himself. He presently rejected it by answering, 'Rich is not quite the word for me, dame. I do work, and I must work. And even if I only get to Casterbridge by midnight I must begin work there at eight tomorrow morning. Yes, het or wet, blow or snow, famine or sword, my day's work tomorrow must be done.'

'Poor man! Then, in spite o' seeming, you be worse off than we?' replied the shepherd's wife.

''Tis the nature of my trade, men and maidens. 'Tis the nature of my trade more than my poverty. . . But really and truly I must up and off, or I shan't get a lodging in the town.' However, the speaker did not move, and directly added, 'There's time for one more draught of friendship before I go; and I'd perform it at once if the mug were not dry.'

'Here's a mug o' small,' said Mrs Fennel. 'Small, we call it, though to be sure 'tis only the first wash o' the combs.'

'No,' said the stranger disdainfully. 'I won't spoil your first kindness by partaking o' your second.'

'Certainly not,' broke in Fennel. 'We don't increase and multiply every day, and I'll fill the mug again.' He went away to the dark place under the stairs where the barrel stood. The shepherdess followed him.

'Why should you do this?' she said reproachfully, as soon as they were alone. 'He's emptied it once, though it held enough for ten people; and now he's not contented wi' the small, but must needs call for more o' the strong! And a stranger unbeknown to any of us. For my part, I don't like the look o' the man at all.'

'But he's in the house, my honey; and 'tis a wet night, and a christening. Daze it, what's a cup of mead more or less? There'll be plenty more next bee-burning.'

'Very well – this time, then,' she answered, looking wistfully at the barrel. 'But what is the man's calling, and where is he one of, that he should come in and join us like this?'

'I don't know. I'll ask him again.'

The catastrophe of having the mug drained dry at one pull by the stranger in cinder-gray was effectually guarded against this time by Mrs Fennel. She poured out his allowance in a small cup, keeping the large one at a discreet distance from him. When he had tossed off his portion the shepherd renewed his inquiry about the stranger's occupation.

The latter did not immediately reply, and the man in the chimney-corner, with sudden demonstrativeness, said, 'Anybody may know my trade – I'm a wheelwright.'

'A very good trade for these parts,' said the shepherd.

'And anybody may know mine – if they've the sense to find it out,' said the shepherd in cinder-gray.

'You may generally tell what a man is by his claws,' observed the hedge-carpenter, looking at his own hands. 'My fingers be as full of thorns as an old pin-cushion is of pins.'

The hands of the man in the chimney-corner instinctively sought the shade, and he gazed into the fire as he resumed his pipe. The man at the table took up the hedge-carpenter's remark, and added smartly, 'True; but the oddity of my trade is that, instead of setting a mark upon me, it sets a mark upon my customers.'

No observation being offered by anybody in elucidation of this enigma the shepherd's wife once more called for a song. The same obstacles presented themselves as at the former time – one had no voice, another had forgotten the first verse. The stranger at the table, whose soul had now risen to a good working temperature, relieved the difficulty by exclaiming that, to start the company, he would sing himself. Thrusting one thumb into the arm-hole of his waistcoat, he waved the other hand in the air, and, with an extemporizing gaze at the shining sheep-crooks above the mantelpiece, began:

'O my trade it is the rarest one,
Simple shepherds all –
My trade is a sight to see;
For my customers I tie, and take them up on high,
And waft 'em to a far countree!'

The room was silent when he had finished the verse – with one exception, that of the man in the chimney-corner, who, at the singer's word, 'Chorus!' joined him in a deep base voice of musical relish –

'And waft 'em to a far countree!'

Oliver Giles, John Pitcher the dairyman, the parish-clerk, the engaged man of fifty, the row of young women against the wall, seemed lost in thought not of the gayest kind. The shepherd looked meditatively on the ground, the shepherdess gazed keenly at the singer, and with some suspicion; she was doubting whether this stranger were merely singing an old song from recollection, or was composing one there and then for the occasion. All were as perplexed at the obscure revelation as the guests at Belshazzar's Feast, except the man in the chimney-corner, who quietly said, 'Second verse, stranger,' and smoked on.

The singer thoroughly moistened himself from his lips inwards, and went on with the next stanza as requested:

'My tools are but common ones,
Simple shepherds all –
My tools are no sight to see:
A little hempen string, and a post whereon to swing,
Are implements enough for me!'

Shepherd Fennel glanced round. There was no longer any doubt that the stranger was answering his question rhythmically. The guests one and all started back with suppressed exclamations. The young woman engaged to the man of fifty fainted half-way, and would have proceeded, but finding him wanting in alacrity for catching her she sat down trembling.

'O, he's the —!' whispered the people in the background, mentioning the name of an ominous public officer. 'He's come to do it! 'Tis to be at Casterbridge jail tomorrow – the man for sheep-stealing – the poor clockmaker we heard of, who used to live away at Shottsford and had no work to do – Timothy Summers, whose family were a-starving, and so he went out of Shottsford by the high-road, and took a sheep in open daylight, defying the farmer and the farmer's wife and the farmer's lad, and every man jack among 'em. He' (and they nodded towards the stranger of the deadly trade) 'is come from up the country to do it because there's not enough to do in his own county-town, and he's got the place here now our own county man's dead; he's going to live in the same cottage under the prison wall.'

The stranger in cinder-gray took no notice of this whispered string of observations, but again wetted his lips. Seeing that his friend in the chimney-corner was the only one who reciprocated his joviality in any way, he held out his cup towards that appreciative comrade, who also held out his own. They clinked together, the eyes of the rest of the room hanging upon the singer's actions. He parted his lips for the third verse; but at that moment another knock was audible upon the door. This time the knock was faint and hesitating.

The company seemed scared; the shepherd looked with consternation towards the entrance, and it was with some effort that he resisted his alarmed wife's deprecatory glance, and uttered for the third time the welcoming words, 'Walk in!'

The door was gently opened, and another man stood upon the mat. He, like those who had preceded him, was a stranger. This time it was a short, small personage, of fair complexion, and dressed in a decent suit of dark clothes.

'Can you tell me the way to—?' he began: when, gazing round the room to observe the nature of the company amongst whom he had fallen, his eyes lighted on the stranger in cinder-gray. It was just at the instant when the latter, who had thrown his mind into his song with such a will that he scarcely heeded the interruption, silenced all whispers and inquiries by bursting into his third verse:

'Tomorrow is my working day,
Simple shepherds all –
Tomorrow is a working day for me:
For the farmer's sheep is slain, and the lad who did it ta'en,
And on his soul may God ha' merc-y!'

The stranger in the chimney-corner, waving cups with the singer so heartily that his mead splashed over on the hearth, repeated in his bass voice as before:

'And on his soul may God ha' merc-y!'

All this time the third stranger had been standing in the doorway. Finding now that he did not come forward or go on speaking, the guests particularly regarded him. They noticed to their surprise that he stood before them the picture of abject terror – his knees trembling, his hand shaking so violently that the door-latch by which he supported himself rattled audibly: his white lips were parted, and his eyes fixed on the merry officer of justice in the middle of the room. A moment more and he had turned, closed the door, and fled.

'What a man can it be?' said the shepherd.

The rest, between the awfulness of their late discovery and the odd conduct of this third visitor, looked as if they knew not what to think, and said nothing. Instinctively they withdrew further and further from the grim gentleman in their midst, whom some of them seemed to take for the Prince of Darkness himself, till they formed a remote circle, an empty space of floor being left between them and him –

'. . . circulus, cujus centrum diabolus'.

The room was so silent – though there were more than twenty people in it – that nothing could be heard but the patter of the rain against the window-shutters, accompanied by the occasional hiss of a stray drop that fell down the chimney into the fire, and the steady puffing of the man in the corner, who had now resumed his pipe of long clay.

The stillness was unexpectedly broken. The distant sound of a gun reverberated through the air – apparently from the direction of the county-town.

'Be jiggered!' cried the stranger who had sung the song, jumping up.

'What does that mean?' asked several.

'A prisoner escaped from the jail – that's what it means.'

All listened. The sound was repeated, and none of them spoke but the man in the chimney-corner, who said quietly, 'I've often been told that in this county they fire a gun at such times; but I never heard it till now.'

'I wonder if it is *my* man?' murmured the personage in cinder-gray.

'Surely it is!' said the shepherd involuntarily. 'And surely we've zeed him! That little man who looked in at the door by now, and quivered like a leaf when he zeed ye and heard your song!'

'His teeth chattered, and the breath went out of his body,' said the dairyman.

'And his heart seemed to sink within him like a stone,' said Oliver Giles.

'And he bolted as if he'd been shot at,' said the hedge-carpenter.

'True – his teeth chattered, and his heart seemed to sink; and he bolted as if he'd been shot at,' slowly summed up the man in the chimney-corner.

'I didn't notice it,' remarked the hangman.

'We were all a-wondering what made him run off in such a fright,' faltered one of the women against the wall, 'and now 'tis explained!'

The firing of the alarm-gun went on at intervals, low and sullenly, and their suspicions became a certainty. The sinister gentleman in cinder-gray roused himself. 'Is there a constable here?' he asked, in thick tones. 'If so, let him step forward.'

The engaged man of fifty stepped quavering out from the wall, his betrothed beginning to sob on the back of the chair.

'You are a sworn constable?'

'I be, sir.'

'Then pursue the criminal at once, with assistance, and bring him back here. He can't have gone far.'

'I will, sir, I will – when I've got my staff. I'll go home and get it, and come sharp here, and start in a body.'

'Staff! – never mind your staff; the man'll be gone!'

'But I can't do nothing without my staff – can I, William, and John, and Charles Jake? No; for there's the king's royal crown a painted on en in yaller and gold, and the lion and the unicorn, so as when I raise en up and hit my prisoner, 'tis made a lawful blow thereby. I wouldn't 'tempt to take up a man without my staff – no, not I. If I hadn't the law to gie me courage, why, instead o'my taking up him he might take up me!'

'Now, I'm a king's man myself, and can give you authority enough for this,' said the formidable officer in gray. 'Now then, all of ye, be ready. Have ye any lanterns?'

'Yes – have ye any lanterns? – I demand it!' said the constable.

'And the rest of you able-bodied—'

'Able-bodied men – yes – the rest of ye!' said the constable.

'Have you some good stout staves and pitchforks—'

'Staves and pitchforks – in the name o' the law! And take 'em in yer hands and go in quest, and do as we in authority tell ye!'

Thus aroused, the men prepared to give chase. The evidence was, indeed, though circumstantial, so convincing, that but little argument was needed to show the shepherd's guests that after what they had seen it would look very much like connivance if they did not instantly pursue the unhappy third stranger, who could not as yet have gone more than a few hundred yards over such uneven country.

A shepherd is always well provided with lanterns; and, lighting these hastily, and with hurdle-staves in their hands, they poured out of the door, taking a direction along the crest of the hill, away from the town, the rain having fortunately a little abated.

Disturbed by the noise, or possibly by unpleasant dreams of her baptism, the child who had been christened began to cry heart-brokenly in the room overhead. These notes of grief came down through the chinks of the floor to the ears of the women below, who jumped up one by one, and seemed glad of the excuse to ascend and comfort the baby, for the incidents of the last half-hour greatly oppressed them. Thus in the space of two or three minutes the room on the ground-floor was deserted quite.

But it was not for long. Hardly had the sound of footsteps died away when a man returned round the corner of the house from the direction the pursuers had taken. Peeping in at the door, and seeing nobody there, he entered leisurely. It was the stranger of the chimney-corner, who had gone out with the rest. The motive of his return was shown by his helping himself to a cut piece of skimmer-cake that lay on a ledge beside where he had sat, and which he had apparently forgotten to take with him. He also poured out half a cup more mead from the quantity that remained, ravenously eating and drinking these as he stood. He had not finished when another figure came in just as quietly – his friend in cinder-gray.

'O – you here?' said the latter, smiling. 'I thought you had gone to help in the capture.' And this speaker also revealed the object of his return by looking solicitously round for the fascinating mug of old mead.

'And I thought you had gone,' said the other, continuing his skimmer-cake with some effort.

'Well, on second thoughts, I felt there were enough without me,' said the first confidentially, 'and such a night as it is, too. Besides, 'tis the business o' the Government to take care of its criminals – not mine.'

'True; so it is. And I felt as you did, that there were enough without me.'

'I don't want to break my limbs running over the humps and hollows of this wild country.'

'Nor I neither, between you and me.'

'These shepherd-people are used to it – simple-minded souls, you know, stirred up to anything in a moment. They'll have him ready for me before the morning, and no trouble to me at all.'

'They'll have him, and we shall have saved ourselves all labour in the matter.'

'True, true. Well, my way is to Casterbridge; and 'tis as much as my legs will do to take me that far. Going the same way?'

'No, I am sorry to say! I have to get home over there' (he nodded indefinitely to the right), 'and I feel as you do, that it is quite enough for my legs to do before bedtime.'

The other had by this time finished the mead in the mug, after which, shaking hands heartily at the door, and wishing each other well, they went their several ways.

In the meantime the company of pursuers had reached the end of the hog's-back elevation which dominated this part of the down. They had decided on no particular plan of action; and, finding that the man of the baleful trade was no longer in their company, they seemed quite unable to form any such plan now. They descended in all directions down the hill, and straightway several of the party fell into the snare set by Nature for all misguided midnight ramblers over this part of the cretaceous formation. The 'lanchets', or flint slopes, which belted the escarpment at intervals of a dozen yards, took the less cautious ones unawares, and losing their footing on the rubbly steep they slid sharply downwards, the lanterns rolling from their hands to the bottom, and there lying on their sides till the horn was scorched through.

When they had again gathered themselves together the shepherd, as the man who knew the country best, took the lead, and guided them round these treacherous inclines. The lanterns, which seemed rather to dazzle their eyes and warn the fugitive than to assist them in the exploration, were extinguished, due silence was observed; and in this more rational order they plunged into the vale. It was a grassy, briery, moist defile, affording some shelter to any person who had sought it; but the party perambulated it in vain, and ascended on the other side. Here they wandered apart, and after an interval closed together again to report progress. At the second time of closing in they found themselves near a lonely ash, the single tree on this part of the coomb, probably sown there by a passing bird some fifty years before. And here, standing a little to one side of the trunk, as motionless as the trunk itself, appeared the man they were in quest of, his outline being well defined against the sky beyond. The band noiselessly drew up and faced him.

'Your money or your life!' said the constable sternly to the still figure.

'No, no,' whispered John Pitcher. ''Tisn't our side ought to say that. That's the doctrine of vagabonds like him, and we be on the side of the law.'

'Well, well,' replied the constable impatiently; 'I must say something, mustn't I? and if you had all the weight o' this undertaking upon your mind, perhaps you'd say the wrong thing too! – Prisoner at the bar, surrender, in the name of the Father – the Crown, I mane!'

The man under the tree seemed now to notice them for the first time, and, giving them no opportunity whatever for exhibiting their courage, he strolled slowly towards them. He was, indeed, the little man, the third stranger; but his trepidation had in a great measure gone.

'Well, travellers,' he said, 'did I hear ye speak to me?'

'You did: you've got to come and be our prisoner at once!' said the constable. 'We arrest 'ee on the charge of not biding in Casterbridge jail in a decent proper manner to be hung tomorrow morning. Neighbours, do your duty, and seize the culpet!'

On hearing the charge the man seemed enlightened, and, saying not another word, resigned himself with preternatural civility to the search-party, who, with their staves in their hands, surrounded him on all sides, and marched him back towards the shepherd's cottage.

It was eleven o'clock by the time they arrived. The light shining from the open door, a sound of men's voices within, proclaimed to them as they approached the house that some new events had arisen in their absence. On entering they discovered the shepherd's living-room to be invaded by two officers from Casterbridge jail, and a well-known magistrate who lived at the nearest country-seat, intelligence of the escape having become generally circulated.

'Gentlemen,' said the constable, 'I have brought back your man – not without risk and danger; but every one must do his duty! He is inside this circle of able-bodied persons, who have lent me useful aid, considering their ignorance of Crown work. Men, bring forward your prisoner!' And the third stranger was led to the light.

'Who is this?' said one of the officials.

'The man,' said the constable.

'Certainly not,' said the turnkey; and the first corroborated his statement.

'But how can it be otherwise?' asked the constable. 'Or why was he so terrified at sight o' the singing instrument of the law who sat there?' Here he related the strange behaviour of the third stranger on entering the house during the hangman's song.

'Can't understand it,' said the officer coolly. 'All I know is that it is not the condemned man. He's quite a different character from this one; a gauntish fellow, with dark hair and eyes, rather good-looking, and with a musical bass voice that if you heard it once you'd never mistake as long as you lived.'

'Why, souls – 'twas the man in the chimney corner!'

'Hey – what?' said the magistrate, coming forward after inquiring particulars from the shepherd in the background. 'Haven't you got the man after all?'

'Well, sir,' said the constable, 'he's the man we were in search of, that's true; and yet he's not the man we were in search of. For the man we were in search of was not the man we wanted, sir, if you understand my everyday way; for 'twas the man in the chimney-corner!'

'A pretty kettle of fish altogether!' said the magistrate. 'You had better start for the other man at once.'

The prisoner now spoke for the first time. The mention of the man in the chimney-corner seemed to have moved him as nothing else could do. 'Sir,' he said, stepping forward to the magistrate, 'take no more trouble about me. The time is come when I may as well speak. I have done nothing; my crime is that the condemned man is my brother. Early this afternoon I left home at Shottsford to tramp it all the way to Casterbridge jail to bid him farewell. I was benighted, and called here to rest and ask the way. When I opened the door I saw before me the very man, my brother, that I thought to see in the condemned cell at Casterbridge. He was in this chimney-corner; and jammed close to him, so that he could not have got out if he had tried, was the executioner who'd come to take his life, singing a song about it and not knowing that it was his victim who was close by, joining in to save appearances. My brother threw a glance of agony at me, and I knew he meant, "Don't reveal what you see; my life depends on it." I was so terror-struck that I could hardly stand, and, not knowing what I did, I turned and hurried away.'

The narrator's manner and tone had the stamp of truth, and his story made a great impression on all around.

'And do you know where your brother is at the present time?' asked the magistrate.

'I do not. I have never seen him since I closed this door.'

'I can testify to that, for we've been between ye ever since,' said the constable.

'Where does he think to fly to? – what is his occupation?'

'He's a watch-and-clock-maker, sir.'

''A said 'a was a wheelwright – a wicked rogue,' said the constable.

'The wheels of clocks and watches he meant, no doubt,' said Shepherd Fennel. 'I thought his hands were palish for's trade.'

'Well, it appears to me that nothing can be gained by retaining this poor man in custody,' said the magistrate; 'your business lies with the other, unquestionably.'

And so the little man was released off-hand; but he looked nothing the less sad on that account, it being beyond the power of magistrate or constable to raze out the written troubles in his brain, for they concerned another whom he regarded with more solicitude than himself. When this was done, and the man had gone his way, the night was found to be so far advanced that it was deemed useless to renew the search before the next morning.

Next day, accordingly, the quest for the clever sheep-stealer became general and keen, to all appearance at least. But the intended punishment was cruelly disproportioned to the transgression, and the sympathy of a great many country-folk in that district was strongly on the side of the fugitive. Moreover, his marvellous coolness and daring in hob-and-nobbing with the hangman, under the unprecedented circumstances of the shepherd's party, won their admiration. So that it may be questioned if all those who ostensibly made themselves so busy in exploring woods and fields and lanes were quite so thorough when it came to the private examination of their own lofts and out-houses. Stories were afloat of a mysterious figure being occasionally seen in some old overgrown trackway or other, remote from turnpike roads; but when a search was instituted in any of these suspected quarters nobody was found. Thus the days and weeks passed without tidings.

In brief, the bass-voiced man of the chimney-corner was never recaptured. Some said that he went across the sea, others that he did not, but buried himself in the depths of a populous city. At any rate, the gentleman in cinder-gray never did his morning's work at Casterbridge, nor met anywhere at all, for business purposes, the genial comrade with whom he had passed an hour of relaxation in the lonely house on the slope of the coomb.

The grass has long been green on the graves of Shepherd Fennel and his frugal wife; the guests who made up the christening party have mainly followed their entertainers to the tomb; the baby in whose honour they all had met is a matron in the sere and yellow leaf. But the arrival of the three strangers at the shepherd's that night, and the details connected therewith, is a story as well known as ever in the country about Higher Crowstairs.

MARCH 1883

A TRADITION OF EIGHTEEN HUNDRED AND FOUR

The widely discussed possibility of an invasion of England through a Channel tunnel has more than once recalled old Solomon Selby's story to my mind.

The occasion on which I numbered myself among his audience was one evening when he was sitting in the yawning chimney-corner of the inn-kitchen, with some others who had gathered there, and I entered for shelter from the rain. Withdrawing the stem of his pipe from the dental notch in which it habitually rested, he leaned back in the recess behind him and smiled into the fire. The smile was neither mirthful nor sad, not precisely humorous nor altogether thoughtful. We who knew him recognized it in a moment: it was his narrative smile. Breaking off our few desultory remarks we drew up closer, and he thus began:

'My father, as you mid know, was a shepherd all his life, and lived out by the Cove four miles yonder, where I was born and lived likewise, till I moved here shortly afore I was married. The cottage that first knew me stood on the top of the down, near the sea; there was no house within a mile and a half of it; it was built o' purpose for the farm-shepherd, and had no other use. They tell me that it is now pulled down, but that you can see where it stood by the mounds of earth and a few broken bricks that are still lying about. It was a bleak and dreary place in winter-time, but in summer it was well enough, though the garden never came to much, because we could not get up a good shelter for the vegetables and currant bushes; and where there is much wind they don't thrive.

'Of all the years of my growing up the ones that bide clearest in my mind were eighteen hundred and three, four, and five. This was for two reasons: I had just then grown to an age when a child's eyes and ears take in and note down everything about him, and there was more at that date to bear in mind than there ever has been since with me. It was, as I need hardly tell ye, the time after the first peace, when Bonaparte was scheming his descent upon England. He had crossed the great Alp mountains, fought in Egypt, drubbed the Turks, the Austrians, and the Proossians, and now thought he'd have a slap at us. On the other side of the Channel, scarce out of sight and hail of a man standing on our English shore, the French army of a hundred and sixty thousand men and fifteen thousand horses had been brought together from all parts, and were drilling every day. Bonaparte had been three years a-making his preparations; and to ferry these soldiers and cannon and horses across he had contrived a couple of thousand flat-bottomed boats. These boats were small things, but wonderfully built. A good few of 'em were so made as to have a little stable on board each for the two horses that were to haul the cannon carried at the stern. To get in order all these, and other things required, he had assembled there five or six thousand fellows that worked at trades – carpenters, blacksmiths, wheelwrights, saddlers, and what not. O 'twas a curious time!

'Every morning Neighbour Boney would muster his multitude of soldiers on the beach, draw 'em up in line, practise 'em in the manoeuvre of embarking, horses and all, till they could do it without a single hitch. My father drove a flock of ewes up into Sussex that year, and as he went along the drover's track over the high downs thereabout he could see this drilling actually going on – the accoutrements of the rank and file glittering in the sun like silver. It was thought and always said by my uncle Job, sergeant of foot (who used to know all about these matters), that Bonaparte meant to cross with oars on a calm night. The grand query with us, was, Where would my gentleman land? Many of the common people thought it would be at Dover; others, who knew how unlikely it was that any skilful general would make a business of landing just where he was expected, said he'd go either east into the River Thames, or west'ard to some convenient place, most likely one of the little bays inside the Isle of Portland, between the Beal and St Alban's Head – and for choice the three-quarter-round Cove screened from every mortal eye, that seemed made o' purpose, out by where we lived, and which I've climmed up with two tubs of brandy across my shoulders on scores o' dark nights in my younger days. Some had heard that a part o' the French fleet would sail right round Scotland, and come up the Channel to a suitable haven. However, there was much doubt upon the matter; and no wonder, for after-years proved that Bonaparte himself could hardly make up his mind upon that great and very particular point, where to land. His uncertainty came about in this wise, that he could get no news as to where and how our troops lay in waiting, and that his knowledge of possible places where flat-bottomed boats might be quietly run ashore, and the men they brought marshalled in order, was dim to the last degree. Being flat-bottomed, they didn't require a harbour for unshipping their cargo of men, but a good shelving beach away from sight, and with a fair open road toward London. How the question posed that great Corsican tyrant (as we used to call him), what pains he took to settle it, and, above all, what a risk he ran on one particular night in trying to do so, were known only to one man here and there; and certainly to no maker of newspapers or printer of books, or my account o't would not have had so many heads shaken over it as it has by gentry who only believe what they see in printed lines.

'The flocks my father had charge of fed all about the downs near our house, overlooking the sea and shore each way for miles. In winter and early spring father was up a deal at nights, watching and tending the lambing. Often he'd go to bed early, and turn out at twelve or one; and on the other hand, he'd sometimes stay up till twelve or one, and then turn in to bed. As soon as I was old enough I used to help him, mostly in the way of keeping an eye upon the ewes while he was gone home to rest. This is what I was doing in a particular month in either the year four or five – I can't certainly fix which, but it was long before I was took away from the sheepkeeping to be bound prentice to a trade. Every night at that time I was at the fold, about half a mile, or it may be a little more, from our cottage, and no living thing at all with me but the ewes and young lambs. Afeared? No; I was never afeared of being alone at these times; for I had been reared in such an out-step place that the lack o' human beings at night made me less fearful than the sight of 'em. Directly I saw a man's shape after dark in a lonely place I was frightened out of my senses.

'One day in that month we were surprised by a visit from my uncle Job, the sergeant in the Sixty-first foot, then in camp on the downs above King George's watering-place, several miles to the west yonder. Uncle Job dropped in about dusk, and went up with my father to the fold for an hour or two. Then he came home, had a drop to drink from the tub of sperrits that the smugglers kept us in for housing their liquor when they'd made a run, and for burning 'em off when there was danger. After that he stretched himself out on the settle to sleep. I went to bed: at one o'clock father came home, and waking me to go and take his place, according to custom, went to bed himself. On my way out of the house I passed Uncle Job on the settle. He opened his eyes, and upon my telling him where I was going he said it was a shame that such a youngster as I should go up there all alone; and when he had fastened up his stock and waist-belt he set off along with me, taking a drop from the sperrit-tub in a little flat bottle that stood in the corner-cupboard.

'By and by we drew up to the fold, saw that all was right, and then, to keep ourselves warm, curled up in a heap of straw that lay inside the thatched hurdles we had set up to break the stroke of the wind when there was any. Tonight, however, there was none. It was one of those very still nights when, if you stand on the high hills anywhere within two or three miles of the sea, you can hear the rise and fall of the tide along the shore, coming and going every few moments like a sort of great snore of the sleeping world. Over the lower ground there was a bit of a mist, but on the hill where we lay the air was clear, and the moon, then in her last quarter, flung a fairly good light on the grass and scattered straw.

'While we lay there Uncle Job amused me by telling me strange stories of the wars he had served in and the wownds he had got. He had already fought the French in the Low Countries, and hoped to fight 'em again. His stories lasted so long that at last I was hardly sure that I was not a soldier myself, and had seen such service as he told of. The wonders of his tales quite bewildered my mind, till I fell asleep and dreamed of battle, smoke, and flying soldiers, all of a kind with the doings he had been bringing up to me.

'How long my nap lasted I am not prepared to say. But some faint sounds over and above the rustle of the ewes in the straw, the bleat of the lambs, and the tinkle of the sheep-bell brought me to my waking senses. Uncle Job was still beside me; but he too had fallen asleep. I looked out from the straw, and saw what it was that had aroused me. Two men, in boat-cloaks, cocked hats, and swords, stood by the hurdles about twenty yards off.

'I turned my ear thitherward to catch what they were saying, but though I heard every word o't, not one did I understand. They spoke in a tongue that was not ours – in French, as I afterward found. But if I could not gain the meaning of a word, I was shrewd boy enough to find out a deal of the talkers' business. By the light o' the moon I could see that one of 'em carried a roll of paper in his hand, while every moment he spoke quick to his comrade, and pointed right and left with the other hand to spots along the shore. There was no doubt that he was explaining to the second gentleman the shapes and features of the coast. What happened soon after made this still clearer to me.

'All this time I had not waked Uncle Job, but now I began to be afeared that they might light upon us, because uncle breathed so heavily through's nose. I put my mouth to his ear and whispered, "Uncle Job."

'"What is it, my boy?" he said, just as if he hadn't been asleep at all.

'"Hush!" says I. "Two French generals—"

'"French?" says he.

'"Yes," says I. "Come to see where to land their army!"

'I pointed 'em out; but I could say no more, for the pair were coming at that moment much nearer to where we lay. As soon as they got as near as eight or ten yards, the officer with a roll in his hand stooped down to a slanting hurdle, unfastened his roll upon it, and spread it out. Then suddenly he sprung a dark lantern open on the paper, and showed it to be a map.

'"What be they looking at?" I whispered to Uncle Job.

'"A chart of the Channel," says the sergeant (knowing about such things).

'The other French officer now stooped likewise, and over the map they had a long consultation, as they pointed here and there on the paper, and then hither and thither at places along the shore beneath us. I noticed that the manner of one officer was very respectful toward the other, who seemed much his superior, the second in rank calling him by a sort of title that I did not know the sense of. The head one, on the other hand, was quite familiar with his friend, and more than once clapped him on the shoulder.

'Uncle Job had watched as well as I, but though the map had been in the lantern-light, their faces had always been in shade. But when they rose from stooping over the chart the light flashed upward, and fell smart upon one of 'em's features. No sooner had this happened than Uncle Job gasped, and sank down as if he'd been in a fit.

'"What is it – what is it, Uncle Job?" said I.

'"O good God!" says he, under the straw.

'"What?" says I.

'"Boney! he groaned out.

'"Who?" says I.

'"Bonaparty," he said. "The Corsican ogre. O that I had got but my new-flinted firelock, that there man should die! But I haven't got my new-flinted firelock, and that there man must live. So lie low, as you value your life!"

'I did lie low, as you mid suppose. But I couldn't help peeping. And then I too, lad as I was, knew that it was the face of Bonaparte. Not know Boney? I should think I did know Boney. I should have known him by half the light o' that lantern. If I had seen a picture of his features once, I had seen it a hundred times. There was his bullet head, his short neck, his round yaller cheeks and chin, his gloomy face, and his great glowing eyes. He took off his hat to blow himself a bit, and there was the forelock in the middle of his forehead, as in all the draughts of him. In moving, his cloak fell a little open, and I could see for a moment his white-fronted jacket and one of the epaulettes.

'But none of this lasted long. In a minute he and his general had rolled up the map, shut the lantern, and turned to go down toward the shore.

'Then Uncle Job came to himself a bit. "Slipped across in the night-time to see how to put his men ashore," he said. "The like o' that man's coolness eyes will never again see! Nephew, I must act in this, and immediate, or England's lost!"

'When they were over the brow, we crope out, and went some little way to look after them. Half-way down they were joined by two others, and six or seven minutes brought them to the shore. Then, from behind a rock, a boat came out into the weak moonlight of the Cove, and they jumped in; it put off instantly, and vanished in a few minutes between the two rocks that stand at the mouth of the Cove as we all know. We climmed back to where we had been before, and I could see, a short way out, a larger vessel, though still not very large. The little boat drew up alongside, was made fast at the stern as I suppose, for the largest sailed away, and we saw no more.

'My uncle Job told his officers as soon as he got back to camp; but what they thought of it I never heard – neither did he. Boney's army never came, and a good job for me; for the Cove below my father's house was where he meant to land, as this secret visit showed. We coastfolk should have been cut down one and all, and I should not have sat here to tell this tale.'

We who listened to old Selby that night have been familiar with his simple gravestone for these ten years past. Thanks to the incredulity of the age his tale has been seldom repeated. But if anything short of the direct testimony of his own eyes could persuade an auditor that Bonaparte had examined these shores for himself with a view to a practicable landing-place, it would have been Solomon Selby's manner of narrating the adventure which befell him on the down.

CHRISTMAS, 1882

THE MELANCHOLY HUSSAR OF THE GERMAN LEGION

I

Here stretch the downs, high and breezy and green, absolutely unchanged since those eventful days. A plough has never disturbed the turf, and the sod that was uppermost then is uppermost now. Here stood the camp; here are distinct traces of the banks thrown up for the horses of the cavalry, and spots where the midden-heaps lay are still to be observed. At night, when I walk across the lonely place, it is impossible to avoid hearing, amid the scourings of the wind over the grass-bents and thistles, the old trumpet and bugle calls, the rattle of the halters; to help seeing rows of spectral tents and the *impedimenta* of the soldiery. From within the canvases come guttural syllables of foreign tongues, and broken songs of the fatherland; for they were mainly regiments of the King's German Legion that slept round the tent-poles hereabout at that time.

It was nearly ninety years ago. The British uniform of the period, with its immense epaulettes, queer-cocked-hat, breeches, gaiters, ponderous cartridge-box, buckled shoes, and what not, would look strange and barbarous now. Ideas have changed; invention has followed invention. Soldiers were monumental objects then. A divinity still hedged kings here and there; and war was considered a glorious thing.

Secluded old manor-houses and hamlets lie in the ravines and hollows among these hills, where a stranger had hardly ever been seen till the King chose to take the baths yearly at the sea-side watering-place a few miles to the south; as a consequence of which battalions descended in a cloud upon the open country around. Is it necessary to add that the echoes of many characteristic tales, dating from that picturesque time, still linger about here in more or less fragmentary form, to be caught by the attentive ear? Some of them I have repeated; most of them I have forgotten; one I have never repeated, and assuredly can never forget.

Phyllis told me the story with her own lips. She was then an old lady of seventy-five, and her auditor a lad of fifteen. She enjoined silence as to her share in the incident, till she should be 'dead, buried, and forgotten'. Her life was prolonged twelve years after the day of her narration, and she has now been dead nearly twenty. The oblivion which in her modesty and humility she courted for herself has only partially fallen on her, with the unfortunate result of inflicting an injustice upon her memory; since such fragments of her story as got abroad at the time, and have been kept alive ever since, are precisely those which are most unfavourable to her character.

It all began with the arrival of the York Hussars, one of the foreign regiments above alluded to. Before that day scarcely a soul had been seen near her father's house for weeks. When a noise like the brushing skirt of a visitor was heard on the doorstep, it proved to be a scudding leaf; when a carriage seemed to be nearing the door, it was her father grinding his sickle on the stone in the garden for his favourite relaxation of trimming the box-tree borders to the plots. A sound like luggage thrown down from the coach was a gun far away at sea; and what looked like a tall man by the gate at dusk was a yew bush cut into a quaint and attenuated shape. There is no such solitude in country places now as there was in those old days.

Yet all the while King George and his Court were at his favourite sea-side resort, not more than five miles off.

The daughter's seclusion was great, but beyond the seclusion of the girl lay the seclusion of the father. If her social condition was twilight, his was darkness. Yet he enjoyed his darkness, while her twilight oppressed her. Dr Grove had been a professional man whose taste for lonely meditation over metaphysical questions had diminished his practice till it no longer paid him to keep it going; after which he had relinquished it and hired at a nominal rent the small, dilapidated, half farm, half manor-house of this obscure inland nook, to make a sufficiency of an income which in a town would have been inadequate for their maintenance. He stayed in his garden the greater part of the day, growing more and more irritable with the lapse of time, and the increasing perception that he had wasted his life in the pursuit of illusions. He saw his friends less and less frequently. Phyllis became so shy that if she met a stranger anywhere in her short rambles she felt ashamed at his gaze, walked awkwardly, and blushed to her shoulders.

Yet Phyllis was discovered even here by an admirer, and her hand most unexpectedly asked in marriage.

The King, as aforesaid, was at the neighbouring town, where he had taken up his abode at Gloucester Lodge; and his presence in the town naturally brought many county people thither. Among these idlers – many of whom professed to have connections and interests with the Court – was one Humphrey Gould, a bachelor; a personage neither young nor old; neither good-looking nor positively plain. Too steady-going to be 'a buck' (as fast and unmarried men were then called), he was an approximately fashionable man of a mild type. This bachelor of thirty found his way to the village on the down: beheld Phyllis; made her father's acquaintance in order to make hers; and by some means or other she sufficiently inflamed his heart to lead him in that direction almost daily; till he became engaged to marry her.

As he was of an old local family, some of whose members were held in respect in the county, Phyllis, in bringing him to her feet, had accomplished what was considered a brilliant move for one in her constrained position. How she had done it was not quite known to Phyllis herself. In those days unequal marriages were regarded rather as a violation of the laws of nature than as a mere infringement of convention, the more modern view, and hence when Phyllis, of the watering-place *bourgeoisie*, was chosen by such a gentlemanly fellow, it was as if she were going to be taken to heaven, though perhaps the uninformed would have seen no great difference in the respective positions of the pair, the said Gould being as poor as a crow.

This pecuniary condition was his excuse – probably a true one – for postponing their union, and as the winter drew nearer, and the King departed for the season, Mr Humphrey Gould set out for Bath, promising to return to Phyllis in a few weeks. The winter arrived, the date of his promise passed, yet Gould postponed his coming, on the ground that he could not very easily leave his father in the city of their sojourn, the elder having no other relative near him. Phyllis, though lonely in the extreme, was content. The man who had asked her in marriage was a desirable husband for her in many ways; her father highly approved of his suit; but this neglect of her was awkward, if not painful, for Phyllis. Love him in the true sense of the word she assured me she never did, but she had a genuine regard for him; admired a certain methodical and dogged way in which he sometimes took his pleasure; valued his knowledge of what the Court was doing, had done, or was about to do; and she was not without a feeling of pride that he had chosen her when he might have exercised a more ambitious choice.

But he did not come; and the spring developed. His letters were regular though formal; and it is not to be wondered that the uncertainty of her position, linked with the fact that there was not much passion in her thoughts of Humphrey, bred an indescribable dreariness in the heart of Phyllis Grove. The spring was soon summer, and the summer brought the King; but still no Humphrey Gould. All this while the engagement by letter was maintained intact.

At this point of time a golden radiance flashed in upon the lives of people here, and charged all youthful thought with emotional interest. This radiance was the aforesaid York Hussars.

2

The present generation has probably but a very dim notion of the celebrated York Hussars of ninety years ago. They were one of the regiments of the King's German Legion, and (though they somewhat degenerated later on) their brilliant uniform, their splendid horses, and above all, their foreign air and mustachios rare appendages then), drew crowds of admirers of both sexes wherever they went. These with other regiments had come to encamp on the downs and pastures, because of the presence of the King in the neighbouring town.

The spot was high and airy, and the view extensive, commanding Portland – the Isle of Slingers – in front, and reaching to St Aldhelm's Head eastward, and almost to the Start on the west.

Phyllis, though not precisely a girl of the village, was as interested as any of them in this military investment. Her father's home stood somewhat apart, and on the highest point of ground to which the lane ascended, so that it was almost level with the top of the church tower in the lower part of the parish. Immediately from the outside of the garden-wall the grass spread away to a great distance, and it was crossed by a path which came close to the wall. Ever since her childhood it had been Phyllis's pleasure to clamber up this fence and sit on the top – a feat not so difficult as it may seem, the walls in this district being built of rubble, without mortar, so that there were plenty of crevices for small toes.

She was sitting up here one day, listlessly surveying the pasture without, when her attention was arrested by a solitary figure walking along the path. It was one of the renowned German Hussars, and he moved onward with his eyes on the ground, and with the manner of one who wished to escape company. His head would probably have been bent like his eyes but for his stiff neck-gear. On nearer view she perceived that his face was marked with deep sadness. Without observing her, he advanced by the footpath till it brought him almost immediately under the wall.

Phyllis was much surprised to see a fine, tall soldier in such a mood as this. Her theory of the military, and of the York Hussars in particular (derived entirely from hearsay, for she had never talked to a soldier in her life), was that their hearts were as gay as their accoutrements.

At this moment the Hussar lifted his eyes and noticed her on her perch, the white muslin neckerchief which covered her shoulders and neck where left bare by her low gown, and her white raiment in general, showing conspicuously in the bright sunlight of this summer day. He blushed a little at the suddenness of the encounter, and without halting a moment from his pace passed on.

All that day the foreigner's face haunted Phyllis; its aspect was so striking, so handsome, and his eyes were so blue, and sad, and abstracted. It was perhaps only natural that on some following day at the same hour she should look over that wall again, and wait till he had passed a second time. On this occasion he was reading a letter, and at the sight of her his manner was that of one who had half expected or hoped to discover her. He almost stopped, smiled, and made a courteous salute. The end of the meeting was that they exchanged a few words. She asked him what he was reading, and he readily informed her that he was re-perusing letters from his mother in Germany; he did not get them often, he said, and was forced to read the old ones a great many times. This was all that passed at the present interview, but others of the same kind followed.

Phyllis used to say that his English, though not good, was quite intelligible to her, so that their acquaintance was never hindered by difficulties of speech. Whenever the subject became too delicate, subtle, or tender, for such words of English as were at his command, the eyes no doubt helped out the tongue, and – though this was later on – the lips helped out the eyes. In short, this acquaintance, unguardedly made, and rash enough on her part, developed and ripened. Like Desdemona, she pitied him, and learnt his history.

His name was Matthäus Tina, and Saarbrück his native town, where his mother was still living. His age was twenty-two, and he had already risen to the grade of corporal, though he had not long been in the army. Phyllis used to assert that no such refined or well-educated young man could have been found in the ranks of the purely English regiments, some of these foreign soldiers having rather the graceful manner and presence of our native officers than of our rank and file.

She by degrees learnt from her foreign friend a circumstance about himself and his comrades which Phyllis would least have expected of the York Hussars. So far from being as gay as its uniform, the regiment was pervaded by a dreadful melancholy, a chronic home-sickness, which depressed many of the men to such an extent that they could hardly attend to their drill. The worst sufferers were the younger soldiers who had not been over here long. They hated England and English life; they took no interest whatever in King George and his island kingdom, and they only wished to be out of it and never to see it any more. Their bodies were here, but their hearts and minds were always far away in their dear fatherland, of which – brave men and stoical as they were in many ways – they would speak with tears in their eyes. One of the worst of the sufferers from this home-woe, as he called it in his own tongue, was Matthäus Tina, whose dreamy musing nature felt the gloom of exile still more intensely from the fact that he had left a lonely mother at home with nobody to cheer her.

Though Phyllis, touched by all this, and interested in his history, did not disdain her soldier's acquaintance, she declined (according to her own account, at least) to permit the young man to overstep the line of mere friendship for a long while – as long, indeed, as she considered herself likely to become the possession of another; though it is probable that she had lost her heart to Matthäus before she was herself aware. The stone wall of necessity made anything like intimacy difficult; and he had never ventured to come, or to ask to come, inside the garden, so that all their conversation had been overtly conducted across this boundary.

3

But news reached the village from a friend of Phyllis's father concerning Mr Humphrey Gould, her remarkably cool and patient betrothed. This gentleman had been heard to say in Bath that he considered his overtures to Miss Phyllis Grove to have reached only the stage of a half-understanding; and in view of his enforced absence on his father's account, who was too great an invalid now to attend to his affairs, he thought it best that there should be no definite promise as yet on either side. He was not sure, indeed, that he might not cast his eyes elsewhere.

This account– though only a piece of hearsay, and as such entitled to no absolute credit – tallied so well with the infrequency of his letters and their lack of warmth, that Phyllis did not doubt its truth for one moment; and from that hour she felt herself free to bestow her heart as she should choose. Not so her father; he declared the whole story to be a fabrication. He had known Mr Gould's family from his boyhood; and if there was one proverb which expressed the matrimonial aspect of that family well, it was 'Love me little, love me long'. Humphrey was an honourable man, who would not think of treating his engagement so lightly. 'Do you wait in patience,' he said; 'all will be right enough in time.'

From these words Phyllis at first imagined that her father was in correspondence with Mr Gould; and her heart sank within her; for in spite of her original intentions she had been relieved to hear that her engagement had come to nothing. But she presently learnt that her father had heard no more of Humphrey Gould than she herself had done; while he would not write and address her affianced directly on the subject, lest it should be deemed an imputation on that bachelor's honour.

'You want an excuse for encouraging one or other of those foreign fellows to flatter you with his unmeaning attentions,' her father exclaimed, his mood having of late been a very unkind one towards her. 'I see more than I say. Don't you ever set foot outside that garden-fence without my permission. If you want to see the camp I'll take you myself some Sunday afternoon.'

Phyllis had not the smallest intention of disobeying him in her actions, but she assumed herself to be independent with respect to her feelings. She no longer checked her fancy for the Hussar, though she was far from regarding him as her lover in the serious sense in which an Englishman might have been regarded as such. The young foreign soldier was almost an ideal being to her, with none of the appurtenances of an ordinary house-dweller; one who had descended she knew not whence, and would disappear she knew not whither; the subject of a fascinating dream – no more.

They met continually now – mostly at dusk – during the brief interval between the going down of the sun and the minute at which the last trumpet-call summoned him to his tent. Perhaps her manner had become less restrained latterly; at any rate that of the Hussar was so; he had grown more tender every day, and at parting after these hurried interviews she reached down her hand from the top of the wall that he might press it. One evening he held it such a while that she exclaimed, 'The wall is white, and somebody in the field may see your shape against it!'

He lingered so long that night that it was with the greatest difficulty that he could run across the intervening stretch of ground and enter the camp in time. On the next occasion of his awaiting her she did not appear in her usual place at the usual hour. His disappointment was unspeakably keen; he remained staring blankly at the spot, like a man in a trance. The trumpets and tattoo sounded, and still he did not go.

She had been delayed purely by an accident. When she arrived she was anxious because of the lateness of the hour, having heard as well as he the sounds denoting the closing of the camp. She implored him to leave immediately.

'No,' he said gloomily. 'I shall not go in yet – the moment you come – I have thought of your coming all day.'

'But you may be disgraced at being after time?'

'I don't mind that. I should have disappeared from the world some time ago if it had not been for two persons – my beloved, here, and my mother in Saarbrück. I hate the army. I care more for a minute of your company than for all the promotion in the world.'

Thus he stayed and talked to her, and told her interesting details of his native place, and incidents of his childhood, till she was in a simmer of distress at his recklessness in remaining. It was only because she insisted on bidding him good-night, and leaving the wall, that he returned to his quarters.

The next time that she saw him he was without the stripes that had adorned his sleeve. He had been broken to the level of private for his lateness that night; and as Phyllis considered herself to be the cause of his disgrace her sorrow was great. But the position was now reversed; it was his turn to cheer her.

'Don't grieve, meine Liebliche!' he said. 'I have got a remedy for whatever comes. First, even supposing I regain my stripes, would your father allow you to marry a non-commissioned officer in the York Hussars?'

She flushed. This practical step had not been in her mind in relation to such an unrealistic person as he was; and a moment's reflection was enough for it. 'My father would not – certainly would not,' she answered unflinchingly. 'It cannot be thought of! My dear friend, please do forget me: I fear I am ruining you and your prospects!'

'Not at all!' said he. 'You are giving this country of yours just sufficient interest to me to make me care to keep alive in it. If my dear land were here also, and my old parent, with you, I could be happy as I am, and would do my best as a soldier. But it is not so. And now listen. This is my plan. That you go with me to my own country, and be my wife there, and live there with my mother and me. I am not a Hanoverian, as you know, though I entered the army as such; my country is by the Saar, and is at peace with France, and if I were once in it I should be free.'

'But how get there?' she asked. Phyllis had been rather amazed than shocked at his proposition. Her position in her father's house was growing irksome and painful in the extreme; his parental affection seemed to be quite dried up. She was not a native of the village, like all the joyous girls around her; and in some way Matthäus Tina had infected her with his own passionate longing for his country, and mother, and home.

'But how?' she repeated, finding that he did not answer. 'Will you buy your discharge?'

'Ah, no,' he said. 'That's impossible in these times. No; I came here against my will; why should I not escape? Now is the time, as we shall soon be striking camp, and I might see you no more. This is my scheme. I will ask you to meet me on the highway two miles off, on some calm night next week that may be appointed. There will be nothing unbecoming in it, or to cause you shame; you will not fly alone with me, for I will bring with me my devoted young friend, Christoph, an Alsatian, who has lately joined the regiment, and who has agreed to assist in this enterprise. We shall have come from yonder harbour, where we shall have examined the boats, and found one suited to our purpose. Christoph has already a chart of the Channel, and we will then go to the harbour, and at midnight cut the boat from her moorings, and row away round the point out of sight; and by the next morning we are on the coast of France, near Cherbourg. The rest is easy, for I have saved money for the land journey, and can get a change of clothes. I will write to my mother, who will meet us on the way.'

He added details in reply to her inquiries, which left no doubt in Phyllis's mind of the feasibility of the undertaking. But its magnitude almost appalled her; and it is questionable if she would ever have gone further in the wild adventure if, on entering the house that night, her father had not accosted her in the most significant terms.

'How about the York Hussars?' he said.

'They are still at the camp; but they are soon going away, I believe.'

'It is useless for you to attempt to cloak your actions in that way. You have been meeting one of those fellows; you have been seen walking with him – foreign barbarians, not much better than the French themselves! I have made up my mind – don't speak a word till I have done, please! – I have made up my mind that you shall stay here no longer while they are on the spot. You shall go to your aunt's.'

It was useless for her to protest that she had never taken a walk with any soldier or man under the sun except himself. Her protestations were feeble, too, for though he was not literally correct in his assertion, he was virtually only half in error.

The house of her father's sister was a prison to Phyllis. She had quite recently undergone experience of its gloom; and when her father went on to direct her to pack what would be necessary for her to take, her heart died within her. In after-years she never attempted to excuse her conduct during this week of agitation; but the result of her self-communing was that she decided to join in the scheme of her lover and his friend, and fly to the country which he had coloured with such lovely hues in her imagination. She always said that the one feature in his proposal which overcame her hesitation was the obvious purity and straightforwardness of his intentions. He showed himself to be so virtuous and kind; he treated her with a respect to which she had never before been accustomed; and she was braced to the obvious risks of the voyage by her confidence in him.

4

It was on a soft, dark evening of the following week that they engaged in the adventure. Tina was to meet her at a point in the highway at which the lane to the village branched off. Christoph was to go ahead of them to the harbour where the boat lay, row it round the Nothe – or Look-out as it was called in those days – and pick them up on the other side of the promontory, which they were to reach by crossing the harbour-bridge on foot, and climbing over the Look-out hill.

As soon as her father had ascended to his room she left the house, and, bundle in hand, proceeded at a trot along the lane. At such an hour not a soul was afoot anywhere in the village, and she reached the junction of the lane with the highway unobserved. Here she took up her position in the obscurity formed by the angle of a fence, whence she could discern every one who approached along the turnpike-road, without being herself seen.

She had not remained thus waiting for her lover longer than a minute – though from the tension of her nerves the lapse of even that short time was trying – when, instead of the expected footsteps, the stage-coach could be heard descending the hill. She knew that Tina would not show himself till the road was clear, and waited impatiently for the coach to pass. Nearing the corner where she was it slackened speed, and, instead of going by as usual, drew up within a few yards of her. A passenger alighted, and she heard his voice. It was Humphrey Gould's.

He had brought a friend with him, and luggage. The luggage was deposited on the grass, and the coach went on its route to the royal watering-place.

'I wonder where that young man is with the horse and trap?' said her former admirer to his companion. 'I hope we shan't have to wait here long. I told him half-past nine o'clock precisely.'

'Have you got her present safe?'

'Phyllis's? O, yes. It is in this trunk. I hope it will please her.'

'Of course it will. What woman would not be pleased with such a handsome peace-offering?'

'Well – she deserves it. I've treated her rather badly. But she has been in my mind these last two days much more than I should care to confess to everybody. Ah, well; I'll say no more about that. It cannot be that she is so bad as they make out. I am quite sure that a girl of her good wit would know better than to get entangled with any of those Hanoverian soldiers. I won't believe it of her, and there's an end on't.'

More words in the same strain were casually dropped as the two men waited; words which revealed to her, as by a sudden illumination, the enormity of her conduct. The conversation was at length cut off by the arrival of the man with the vehicle. The luggage was placed in it, and they mounted, and were driven on in the direction from which she had just come.

Phyllis was so conscience-stricken that she was at first inclined to follow them; but a moment's reflection led her to feel that it would only be bare justice to Matthäus to wait till he arrived, and explain candidly that she had changed her mind – difficult as the struggle would be when she stood face to face with him. She bitterly reproached herself for having believed reports which represented Humphrey Gould as false to his engagement, when, from what she now heard from his own lips, she gathered that he had been living full of trust in her. But she knew well enough who had won her love. Without him her life seemed a dreary prospect, yet the more she looked at his proposal the more she feared to accept it – so wild as it was, so vague, so venturesome. She had promised Humphrey Gould, and it was only his assumed faithlessness which had led her to treat that promise as nought. His solicitude in bringing her these gifts touched her; her promise must be kept, and esteem must take the place of love. She would preserve her self-respect. She would stay at home, and marry him, and suffer.

Phyllis had thus braced herself to an exceptional fortitude when, a few minutes later, the outline of Matthäus Tina appeared behind a field-gate, over which he lightly leapt as she stepped forward. There was no evading it, he pressed her to his breast.

'It is the first and last time!' she wildly thought as she stood encircled by his arms.

How Phyllis got through the terrible ordeal of that night she could never clearly recollect. She always attributed her success in carrying out her resolve to her lover's honour, for as soon as she declared to him in feeble words that she had changed her mind, and felt that she could not, dared not, fly with him, he forbore to urge her, grieved as he was at her decision. Unscrupulous pressure on his part, seeing how romantically she had become attached to him, would no doubt have turned the balance in his favour. But he did nothing to tempt her unduly or unfairly.

On her side, fearing for his safety, she begged him to remain. This, he declared, could not be. 'I cannot break faith with my friend,' said he. Had he stood alone he would have abandoned his plan. But Christoph, with the boat and compass and chart, was waiting on the shore; the tide would soon turn; his mother had been warned of his coming; go he must.

Many precious minutes were lost while he tarried, unable to tear himself away. Phyllis held to her resolve, though it cost her many a bitter pang. At last they parted, and he went down the hill. Before his footsteps had quite died away she felt a desire to behold at least his outline once more, and running noiselessly after him regained view of his diminishing figure. For one moment she was sufficiently excited to be on the point of rushing forward and linking her fate with his. But she could not. The courage which at the critical instant failed Cleopatra of Egypt could scarcely be expected of Phyllis Grove.

A dark shape, similar to his own, joined him in the highway. It was Christoph, his friend. She could see no more; they had hastened on in the direction of the town and harbour, four miles ahead. With a feeling akin to despair she turned and slowly pursued her way homeward.

Tattoo sounded in the camp; but there was no camp for her now. It was as dead as the camp of the Assyrians after the passage of the Destroying Angel.

She noiselessly entered the house, seeing nobody, and went to bed. Grief, which kept her awake at first, ultimately wrapped her in a heavy sleep. The next morning her father met her at the foot of the stairs.

'Mr Gould is come!' he said triumphantly.

Humphrey was staying at the inn, and had already called to inquire for her. He had brought her a present of a very handsome looking-glass in a frame of *repoussé* silverwork, which her father held in his hand. He had promised to call again in the course of an hour, to ask Phyllis to walk with him.

Pretty mirrors were rarer in country-houses at that day than they are now, and the one before her won Phyllis's admiration. She looked into it, saw how heavy her eyes were, and endeavoured to brighten them. She was in that wretched state of mind which leads a woman to move mechanically onward in what she conceives to be her allotted path. Mr Humphrey had, in his undemonstrative way, been adhering all along to the old understanding; it was for her to do the same, and to say not a word of her own lapse. She put on her bonnet and tippet, and when he arrived at the hour named she was at the door awaiting him.

5

Phyllis thanked him for his beautiful gift; but the talking was soon entirely on Humphrey's side as they walked along. He told her of the latest movements of the world of fashion – a subject which she willingly discussed to the exclusion of anything more personal – and his measured language helped to still her disquieted heart and brain. Had not her own sadness been what it was she must have observed his embarrassment. At last he abruptly changed the subject.

'I am glad you are pleased with my little present,' he said. 'The truth is that I brought it to propitiate 'ee, and to get you to help me out of a mighty difficulty.'

It was inconceivable to Phyllis that this independent bachelor – whom she admired in some respects – could have a difficulty.

'Phyllis – I'll tell you my secret at once; for I have a monstrous secret to confide before I can ask your counsel. The case is, then, that I am married: yes, I have privately married a dear young belle; and if you knew her, and I hope you will, you would say everything in her praise. But she is not quite the one that my father would have chose for me – you know the paternal idea as well as I – and I have kept it secret. There will be a terrible noise, no doubt; but I think that with your help I may get over it. If you would only do me this good turn – when I have told my father, I mean – say that you never could have married me, you know, or something of that sort – 'pon my life it will help to smooth the way vastly. I am so anxious to win him round to my point of view, and not to cause any estrangement.'

What Phyllis replied she scarcely knew, or how she counselled him as to his unexpected situation. Yet the relief that his announcement brought her was perceptible. To have confided her trouble in return was what her aching heart longed to do; and had Humphrey been a woman she would instantly have poured out her tale. But to him she feared to confess; and there was a real reason for silence, till a sufficient time had elapsed to allow her lover and his comrade to get out of harm's way.

As soon as she reached home again she sought a solitary place, and spent the time in half regretting that she had not gone away, and in dreaming over the meetings with Matthäus Tina from their beginning to their end. In his own country, amongst his own countrywomen, he would possibly soon forget her, even to her very name.

Her listlessness was such that she did not go out of the house for several days. There came a morning which broke in fog and mist, behind which the dawn could be discerned in greenish grey; and the outlines of the tents, and the rows of horses at the ropes. The smoke from the canteen fires drooped heavily.

The spot at the bottom of the garden where she had been accustomed to climb the wall to meet Matthäus was the only inch of English ground in which she took any interest; and in spite of the disagreeable haze prevailing she walked out there till she reached the well-known corner. Every blade of grass was weighted with little liquid globes, and slugs and snails had crept out upon the plots. She could hear the usual faint noises from the camp, and in the other direction the trot of farmers on the road to the town, for it was market-day. She observed that her frequent visits to this corner had quite trodden down the grass in the angle of the wall, and left marks of garden soil on the stepping-stones by which she had mounted to look over the top. Seldom having gone there till dusk, she had not considered that her traces might be visible by day. Perhaps it was these which had revealed her trysts to her father.

While she paused in melancholy regard, she fancied that the customary sounds from the tents were changing their character. Indifferent as Phyllis was to camp doings now, she mounted by the steps to the old place. What she beheld at first awed and perplexed her; then she stood rigid, her fingers hooked to the wall, her eyes staring out of her head, and her face as if hardened to stone.

On the open green stretching before her all the regiments in the camp were drawn up in line, in the mid-front of which two empty coffins lay on the ground. The unwonted sounds which she had noticed came from an advancing procession. It consisted of the band of the York Hussars playing a dead march; next two soldiers of that regiment in a mourning coach, guarded on each side, and accompanied by two priests. Behind came a crowd of rustics who had been attracted by the event. The melancholy procession marched along the front of the line, returned to the centre, and halted beside the coffins, where the two condemned men were blindfolded, and each placed kneeling on his coffin; a few minutes' pause was now given while they prayed.

A firing-party of twenty-four men stood ready with levelled carbines. The commanding officer, who had his sword drawn, waved it through some cuts of the sword-exercise till he reached the downward stroke, whereat the firing-party discharged their volley. The two victims fell, one upon his face across his coffin, the other backwards.

As the volley resounded there arose a shriek from the wall of Dr

Grove's garden, and some one fell down inside; but nobody among the spectators without noticed it at the time. The two executed Hussars were Matthäus Tina and his friend Christoph. The soldiers on guard placed the bodies in the coffins almost instantly; but the colonel of the regiment, an Englishman, rode up and exclaimed in a stern voice: 'Turn them out – as an example to the men!'

The coffins were lifted endwise, and the dead Germans flung out upon their faces on the grass. Then all the regiments wheeled in sections, and marched past the spot in slow time. When the survey was over the corpses were again coffined, and borne away.

Meanwhile Dr Grove, attracted by the noise of the volley, had rushed out into his garden, where he saw his wretched daughter lying motionless against the wall. She was taken indoors, but it was long before she recovered consciousness; and for weeks they despaired of her reason.

It transpired that the luckless deserters from the York Hussars had cut the boat from her moorings in the adjacent harbour, according to their plan, and with two other comrades who were smarting under ill-treatment from their colonel, had sailed in safety across the Channel. But mistaking their bearings they steered into Jersey, thinking that island the French coast. Here they were perceived to be deserters, and delivered up to the authorities. Matthäus and Chrstoph interceded for the other two at the court-martial, saying that it was entirely by the former's representations that these were induced to go. Their sentence was accordingly commuted to flogging, the death punishment being reserved for their leaders.

The visitor to the well-known old Georgian watering-place, who may care to ramble to the neighbouring village under the hills, and examine the register of burials, will there find two entries in these words:

> Matth: Tina (Corpl) in His Majesty's Regmt of York Hussars, and Shot for Desertion, was Buried June 30th, 1801, aged 22 years. Born in the town of Sarrbruk, Germany.

> Christoph Bless, belonging to His Majesty's Regmt of York Hussars, who was Shot for Desertion, was Buried June 30th, 1801, aged 22 years. Born at Lothaargen, Alsatia.

Their graves were dug at the back of the little church, near the wall. There is no memorial to mark the spot, but Phyllis pointed it out to me. While she lived she used to keep their mounds neat; but now they are overgrown with nettles, and sunk nearly flat. The older villagers, however, who know of the episode from their parents, still recollect the place where the soldiers lie. Phyllis lies near.

OCTOBER 1889

THE WITHERED ARM

I. A LORN MILKMAID

It was an eighty-cow dairy, and the troop of milkers, regular and supernumerary, were all at work; for, though the time of year was as yet but early April, the feed lay entirely in water-meadows, and the cows were 'in full pail'. The hour was about six in the evening, and three-fourths of the large, red, rectangular animals having been finished off, there was opportunity for a little conversation.

'He do bring home his bride tomorrow, I hear. They've come as far as Anglebury today.'

The voice seemed to proceed from the belly of the cow called Cherry, but the speaker was a milking-woman, whose face was buried in the flank of that motionless beast.

'Hav' anybody seen her?' said another.

There was a negative response from the first. 'Though they say she's a rosy-cheeked, tisty-tosty little body enough,' she added; and as the milkmaid spoke she turned her face so that she could glance past her cow's tail to the other side of the barton, where a thin, fading woman of thirty milked somewhat apart from the rest.

'Years younger than he, they say,' continued the second, with also a glance of reflectiveness in the same direction.

'How old do you call him, then?'

'Thirty or so.'

'More like forty,' broke in an old milkman near, in a long white pinafore or 'wropper', and with the brim of his hat tied down, so that he looked like a woman. ''A was born before our Great Weir was builded, and I hadn't man's wages when I laved water there.'

The discussion waxed so warm that the purr of the milk-streams became jerky, till a voice from another cow's belly cried with authority, 'Now then, what the Turk do it matter to us about Farmer Lodge's age, or Farmer Lodge's new mis'ess? I shall have to pay him nine pound a year for the rent of every one of these milchers, whatever his age or hers. Get on with your work, or 'twill be dark afore we have done. The evening is pinking in a'ready.' This speaker was the dairyman himself, by whom the milkmaids and men were employed.

Nothing more was said publicly about Farmer Lodge's wedding, but the first woman murmured under her cow to her next neighbour, ''Tis hard for *she*,' signifying the thin worn milkmaid aforesaid.

'O no,' said the second. 'He ha'n't spoke to Rhoda Brook for years.'

When the milking was done they washed their pails and hung them on a many-forked stand made as usual of the peeled limb of an oak tree, set upright in the earth, and resembling a colossal antlered horn. The majority then dispersed in various directions homeward. The thin woman who had not spoken was joined by a boy of twelve or thereabout, and the twain went away up the field also.

Their course lay apart from that of the others, to a lonely spot high above the water-meads, and not far from the border of Egdon Heath, whose dark countenance was visible in the distance as they drew nigh to their home.

'They've just been saying down in barton that your father brings his young wife home from Anglebury tomorrow,' the woman observed. 'I shall want to send you for a few things to market, and you'll be pretty sure to meet 'em.'

'Yes, mother,' said the boy. 'Is father married then?'

'Yes. . . You can give her a look, and tell me what she's like, if you do see her.'

'Yes, mother.'

'If she's dark or fair, and if she's tall – as tall as I. And if she seems like a woman who has ever worked for a living, or one that has been always well off, and has never done anything, and shows marks of the lady on her, as I expect she do.'

'Yes.'

They crept up the hill in the twilight and entered the cottage. It was built of mud-walls, the surface of which had been washed by many rains into channels and depressions that left none of the original flat face visible; while here and there in the thatch above a rafter showed like a bone protruding through the skin.

She was kneeling down in the chimney-corner, before two pieces of turf laid together with the heather inwards, blowing at the red-hot ashes with her breath till the turves flamed. The radiance lit her pale cheek, and made her dark eyes, that had once been handsome, seem handsome anew. 'Yes,' she resumed, 'see if she is dark or fair, and if you can notice if her hands be white; if not, see if they look as though she had ever done housework, or are milker's hands like mine.'

The boy again promised, inattentively this time, his mother not observing that he was cutting a notch with his pocket-knife in the beech-backed chair.

2. THE YOUNG WIFE

The road from Anglebury to Holmstoke is in general level; but there is one place where a sharp ascent breaks its monotony. Farmers homeward-bound from the former market-town, who trot all the rest of the way, walk their horses up this short incline.

The next evening while the sun was yet bright a handsome new gig, with a lemon-coloured body and red wheels, was spinning westward along the level highway at the heels of a powerful mare. The driver was a yeoman in the prime of life, cleanly shaven like an actor, his face being toned to that bluish vermilion hue which so often graces a thriving farmer's features when returning home after successful dealings in the town. Beside him sat a woman, many years his junior – almost, indeed, a girl. Her face too was fresh in colour, but it was of a totally different quality – soft and evanescent, like the light under a heap of rose-petals.

Few people travelled this way, for it was not a main road, and the long white riband of gravel that stretched before them was empty, save of one small scarce-moving speck, which presently resolved itself into the figure of a boy, who was creeping on at a snail's pace, and continually looking behind him – the heavy bundle he carried being some excuse for, if not the reason of, his dilatoriness. When the bouncing gig-party slowed at the bottom of the incline above mentioned, the pedestrian was only a few yards in front. Supporting the large bundle by putting one hand on his hip, he turned and looked straight at the farmer's wife as though he would read her through and through, pacing along abreast of the horse.

The low sun was full in her face, rendering every feature, shade, and contour distinct, from the curve of her little nostril to the colour of her eyes. The farmer, though he seemed annoyed at the boy's persistent presence, did not order him to get out of the way; and thus the lad preceded them, his hard gaze never leaving her, till they reached the top of the ascent, when the farmer trotted on with relief in his lineaments – having taken no outward notice of the boy whatever.

'How that poor lad stared at me!' said the young wife.

'Yes, dear; I saw that he did.'

'He is one of the village, I suppose?'

'One of the neighbourhood. I think he lives with his mother a mile or two off.'

'He knows who we are, no doubt?'

'O yes. You must expect to be stared at just at first, my pretty Gertrude.'

'I do, – though I think the poor boy may have looked at us in the hope we might relieve him of his heavy load, rather than from curiosity.'

'O no,' said her husband off-handedly. 'These country lads will carry a hundredweight once they get it on their backs; besides, his pack had more size than weight in it. Now, then, another mile and I shall be able to show you our house in the distance – if it is not too dark before we get there.' The wheels spun round, and particles flew from their periphery as before, till a white house of ample dimensions revealed itself, with farm-buildings and ricks at the back.

Meanwhile the boy had quickened his pace, and turning up a by-lane some mile and half short of the white farmstead, ascended towards the leaner pastures, and so on to the cottage of his mother.

She had reached home after her day's milking at the outlying dairy, and was washing cabbage at the doorway in the declining light. 'Hold up the net a moment,' she said, without preface, as the boy came up.

He flung down his bundle, held the edge of the cabbage-net, and as she filled its meshes with the dripping leaves she went on, 'Well, did you see her?'

'Yes; quite plain.'

'Is she ladylike?'

'Yes; and more. A lady complete.'

'Is she young?'

'Well, she's growed up, and her ways be quite a woman's.'

'Of course. What colour is her hair and face?'

'Her hair is lightish, and her face is comely as a live doll's.'

'Her eyes, then, are not dark like mine?'

'No – of a bluish turn, and her mouth is very nice and red; and when she smiles, her teeth show white.'

'Is she tall?' said the woman sharply.

'I couldn't see. She was sitting down.'

'Then do you go to Holmstoke church tomorrow morning: she's sure to be there. Go early and notice her walking in, and come home and tell me if she's taller than I.'

'Very well, mother. But why don't you go and see for yourself?'

'*I* go to see her! I wouldn't look up at her if she were to pass my window this instant. She was with Mr Lodge, of course. What did he say or do?'

'Just the same as usual.'

'Took no notice of you?'

'None.'

Next day the mother put a clean shirt on the boy, and started him off for Holmstoke church. He reached the ancient little pile when the door was just being opened and he was the first to enter. Taking his seat by the font, he watched all the parishioners file in. The well-to-do Farmer Lodge came nearly last, and his young wife, who accompanied him, walked up the aisle with the shyness natural to a modest woman who had appeared thus for the first time. As all other eyes were fixed upon her, the youth's stare was not noticed now.

When he reached home his mother said, 'Well?' before he had entered the room.

'She is not tall. She is rather short,' he replied.

'Ah!' said his mother, with satisfaction.

'But she's very pretty – very. In fact she's lovely.' The youthful freshness of the yeoman's wife had evidently made an impression even on the somewhat hard nature of the boy.

'That's all I want to hear,' said his mother quickly. 'Now, spread the tablecloth. The hare you wired is very tender; but mind that nobody catches you. – You've never told me what sort of hands she had.'

'I have never seen 'em. She never took off her gloves.'

'What did she wear this morning?'

'A white bonnet and a silver-coloured gownd. It whewed and whistled so loud when it rubbed against the pews that the lady coloured up more than ever for very shame at the noise, and pulled it in to keep it from touching; but when she pushed into her seat, it whewed more than ever. Mr Lodge, he seemed pleased, and his waistcoat stuck out, and his great golden seals hung like a lord's; but she seemed to wish her noisy gownd anywhere but on her.'

'Not she! However, that will do now.'

These descriptions of the newly-married couple were continued from time to time by the boy at his mother's request, after any chance encounter he had had with them. But Rhoda Brook, though she might easily have seen young Mrs Lodge for herself by walking a couple of miles, would never attempt an excursion towards the quarter where the farmhouse lay. Neither did she, at the daily milking in the dairyman's yard on Lodge's outlying second farm, ever speak on the subject of the recent marriage. The dairyman, who rented the cows of Lodge, and knew perfectly the tall milkmaid's history, with manly kindliness always kept the gossip in the cow-barton from annoying Rhoda. But the atmosphere thereabout was full of the subject during the first days of Mrs Lodge's arrival, and from her boy's description and the casual words of the other milkers, Rhoda Brook could raise a mental image of the unconscious Mrs Lodge that was realistic as a photograph.

3. A VISION

One night, two or three weeks after the bridal return, when the boy was gone to bed, Rhoda sat a long time over the turf ashes that she had raked out in front of her to extinguish them. She contemplated so intently the new wife, as presented to her in her mind's eye over the embers, that she forgot the lapse of time. At last, wearied with her day's work, she too retired.

But the figure which had occupied her so much during this and the previous days was not to be banished at night. For the first time Gertrude Lodge visited the supplanted woman in her dreams. Rhoda Brook dreamed – since her assertion that she really saw, before falling asleep, was not to be believed – that the young wife, in the pale silk dress and white bonnet, but with features shockingly distorted, and wrinkled as by age, was sitting upon her chest as she lay. The pressure of Mrs Lodge's person grew heavier; the blue eyes peered cruelly into her face, and then the figure thrust forward its left hand mockingly, so as to make the wedding-ring it wore glitter in Rhoda's eyes. Maddened mentally, and nearly suffocated by pressure, the sleeper struggled; the incubus, still regarding her, withdrew to the foot of the bed, only, however, to come forward by degrees, resume her seat, and flash her left hand as before.

Gasping for breath, Rhoda, in a last desperate effort, swung out her right hand, seized the confronting spectre by its obtrusive left arm, and whirled it backward to the floor, starting up herself as she did so with a low cry.

'O, merciful heaven!' she cried, sitting on the edge of the bed in a cold sweat; 'that was not a dream – she was here!'

She could feel her antagonist's arm with her grasp even now – the very flesh and bone of it, as it seemed. She looked on the floor whither she had whirled the spectre, but there was nothing to be seen.

Rhoda Brook slept no more that night, and when she went milking at the next dawn they noticed how pale and haggard she looked. The milk that she drew quivered into the pail: her hand had not calmed even yet, and still retained the feel of the arm. She came home to breakfast as wearily as if it had been supper-time.

'What was that noise in your chimmer, mother, last night?' said her son. 'You fell off the bed, surely?'

'Did you hear anything fall? At what time?'

'Just when the clock struck two.'

She could not explain, and when the meal was done went silently about her household work, the boy assisting her, for he hated going afield on the farms, and she indulged his reluctance. Between eleven and twelve the garden-gate clicked, and she lifted her eyes to the window. At the bottom of the garden, within the gate, stood the woman of her vision. Rhoda seemed transfixed.

'Ah, she said she would come!' exclaimed the boy, also observing her.

'Said so – when? How does she know us?'

'I have seen and spoken to her. I talked to her yesterday.'

'I told you,' said the mother, flushing indignantly, 'never to speak to anybody in that house, or go near the place.'

'I did not speak to her till she spoke to me. And I did not go near the place. I met her in the road.'

'What did you tell her?'

'Nothing. She said, "Are you the poor boy who had to bring the heavy load from market?" And she looked at my boots, and said they would not keep my feet dry if it came on wet, because they were so cracked. I told her I lived with my mother, and we had enough to do to keep ourselves, and that's how it was; and she said then, "I'll come and bring you some better boots, and see your mother." She gives away things to other folks in the meads besides us.'

Mrs Lodge was by this time close to the door – not in her silk, as Rhoda had dreamt of in the bed-chamber, but in a morning hat, and gown of common light material, which became her better than silk. On her arm she carried a basket.

The impression remaining from the night's experience was still strong. Brook had almost expected to see the wrinkles, the scorn, and the cruelty on her visitor's face. She would have escaped an interview had escape been possible. There was, however, no back door to the cottage, and in an instant the boy had lifted the latch to Mrs Lodge's gentle knock.

'I see I have come to the right house,' said she, glancing at the lad, and smiling. 'But I was not sure till you opened the door.'

The figure and action were those of the phantom; but her voice was so indescribably sweet, her glance so winning, her smile so tender, so unlike that of Rhoda's midnight visitant, that the latter could hardly believe the evidence of her senses. She was truly glad that she had not hidden away in sheer aversion, as she had been inclined to do. In her basket Mrs Lodge brought the pair of boots that she had promised to the boy, and other useful articles.

At these proofs of a kindly feeling towards her and hers Rhoda's heart reproached her bitterly. This innocent young thing should have her blessing and not her curse. When she left them a light seemed gone from the dwelling. Two days later she came again to know if the boots fitted, and less than a fortnight after that paid Rhoda another call. On this occasion the boy was absent.

'I walk a good deal,' said Mrs Lodge, 'and your house is the nearest outside our own parish. I hope you are well. You don't look quite well.'

Rhoda said she was well enough, and, indeed, though the paler of the two, there was more of the strength that endures in her well-defined features and large frame than in the soft-cheeked young woman before her. The conversation became quite confidential as regarded their powers and weaknesses; and when Mrs Lodge was leaving, Rhoda said, 'I hope you will find this air agree with you, ma'am, and not suffer from the damp of the water-meads.'

The younger one replied that there was not much doubt of it, her general health being usually good. 'Though, now you remind me,' she added, 'I have one little ailment which puzzles me. It is nothing serious, but I cannot make it out.'

She uncovered her left hand and arm, and their outline confronted Rhoda's gaze as the exact original of the limb she had beheld and seized in her dream. Upon the pink round surface of the arm were faint marks of an unhealthy colour, as if produced by a rough grasp. Rhoda's eyes became riveted on the discolorations; she fancied that she discerned in them the shape of her own four fingers.

'How did it happen?' she said mechanically.

'I cannot tell,' replied Mrs Lodge, shaking her head. 'One night when I was sound asleep, dreaming I was away in some strange place, a pain suddenly shot into my arm there, and was so keen as to awaken me. I must have struck it in the daytime, I suppose, though I don't remember doing so.' She added, laughing, 'I tell my dear husband that it looks just as if he had flown into a rage and struck me there. O, I daresay it will soon disappear.'

'Ha, ha! Yes. . . On what night did it come?'

Mrs Lodge considered, and said it would be a fortnight ago on the morrow. 'When I awoke I could not remember where I was,' she added, 'till the clock striking two reminded me.'

She had named the night and the hour and Rhoda's spectral encounter, and Brook felt like a guilty thing. The artless disclosure startled her; she did not reason on the freaks of coincidence, and all the scenery of that ghastly night returned with double vividness to her mind.

'O, can it be,' she said to herself, when her visitor had departed, 'that I exercise a malignant power over people against my own will?' She knew that she had been slily called a witch since her fall; but never having understood why that particular stigma had been attached to her, it had passed disregarded. Could this be the explanation, and had such things as this ever happened before?

4. A SUGGESTION

The summer drew on, and Rhoda Brook almost dreaded to meet Mrs Lodge again, notwithstanding that her feeling for the young wife amounted wellnigh to affection. Something in her own individuality seemed to convict Rhoda of crime. Yet a fatality sometimes would direct the steps of the latter to the outskirts of Holmstoke whenever she left her house for any other purpose than her daily work, and hence it happened that their next encounter was out of doors. Rhoda could not avoid the subject which had so mystified her, and after the first few words she stammered, 'I hope your – arm is well again, ma'am?' She had perceived with consternation that Gertrude Lodge carried her left arm stiffly.

'No; it is not quite well. Indeed, it is no better at all; it is rather worse. It pains me dreadfully sometimes.'

'Perhaps you had better go to a doctor, ma'am.'

She replied that she had already seen a doctor. Her husband had insisted upon her going to one. But the surgeon had not seemed to understand the afflicted limb at all; he had told her to bathe it in hot water, and she had bathed it, but the treatment had done no good.

'Will you let me see it?' said the milkwoman.

Mrs Lodge pushed up her sleeve and disclosed the place, which was a few inches above the wrist. As soon as Rhoda Brook saw it, she could hardly preserve her composure. There was nothing of the nature of a wound, but the arm at that point had a shrivelled look, and the outline of the four fingers appeared more distinct than at the former time. Moreover, she fancied that they were imprinted in precisely the relative position of her clutch upon the arm in the trance: the first finger towards Gertrude's wrist, and the fourth towards her elbow.

What the impress resembled seemed to have struck Gertrude herself since their last meeting. 'It looks almost like finger-marks,' she said; adding with a faint laugh, 'My husband says it is as if some witch, or the devil himself, had taken hold of me there, and blasted the flesh.'

Rhoda shivered. 'That's fancy,' she said hurriedly. 'I wouldn't mind it, if I were you.'

'I shouldn't so much mind it,' said the younger, with hesitation, 'if – if I hadn't a notion that it makes my husband – dislike me – no, love me less. Men think so much of personal appearance.'

'Some do – he for one.'

'Yes; and he was very proud of mine, at first.'

'Keep your arm covered from his sight.'

'Ah – he knows the disfigurement is there!' She tried to hide the tears that filled her eyes.

'Well, ma'am, I earnestly hope it will go away soon.'

And so the milkwoman's mind was chained anew to the subject by a horrid sort of spell as she returned home. The sense of having been guilty of an act of malignity increased, affect as she might to ridicule her superstition. In her secret heart Rhoda did not altogether object to a slight diminution of her successor's beauty, by whatever means it had come about; but she did not wish to inflict upon her physical pain. For though this pretty young woman had rendered impossible any reparation which Lodge might have made Rhoda for his past conduct, everything like resentment at the unconscious usurpation had quite passed away from the elder's mind.

If the sweet and kindly Gertrude Lodge only knew of the dream-scene in the bed-chamber, what would she think? Not to inform her of it seemed treachery in the presence of her friendliness; but tell she could not of her own accord – neither could she devise a remedy.

She mused upon the matter the greater part of the night, and the next day, after the morning milking, set out to obtain another glimpse of Gertrude Lodge if she could, being held to her by a gruesome fascination. By watching the house from a distance the milkmaid was presently able to discern the farmer's wife in a ride she was taking alone – probably to join her husband in some distant field. Mrs Lodge perceived her, and cantered in her direction.

'Good morning, Rhoda!' Gertrude said, when she had come up. 'I was going to call.'

Rhoda noticed that Mrs Lodge held the reins with some difficulty.

'I hope – the bad arm,' said Rhoda.

'They tell me there is possibly one way by which I might be able to find out the cause, and so perhaps the cure, of it,' replied the other anxiously. 'It is by going to some clever man over in Egdon Heath. They did not know if he was still alive – and I cannot remember his name at this moment; but they said that you knew more of his movements than anybody else hereabout, and could tell me if he were still to be consulted. Dear me – what was his name? But you know.'

'Not Conjuror Trendle?' said her thin companion, turning pale.

'Trendle – yes. Is he alive?'

'I believe so,' said Rhoda, with reluctance.

'Why do you call him conjuror?'

'Well – they say – they used to say he was a – he had powers other folks have not.'

'Oh, how could my people be so superstitious as to recommend a man of that sort! I thought they meant some medical man. I shall think no more of him.'

Rhoda looked relieved, and Mrs Lodge rode on. The milk-woman had inwardly seen, from the moment she heard of her having been mentioned as a reference for this man, that there must exist a sarcastic feeling among the workfolk that a sorceress would know the whereabouts of the exorcist. They suspected her, then. A short time ago this would have given no concern to a woman of her common sense. But she had a haunting reason to be superstitious now; and she had been seized with sudden dread that this Conjuror Trendle might name her as the malignant influence which was blasting the fair person of Gertrude and so lead her friend to hate her for ever, and to treat her as some fiend in human shape.

But all was not over. Two days after, a shadow intruded into the window-pattern thrown on Rhoda Brook's floor by the afternoon sun. The woman opened the door at once, almost breathlessly.

'Are you alone?' said Gertrude. She seemed to be no less harassed and anxious than Brook herself.

'Yes,' said Rhoda.

The place on my arm seems worse, and troubles me!' the young farmer's wife went on. 'It is so mysterious! I do hope it will not be an incurable wound. I have again been thinking of what they said about Conjuror Trendle. I don't really believe in such men, but I should not mind just visiting him, for curiosity – though on no account must my husband know. Is it far to where he lives?'

'Yes – five miles,' said Rhoda backwardly. 'In the heart of Egdon.'

'Well, I should have to walk. Could you not go with me to show me the way – say tomorrow afternoon?'

'O, not I – that is,' the milkwoman murmured, with a start of dismay. Again the dread seized her that something to do with her fierce act in the dream might be revealed, and her character in the eyes of the most useful friend she had ever had be ruined irretrievably.

Mrs Lodge urged, and Rhoda finally assented, though with much misgiving. Sad as the journey would be to her, she could not conscientiously stand in the way of a possible remedy for her patron's strange affliction. It was agreed that, to escape suspicion of their mystic intent, they should meet at the edge of the heath at the corner of a plantation which was visible from the spot where they now stood.

5. CONJUROR TRENDLE

By the next afternoon Rhoda would have done anything to escape this inquiry. But she had promised to go. Moreover, there was a horrid fascination at times in becoming instrumental in throwing such possible light on her own character as would reveal her to be something greater in the occult world than she had ever herself suspected.

She started just before the time of day mentioned between them, and half-an-hour's brisk walking brought her to the south-eastern extension of the Egdon tract of country, where the fir plantation was. A slight figure, cloaked and veiled, was already there. Rhoda recognized, almost with a shudder, that Mrs Lodge bore her left arm in a sling.

They hardly spoke to each other, and immediately set out on their climb into the interior of this solemn country, which stood high above the rich alluvial soil they had left half-an-hour before. It was a long walk; thick clouds made the atmosphere dark, though it was as yet only early afternoon; and the wind howled dismally over the slopes of the heath – not improbably the same heath which had witnessed the agony of the Wessex King Ina, presented to after-ages as Lear. Gertrude Lodge talked most, Rhoda replying with monosyllabic preoccupation. She had a strange dislike to walking on the side of her companion where hung the afflicted arm, moving round to the other when inadvertently near it. Much heather had been brushed by their feet when they descended upon a cart-track, beside which stood the house of the man they sought.

He did not profess his remedial practices openly, or care anything about their continuance, his direct interests being those of a dealer in furze, turf, 'sharp sand' and other local products. Indeed, he affected not to believe largely in his own powers, and when warts that had been shown him for cure miraculously disappeared – which it must be owned they infallibly did – he would say lightly, 'O, I only drink a glass of grog upon 'em at your expense – perhaps it's all chance,' and immediately turn the subject.

He was at home when they arrived, having in fact seen them descending into his valley. He was a grey-bearded man, with a reddish face, and he looked singularly at Rhoda the first moment he beheld her. Mrs Lodge told him her errand; and then with words of self-disparagement he examined her arm.

'Medicine can't cure it,' he said promptly. ''Tis the work of an enemy.'

Rhoda shrank into herself, and drew back.

'An enemy? What enemy?' asked Mrs Lodge.

He shook his head. 'That's best known to yourself,' he said. 'If you like, I can show the person to you, though I shall not myself know who it is. I can do no more; and don't wish to do that.'

She pressed him; on which he told Rhoda to wait outside where she stood, and took Mrs Lodge into the room. It opened immediately from the door; and, as the latter remained ajar, Rhoda Brook could see the proceedings without taking part in them. He brought a tumbler from the dresser, nearly filled it with water, and fetching an egg, prepared it in some private way; after which he broke it on the edge of the glass, so that the white went in and the yolk remained. As it was getting gloomy, he took the glass and its contents to the window, and told Gertrude to watch the mixture closely. They leant over the table together, and the milkwoman could see the opaline hue of the egg-fluid changing form as it sank in the water, but she was not near enough to define the shape that it assumed.

'Do you catch the likeness of any face or figure as you look?' demanded the conjuror of the young woman.

She murmured a reply, in tones so low as to be inaudible to Rhoda, and continued to gaze intently into the glass. Rhoda turned, and walked a few steps away.

When Mrs Lodge came out, and her face was met by the light, it appeared exceedingly pale – as pale as Rhoda's – against the sad dun shades of the upland's garniture. Trendle shut the door behind her, and they at once started homeward together. But Rhoda perceived that her companion had quite changed.

'Did he charge much?' she asked tentatively.

'O no – nothing. He would not take a farthing,' said Gertrude.

'And what did you see?' inquired Rhoda.

'Nothing I – care to speak of.' The constraint in her manner was remarkable; her face was so rigid as to wear an oldened aspect, faintly suggestive of the face in Rhoda's bed-chamber.

'Was it you who first proposed coming here?' Mrs Lodge suddenly inquired, after a long pause. 'How very odd, if you did!'

'No. But I am not sorry we have come, all things considered,' she replied. For the first time a sense of triumph possessed her, and she did not altogether deplore that the young thing at her side should learn that their lives had been antagonized by other influences than their own.

The subject was no more alluded to during the long and dreary walk home. But in some way or other a story was whispered about the manydairied lowland that winter that Mrs Lodge's gradual loss of the use of her left arm was owing to her being 'overlooked' by Rhoda Brook. The latter kept her own counsel about the incubus, but her face grew sadder and thinner; and in the spring she and her boy disappeared from the neighbourhood of Holmstoke.

6. A SECOND ATTEMPT

Half a dozen years passed away, and Mr and Mrs Lodge's married experience sank into prosiness, and worse. The farmer was usually gloomy and silent; the woman whom he had wooed for her grace and beauty was contorted and disfigured in the left limb; moreover, she had brought him no child, which rendered it likely that he would be the last of a family who had occupied that valley for some two hundred years. He thought of Rhoda Brook and her son; and feared this might be a judgment from heaven upon him.

The once blithe-hearted and enlightened Gertrude was changing into an irritable, superstitious woman, whose whole time was given to experimenting upon her ailment with every quack remedy she came across. She was honestly attached to her husband, and was ever secretly hoping against hope to win back his heart again by regaining some at least of her personal beauty. Hence it arose that her closet was lined with bottles, packets, and ointment-pots of every description – nay, bunches of mystic herbs, charms, and books of necromancy, which in her schoolgirl time she would have ridiculed as folly.

'Damned if you won't poison yourself with these apothecary messes and witch mixtures some time or other,' said her husband, when his eyes chanced to fall upon the multitudinous array.

She did not reply, but turned her sad, soft glance upon him in such heart-swollen reproach that he looked sorry for his words, and added, 'I only meant it for your good, you know, Gertrude.'

'I'll clear out the whole lot, and destroy them,' said she huskily, 'and try such remedies no more!'

'You want somebody to cheer you,' he observed. 'I once thought of adopting a boy; but he is too old now. And he is gone away I don't know where.'

She guessed to whom he alluded; for Rhoda Brook's story had in the course of years become known to her; though not a word had ever passed between her husband and herself on the subject. Neither had she ever spoken to him of her visit to Conjuror Trendle, and of what was revealed to her, or she thought was revealed to her, by that solitary heathman.

She was now five and twenty; but she seemed older. 'Six years of marriage, and only a few months of love,' she sometimes whispered to herself. And then she thought of the apparent cause, and said, with a tragic glance at her withering limb, 'If I could only again be as I was when he first saw me!'

She obediently destroyed her nostrums and charms; but there remained a hankering wish to try something else – some other sort of cure altogether. She had never revisited Trendle since she had been conducted to the house of the solitary by Rhoda against her will; but it now suddenly occurred to Gertrude that she would, in a last desperate effort at deliverance from this seeming curse, again seek out the man, if he yet lived. He was entitled to a certain credence, for the indistinct form he had raised in the glass had undoubtedly resembled the only woman in the world who – as she now knew, though not then – could have a reason for bearing her ill-will. The visit should be paid.

This time she went alone, though she nearly got lost on the heath, and roamed a considerable distance out of her way. Trendle's house was reached at last, however; he was not indoors, and instead of waiting at the cottage, she went to where his bent figure was pointed out to her at work a long way off. Trendle remembered her, and laying down the handful of furze-roots which he was gathering and throwing into a heap, he offered to accompany her in her homeward direction, as the distance was considerable and the days were short. So they walked together, his head bowed nearly to the earth, and his form of a colour with it.

'You can send away warts and other excrescences, I know,' she said; 'why can't you send away this?' And the arm was uncovered.

'You think too much of my powers!' said Trendle; 'and I am old and weak now, too. No, no; it is too much for me to attempt in my own person. What have ye tried?'

She named to him some of the hundred medicaments and counter-spells which she had adopted from time to time. He shook his head.

'Some were good enough,' he said approvingly; 'but not many of them for such as this. This is of the nature of a blight, not of the nature of a wound, and if you ever do throw it off, it will be all at once.'

'If I only could!'

'There is only one chance of doing it known to me. It has never failed in kindred afflictions – that I can declare. But it is hard to carry out, and especially for a woman.'

'Tell me!' said she.

'You must touch with the limb the neck of a man who's been hanged.'

She started a little at the image he had raised.

'Before he's cold – just after he's cut down,' continued the conjuror impassively.

'How can that do good?'

'It will turn the blood and change the constitution. But, as I say, to do it is hard. You must go to the jail when there's a hanging, and wait for him when he's brought off the gallows. Lots have done it, though perhaps not such pretty women as you. I used to send dozens for skin complaints. But that was in former times. The last I sent was in '13 – near twelve years ago.'

He had no more to tell her, and, when he had put her into a straight track homeward, turned and left her, refusing all money as at first.

7. A RIDE

The communication sank deep into Gertrude's mind. Her nature was rather a timid one; and probably of all remedies that the white wizard could have suggested there was not one which would have filled her with so much aversion as this, not to speak of the immense obstacles in the way of its adoption.

Casterbridge, the county-town, was a dozen or fifteen miles off; and though in those days, when men were executed for horse-stealing, arson, and burglary, an assize seldom passed without a hanging, it was not likely that she could get access to the body of the criminal unaided. And the fear of her husband's anger made her reluctant to breathe a word of Trendle's suggestion to him or to anybody about him.

She did nothing for months, and patiently bore her disfigurement as before. But her woman's nature, craving for renewed love, through the medium of renewed beauty (she was but twenty-five), was ever stimulating her to try what, at any rate, could hardly do her any harm. 'What came by a spell will go by a spell surely,' she would say. Whenever her imagination pictured the act she shrank in terror from the possibility of it; then the words of the conjuror, 'It will turn your blood,' were seen to be capable of a scientific no less than a ghastly interpretation; the mastering desire returned, and urged her on again.

There was at this time but one county paper, and that her husband only occasionally borrowed. But old-fashioned days had old-fashioned means, and news was extensively conveyed by word of mouth from market to market, or from fair to fair, so that, whenever such an event as execution was about to take place, few within a radius of twenty miles were ignorant of the coming sight; and so far as Holmstoke was concerned, some enthusiasts had been known to walk all the way to Casterbridge and back in one day, solely to witness the spectacle. The next assizes were in March; and when Gertrude Lodge heard that they had been held, she inquired stealthily at the inn as to the result, as soon as she could find opportunity.

She was, however, too late. The time at which the sentences were to be carried out had arrived, and to make the journey and obtain admission at such short notice required at least her husband's assistance. She dared not tell him, for she had found by delicate experiment that these smouldering village beliefs made him furious if mentioned, partly because he half entertained them himself. It was therefore necessary to wait for another opportunity.

Her determination received a fillip from learning that two epileptic children had attended from this very village of Holmstoke many years before with beneficial results, though the experiment had been strongly condemned by the neighbouring clergy. April, May, June passed; and it is no overstatement to say that by the end of the last-named month Gertrude wellnigh longed for the death of a fellow-creature. Instead of her formal prayers each night, her unconscious prayer was, 'O Lord, hang some guilty or innocent person soon!'

This time she made earlier inquiries, and was altogether more systematic in her proceedings. Moreover, the season was summer, between the haymaking and the harvest, and in the leisure thus afforded him her husband had been holiday-taking away from home.

The assizes were in July, and she went to the inn as before. There was to be one execution – only one – for arson.

Her greatest problem was not how to get to Casterbridge, but what means she should adopt for obtaining admission to the jail. Though access for such purposes had formerly never been denied, the custom had fallen into desuetude; and in contemplating her possible difficulties, she was again almost driven to fall back upon her husband. But, on sounding him about the assizes, he was so uncommunicative, so more than usually cold, that she did not proceed, and decided that whatever she did she would do alone.

Fortune, obdurate hitherto, showed her unexpected favour. On the Thursday before the Saturday fixed for the execution, Lodge remarked to her that he was going away from home for another day or two on business at a fair, and that he was sorry he could not take her with him.

She exhibited on this occasion so much readiness to stay at home that he looked at her in surprise. Time had been when she would have shown deep disappointment at the loss of such a jaunt. However, he lapsed into his usual taciturnity, and on the day named left Holmstoke.

It was now her turn. She at first had thought of driving, but on reflection held that driving would not do, since it would necessitate her keeping to the turnpike-road, and so increase by tenfold the risk of her ghastly errand being found out. She decided to ride, and avoid the beaten track, notwithstanding that in her husband's stables there was no animal just at present which by any stretch of imagination could be considered a lady's mount, in spite of his promise before marriage to always keep a mare for her. He had, however, many cart-horses, fine ones of their kind; and among the rest was a serviceable creature, an equine Amazon, with a back as broad as a sofa, on which Gertrude had occasionally taken an airing when unwell. This horse she chose.

On Friday afternoon one of the men brought it round. She was dressed, and before going down looked at her shrivelled arm. 'Ah!' she said to it, 'if it had not been for you this terrible ordeal would have been saved me!'

When strapping up the bundle in which she carried a few articles of clothing, she took occasion to say to the servant, 'I take these in case I should not get back tonight from the person I am going to visit. Don't be alarmed if I am not in by ten, and close up the house as usual. I shall be at home tomorrow for certain.' She meant then to tell her husband privately; the deed accomplished was not like the deed projected. He would almost certainly forgive her.

And then the pretty palpitating Gertrude Lodge went from her husband's homestead; but though her goal was Casterbridge she did not take the direct route thither through Stickleford. Her cunning course at first was in precisely the opposite direction. As soon as she was out of sight, however, she turned to the left, by a road which led into Egdon, and on entering the heath wheeled round, and set out in the true course, due westerly. A more private way down the county could not be imagined; and so to direction, she had merely to keep her horse's head to a point a little to the right of the sun. She knew that she would light upon a furze-cutter or cottager of some sort from time to time, from whom she might correct her bearing.

Though the date was comparatively recent, Egdon was much less fragmentary in character than now. The attempts – successful and otherwise – at cultivation on the lower slopes, which intrude and break up the original heath into small detached heaths, had not been carried far; Enclosure Acts had not taken effect, and the banks and fences which now exclude the cattle of those villagers who formerly enjoyed rights of commonage thereon, and the carts of those who had turbary privileges which kept them in firing all the year round, were not erected. Gertrude, therefore, rode along with no other obstacles than the prickly furzebushes, the mats of heather, the white water-courses, and the natural steeps and declivities of the ground.

Her horse was sure, if heavy-footed and slow, and though a draught animal, was easy-paced; had it been otherwise, she was not a woman who could have ventured to ride over such a bit of country with a half-dead arm. It was therefore nearly eight o'clock when she drew rein to breathe her bearer on the last outlying high point of heath-land towards Casterbridge, previous to leaving Egdon for the cultivated valleys.

She halted before a pool called Rushy-pond, flanked by the ends of two hedges; a railing ran through the centre of the pond, dividing it in half. Over the railing she saw the low green country; over the green trees the roofs of the town; over the roofs a white flat façade, denoting the entrance to the county jail. On the roof of this front specks were moving about; they seemed to be workmen erecting something. Her flesh crept. She descended slowly, and was soon amid corn-fields and pastures. In another half-hour, when it was almost dusk, Gertrude reached the White Hart, the first inn of the town on that side.

Little surprise was excited by her arrival; farmers' wives rode on horseback then more than they do now; though, for that matter, Mrs Lodge was not imagined to be a wife at all; the innkeeper supposed her some harum-skarum young woman who had come to attend 'hang-fair' next day. Neither her husband nor herself ever dealt in Casterbridge market, so that she was unknown. While dismounting she beheld a crowd of boys standing at the door of a harness-maker's shop just above the inn, looking inside it with deep interest.

'What is going on there?' she asked of the ostler.

'Making the rope for tomorrow.'

She throbbed responsively, and contracted her arm.

''Tis sold by the inch afterwards,' the man continued. 'I could get you a bit, miss, for nothing, if you'd like?'

She hastily repudiated any such wish, all the more from a curious creeping feeling that the condemned wretch's destiny was becoming interwoven with her own; and having engaged a room for the night, sat down to think.

Up to this time she had formed but the vaguest notions about her means of obtaining access to the prison. The words of the cunning-man returned to her mind. He had implied that she should use her beauty, impaired though it was, as a pass-key. In her inexperience she knew little about jail functionaries; she had heard of a high-sheriff and an under-sheriff, but dimly only. She knew, however, that there must be a hangman, and to the hangman she determined to apply.

8. A WATER-SIDE HERMIT

At this date, and for several years after, there was a hangman to almost every jail. Gertrude found, on inquiry, that the Casterbridge official dwelt in a lonely cottage by a deep slow river flowing under the cliff on which the prison buildings were situate – the stream being the self-same one, though she did not know it, which watered the Stickleford and Holmstoke meads lower down in its course.

Having changed her dress, and before she had eaten or drunk – for she could not take her ease till she had ascertained some particulars – Gertrude pursued her way by a path along the water-side to the cottage indicated. Passing thus the outskirts of the jail, she discerned on the level roof over the gateway three rectangular lines against the sky, where the specks had been moving in her distant view; she recognized what the erection was, and passed quickly on. Another hundred yards brought her to the executioner's house, which a boy pointed out. It stood close to the same stream, and was hard by a weir, the waters of which emitted a steady roar.

While she stood hesitating the door opened, and an old man came forth, shading a candle with one hand. Locking the door on the outside, he turned to a flight of wooden steps fixed against the end of the cottage, and began to ascend them, this being evidently the staircase to his bedroom. Gertrude hastened forward, but by the time she reached the foot of the ladder he was at the top. She called to him loudly enough to be heard above the roar of the weir; he looked down and said, 'What d'ye want here?'

'To speak to you a minute.'

The candlelight, such as it was, fell upon her imploring, pale, upturned face, and Davies (as the hangman was called) backed down the ladder. 'I was just going to bed,' he said. '"Early to bed and early to rise", but I don't mind stopping a minute for such a one as you. Come into house.' He reopened the door, and preceded her to the room within.

The implements of his daily work, which was that of a jobbing gardener, stood in a corner, and seeing probably that she looked rural, he said, 'If you want me to undertake country work I can't come, for I never leave Casterbridge for gentle nor simple – not I. My real calling is officer of justice,' he added formally.

'Yes, yes! That's it. Tomorrow!'

'Ah! I thought so. Well, what's the matter about that? 'Tis no use to come here about the knot – folks do come continually, but I tell 'em one knot is as merciful as another if ye keep it under the ear. Is the unfortunate man a relation; or, I should say, perhaps' (looking at her dress) 'a person who's been in your employ?'

'No. What time is the execution?'

'The same as usual – twelve o'clock, or as soon after as the London mail-coach gets in. We always wait for that, in case of a reprieve.'

'O – a reprieve – I hope not!' she said involuntarily.

'Well, – hee, hee! – as a matter of business, so do I! But still, if ever a young fellow deserved to be let off, this one does; only just turned eighteen, and only present by chance when the rick was fired. Howsomever, there's not much risk of it, as they are obliged to make an example of him, there having been so much destruction of property that way lately.'

'I mean,' she explained, 'that I want to touch him for a charm, a cure of an affliction, by the advice of a man who has proved the virtue of the remedy.'

'O yes, miss! Now I understand. I've had such people come in past years. But it didn't strike me that you looked of a sort to require blood-turning. What's the complaint? The wrong kind for this, I'll be bound.'

'My arm.' She reluctantly showed the withered skin.

'Ah! – 'tis all a-scram!' said the hangman, examining it.

'Yes,' said she.

'Well,' he continued, with interest, 'that *is* the class o' subject, I'm bound to admit! I like the look of the wownd; it is truly as suitable for the cure as any I ever saw. 'Twas a knowing-man that sent 'ee, whoever he was.'

'You can contrive for me all that's necessary?' she said breathlessly.

'You should really have gone to the governor of the jail, and your doctor with 'ee, and given your name and address – that's how it used to be done, if I recollect. Still, perhaps, I can manage it for a trifling fee.'

'O, thank you! I would rather do it this way, as I should like it kept private.'

'Lover not to know, eh?'

'No – husband.'

'Aha! Very well. I'll get 'ee a touch of the corpse.'

'Where is it now?' she said, shuddering.

'It? – *he*, you mean; he's living yet. Just inside that little small winder up there in the glum.' He signified the jail on the cliff above.

She thought of her husband and her friends. 'Yes, of course,' she said; 'and how am I to proceed?'

He took her to the door. 'Now, do you be waiting at the little wicket in the wall, that you'll find up there in the lane, not later than one o'clock. I will open it from the inside, as I shan't come home to dinner till he's cut down. Good-night. Be punctual; and if you don't want anybody to know 'ee, wear a veil. Ah – once I had such a daughter as you!'

She went away, and climbed the path above, to assure herself that she would be able to find the wicket next day. Its outline was soon visible to her – a narrow opening in the outer wall of the prison precincts. The steep was so great that, having reached the wicket, she stopped a moment to breathe; and, looking back upon the water-side cot, saw the hangman again ascending his outdoor staircase. He entered the loft or chamber to which it led, and in a few minutes extinguished his light.

The town clock struck ten, and she returned to the White Hart as she had come.

9. A RENCOUNTER

It was one o'clock on Saturday. Gertrude Lodge, having been admitted to the jail as above described, was sitting in a waiting-room within the second gate, which stood under a classic archway of ashlar, then comparatively modern, and bearing the inscription, 'COVNTY JAIL: 1793'. This had been the façade she saw from the heath the day before. Near at hand was a passage to the roof on which the gallows stood.

The town was thronged, and the market suspended; but Gertrude had seen scarcely a soul. Having kept her room till the hour of the appointment, she had proceeded to the spot by a way which avoided the open space below the cliff where the spectators had gathered; but she could, even now, hear the multitudinous babble of their voices, out of which rose at intervals the hoarse croak of a single voice uttering the words, 'Last dying speech and confession!' There had been no reprieve, and the execution was over; but the crowd still waited to see the body taken down.

Soon the persistent woman heard a trampling overhead, then a hand beckoned to her, and, following directions, she went out and crossed the inner paved court beyond the gatehouse, her knees trembling so that she could scarcely walk. One of her arms was out of its sleeve, and only covered by her shawl.

On the spot at which she had now arrived were two trestles, and before she could think of their purpose she heard heavy feet descending stairs somewhere at her back. Turn her head she would not, or could not, and, rigid in this position, she was conscious of a rough coffin passing her shoulder, borne by four men. It was open, and in it lay the body of a young man, wearing the smockfrock of a rustic, and fustian breeches. The corpse had been thrown into the coffin so hastily that the skirt of the smockfrock was hanging over. The burden was temporarily deposited on the trestles.

By this time the young woman's state was such that a gray mist seemed to float before her eyes, on account of which, and the veil she wore, she could scarcely discern anything: it was as though she had nearly died, but was held up by a sort of galvanism.

'Now!' said a voice close at hand, and she was just conscious that the word had been addressed to her.

By a last strenuous effort she advanced, at the same time hearing persons approaching behind her. She bared her poor curst arm; and Davies, uncovering the face of the corpse, took Gertrude's hand, and held it so that her arm lay across the dead man's neck, upon a line the colour of an unripe blackberry, which surrounded it.

Gertrude shrieked: 'the turn o' the blood', predicted by the conjuror, had taken place. But at that moment a second shriek rent the air of the enclosure: it was not Gertrude's, and its effect upon her was to make her start round.

Immediately behind her stood Rhoda Brook, her face drawn, and her eyes red with weeping. Behind Rhoda stood Gertrude's own husband; his countenance lined, his eyes dim, but without a tear.

'D—n you! what are you doing here?' he said hoarsely.

'Hussy – to come between us and our child now!' cried Rhoda. 'This is the meaning of what Satan showed me in the vision! You are like her at last!' And clutching the bare arm of the younger woman, she pulled her unresistingly back against the wall. Immediately Brook had loosened her hold the fragile young Gertrude slid down against the feet of her husband. When he lifted her up she was unconscious.

The mere sight of the twain had been enough to suggest to her that the dead young man was Rhoda's son. At that time the relatives of an executed convict had the privilege of claiming the body for burial, if they chose to do so; and it was for this purpose that Lodge was awaiting the inquest with Rhoda. He had been summoned by her as soon as the young man was taken in the crime, and at different times since; and he had attended in court during the trial. This was the 'holiday' he had been indulging in of late. The two wretched parents had wished to avoid exposure; and hence had come themselves for the body, a waggon and sheet for its conveyance and covering being in waiting outside.

Gertrude's case was so serious that it was deemed advisable to call to her the surgeon who was at hand. She was taken out of the jail into the town; but she never reached home alive. Her delicate vitality, sapped perhaps by the paralyzed arm, collapsed under the double shock that followed the severe strain, physical and mental, to which she had subjected herself during the previous twenty-four hours. Her blood had been 'turned' indeed – too far. Her death took place in the town three days after.

Her husband was never seen in Casterbridge again; once only in the old market-place at Anglebury, which he had so much frequented, and very seldom in pubiic anywhere. Burdened at first with moodiness and remorse, he eventually changed for the better, and appeared as a chastened and thoughtful man. Soon after attending the funeral of his poor young wife he took steps towards giving up the farms in Holmstoke and the adjoining parish, and, having sold every head of his stock, he went away to Port-Bredy, at the other end of the county, living there in solitary lodgings till his death two years later of a painless decline. It was then found that he had bequeathed the whole of his not inconsiderable property to a reformatory for boys, subject to the payment of a small annuity to Rhoda Brook, if she could be found to claim it.

For some time she could not be found; but eventually she reappeared in her old parish, – absolutely refusing, however, to have anything to do with the provision made for her. Her monotonous milking at the dairy was resumed, and followed for many long years, till her form became bent, and her once abundant dark hair white and worn away at the forehead – perhaps by long pressure against the cows. Here, sometimes, those who knew her experiences would stand and observe her, and wonder what sombre thoughts were beating inside that impassive, wrinkled brow, to the rhythm of the alternating milk-streams.

Blackwood's Magazine,
JANUARY 1888

FELLOW-TOWNSMEN

I

The shepherd on the east hill could shout out lambing intelligence to the shepherd on the west hill, over the intervening town chimneys, without great inconvenience to his voice, so nearly did the steep pastures encroach upon the burghers' backyards. And at night it was possible to stand in the very midst of the town and hear from their native paddocks on the lower levels of greensward the mild lowing of the farmer's heifers, and the profound, warm blowings of breath in which those creatures indulge. But the community which had jammed itself in the valley thus flanked formed a veritable town, with a real mayor and corporation, and a staple manufacture.

During a certain damp evening five-and-thirty years ago, before the twilight was far advanced, a pedestrian of professional appearance, carrying a small bag in his hand and an elevated umbrella, was descending one of these hills by the turnpike road when he was overtaken by a phaeton.

'Hullo, Downe – is that you?' said the driver of the vehicle, a young man of pale and refined appearance. 'Jump up here with me, and ride down to your door.'

The other turned a plump, cheery, rather self-indulgent face over his shoulder towards the hailer.

'O, good evening, Mr Barnet – thanks,' he said, and mounted beside his acquaintance.

They were fellow-burgesses of the town which lay beneath them, but though old and very good friends they were differently circumstanced. Barnet was a richer man than the struggling young lawyer Downe, a fact which was to some extent perceptible in Downe's manner towards his companion, though nothing of it ever showed in Barnet's manner towards the solicitor. Barnet's position in the town was none of his own making; his father had been a very successful flax-merchant in the same place, where the trade was still carried on as briskly as the small capacities of its quarters would allow. Having acquired a fair fortune, old Mr Barnet had retired from business, bringing up his son as a gentleman-burgher, and, it must be added, as a well-educated, liberal-minded young man.

'How is Mrs Barnet?' asked Downe.

'Mrs Barnet was very well when I left home,' the other answered constrainedly, exchanging his meditative regard of the horse for one of self-consciousness.

Mr Downe seemed to regret his inquiry, and immediately took up another thread of conversation. He congratulated his friend on his election as a councilman; he thought he had not seen him since that event took place; Mrs Downe had meant to call and congratulate Mrs Barnet, but he feared that she had failed to do so as yet.

Barnet seemed hampered in his replies. 'We should have been glad to see you. I – my wife would welcome Mrs Downe at any time, as you know. . . Yes, I am a member of the corporation – rather an inexperienced member, some of them say. It is quite true; and I should have declined the honour as premature – having other things on my hands just now, too – if it had not been pressed upon me so very heartily.'

'There is one thing you have on your hands which I can never quite see the necessity for,' said Downe, with good-humoured freedom. 'What the deuce do you want to build that new mansion for, when you have already got such an excellent house as the one you live in?'

Barnet's face acquired a warmer shade of colour; but as the question had been idly asked by the solicitor while regarding the surrounding flocks and fields, he answered after a moment with no apparent embarrassment –

'Well, we wanted to get out of the town, you know; the house I am living in is rather old and inconvenient.'

Mr Downe declared that he had chosen a pretty site for the new building. They would be able to see for miles and miles from the windows. Was he going to give it a name? He supposed so.

Barnet thought not. There was no other house near that was likely to be mistaken for it. And he did not care for a name.

'But I think it has a name!' Downe observed: 'I went past – when was it? – this morning; and I saw something, – "Château Ringdale", I think it was, stuck up on a board!'

'It was an idea she – we had for a short time,' said Barnet hastily. 'But we have decided finally to do without a name – at any rate such a name as that. It must have been a week ago that you saw it. It was taken down last Saturday. . . Upon that matter I am firm!' he added grimly.

Downe murmured in an unconvinced tone that he thought he had seen it yesterday.

Talking thus they drove into the town. The street was unusually still for the hour of seven in the evening; an increasing drizzle from the sea had prevailed since the afternoon, and now formed a gauze across the yellow lamps, and trickled with a gentle rattle down the heavy roofs of stone tile, that bent the house-ridges hollow-backed with its weight, and in some instances caused the walls to bulge outwards in the upper story. Their route took them past the little town-hall, the Black-Bull Hotel, and onward to the junction of a small street on the right, consisting of a row of those two-and-two windowed brick residences of no particular age, which are exactly alike wherever found, except in the people they contain.

'Wait – I'll drive you up to your door,' said Barnet, when Downe prepared to alight at the corner. He thereupon turned into the narrow street, when the faces of three little girls could be discerned close to the panes of a lighted window a few yards ahead, surmounted by that of a young matron, the gaze of all four being directed eagerly up the empty street. 'You are a fortunate fellow, Downe,' Barnet continued, as mother and children disappeared from the window to run to the door. 'You must be happy if any man is. I would give a hundred such houses as my new one to have a home like yours.'

'Well – yes, we get along pretty comfortably,' replied Downe complacently.

'That house, Downe, is none of my ordering,' Barnet broke out, revealing a bitterness hitherto suppressed, and checking the horse a moment to finish his speech before delivering up his passenger. 'The house I have already is good enough for me, as you supposed. It is my own freehold; it was built by my grandfather, and is stout enough for a castle. My father was born there, lived there, and died there. I was born there, and have always lived there; yet I must needs build a new one.'

'Why do you?' said Downe.

'Why do I? To preserve peace in the household. I do anything for that; but I don't succeed. I was firm in resisting "Château Ringdale", however; not that I would not have put up with the absurdity of the name, but it was too much to have your house christened after Lord Ringdale, because your wife once had a fancy for him. If you only knew everything, you would think all attempt at reconciliation hopeless. In your happy home you have had no such experiences; and God forbid that you ever should. See, here they are all ready to receive you!'

'Of course! And so will your wife be waiting to receive you,' said Downe. 'Take my word for it she will! And with a dinner prepared for you far better than mine.'

'I hope so,' Barnet replied dubiously.

He moved on to Downe's door, which the solicitor's family had already opened. Downe descended, but being encumbered with his bag and umbrella, his foot slipped, and he fell upon his knees in the gutter.

'O, my dear Charles!' said his wife, running down the steps; and, quite ignoring the presence of Barnet, she seized hold of her husband, pulled him to his feet, and kissed him, exclaiming, 'I hope you are not hurt, darling!' The children crowded round, chiming in piteously, 'Poor papa!'

'He's all right,' said Barnet, perceiving that Downe was only a little muddy, and looking more at the wife than at the husband. Almost at any other time – certainly during his fastidious bachelor years – he would have thought her a too demonstrative woman; but those recent circumstances of his own life to which he had just alluded made Mrs Downe's solicitude so affecting that his eye grew damp as he witnessed it. Bidding the lawyer and his family good-night he left them, and drove slowly into the main street towards his own house.

The heart of Barnet was sufficiently impressionable to be influenced by Downe's parting prophecy that he might not be so unwelcome home as he imagined: the dreary night might, at least on this one occasion, make Downe's forecast true. Hence it was in a suspense that he could hardly have believed possible that he halted at his door. On entering his wife was nowhere to be seen, and he inquired for her. The servant informed him that her mistress had the dressmaker with her, and would be engaged for some time.

'Dressmaker at this time of day!'

'She dined early, sir, and hopes you will excuse her joining you this evening.'

'But she knew I was coming tonight?'

'O yes, sir.'

'Go up and tell her I am come.'

The servant did so; but the mistress of the house merely transmitted her former words.

Barnet said nothing more, and presently sat down to his lonely meal, which was eaten abstractedly, the domestic scene he had lately witnessed still impressing him by its contrast with the situation here. His mind fell back into past years upon a certain pleasing and gentle being whose face would loom out of their shades at such times as these. Barnet turned in his chair, and looked with unfocused eyes in a direction southward from where he sat, as if he saw not the room but a long way beyond. 'I wonder if she lives there still!' he said.

2

He rose with a sudden rebelliousness, put on his hat and coat, and went out of the house, pursuing his way along the glistening pavement while eight o'clock was striking from St Mary's tower, and the apprentices and shopmen were slamming up the shutters from end to end of the town. In two minutes only those shops which could boast of no attendant save the master or the mistress remained with open eyes. These were ever somewhat less prompt to exclude customers than the others: for their owners' ears the closing hour had scarcely the cheerfulness that it possessed for the hired servants of the rest. Yet the night being dreary the delay was not for long, and their windows, too, blinked together one by one.

During this time Barnet had proceeded with decided step in a direction at right angles to the broad main thoroughfare of the town, by a long street leading due southward. Here, though his family had no more to do with the flax manufacture, his own name occasionally greeted him on gates and warehouses, being used allusively by small rising tradesmen as a recommendation, in such words as 'Smith, from Barnet & Co.' – 'Robinson, late manager at Barnet's'. The sight led him to reflect upon his father's busy life, and he questioned if it had not been far happier than his own.

The houses along the road became fewer, and presently open ground appeared between them on either side, the track on the right hand rising to a higher level till it merged in a knoll. On the summit a row of builders' scaffold-poles probed the indistinct sky like spears, and at their bases could be discerned the lower courses of a building lately begun. Barnet slackened his pace and stood for a few moments without leaving the centre of the road, apparently not much interested in the sight, till suddenly his eye was caught by a post in the fore part of the ground bearing a white board at the top. He went to the rails, vaulted over, and walked in far enough to discern painted upon the board 'Château Ringdale'.

A dismal irony seemed to lie in the words, and its effect was to irritate him. Downe, then, had spoken truly. He stuck his umbrella into the sod, and seized the post with both hands, as if intending to loosen and throw it down. Then, like one bewildered by an opposition which would exist none the less though its manifestations were removed, he allowed his arms to sink to his side.

'Let it be,' he said to himself. 'I have declared there shall be peace – if possible.'

Taking up his umbrella, he quietly left the enclosure, and went on his way, still keeping his back to the town. He had advanced with more decision since passing the new building, and soon a hoarse murmur rose upon the gloom; it was the sound of the sea. The road led to the harbour, at a distance of a mile from the town, from which the trade of the district was fed. After seeing the obnoxious name-board Barnet had forgotten to open his umbrella, and the rain tapped smartly on his hat, and occasionally stroked his face as he went on.

Though the lamps were still continued at the roadside they stood at wider intervals than before, and the pavement had given place to rough gravel. Every time he came to a lamp an increasing shine made itself visible upon his shoulders, till at last they quite glistened with wet. The murmur from the shore grew stronger, but it was still some distance off when he paused before one of the smallest of the detached houses by the wayside, standing in its own garden, the latter being divided from the road by a row of wooden palings. Scrutinizing the spot to ensure that he was not mistaken, he opened the gate and gently knocked at the cottage door.

When he had patiently waited minutes enough to lead any man in ordinary cases to knock again, the door was heard to open, though it was impossible to see by whose hand, there being no light in the passage. Barnet said at random, 'Does Miss Savile live here?'

A youthful voice assured him that she did live there, and by a sudden afterthought asked him to come in. It would soon get a light, it said: but the night being wet, mother had not thought it worth while to trim the passage lamp.

'Don't trouble yourself to get a light for me,' said Barnet hastily; 'it is not necessary at all. Which is Miss Savile's sitting-room?'

The young person, whose white pinafore could just be discerned, signified a door in the side of the passage, and Barnet went forward at the same moment, so that no light should fall upon his face. On entering the room he closed the door behind him, pausing till he heard the retreating footsteps of the child.

He found himself in an apartment which was simply and neatly, though not poorly furnished; everything, from the miniature chiffonnier to the shining little daguerreotype which formed the central ornament of the mantelpiece, being in scrupulous order. The picture was enclosed by a frame of embroidered card-board – evidently the work of feminine hands – and it was the portrait of a thin-faced, elderly lieutenant in the navy. From behind the lamp on the table a female form now rose into view, that of a young girl, and a resemblance between her and the portrait was early discoverable. She had been so absorbed in some occupation on the other side of the lamp as to have barely found time to realize her visitor's presence.

They both remained standing for a few seconds without speaking. The face that confronted Barnet had a beautiful outline; the Raffaelesque oval of its contour was remarkable for an English countenance, and that countenance housed in a remote country-road to an unheard-of harbour. But her features did not do justice to this splendid beginning: Nature had recollected that she was not in Italy; and the young lady's lineaments, though not so inconsistent as to make her plain, would have been accepted rather as pleasing than as correct. The preoccupied expression which, like images on the retina, remained with her for a moment after the state that caused it had ceased, now changed into a reserved, half-proud, and slightly indignant look, in which the blood diffused itself quickly across her cheek, and additional brightness broke the shade of her rather heavy eyes.

'I know I have no business here,' he said, answering the look. 'But I had a great wish to see you, and inquire how you were. You can give your hand to me, seeing how often I have held it in past days?'

'I would rather forget than remember all that, Mr Barnet,' she answered, as she coldly complied with the request. 'When I think of the circumstances of our last meeting, I can hardly consider it kind of you to allude to such a thing as our past – or, indeed, to come here at all.'

'There was no harm in it surely? I don't trouble you often, Lucy.'

'I have not had the honour of a visit from you for a very long time, certainly, and I did not expect it now,' she said, with the same stiffness in her air. 'I hope Mrs Barnet is very well?'

'Yes, yes!' he impatiently returned. 'At least, I suppose so – though I only speak from inference!'

'But she is your wife, sir,' said the young girl tremulously.

The unwonted tones of a man's voice in that feminine chamber had startled a canary that was roosting in its cage by the window; the bird awoke hastily, and fluttered against the bars. She went and stilled it by laying her face against the cage and murmuring a coaxing sound. It might partly have been done to still herself.

'I didn't come to talk of Mrs Barnet,' he pursued; 'I came to talk of you, of yourself alone; to inquire how you are getting on since your great loss.' And he turned towards the portrait of her father.

'I am getting on fairly well, thank you'.

The force of her utterance was scarcely borne out by her look; but Barnet courteously reproached himself for not having guessed a thing so natural; and to dissipate all embarrassment added, as he bent over the table, 'What were you doing when I came? – painting flowers, and by candlelight?'

'O no,' she said, 'not painting them – only sketching the outlines. I do that at night to save time – I have to get three dozen done by the end of the month.'

Barnet looked as if he regretted it deeply. 'You will wear your poor eyes out,' he said, with more sentiment than he had hitherto shown. 'You ought not to do it. There was a time when I should have said you must not. Well – I almost wish I had never seen light with my own eyes when I think of that.'

'Is this a time or place for recalling such matters?' she asked, with dignity. 'You used to have a gentlemanly respect for me, and for yourself. Don't speak any more as you have spoken, and don't come again. I cannot think that this visit is serious, or was closely considered by you.'

'Considered: well, I came to see you as an old and good friend – not to mince matters, to visit a woman I loved. Don't be angry! I could not help doing it, so many things brought you into my mind. . . This evening I fell in with an acquaintance, and when I saw how happy he was with his wife and family welcoming him home, though with only one-tenth of my income and chances, and thought what might have been in my case, it fairly broke down my discretion, and off I came here. Now I am here I feel that I am wrong to some extent. But the feeling that I should like to see you, and talk of those we used to know in common, was very strong.'

'Before that can be the case a little more time must pass,' said Miss Savile quietly; 'a time long enough for me to regard with some calmness what at present I remember far too impatiently – though it may be you almost forget it. Indeed, you must have forgotten it long before you acted as you did.' Her voice grew stronger and more vivacious as she added: 'But I am doing my best to forget it too, and I know I shall succeed from the progress I have made already!'

She had remained standing till now, when she turned and sat down, facing half away from him.

Barnet watched her moodily. 'Yes, it is only what I deserve,' he said. 'Ambition pricked me on – no, it was not ambition, it was wrongheadedness! Had I but reflected . . .' He broke out vehemently: 'But always remember this, Lucy: if you had written to me only one little line after that misunderstanding, I declare I should have come back to you. That ruined me!' He slowly walked as far as the little room would allow him to go, and remained with his eyes on the skirting.

'But, Mr Barnet, how could I write to you? There was no opening for my doing so.'

'Then there ought to have been,' said Barnet, turning. 'That was my fault!'

'Well, I don't know anything about that; but as there had been nothing said by me which required any explanation by letter, I did not send one. Everything was so indefinite, and feeling your position to be so much wealthier than mine, I fancied I might have mistaken your meaning. And when I heard of the other lady – a woman of whose family even you might be proud – I thought how foolish I had been, and said nothing.'

'Then I suppose it was destiny – accident – I don't know what, that separated us, dear Lucy. Anyhow, you were the woman I ought to have made my wife – and I let you slip, like the foolish man that I was!'

'O Mr Barnet,' she said, almost in tears, 'don't revive the subject to me; I am the wrong one to console you – think, sir, – you should not be here – it would be so bad for me if it were known!'

'It would – it would, indeed,' he said hastily. 'I am not right in doing this, and I won't do it again.'

'It is a very common folly of human nature, you know, to think the course you did *not* adopt must have been the best,' she continued, with gentle solicitude, as she followed him to the door of the room. 'And you don't know that I should have accepted you, even if you had asked me to be your wife.' At this his eye met hers, and she dropped her gaze. She knew that her voice belied her. There was a silence till she looked up to add, in a voice of soothing playfulness, 'My family was so much poorer than yours, even before I lost my dear father, that – perhaps your companions would have made it unpleasant for us on account of my deficiencies.'

'Your disposition would soon have won them round,' said Barnet.

She archly expostulated: 'Now, never mind my disposition; try to make it up with your wife! Those are my commands to you. And now you are to leave me at once.'

'I will. I must make the best of it all, I suppose,' he replied, more cheerfully than he had as yet spoken. 'But I shall never again meet with such a dear girl as you!' And he suddenly opened the door and left her alone. When his glance again fell on the lamps that were sparsely ranged along the dreary level road, his eyes were in a state which showed straw-like motes of light radiating from each flame into the surrounding air.

On the other side of the way Barnet observed a man under an umbrella, walking parallel with himself. Presently this man left the footway, and gradually converged on Barnet's course. The latter then saw that it was Charlson, a surgeon of the town, who owed him money. Charlson was a man not without ability; yet he did not prosper. Sundry circumstances stood in his way as a medical practitioner: he was needy; he was not a coddle; he gossiped with men instead of with women; he had married a stranger instead of one of the town young ladies; and he was given to conversational buffoonery. Moreover, his look was quite erroneous. Those only proper features in the family doctor, the quiet eye, and the thin straight passionless lips which never curl in public either for laughter or for scorn, were not his; he had a full-curved mouth, and a bold black eye that made timid people nervous. His companions were what in old times would have been called boon companions – an expression which, though of irreproachable root, suggests fraternization carried to the point of unscrupulousness. All this was against him in the little town of his adoption.

Charlson had been in difficulties, and to oblige him Barnet had put his name to a bill; and, as he had expected, was called upon to meet it when it fell due. It had been only a matter of fifty pounds, which Barnet could well afford to lose, and he bore no ill-will to the thriftless surgeon on account of it. But Charlson had a little too much brazen indifferentism in his composition to be altogether a desirable acquaintance.

'I hope to be able to make that little bill-business right with you in the course of three weeks, Mr Barnet,' said Charlson with hail-fellow friendliness.

Barnett replied good-naturedly that there was no hurry.

This particular three weeks had moved on in advance of Charlson's present with the precision of a shadow for some considerable time.

'I've had a dream,' Charlson continued. Barnet knew from his tone that the surgeon was going to begin his characteristic nonsense, and did not encourage him. 'I've had a dream,' repeated Charlson, who required no encouragement. 'I dreamed that a gentleman, who has been very kind to me, married a haughty lady in haste, before he had quite forgotten a nice little girl he knew before, and that one wet evening, like the present, as I was walking up the harbour-road, I saw him come out of that dear little girl's present abode.'

Barnet glanced towards the speaker. The rays from a neighbouring lamp struck through the drizzle under Charlson's umbrella, so as just to illumine his face against the shade behind, and show that his eye was turned up under the outer corner of its lid, whence it leered with impish jocoseness as he thrust his tongue into his cheek.

'Come,' said Barnet gravely, 'we'll have no more of that.'

'No, no – of course not,' Charlson hastily answered, seeing that his humour had carried him too far, as it had done many times before. He was profuse in his apologies, but Barnet did not reply. Of one thing he was certain – that scandal was a plant of quick root, and that he was bound to obey Lucy's injunction for Lucy's own sake.

3

He did so, to the letter; and though, as the crocus followed the snowdrop and the daffodil the crocus in Lucy's garden, the harbour-road was a not unpleasant place to walk in, Barnet's feet never trod its stones, much less approached her door. He avoided a saunter that way as he would have avoided a dangerous dream, and took his airings a long distance northward, among severely square and brown ploughed fields, where no other townsman came. Sometimes he went round by the lower lanes of the borough, where the rope-walks stretched in which his family formerly had share, and looked at the rope-makers walking backwards, over-hung by apple-trees and bushes, and intruded on by cows and calves, as if trade had established itself there at considerable inconvenience to Nature.

One morning, when the sun was so warm as to raise a steam from the south-eastern slopes of those flanking hills that looked so lovely above the old roofs, but made every low-chimneyed house in the town as smoky as Tophet, Barnet glanced from the windows of the town-council room for lack of interest in what was proceeding within. Several members of the corporation were present, but there was not much business doing, and in a few minutes Downe came leisurely across to him, saying that he seldom saw Barnet now.

Barnet owned that he was not often present.

Downe looked at the crimson curtain which hung down beside the panes, reflecting its hot hues into their faces, and then out of the window. At that moment there passed along the street a tall commanding lady, in whom the solicitor recognized Barnet's wife. Barnet had done the same thing, and turned away.

'It will be all right some day,' said Downe, with cheering sympathy.

'You have heard, then, of her last outbreak?'

Downe depressed his cheerfulness to its very reverse in a moment. 'No, I have not heard of anything serious,' he said, with as long a face as one naturally round could be turned into at short notice. 'I only hear vague reports of such things.'

'You may think it will be all right,' said Barnet drily 'But I have a different opinion. . . No, Downe, we must look the thing in the face. Not poppy nor mandragora – however, how are your wife and children?'

Downe said that they were all well, thanks; they were out that morning somewhere; he was just looking to see if they were walking that way. Ah, there they were, just coming down the street; and Downe pointed to the figures of two children with a nursemaid, and a lady walking behind them.

'You will come out and speak to her?' he asked.

'Not this morning. The fact is I don't care to speak to anybody just now.'

'You are too sensitive, Mr Barnet. At school I remember you used to get as red as a rose if anybody uttered a word that hurt your feelings.'

Barnet mused. 'Yes,' he admitted, 'there is a grain of truth in that. It is because of that I often try to make peace at home. Life would be tolerable then at any rate, even if not particularly bright.'

'I have thought more than once of proposing a little plan to you,' said Downe with some hesitation. 'I don't know whether it will meet your views, but take it or leave it, as you choose. In fact, it was my wife who suggested it: that she would be very glad to call on Mrs Barnet and get into her confidence. She seems to think that Mrs Barnet is rather alone in the town, and without advisers. Her impression is that your wife will listen to reason. Emily has a wonderful way of winning the hearts of people of her own sex.'

'And of the other sex too, I think. She is a charming woman, and you were a lucky fellow to find her.'

'Well, perhaps I was,' simpered Downe, trying to wear an aspect of being the last man in the world to feel pride. 'However, she will be likely to find out what ruffles Mrs Barnet. Perhaps it is some misunderstanding, you know – something that she is too proud to ask you to explain, or some little thing in your conduct that irritates her because she does not fully comprehend you. The truth is, Emily would have been more ready to make advances if she had been quite sure of her fitness for Mrs Barnet's society, who has of course been accustomed to London people of good position, which made Emily fearful of intruding.'

Barnet expressed his warmest thanks for the well-intentioned propositon. There was reason in Mrs Downe's fear – that he owned. 'But do let her call,' he said. 'There is no woman in England I would so soon trust on such an errand. I am afraid there will not be any brilliant result; still, I shall take it as the kindest and nicest thing if she will try it, and not be frightened at a repulse.'

When Barnet and Downe had parted, the former went to the Town Savings-Bank, of which he was a trustee, and endeavoured to forget his troubles in the contemplation of low sums of money, and figures in a network of red and blue lines. He sat and watched the working-people making their deposits, to which at intervals he signed his name. Before he left in the afternoon Downe put his head inside the door.

'Emily has seen Mrs Barnet,' he said in a low voice. 'She has got Mrs Barnet's promise to take her for a drive down to the shore tomorrow, if it is fine. Good afternoon!'

Barnet shook Downe by the hand without speaking, and Downe went away.

4

The next day was as fine as the arrangement could possibly require. As the sun passed the meridian and declined westward, the tall shadows from the scaffold-poles of Barnet's rising residence streaked the ground as far as to the middle of the highway. Barnet himself was there inspecting the progress of the works for the first time during several weeks. A building in an old-fashioned town five-and-thirty years ago did not, as in the modern fashion, rise from the sod like a booth at a fair. The foundations and lower courses were put in and allowed to settle for many weeks before the superstructure was built up, and a whole summer of drying was hardly sufficient to do justice to the important issues involved. Barnet stood within a window-niche which had as yet received no frame, and thence looked down a slope into the road. The wheels of a chaise were heard, and then his handsome Xantippe, in the company of Mrs Downe, drove past on their way to the shore. They were driving slowly; there was a pleasing light in Mrs Downe's face, which seemed faintly to reflect itself upon the countenance of her companion – that *politesse du cœur* which was so natural to her having possibly begun already to work results. But whatever the situation, Barnet resolved not to interfere, or do anything to hazard the promise of the day. He might well afford to trust the issue to another when he could never direct it but to ill himself. His wife's clenched rein-hand in its lemon-coloured glove, her stiff erect figure, clad in velvet and lace, and her boldly-outlined face, passed on, exhibiting their owner as one fixed for ever above the level of her companion – socially by her early breeding, and materially by her higher cushion.

Barnet decided to allow them a proper time to themselves, and then stroll down to the shore and drive them home. After lingering on at the house for another hour he started with this intention. A few hundred yards below 'Château Ringdale' stood the cottage in which the late lieutenant's daughter had her lodging. Barnet had not been so far that way for a long time, and as he approached the forbidden ground a curious warmth passed into him, which led him to perceive that, unless he were careful, he might have to fight the battle with himself about Lucy over again. A tenth of his present excuse would, however, have justified him in travelling by that road today.

He came opposite the dwelling, and turned his eyes for a momentary glance into the little garden that stretched from the palings to the door. Lucy was in the enclosure; she was walking and stooping to gather some flowers, possibly for the purpose of painting them, for she moved about quickly, as if anxious to save time. She did not see him; he might have passed unnoticed; but a sensation which was not in strict unison with his previous sentiments that day led him to pause in his walk and watch her. She went nimbly round and round the beds of anemones, tulips, jonquils, polyanthuses, and other old-fashioned flowers, looking a very charming figure in her half-mourning bonnet, and with an incomplete nosegay in her left hand. Raising herself to pull down a lilac blossom she observed him.

'Mr Barnet!' she said, innocently smiling. 'Why, I have been thinking of you many times since Mrs Barnet went by in the pony-carriage, and now here you are!'

'Yes, Lucy,' he said.

Then she seemed to recall particulars of their last meeting, and he believed that she flushed, though it might have been only the fancy of his own supersensitiveness.

'I am going to the harbour,' he added.

'Are you?' Lucy remarked simply. 'A great many people begin to go there now the summer is drawing on.'

Her face had come more into his view as she spoke, and he noticed how much thinner and paler it was than when he had seen it last. 'Lucy, how weary you look! tell me, can I help you?' he was going to cry out. – 'If I do,' he thought, 'it will be the ruin of us both!' He merely said that the afternoon was fine, and went on his way.

As he went a sudden blast of air came over the hill as if in contradiction to his words, and spoilt the previous quiet of the scene. The wind had already shifted violently, and now smelt of the sea.

The harbour-road soon began to justify its name. A gap appeared in the rampart of hills which shut out the sea, and on the left of the opening rose a vertical cliff, coloured a burning orange by the sunlight, the companion cliff on the right being livid in shade. Between these cliffs, like the Libyan bay which sheltered the shipwrecked Trojans, was a little haven, seemingly a beginning made by Nature herself of a perfect harbour, which appealed to the passer-by as only requiring a little human industry to finish it and make it famous, the ground on each side as far back as the daisied slopes that bounded the interior valley being a mere layer of blown sand. But the Port-Bredy burgesses a mile inland had, in the course of ten centuries, responded many times to that mute appeal, with the result that the tides had invariably choked up their works with sand and shingle as soon as completed. There were but few houses here: a rough pier, a few boats, some stores, an inn, a residence or two, a ketch unloading in the harbour, were the chief features of the settlement. On the open ground by the shore stood his wife's pony-carriage, empty, the boy in attendance holding the horse.

When Barnet drew nearer, he saw an indigo-coloured spot moving swiftly along beneath the radiant base of the eastern cliff, which proved to be a man in a jersey, running with all his might. He held up his hand to Barnet, as it seemed, and they approached each other. The man was local, but a stranger to him.

'What is it, my man?' said Barnet.

'A terrible calamity!' the boatman hastily explained. Two ladies had been capsized in a boat – they were Mrs Downe and Mrs Barnet of the old town; they had driven down there that afternoon – they had alighted, and it was so fine, that, after walking about a little while, they had been tempted to go out for a short sail round the cliff. Just as they were putting in to the shore, the wind shifted with a sudden gust, the boat listed over, and it was thought they were both drowned. How it could have happened was beyond his mind to fathom, for John Green knew how to sail a boat as well as any man there.

'Which is the way to the place?' said Barnet.

It was just round the cliff.

'Run to the carriage and tell the boy to bring it to the place as soon as you can. Then go to the Harbour Inn and tell them to ride to town for a doctor. Have they been got out of the water?'

'One lady has.'

'Which?'

'Mrs Barnet. Mrs Downe, it is feared, has fleeted out to sea.'

Barnet ran on to that part of the shore which the cliff had hitherto obscured from his view, and there discerned, a long way ahead, a group of fishermen standing. As soon as he came up one or two recognized him, and, not liking to meet his eye, turned aside with misgiving. He went amidst them and saw a small sailing-boat lying draggled at the water's edge; and, on the sloping shingle beside it, a soaked and sandy woman's form in the velvet dress and yellow gloves of his wife.

5

All had been done that could be done. Mrs Barnet was in her own house under medical hands, but the result was still uncertain. Barnet had acted as if devotion to his wife were the dominant passion of his existence. There had been much to decide – whether to attempt restoration of the apparently lifeless body as it lay on the shore – whether to carry her to the Harbour Inn – whether to drive with her at once to his own house. The first course, with no skilled help or appliances near at hand, had seemed hopeless. The second course would have occupied nearly as much time as a drive to the town, owing to the intervening ridges of shingle, and the necessity of crossing the harbour by boat to get to the house, added to which much time must have elapsed before a doctor could have arrived down there. By bringing her home in the carriage some precious moments had slipped by; but she had been laid in her own bed in seven minutes, a doctor called to her side, and every possible restorative brought to bear upon her.

At what a tearing pace he had driven up that road, through the yellow evening sunlight, the shadows flapping irksomely into his eyes as each wayside object rushed past between him and the west! Tired workmen with their baskets at their backs had turned on their homeward journey to wonder at his speed. Half-way between the shore and Port-Bredy town he had met Charlson, who had been the first surgeon to hear of the accident. He was accompanied by his assistant in a gig. Barnet had sent on the latter to the coast in case that Downe's poor wife should by that time have been reclaimed from the waves, and had brought Charlson back with him to the house.

Barnet's presence was not needed here, and he felt it to be his next duty to set off at once and find Downe, that no other than himself might break the news to him.

He was quite sure that no chance had been lost for Mrs Downe by his leaving the shore. By the time that Mrs Barnet had been laid in the carriage a much larger group had assembled to lend assistance in finding her friend, rendering his own help superfluous. But the duty of breaking the news was made doubly painful by the circumstance that the catastrophe which had befallen Mrs Downe was solely the result of her own and her husband's loving kindness towards himself.

He found Downe in his office. When the solicitor comprehended the intelligence he turned pale, stood up, and remained for a moment perfectly still, as if bereft of his faculties; then his shoulders heaved, he pulled out his handkerchief and began to cry like a child. His sobs might have been heard in the next room. He seemed to have no idea of going to the shore, of or doing anything; but when Barnet took him gently by the hand and proposed to start at once, he quietly acquiesced, neither uttering any further word nor making any effort to repress his tears.

Barnet accompanied him to the shore, where, finding that no trace had as yet been seen of Mrs Downe, and that his stay would be of no avail, he left Downe with his friends and the young doctor, and once more hastened back to his own house.

At the door he met Charlson. 'Well!' Barnet said.

'I have just come down,' said the doctor; 'we have done everything, but without result. I sympathize with you in your bereavement.'

Barnet did not appreciate Charlson's sympathy, which sounded to his ears as something of a mockery from the lips of a man who knew what Charlson knew about his domestic relations. Indeed, there seemed an odd spark in Charlson's full black eye as he said the words; but that might have been imaginary.

'And, Mr Barnet,' Charlson resumed, 'that little matter between us – I hope to settle it finally in three weeks at least.'

'Never mind that now,' said Barnet abruptly. He directed the surgeon to go to the harbour in case his services might even now be necessary there: and himself entered the house.

The servants were coming from his wife's chamber, looking helplessly at each other and at him. He passed them by and entered the room, where he stood regarding the shape on the bed for a few minutes, after which he walked into his own dressing-room adjoining, and there paced up and down. In a minute or two he noticed what a strange and total silence had come over the upper part of the house; his own movements, muffled as they were by the carpet, seemed noisy, and his thoughts to disturb the air like articulate utterances. His eye glanced through the window. Far down the road to the harbour a roof detained his gaze: out of it rose a red chimney, and out of the red chimney a curl of smoke, as from a fire newly kindled. He had often seen such a sight before. In that house lived Lucy Savile; and the smoke was from the fire which was regularly lighted at this time to make her tea.

After that he went back to the bedroom, and stood there some time regarding his wife's silent form. She was a woman some years older than himself, but had not by any means overpassed the maturity of good looks and vigour. Her passionate features, well-defined, firm, and statuesque in life, were doubly so now: her mouth and brow, beneath her purplish-black hair, showed only too clearly that the turbulency of character which had made a bear-garden of his house had been no temporary phase of her existence. While he reflected, he suddenly said to himself, I wonder if all has been done?

The thought was led up to by his having fancied that his wife's features lacked in its completeness the expression which he had been accustomed to associate with the faces of those whose spirits have fled for ever. The effacement of life was not so marked but that, entering uninformed, he might have supposed her sleeping. Her complexion was that seen in the numerous faded portraits by Sir Joshua Reynolds; it was pallid in comparison with life, but there was visible on a close inspection the remnant of what had once been a flush; the keeping between the cheeks and the hollows of the face being thus preserved, although positive colour was gone. Long orange rays of evening sun stole in through chinks in the blind, striking on the large mirror, and being thence reflected upon the crimson hangings and woodwork of the heavy bedstead, so that the general tone of light was remarkably warm; and it was probable that something might be due to this circumstance. Still the fact impressed him as strange. Charlson had been gone more than a quarter of an hour: could it be possible that he had left too soon, and that his attempts to restore her had operated so sluggishly as only now to have made themselves felt? Barnet laid his hand upon her chest, and fancied that ever and anon a faint flutter of palpitation, gentle as that of a butterfly's wing, disturbed the stillness there – ceasing for a time, then struggling to go on, then breaking down in weakness and ceasing again.

Barnet's mother had been an active practitioner of the healing art among her poorer neighbours, and her inspirations had all been derived from an octavo volume of Domestic Medicine, which at this moment was lying, as it had lain for many years, on a shelf in Barnet's dressing-room. He hastily fetched it, and there read under the head 'Drowning':

> Exertions for the recovery of any person who has not been immersed for a longer period than half-an-hour should be continued for at least four hours, as there have been many cases in which returning life has made itself visible even after a longer interval.
>
> Should, however, a weak action of any of the organs show itself when the case seems almost hopeless, our efforts must be redoubled; the feeble spark in this case requires to be solicited; it will certainly disappear under a relaxation of labour.

Barnet looked at his watch; it was now barely two hours and a half from the time when he had first heard of the accident. He threw aside the book and turned quickly to reach a stimulant which had previously been used. Pulling up the blind for more light, his eye glanced out of the window. There he saw that red chimney still smoking cheerily, and that roof, and through the roof that somebody. His mechanical movements stopped, his hand remained on the blind-cord, and he seemed to become breathless, as if he had suddenly found himself treading a high rope.

While he stood a sparrow lighted on the window-sill, saw him, and flew away. Next a man and a dog walked over one of the green hills which bulged above the roofs of the town. But Barnet took no notice.

We may wonder what were the exact images that passed through his mind during those minutes of gazing upon Lucy Savile's house, the sparrow, the man and the dog, and Lucy Savile's house again. There are honest men who will not admit to their thoughts, even as idle hypotheses, views of the future that assume as done a deed which they would recoil from doing; and there are other honest men for whom morality ends at the surface of their own heads, who will deliberate what the first will not so much as suppose. Barnet had a wife whose presence distracted his home; she now lay as in death; by merely doing nothing – by letting the intelligence which had gone forth to the world lie undisturbed – he would effect such a deliverance for himself as he had never hoped for, and open up an opportunity of which till now he had never dreamed. Whether the conjuncture had arisen through any unscrupulous, ill-considered impulse of Charlson to help out of a strait the friend who was so kind as never to press him for what was due could not be told; there was nothing to prove it; and it was a question which could never be asked. The triangular situation – himself – his wife – Lucy Savile – was the one clear thing.

From Barnet's actions we may infer that he *supposed* such and such a result, for a moment, but did not deliberate. He withdrew his hazel eyes from the scene without, calmly turned, rang the bell for assistance, and vigorously exerted himself to learn if life still lingered in that motionless frame. In a short time another surgeon was in attendance; and then Barnet's surmise proved to be true. The slow life timidly heaved again; but much care and patience were needed to catch and retain it, and a considerable period elapsed before it could be said with certainty that Mrs Barnet lived. When this was the case, and there was no further room for doubt, Barnet left the chamber. The blue evening smoke from Lucy's chimney had died down to an imperceptible stream, and as he walked about downstairs he murmured to himself, 'My wife was dead, and she is alive again.'

It was not so with Downe. After three hours' immersion his wife's body had been recovered, life, of course, being quite extinct. Barnet, on descending, went straight to his friend's house, and there learned the result. Downe was helpless in his wild grief, occasionally even hysterical. Barnet said little, but finding that some guiding hand was necessary in the sorrow-stricken household, took upon him to supervise and manage till Downe should be in a state of mind to do so for himself.

6

One September evening, four months later, when Mrs Barnet was in perfect health, and Mrs Downe but a weakening memory, an errand-boy paused to rest himself in front of Mr Barnet's old house, depositing his basket on one of the window-sills. The street was not yet lighted, but there were lights in the house, and at intervals a flitting shadow fell upon the blind at his elbow. Words also were audible from the same apartment, and they seemed to be those of persons in violent altercation. But the boy could not gather their purport, and he went on his way.

Ten minutes afterwards the door of Barnet's house opened, and a tall closely-veiled lady in a travelling-dress came out and descended the freestone steps. The servant stood in the doorway watching her as she went with a measured tread down the street. When she had been out of sight for some minutes Barnet appeared at the door from within.

'Did your mistress leave word where she was going?' he asked.

'No, sir.'

'Is the carriage ordered to meet her anywhere?'

'No, sir.'

'Did she take a latch-key?'

'No, sir.'

Barnet went in again, sat down in his chair, and leaned back. Then in solitude and silence he brooded over the bitter emotions that filled his heart. It was for this that he had gratuitously restored her to life, and made his union with another impossible! The evening drew on, and nobody came to disturb him. At bedtime he told the servants to retire, that he would sit up for Mrs Barnet himself; and when they were gone he leaned his head upon his hand and mused for hours.

The clock struck one, two; still his wife came not, and, with impatience added to depression, he went from room to room till another weary hour had passed. This was not altogether a new experience for Barnet; but she had never before so prolonged her absence. At last he sat down again and fell asleep.

He awoke at six o'clock to find that she had not returned. In searching about the rooms he discovered that she had taken a case of jewels which had been hers before her marriage. At eight a note was brought him; it was from his wife, in which she stated that she had gone by the coach to the house of a distant relative near London, and expressed a wish that certain boxes, articles of clothing, and so on, might be sent to her forthwith. The note was brought to him by a waiter at the Black-Bull Hotel, and had been written by Mrs Barnet immediately before she took her place in the stage.

By the evening this order was carried out, and Barnet, with a sense of relief, walked out into the town. A fair had been held during the day, and the large clear moon which rose over the most prominent hill flung its light upon the booths and standings that still remained in the street, mixing its rays curiously with those from the flaring naphtha lamps. The town was full of country-people who had come in to enjoy themselves, and on this account Barnet strolled through the streets unobserved. With a certain recklessness he made for the harbour-road, and presently found himself by the shore, where he walked on till he came to the spot near which his friend the kindly Mrs Downe had lost her life, and his own wife's life had been preserved. A tremulous pathway of bright moonshine now stretched over the water which had engulfed them, and not a living soul was near.

Here he ruminated on their characters, and next on the young girl in whom he now took a more sensitive interest than at the time when he had been free to marry her. Nothing, so far as he was aware, had ever appeared in his own conduct to show that such an interest existed. He had made it a point of the utmost strictness to hinder that feeling from influencing in the faintest degree his attitude towards his wife; and this was made all the more easy for him by the small demand Mrs Barnet made upon his attentions, for which she ever evinced the greatest contempt; thus unwittingly giving him the satisfaction of knowing that their severance owed nothing to jealousy, or, indeed, to any personal behaviour of his at all. Her concern was not with him or his feelings, as she frequently told him; but that she had, in a moment of weakness, thrown herself away upon a common burgher when she might have aimed at, and possibly brought down, a peer of the realm. Her frequent depreciation of Barnet in these terms had at times been so intense that he was sorely tempted to retaliate on her egotism by owning that he loved at the same low level on which he lived; but prudence had prevailed, for which he was now thankful.

Something seemed to sound upon the shingle behind him over and above the raking of the wave. He looked round, and a slight girlish shape appeared quite close to him. He could not see her face because it was in the direction of the moon.

'Mr Barnet?' the rambler said, in timid surprise. The voice was the voice of Lucy Savile.

'Yes,' said Barnet. 'How can I repay you for this pleasure?'

'I only came because the night was so clear. I am now on my way home.'

'I am glad we have met. I want to know if you will let me do something for you, to give me an occupation, as an idle man? I am sure I ought to help you, for I know you are almost without friends.'

She hesitated. 'Why should you tell me that?' she said.

'In the hope that you will be frank with me.'

'I am not altogether without friends here. But I am going to make a little change in my life – to go out as a teacher of freehand drawing and practical perspective, of course I mean on a comparatively humble scale, because I have not been specially educated for that profession. But I am sure I shall like it much.'

'You have an opening?'

'I have not exactly got it, but I have advertised for one.'

'Lucy, you must let me help you!'

'Not at all.'

'You need not think it would compromise you, or that I am indifferent to delicacy. I bear in mind how we stand. It is very unlikely that you will succeed as teacher of the class you mention, so let me do something of a different kind for you. Say what you would like and it shall be done.'

'No; if I can't be a drawing-mistress or governess, or something of that sort, I shall go to India and join my brother.'

'I wish I could go abroad, anywhere, everywhere with you, Lucy, and leave this place and its associations for ever!'

She played with the end of her bonnet-string, and hastily turned aside. 'Don't ever touch upon that kind of topic again,' she said, with a quick severity not free from anger. 'It simply makes it impossible for me to see you, much less receive any guidance from you. No, thank you, Mr Barnet; you can do nothing for me at present; and as I suppose my uncertainty will end in my leaving for India, I fear you never will. If ever I think you *can* do anything, I will take the trouble to ask you. Till then, good-bye.'

The tone of her latter words was equivocal, and while he remained in doubt whether a gentle irony was or was not inwrought with their sound, she swept lightly round and left him alone. He saw her form get smaller and smaller along the damp belt of sea-sand between ebb and flood, and when she had vanished round the cliff into the harbour-road he himself followed in the same direction.

That her hopes from an advertisement should be the single thread which held Lucy Savile in England was too much for Barnet. On reaching the town he went straight to the residence of Downe, now a widower with four children. The young motherless brood had been sent to bed about a quarter of an hour earlier, and when Barnet entered he found Downe sitting alone. It was the same room as that from which the family had been looking out for Downe at the beginning of the year, when Downe had slipped into the gutter and his wife had been so enviably tender towards him. The old neatness had gone from the house; articles lay in places which could show no reason for their presence, as if momentarily deposited there some months ago, and forgotten ever since; there were no flowers; things were jumbled together on the furniture which should have been in cupboards; and the place in general had that stagnant, unrenovated air which usually pervades the maimed home of the widower.

Downe soon renewed his customary full-worded lament over his wife, and even when he had worked himself up to tears, went on volubly, as if a listener were a luxury to be enjoyed whenever he could be caught.

'She was a treasure beyond compare, Mr Barnet! I shall never see such another. Nobody now to nurse me – nobody to console me in those daily troubles, you know, Barnet, which make consolation so necessary to a nature like mine. It would be unbecoming to repine, for her spirit's home was elsewhere – the tender light in her eyes always showed it; but it is a long dreary time that I have before me, and nobody else can ever fill the void left in my heart by her loss – nobody – nobody!' And Downe wiped his eyes again.

'She was a good woman in the highest sense,' gravely answered Barnet, who, though Downe's words drew genuine compassion from his heart, could not help feeling that a tender reticence would have been a finer tribute to Mrs Downe's really sterling virtues than such a second-class lament as this.

'I have something to show you,' Downe resumed, producing from a drawer a sheet of paper on which was an elaborate design for a canopied tomb. 'This has been sent me by the architect, but it is not exactly what I want.'

'You have got Jones to do it, I see, the man who is carrying out my house,' said Barnet, as he glanced at the signature to the drawing.

'Yes, but it is not quite what I want. I want something more striking – more like a tomb I have seen in St Paul's Cathedral. Nothing less will do justice to my feelings, and how far short of them that will fall!'

Barnet privately thought the design a sufficiently imposing one as it stood, even extravagantly ornate; but, feeling that he had no right to criticize, he said gently, 'Downe, should you not live more in your children's lives at the present time, and soften the sharpness of regret for your own past by thinking of their future?'

'Yes, yes; but what can I do more?' asked Downe, wrinkling his forehead hopelessly.

It was with anxious slowness that Barnet produced his reply – the secret object of his visit tonight. 'Did you not say one day that you ought by right to get a governess for the children?'

Downe admitted that he had said so, but that he could not see his way to it. 'The kind of woman I should like to have,' he said, 'would be rather beyond my means. No; I think I shall send them to school in the town when they are old enough to go out alone.'

'Now, I know of something better than that. The late Lieutenant Savile's daughter, Lucy, wants to do something for herself in the way of teaching. She would be inexpensive, and would answer your purpose as well as anybody for six or twelve months. She would probably come daily if you were to ask her, and so your housekeeping arrangements would not be much affected.'

'I thought she had gone away,' said the solicitor, musing. 'Where does she live?'

Barnet told him, and added that, if Downe should think of her as suitable, he would do well to call as soon as possible, or she might be on the wing. 'If you do see her,' he said, 'it would be advisable not to mention my name. She is rather stiff in her ideas of me, and it might prejudice her against a course if she knew that I recommended it.'

Downe promised to give the subject his consideration, and nothing more was said about it just then. But when Barnet rose to go, which was not till nearly bedtime, he reminded Downe of the suggestion and went up the street to his own solitary home with a sense of satisfaction at his promising diplomacy in a charitable cause.

7

The walls of his new house were carried up nearly to their full height. By a curious though not infrequent reaction, Barnet's feelings about that unnecessary structure had undergone a change; he took considerable interest in its progress as a long-neglected thing, his wife before her departure having grown quite weary of it as a hobby. Moreover, it was an excellent distraction for a man in the unhappy position of having to live in a provincial town with nothing to do. He was probably the first of his line who had ever passed a day without toil, and perhaps something like an inherited instinct disqualifies such men for a life of pleasant inaction, such as lies in the power of those whose leisure is not a personal accident, but a vast historical accretion which has become part of their natures.

Thus Barnet got into a way of spending many of his leisure hours on the site of the new building, and he might have been seen on most days at this time trying the temper of the mortar by punching the joints with his stick, looking at the grain of a floor-board, and meditating where it grew, or picturing under what circumstances the last fire would be kindled in the at present sootless chimneys. One day when thus occupied he saw three children pass by in the company of a fair young woman, whose sudden appearance caused him to flush perceptibly.

'Ah, she is there,' he thought. 'That's a blessed thing.'

Casting an interested glance over the rising building and the busy workmen, Lucy Savile and the little Downes passed by; and after that time it became a regular though almost unconscious custom of Barnet to stand in the half-completed house and look from the ungarnished windows at the governess as she tripped towards the sea-shore with her young charges, which she was in the habit of doing on most fine afternoons. It was on one of these occasions, when he had been loitering on the first-floor landing, near the hole left for the staircase, not yet erected, that there appeared above the edge of the floor a little hat, followed by a little head.

Barnet withdrew through a doorway, and the child came to the top of the ladder, stepping on to the floor and crying to her sisters and Miss Savile to follow. Another head rose above the floor, and another, and then Lucy herself came into view. The troop ran hither and thither through the empty, shaving-strewn rooms, and Barnet came forward.

Lucy uttered a small exclamation: she was very sorry that she had intruded; she had not the least idea that Mr Barnet was there: the children had come up, and she had followed.

Barnet replied that he was only too glad to see them there. 'And now, let me show you the rooms,' he said.

She passively assented, and he took her round. There was not much to show in such a bare skeleton of a house, but he made the most of it, and explained the different ornamental fittings that were soon to be fixed here and there. Lucy made but few remarks in reply, though she seemed pleased with her visit, and stole away down the ladder, followed by her companions.

After this the new residence became yet more of a hobby for Barnet. Downe's children did not forget their first visit, and when the windows were glazed, and the handsome staircase spread its broad low steps into the hall, they came again, prancing in unwearied succession through every room from ground-floor to attics, while Lucy stood waiting for them at the door. Barnet, who rarely missed a day in coming to inspect progress, stepped out from the drawing-room.

'I could not keep them out,' she said, with an apologetic blush. 'I tried to do so very much; but they are rather wilful, and we are directed to walk this way for the sea air.'

'Do let them make the house their regular playground, and you yours,' said Barnet. 'There is no better place for children to romp and take their exercise in than an empty house, particularly in muddy or damp weather such as we shall get a good deal of now; and this place will not be furnished for a long time – perhaps never. I am not at all decided about it.'

'O, but it must!' replied Lucy, looking round at the hall.' The rooms are excellent, twice as high as ours, and the views from the windows are so lovely.'

'I daresay, I daresay,' he said absently.

'Will all the furniture be new?' she asked.

'All the furniture be new – that's a thing I have not thought of. In fact, I only come here and look on. My father's house would have been large enough for me, but another person had a voice in the matter, and it was settled that we should build. However, the place grows upon me; its recent associations are cheerful, and I am getting to like it fast.'

A certain uneasiness in Lucy's manner showed that the conversation was taking too personal a turn for her. 'Still, as modern tastes develop, people require more room to gratify them in,' she said, withdrawing to call the children; and serenely bidding him good-afternoon she went on her way.

Barnet's life at this period was singularly lonely, and yet he was happier than he could have expected. His wife's estrangement and absence, which promised to be permanent, left him free as a boy in his movements, and the solitary walks that he took gave him ample opportunity for chastened reflection on what might have been his lot if he had only shown wisdom enough to claim Lucy Savile when there was no bar between their lives, and she was to be had for the asking. He would occasionally call at the house of his friend Downe; but there was scarcely enough in common between their two natures to make them more than friends of that excellent sort whose personal knowledge of each other's history and character is always in excess of intimacy, whereby they are not so likely to be severed by a clash of sentiment as in cases where intimacy springs up in excess of knowledge. Lucy was never visible at these times, being either engaged in the school-room, or in taking an airing out of doors; but, knowing that she was now comfortable, and had given up the, to him, depressing idea of going off to the other side of the globe, he was quite content.

The new house had so far progressed that the gardeners were beginning to grass down the front. During an afternoon which he was passing in marking the curve for the carriage-drive, he beheld her coming in boldly towards him from the road. Hitherto Barnet had only caught her on the premises by stealth; and this advance seemed to show that at last her reserve had broken down.

A smile gained strength upon her face as she approached, and it was quite radiant when she came up, and said, without a trace of embarrassment, 'I find I owe you a hundred thanks – and it comes to me quite as a surprise! It was through your kindness that I was engaged by Mr Downe. Believe me, Mr Barnet, I did not know it until yesterday, or I should have thanked you long and long ago!'

'I had offended you – just a trifle – at the time, I think?' said Barnet, smiling, 'and it was best that you should not know.'

'Yes, yes,' she returned hastily. 'Don't allude to that; it is past and over, and we will let it be. The house is finished almost, is it not? How beautiful it will look when the evergreens are grown! Do you call the style Palladian, Mr Barnet?'

'I – really don't quite know what it is. Yes, it must be Palladian, certainly. But I'll ask Jones, the architect; for, to tell the truth, I had not thought much about the style: I had nothing to do with choosing it, I am sorry to say.'

She would not let him harp on this gloomy refrain, and talked on bright matters till she said, producing a small roll of paper which he had noticed in her hand all the while, 'Mr Downe wished me to bring you this revised drawing of the late Mrs Downe's tomb, which the architect has just sent him. He would like you to look it over.'

The children came up with their hoops, and she went off with them down the harbour-road as usual. Barnet had been glad to get those words of thanks; he had been thinking for many months that he would like her to know of his share in finding her a home such as it was; and what he could not do for himself, Downe had now kindly done for him. He returned to his desolate house with a lighter tread; though in reason he hardly knew why his tread should be light.

On examining the drawing, Barnet found that, instead of the vast altar-tomb and canopy Downe had determined on at their last meeting, it was to be a more modest memorial even than had been suggested by the architect; a coped tomb of good solid construction, with no useless elaboration at all. Barnet was truly glad to see that Downe had come to reason of his own accord; and he returned the drawing with a note of approval.

He followed up the house-work as before, and as he walked up and down the rooms, occasionally gazing from the windows over the bulging green hills and the quiet harbour that lay between them, he murmured words and fragments of words which, if listened to, would have revealed all the secrets of his existence. Whatever his reason in going there, Lucy did not call again: the walk to the shore seemed to be abandoned: he must have thought it as well for both that it should be so, for he did not go anywhere out of his accustomed ways to endeavour to discover her.

8

The winter and the spring had passed, and the house was complete. It was a fine morning in the early part of June, and Barnet, though not in the habit of rising early, had taken a long walk before breakfast; returning by way of the new building. A sufficiently exciting cause of his restlessness today might have been the intelligence which had reached him the night before, that Lucy Savile was going to India after all, and notwithstanding the representations of her friends that such a journey was unadvisable in many ways for an unpractised girl, unless some more definite advantage lay at the end of it than she could show to be the case. Barnet's walk up the slope to the building betrayed that he was in a dissatisfied mood. He hardly saw that the dewy time of day lent an unusual freshness to the bushes and trees which had so recently put on their summer habit of heavy leafage, and made his newly-laid lawn look as well established as an old manorial meadow. The house had been so adroitly placed between six tall elms which were growing on the site beforehand, that they seemed like real ancestral trees; and the rooks, young and old, cawed melodiously to their visitor.

The door was not locked, and he entered. No workmen appeared to be present, and he walked from sunny window to sunny window of the empty rooms, with a sense of seclusion which might have been very pleasant but for the antecedent knowledge that his almost paternal care of Lucy Savile was to be thrown away by her wilfulness. Footsteps echoed through an adjoining room; and bending his eyes in that direction, he perceived Mr Jones, the architect. He had come to look over the building before giving the contractor his final certificate. They walked over the house together. Everything was finished except the papering: there were the latest improvements of the period in bell-hanging, ventilating, smoke-jacks, fire-grates, and French windows. The business was soon ended, and Jones, having directed Barnet's attention to a book of wall-paper patterns which lay on a bench for his choice, was leaving to keep another engagement, when Barnet said, 'Is the tomb finished yet for Mrs Downe?'

'Well – yes: it is at last,' said the architect, coming back and speaking as if he were in a mood to make a confidence. 'I have had no end of trouble in the matter, and, to tell the truth, I am heartily glad it is over.'

Barnet expressed his surprise. 'I thought poor Downe had given up those extravagant notions of his? Then he has gone back to the altar and canopy after all? Well, he is to be excused, poor fellow!'

'O no – he had not at all gone back to them – quite the reverse,' Jones hastened to say. 'He has so reduced design after design that the whole thing has been nothing but waste labour for me; till in the end it has become a common headstone, which a mason put up in half a day.'

'A common headstone?' said Barnet.

'Yes. I held out for some time for the addition of a footstone at least. But he said, "O no – he couldn't afford it."'

'Ah, well – his family is growing up, poor fellow, and his expenses are getting serious.'

'Yes, exactly,' said Jones, as if the subject were none of his. And again directing Barnet's attention to the wall-papers, the bustling architect left him to keep some other engagement.

'A common headstone,' murmured Barnet, left again to himself. He mused a minute or two, and next began looking over and selecting from the patterns; but had not long been engaged in the work when he heard another footstep on the gravel without, and somebody enter the open porch.

Barnet went to the door – it was his manservant in search of him.

'I have been trying for some time to find you, sir,' he said. 'This letter has come by the post, and it is marked immediate. And there's this one from Mr Downe, who called just now wanting to see you.' He searched his pocket for the second.

Barnet took the first letter – it had a black border, and bore the London postmark. It was not in his wife's handwriting, or in that of any person he knew; but conjecture soon ceased as he read the page, wherein he was briefly informed that Mrs Barnet had died suddenly on the previous day, at the furnished villa she had occupied near London.

Barnet looked vaguely round the empty hall, at the blank walls, out of the doorway. Drawing a long palpitating breath, and with eyes downcast, he turned and climbed the stairs slowly, like a man who doubted their stability. The fact of his wife having, as it were, died once already, and lived on again, had entirely dislodged the possibility of her actual death from his conjecture. He went to the landing, leant over the balusters, and after a reverie, of whose duration he had but the faintest notion, turned to the window and stretched his gaze to the cottage further down the road, which was visible from his landing, and from which Lucy still walked to the solicitor's house by a cross path. The faint words that came from his moving lips were simply, 'At last!'

Then, almost involuntarily, Barnet fell down on his knees and murmured some incoherent words of thanksgiving. Surely his virtue in restoring his wife to life had been rewarded! But, as if the impulse struck uneasily on his conscience, he quickly rose, brushed the dust from his trousers, and set himself to think of his next movements. He could not start for London for some hours; and as he had no preparations to make that could not be made in half-an-hour, he mechanically descended and resumed his occupation of turning over the wall-papers. They had all got brighter for him, those papers. It was all changed – who would sit in the rooms that they were to line? He went on to muse upon Lucy's conduct in so frequently coming to the house with the children; her occasional blush in speaking to him; her evident interest in him. What woman can in the long run avoid being interested in a man whom she knows to be devoted to her? If human solicitation could ever effect anything, there should be no going to India for Lucy now. All the papers previously chosen seemed wrong in their shades, and he began from the beginning to choose again.

While entering on the task he heard a forced 'Ahem!' from without the porch, evidently uttered to attract his attention, and footsteps again advancing to the door. His man, whom he had quite forgotten in his mental turmoil, was still waiting there.

'I beg your pardon, sir,' the man said from round the doorway; 'but here's the note from Mr Downe that you didn't take. He called just after you went out, and as he couldn't wait, he wrote this on your study-table.'

He handed in the letter – no black-bordered one now, but a practical-looking note in the well-known writing of the solicitor.

DEAR BARNET – it ran – 'Perhaps you will be prepared for the information I am about to give – that Lucy Savile and myself are going to be married this morning. I have hitherto said nothing as to my intention to any of my friends, for reasons which I am sure you will fully appreciate. The crisis has been brought about by her expressing her intention to join her brother in India. I then discovered that I could not do without her.

'It is to be quite a private wedding; but it is my particular wish that you come down here quietly at ten, and go to church with us; it will add greatly to the pleasure I shall experience in the ceremony, and, I believe, to Lucy's also. I have called on you very early to make the request, in the belief that I should find you at home; but you are beforehand with me in your early rising. – Yours sincerely,

C. Downe'

'Need I wait, sir?' said the servant after a dead silence.

'That will do, William. No answer,' said Barnet calmly.

When the man had gone Barnet re-read the letter. Turning eventually to the wall-papers, which he had been at such pains to select, he deliberately tore them into halves and quarters, and threw them into the empty fireplace. Then he went out of the house, locked the door, and stood in the front awhile. Instead of returning into the town, he went down the harbour-road and thoughtfully lingered about by the sea, near the spot where the body of Downe's late wife had been found and brought ashore.

Barnet was a man with a rich capacity for misery, and there is no doubt that he exercised it to its fullest extent now. The events that had, as it were, dashed themselves together into one half-hour of this day showed that curious refinement of cruelty in their arrangement which often proceeds from the bosom of the whimsical god at other times known as blind Circumstance. That his few minutes of hope, between the reading of the first and second letters, had carried him to extraordinary heights of rapture was proved by the immensity of his suffering now. The sun blazing into his face would have shown a close watcher that a horizontal line, which had never been seen before, but which was never to be gone thereafter, was somehow gradually forming itself in the smooth of his forehead. His eyes, of a light hazel, had a curious look which can only be described by the word bruised; the sorrow that looked from them being largely mixed with the surprise of a man taken unawares.

The secondary particulars of his present position, too, were odd enough, though for some time they appeared to engage little of his attention. Not a soul in the town knew, as yet, of his wife's death; and he almost owed Downe the kindness of not publishing it till the day was over: the conjuncture, taken with that which had accompanied the death of Mrs Downe, being so singular as to be quite sufficient to darken the pleasure of the impressionable solicitor to a cruel extent, if made known to him. But as Barnet could not set out on his journey to London, where his wife lay, for some hours (there being at this date no railway within a distance of many miles), no great reason existed why he should leave the town.

Impulse in all its forms characterized Barnet, and when he heard the distant clock strike the hour of ten his feet began to carry him up the harbour-road with the manner of a man who must do something to bring himself to life. He passed Lucy Savile's old house, his own new one, and came in view of the church. Now he gave a percpetible start, and his mechanical condition went away. Before the church-gate were a couple of carriages, and Barnet then could perceive that the marriage between Downe and Lucy was at that moment being solemnized within. A feeling of sudden, proud self-confidence, an indocile wish to walk unmoved in spite of grim environments, plainly possessed him, and when he reached the wicket-gate he turned in without apparent effort. Pacing up the paved footway he entered the church and stood for awhile in the nave passage. A group of people were standing round the vestry door; Barnet advanced through these and stepped into the vestry.

There they were, busily signing their names. Seeing Downe about to look round Barnet averted his somewhat disturbed face for a second or two; when he turned again front to front he was calm and quite smiling; it was a creditable triumph over himself, and deserved to be remembered in his native town. He greeted Downe heartily, offering his congratulations.

It seemed as if Barnet expected a half-guilty look upon Lucy's face; but no; save the natural flush and flurry engendered by the service just performed, there was nothing whatever in her bearing which showed a disturbed mind: her gray-brown eyes carried in them now as at other times the well-known expression of commonsensed rectitude which never went so far as to touch on hardness. She shook hands with him, and Downe said warmly, 'I wish you could have come sooner: I called on purpose to ask you. You'll drive back with us now?'

'No, no,' said Barnet; 'I am not at all prepared; but I thought I would look in upon you for a moment, even though I had not time to go home and dress. I'll stand back and see you pass out, and observe the effect of the spectacle upon myself as one of the public.'

Then Lucy and her husband laughed, and Barnet laughed and retired; and the quiet little party went gliding down the nave and towards the porch, Lucy's new silk dress sweeping with a smart rustle round the base-mouldings of the ancient font, and Downe's little daughters following in a state of round-eyed interest in their position, and that of Lucy, their teacher and friend.

So Downe was comforted after his Emily's death, which had taken place twelve months, two weeks, and three days before that time.

When the two flys had driven off and the spectators had vanished, Barnet followed to the door, and went out into the sun. He took no more trouble to preserve a spruce exterior; his step was unequal, hesitating, almost convulsive; and the slight changes of colour which went on in his face seemed refracted from some inward flame. In the churchyard he became pale as a summer cloud, and finding it not easy to proceed he sat down on one of the tombstones and supported his head with his hand.

Hard by was a sexton filling up a grave which he had not found time to finish on the previous evening. Observing Barnet, he went up to him, and recognizing him, said, 'Shall I help you home, sir?'

'O no, thank you,' said Barnet, rousing himself and standing up. The sexton returned to his grave, followed by Barnet, who, after watching him awhile, stepped into the grave, now nearly filled, and helped to tread in the earth.

The sexton apparently thought his conduct a little singular, but he made no observation, and when the grave was full, Barnet suddenly stopped, looked far away, and with a decided step proceeded to the gate and vanished. The sexton rested on his shovel and looked after him for a few moments, and then began banking up the mound.

In those short minutes of treading in the dead man Barnet had formed a design, but what it was the inhabitants of that town did not for some long time imagine. He went home, wrote several letters of business, called on his lawyer, an old man of the same place who had been the legal adviser of Barnet's father before him, and during the evening overhauled a large quantity of letters and other documents in his possession. By eleven o'clock the heap of papers in and before Barnet's grate had reached formidable dimensions, and he began to burn them. This, owing to their quantity, it was not so easy to do as he had expected, and he sat long into the night to complete the task.

The next morning Barnet departed for London, leaving a note for Downe to inform him of Mrs Barnet's sudden death, and that he was gone to bury her; but when a thrice-sufficient time for that purpose had elapsed, he was not seen again in his accustomed walks, or in his new house, or in his old one. He was gone for good, nobody knew whither. It was soon discovered that he had empowered his lawyer to dispose of all his property, real and personal, in the borough, and pay in the proceeds to the account of an unknown person at one of the large London banks. The person was by some supposed to be himself under an assumed name; but few, if any, had certain knowledge of that fact.

The elegant new residence was sold with the rest of his possessions; and its purchaser was no other than Downe, now a thriving man in the borough, and one whose growing family and new wife required more roomy accommodation than was afforded by the little house up the narrow side street. Barnet's old habitation was bought by the trustees of the Congregational Baptist body in that town, who pulled down the time-honoured dwelling and built a new chapel on its site. By the time the last hour of that, to Barnet, eventful year had chimed, every vestige of him had disappeared from the precincts of his native place, and the name became extinct in the borough of Port-Bredy, after having been a living force therein for more than two hundred years.

9

Twenty-one years and six months do not pass without setting a mark even upon durable stone and triple brass; upon humanity such a period works nothing less than transformation. In Barnet's old birthplace vivacious young children with bones like india-rubber had grown up to be stable men and women, men and women had dried in the skin, stiffened, withered, and sunk into decrepitude; while selections from every class had been consigned to the outlying cemetery. Of inorganic differences the greatest was that a railway had invaded the town, tying it on to a main line at a junction a dozen miles off. Barnet's house on the harbour-road, once so insistently new, had acquired a respectable mellowness, with ivy, Virginia creepers, lichens, damp patches, and even constitutional infirmities of its own like its elder fellows. Its architecture, once so very improved and modern, had already become stale in style, without having reached the dignity of being old-fashioned. Trees about the harbour-road had increased in circumference or disappeared under the saw; while the church had had such a tremendous practical joke played upon it by some facetious restorer or other as to be scarce recognizable by its dearest old friends.

During this long interval George Barnet had never once been seen or heard of in the town of his fathers.

It was the evening of a market-day, and some half-dozen middle-aged farmers and dairymen were lounging round the bar of the Black-Bull Hotel, occasionally dropping a remark to each other, and less frequently to the two barmaids who stood within the pewter-topped counter in a perfunctory attitude of attention, these latter sighing and making a private observation to one another at odd intervals, on more interesting experiences than the present.

'Days get shorter,' said one of the dairymen, as he looked towards the street, and noticed that the lamplighter was passing by.

The farmers merely acknowledged by their countenances the propriety of this remark, and finding that nobody else spoke, one of the barmaids said 'yes', in a tone of painful duty.

'Come fair-day we shall have to light up before we start for home-along.'

'That's true,' his neighbour conceded, with a gaze of blankness.

'And after that we shan't see much further difference all's winter.'

The rest were not unwilling to go even so far as this.

The barmaid sighed again, and raised one of her hands from the counter on which they rested to scratch the smallest surface of her face with the smallest of her fingers. She looked towards the door, and presently remarked, 'I think I hear the 'bus coming in from station.'

The eyes of the dairymen and farmers turned to the glass door dividing the hall from the porch, and in a minute or two the omnibus drew up outside. Then there was a lumbering down of luggage, and then a man came into the hall, followed by a porter with a portmanteau on his poll, which he deposited on a bench.

The stranger was an elderly person, with curly ashen-white hair, a deeply-creviced outer corner to each eyelid, and a countenance baked by innumerable suns to the colour of terra-cotta, its hue and that of his hair contrasting like heat and cold respectively. He walked meditatively and gently, like one who was fearful of disturbing his own mental equilibrium. But whatever lay at the bottom of his breast had evidently made him so accustomed to its situation there that it caused him little practical inconvenience.

He paused in silence while, with his dubious eyes fixed on the barmaids, he seemed to consider himself. In a moment or two he addressed them, and asked to be accommodated for the night. As he waited he looked curiously round the hall, but said nothing. As soon as invited he disappeared up the staircase, preceded by a chambermaid and candle, and followed by a lad with his trunk. Not a soul had recognized him.

A quarter of an hour later, when the farmers and dairymen had driven off to their homesteads in the country, he came downstairs, took a biscuit and one glass of wine, and walked out into the town, where the radiance from the shop-windows had grown so in volume of late years as to flood with cheerfulness every standing cart, barrow, stall, and idler that occupied the wayside, whether shabby or genteel. His chief interest at present seemed to lie in the names painted over the shop-fronts and on doorways, as far as they were visible; these now differed to an ominous extent from what they had been one-and-twenty years before.

The traveller passed on till he came to the bookseller's, where he looked in through the glass door. A fresh-faced young man was standing behind the counter, otherwise the shop was empty. The gray-haired observer entered, asked for some periodical by way of paying for admission, and with his elbow on the counter began to turn over the pages he had bought, though that he read nothing was obvious.

At length he said, 'Is old Mr Watkins still alive?' in a voice which had a curious youthful cadence in it even now.

'My father is dead, sir,' said the young man.

'Ah, I am sorry to hear it,' said the stranger. 'But it is so many years since I last visited this town that I could hardly expect it should be otherwise.' After a short silence he continued – 'And is the firm of Barnet, Browse and Company still in existence? – they used to be large flax-merchants and twine-spinners here?'

'The firm is still going on, sir, but they have dropped the name of Barnet. I believe that was a sort of fancy name – at least, I never knew of any living Barnet. 'Tis now Browse and Co.'

'And does Andrew Jones still keep on as architect?'

'He's dead, sir.'

'And the vicar of St Mary's – Mr Melrose?'

'He's been dead a great many years.'

'Dear me!' He paused yet longer, and cleared his voice. 'Is Mr Downe, the solicitor, still in practice?'

'No, sir, he's dead. He died about seven years ago.'

Here it was a longer silence still; and an attentive observer would have noticed that the paper in the stranger's hand increased its imperceptible tremor to a visible shake. That gray-haired gentleman noticed it himself, and rested the paper on the counter. 'Is *Mrs* Downe still alive?' he asked, closing his lips firmly as soon as the words were out of his mouth, and dropping his eyes.

'Yes, sir, she's alive and well. She's living at the old place.'

'In East Street?'

'O no; at Château Ringdale. I believe it has been in the family for some generations.'

'She lives with her children, perhaps?'

'No; she has no children of her own. There were some Miss Downes; I think they were Mr Downe's daughters by a former wife; but they are married and living in other parts of the town. Mrs Downe lives alone.'

'Quite alone?'

'Yes, sir; quite alone.'

The newly-arrived gentleman went back to the hotel and dined; after which he made some change in his dress, shaved back his beard to the fashion that had prevailed twenty years earlier, when he was young and interesting, and once more emerging, bent his steps in the direction of the harbour-road. Just before getting to the point where the pavement ceased and the houses isolated themselves, he overtook a shambling, stooping, unshaven man, who at first sight appeared like a professional tramp, his shoulders having a perceptible greasiness as they passed under the gaslight. Each pedestrian momentarily turned and regarded the other, and the tramp-like gentleman started back.

'Good – why – is that Mr Barnet? 'Tis Mr Barnet, surely!'

'Yes; and you are Charlson?'

'Yes – ah – you notice my appearance. The Fates have rather ill-used me. By-the-bye, that fifty pounds. I never paid it, did I? . . . But I was not ungrateful!' Here the stooping man laid one hand emphatically on the palm of the other. 'I gave you a chance, Mr George Barnet, which many men would have thought full value received – the chance to marry your Lucy. As far as the world was concerned, your wife was a *drowned woman*, hey?'

'Heaven forbid all that, Charlson!'

'Well, well, 'twas a wrong way of showing gratitude, I suppose. And now a drop of something to drink for old acquaintance' sake! And, Mr Barnet, she's again free – there's a chance now if you care for it – ha, ha!' And the speaker pushed his tongue into his hollow cheek and slanted his eye in the old fashion.

'I know all,' said Barnet quickly; and slipping a small present into the hands of the needy, saddening man, he stepped ahead and was soon in the outskirts of the town.

He reached the harbour-road, and paused before the entrance to a well-known house. It was so highly bosomed in trees and shrubs planted since the erection of the building that one would scarcely have recognized the spot as that which had been a mere neglected slope till chosen as a site for a dwelling. He opened the swing-gate, closed it noiselessly, and gently moved into the semicircular drive, which remained exactly as it had been marked out by Barnet on the morning when Lucy Savile ran in to thank him for procuring her the post of governess to Downe's children. But the growth of trees and bushes which revealed itself at every step was beyond all expectation; sun-proof and moon-proof bowers vaulted the walks, and the walls of the house were uniformly bearded with creeping plants as high as the first-floor windows.

After lingering for a few minutes in the dusk of the bending boughs, the visitor rang the door-bell, and on the servant appearing, he announced himself as 'an old friend of Mrs Downe's'.

The hall was lighted, but not brightly, the gas being turned low, as if visitors were rare. There was a stagnation in the dwelling; it seemed to be waiting. Could it really be waiting for him? The partitions which had been probed by Barnet's walking-stick when the mortar was green, were now quite brown with the antiquity of their varnish, and the ornamental woodwork of the staircase, which had glistened with a pale yellow newness when first erected, was now of a rich wine-colour. During the servant's absence the following colloquy could be dimly heard through the nearly closed door of the drawing-room.

'He didn't give his name?'

'He only said "an old friend", ma'am.'

'What kind of gentleman is he?'

'A staidish gentleman, with gray hair.'

The voice of the second speaker seemed to affect the listener greatly. After a pause, the lady said, 'Very well, I will see him.'

And the stranger was shown in face to face with the Lucy who had once been Lucy Savile. The round cheek of that formerly young lady had, of course, alarmingly flattened its curve in her modern representative; a pervasive grayness overspread her once dark brown hair, like morning rime on heather. The parting down the middle was wide and jagged; once it had been a thin white line, a narrow crevice between two high banks of shade. But there was still enough left to form a handsome knob behind, and some curls beneath inwrought with a few hairs like silver wires were very becoming. In her eyes the only modification was that their originally mild rectitude of expression had become a little more stringent than heretofore. Yet she was still girlish – a girl who had been gratuitously weighted by destiny with a burden of five-and-forty years instead of her proper twenty.

'Lucy, don't you know me?' he said, when the servant had closed the door.

'I knew you the instant I saw you!' she returned cheerfully. 'I don't know why, but I always thought you would come back to your old town again.'

She gave him her hand, and then they sat down. 'They said you were dead,' continued Lucy, 'but I never thought so. We should have heard of it for certain if you had been.'

'It is a very long time since we met.'

'Yes; what you must have seen, Mr Barnet, in all these roving years, in comparison with what I have seen in this quiet place!' Her face grew more serious. 'You know my husband has been dead a long time? I am a lonely old woman now, considering what I have been; though Mr Downe's daughters – all married – manage to keep me pretty cheerful.'

'And I am a lonely old man, and have been any time these twenty years.'

'But where have you kept yourself? And why did you go off so mysteriously?'

'Well, Lucy, I have kept myself a little in America, and a little in

Australia, a little in India, a little at the Cape, and so on; I have not stayed in any place for a long time, as it seems to me, and yet more than twenty years have flown. But when people get to my age two years go like one! – Your second question, why did I go away so mysteriously, is surely not necessary. You guessed why, didn't you?'

'No, I never once guessed,' she said simply; 'nor did Charles, nor did anybody as far as I know.'

'Well, indeed! Now think it over again, and then look at me, and say if you can't guess?'

She looked him in the face with an inquiring smile. 'Surely not because of me?' she said, pausing at the commencement of surprise.

Barnet nodded, and smiled again; but his smile was sadder than hers.

'Because I married Charles?' she asked.

'Yes; solely because you married him on the day I was free to ask you to marry me. My wife died four-and-twenty hours before you went to church with Downe. The fixing of my journey at that particular moment was because of her funeral; but once away I knew I should have no inducement to come back, and took my steps accordingly.'

Her face assumed an aspect of gentle reflection, and she looked up and down his form with great interest in her eyes. 'I never thought of it!' she said. 'I knew, of course, that you had once implied some warmth of feeling towards me, but I concluded that it passed off. And I have always been under the impression that your wife was alive at the time of my marriage. Was it not stupid of me! – But you will have some tea or something? I have never dined late, you know, since my husband's death. I have got into the way of making a regular meal of tea. You will have some tea with me, will you not?'

The travelled man assented quite readily, and tea was brought in. They sat and chatted over the tray, regardless of the flying hour. 'Well, well!' said Barnet presently, as for the first time he leisurely surveyed the room; 'how like it all is, and yet how different! Just where your piano stands was a board on a couple of trestles, bearing the patterns of wall-papers, when I was last here. I was choosing them – standing in this way, as it might be. Then my servant came in at the door, and handed me a note, so. It was from Downe, and announced that you were just going to be married to him. I chose no more wall-papers – tore up all those I had selected, and left the house. I never entered it again till now.'

'Ah, at last I understand it all,' she murmured.

They had both risen and gone to the fireplace. The mantel came almost on a level with her shoulder, which gently rested against it, and Barnet laid his hand upon the shelf close beside her shoulder. 'Lucy,' he said, 'better late than never. Will you marry me now?'

She started back, and the surprise which was so obvious in her wrought even greater surprise in him that it should be so. It was difficult to believe that she had been quite blind to the situation, and yet all reason and common sense went to prove that she was not acting.

'You take me quite unawares by such a question!' she said, with a forced laugh of uneasiness. It was the first time she had shown any embarrassment at all. 'Why,' she added, 'I couldn't marry you for the world.'

'Not after all this! Why not?'

'It is – I would – I really think I may say it – I would upon the whole rather marry you, Mr Barnet, than any other man I have ever met, if I ever dreamed of marriage again. But I don't dream of it – it is quite out of my thoughts; I have not the least intention of marrying again.'

'But – on my account – couldn't you alter your plans a little? Come!'

'Dear Mr Barnet,' she said with a little flutter, 'I would on your account if on anybody's in existence. But you don't know in the least what it is you are asking – such an impracticable thing – I won't say ridiculous, of course, because I see that you are really in earnest, and earnestness is never ridiculous to my mind.'

'Well, yes,' said Barnet more slowly, dropping her hand, which he had taken at the moment of pleading, 'I am in earnest. The resolve, two months ago, at the Cape, to come back once more was, it is true, rather sudden, and as I see now, not well considered. But I am in earnest in asking.'

'And I in declining. With all good feeling and all kindness, let me say that I am quite opposed to the idea of marrying a second time.'

'Well, no harm has been done,' he answered, with the same subdued and tender humorousness that he had shown on such occasions in early life. 'If you really won't accept me, I must put up with it, I suppose.' His eye fell on the clock as he spoke. 'Had you any notion that it was so late?' he asked. 'How absorbed I have been!'

She accompanied him to the hall, helped him to put on his overcoat, and let him out of the house herself.

'Good-night,' said Barnet, on the doorstep, as the lamp shone in his face. 'You are not offended with me?'

'Certainly not. Nor you with me?'

'I'll consider whether I am or not,' he pleasantly replied. 'Good-night.'

She watched him safely through the gate; and when his footsteps had died away upon the road, closed the door softly and returned to the room.

Here the modest widow long pondered his speeches, with eyes dropped to an unusually low level. Barnet's urbanity under the blow of her refusal greatly impressed her. After having his long period of probabion rendered useless by her decision, he had shown no anger, and had philosophically taken her words as if he deserved no better ones. It was very gentlemanly of him, certainly; it was more than gentlemanly: it was heroic and grand. The more she meditated, the more she questioned the virtue of her conduct in checking him so peremptorily; and went to her bedroom in a mood of dissatisfaction. On looking in the glass she was reminded that there was not so much remaining of her former beauty as to make his frank declaration an impulsive natural homage to her cheeks and eyes; it must undoubtedly have arisen from an old staunch feeling of his, deserving tenderest consideration. She recalled to her mind with much pleasure that he had told her he was staying at the Black-Bull Hotel; so that if, after waiting a day or two, he should not, in his modesty, call again, she might then send him a nice little note. To alter her views for the present was far from her intention; but she would allow herself to be induced to reconsider the case, as any generous woman ought to do.

The morrow came and passed, and Mr Barnet did not drop in. At every knock, light youthful hues flew across her cheek; and she was abstracted in the presence of her other visitors. In the evening she walked about the house, not knowing what to do with herself; the conditions of existence seemed totally different from those which ruled only four-and-twenty short hours ago. What had been at first a tantalizing, elusive sentiment was getting acclimatized within her as a definite hope, and her person was so informed by that emotion that she might almost have stood as its emblematical representative by the time the clock struck ten. In short, an interest in Barnet precisely resembling that of her early youth led her present heart to belie her yesterday's words to him, and she longed to see him again.

The next day she walked out early, thinking she might meet him in the street. The growing beauty of her romance absorbed her, and she went from the street to the fields, and from the fields to the shore, without any consciousness of distance, till reminded by her weariness that she could go no further. He had nowhere appeared. In the evening she took a step which under the circumstances seemed justifiable; she wrote a note to him at the hotel, inviting him to tea with her at six precisely, and signing her note 'Lucy'.

In a quarter of an hour the messenger came back. Mr Barnet had left the hotel early in the morning of the day before, but he had stated that he would probably return in the course of the week.

The note was sent back, to be given to him immediately on his arrival.

There was no sign from the inn that this desired event had occurred, either on the next day or the day following. On both nights she had been restless, and had scarcely slept half-an-hour.

On the Saturday, putting off all diffidence, Lucy went herself to the Black-Bull, and questioned the staff closely.

Mr Barnet had cursorily remarked when leaving that he might return on the Thursday or Friday, but they were directed not to reserve a room for him unless he should write.

He had left no address.

Lucy sorrowfully took back her note, went home, and resolved to wait.

She did wait – years and years – but Barnet never reappeared.

APRIL 1880

INTERLOPERS AT THE KNAP

I

The north road from Casterbridge is tedious and lonely, especially in winter-time. Along a part of its course it connects with Long-Ash Lane, a monotonous track without a village or hamlet for many miles, and with very seldom a turning. Unapprized wayfarers who are too old, or too young, or in other respects too weak for the distance to be traversed, but who, nevertheless, have to walk it, say, as they look wistfully ahead, 'Once at the top of that hill, and I must surely see the end of Long-Ash Lane!' But they reach the hilltop, and Long-Ash Lane stretches in front as mercilessly as before.

Some few years ago a certain farmer was riding through this lane in the gloom of a winter evening. The farmer's friend, a dairyman, was riding beside him. A few paces in the rear rode the farmer's man. All three were well horsed on strong, round-barrelled cobs; and to be well horsed was to be in better spirits about Long-Ash Lane than poor pedestrians could attain to during its passage.

But the farmer did not talk much to his friend as he rode along. The enterprise which had brought him there filled his mind; for in truth it was important. Not altogether so important was it, perhaps, when estimated by its value to society at large; but if the true measure of a deed be proportionate to the space it occupies in the heart of him who undertakes it, Farmer Charles Darton's business tonight could hold its own with the business of kings.

He was a large farmer. His turnover, as it is called, was probably thirty thousand pounds a year. He had a great many draught horses, a great many milch cows, and of sheep a multitude. This comfortable position was, however, none of his own making. It had been created by his father, a man of a very different stamp from the present representative of the line.

Darton, the father, had been a one-idea'd character, with a buttoned-up pocket and a chink-like eye brimming with commercial subtlety. In Darton the son, this trade subtlety had become transmuted into emotional, and the harshness had disappeared; he would have been called a sad man but for his constant care not to divide himself from lively friends by piping notes out of harmony with theirs. Contemplative, he allowed his mind to be a quiet meeting-place for memories and hopes. So that, naturally enough, since succeeding to the agricultural calling, and up to his present age of thirty-two, he had neither advanced nor receded as a capitalist – a stationary result which did not agitate one of his unambitious, unstrategic nature, since he had all that he desired. The motive of his expedition tonight showed the same absence of anxious regard for Number One.

The party rode on in the slow, safe trot proper to night-time and bad roads, Farmer Darton's head jigging rather unromantically up and down against the sky, and his motions being repeated with bolder emphasis by his friend Japheth Johns; while those of the latter were travestied in jerks still less softened by art in the person of the lad who attended them. A pair of whitish objects hung one on each side of the latter, bumping against him at each step, and still further spoiling the grace of his seat. On close inspection they might have been perceived to be open rush baskets – one containing a turkey, and the other some bottles of wine.

'D'ye feel ye can meet your fate like a man, neighbour Darton?' asked Johns, breaking a silence which had lasted while five-and-twenty hedgerow trees had glided by.

Mr Darton with a half-laugh murmured, 'Ay – call it my fate! Hanging and wiving go by destiny.' And then they were silent again.

The darkness thickened rapidly, at intervals shutting down on the land in a perceptible flap, like the wave of a wing. The customary close of day was accelerated by a simultaneous blurring of the air. With the fall of night had come a mist just damp enough to incommode, but not sufficient to saturate them. Countrymen as they were – born, as may be said, with only an open door between them and the four seasons – they regarded the mist but as an added obscuration, and ignored its humid quality.

They were travelling in a direction that was enlivened by no modern current of traffic, the place of Darton's pilgrimage being an old-fashioned village – one of the Hintocks (several villages of that name, with a distinctive prefix or affix, lying thereabout) – where the people make the best cider and cider-wine in all Wessex, and where the dunghills smell of pomace instead of stable refuse as elsewhere. The lane was sometimes so narrow that the brambles of the hedge, which hung forward like anglers' rods over a stream, scratched their hats and hooked their whiskers as they passed. Yet this neglected lane had been a highway to Queen Elizabeth's subjects and the cavalcades of the past. Its day was over now, and its history as a national artery done for ever.

'Why I have decided to marry her,' resumed Darton (in a measured musical voice of confidence which revealed a good deal of his composition), as he glanced round to see that the lad was not too near, 'is not only that I like her, but that I can do no better, even from a fairly practical point of view. That I might ha' looked higher is possibly true, though it is really all nonsense. I have had experience enough in looking above me. "No more superior women for me," said I – you know when. Sally is a comely, independent, simple character, with no make-up about her, who'll think me as much a superior to her as I used to think – you know who I mean – was to me.'

'Ay', said Johns. 'However, I shouldn't call Sally Hall simple. Primary, because no Sally is; secondary, because if some could be, this one wouldn't. 'Tis a wrong denomination to apply to a woman, Charles, and affects me, as your best man, like cold water. 'Tis like recommending a stage play by saying there's neither murder, villainy, nor harm of any sort in it, when that's what you've paid your half-crown to see.'

'Well; may your opinion do you good. Mine's a different one.' And turning the conversation from the philosophical to the practical, Darton expressed a hope that the said Sally had received what he'd sent on by the carrier that day.

Johns wanted to know what that was.

'It is a dress,' said Darton. 'Not exactly a wedding-dress; though she may use it as one if she likes. It is rather serviceable than showy – suitable for the winter weather.'

'Good,' said Johns. 'Serviceable is a wise word in a bridegroom. I commend 'ee, Charles.'

'For,' said Darton, 'why should a woman dress up like a rope-dancer because she's going to do the most solemn deed of her life except dying?'

'Faith, why? But she will, because she will, I suppose,' said Dairyman Johns.

'H'm,' said Darton.

The lane they followed had been nearly straight for several miles, but they now left it for a smaller one which after winding uncertainly for some distance forked into two. By night country roads are apt to reveal ungainly qualities which pass without observation during day; and though Darton had travelled this way before, he had not done so frequently, Sally having been wooed at the house of a relative near his own. He never remembered seeing at this spot a pair of alternative ways looking so equally probable as these two did now. Johns rode on a few steps.

'Don't be out of heart, sonny,' he cried. 'Here's a handpost. Ezra –

come and climm this post, and tell us the way.'

The lad dismounted, and jumped into the hedge where the post stood under a tree.

'Unstrap the baskets, or you'll smash up that wine!' cried Darton, as the young man began spasmodically to climb the post, baskets and all.

'Was there ever less head in a brainless world?' said Johns. 'Here, simple Ezzy, I'll do it.' He leapt off, and with much puffing climbed the post, striking a match when he reached the top, and moving the light along the arm, the lad standing and gazing at the spectacle.

'I have faced tantalization these twenty years with a temper as mild as milk!' said Japheth; 'but such things as this don't come short of devilry!' And flinging the match away, he slipped down to the ground.

'What's the matter?' asked Darton.

'Not a letter, sacred or heathen – not so much as would tell us the way to the town of Smokeyhole – ever I should sin to say it! Either the moss and mildew have eat away the words, or we have arrived in a land where the natyves have lost the art o' writing, and should ha' brought our compass like Christopher Columbus.'

'Let us take the straightest road,' said Darton placidly; 'I shan't be sorry to get there – 'tis a tiresome ride. I would have driven if I had known.'

'Nor I neither, sir,' said Ezra. 'These straps plough my shoulder like a zull. If 'tis much further to your lady's home, Maister Darton, I shall ask to be let carry half of these good things in my innerds – hee, hee!'

'Don't you be such a reforming radical, Ezra,' said Johns sternly. 'Here, I'll take the turkey.'

This being done, they went forward by the right-hand lane, which ascended a hill, the left winding away under a plantation. The pit-a-pit of their horses' hoofs lessened up the slope; and the ironical directing-post stood in solitude as before, holding out its blank arms to the raw breeze, which brought a snore from the wood as if Skrymir the Giant were sleeping there.

2

Three miles to the left of the travellers, along the road they had not followed, rose an old house with mullioned windows of Ham-hill stone, and chimneys of lavish solidity. It stood at the top of a slope beside King's-Hintock village-street, only a mile or two from King's-Hintock Court, yet quite shut away from that mansion and its precincts. Immediately in front of it grew a large sycamore tree, whose bared roots formed a convenient staircase from the road below to the front door of the dwelling. Its situation gave the house what little distinctive name it possessed, namely, 'The Knap'. Some forty yards off a brook dribbled past, which, for its size, made a great deal of noise. At the back was a dairy barton, accessible for vehicles and live-stock by a side 'drong'. Thus much only of the character of the homestead could be divined out of doors at this shady evening-time.

But within there was plenty of light to see by, as plenty was construed at Hintock. Beside a Tudor fireplace, whose moulded four-centred arch was nearly hidden by a figured blue-cloth blower, were seated two women – mother and daughter – Mrs Hall, and Sarah, or Sally; for this was a part of the world where the latter modification had not as yet been effaced as a vulgarity by the march of intellect. The owner of the name was the young woman by whose means Mr Darton proposed to put an end to his bachelor condition on the approaching day.

The mother's bereavement had been so long ago as not to leave much mark of its occurrence upon her now, either in face or clothes. She had resumed the mob-cap of her early married life, enlivening its whiteness by a few rose-du-Barry ribbons. Sally required no such aids to pinkness. Roseate good-nature lit up her gaze; her features showed curves of decision and judgment; and she might have been regarded without much mistake as a warm-hearted, quick-spirited, handsome girl.

She did most of the talking, her mother listening with a half-absent air, as she picked up fragments of red-hot wood ember with the tongs, and piled them upon the brands. But the number of speeches that passed was very small in proportion to the meanings exchanged. Long experience together often enabled them to see the course of thought in each other's minds without a word being spoken. Behind them, in the centre of the room, the table was spread for supper, certain whiffs of air laden with fat vapours, which ever and anon entered from the kitchen, denoting its preparation there.

'The new gown he was going to send you stays about on the way like himself,' Sally's mother was saying.

'Yes, not finished, I daresay,' cried Sally independently. 'Lord, I shouldn't be amazed if it didn't come at all! Young men make such kind promises when they are near you, and forget 'em when they go away. But he doesn't intend it as a wedding-gown – he gives it to me merely as a gown to wear when I like – a travelling-dress is what it would be called by some. Come rathe or come late it don't much matter, as I have a dress of my own to fall back upon. But what time is it?'

She went to the family clock and opened the glass, for the hour was not otherwise discernible by night, and indeed at all times was rather a thing to be investigated than beheld, so much more wall than window was there in the apartment. 'It is nearly eight,' said she.

'Eight o'clock, and neither dress nor man,' said Mrs Hall.

'Mother, if you think to tantalize me by talking like that, you are much mistaken! Let him be as late as he will – or stay away altogether – I don't care,' said Sally. But a tender minute quaver in the negation showed that there was something forced in that statement.

Mrs Hall perceived it, and drily observed that she was not so sure about Sally not caring. 'But perhaps you don't care so much as I do, after all,' she said. 'For I see what you don't, that it is a good and flourishing match for you; a very honourable offer in Mr Darton. And I think I see a kind husband in him. So pray God 'twill go smooth, and wind up well.'

Sally would not listen to misgivings. Of course it would go smoothly, she asserted. 'How you are up and down, mother!' she went on. 'At this moment, whatever hinders him, we are not so anxious to see him as he is to be here, and his thought runs on before him, and settles down upon us like the star in the east. Hark!' she exclaimed, with a breath of relief, her eyes sparkling. 'I hear something. Yes – here they are!'

The next moment her mother's slower ear also distinguished the familiar reverberation occasioned by footsteps clambering up the roots of the sycamore.

'Yes, it sounds like them at last,' she said. 'Well, it is not so very late after all, considering the distance.'

The footfall ceased, and they arose, expecting a knock. They began to think it might have been, after all, some neighbouring villager under Bacchic influence, giving the centre of the road a wide berth, when their doubts were dispelled by the new-comer's entry into the passage. The door of the room was gently opened, and there appeared, not the pair of travellers with whom we have already made acquaintance, but a pale-faced man in the garb of extreme poverty – almost in rags.

O, it's a tramp – gracious me!' said Sally, starting back.

His cheeks and eye-orbits were deep concaves – rather, it might be, from natural weakness of constitution than irregular living, though there were indications that he had led no careful life. He gazed at the two women fixedly for a moment: then with an abashed, humiliated demeanour, dropped his glance to the floor, and sank into a chair without uttering a word.

Sally was in advance of her mother, who had remained standing by the fire. She now tried to discern the visitor across the candles.

'Why – mother,' said Sally faintly, turning back to Mrs Hall. 'It is Phil, from Australia!'

Mrs Hall started, and grew pale, and a fit of coughing seized the man with the ragged clothes. 'To come home like this!' she said. 'O, Philip – are you ill?'

'No, no, mother,' replied he impatiently, as soon as he could speak.

'But for God's sake how do you come here – and just now, too?'

'Well, I am here,' said the man. 'How it is I hardly know. I've come home, mother, because I was driven to it. Things were against me out there, and went from bad to worse.'

'Then why didn't you let us know? – you've not writ a line for the last two or three years.'

The son admitted sadly that he had not. He said that he had hoped and thought he might fetch up again, and be able to send good news. Then he had been obliged to abandon that hope, and had finally come home from sheer necessity – previously to making a new start. 'Yes, things are very bad with me,' he repeated, perceiving their commiserating glances at his clothes.

They brought him nearer the fire, took his hat from his thin hand, which was so small and smooth as to show that his attempts to fetch up again had not been in a manual direction. His mother resumed her inquiries, and dubiously asked if he had chosen to come that particular night for any special reason.

For no reason, he told her. His arrival had been quite at random. Then Philip Hall looked round the room, and saw for the first time that the table was laid somewhat luxuriously, and for a larger number than themselves; and that an air of festivity pervaded their dress. He asked quickly what was going on.

'Sally is going to be married in a day or two,' replied the mother; and she explained how Mr Darton, Sally's intended husband, was coming there that night with the groomsman, Mr Johns, and other details. 'We thought it must be their step when we heard you,' said Mrs Hall.

The needy wanderer looked again on the floor. 'I see – I see,' he murmured. 'Why, indeed, should I have come tonight? Such folk as I are not wanted here at these times, naturally. And I have no business here – spoiling other people's happiness.'

'Phil,' said his mother, with a tear in her eye, but with a thinness of lip and severity of manner which were presumably not more than past events justified; 'since you speak like that to me, I'll speak honestly to you. For these three years you have taken no thought for us. You left home with a good supply of money, and strength and education, and you ought to have made good use of it all. But you come back like a beggar; and that you come in a very awkward time for us cannot be denied. Your return tonight may do us much harm. But mind – you are welcome to this home as long as it is mine. I don't wish to turn you adrift. We will make the best of a bad job; and I hope you are not seriously ill?'

'O no. I have only this infernal cough.'

She looked at him anxiously. 'I think you had better go to bed at once,' she said.

'Well – I shall be out of the way there,' said the son wearily. 'Having ruined myself don't let me ruin you by being seen in these togs, for Heaven's sake. Who do you say Sally is going to be married to – a Farmer Darton?'

'Yes – a gentleman-farmer – quite a wealthy man. Far better in station than she could have expected. It is a good thing, altogether.'

'Well done, little Sal!' said her brother, brightening and looking up at her with a smile. 'I ought to have written; but perhaps I have thought of you all the more. But let me get out of sight, I would rather go and jump into the river than be seen here. But have you anything I can drink? I am confoundedly thirsty with my long tramp.'

'Yes, yes, we will bring something upstairs to you,' said Sally, with grief in her face.

'Ay, that will do nicely. But, Sally and mother—' He stopped, and they waited. 'Mother, I have not told you all,' he resumed slowly, still looking on the floor between his knees. 'Sad as what you see of me is, there's worse behind.'

His mother gazed upon him in grieved suspense, and Sally went and leant upon the bureau, listening for every sound, and sighing. Suddenly she turned round, saying, 'Let them come, I don't care! Philip, tell the worst, and take your time.'

'Well, then,' said the unhappy Phil, 'I am not the only one in this mess. Would to Heaven I were! But—'

'O, Phil!'

'I have a wife as destitute as I.'

'A wife?' said his mother.

'Unhappily!'

'A wife! Yes, that is the way with sons!'

'And besides—' said he.

'Besides! O, Philip, surely—'

'I have two little children.'

'Wife and children!' whispered Mrs Hall, sinking down confounded.

'Poor little things!' said Sally involuntarily.

His mother turned again to him. 'I suppose these helpless beings are left in Australia?'

'No. They are in England.'

'Well, I can only hope you've left them in a respectable place.'

'I have not left them at all. They are here – within a few yards of us. In short, they are in the stable.'

'Where?'

'In the stable. I did not like to bring them indoors till I had seen you, mother, and broken the bad news a bit to you. They were very tired, and are resting out there on some straw.'

Mrs Hall's fortitude visibly broke down. She had been brought up not without refinement, and was even more moved by such a collapse of genteel aims as this than a substantial dairyman's widow would in ordinary have been moved. 'Well, it must be borne,' she said, in a low voice, with her hands tightly joined. 'A starving son, a starving wife, starving children! Let it be. But why is this come to us now, today, tonight? Could no other misfortune happen to helpless women than this, which will quite upset my poor girl's chance of a happy life? Why have you done us this wrong, Philip? What respectable man will come here, and marry open-eyed into a family of vagabonds?'

'Nonsense, mother!' said Sally vehemently, while her face flushed. 'Charley isn't the man to desert me. But if he should be, and won't marry me because Phil's come, let him go and marry elsewhere. I won't be ashamed of my own flesh and blood for any man in England – not I!' And then Sally turned away and burst into tears.

'Wait till you are twenty years older and you will tell a different tale,' replied her mother.

The son stood up. 'Mother,' he said bitterly, 'as I have come, so I will go. All I ask of you is that you will allow me and mine to lie in your stable tonight. I give you my word that we'll be gone by break of day, and trouble you no further!'

Mrs Hall, the mother, changed at that. 'O no,' she answered hastily; 'never shall it be said that I sent any of my own family from my door. Bring 'em in, Philip, or take me out to them.'

'We will put 'em all into the large bedroom,' said Sally, brightening, 'and make up a large fire. Let's go and help them in, and call Rebekah.' (Rebekah was the woman who assisted at the dairy and housework; she lived in a cottage hard by with her husband, who attended to the cows.)

Sally went to fetch a lantern from the back-kitchen, but her brother said, 'You won't want a light. I lit the lantern that was hanging there.'

'What must we call your wife?' asked Mrs Hall.

'Helena,' said Philip.

With shawls over their heads they proceeded towards the back door.

'One minute before you go,' interrupted Philip. 'I – I haven't confessed all.'

'Then Heaven help us!' said Mrs Hall, pushing to the door and clasping her hands in calm despair.

'We passed through Evershead as we came,' he continued, 'and I just looked in at the "Sow-and-Acorn" to see if old Mike still kept on there as usual. The carrier had come in from Sherton Abbas at that moment, and guessing that I was bound for this place – for I think he knew me – he asked me to bring on a dressmaker's parcel for Sally that was marked "immediate". My wife had walked on with the children. 'Twas a flimsy parcel and the paper was torn, and I found on looking at it that it was a thick warm gown. I didn't wish you to see poor Helena in a shabby state. I was ashamed that you should – 'twas not what she was born to. I untied the parcel in the road, took it on to her where she was waiting in the Lower Barn, and told her I had managed to get it for her, and that she was to ask no question. She, poor thing, must have supposed I obtained it on trust, through having reached a place where I was known, for she put it on gladly enough. She has it on now. Sally has other gowns, I daresay.'

Sally looked at her mother, speechless.

'You have others. I daresay!' repeated Phil, with a sick man's impatience. 'I thought to myself, "Better Sally cry than Helena freeze." Well, is the dress of great consequence? 'Twas nothing very ornamental, as far as I could see.'

'No – no; not of consequence,' returned Sally sadly, adding in a gentle voice, 'You will not mind if I lend her another instead of that one, will you?'

Philip's agitation at the confession had brought on another attack of the cough, which seemed to shake him to pieces. He was so obviously unfit to sit in a chair that they helped him upstairs at once; and having hastily given him a cordial and kindled the bedroom fire, they descended to fetch their unhappy new relations.

3

It was with strange feelings that the girl and her mother, lately so cheerful, passed out of the back door into the open air of the barton, laden with hay scents and the herby breath of cows. A fine sleet had begun to fall, and they trotted across the yard quickly. The stable-door was open; a light shone from it – from the lantern which always hung there, and which Philip had lighted, as he said. Softly nearing the door, Mrs Hall pronounced the name 'Helena!'

There was no answer for the moment. Looking in she was taken by surprise. Two people appeared before her. For one, instead of the drabbish woman she had expected, Mrs Hall saw a pale, dark-eyed, ladylike creature, whose personality ruled her attire rather than was ruled by it. She was in a new and handsome gown, Sally's own, and an old bonnet. She was standing up, agitated; her hand was held by her companion – none else than Sally's affianced, Farmer Charles Darton, upon whose fine figure the pale stranger's eyes were fixed, as his were fixed upon her. His other hand held the rein of his horse, which was standing saddled as if just led in.

At sight of Mrs Hall they both turned, looking at her in a way neither quite conscious nor unconscious, and without seeming to recollect that words were necessary as a solution to the scene. In another moment Sally entered also, when Mr Darton dropped his companion's hand, led the horse aside, and came to greet his betrothed and Mrs Hall.

'Ah!' he said, smiling – with something like forced composure – 'this is a roundabout way of arriving, you will say, my dear Mrs Hall. But we lost our way, which made us late. I saw a light here, and led in my horse at once – my friend Johns and my man have gone onward to the little inn with theirs, not to crowd you too much. No sooner had I entered than I saw that this lady had taken temporary shelter here – and found I was intruding.'

'She is my daughter-in-law,' said Mrs Hall calmly. 'My son, too, is in the house, but he has gone to bed unwell.'

Sally had stood staring wonderingly at the scene until this moment, hardly recognizing Darton's shake of the hand. The spell that bound her was broken by her perceiving the two little children seated on a heap of hay. She suddenly went forward, spoke to them, and took one on her arm and the other in her hand.

'And two children?' said Mr Darton, showing thus that he had not been there long enough as yet to understand the situation.

'My grandchildren,' said Mrs Hall, with as much affected ease as before.

Philip Hall's wife, in spite of this interruption to her first rencounter, seemed scarcely so much affected by it as to feel anyone's presence in addition to Mr Darton's. However, arousing herself by a quick reflection, she threw a sudden critical glance of her sad eyes upon Mrs Hall, and, apparently finding her satisfactory, advanced to her in a meek initiative. Then Sally and the stranger spoke some friendly words to each other, and Sally went on with the children into the house. Mrs Hall and Helena followed, and Mr Darton followed these, looking at Helena's dress and outline, and listening to her voice like a man in a dream.

By the time the others reached the house Sally had already gone upstairs with the tired children. She rapped against the wall for Rebekah to come in and help to attend to them, Rebekah's house being a little 'spit-and-daub' cabin leaning against the substantial stonework of Mrs Hall's taller erection. When she came a bed was made up for the little ones, and some supper given to them. On descending the stairs after seeing this done Sally went to the sitting-room. Young Mrs Hall entered it just in advance of her, having in the interim retired with her mother-in-law to take off her bonnet, and otherwise make herself presentable. Hence it was evident that no further communication could have passed between her and Mr Darton since their brief interview in the stable.

Mr Japheth Johns now opportunely arrived, and broke up the restraint of the company, after a few orthodox meteorological commentaries had passed between him and Mrs Hall by way of introduction. They at once sat down to supper, the present of wine and turkey not being produced for consumption tonight, lest the premature display of those gifts should seem to throw doubt on Mrs Hall's capacities as a provider.

'Drink hearty, Mr Johns – drink hearty,' said the matron magnanimously. 'Such as it is there's plenty of. But perhaps cider-wine is not to your taste? – though there's body in it.'

'Quite the contrairy, ma'am – quite the contrairy,' said the dairyman. 'For though I inherit the malt-liquor principle from my father, I am a cider-drinker on my mother's side. She came from these parts, you know. And there's this to be said for't – 'tis a more peaceful liquor, and don't lie about a man like your hotter drinks. With care, one may live on it a twelve-month without knocking down a neighbour, or getting a black eye from an old acquaintance.'

The general conversation thus begun was continued briskly, though it was in the main restricted to Mrs Hall and Japheth, who in truth required but little help from anybody. There being slight call upon Sally's tongue, she had ample leisure to do what her heart most desired, namely, watch her intended husband and her sister-in-law with a view of elucidating the strange momentary scene in which her mother and herself had surprised them in the stable. If that scene meant anything, it meant, at least, that they had met before. That there had been no time for explanations Sally could see, for their manner was still one of suppressed amazement at each other's presence there. Darton's eyes, too, fell continually on the gown worn by Helena as if this were an added riddle to his perplexity; though to Sally it was the one feature in the case which was no mystery. He seemed to feel that fate had impishly changed his *vis-à-vis* in the lover's jig he was about to foot; that while the gown had been expected to enclose a Sally, a Helena's face looked out from the bodice; that some long-lost hand met his own from the sleeves.

Sally could see that whatever Helena might know of Darton, she knew nothing of how the dress entered into his embarrassment. And at moments the young girl would have persuaded herself that Darton's looks at her sister-in-law were entirely the fruit of the clothes query. But surely at other times a more extensive range of speculation and sentiment was expressed by her lover's eye than that which the changed dress would account for.

Sally's independence made her one of the least jealous of women. But there was something in the relations of these two visitors which ought to be explained.

Japheth Johns continued to converse in his well-known style, interspersing his talk with some private reflections on the position of Darton and Sally, which, though the sparkle in his eye showed them to be highly entertaining to himself, were apparently not quite communicable to the company. At last he withdrew for the night, going off to the roadside inn half-a-mile ahead, whither Darton promised to follow him in a few minutes.

Half-an-hour passed, and then Mr Darton also rose to leave, Sally and her sister-in-law simultaneously wishing him good-night as they retired upstairs to their rooms. But on his arriving at the front door with Mrs Hall a sharp shower of rain began to come down, when the widow suggested that he should return to the fireside till the storm ceased.

Darton accepted her proposal, but insisted that, as it was getting late, and she was obviously tired, she should not sit up on his account, since he could let himself out of the house, and would quite enjoy smoking a pipe by the hearth alone. Mrs Hall assented; and Darton was left by himself. He spread his knees to the brands, lit up his tobacco as he had said, and sat gazing into the fire, and at the notches of the chimney-crook which hung above.

An occasional drop of rain rolled down the chimney with a hiss, and still he smoked on; but not like a man whose mind was at rest. In the long run, however, despite his meditations, early hours afield and a long ride in the open air produced their natural result. He began to doze.

How long he remained in his half-unconscious state he did not know. He suddenly opened his eyes. The back-brand had burnt itself in two, and ceased to flame; the light which he had placed on the mantelpiece had nearly gone out. But in spite of these deficiencies there was a light in the apartment, and it came from elsewhere. Turning his head he saw Philip

Hall's wife standing at the entrance of the room with a bed-candle in one hand, a small brass tea-kettle in the other, and *his* gown, as it certainly seemed, still upon her.

'Helena!' said Darton, starting up.

Her countenance expressed dismay, and her first words were an apology. 'I – did not know you were here, Mr Darton,' she said, while a blush flashed to her cheek. 'I thought every one had retired – I was coming to make a little water boil; my husband seems to be worse. But perhaps the kitchen fire can be lighted up again.'

'Don't go on my account. By all means put it on here as you intended,' said Darton. 'Allow me to help you.' He went forward to take the kettle from her hand, but she did not allow him, and placed it on the fire herself.

They stood some way apart, one on each side of the fireplace, waiting till the water should boil, the candle on the mantel between them, and Helena with her eyes on the kettle. Darton was the first to break the silence. 'Shall I call Sally?' he said.

'O no,' she quickly returned. 'We have given trouble enough already. We have no right here. But we are the sport of fate, and were obliged to come.'

'No right here!' said he in surprise.

'None. I can't explain it now,' answered Helena. 'This kettle is very slow.'

There was another pause; the proverbial dilatoriness of watched pots was never more clearly exemplified.

Helena's face was of that sort which seems to ask for assistance without the owner's knowledge – the very antipodes of Sally's, which was self-reliance expressed. Darton's eyes travelled from the kettle to Helena's face, then back to the kettle, then to the face for rather a longer time. 'So I am not to know anything of the mystery that has distracted me all the evening?' he said. 'How is it that a woman, who refused me because (as I supposed) my position was not good enough for her taste, is found to be the wife of a man who certainly seems to be worse off than I?'

'He had the prior claim,' said she.

'What! you knew him at that time?'

'Yes, yes! And he went to Australia, and sent for me, and I joined him out there!'

'Ah – that was the mystery!'

'Please say no more,' she implored. 'Whatever my errors, I have paid for them during the last five years!'

The heart of Darton was subject to sudden overflowings. He was kind to a fault. 'I am sorry from my soul,' he said, involuntarily approaching her. Helena withdrew a step or two, at which he became conscious of his movement, and quickly took his former place. Here he stood without speaking, and the little kettle began to sing.

'Well, you might have been my wife if you had chosen,' he said at last. 'But that's all past and gone. However, if you are in any trouble or poverty I shall be glad to be of service, and as your relation by marriage I shall have a right to be. Does your uncle know of your distress?'

'My uncle is dead. He left me without a farthing. And now we have two children to maintain.'

'What, left you nothing? How could he be so cruel as that?'

'I disgraced myself in his eyes.'

'Now,' said Darton earnestly, 'let me take care of the children, at least while you are so unsettled. *You* belong to another, so I cannot take care of you.'

'Yes, you can,' said a voice; and suddenly a third figure stood beside them. It was Sally. 'You can, since you seem to wish to,' she repeated. 'She no longer belongs to another. . . My poor brother is dead!'

Her face was red, her eyes sparkled, and all the woman came to the front. 'I have heard it!' she went on to him passionately. 'You can protect her now as well as the children!' She turned then to her agitated sister-in-law. 'I heard something,' said Sally (in a gentle murmur, differing much from her previous passionate words), 'and I went into his room. It must have been the moment you left. He went off so quickly, and weakly, and it was so unexpected, that I couldn't leave even to call you.'

Darton was just able to gather from the confused discourse which followed that, during his sleep by the fire, Sally's brother whom he had never seen had become worse; and that during Helena's absence for water the end had unexpectedly come. The two young women hastened upstairs, and he was again left alone.

After standing there a short time he went to the front door and looked out; till, softly closing it behind him, he advanced and stood under the large sycamore-tree. The stars were flickering coldly, and the dampness which had just descended upon the earth in rain now sent up a chill from it. Darton was in a strange position, and he felt it. The unexpected appearance, in deep poverty, of Helena – a young lady, daughter of a deceased naval officer, who had been brought up by her uncle, a solicitor, and had refused Darton in marriage years ago – the passionate, almost angry demeanour of Sally at discovering them, the abrupt announcement that Helena was a widow; all this coming together was a conjuncture difficult to cope with in a moment, and made him question whether he ought to leave the house or offer assistance. But for Sally's manner he would unhesitatingly have done the latter.

He was still standing under the tree when the door in front of him opened, and Mrs Hall came out. She went round to the garden-gate at the side without seeing him. Darton followed her, intending to speak. Pausing outside, as if in thought, she proceeded to a spot where the sun came earliest in spring-time, and where the north wind never blew; it was where the row of beehives stood under the wall. Discerning her object, he waited till she had accomplished it.

It was the universal custom thereabout to wake the bees by tapping at their hives whenever a death occurred in the household, under the belief that if this were not done the bees themselves would pine away and perish during the ensuing year. As soon as an interior buzzing responded to her tap at the first hive Mrs Hall went on to the second, and thus passed down the row. As soon as she came back he met her.

'What can I do in this trouble, Mrs Hall?' he said.

'O – nothing, thank you, nothing,' she said in a tearful voice, now just perceiving him. 'We have called Rebekah and her husband, and they will do everything necessary.' She told him in a few words the particulars of her son's arrival, broken in the health – indeed, at death's very door, though they did not suspect it – and suggested, as the result of a conversation between her and her daughter, that the wedding should be postponed.

'Yes, of course,' said Darton. 'I think now to go straight to the inn and tell Johns what has happened.' It was not till after he had shaken hands with her that he turned hesitatingly and added, 'Will you tell the mother of his children that, as they are now left fatherless, I shall be glad to take the eldest of them, if it would be any convenience to her and to you?'

Mrs Hall promised that her son's widow should be told of the offer, and they parted. He retired down the rooty slope and disappeared in the direction of the inn, where he informed Johns of the circumstances. Meanwhile Mrs Hall had entered the house. Sally was downstairs in the sitting-room alone, and her mother explained to her that Darton had readily assented to the postponement.

'No doubt he has,' said Sally, with sad emphasis. 'It is not put off for a week, or a month, or a year. I shall never marry him, and she will!'

4

Time passed, and the household on the Knap became again serene under the composing influences of daily routine. A desultory, very desultory, correspondence dragged on between Sally Hall and Darton, who, not quite knowing how to take her petulant words on the night of her brother's death, had continued passive thus long. Helena and her children remained at the dairy-house, almost of necessity, and Darton therefore deemed it advisable to stay away.

One day, seven months later on, when Mr Darton was as usual at his farm, twenty miles from King's-Hintock, a note reached him from Helena. She thanked him for his kind offer about her children, which her mother-in-law had duly communicated, and stated that she would be glad to accept it as regarded the eldest, the boy. Helena had, in truth, good need to do so, for her uncle had left her penniless, and all application to some relatives in the north had failed. There was, besides, as she said, no good school near Hintock to which she could send the child.

On a fine summer day the boy came. He was accompanied half-way by Sally and his mother – to the 'White Horse', the fine old Elizabethan inn at Chalk Newton,[1] where he was handed over to Darton's bailiff in a shining spring-cart, who met them there.

He was entered as a day-scholar at a popular school at Casterbridge, three or four miles from Darton's, having first been taught by Darton to ride a forest-pony, on which he cantered to and from the aforesaid fount of knowledge, and (as Darton hoped) brought away a promising headful of the same at each diurnal expedition. The thoughtful taciturnity into which Darton had latterly fallen was quite dissipated by the presence of this boy.

When the Christmas holidays came it was arranged that he should spend them with his mother. The journey was, for some reason or other, performed in two stages, as at his coming, except that Darton in person took the place of the bailiff, and that the boy and himself rode on horseback.

Reaching the renowned 'White Horse', Darton inquired if Miss and young Mrs Hall were there to meet little Philip (as they had agreed to be). He was answered by the appearance of Helena alone at the door.

'At the last moment Sally would not come,' she faltered.

That meeting practically settled the point towards which these long-severed persons were converging. But nothing was broached about it for some time yet. Sally Hall had, in fact, imparted the first decisive motion to events by refusing to accompany Helena. She soon gave them a second move by writing the following note:

[1] It is now pulled down, and its site occupied by a modern one in red brick (1912)

[*Private*]

DEAR CHARLES, – Living here so long and intimately with Helena, I have naturally learnt her history, especially that of it which refers to you. I am sure she would accept you as a husband at the proper time, and I think you ought to give her the opportunity. You inquire in an old note if I am sorry that I showed temper (which it *wasn't*) that night when I heard you talking to her. No, Charles, I am not sorry at all for what I said then. –
Yours sincerely,

SALLY HALL

Thus set in train, the transfer of Darton's heart back to its original quarters proceeded by mere lapse of time. In the following July, Darton went to his friend Japheth to ask him at last to fulfil the bridal office which had been in abeyance since the previous January twelvemonths.

'With all my heart, man o' constancy!' said Dairyman Johns warmly. 'I've lost most of my genteel fair complexion haymaking this hot weather, 'tis true, but I'll do your business as well as them that look better. There be scents and good hair-oil in the world yet, thank God, and they'll take off the roughest o' my edge. I'll compliment her. "Better late than never, Sally Hall," I'll say.'

'It is not Sally,' said Darton hurriedly. 'It is young Mrs Hall.'

Japheth's face, as soon as he really comprehended, became a picture of reproachful dismay. 'Not Sally?' he said. 'Why not Sally? I can't believe it! Young Mrs Hall! Well, well – where's your wisdom?'

Darton shortly explained particulars; but Johns would not be reconciled. 'She was a woman worth having if ever woman was,' he cried. 'And now to let her go!'

'But I suppose I can marry where I like,' said Darton.

'H'm,' replied the dairyman, lifting his eyebrows expressively. 'This don't become you, Charles – it really do not. If I had done such a thing you would have sworn I was a curst no'thern fool to be drawn off the scent by such a red-herring doll-oll-oll.'

Farmer Darton responded in such sharp terms to the laconic opinion that the two friends finally parted in a way they had never parted before. Johns was to be no groomsman to Darton after all. He had flatly declined. Darton went off sorry, and even unhappy, particularly as Japheth was about to leave that side of the county, so that the words which had divided them were not likely to be explained away or softened down.

A short time after the interview Darton was united to Helena at a simple matter-of-fact wedding, and she and her little girl joined the boy who had already grown to look on Darton's house as home.

For some months the farmer experienced an unprecedented happiness and satisfaction. There had been a flaw in his life, and it was as neatly mended as was humanly possible. But after a season the stream of events followed less clearly, and there were shades in his reveries. Helena was a fragile woman, of little staying-power, physically or morally, and since the time that he had originally known her – eight or ten years before – she had been severely tried. She had loved herself out, in short, and was now occasionally given to moping. Sometimes she spoke regretfully of the gentilities of her early life, and instead of comparing her present state with her condition as the wife of the unlucky Hall, she mused rather on what it had been before she took the first fatal step of clandestinely marrying him. She did not care to please such people as those with whom she was thrown as a thriving farmer's wife. She allowed the pretty trifles of agricultural domesticity to glide by her as sorry details, and had it not been for the children Darton's house would have seemed but little brighter than it had been before.

This led to occasional unpleasantness, until Darton sometimes declared to himself that such endeavours as his to rectify early deviations of the heart by harking back to the old point mostly failed of success. 'Perhaps Johns was right,' he would say. 'I should have gone on with Sally. Better go with the tide and make the best of its course than stem it at the risk of a capsize.' But he kept these unmelodious thoughts to himself, and was outwardly considerate and kind.

This somewhat barren tract of his life had extended to less than a year and a half when his ponderings were cut short by the loss of the woman they concerned. When she was in her grave he thought better of her than when she had been alive; the farm was a worse place without her than with her, after all. No woman short of divine could have gone through such an experience as hers with her first husband without becoming a little soured. Her stagnant sympathies, her sometimes unreasonable manner, had covered a heart frank and well-meaning, and originally hopeful and warm. She left him a tiny red infant in white wrappings. To make life as easy as possible to this touching object became at once his care.

As this child learnt to walk and talk Darton learnt to see feasibility in a scheme which pleased him. Revolving the experiment which he had hitherto made upon life, he fancied he had gained wisdom from his mistakes and caution from his miscarriages.

What the scheme was needs no penetration to discover. Once more he had opportunity to recast and rectify his ill-wrought situations by returning to Sally Hall, who still lived quietly on under her mother's roof at Hintock. Helena had been a woman to lend pathos and refinement to a home; Sally was the woman to brighten it. She would not, as Helena did, despise the rural simplicities of a farmer's fireside. Moreover, she had a pre-eminent qualification for Darton's household; no other woman could make so desirable a mother to her brother's two children and Darton's one as Sally – while Darton, now that Helena had gone, was a more promising husband for Sally than he had ever been when liable to reminders from an uncured sentimental wound.

Darton was not a man to act rapidly, and the working out of his reparative designs might have been delayed for some time. But there came a winter evening precisely like the one which had darkened over that former ride to Hintock, and he asked himself why he should postpone longer, when the very landscape called for a repetition of that attempt.

He told his man to saddle the mare, booted and spurred himself with a younger horseman's nicety, kissed the two youngest children, and rode off. To make the journey a complete parallel to the first, he would fain have had his old acquaintance Japheth Johns with him. But Johns, alas! was missing. His removal to the other side of the county had left unrepaired the breach which had arisen between him and Darton; and though Darton had forgiven him a hundred times, as Johns had probably forgiven Darton, the effort of reunion in present circumstances was one not likely to be made.

He screwed himself up to as cheerful a pitch as he could without his former crony, and became content with his own thoughts as he rode, instead of the words of a companion. The sun went down; the boughs appeared scratched in like an etching against the sky; old crooked men with faggots at their backs said 'Good-night, sir,' and Darton replied 'Good-night' right heartily.

By the time he reached the forking roads it was getting as dark as it had been on the occasion when Johns climbed the directing-post. Darton made no mistake this time. 'Nor shall I be able to mistake, thank Heaven, when I arrive,' he murmured. It gave him peculiar satisfaction to think that the proposed marriage, like his first, was of the nature of setting in order things long awry, and not a momentary freak of fancy.

Nothing hindered the smoothness of his journey, which seemed not half its former length. Though dark, it was only between five and six o'clock when the bulky chimneys of Mrs Hall's residence appeared in view behind the sycamore tree. On second thoughts he retreated and put up at the ale-house as in former time; and when he had plumed himself before the inn mirror, called for something to drink, and smoothed out the incipient wrinkles of care, he walked on to the Knap with a quick step.

5

That evening Sally was making 'pinners' for the milkers, who were now increased by two, for her mother and herself no longer joined in milking the cows themselves. But upon the whole there was little change in the household economy, and not much in its appearance, beyond such minor particulars as that the crack over the window, which had been a hundred years coming, was a trifle wider; that the beams were a shade blacker; that the influence of modernism had supplanted the open chimney-corner by a grate; that Rebekah, who had worn a cap when she had plenty of hair, had left it off now she had scarce any, because it was reported that caps were not fashionable; and that Sally's face had naturally assumed a more womanly and experienced cast.

Mrs Hall was actually lifting coals with the tongs, as she had used to do.

'Five years ago this very night, if I am not mistaken—' she said, laying on an ember.

'Not this very night – though 'twas one night this week,' said the correct Sally.

'Well, 'tis near enough. Five years ago Mr Darton came to marry you, and my poor boy Phil came home to die.' She sighed. 'Ah, Sally,' she presently said, 'if you had managed well Mr Darton would have had you, Helena or none.'

'Don't be sentimental about that, mother,' begged Sally. 'I didn't care to manage well in such a case. Though I liked him, I wasn't so anxious. I would never have married the man in the midst of such a hitch as that was,' she added with decision; 'and I don't think I would if he were to ask me now.'

'I am not sure about that, unless you have another in your eye.'

'I wouldn't; and I'll tell you why. I could hardly marry him for love at this time o' day. And as we've quite enough to live on if we give up the dairy tomorrow, I should have no need to marry for any meaner reason. . . I am quite happy enough as I am, and there's an end of it.'

Now it was not long after this dialogue that there came a mild rap at the door, and in a moment there entered Rebekah, looking as though a ghost had arrived. The fact was that that accomplished skimmer and churner (now a resident in the house) had overheard the desultory observations between mother and daughter, and on opening the door to Mr Darton thought the coincidence must have a grisly meaning in it. Mrs Hall welcomed the farmer with warm surprise, as did Sally, and for a moment they rather wanted words.

'Can you push up the chimney-crook for me, Mr Darton? – the notches hitch,' said the matron. He did it, and the homely little act bridged over the awkward consciousness that he had been a stranger for four years.

Mrs Hall soon saw what he had come for, and left the principals together while she went to prepare him a late tea, smiling at Sally's recent hasty assertions of indifference, when she saw how civil Sally was. When tea was ready she joined them. She fancied that Darton did not look so confident as when he had arrived; but Sally was quite light-hearted, and the meal passed pleasantly.

About seven he took his leave of them. Mrs Hall went as far as the door to light him down the slope. On the doorstep he said frankly –

'I came to ask your daughter to marry me; chose the night and everything, with an eye to a favourable answer. But she won't.'

'Then she's a very ungrateful girl!' emphatically said Mrs Hall.

Darton paused to shape his sentence, and asked, 'I – I suppose there's nobody else more favoured?'

'I can't say that there is, or that there isn't,' answered Mrs Hall. 'She's private in some things. I'm on your side, however, Mr Darton, and I'll talk to her.'

'Thank 'ee, thank 'ee!' said the farmer in a gayer accent; and with this assurance the not very satisfactory visit came to an end. Darton descended the roots of the sycamore, the light was withdrawn, and the door closed. At the bottom of the slope he nearly ran against a man about to ascend.

'Can a jack-o'-lent believe his few senses on such a dark night, or can't he?' exclaimed one whose utterance Darton recognized in a moment, despite its unexpectedness. 'I dare not swear he can, though I fain would!' The speaker was Johns.

Darton said he was glad of this opportunity, bad as it was, of putting an end to the silence of years, and asked the dairyman what he was travelling that way for.

Japheth showed the old jovial confidence in a moment. 'I'm going to see your – relations – as they always seem to me,' he said – 'Mrs Hall and Sally. Well, Charles, the fact is I find the natural barbarousness of man is much increased by a bachelor life, and, as your leavings were always good enough for me, I'm trying civilization here.' He nodded towards the house.

'Not with Sally – to marry her?' said Darton, feeling something like a rill of ice water between his shoulders.

'Yes, by the help of Providence and my personal charms. And I think I shall get her. I am this road every week – my present dairy is only four miles off, you know, and I see her through the window. 'Tis rather odd that I was going to speak practical tonight to her for the first time. You've just called?'

'Yes, for a short while. But she didn't say a word about you.'

'A good sign, a good sign. Now that decides me. I'll swing the mallet and get her answer this very night as I planned.'

A few more remarks, and Darton, wishing his friend joy of Sally in a slightly hollow tone of jocularity, bade him good-bye. Johns promised to write particulars, and ascended, and was lost in the shade of the house and tree. A rectangle of light appeared when Johns was admitted, and all was dark again.

'Happy Japheth!' said Darton. 'This then is the explanation!'

He determined to return home that night. In a quarter of an hour he passed out of the village, and the next day went about his swede-lifting and storing as if nothing had occurred.

He waited and waited to hear from Johns whether the wedding-day was fixed: but no letter came. He learnt not a single particular till, meeting Johns one day at a horse-auction, Darton exclaimed genially – rather more genially than he felt – 'When is the joyful day to be?'

To his great surprise a reciprocity of gladness was not conspicuous in Johns. 'Not at all,' he said, in a very subdued tone. ''Tis a bad job; she won't have me.'

Darton held his breath till he said with treacherous solicitude, 'Try again – 'tis coyness.'

'O no,' said Johns decisively. 'There's been none of that. We talked it over dozens of times in the most fair and square way. She tells me plainly, I don't suit her. 'Twould be simply annoying her to ask her again. Ah, Charles, you threw a prize away when you let her slip five years ago.'

'I did – I did,' said Darton.

He returned from that auction with a new set of feelings in play. He had certainly made a surprising mistake in thinking Johns his successful rival. It really seemed as if he might hope for Sally after all.

This time, being rather pressed by business, Darton had recourse to pen-and-ink, and wrote her as manly and straightforward a proposal as any woman could wish to receive. The reply came promptly:

> DEAR MR DARTON, – I am as sensible as any woman can be of the goodness that leads you to make me this offer a second time. Better women than I would be proud of the honour, for when I read your nice long speeches on mangold-wurzel, and such-like topics, at the Casterbridge Farmers' Club, I do feel it an honour, I assure you. But my answer is just the same as before. I will not try to explain what, in truth, I cannot explain – my reasons; I will simply say that I must decline to be married to you. With good wishes as in former times, I am, your faithful friend,
>
> SALLY HALL

Darton dropped the letter hopelessly. Beyond the negative, there was just a possibility of sarcasm in it – 'nice long speeches on mangold-wurzel' had a suspicious sound. However, sarcasm or none, there was the answer, and he had to be content.

He proceeded to seek relief in a business which at this time engrossed much of his attention – that of clearing up a curious mistake just current in the county, that he had been nearly ruined by the recent failure of a local bank. A farmer named Darton had lost heavily, and the similarity of name had probably led to the error. Belief in it was so persistent that it demanded several days of letter-writing to set matters straight, and persuade the world that he was as solvent as ever he had been in his life. He had hardly concluded this worrying task when, to his delight, another letter arrived in the handwriting of Sally.

Darton tore it open; it was very short.

> DEAR MR DARTON, – We have been so alarmed these last few days by the report that you were ruined by the stoppage of ——'s Bank, that, now it is contradicted, I hasten, by my mother's wish, to say how truly glad we are to find there is no foundation for the report. After your kindness to my poor brother's children, I can do no less than write at such a moment. We had a letter from each of them a few days ago. – Your faithful friend,
>
> SALLY HALL

'Mercenary little woman!' said Darton to himself with a smile.' Then that was the secret of her refusal this time – she thought I was ruined.'

Now, such was Darton, that as hours went on he could not help feeling too generously towards Sally to condemn her in this. What did he want in a wife? he asked himself. Love and integrity. What next? Worldly wisdom. And was there really more than worldly wisdom in her refusal to go aboard a sinking ship? She now knew it was otherwise. 'Begad,' he said, 'I'll try her again.'

The fact was he had so set his heart upon Sally, and Sally alone, that nothing was to be allowed to baulk him, and his reasoning was purely formal.

Anniversaries having been unpropitious, he waited on till a bright day late in May – a day when all animate nature was fancying, in its trusting, foolish way, that it was going to bask under blue sky for evermore. As he rode through Long-Ash Lane it was scarce recognizable as the track of his two winter journeys. No mistake could be made now, even with his eyes shut. The cuckoo's note was at its best, between April tentativeness and midsummer decrepitude, and the reptiles in the sun behaved as winningly as kittens on a hearth. Though afternoon, and about the same time as on the last occasion, it was broad day and sunshine when he entered Hintock, and the details of the Knap dairy-house were visible far up the road. He saw Sally in the garden, and was set vibrating. He had first intended to go on to the inn; but 'No,' he said; 'I'll tie my horse to the garden-gate. If all goes well it can soon be taken round; if not, I mount and ride away.'

The tall shade of the horseman darkened the room in which Mrs Hall sat, and made her start, for he had ridden by a side path to the top of the slope, where riders seldom came. In a few seconds he was in the garden with Sally.

Five – ay, three minutes – did the business at the back of that row of bees. Though spring had come and heavenly blue consecrated the scene, Darton succeeded not. '*No*,' said Sally firmly. 'I will never, never marry you, Mr Darton. I would have done it once; but now I never can.'

'But—!' implored Mr Darton. And with a burst of real eloquence he went on to declare all sorts of things that he would do for her. He would drive her to see her mother every week – take her to London – settle so much money upon her – Heaven knows what he did not promise, suggest, and tempt her with. But it availed nothing. She interposed with a stout negative which closed the course of his argument like an iron gate across a highway. Darton paused.

'Then,' said he simply, 'you hadn't heard of my supposed failure when you declined last time?'

'I had not,' she said. 'That you believed me capable of refusing you for such a reason does not help your cause.'

'And 'tis not because of any soreness from my slighting you years ago?'

'No. That soreness is long past.'

'Ah – then you despise me, Sally!'

'No,' she slowly answerd. 'I don't altogether despise you. I don't think you quite such a hero as I once did – that's all. The truth is, I am happy enough as I am, and I don't mean to marry at all. Now, may *I* ask a favour, sir?' She spoke with an ineffable charm, which, whenever he thought of it, made him curse his loss of her as long as he lived.

'To any extent.'

'Please do not put this question to me any more. Friends as long as you like, but lovers and married never.'

'I never will,' said Darton. 'Not if I live a hundred years.'

And he never did. That he had worn out his welcome in her heart was only too plain.

When his step-children had grown up and were placed out in life all communication between Darton and the Hall family ceased. It was only by chance that, years after, he learnt that Sally, notwithstanding the solicitations her attractions drew down upon her, had refused several offers of marriage, and steadily adhered to her purpose of leading a single life.

MAY 1884

THE DISTRACTED PREACHER

I. HOW HIS COLD WAS CURED

Something delayed the arrival of the Wesleyan minister, and a young man came temporarily in his stead. It was on the thirteenth of January 183– that Mr Stockdale, the young man in question, made his humble entry into the village, unknown, and almost unseen. But when those of the inhabitants who styled themselves of his connection became acquainted with him, they were rather pleased with the substitute than otherwise, though he had scarcely as yet acquired ballast of character sufficient to steady the consciences of the hundred-and-forty Methodists of pure blood who, at this time, lived in Nether-Moynton, and to give in addition supplementary support to the mixed race which went to church in the morning and chapel in the evening, or when there was a tea – as many as a hundred-and-ten people more, all told, and including the parish clerk in the winter-time, when it was too dark for the vicar to observe who passed up the street at seven o'clock – which, to be just to him, he was never anxious to do.

It was owing to this overlapping of creeds that the celebrated population-puzzle arose among the denser gentry of the district around Nether-Moynton: how could it be that a parish containing fifteen score of strong full-grown Episcopalians, and nearly thirteen score of well-matured Dissenters, numbered barely two-and-twenty score adults in all?

The young man being personally interesting, those with whom he came in contact were content to waive for a while the graver question of his sufficiency. It is said that at this time of his life his eyes were affectionate, though with a ray of levity; that his hair was curly, and his figure tall; that he was, in short, a very lovable youth, who won upon his female hearers as soon as they saw and heard him, and caused them to say, 'Why didn't we know of this before he came, that we might have gi'ed him a warmer welcome!'

The fact was that, knowing him to be only provisionally selected, and expecting nothing remarkable in his person or doctrine, they and the rest of his flock in Nether-Moynton had felt almost as indifferent about his advent as if they had been the soundest church-going parishioners in the country, and he their true and appointed parson. Thus when Stockdale set foot in the place nobody had secured a lodging for him, and though his journey had given him a bad cold in the head he was forced to attend to that business himself. On inquiry he learnt that the only possible accommodation in the village would be found at the house of one Mrs Lizzy Newberry, at the upper end of the street.

It was a youth who gave this information, and Stockdale asked him who Mrs Newberry might be.

The boy said that she was a widow-woman, who had got no husband, because he was dead. Mr Newberry, he added, had been a well-to-do man enough, as the saying was, and a farmer; but he had gone off in a decline. As regarded Mrs Newberry's serious side, Stockdale gathered that she was one of the trimmers who went to church and chapel both.

'I'll go there,' said Stockdale, feeling that, in the absence of purely sectarian lodgings, he could do no better.

'She's a little particular, and won't hae gover'ment folks, or curates, or the pa'sons's friends, or such like,' said the lad dubiously.

'Ah, that may be a promising sign: I'll call. Or no; just you go up and ask first if she can find room for me. I have to see one or two persons on another matter. You will find me down at the carrier's.'

In a quarter of an hour the lad came back, and said that Mrs Newberry would have no objection to accommodate him, whereupon Stockdale called at the house. It stood within a garden-hedge, and seemed to be roomy and comfortable. He saw an elderly woman, with whom he made arrangements to come the same night, since there was no inn in the place, and he wished to house himself as soon as possible; the village being a local centre from which he was to radiate at once to the different small chapels in the neighbourhood. He forthwith sent his luggage to Mrs Newberry's from the carrier's, where he had taken shelter, and in the evening walked up to his temporary home.

As he now lived there, Stockdale felt it unnecessary to knock at the door, and entering quietly he had the pleasure of hearing footsteps scudding away like mice into the back quarters. He advanced to the parlour, as the front room was called, though its stone floor was scarcely disguised by the carpet, which only overlaid the trodden areas, leaving sandy deserts under the furniture. But the room looked snug and cheerful. The firelight shone out brightly, trembling on the bulging mouldings of the table-legs, playing with brass knobs and handles, and lurking in great strength on the under surface of the chimney-piece. A deep armchair, covered with horsehair, and studded with a countless throng of brass nails, was pulled up on one side of the fireplace. The tea-things were on the table, the teapot cover was open, and a little handbell had been laid at that precise point towards which a person seated in the great chair might be expected instinctively to stretch his hand.

Stockdale sat down, not objecting to his experience of the room thus far, and began his residence by tinkling the bell. A little girl crept in at the summons, and made tea for him. Her name, she said, was Marther Sarer, and she lived out there, nodding towards the road and village generally. Before Stockdale had got far with his meal a tap sounded on the door behind him, and on his telling the inquirer to come in, a rustle of garments caused him to turn his head. He saw before him a fine and extremely well-made young woman, with dark hair, a wide, sensible, beautiful forehead, eyes that warmed him before he knew it, and a mouth that was in itself a picture to all appreciative souls.

'Can I get you anything else for tea?' she said, coming forward a step or two, an expression of liveliness on her features, and her hand waving the door by its edge.

'Nothing, thank you,' said Stockdale, thinking less of what he replied than of what might be her relation to the household.

'You are quite sure?' said the young woman, apparently aware that he had not considered his answer.

He conscientiously examined the tea-things, and found them all there. 'Quite sure, Miss Newberry,' he said.

'It is Mrs Newberry,' she said. 'Lizzy Newberry. I used to be Lizzy Simpkins.'

'O, I beg your pardon, Mrs Newberry.' And before he had occasion to say more she left the room.

Stockdale remained in some doubt till Martha Sarah came to clear the table. 'Whose house is this, my little woman?' said he.

'Mrs Lizzy Newberry's, sir.'

'Then Mrs Newberry is not the old lady I saw this afternoon?'

'No. That's Mrs Newberry's mother. It was Mrs Newberry who comed in to you just by now, because she wanted to see if you was good-looking.'

Later in the evening, when Stockdale was about to begin supper, she came again. 'I have come myself, Mr Stockdale,' she said. The minister stood up in acknowledgment of the honour. 'I am afraid little Marther might not make you understand. What will you have for supper? – there's cold rabbit, and there's a ham uncut.'

Stockdale said he could get on nicely with those viands, and supper was laid. He had no more than cut a slice when tap-tap came to the door again. The minister had already learnt that this particular rhythm in taps denoted the fingers of his enkindling landlady, and the doomed young fellow buried his first mouthful under a look of receptive blandness.

'We have a chicken in the house, Mr Stockdale – I quite forgot to mention it just now. Perhaps you would like Marther Sarer to bring it up?'

Stockdale had advanced far enough in the art of being a young man to say that he did not want the chicken, unless she brought it up herself; but when it was uttered he blushed at the daring gallantry of the speech, perhaps a shade too strong for a serious man and a minister. In three minutes the chicken appeared, but, to his great surprise, only in the hands of Martha Sarah. Stockdale was disappointed, which perhaps it was intended that he should be.

He had finished supper, and was not in the least anticipating Mrs Newberry again that night, when she tapped and entered as before. Stockdale's gratified look told that she had lost nothing by not appearing when expected. It happened that the cold in the head from which the young man suffered had increased with the approach of night, and before she had spoken he was seized with a violent fit of sneezing which he could not anyhow repress.

Mrs Newberry looked full of pity. 'Your cold is very bad tonight, Mr Stockdale.'

Stockdale replied that it was rather troublesome.

'And I've a good mind—' she added archly, looking at the cheerless glass of water on the table, which the abstemious minister was going to drink.

'Yes, Mrs Newberry?'

'I've a good mind that you should have something more likely to cure it than that cold stuff.'

'Well,' said Stockdale, looking down at the glass, 'as there is no inn here, and nothing better to be got in the village, of course it will do.'

To this she replied, 'There is something better, not far off, though not in the house. I really think you must try it, or you may be ill. Yes, Mr Stockdale, you shall.' She held up her finger, seeing that he was about to speak. 'Don't ask what it is; wait, and you shall see.'

Lizzy went away, and Stockdale waited in a pleasant mood. Presently she returned with her bonnet and cloak on, saying, 'I am so sorry, but you must help me to get it. Mother has gone to bed. Will you wrap yourself up, and come this way, and please bring that cup with you?'

Stockdale, a lonely young fellow, who had for weeks felt a great craving for somebody on whom to throw away superfluous interest, and even tenderness, was not sorry to join her, and followed his guide through the back door across the garden, to the bottom, where the boundary was a wall. This wall was low, and beyond it Stockdale discerned in the night shades several grey headstones, and the outlines of the church roof and tower.

'It is easy to get up this way,' she said, stepping upon a bank which abutted on the wall; then putting her foot on the top of the stonework, and descending by a spring inside, where the ground was much higher, as is the manner of graveyards to be. Stockdale did the same, and followed her in the dusk across the irregular ground till they came to the tower door, which, when they had entered, she softly closed behind them.

'You can keep a secret?' she said, in a musical voice.

'Like an iron chest!' said he fervently.

Then from under her cloak she produced a small lighted lantern, which the minister had not noticed that she carried at all. The light showed them to be close to the singing-gallery stairs, under which lay a heap of lumber of all sorts, but consisting mostly of decayed framework, pews, panels, and pieces of flooring, that from time to time had been removed from their original fixings in the body of the edifice and replaced by new.

'Perhaps you will drag some of those boards aside?' she said, holding the lantern over her head to light him better. 'Or will you take the lantern while I move them?'

'I can manage it,' said the young man, and acting as she ordered, he uncovered, to his surprise, a row of little barrels bound with wood hoops, each barrel being about as large as the nave of a heavy waggon-wheel. When they were laid open Lizzy fixed her eyes on him, as if she wondered what he would say.

'You know what they are?' she asked, finding that he did not speak.

'Yes, barrels,' said Stockdale simply. He was an inland man, the son of highly respectable parents, and brought up with a single eye to the ministry, and the sight suggested nothing beyond the fact that such articles were there.

'You are quite right, they are barrels,' she said, in an emphatic tone of candour that was not without a touch of irony.

Stockdale looked at her with an eye of sudden misgiving. 'Not smugglers' liquor?' he said.

'Yes,' said she. 'They are tubs of spirit that have accidentally floated over in the dark from France.'

In Nether-Moynton and its vicinity at this date people always smiled at the sort of sin called in the outside world illicit trading; and these little kegs of gin and brandy were as well known to the inhabitants as turnips. So that Stockdale's innocent ignorance, and his look of alarm when he guessed the sinister mystery, seemed to strike Lizzy first as ludicrous, and then as very awkward for the good impression that she wished to produce upon him.

'Smuggling is carried on here by some of the people,' she said in a gentle, apologetic voice. 'It has been their practice for generations, and they think it no harm. Now, will you roll out one of the tubs?'

'What to do with it?' said the minister.

'To draw a little from it to cure your cold,' she answered. 'It is so 'nation strong that it drives away that sort of thing in a jiffy. O, it is all right about our taking it. I may have what I like; the owner of the tubs says so. I ought to have had some in the house, and then I shouldn't ha' been put to this trouble; but I drink none myself, and so I often forget to keep it indoors.'

'You are allowed to help yourself, I suppose, that you may not inform where their hiding-place is?'

'Well, no; not that particularly; but I may take any if I want it. So help yourself.'

'I will, to oblige you, since you have a right to it,' murmured the minister; and though he was not quite satisfied with his part in the performance, he rolled one of the 'tubs' out from the corner into the middle of the tower floor. 'How do you wish me to get it out – with a gimlet, I suppose?'

'No, I'll show you,' said his interesting companion; and she held up with her other hand a shoemaker's awl and a hammer. 'You must never do these things with a gimlet, because the wood-dust gets in; and when the buyers pour out the brandy that would tell them that the tub had been broached. An awl makes no dust, and the hole nearly closes up again. Now tap one of the hoops forward.'

Stockdale took the hammer and did so.

'Now make the hole in the part that was covered by the hoop.'

He made the hole as directed. 'It won't run out,' he said.

'O yes it will,' said she. 'Take the tub between your knees, and squeeze the heads; and I'll hold the cup.'

Stockdale obeyed; and the pressure taking effect upon the tub, which seemed to be thin, the spirit spirted out in a stream. When the cup was full he ceased pressing, and the flow immediately stopped. 'Now we must fill up the keg with water,' said Lizzy, 'or it will cluck like forty hens when it is handled, and show that 'tis not full.'

'But they tell you you may take it?'

'Yes, the *smugglers*; but the *buyers* must not know that the smugglers have been kind to me at their expense.'

'I see,' said Stockdale doubtfully. 'I much question the honesty of this proceeding.'

By her direction he held the tub with the hole upwards, and while he went through the process of alternately pressing and ceasing to press, she produced a bottle of water, from which she took mouthfuls, conveying each to the keg by putting her pretty lips to the hole, where it was sucked in at each recovery of the cask from pressure. When it was again full he plugged the hole, knocked the hoop down to its place, and buried the tub in the lumber as before.

'Aren't the smugglers afraid that you will tell?' he asked, as they recrossed the churchyard.

'O no; they are not afraid of that. I couldn't do such a thing.'

'They have put you into a very awkward corner,' said Stockdale emphatically. 'You must, of course, as an honest person, sometimes feel that it is your duty to inform – really you must.'

'Well, I have never particularly felt it as a duty; and, besides, my first husband—' She stopped, and there was some confusion in her voice. Stockdale was so honest and unsophisticated that he did not at once discern why she paused: but at last he did perceive that the words were a slip, and that no woman would have uttered 'first husband' by accident unless she had thought pretty frequently of a second. He felt for her confusion, and allowed her time to recover and proceed. 'My husband,' she said, in a self-corrected tone, 'used to know of their doings, and so did my father, and kept the secret. I cannot inform, in fact, against anybody.'

'I see the hardness of it,' he continued, like a man who looked far into the moral of things. 'And it is very cruel that you should be tossed and tantalized between your memories and your conscience. I do hope, Mrs Newberry, that you will soon see your way out of this unpleasant position'.

'Well, I don't just now,' she murmured.

By this time they had passed over the wall and entered the house, where she brought him a glass and hot water, and left him to his own reflections. He looked after her vanishing form, asking himself whether he, as a respectable man, and a minister, and a shining light, even though as yet only of the halfpenny-candle sort, were quite justified in doing this thing. A sneeze settled the question; and he found that when the fiery liquid was lowered by the addition of twice or thrice the quantity of water, it was one of the prettiest cures for a cold in the head that he had ever known, particularly at this chilly time of the year.

Stockdale sat in the deep chair about twenty minutes sipping and meditating, till he at length took warmer views of things, and longed for the morrow, when he would see Mrs Newberry again. He then felt that, though chronologically at a short distance, it would in an emotional sense be very long before tomorrow came, and walked restlessly round the room. His eye was attracted by a framed and glazed sampler in which a running ornament of fir-trees and peacocks surrounded the following pretty bit of sentiment:

Rose-leaves smell when roses thrive,
Here's my work while I'm alive;
Rose-leaves smell when shrunk and shed,
Here's my work when I am dead.

Lizzy Simpkins. Fear God. Honour the King.
Aged 11 years.

''Tis hers,' he said to himself. 'Heavens, how I like that name!'

Before he had done thinking that no other name from Abigail to Zenobia would have suited his young landlady so well, tap-tap came again upon the door; and the minister started as her face appeared yet another time, looking so disinterested that the most ingenious would have refrained from asserting that she had come to affect his feelings by her seductive eyes.

'Would you like a fire in your room, Mr Stockdale, on account of your cold?'

The minister, being still a little pricked in the conscience for countenancing her in watering the spirits, saw here a way to self-chastisement. 'No, I thank you,' he said firmly; 'it is not necessary. I have never been used to one in my life, and it would be giving way to luxury too far.'

'Then I won't insist,' she said, and disconcerted him by vanishing instantly.

Wondering if she was vexed by his refusal, he wished that he had chosen to have a fire, even though it should have scorched him out of bed and endangered his self-discipline for a dozen days. However, he consoled himself with what was in truth a rare consolation for a budding lover, that he was under the same roof with Lizzy; her guest, in fact, to take a poetical view of the term lodger; and that he would certainly see her on the morrow.

The morrow came, and Stockdale rose early, his cold quite gone. He had never in his life so longed for the breakfast-hour as he did that day, and punctually at eight o'clock, after a short walk to reconnoitre the premises, he re-entered the door of his dwelling. Breakfast passed, and Martha Sarah attended, but nobody came voluntarily as on the night before to inquire if there were other wants which he had not mentioned, and which she would attempt to gratify. He was disappointed, and went out, hoping to see her at dinner. Dinner-time came; he sat down to the meal, finished it, lingered on for a whole hour, although two new teachers were at that moment waiting at the chapel-door to speak to him by appointment. It was useless to wait longer, and he slowly went his way down the lane, cheered by the thought that, after all, he would see her in the evening, and perhaps engage again in the delightful tub-broaching in the neighbouring church tower, which proceeding he resolved to render more moral by steadfastly insisting that no water should be introduced to fill up, though the tub should cluck like all the hens in Christendom. But nothing could disguise the fact that it was a queer business; and his countenance fell when he thought how much more his mind was interested in that matter than in his serious duties.

However, compunction vanished with the decline of day. Night came, and his tea and supper; but no Lizzy Newberry, and no sweet temptations. At last the minister could bear it no longer, and said to his quaint little attendant, 'Where is Mrs Newberry today?' judiciously handing a penny as he spoke.

'She's busy,' said Martha.

'Anything serious happened?' he asked, handing another penny, and revealing yet additional pennies in the background.

'O no – nothing at all!' said she, with breathless confidence. 'Nothing ever happens to her. She's only biding upstairs in bed because 'tis her way sometimes.'

Being a young man of some honour he would not question further, and assuming that Lizzy must have a bad headache, or other slight ailment, in spite of what the girl had said, he went to bed dissatisfied, not even setting eyes on old Mrs Simpkins. 'I said last night that I should see her tomorrow,' he reflected; 'but that was not to be!'

Next day he had better fortune, or worse, meeting her at the foot of the stairs in the morning, and being favoured by a visit or two from her during the day – once for the purpose of making kindly inquiries about his comfort, as on the first evening, and at another time to place a bunch of winter-violets on his table, with a promise to renew them when they drooped. On these occasions there was something in her smile which showed how conscious she was of the effect she produced, though it must be said that it was rather a humorous than a designing consciousness, and savoured more of pride than of vanity.

As for Stockdale, he clearly perceived that he possessed unlimited capacity for backsliding, and wished that tutelary saints were not denied to Dissenters. He set a watch upon his tongue and eyes for the space of one hour and a half, after which he found it was useless to struggle further, and gave himself up to the situation. 'The other minister will be here in a month,' he said to himself when sitting over the fire. 'Then I shall be off, and she will distract my mind no more! . . . And then, shall I go on living by myself for ever? No; when my two years of probation are finished, I shall have a furnished house to live in, with a varnished door and a brass knocker; and I'll march straight back to her, and ask her flat, as soon as the last plate is on the dresser!'

Thus a titillating fortnight was passed by young Stockdale, during which time things proceeded much as such matters have done ever since the beginning of history. He saw the object of attachment several times one day, did not see her at all the next, met her when he least expected to do so, missed her when hints and signs as to where she should be at a given hour almost amounted to an appointment. This mild coquetry was perhaps fair enough under the circumstances of their being so closely lodged, and Stockdale put up with it as philosophically as he was able. Being in her own house she could, after vexing him or disappointing him of her presence, easily win him back by suddenly surrounding him with those little attentions which her position as his landlady put it in her power to bestow. When he had waited indoors half the day to see her, and on finding that she would not be seen, had gone off in a huff to the dreariest and dampest walk he could discover, she would restore equilibrium in the evening with 'Mr Stockdale, I have fancied you must feel draught o' nights from your bedroom window, and so I have been putting up thicker curtains this afternoon while you were out'; or, 'I noticed that you sneezed twice again this morning, Mr Stockdale. Depend upon it that cold is hanging about you yet; I am sure it is – I have thought of it continually; and you must let me make a posset for you.'

Sometimes in coming home he found his sitting-room rearranged, chairs placed where the table had stood, and the table ornamented with the few fresh flowers and leaves that could be obtained at this season, so as to add a novelty to the room. At times she would be standing on a chair outside the house, trying to nail up a branch of the monthly rose which the winter wind had blown down; and of course he stepped forward to assist her, when their hands got mixed in passing the shreds and nails. Thus they became friends again after a disagreement. She would utter on these occasions some pretty and deprecatory remark on the necessity of her troubling him anew; and he would straightway say that he would do a hundred times as much for her if she should so require.

2. HOW HE SAW TWO OTHER MEN

Matters being in this advancing state, Stockdale was rather surprised one cloudy evening, while sitting in his room, at hearing her speak in low tones of expostulation to some one at the door. It was nearly dark, but the shutters were not yet closed, nor the candles lighted; and Stockdale was tempted to stretch his head towards the window. He saw outside the door a young man in clothes of a whitish colour, and upon reflection judged their wearer to be the well-built and rather handsome miller who lived below. The miller's voice was alternately low and firm, and sometimes it reached the level of positive entreaty; but what the words were Stockdale could in no way hear.

Before the colloquy had ended, the minister's attention was attracted by a second incident. Opposite Lizzy's home grew a clump of laurels, forming a thick and permanent shade. One of the laurel boughs now quivered against the light background of sky, and in a moment the head of a man peered out, and remained still. He seemed to be also much interested in the conversation at the door, and was plainly lingering there to watch and listen. Had Stockdale stood in any other relation to Lizzy than that of a lover, he might hve gone out and investigated the meaning of this: but being as yet but an unprivileged ally, he did nothing more than stand up and show himself against the firelight, whereupon the listener disappeared, and Lizzy and the miller spoke in lower tones.

Stockdale was made so uneasy by the circumstance, that as soon as the miller was gone, he said, 'Mrs Newberry, are you aware that you were watched just now, and your conversation heard?'

'When?' she said.

'When you were talking to that miller. A man was looking from the laurel-tree as jealously as if he could have eaten you.'

She showed more concern than the trifling event seemed to demand, and he added, 'Perhaps you were talking of things you did not wish to be overheard?'

'I was talking only on business,' she said.

'Lizzy, be frank!' said the young man. 'If it was only on business, why should anybody wish to listen to you?'

She looked curiously at him. 'What else do you think it could be, then?'

'Well – the only talk between a young woman and man that is likely to amuse an eavesdropper.'

'Ah yes,' she said, smiling in spite of her preoccupation. 'Well, my cousin Owlett has spoken to me about matrimony, every now and then, that's true; but he was not speaking of it then. I wish he had been speaking of it, with all my heart. It would have been much less serious for me.'

'O Mrs Newberry!'

'It would. Not that I should ha' chimed in with him, of course. I wish it for other reasons. I am glad, Mr Stockdale, that you have told me of that listener. It is a timely warning, and I must see my cousin again.'

'But don't go away till I have spoken,' said the minister. 'I'll out with it at once, and make no more ado. Let it be Yes or No between us, Lizzy; please do!' And he held out his hand, in which she freely allowed her own to rest, but without speaking.

'You mean Yes by that?' he asked, after waiting a while.

'You may be my sweetheart, if you will.'

'Why not say at once you will wait for me until I have a house and can come back to marry you.'

'Because I am thinking – thinking of something else,' she said with embarrassment. 'It all comes upon me at once, and I must settle one thing at a time.'

'At any rate, dear Lizzy, you can assure me that the miller shall not be allowed to speak to you except on business? You have never directly encouraged him?'

She parried the question by saying, 'You see, he and his party have been in the habit of leaving things on my premises sometimes, and as I have not denied him, it makes him rather forward.'

'Things – what things?'

'Tubs – they are called Things here.'

'But why don't you deny him, my dear Lizzy?'

'I cannot well.'

'You are too timid. It is unfair of him to impose so upon you, and get your good name into danger by his smuggling tricks. Promise me that the next time he wants to leave his tubs here you will let me roll them into the street?'

She shook her head. 'I would not venture to offend the neighbours so much as that,' said she, 'or do anything that would be so likely to put poor Owlett into the hands of the Customs-men.'

Stockdale sighed, and said that he thought hers a mistaken generosity when it extended to assisting those who cheated the king of his dues. 'At any rate, you will let me make him keep his distance as your lover, and tell him flatly that you are not for him?'

'Please not, at present,' she said. 'I don't wish to offend my old neighbours. It is not only Mr Owlett who is concerned.'

'This is too bad,' said Stockdale impatiently.

'On my honour, I won't encourage him as my lover,' Lizzy answered earnestly. 'A reasonable man will be satisfied with that.'

'Well, so I am,' said Stockdale, his countenance clearing.

3. THE MYSTERIOUS GREATCOAT

Stockdale now began to notice more particularly a feature in the life of his fair landlady, which he had casually observed but scarcely ever thought of before. It was that she was markedly irregular in her hours of rising. For a week or two she would be tolerably punctual, reaching the ground-floor within a few minutes of half-past seven. Then suddenly she would not be visible till twelve at noon, perhaps for three or four days in succession; and twice he had certain proof that she did not leave her room till half-past three in the afternoon. The second time that this extreme lateness came under his notice was on a day when he had particularly wished to consult with her about his future movements; and he concluded, as he always had done, that she had a cold, headache, or other ailment, unless she had kept herself invisible to avoid meeting and talking to him, which he could hardly believe. The former supposition was disproved, however, by her innocently saying, some days later, when they were speaking on a question of health, that she had never had a moment's heaviness, headache, or illness of any kind since the previous January twelvemonth.

'I am glad to hear it,' said he. 'I thought quite otherwise.'

'What, do I look sickly?' she asked, turning up her face to show the impossibility of his gazing on it and holding such a belief for a moment.

'Not at all; I merely thought so from your being sometimes obliged to keep your room through the best part of the day.'

'O, as for that – it means nothing,' she murmured, with a look which some might have called cold, and which was the worst look that he liked to see upon her. 'It is pure sleepiness, Mr Stockdale.'

'Never!'

'It is, I tell you. When I stay in my room till half-past three in the afternoon, you may always be sure that I slept soundly till three, or I shouldn't have stayed there.'

'It is dreadful,' said Stockdale, thinking of the disastrous effects of such indulgence upon the household of a minister, should it become a habit of everyday occurrence.

'But then,' she said, divining his good and prescient thoughts, 'it only happens when I stay awake all night. I don't go to sleep till five or six in the morning sometimes.'

'Ah, that's another matter,' said Stockdale. 'Sleeplessness to such an alarming extent is real illness. Have you spoken to a doctor?'

'O no – there is no need for doing that – it is all natural to me.' And she went away without further remark.

Stockdale might have waited a long time to know the real cause of her sleeplessness, had it not happened that one dark night he was sitting in his bedroom jotting down notes for a sermon, which occupied him perfunctorily for a considerable time after the other members of the household had retired. He did not get to bed till one o'clock. Before he had fallen asleep he heard a knocking at the front door, first rather timidly performed, and then louder. Nobody answered it, and the person knocked again. As the house still remained undisturbed, Stockdale got out of bed, went to his window, which overlooked the door, and opening it, asked who was there.

A young woman's voice replied that Susan Wallis was there, and that she had come to ask if Mrs Newberry could give her some mustard to make a plaster with, as her father was taken very ill on the chest.

The minister, having neither bell nor servant, was compelled to act in person. 'I will call Mrs Newberry,' he said. Partly dressing himself, he went along the passage and tapped at Lizzy's door. She did not answer, and, thinking of her erratic habits in the matter of sleep, he thumped the door persistently, when he discovered, by its moving ajar under his knocking, that it had only been gently pushed to. As there was now a sufficient entry for the voice, he knocked no longer, but said in firm tones, 'Mrs Newberry, you are wanted.'

The room was quite silent; not a breathing, not a rustle, came from any part of it. Stockdale now sent a positive shout through the open space of the door: 'Mrs Newberry!' – still no answer, or movement of any kind within. Then he heard sounds from the opposite room, that of Lizzy's mother, as if she had been aroused by his uproar though Lizzy had not, and was dressing herself hastily. Stockdale softly closed the younger woman's door and went on to the other, which was opened by Mrs Simpkins before he could reach it. She was in her ordinary clothes, and had a light in her hand.

'What's the person calling about?' she said in alarm.

Stockdale told the girl's errand, adding seriously, 'I cannot wake Mrs Newberry.'

'It is no matter,' said her mother. 'I can let the girl have what she wants as well as my daughter.' And she came out of the room and went downstairs.

Stockdale retired towards his own apartment, saying, however, to Mrs Simpkins from the landing, as if on second thoughts, 'I suppose there is nothing the matter with Mrs Newberry, that I could not wake her?'

'O no,' said the old lady hastily. 'Nothing at all.'

Still the minister was not satisfied. 'Will you go in and see?' he said. 'I should be much more at ease.'

Mrs Simpkins returned up the staircase, went to her daughter's room, and came out again almost instantly. 'There is nothing at all the matter with Lizzy,' she said; and descended again to attend to the applicant, who, having seen the light, had remained quiet during this interval.

Stockdale went into his room and lay down as before. He heard Lizzy's mother open the front door, admit the girl, and then the murmured discourse of both as they went to the store-cupboard for the medicament required. The girl departed, the door was fastened, Mrs Simpkins came upstairs, and the house was again in silence. Still the minister did not fall asleep. He could not get rid of a singular suspicion, which was all the more harassing in being, if true, the most unaccountable thing within his experience. That Lizzy Newberry was in her bedroom when he made such a clamour at the door he could not possibly convince himself, notwithstanding that he had heard her come upstairs at the usual time, go into her chamber, and shut herself up in the usual way. Yet all reason was so much against her being elsewhere, that he was constrained to go back again to the unlikely theory of a heavy sleep, though he had heard neither breath nor movement during a shouting and knocking loud enough to rouse the Seven Sleepers.

Before coming to any positive conclusion he fell asleep himself and did not awake till day. He saw nothing of Mrs Newberry in the morning, before he went out to meet the rising sun, as he liked to do when the weather was fine; but as this was by no means unusual, he took no notice of it. At breakfast-time he knew that she was not far off by hearing her in the kitchen, and though he saw nothing of her person, that back apartment being rigorously closed against his eyes, she seemed to be talking, ordering, and bustling about among the pots and skimmers in so ordinary a manner, that there was no reason for his wasting more time in fruitless surmise.

The minister suffered from these distractions, and his extemporized sermons were not improved thereby. Already he often said Romans for Corinthians in the pulpit, and gave out hymns in strange cramped metres, that hitherto had always been skipped, because the congregation could not raise a tune to fit them. He fully resolved that as soon as his few weeks of stay approached their end he would cut the matter short, and commit himself by proposing a definite engagement, repenting at leisure if necessary.

With this end in view, he suggested to her on the evening after her mysterious sleep that they should take a walk together just before dark, the latter part of the proposition being introduced that they might return home unseen. She consented to go; and away they went over a stile, to a shrouded footpath suited for the occasion. But, in spite of attempts on both sides, they were unable to infuse much spirit into the ramble. She looked rather paler than usual, and sometimes turned her head away.

'Lizzy,' said Stockdale reproachfully, when they had walked in silence a long distance.

'Yes,' said she.

'You yawned – much my company is to you!' He put it in that way, but he was really wondering whether her yawn could possibly have more to do with physical weariness from the night before than mental weariness of that present moment. Lizzy apologized, and owned that she was rather tired, which gave him an opening for a direct question on the point; but his modesty would not allow him to put it to her; and he uncomfortably resolved to wait.

The month of February passed with alternations of mud and frost, rain and sleet, east winds and north-westerly gales. The hollow places in the ploughed fields showed themselves as pools of water, which had settled there from the higher levels, and had not yet found time to soak away. The birds began to get lively, and a single thrush came just before sunset each evening, and sang hopefully on the large elm-tree which stood nearest to Mrs Newberry's house. Cold blasts and brittle earth had given place to an oozing dampness more unpleasant in itself than frost; but it suggested coming spring, and its unpleasantness was of a bearable kind.

Stockdale had been going to bring about a practical understanding with Lizzy at least half a dozen times; but, what with the mystery of her apparent absence on the night of the neighbour's call, and her curious way of lying in bed at unaccountable times, he felt a check within him whenever he wanted to speak out. Thus they still lived on as indefinitely affianced lovers, each of whom hardly acknowledged the other's claim to the name of chosen one. Stockdale persuaded himself that his hesitation was owing to the postponement of the ordained minister's arrival, and the consequent delay in his own departure, which did away with all necessity for haste in his courtship; but perhaps it was only that his discretion was reasserting itself, and telling him that he had better get clearer ideas of Lizzy before arranging for the grand contract of his life with her. She, on her part, always seemed ready to be urged further on that question than he had hitherto attempted to go; but she was none the less independent, and to a degree which would have kept from flagging the passion of a far more mutable man.

On the evening of the first of March he went casually into his bedroom about dusk, and noticed lying on a chair a greatcoat, hat, and breeches. Having no recollection of leaving any clothes of his own in that spot, he went and examined them as well as he could in the twilight, and found that they did not belong to him. He paused for a moment to consider how they might have got there. He was the only man living in the house; and yet these were not his garments, unless he had made a mistake. No, they were not his. He called up Martha Sarah.

'How did these things come in my room?' he said, flinging the objectionable articles to the floor.

Martha said that Mrs Newberry had given them to her to brush, and that she had brought them up there thinking they must be Mr Stockdale's, as there was no other gentleman a-lodging there.

'Of course you did,' said Stockdale. 'Now take them down to your mis'ess, and say they are some clothes I have found here and know nothing about.'

As the door was left open he heard the conversation downstairs. 'How stupid!' said Mrs Newberry, in a tone of confusion. 'Why, Marther Sarer, I did not tell you to take 'em to Mr Stockdale's room!'

'I thought they must be his as they was so muddy,' said Martha humbly.

'You should have left 'em on the clothes-horse,' said the young mistress severely; and she came upstairs with the garments on her arm, quickly passed Stockdale's room, and threw them forcibly into a closet at the end of a passage. With this the incident ended, and the house was silent again.

There would have been nothing remarkable in finding such clothes in a widow's house had they been clean; or moth-eaten, or creased, or mouldy from long lying by; but that they should be splashed with recent mud bothered Stockdale a good deal. When a young pastor is in the aspen stage of attachment, and open to agitation at the merest trifles, a really substantial incongruity of this complexion is a disturbing thing. However, nothing further occurred at that time; but he became watchful, and given to conjecture, and was unable to forget the circumstance.

One morning, on looking from his window, he saw Mrs Newberry herself brushing the tails of a long drab greatcoat, which, if he mistook not, was the very same garment as the one that had adorned the chair of his room. It was densely splashed up to the hollow of the back with neighbouring Nether-Moynton mud, to judge by its colour, the spots being distinctly visible to him in the sunlight. The previous day or two having been wet, the inference was irresistible that the wearer had quite recently been walking some considerable distance about the lanes and fields. Stockdale opened the window and looked out, and Mrs Newberry turned her head. Her face became slowly red; she never had looked prettier, or more incomprehensible. He waved his hand affectionately, and said good-morning; she answered with embarrassment, having ceased her occupation on the instant that she saw him, and rolled up the coat half-cleaned.

Stockdale shut the window. Some simple explanation of her proceeding was doubtless within the bounds of possibility; but he himself could not think of one; and he wished that she had placed the matter beyond conjecture by voluntarily saying something about it there and then.

But, though Lizzy had not offered an explanation at the moment, the subject was brought forward by her at the next time of their meeting. She was chatting to him concerning some other event, and remarked that it happened about the time when she was dusting some old clothes that had belonged to her poor husband.

'You keep them clean out of respect to his memory?' said Stockdale tentatively.

'I air and dust them sometimes,' she said, with the most charming innocence in the world.

'Do dead men come out of their graves and walk in mud?' murmured the minister, in a cold sweat at the deception that she was practising.

'What did you say?' asked Lizzy.

'Nothing, nothing,' said he mournfully. 'Mere words – a phrase that will do for my sermon next Sunday.' It was too plain that Lizzy was unaware that he had seen fresh pedestrian splashes upon the skirts of the tell-tale overcoat, and that she imagined him to believe it had come direct from some chest or drawer.

The aspect of the case was now considerably darker. Stockdale was so much depressed by it that he did not challenge her explanation, or threaten to go off as a missionary to benighted islanders, or reproach her in any way whatever. He simply parted from her when she had done talking, and lived on in perplexity, till by degrees his natural manner became sad and constrained.

4. AT THE TIME OF THE NEW MOON

The following Thursday was changeable, damp, and gloomy; and the night threatened to be windy and unpleasant. Stockdale had gone away to Knollsea in the morning, to be present at some commemoration service there, and on his return he was met by the attractive Lizzy in the passage.

Whether influenced by the tide of cheerfulness which had attended him that day, or by the drive through the open air, or whether from a natural disposition to let bygones alone, he allowed himself to be fascinated into forgetfulness of the greatcoat incident, and upon the whole passed a pleasant evening; not so much in her society as within sound of her voice, as she sat talking in the back parlour to her mother, till the latter went to bed. Shortly after this Mrs Newberry retired, and then Stockdale prepared to go upstairs himself. But before he left the room he remained standing by the dying embers a while, thinking long of one thing and another; and was only aroused by the flickering of his candle in the socket as it suddenly declined and went out. Knowing that there were a tinder-box, matches, and another candle in his bedroom, he felt his way upstairs without a light. On reaching his chamber he laid his hand on every possible ledge and corner for the tinder-box, but for a long time in vain. Discovering it at length, Stockdale produced a spark, and was kindling the brimstone, when he fancied that he heard a movement in the passage. He blew harder at the lint, the match flared up, and looking by aid of the blue light through the door, which had been stnding open all this time, he was surprised to see a male figure vanishing round the top of the staircase with the evident intention of escaping unobserved. The personage wore the clothes which Lizzy had been brushing, and something in the outline and gait suggested to the minister that the wearer was Lizzy herself.

But he was not sure of this; and, greatly excited, Stockdale determined to investigate the mystery, and to adopt his own way for doing it. He blew out the match without lighting the candle, went into the passage, and proceeded on tiptoe towards Lizzy's room. A faint gray square of light in the direction of the chamber-window as he approached told him that the door was open, and at once suggested that the occupant was gone. He turned and brought down his fist upon the handrail of the staircase: 'It was she; in her late husband's coat and hat!'

Somewhat relieved to find that there was no intruder in the case, yet none the less surprised, the minister crept down the stairs, softly put on his boots, overcoat, and hat, and tried the front door. It was fastened as usual; he went to the back door, found this unlocked, and emerged into the garden. The night was mild and moonless, and rain had lately been falling, though for the present it had ceased. There was a sudden dropping from the trees and bushes every now and then, as each passing wind shook their boughs. Among these sounds Stockdale heard the faint fall of feet upon the road outside, and he guessed from the step that it was Lizzy's. He followed the sound, and, helped by the circumstance of the wind blowing from the direction in which the pedestrian moved, he got nearly close to her, and kept there, without risk of being overheard. While he thus followed her up the street or lane, as it might indifferently be called, there being more hedge than houses on either side, a figure came forward to her from one of the cottage doors. Lizzy stopped; the minister stepped upon the grass and stopped also.

'Is that Mrs Newberry?' said the man who had come out, whose voice Stockdale recognized as that of one of the most devout members of his congregation.

'It is,' said Lizzy.

'I be quite ready – I've been here this quarter-hour.'

'Ah, John,' said she, 'I have bad news; there is danger tonight for our venture.'

'And d'ye tell o't! I dreamed there might be.'

'Yes,' she said hurriedly; 'and you must go at once round to where the chaps are waiting, and tell them they will not be wanted till tomorrow night at the same time. I go to burn the lugger off.'

'I will,' he said; and instantly went off through a gate, Lizzy continuing her way.

On she tripped at a quickening pace till the lane turned into the turnpike-road, which she crossed, and got into the track for Ringsworth. Here she ascended the hill without the least hesitation, passed the lonely hamlet of Holworth, and went down the vale on the other side. Stockdale had never taken any extensive walks in this direction, but he was aware that if she persisted in her course much longer she would draw near to the coast, which was here between two and three miles distant from Nether-Moynton; and as it had been about a quarter-past eleven o'clock when they set out, her intention seemed to be to reach the shore about midnight.

Lizzy soon ascended a small mound, which Stockdale at the same time adroitly skirted on the left; and a dull monotonous roar burst upon his ear. The hillock was about fifty yards from the top of the cliffs, and by day it apparently commanded a full view of the bay. There was light enough in the sky to show her disguised figure against it when she reached the top, where she paused, and afterwards sat down. Stockdale, not wishing on any account to alarm her at this moment, yet desirous of being near her, sank upon his hands and knees, crept a little higher up, and there stayed still.

The wind was chilly, the ground damp, and his position one in which he did not care to remain long. However, before he had decided to leave it, the young man heard voices behind him. What they signified he did not know; but, fearing that Lizzy was in danger, he was about to run forward and warn her that she might be seen, when she crept to the shelter of a little bush which maintained a precarious existence in that exposed spot; and her form was absorbed in its dark and stunted outline as if she had become part of it. She had evidently heard the men as well as he. They passed near him, talking in loud and careless tones, which could be heard above the uninterrupted washings of the sea, and which suggested that they were not engaged in any business at their own risk. This proved to be the fact; some of their words floated across to him, and caused him to forget at once the coldness of his situation.

'What's the vessel?'

'A lugger, about fifty tons.'

'From Cherbourg, I suppose?'

'Yes, 'a b'lieve.'

'But it don't all belong to Owlett?'

'O no. He's only got a share. There's another or two in it – a farmer and such like, but the names I don't know.'

The voices died away, and the heads and shoulders of the men diminished towards the cliff, and dropped out of sight.

'My darling has been tempted to buy a share by that unbeliever Owlett,' groaned the minister, his honest affection for Lizzy having quickened to its intensest point during these moments of risk to her person and name. 'That's why she's here,' he said to himself. 'O, it will be the ruin of her!'

His perturbation was interrupted by the sudden bursting out of a bright and increasing light from the spot where Lizzy was in hiding. A few seconds later, and before it had reached the height of a blaze, he heard her rush past him down the hollow like a stone from a sling, in the direction of home. The light now flared high and wide, and showed its position clearly. She had kindled a bough of furze and stuck it into the bush under which she had been crouching; the wind fanned the flame, which crackled fiercely, and threatened to consume the bush as well as the bough. Stockdale paused just long enough to notice thus much, and then followed rapidly the route taken by the young woman. His intention was to overtake her, and reveal himself as a friend; but run as he would he could see nothing of her. Thus he flew across the open country about Holworth, twisting his legs and ankles in unexpected fissures and descents, till, on coming to the gate between the downs and the road, he was forced to pause to get breath. There was no audible movement either in front or behind him, and he now concluded that she had not outrun him, but that, hearing him at her heels, and believing him one of the excise party, she had hidden herself somewhere on the way, and let him pass by.

He went on at a more leisurely pace towards the village. On reaching the house he found his surmise to be correct, for the gate was on the latch, and the door unfastened, just as he had left them. Stockdale closed the door behind him, and waited silently in the passage. In about ten minutes he heard the same light footstep that he had heard in going out; it paused at the gate, which opened and shut softly, and then the door-latch was lifted, and Lizzy came in.

Stockdale went forward and said at once, 'Lizzy, don't be frightened. I have been waiting up for you.'

She started, though she had recognized the voice. 'It is Mr Stockdale, isn't it?' she said.

'Yes,' he answered, becoming angry now that she was safe indoors, and not alarmed. 'And a nice game I've found you out in tonight. You are in man's clothes, and I am ashamed of you!'

Lizzy could hardly find a voice to answer this unexpected reproach.

'I am only partly in man's clothes,' she faltered, shrinking back to the wall. 'It is only his greatcoat and hat and breeches that I've got on, which is no harm, as he was my own husband; and I do it only because a cloak blows about so, and you can't use your arms. I have got my own dress under just the same – it is only tucked in! Will you go away upstairs and let me pass? I didn't want you to see me at such a time as this!'

'But I have a right to see you! How do you think there can be anything between us now?' Lizzy was silent. 'You are a smuggler,' he continued sadly.

'I have only a share in the run,' she said.

'That makes no difference. Whatever did you engage in such a trade as that for, and keep it such a secret from me all this time?'

'I don't do it always. I only do it in winter-time when 'tis new moon.'

'Well, I suppose that's because it can't be done anywhen else. . . You have regularly upset me, Lizzy.'

'I am sorry for that,' Lizzy meekly replied.

'Well now,' said he more tenderly, 'no harm is done as yet. Won't you for the sake of me give up this blameable and dangerous practice altogether?'

'I must do my best to save this run,' said she, getting rather husky in the throat. 'I don't want to give you up – you know that; but I don't want to lose my venture. I don't know what to do now! Why I have kept it so secret from you is that I was afraid you would be angry if you knew.'

'I should think so! I suppose if I had married you without finding this out you'd have gone on with it just the same?'

'I don't know. I did not think so far ahead. I only went tonight to burn the folks off, because we found that the Preventive-men knew where the tubs were to be landed.'

'It is a pretty mess to be in altogether, is this,' said the distracted young minster. 'Well, what will you do now?'

Lizzy slowly murmured the particulars of their plan, the chief of which were that they meant to try their luck at some other point of the shore the next night; that three landing-places were always agreed upon before the run was attempted, with the understanding that, if the vessel was 'burnt off' from the first point, which was Ringsworth, as it had been by her tonight, the crew should attempt to make the second, which was Lulwind Cove, on the second night; and if there, too, danger threatened, they should on the third night try the third place, which was behind a headland further west.

'Suppose the officers hinder them landing there, too?' he said, his attention to this interesting programme displacing for a moment his concern at her share in it.

'Then we shan't try anywhere else all this dark – that's what we call the time between moon and moon – and perhaps they'll string the tubs to a stray-line, and sink 'em a little-ways from shore, and take the bearings; and then when they have a chance they'll go to creep for 'em.'

'What's that?'

'O, they'll go out in a boat and drag a creeper – that's a grapnel – along the bottom till it catch hold of the stray-line.'

The minister stood thinking; and there was no sound within doors but the tick of the clock on the stairs, and the quick breathing of Lizzy, partly from her walk and partly from agitation, as she stood close to the wall, not in such complete darkness but that he could discern against its whitewashed surface the greatcoat, breeches, and broad hat which covered her.

'Lizzy, all this is very wrong,' he said. 'Don't you remember the lesson of the tribute-money? "Render unto Caesar the things that are Caesar's." Surely you have heard that read times enough in your growing up?'

'He's dead,' she pouted.

'But the spirit of the text is in force just the same.'

'My father did it, and so did my grandfather, and almost everybody in Nether-Moynton lives by it, and life would be so dull if it wasn't for that, that I should not care to live at all.'

'I am nothing to live for, of course,' he replied bitterly. 'You would not think it worth while to give up this wild business and live for me alone?'

'I have never looked at it like that.'

'And you won't promise and wait till I am ready?'

'I cannot give you my word tonight.' And, looking thoughtfully down, she gradually moved and moved away, going into the adjoining room, and closing the door between them. She remained there in the dark till he was tired of waiting, and had gone up to his own chamber.

Poor Stockdale was dreadfully depressed all the next day by the discoveries of the night before. Lizzy was unmistakably a fascinating young woman, but as a minister's wife she was hardly to be contemplated. 'If I had only stuck to father's little grocery business, instead of going in for the ministry, she would have suited me beautifully!' he said sadly, until he remembered that in that case he would never have come from his distant home to Nether-Moynton, and never have known her.

The estrangement between them was not complete, but it was sufficient to keep them out of each other's company. Once during the day he met her in the garden-path, and said, turning a reproachful eye upon her, 'Do you promise, Lizzy?' But she did not reply. The evening drew on, and he knew well enough that Lizzy would repeat her excursion at night – her half-offended manner had shown that she had not the slightest intention of altering her plans at present. He did not wish to repeat his own share of the adventure; but, act as he would, his uneasiness on her account increased with the decline of day. Supposing that an accident should befall her, he would never forgive himself for not being there to help, much as he disliked the idea of seeming to countenance such unlawful escapades.

5. HOW THEY WENT TO LULWIND COVE

As he had expected, she left the house at the same hour at night, this time passing his door without stealth, as if she knew very well that he would be watching, and were resolved to brave his displeasure. He was quite ready, opened the door quickly, and reached the back door almost as soon as she.

'Then you will go, Lizzy?' he said as he stood on the step beside her, who now again appeared as a little man with a face altogether unsuited to his clothes.

'I must,' she said, repressed by his stern manner.

'Then I shall go, too,' said he.

'And I am sure you will enjoy it!' she exclaimed in more buoyant tones. 'Everybody does who tries it.'

'God forbid that I should!' he said. 'But I must look after you.'

They opened the wicket and went up the road abreast of each other, but at some distance apart, scarcely a word passing between them. The evening was rather less favourable to smuggling enterprise than the last had been, the wind being lower, and the sky somewhat clear towards the north.

'It is rather lighter,' said Stockdale.

''Tis, unfortunately,' said she. 'But it is only from those few stars over there. The moon was new today at four o'clock, and I expected clouds. I hope we shall be able to do it this dark, for when we have to sink 'em for long it makes the stuff taste bleachy, and folks don't like it so well.'

Her course was different from that of the preceding night, branching off to the left over Lord's Barrow as soon as they had got out of the lane and crossed the highway. By the time they reached Chaldon Down, Stockdale, who had been in perplexed thought as to what he should say to her, decided that he would not attempt expostulation now, while she was excited by the adventure, but wait till it was over, and endeavour to keep her from such practices in future. It occurred to him once or twice, as they rambled on, that should they be surprised by the Preventive-guard, his situation would be more awkward than hers, for it would be difficult to prove his true motive in coming to the spot; but the risk was a slight consideration beside his wish to be with her.

They now arrived at a ravine which lay on the outskirts of Chaldon, a village two miles on their way towards the point of the shore they sought. Lizzy broke the silence this time: 'I have to wait here to meet the carriers. I don't know if they have come yet. As I told you, we go to Lulwind Cove tonight, and it is two miles further than Ringsworth.'

It turned out that the men had already come; for while she spoke two or three dozen heads broke the line of the slope, and a company of them at once descended from the bushes where they had been lying in wait. These carriers were men whom Lizzy and other proprietors regularly employed to bring the tubs from the boat to a hiding-place inland. They were all young fellows of Nether-Moynton, Chaldon, and the neighbourhood, quiet and inoffensive persons, even though some held heavy sticks, who simply engaged to carry the cargo for Lizzy and her cousin Owlett, as they would have engaged in any other labour for which they were fairly well paid.

At a word from her they closed in together. 'You had better take it now,' she said to them; and handed to each a packet. It contained six shillings, their renumeration for the night's undertaking, which was paid beforehand without reference to success or failure; but, besides this, they had the privilege of selling as agents when the run was successfully made. As soon as it was done, she said to them, 'The place is the old one, Dagger's Grave, near Lulwind Cove'; the men till that moment not having been told whither they were bound, for obvious reasons. 'Mr Owlett will meet you there,' added Lizzy. 'I shall follow behind, to see that we are not watched.'

The carriers went on, and Stockdale and Mrs Newberry followed at a distance of a stone's throw. 'What do these men do by day?' he said.

'Twelve or fourteen of them are labouring men. Some are brick-makers, some carpenters, some shoemakers, some thatchers. They are all known to me very well. Nine of 'em are of your own congregation.'

'I can't help that,' said Stockdale.

'O, I know you can't. I only told you. The others are more church-inclined, because they supply the pa'son with all the spirits he requires, and they don't wish to show unfriendliness to a customer.'

'How do you choose 'em?' said Stockdale.

'We choose 'em for their closeness, and because they are strong and surefooted, and able to carry a heavy load a long way without being tired.'

Stockdale sighed as she enumerated each particular, for it proved how far involved in the business a woman must be who was so well acquainted with its conditions and needs. And yet he felt more tenderly towards her at this moment than he had felt all the foregoing day. Perhaps it was that her experienced manner and bold indifference stirred his admiration in spite of himself.

'Take my arm, Lizzy,' he murmured.

'I don't want it,' she said. 'Besides, we may never be to each other again what we once have been.'

'That depends upon you,' said he, and they went on again as before.

The hired carriers paced along over Chaldon Down with as little hesitation as if it had been day, avoiding the cartway, and leaving the village of East Chaldon on the left, so as to reach the crest of the hill at a lonely trackless place not far from the ancient earthwork called Round Pound. A quarter-hour more of brisk walking brought them within sound of the sea, to the place called Dagger's Grave, not many hundred yards from Lulwind Cove. Here they paused, and Lizzy and Stockdale came up with them, when they went on together to the verge of the cliff. One of the men now produced an iron bar, which he drove firmly into the soil a yard from the edge, and attached to it a rope that he had uncoiled from his body. They all began to descend, partly stepping, partly sliding down the incline, as the rope slipped through their hands.

'You will not go to the bottom, Lizzy?' said Stockdale anxiously.

'No. I stay here to watch,' she said. 'Mr Owlett is down there.'

The men remained quite silent when they reached the shore; and the next thing audible to the two at the top was the dip of heavy oars, and the dashing of waves against a boat's bow. In a moment the keel gently touched the shingle, and Stockdale heard the footsteps of the thirty-six carriers running forwards over the pebbles towards the point of landing.

There was a sousing in the water as of a brood of ducks plunging in, showing that the men had not been particular about keeping their legs, or even their waists, dry from the brine: but it was impossible to see what they were doing, and in a few minutes the shingle was trampled again. The iron bar sustaining the rope, on which Stockdale's hand rested, began to swerve a little, and the carriers one by one appeared climbing up the sloping cliff, dripping audibly as they came, and sustaining themselves by the guide-rope. Each man on reaching the top was seen to be carrying a pair of tubs, one on his back and one on his chest, the two being slung together by cords passing round the chine hoops, and resting on the carrier's shoulders. Some of the stronger men carried three by putting an extra one on the top behind, but the customary load was a pair, these being quite weighty enough to give their bearer the sensation of having chest and backbone in contact after a walk of four or five miles.

'Where is Mr Owlett?' said Lizzy to one of them.

'He will not come up this way,' said the carrier. 'He's to bide on shore till we be safe off.' Then, without waiting for the rest, the foremost men plunged across the down, and, when the last had ascended, Lizzy pulled up the rope, wound it round her arm, wriggled the bar from the sod, and turned to follow the carriers.

'You are very anxious about Owlett's safety,' said the minister.

'Was there ever such a man!' said Lizzy. 'Why, isn't he my cousin?'

'Yes. Well, it is a bad night's work,' said Stockdale heavily. 'But I'll carry the bar and rope for you.'

'Thank God, the tubs have got so far all right,' said she.

Stockdale shook his head, and taking the bar, walked by her side towards the downs; and the moan of the sea was heard no more.

'Is this what you meant the other day when you spoke of having business with Owlett?' the young man asked.

'This is it,' she replied. 'I never see him on any other matter.'

'A partnership of that kind with a young man is very odd.'

'It was begun by my father and his, who were brother-laws.'

Her companion could not blind himself to the fact that where tastes and pursuits were so akin as Lizzy's and Owlett's, and where risks were shared, as with them, in every undertaking, there would be a peculiar appropriateness in her answering Owlett's standing question on matrimony in the affirmative. This did not soothe Stockdale, its tendency being rather to stimulate in him an effort to make the pair as inappropriate as possible, and win her away from this nocturnal crew to correctness of conduct and a minister's parlour in some far-removed inland county.

They had been walking near enough to the file of carriers for Stockdale to perceive that, when they got into the road to the village, they split up into two companies of unequal size, each of which made off in a direction of its own. One company, the smaller of the two, went towards the church, and by the time that Lizzy and Stockdale reached their own house these men had scaled the churchyard wall, and were proceeding noiselessly over the grass within.

'I see that Mr Owlett has arranged for one batch to be put in the church again,' observed Lizzy. 'Do you remember my taking you there the first night you came?'

'Yes, of course,' said Stockdale. 'No wonder you had permission to broach the tubs – they were his, I suppose?'

'No, they were not – they were mine; I had permission from myself. The day after that they went several miles inland in a waggon-load of manure, and sold very well.'

At this moment the group of men who had made off to the left some time before began leaping one by one from the hedge opposite Lizzy's house, and the first man, who had no tubs upon his shoulders, came forward.

'Mrs Newberry, isn't it?' he said hastily.

'Yes, Jim,' said she. 'What's the matter?'

'I find that we can't put any in Badger's Clump tonight, Lizzy,' said Owlett. 'The place is watched. We must sling the apple-tree in the orchet if there's time. We can't put any more under the church lumber than I have sent on there, and my mixen hev already more in en than is safe.'

'Very well,' she said. 'Be quick about it – that's all. What can I do?'

'Nothing at all, please. Ah, it is the minister! – you two that can't do anything had better get indoors and not be zeed.'

While Owlett thus conversed, in a tone so full of contraband anxiety and so free from lover's jealousy, the men who followed him had been descending one by one from the hedge; and it unfortunately happened that when the hindmost took his leap, the cord slipped which sustained his tubs; the result was that both the kegs fell into the road, one of them being stove in by the blow.

''Od drown it all!' said Owlett, rushing back.

'It is worth a good deal, I suppose?' said Stockdale.

'O no – about two guineas and half to us now,' said Lizzy excitedly. 'It isn't that – it is the smell! It is so blazing strong before it has been lowered by water, that it smells dreadfully when spilt in the road like that! I do hope Latimer won't pass by till it is gone off.'

Owlett and one or two others picked up the burst tub and began to scrape and trample over the spot, to disperse the liquor as much as possible; and then they all entered the gate of Owlett's orchard, which adjoined Lizzy's garden on the right. Stockdale did not care to follow them, for several on recognizing him had looked wonderingly at his presence, though they said nothing. Lizzy left his side and went to the bottom of the garden, looking over the hedge into the orchard, where the men could be dimly seen bustling about, and apparently hiding the tubs. All was done noiselessly, and without a light; and when it was over they dispersed in different directions, those who had taken their cargoes to the church having already gone off to their homes.

Lizzy returned to the garden-gate, over which Stockdale was still abstractedly leaning. 'It is all finished: I am going indoors now,' she said gently. 'I will leave the door ajar for you.'

'O no – you needn't,' said Stockdale; 'I am coming too.'

But before either of them had moved, the faint clatter of horses' hoofs broke upon the ear, and it seemed to come from the point where the track across the down joined the hard road.

'They are just too late!' cried Lizzy exultingly.

'Who?' said Stockdale.

'Latimer, the riding-officer, and some assistant of his. We had better go indoors.'

They entered the house, and Lizzy bolted the door. 'Please don't get a light, Mr Stockdale,' she said.

'Of course I will not,' said he.

'I thought you might be on the side of the king,' said Lizzy, with faintest sarcasm.

'I am,' said Stockdale. 'But, Lizzy Newberry, I love you, and you know it perfectly well, and you ought to know, if you do not, what I have suffered in my conscience on your account these last few days!'

'I guess very well,' she said hurriedly. 'Yet I don't see why. Ah, you are better than I!'

The trotting of the horses seemed to have again died away, and the pair of listeners touched each other's fingers in the cold 'Good-night' of those whom something seriously divided. They were on the landing, but before they had taken three steps apart, the tramp of the horsemen suddenly revived, almost close to the house. Lizzy turned to the staircase window, opened the casement about an inch, and put her face close to the aperture. 'Yes, one of 'em is Latimer,' she whispered. 'He always rides a white horse. One would think it was the last colour for a man in that line.'

Stockdale looked, and saw the white shape of the animal as it passed by; but before the riders had gone another ten yards Latimer reined in his horse, and said something to his companion which neither Stockdale nor Lizzy could hear. Its drift was, however, soon made evident, for the other man stopped also; and sharply turning the horses' heads they cautiously retraced their steps. When they were again opposite Mrs Newberry's garden, Latimer dismounted, and the man on the dark horse did the same.

Lizzy and Stockdale, intently listening and observing the proceedings, naturally put their heads as close as possible to the slit formed by the slightly opened casement; and thus it occurred that at last their cheeks came positively into contact. They went on listening, as if they did not know of the singular incident which had happened to their faces, and the pressure of each to each rather increased than lessened with the lapse of time.

They could hear the Customs-men sniffing the air like hounds as they paced slowly along. When they reached the spot where the tub had burst, both stopped on the instant.

'Ay, ay, 'tis quite strong here,' said the second officer. 'Shall we knock at the door?'

'Well, no,' said Latimer. 'Maybe this is only a trick to put us off the scent. They wouldn't kick up this stink anywhere near their hiding-place. I have known such things before.'

'Anyhow, the things, or some of 'em, must have been brought this way,' said the other.

'Yes,' said Latimer musingly. 'Unless 'tis all done to tole us the wrong way. I have a mind that we go home for tonight without saying a word, and come the first thing in the morning with more hands. I know they have storages about here, but we can do nothing by this owl's light. We will look round the parish and see if everybody is in bed, John; and if all is quiet, we will do as I say.'

They went on, and the two inside the window could hear them passing leisurely through the whole village, the street of which curved round at the bottom and entered the turnpike road at another junction. This way the officers followed, and the amble of their horses died quite away.

'What will you do?' said Stockdale, withdrawing from his position.

She knew that he alluded to the coming search by the officers to divert her attention from their own tender incident by the casement, which he wished to be passed over as a thing rather dreamt of than done. 'O, nothing,' she replied, with as much coolness as she could command under her disappointment at his manner. 'We often have such storms as this.

You would not be frightened if you knew what fools they are. Fancy riding o' horseback through the place; of course they will hear and see nobody while they make that noise; but they are always afraid to get off, in case some of our fellows should burst out upon 'em, and tie them up to the gate-post, as they have done before now. Good-night, Mr Stockdale.'

She closed the window and went to her room, where a tear fell from her eyes; and that not because of the alertness of the riding-officers.

6. THE GREAT SEARCH AT NETHER-MOYNTON

Stockdale was so excited by the events of the evening, and the dilemma that he was placed in between conscience and love, that he did not sleep, or even doze, but remained as broadly awake as at noonday. As soon as the gray light began to touch ever so faintly the whiter objects in his bedroom he arose, dressed himself and went downstairs into the road.

The village was already astir. Several of the carriers had heard the well-known canter of Latimer's horse while they were undressing in the dark that night, and had already communicated with each other and Owlett on the subject. The only doubt seemed to be about the safety of those tubs which had been left under the church gallery-stairs, and after a short discussion at the corner of the mill, it was agreed that these should be removed before it got lighter, and hidden in the middle of a double hedge bordering the adjoining field. However, before anything could be carried into effect, the footsteps of many men were heard coming down the lane from the highway.

'Damn it, here they be,' said Owlett, who, having already drawn the hatch and started his mill for the day, stood stolidly at the mill-door covered with flour, as if the interest of his whole soul was bound up in the shaking walls around him.

The two or three with whom he had been talking dispersed to their usual work, and when the Customs-officers, and the formidable body of men they had hired, reached the village cross, between the mill and Mrs Newberry's house, the village wore the natural aspect of a place beginning its morning labours.

'Now,' said Latimer to his associates, who numbered thirteen men in all, 'what I know is that the things are somewhere in this here place. We have got the day before us and 'tis hard if we can't light upon 'em and get 'em to Budmouth Custom-house before night. First we will try the fuel houses, and then we'll work our way into the chimmers, and then to the ricks and stables, and so creep round. You have nothing but your noses to guide ye, mind, so use 'em today if you never did in your lives before.'

Then the search began. Owlett, during the early part, watched from his mill-window, Lizzy from the door of her house, with the greatest self-possession. A farmer down below, who also had a share in the run, rode about with one eye on his fields and the other on Latimer and his myrmidons, prepared to put them off the scent if he should be asked a question. Stockdale, who was no smuggler at all, felt more anxiety than the worst of them, and went about his studies with a heavy heart, coming frequently to the door to ask Lizzy some question or other on the consequences to her of the tubs being found.

'The consequences,' she said quietly, 'are simply that I shall lose 'em. As I have none in the house or garden, they can't touch me personally.'

'But you have some in the orchard?'

'Mr Owlett rents that of me, and he lends it to others. So it will be hard to say who put any tubs there if they should be found.'

There was never such a tremendous sniffing known as that which took place in Nether-Moynton parish and its vicinity this day. All was done methodically, and mostly on hands and knees. At different hours of the day they had different plans. From daybreak to breakfast-time the officers used their sense of smell in a direct and straightforward manner only, pausing nowhere but at such places as the tubs might be supposed to be secreted in at that very moment, pending their removal on the following night. Among the places tested and examined were:

Hollow trees	Cupboards	Culverts
Potato-graves	Clock-cases	Hedgerows
Fuel-houses	Chimney-flues	Faggot-ricks
Bedrooms	Rainwater-butts	Haystacks
Apple-lofts	Pigsties	Coppers and ovens

After breakfast they recommenced with renewed vigour, taking a new line; that is to say, directing their attention to clothes that might be supposed to have come in contact with the tubs in their removal from the shore, such garments being usually tainted with the spirit, owing to its oozing between the staves. They now sniffed at –

Smock-frocks	Smiths' and shoemakers' aprons
Old shirts and waistcoats	Knee-naps and hedging-gloves
Coats and hats	Tarpaulins
Breeches and leggings	Market-cloaks
Women's shawls and gowns	Scarecrows

And as soon as the midday meal was over, they pushed their search into places where the spirits might have been thrown away in alarm:

Horse-ponds	Mixens	Sinks in yards
Stable-drains	Wet ditches	Road-scrapings, and
Cinder-heaps	Cesspools	Back-door gutters

But still these indefatigable Custom-house men discovered nothing more than the original tell-tale smell in the road opposite Lizzy's house, which even yet had not passed off.

'I'll tell ye what it is, men,' said Latimer, about three o'clock in the afternoon, 'we must begin over again. Find them tubs I will.'

The men who had been hired for the day, looked at their hands and knees, muddy with creeping on all fours so frequently, and rubbed their noses, as if they had almost had enough of it; for the quantity of bad air which had passed into each one's nostril had rendered it nearly as insensible as a flue. However, after a moment's hesitation, they prepared to start anew, except three, whose power of smell had quite succumbed under the excessive wear and tear of the day.

By this time not a male villager was to be seen in the parish. Owlett was not at his mill, the farmers were not in their fields, the parson was not in his garden, the smith had left his forge, and the wheelwright's shop was silent.

'Where the divil are the folk gone?' said Latimer, waking up to the fact of their absence, and looking round. 'I'll have 'em up for this! Why don't they come and help us? There's not a man about the place but the Methodist parson, and he's an old woman. I demand assistance in the king's name!'

'We must find the jineral public afore we can demand that,' said his lieutenant.

'Well, well, we shall do better without 'em,' said Latimer, who changed his moods at a moment's notice. 'But there's great cause of suspicion in this silence and this keeping out of sight, and I'll bear it in mind. Now we will go across to Owlett's orchard and see what we can find there.'

Stockdale, who heard this discussion from the garden-gate, over which he had been leaning, was rather alarmed, and thought it a mistake of the villagers to keep so completely out of the way. He himself, like the Preventives, had been wondering for the last half-hour what could have become of them. Some labourers were of necessity engaged in distant fields, but the master-workmen should have been at home; though one and all, after just showing themselves at their shops, had apparently gone off for the day. He went in to Lizzy, who sat at a back window sewing, and said, 'Lizzy, where are the men?'

Lizzy laughed. 'Where they mostly are when they're run so hard as this.' She cast her eyes to heaven. 'Up there,' she said.

Stockdale looked up. 'What – on the top of the church tower?' he asked, seeing the direction of her glance.

'Yes.'

'Well, I expect they will soon have to come down,' said he gravely. 'I have been listening to the officers, and they are going to search the orchard over again, and then every nook in the church.'

Lizzy looked alarmed for the first time. 'Will you go and tell our folk?' she said. 'They ought to be let know.' Seeing his conscience struggling within him like a boiling pot, she added, 'No, never mind, I'll go myself.'

She went out, descended the garden, and climbed over the churchyard wall at the same time that the Preventive-men were ascending the road to the orchard. Stockdale could do no less than follow her. By the time that she reached the tower entrance he was at her side, and they entered together.

Nether-Moynton church-tower was, as in many villages, without a turret, and the only way to the top was by going up to the singers' gallery, and thence ascending by a ladder to a square trap-door in the floor of the bell-loft, above which a permanent ladder was fixed, passing through the bells to a hole in the roof. When Lizzy and Stockdale reached the gallery and looked up, nothing but the trap-door and the five holes for the bell-ropes appeared. The ladder was gone.

'There's no getting up,' said Stockdale.

'O yes, there is,' said she. 'There's an eye looking at us at this moment through a knot-hole in that trap-door.'

And as she spoke the trap opened, and the dark line of the ladder was seen descending against the whitewashed wall. When it touched the bottom Lizzy dragged it to its place, and said, 'If you'll go up, I'll follow.'

The young man ascended, and presently found himself among consecrated bells for the first time in his life, nonconformity having been in the Stockdale blood for some generations. He eyed them uneasily, and looked round for Lizzy. Owlett stood here, holding the top of the ladder.

'What, be you really one of us?' said the miller.

'It seems so,' said Stockdale sadly.

'He's not,' said Lizzy, who overheard. 'He's neither for nor against us. He'll do us no harm.'

She stepped up beside them, and then they went on to the next stage, which when they had clambered over the dusty bell-carriages, was of easy ascent, leading towards the hole through which the pale sky appeared, and into the open air. Owlett remained behind for a moment, to pull up the lower ladder.

'Keep down your heads,' said a voice, as soon as they set foot on the flat.

Stockdale here beheld all the missing parishioners, lying on their stomachs on the tower roof, except a few who, elevated on their hands and knees, were peeping through the embrasures of the parapet. Stockdale did the same, and saw the village lying like a map below him, over which moved the figures of the Customs-men, each foreshortened to a crablike object, the crown of his hat forming a circular disc in the centre of him. Some of the men had turned their heads when the young preacher's figure arose among them.

'What, Mr Stockdale?' said Matt Grey, in a tone of surprise.

'I'd as lief that it hadn't been,' said Jim Clarke. 'If the pa'son should see him a-trespassing here in his tower, 'twould be none the better for we, seeing how 'a do hate chapel-members. He'd never buy a tub of us again, and he's as good a customer as we have got this side o' Warm'll.'

'Where is the pa'son?' said Lizzy.

'In his house, to be sure, that he mid see nothing of what's going on – where all good folks ought to be, and this young man likewise.'

'Well, he has brought some news,' said Lizzy. 'They are going to search the orchard and church; can we do anything if they should find?'

'Yes,' said her cousin Owlett. 'That's what we've been talking o', and we have settled our line. Well, be dazed!'

The exclamation was claused by his perceiving that some of the searchers, having got into the orchard, and begun stooping and creeping hither and thither, were pausing in the middle, where a tree smaller than the rest was growing. They drew closer, and bent lower than ever upon the ground.

'O, my tubs!' said Lizzy faintly, as she peered through the parapet at them.

'They have got 'em, 'a b'lieve,' said Owlett.

The interest in the movements of the officers was so keen that not a single eye was looking in any other direction; but at that moment a shout from the church beneath them attracted the attention of the smugglers, as it did also of the party in the orchard, who sprang to their feet and went towards the churchyard wall. At the same time those of the Government. men who had entered the church unperceived by the smugglers cried aloud, 'Here be some of 'em at last.'

The smugglers remained in a blank silence, uncertain whether 'some of 'em' meant tubs or men; but again peeping cautiously over the edge of the tower they learnt that tubs were the things descried; and soon these fated articles were brought one by one into the middle of the churchyard from their hiding-place under the gallery-stairs.

'They are going to put 'em on Hinton's vault till they find the rest!' said Lizzy hopelessly. The Customs-men had, in fact, begun to pile up the tubs on a large stone slab which was fixed there; and when all were brought out from the tower, two or three of the men were left standing by them, the rest of the party again proceeding to the orchard.

The interest of the smugglers in the next manoeuvres of their enemies became painfully intense. Only about thirty tubs had been secreted in the lumber of the tower, but seventy were hidden in the orchard, making up all that they had brought ashore as yet, the remainder of the cargo having been tied to a sinker and dropped overboard for another night's operations. The Preventives, having re-entered the orchard, acted as if they were positive that here lay hidden the rest of the tubs, which they were determined to find before nightfall. They spread themselves out round the field, and advancing on all fours as before, went anew round every apple-tree in the enclosure. The young tree in the middle again led them to pause, and at length the whole company gathered there in a way which signified that a second chain of reasoning had led to the same results as the first.

When they had examined the sod hereabouts for some minutes, one of the men rose, ran to a disused part of the church where tools were kept, and returned with the sexton's pickaxe and shovel, with which they set to work.

'Are they really buried there?' said the minister, for the grass was so green and uninjured that it was difficult to believe it had been disturbed. The smugglers were too interested to reply, and presently they saw, to their chagrin, the officers stand several on each side of the tree; and, stooping and applying their hands to the soil, they bodily lifted the tree and the turf around it. The apple-tree now showed itself to be growing in a shallow box, with handles for lifting at each of the four sides. Under the site of the tree a square hole was revealed, and an officer went and looked down.

'It is all up now,' said Owlett quietly. 'And now all of ye get down before they notice we are here; and be ready for our next move. I had better bide here till dark, or they may take me on suspicion, as 'tis on my ground. I'll be with ye as soon as daylight begins to pink in.'

'And I!' said Lizzy.

'You please look to the linch-pins and screws; then go indoors and know nothing at all. The chaps will do the rest.'

The ladder was replaced, and all but Owlett descended, the men passing off one by one at the back of the church, and vanishing on their respective errands. Lizzy walked boldly along the street, followed closely by the minister.

'You are going indoors, Mrs Newberry?' he said.

She knew from the words 'Mrs Newberry' that the division between them had widened yet another degree.

'I am not going home,' she said. 'I have a little thing to do before I go in. Martha Sarah will get your tea.'

'O, I don't mean on that account,' said Stockdale. 'What *can* you have to do further in this unhallowed affair?'

'Only a little,' she said.

'What is that? I'll go with you.'

'No, I shall go by myself. Will you please go indoors? I shall be there in less than an hour.'

'You are not going to run any danger, Lizzy?' said the young man, his tenderness reasserting itself.

'None whatever – worth mentioning,' answered she, and went down towards the Cross.

Stockdale entered the garden-gate, and stood behind it looking on. The Preventive-men were still busy in the orchard, and at last he was tempted to enter and watch their proceedings. When he came closer he found that the secret cellar, of whose existence he had been totally unaware, was formed by timbers placed across from side to side about a foot under the ground, and grassed over.

The officers looked up at Stockdale's fair and downy countenance, and evidently thinking him above suspicion, went on with their work again. As soon as all the tubs were taken out they began tearing up the turf, pulling out the timbers, and breaking in the sides, till the cellar was wholly dismantled and shapeless, the apple-tree lying with its roots high to the air. But the hole which had in its time held so much contraband merchandize was never completely filled up, either then or afterwards, a depression in the greensward marking the spot to this day.

7. THE WALK TO WARM'ELL CROSS AND AFTERWARDS

As the goods had all to be carried to Budmouth that night, the next object of the Custom-house officers was to find horses and carts for the journey, and they went about the village for that purpose. Latimer strode hither and thither with a lump of chalk in his hand, marking broad-arrows so vigorously on every vehicle and set of harness that he came across, that it seemed as if he would chalk broad-arrows on the very hedges and roads. The owner of every conveyance so marked was bound to give it up for

Government purposes. Stockdale, who had had enough of the scene, turned indoors thoughtful and depressed. Lizzy was already there, having come in at the back, though she had not yet taken off her bonnet. She looked tired, and her mood was not much brighter than his own. They had but little to say to each other; and the minister went away and attempted to read; but at this he could not succeed, and he shook the little bell for tea.

Lizzy herself brought in the tray, the girl having run off into the village during the afternoon, too full of excitement at the proceedings to remember her state of life. However, almost before the sad lovers had said anything to each other, Martha came in in a steaming state.

'O, there's such a stoor, Mrs Newberry and Mr Stockdale! The king's officers can't get the carts ready nohow at all! They pulled Thomas Artnell's, and William Rogers's, and Stephen Sprake's carts into the road, and off came the wheels, and down fell the carts; and they found there was no linch-pins in the arms; and then they tried Samuel Shane's waggon, and found that the screws were gone from he, and at last they looked at the dairyman's cart, and he's not got none neither! They have gone now to the blacksmith's to get some made, but he's nowhere to be found!'

Stockdale looked at Lizzy, who blushed very slightly, and went out of the room, followed by Martha Sarah. But before they had got through the passage there was a rap at the front door, and Stockdale recognized Latimer's voice addressing Mrs Newberry, who had turned back.

'For God's sake, Mrs Newberry, have you seen Hardman the blacksmith up this way? If we could get hold of him, we'd e'en a'most drag him by the hair of his head to his anvil, where he ought to be.'

'He's an idle man, Mr Latimer,' said Lizzy archly. 'What do you want him for?'

'Why, there isn't a horse in the place that has got more than three shoes on, and some have only two. The waggon-wheels be without strakes, and there's no linch-pins to the carts. What with that, and the bother about every set of harness being out of order, we shan't be off before nightfall – upon my soul we shan't. 'Tis a rough lot, Mrs Newberry, that you've got about you here; but they'll play at this game once too often, mark my words they will! There's not a man in the parish that don't deserve to be whipped.'

It happened that Hardman was at that moment a little further up the lane, smoking his pipe behind a holly-bush. When Latimer had done speaking he went on in this direction, and Hardman, hearing the riding-officer's steps, found curiosity too strong for prudence. He peeped out from the bush at the very moment that Latimer's glance was on it. There was nothing left for him to do but to come forward with unconcern.

'I've been looking for you for the last hour!' said Latimer with a glare in his eye.

'Sorry to hear that,' said Hardman. 'I've been out for a stroll, to look for more hid tubs, to deliver 'em up to Gover'ment.'

'O yes, Hardman we know it,' said Latimer, with withering sarcasm. 'We know that you'll deliver 'em up to Gover'ment. We know that all the parish is helping us, and have been all day! Now you please walk along with me down to your shop, and kindly let me hire ye in the king's name.'

They went down the lane together, and presently there resounded from the smithy the ring of a hammer not very briskly swung. However, the carts and horses were got into some sort of travelling condition, but it was not until after the clock had struck six, when the muddy roads were glistening under the horizontal light of the fading day. The smuggled tubs were soon packed into the vehicles, and Latimer, with three of his assistants, drove slowly out of the village in the direction of the port of Budmouth, some considerable number of miles distant, the other men of the Preventive-guard being left to watch for the remainder of the cargo, which they knew to have been sunk somewhere between Ringsworth and Lulwind Cove, and to unearth Owlett, the only person clearly implicated by the discovery of the cave.

Women and children stood at the doors as the carts, each chalked with the Government pitchfork, passed in the increasing twilight; and as they stood they looked at the confiscated property with a melancholy expression that told only too plainly the relation which they bore to the trade.

'Well, Lizzy,' said Stockdale, when the crackle of the wheels had nearly died away. 'This is a fit finish to your adventure. I am truly thankful that you have got off without suspicion, and the loss only of the liquor. Will you sit down and let me talk to you?'

'By and by,' she said. 'But I must go out now.'

'Not to that horrid shore again?' he said blankly.

'No, not there. I am only going to see the end of this day's business.'

He did not answer to this, and she moved towards the door slowly, as if waiting for him to say something more.

'You don't offer to come with me,' she added at last. 'I suppose that's because you hate me after all this!'

'Can you say it, Lizzy, when you know I only want to save you from such practices? Come with you! – of course I will, if it is only to take care of you. But why will you go out again?'

'Because I cannot rest indoors. Something is happening, and I must know what. Now, come!' And they went into the dusk together.

When they reached the turnpike-road she turned to the right, and he soon perceived that they were following the direction of the Preventive-men and their load. He had given her his arm, and every now and then she suddenly pulled it back, to signify that he was to halt a moment and listen. They had walked rather quickly along the first quarter of a mile, and on the second or third time of standing still she said, 'I hear them ahead – don't you?'

'Yes,' he said; 'I hear the wheels. But what of that?'

'I only want to know if they get clear away from the neighbourhood.'

'Ah,' said he, a light breaking upon him. 'Something desperate is to be attempted! – and now I remember there was not a man about the village when we left.'

'Hark!' she murmured. The noise of the cart-wheels had stopped, and given place to another sort of sound.

''Tis a scuffle!' said Stockdale. 'There'll be murder! Lizzy, let go my arm; I am going on. On my conscience, I must not stay here and do nothing!'

'There'll be no murder, and not even a broken head,' she said. 'Our men are thirty to four of them: no harm will be done at all.'

'Then there *is* an attack!' exclaimed Stockdale; 'and you knew it was to be. Why should you side with men who break the laws like this?'

'Why should you side with men who take from country traders what they have honestly bought wi' their own money in France?' said she firmly.

'They are not honestly bought,' said he.

'They are,' she contradicted. 'I and Mr Owlett and the others paid thirty shillings for every one of the tubs before they were put on board at Cherbourg, and if a king who is nothing to us sends his people to steal our property we have a right to steal it back again.'

Stockdale did not stop to argue the matter but went quickly in the direction of the noise, Lizzy keeping at his side. 'Don't you interfere, will you, dear Richard?' she said anxiously, as they drew near. 'Don't let us go any closer: 'tis at Warm'ell Cross where they are seizing 'em. You can do no good, and you may meet with a hard blow!'

'Let us see first what is going on,' he said. But before they had got much further the noise of the cart-wheels began again; and Stockdale soon found that they were coming towards him. In another minute the three carts came up, and Stockdale and Lizzy stood in the ditch to let them pass.

Instead of being conducted by four men, as had happened when they went out of the village, the horses and carts were now accompanied by a body of from twenty to thirty, all of whom, as Stockdale perceived to his astonishment, had blackened faces. Among them walked six or eight huge female figures, whom, from their wide strides, Stockdale guessed to be men in disguise. As soon as the party discerned Lizzy and her companion four or five fell back, and when the carts had passed, came close to the pair.

'There is no walking up this way for the present,' said one of the gaunt women, who wore curls a foot long, dangling down the sides of her face, in the fashion of the time. Stockdale recognized this lady's voice as Owlett's.

'Why not?' said Stockdale. 'This is the public highway.'

'Now look here, youngster,' said Owlett. 'O, 'tis the Methodist parson! – what, and Mrs Newberry! Well, you'd better not go up that way, Lizzy. They've all run off, and folks have got their own again.'

The miller then hastened on and joined his comrades. Stockdale and Lizzy also turned back. 'I wish all this hadn't been forced upon us,' she said regretfully. 'But if those Coast-men had got off with the tubs, half the people in the parish would have been in want for the next month or two.'

Stockdale was not paying much attention to her words, and he said, 'I don't think I can go back like this. Those four poor Preventives may be murdered for all I know.'

'Murdered!' said Lizzy impatiently. 'We don't do murder here.'

'Well, I shall go as far as Warm'ell Cross to see,' said Stockdale decisively; and, without wishing her safe home or anything else, the minister turned back. Lizzy stood looking at him till his form was absorbed in the shades; and then, with sadness, she went in the direction of Nether-Moynton.

The road was lonely, and after nightfall at this time of the year there was often not a passer for hours. Stockdale pursued his way without hearing a sound beyond that of his own footsteps; and in due time he passed beneath the trees of the plantation which surrounded the Warm'ell Cross-road. Before he had reached the point of intersection he heard voices from the thicket.

'Hoi-hoi-hoi! Help, help!'

The voices were not at all feeble or despairing, but they were unmistakably anxious. Stockdale had no weapon, and before plunging into the pitchy darkness of the plantation he pulled a stake from the hedge, to use in case of need. When he got among the trees he shouted – 'What's the matter – where are you?'

'Here,' answered the voices; and, pushing through the brambles in that direction, he came near the objects of his search.

'Why don't you come forward?' said Stockdale.

'We be tied to the trees!'

'Who are you?'

'Poor Will Latimer the Customs-officer!' said one plaintively. 'Just come and cut these cords, there's a good man. We were afraid nobody would pass by tonight.'

Stockdale soon loosened them, upon which they stretched their limbs and stood at their ease.

'The rascals!' said Latimer, getting now into a rage, though he had seemed quite meek when Stockdale first came up. ''Tis the same set of fellows. I know they were Moynton chaps to a man.'

'But we can't swear to 'em,' said another. 'Not one of 'em spoke.'

'What are you going to do?' said Stockdale.

'I'd fain go back to Moynton, and have at 'em again!' said Latimer.

'So would we!' said his comrades.

'Fight till we die!' said Latimer.

'We will, we will!' said his men.

'But,' said Latimer, more frigidly, as they came out of the plantation, 'we don't *know* that these chaps with black faces were Moynton men? And proof is a hard thing.'

'So it is,' said the rest.

'And therefore we won't do nothing at all,' said Latimer, with complete dispassionateness. 'For my part, I'd sooner be them than we. The clitches of my arms are burning like fire from the cords those two strapping women tied round 'em. My opinion is, now I have had time to think o't, that you may serve your Gover'ment at too high a price. For these two nights and days I have not had an hour's rest; and, please God, here's for home-along.'

The other officers agreed heartily to this course; and, thanking Stockdale for his timely assistance, they parted from him at the Cross, taking themselves the western road, and Stockdale going back to Nether-Moynton.

During that walk the minister was lost in reverie of the most painful kind. As soon as he got into the house, and before entering his own rooms, he advanced to the door of the little back parlour in which Lizzy usually sat with her mother. He found her there alone. Stockdale went forward, and, like a man in a dream, looked down upon the table that stood between him and the young woman, who had her bonnet and cloak still on. As he did not speak, she looked up from her chair at him, with misgiving in her eye.

'Where are they gone?' he then said listlessly.

'Who? – I don't know. I have seen nothing of them since. I came straight in here.'

'If your men can manage to get off with those tubs, it will be a great profit to you, I suppose?'

'A share will be mine, a share my cousin Owlett's, a share to each of the two farmers, and a share divided amongst the men who helped us.'

'And you still think,' he went on slowly, 'that you will not give this business up?'

Lizzy rose, and put her hand upon his shoulder. 'Don't ask that,' she whispered. 'You don't know what you are asking. I must tell you, though I meant not to do it. What I make by that trade is all I have to keep my mother and myself with.'

He was astonished. 'I did not dream of such a thing,' he said. 'I would rather have scraped the roads, had I been you. What is money compared with a clear conscience?'

'My conscience is clear. I know my mother, but the king I have never seen. His dues are nothing to me. But it is a great deal to me that my mother and I should live.'

'Marry me, and promise to give it up. I will keep your mother.'

'It is good of you,' she said, moved a little. 'Let me think of it by myself. I would rather not answer now.'

She reserved her answer till the next day, and came into his room with a solemn face. 'I cannot do what you wished!' she said passionately. 'It is too much to ask. My whole life ha' been passed in this way.' Her words and manner showed that before entering she had been struggling with herself in private, and that the contention had been strong.

Stockdale turned pale, but he spoke quietly. 'Then, Lizzy, we must part. I cannot go against my principles in this matter, and I cannot make my profession a mockery. You know how I love you, and what I would do for you; but this one thing I cannot do.'

'But why should you belong to that profession?' she burst out. 'I have got this large house; why can't you marry me, and live here with us, and not be a Methodist preacher any more? I assure you, Richard, it is no harm, and I wish you could only see it as I do! We only carry it on in winter: in summer it is never done at all. It stirs up one's dull life at this time o' the year, and gives excitement, which I have got so used to now that I should hardly know how to do 'ithout it. At nights, when the wind blows, instead of being dull and stupid, and not noticing whether it do blow or not, your mind is afield, even if you are not afield yourself; and you are wondering how the chaps are getting on; and you walk up and down the room, and look out o' window, and then you go out yourself, and know your way about as well by night as by day, and have hair-breadth escapes from old Latimer and his fellows, who are too stupid ever to really frighten us, and only make us a bit nimble.'

'He frightened you a little last night, anyhow: and I would advise you to drop it before it is worse.'

She shook her head. 'No, I must go on as I have begun. I was born to it. It is in my blood, and I can't be cured. O, Richard, you cannot think what a hard thing you have asked, and how sharp you try me when you put me between this and my love for 'ee!'

Stockdale was leaning with his elbow on the mantelpiece, his hands over his eyes. 'We ought never to have met, Lizzy,' he said. 'It was an ill day for us! I little thought there was anything so hopeless and impossible in our engagement as this. Well, it is too late now to regret consequences in this way. I have had the happiness of seeing you and knowing you at least.'

'You dissent from Church, and I dissent from State,' she said. 'And I don't see why we are not well matched.'

He smiled sadly, while Lizzy remained looking down, her eyes beginning to overflow.

That was an unhappy evening for both of them, and the days that followed were unhappy days. Both she and he went mechanically about their employments, and his depression was marked in the village by more than one of his denomination with whom he came in contact. But Lizzy, who passed her days indoors, was unsuspected of being the cause: for it was generally understood that a quiet engagement to marry existed between her and her cousin Owlett, and had existed for some time.

Thus uncertainly the week passed on; till one morning Stockdale said to her: 'I have had a letter, Lizzy. I must call you that till I am gone.'

'Gone?' said she blankly.

'Yes,' he said. 'I am going from this place. I felt it would be better for us both that I should not stay after what has happened. In fact, I couldn't stay here, and look on you from day to day, without becoming weak and faltering in my course. I have just heard of an arrangement by which the other minister can arrive here in about a week; and let me go elsewhere.'

That he had all this time continued so firmly fixed in his resolution came upon her as a grievous surprise. 'You never loved me!' she said bitterly.

'I might say the same,' he returned; 'but I will not. Grant me one favour. Come and hear my last sermon on the day before I go.'

Lizzy, who was a church-goer on Sunday mornings, frequently attended Stockdale's chapel in the evening with the rest of the double-minded; and she promised.

It became known that Stockdale was going to leave, and a good many people outside his own sect were sorry to hear it. The intervening days flew rapidly away, and on the evening of the Sunday which preceded the morning of his departure Lizzy sat in the chapel to hear him for the last time. The little building was full to overflowing, and he took up the subject which all had expected, that of the contraband trade so extensively practised among them. His hearers, in laying his words to their own hearts, did not perceive that they were most particularly directed against Lizzy, till the sermon waxed warm, and Stockdale nearly broke down with emotion. In truth his own earnestness, and her sad eyes looking up at him, were too much for the young man's equanimity. He hardly knew how he ended. He saw Lizzy, as through a mist, turn and go away with the rest of the congregation; and shortly afterwards followed her home.

She invited him to supper, and they sat down alone, her mother having, as was usual with her on Sunday nights, gone to bed early.

'We will part friends, won't we?' said Lizzy, with forced gaiety, and never alluding to the sermon: a reticence which rather disappointed him.

'We will,' he said, with a forced smile on his part; and they sat down.

It was the first meal that they had even shared together in their lives, and probably the last that they would so share. When it was over, and the indifferent conversation could no longer be continued, he arose and took her hand. 'Lizzy,' he said, 'do you say we must part – do you?'

'You do,' she said solemnly. 'I can say no more.'

'Nor I,' said he. 'If that is your answer, good-bye!'

Stockdale bent over her and kissed her, and she involuntarily returned his kiss. 'I shall go early,' he said hurriedly. 'I shall not see you again.'

And he did leave early. He fancied, when stepping forth into the gray morning light, to mount the van which was to carry him away, that he saw a face between the parted curtains of Lizzy's window, but the light was faint, and the panes glistened with wet; so he could not be sure. Stockdale mounted the vehicle, and was gone; and on the following Sunday the new minister preached in the chapel of the Moynton Wesleyans.

One day, two years after the parting, Stockdale, now settled in a midland town, came into Nether-Moynton by carrier in the original way. Jogging along in the van that afternoon he had put questions to the driver, and the answers that he received interested the minister deeply. The result of them was that he went without the least hesitation to the door of his former lodging. It was about six o'clock in the evening, and the same time of year as when he had left; now, too, the ground was damp and glistening, the west was bright, and Lizzy's snowdrops were raising their heads in the border under the wall.

Lizzy must have caught sight of him from the window, for by the time that he reached the door she was there holding it open: and then, as if she had not sufficiently considered her act of coming out, she drew herself back, saying with some constraint, 'Mr Stockdale!'

'You knew it was,' said Stockdale, taking her hand. 'I wrote to say I should call.'

'Yes, but you did not say when,' she answered.

'I did not. I was not quite sure when my business would lead me to these parts.'

'You only came because business brought you near?'

'Well, that is the fact; but I have often thought I should like to come on purpose to see you. . . But what's all this that has happened? I told you how it would be, Lizzy, and you would not listen to me.'

'I would not,' she said sadly. 'But I had been brought up to that life; and it was second nature to me. However, it is all over now. The officers have blood-money for taking a man dead or alive, and the trade is going to nothing. We were hunted down like rats.'

'Owlett is quite gone, I hear.'

'Yes. He is in America. We had a dreadful struggle that last time, when they tried to take him. It is a perfect miracle that he lived through it; and it is a wonder that I was not killed. I was shot in the hand. It was not by aim; the shot was really meant for my cousin; but I was behind, looking on as usual, and the bullet came to me. It bled terribly, but I got home without fainting; and it healed after a time. You know how he suffered?'

'No,' said Stockdale. 'I only heard that he just escaped with his life.'

'He was shot in the back; but a rib turned the ball. He was badly hurt. We would not let him be took. The men carried him all night across the meads to Kingsbere, and hid him in a barn, dressing his wound as well as they could, till he was so far recovered as to be able to get about. Then he was caught, and tried with the others at the assizes; but they all got off.[1] He had given up his mill for some time; and at last he went to Bristol, and took a passage to America, where he's settled.'

'What do you think of smuggling now?' said the minister gravely.

'I own that we were wrong,' said she. 'But I have suffered for it. I am very poor now, and my mother has been dead these twelve months. . . But won't you come in, Mr Stockdale?'

Stockdale went in; and it is to be supposed that they came to an understanding; for a fortnight later there was a sale of Lizzy's furniture, and after that a wedding at a chapel in a neighbouring town.

He took her away from her old haunts to the home that he had made for himself in his native county, where she studied her duties as a minister's wife with praiseworthy assiduity. It is said that in after years she wrote an excellent tract called *Render unto Caesar; or, The Repentant Villagers*, in which her own experience was anonymously used as the introductory story. Stockdale got it printed, after making some corrections, and putting in a few powerful sentences of his own; and many hundreds of copies were distributed by the couple in the course of their married life.

APRIL 1879

NOTE – The ending of this story with the marriage of Lizzy and the minister was almost *de rigueur* in an English magazine at the time of writing. But at this late date, thirty years after, it may not be amiss to give the ending that would have been preferred by the writer to the convention used above. Moreover it corresponds more closely with the true incidents of which the tale is a vague and flickering shadow. Lizzy did not, in fact, marry the minister, but – much to her credit in the author's opinion – stuck to Jim the smuggler, and emigrated with him

[1] See the Preface to *Wessex Tales*.

after their marriage, an expatrial step rather forced upon him by his adventurous antecedents. They both died in Wisconsin between 1850 and 1860.

MAY 1912

A GROUP OF NOBLE DAMES

'. . . Store of ladies, whose bright eyes
Rain influence.' – *L'Allegro*

PREFACE TO 'A GROUP OF NOBLE DAMES'

The pedigrees of our county families, arranged in diagrams on the pages of county histories, mostly appear at first sight to be as barren of any touch of nature as a table of logarithms. But given a clue – the faintest tradition of what went on behind the scenes, and this dryness as of dust may be transformed into a palpitating drama. More, the careful comparison of dates alone – that of birth with marriage, of marriage with death, of one marriage, birth, or death with a kindred marriage, birth, or death – will often effect the same transformation, and anybody practised in raising images from such genealogies finds himself unconsciously filling into the framework the motives, passions, and personal qualities which would appear to be the single explanation possible of some extraordinary conjunction in times, events, and personages that occasionally marks these reticent family records.

Out of such pedigrees and supplementary material most of the following stories have arisen and taken shape.

I would make this preface an opportunity of expressing my sense of the courtesy and kindness of several bright-eyed Noble Dames yet in the flesh, who, since the first publication of these tales in periodicals, six or seven years ago, have given me interesting comments and conjectures on such of the narratives as they have recognized to be connected with their own families, residences, or traditions; in which they have shown a truly philosophic absence of prejudice in their regard of those incidents whose relation has tended more distinctly to dramatize than to eulogize their ancestors. The outlines they have also given of other singular events in their family histories for use in a second 'Group of Noble Dames' will, I fear, never reach the printing-press through me; but I shall store them up in memory of my informants' good nature.

The tales were first collected and published in their present form in 1891.

T.H.

JUNE 1896

PART FIRST
Before Dinner

DAME THE FIRST
THE FIRST COUNTESS OF WESSEX

BY THE LOCAL HISTORIAN

King's-Hintock Court (said the narrator, turning over his memoranda for reference) – King's-Hintock Court is, as we know, one of the most imposing of the mansions that overlook our beautiful Blackmoor or Blakemore Vale. On the particular occasion of which I have to speak this building stood, as it had often stood before, in the perfect silence of a calm clear night, lighted only by the cold shine of the stars. The season was winter, in days long ago, the eighteenth century having run but little more than a third of its length. North, south, and west, not a casement was unfastened, not a curtain undrawn; eastward, one window on the upper floor was open, and a girl of twelve or thirteen was leaning over the sill. That she had not taken up the position for purposes of observation was apparent at a glance, for she kept her eyes covered with her hands.

The room occupied by the girl was an inner one of a suite, to be reached only by passing through a large bedchamber adjoining. From this apartment voices in altercation were audible, everything else in the building being so still. It was to avoid listening to these voices that the girl had left her little cot, thrown a cloak round her head and shoulders, and stretched into the night air.

But she could not escape the conversation, try as she would. The words reached her in all their painfulness, one sentence in masculine tones, those of her father, being repeated many times.

'I tell 'ee there shall be no such betrothal! I tell 'ee there shan't! A child like her!'

She knew the subject of dispute to be herself. A cool feminine voice, her mother's, replied:

'Have done with you, and be wise. He is willing to wait a good five or six years before the marriage takes place, and there's not a man in the county to compare with him.'

'It shall not be! He is over thirty. It is wickedness.'

'He is just thirty and the best and finest man alive – a perfect match for her.'

'He is poor!'

'But his father and elder brothers are made much of at Court – none so constantly at the palace as they; and with her fortune, who knows? He may be able to get a barony.'

'I believe you are in love with en yourself!'

'How can you insult me so, Thomas! And is it not monstrous for you to talk of my wickedness when you have a like scheme in your own head? You know you have. Some bumpkin of your own choosing – some petty gentleman who lives down at that outlandish place of yours, Falls-Park – one of your pot-companions' sons—'

There was an outburst of imprecation on the part of her husband in lieu of further argument. As soon as he could utter a connected sentence he said: 'You crow and you domineer, mistress, because you are heiress-general here. You are in your own house; you are on your own land. But let me tell 'ee that if I did come here to you instead of taking you to me, it was done at the dictates of convenience merely. Hell! I'm no beggar! Han't I a place of my own? Han't I an avenue as long as thine? Han't I beeches that will more than match thy oaks? I should have lived in my own quiet house and land, contented, if you had not called me off with your airs and graces. Faith, I'll go back there; I'll not stay with thee longer! If it had not been for our Betty I should have gone long ago!'

After this there were no more words; but presently, hearing the sound of a door opening and shutting below, the girl again looked from the window. Footsteps crunched on the gravel-walk, and a shape in a drab greatcoat, easily distinguishable as her father, withdrew from the house. He moved to the left, and she watched him diminish down the long east front till he had turned the corner and vanished. He must have gone round to the stables.

She closed the window and shrank into bed, where she cried herself to sleep. This child, their only one, Betty, beloved ambitiously by her mother, and with uncalculating passionateness by her father, was frequently made wretched by such episodes as this; though she was too young to care very deeply, for her own sake, whether her mother betrothed her to the gentleman discussed or not.

The Squire had often gone out of the house in this manner, declaring that he would never return, but he had always reappeared in the morning. The present occasion, however, was different in the issue: next day she was told that her father had ridden to his estate at Falls-Park early in the morning on business with his agent, and might not come back for some days.

*

Falls-Park was over twenty miles from King's-Hintock Court, and was altogether a more modest centre-piece to a more modest possession than the latter. But as Squire Dornell came in view of it that February morning, he thought that he had been a fool ever to leave it, though it was for the sake of the greatest heiress in Wessex. Its Palladian front, of the period of the first Charles, derived from its regular features a dignity which the great, many-gabled, heterogeneous mansion of his wife could not eclipse. Altogether he was sick at heart, and the gloom which the densely-timbered park threw over the scene did not tend to remove the depression of this rubicund man of eight-and-forty, who sat so heavily upon his gelding. The child, his darling Betty: there lay the root of his trouble. He was unhappy when near his wife, he was unhappy when away from his little girl; and from this dilemma there was no practicable escape. As a consequence he indulged rather freely in the pleasures of the table, became what was called a three-bottle man, and, in his wife's estimation, less and less presentable to her polite friends from town.

He was received by the two or three old servants who were in charge of the lonely place, where a few rooms only were kept habitable for his use or that of his friends when hunting; and during the morning he was made more comfortable by the arrival of his faithful servant Tupcombe from King's-Hintock. But after a day or two spent here in solitude he began to feel that he had made a mistake in coming. By leaving King's-Hintock in his anger he had thrown away his best opportunity of counter-acting his wife's preposterous notion of promising his poor little Betty's hand to a man she had hardly seen. To protect her from such a repugnant bargain he should have remained on the spot. He felt it almost as a misfortune that the child would inherit so much wealth. She would be a mark for all the adventurers in the kingdom. Had she been only the heiress to his own unassuming little place at Falls, how much better would have been her chances of happiness!

His wife had divined truly when she insinuated that he himself had a lover in view for this pet child. The son of a dear deceased friend of his, who lived not two miles from where the Squire now was, a lad a couple of years his daughter's senior, seemed in her father's opinion the one person in the world likely to make her happy. But as to breathing such a scheme to either of the young people with the indecent haste that his wife had shown, he would not dream of it; years hence would be soon enough for that. They had already seen each other, and the Squire fancied that he noticed a tenderness on the youth's part which promised well. He was strongly tempted to profit by his wife's example, and forestall her match-making by throwing the two young people together there at Falls. The girl, though marriageable in the views of those days, was too young to be in love, but the lad was fifteen, and already felt an interest in her.

Still better than keeping watch over her at King's-Hintock, where she was necessarily much under her mother's influence, would it be to get the child to stay with him at Falls for a time, under his exclusive control. But how accomplish this without using main force? The only possible chance was that his wife might, for appearance' sake, as she had done before, consent to Betty paying him a day's visit, when he might find means of detaining her till Reynard, the suitor whom his wife favoured, had gone abroad, which he was expected to do the following week. Squire Dornell determined to return to King's-Hintock and attempt the enterprise. If he were refused, it was almost in him to pick up Betty bodily and carry her off.

The journey back, vague and Quixotic as were his intentions, was performed with a far lighter heart than his setting forth. He would see Betty, and talk to her, come what might of his plan.

So he rode along the dead level which stretches between the hills skirting Falls-Park and those bounding the town of Ivell, trotted through that borough, and out by the King's-Hintock highway, till, passing the village, he entered the mile-long drive through the park to the Court. The drive being open, without an avenue, the Squire could discern the north front and door of the Court a long way off, and was himself visible from the windows on that side; for which reason he hoped that Betty might perceive him coming, as she sometimes did on his return from an outing, and run to the door or wave her handkerchief.

But there was no sign. He inquired for his wife as soon as he set foot to earth.

'Mistress is away. She was called to London, sir.'

'And Mistress Betty?' said the Squire blankly.

'Gone likewise, sir, for a little change. Mistress has left a letter for you.'

The note explained nothing, merely stating that she had posted to London on her own affairs, and had taken the child to give her a holiday. On the fly-leaf were some words from Betty herself to the same effect, evidently written in a state of high jubilation at the idea of her jaunt. Squire Dornell murmured a few expletives, and submitted to his disappointment. How long his wife meant to stay in town she did not say; but on investigation he found that the carriage had been packed with sufficient luggage for a sojourn of two or three weeks.

King's-Hintock Court was in consequence as gloomy as Falls-Park had been. He had lost all zest for hunting of late, and had hardly attended a meet that season. Dornell read and re-read Betty's scrawl, and hunted up some other such notes of hers to look over, this seeming to be the only pleasure there was left for him. That they were really in London he learnt in a few days by another letter from Mrs Dornell, in which she explained that they hoped to be home in about a week, and that she had had no idea he was coming back to King's-Hintock so soon, or she would not have gone away without telling him.

Squire Dornell wondered if, in going or returning, it had been her plan to call at the Reynards' place near Melchester, through which city their journey lay. It was possible that she might do this in furtherance of her project, and the sense that his own might become the losing game was harassing.

He did not know how to dispose of himself, till it occurred to him that, to get rid of his intolerable heaviness, he would invite some friends to dinner and drown his cares in grog and wine. No sooner was the carouse decided upon than he put it in hand; those invited being mostly neighbouring landholders, all smaller men than himself, members of the hunt; also the doctor from Evershead, and the like – some of them rollicking blades whose presence his wife would not have countenanced had she been at home. 'When the cat's away—!' said the Squire.

They arrived, and there were indications in their manner that they meant to make a night of it. Baxby of Sherton Castle was late, and they waited a quarter of an hour for him, he being one of the liveliest of Dornell's friends; without whose presence no such dinner as this would be considered complete, and, it may be added, with whose presence no dinner which included both sexes could be conducted with strict propriety. He had just returned from London, and the Squire was anxious to talk to him – for no definite reason; but he had lately breathed the atmosphere in which Betty was.

At length they heard Baxby driving up to the door, whereupon the host and the rest of his guests crossed over to the dining-room. In a moment Baxby came hastily in at their heels, apologizing for his lateness.

'I only came back last night, you know,' he said; 'and the truth o't is, I had as much as I could carry.' He turned to the Squire. 'Well, Dornell – so cunning reynard has stolen your little ewe lamb? Ha, ha!'

'What?' said Squire Dornell vacantly, across the dining-table, round which they were all standing, the cold March sunlight streaming in upon his full, clean-shaven face.

'Surely th'st know what all the town knows? – you've had a letter by this time? – that Stephen Reynard has married your Betty? Yes, as I'm a living man. It was a carefully-arranged thing: they parted at once, and are not to meet for five or six years. But, Lord, you must know!'

A thud on the floor was the only reply of the Squire. They quickly turned. He had fallen down like a log behind the table, and lay motionless on the oak boards.

Those at hand hastily bent over him, and the whole group were in confusion. They found him to be quite unconscious, though puffing and panting like a blacksmith's bellows. His face was livid, his veins swollen, and beads of perspiration stood upon his brow.

'What's happened to him?' said several.

'An apoplectic fit,' said the doctor from Evershead, gravely.

He was only called in at the Court for small ailments, as a rule, and felt the importance of the situation. He lifted the Squire's head, loosened his cravat and clothing, and rang for the servants, who took the Squire upstairs.

There he lay as if in a drugged sleep. The surgeon drew a basinful of blood from him, but it was nearly six o'clock before he came to himself. The dinner was completely disorganized, and some had gone home long ago; but two or three remained.

'Bless my soul,' Baxby kept repeating, 'I didn't know things had come to this pass between Dornell and his lady! I thought the feast he was spreading today was in honour of the event, though privately kept for the present! His little maid married without his knowledge!'

As soon as the Squire recovered consciousness he gasped: ''Tis abduction! 'Tis a capital felony! He can be hung! Where is Baxby? I am very well now. What items have ye heard, Baxby?'

The bearer of the untoward news was extremely unwilling to agitate Dornell further, and would say little more at first. But an hour after, when the Squire had partially recovered and was sitting up, Baxby told as much as he knew, the most important particular being that Betty's mother was present at the marriage, and showed every mark of approval. 'Everything appeared to have been done so regularly that I, of course, thought you knew all about it,' he said.

'I knew no more than the underground dead that such a step was in the wind! A child just gone thirteen! How Sue hath outwitted me! Did Reynard go up to Lon'on with 'em, d'ye know?'

'I can't say. All I know is that your lady and daughter were walking along the street, with the footman behind 'em; that they entered a jeweller's shop, where Reynard was standing; and that there, in the presence o' the shopkeeper and your man, who was called in on purpose, your Betty said to Reynard – so the story goes: 'pon my soul I don't vouch for the truth of it – she said, "Will you marry me?" or, "I want to marry you: will you have me – now or never?" she said.'

'What she said means nothing,' murmured the Squire, with wet eyes. 'Her mother put the words into her mouth to avoid the serious consequences that would attach to any suspicion of force. The words be not the child's – she didn't dream of marriage – how should she, poor little maid! Go on.'

'Well, be that as it will, they were all agreed apparently. They bought the ring on the spot, and the marriage took place at the nearest church within half-an-hour.'

A day or two later there came a letter from Mrs Dornell to her husband, written before she knew of his stroke. She related the circumstances of the marriage in the gentlest manner, and gave cogent reasons and excuses for consenting to the premature union, which was now an accomplished fact indeed. She had no idea, till sudden pressure was put upon her, that the contract was expected to be carried out so soon, but being taken half unawares she had consented, having learned that Stephen Reynard, now their son-in-law, was becoming a great favourite at Court, and that he would in all likelihood have a peerage granted him before long. No harm could come to their dear daughter by this early marriage-contract, seeing that her life would be continued under their own eyes, exactly as before, for some years. In fine, she had felt that no other such fair opportunity for a good marriage with a shrewd courtier and wise man of the world, who was at the same time noted for his excellent personal qualities, was within the range of probability, owing to the rusticated lives they led at King's-Hintock. Hence she had yielded to Stephen's solicitation, and hoped her husband would forgive her. She wrote, in short, like a woman who, having had her way as to the deed, is prepared to make any concession as to words and subsequent behaviour.

All this Dornell took at its true value, or rather, perhaps, at less than its true value. As his life depended upon his not getting into a passion, he controlled his perturbed emotions as well as he was able, going about the house sadly and utterly unlike his former self. He took every precaution to prevent his wife knowing of the incidents of his sudden illness, from a sense of shame at having a heart so tender; a ridiculous quality, no doubt, in her eyes, now that she had become so imbued with town ideas. But rumours of his seizure somehow reached her, and she let him know that she was about to return to nurse him. He thereupon packed up and went off to his own place at Falls-Park.

Here he lived the life of a recluse for some time. He was still too unwell to entertain company, or to ride to hounds or elsewhither; but more than this, his aversion to the faces of strangers and acquaintances who knew by that time of the trick his wife had played him, operated to hold him aloof.

Nothing could influence him to censure Betty for her share in the exploit. He never once believed that she had acted voluntarily. Anxious to know how she was getting on, he despatched the trusty servant Tupcombe to Evershead village, close to King's-Hintock, timing his journey so that he should reach the place under cover of dark. The emissary arrived without notice, being out of livery, and took a seat in the chimney-corner of the Sow-and-Acorn.

The conversation of the droppers-in was always of the nine days' wonder – the recent marriage. The smoking listener learnt that Mrs Dornell and the girl had returned to King's-Hintock for a day or two, that Reynard had set out for the Continent, and that Betty had since been packed off to school. She did not realize her position as Reynard's child-wife – so the story went – and though somewhat awe-stricken at first by the ceremony, she had soon recovered her spirits on finding that her freedom was in no way to be interfered with.

After that, formal messages began to pass between Dornell and his wife, the latter being now as persistently conciliating as she was formerly masterful. But her rustic, simple, blustering husband still held personally aloof. Her wish to be reconciled – to win his forgiveness for her stratagem – moreover, a genuine tenderness and desire to soothe his sorrow, which welled up in her at times, brought her at last to his door at Falls-Park one day.

They had not met since that night of altercation, before her departure for London and his subsequent illness. She was shocked at the change in him. His face had become expressionless, as blank as that of a puppet, and what troubled her still more was that she found him living in one room, and indulging freely in stimulants, in absolute disobedience to the physician's order. The fact was obvious that he could no longer be allowed to live thus uncouthly.

So she sympathized, and begged his pardon, and coaxed. But though after this date there was no longer such a complete estrangement as before, they only occasionally saw each other, Dornell for the most part making Falls his headquarters still.

Three or four years passed thus. Then she came one day, with more animation in her manner, and at once moved him by the simple statement that Betty's schooling had ended; she had returned, and was grieved because he was away. She had sent a message to him in these words: 'Ask father to come home to his dear Betty.'

'Ah! Then she is very unhappy!' said Squire Dornell.

His wife was silent.

''Tis that accursed marriage!' continued the Squire.

Still his wife would not dispute with him. 'She is outside in the carriage,' said Mrs Dornell gently.

'What – Betty?'

'Yes.'

'Why didn't you tell me?' Dornell rushed out, and there was the girl awaiting his forgiveness, for she supposed herself, no less than her mother, to be under his displeasure.

Yes, Betty had left school, and had returned to King's-Hintock. She was nearly seventeen, and had developed to quite a young woman. She looked not less a member of the household for her early marriage-contract, which she seemed, indeed, to have almost forgotten. It was like a dream to her; that clear cold March day, the London church, with its gorgeous pews, and green-baize linings, and the great organ in the west gallery – so different from their own little church in the shrubbery of King's-Hintock Court – the man of thirty, to whose face she had looked up with so much awe, and with a sense that he was rather ugly and formidable; the man whom, though they corresponded politely, she had never seen since; one to whose existence she was now so indifferent that if informed of his death, and that she would never see him more, she would merely have replied, 'Indeed!' Betty's passions as yet still slept.

'Hast heard from thy husband lately?' said Squire Dornell, when they were indoors, with an ironical laugh of fondness which demanded no answer.

The girl winced, and he noticed that his wife looked appealingly at him. As the conversation went on, and there were signs that Dornell would express sentiments that might do harm to a position which they could not alter, Mrs Dornell suggested that Betty should leave the room till her father and herself had finished their private conversation; and this Betty obediently did.

Dornell renewed his animadversions freely. 'Did you see how the sound of his name frightened her?' he presently added. 'If you didn't, I did. Zounds! what a future is in store for the poor little unfortunate wench o' mine! I tell 'ee, Sue, 'twas not a marriage at all, in morality, and if I were a woman in such a position, I shouldn't feel it as one. She might, without a sign of sin, love a man of her choice as well now as if she were chained up to no other at all. There, that's my mind, and I can't help it. Ah, Sue, my man was best! He'd ha' suited her.'

'I don't believe it,' she replied incredulously.

'You should see him; then you would. He's growing up a fine fellow, I can tell 'ee.'

'Hush! not so loud!' she answered, rising from her seat and going to the door of the next room, whither her daughter had betaken herself. To Mrs Dornell's alarm, there sat Betty in a reverie, her round eyes fixed on vacancy, musing so deeply that she did not perceive her mother's entrance. She had heard every word, and was digesting the new knowledge.

Her mother felt that Falls-Park was dangerous ground for a young girl of the susceptible age, and in Betty's peculiar position, while Dornell talked and reasoned thus. She called Betty to her, and they took leave. The Squire would not clearly promise to return and make King's-Hintock Court his permanent abode; but Betty's presence there, as at former times, was sufficient to make him agree to pay them a visit soon.

All the way home Betty remained preoccupied and silent. It was too plain to her anxious mother that Squire Dornell's free views had been a sort of awakening to the girl.

The interval before Dornell redeemed his pledge to come and see them was unexpectedly short. He arrived one morning about twelve o'clock, driving his own pair of black-bays in the curricle-phaeton with yellow panels and red wheels, just as he had used to do, and his faithful old Tupcombe on horseback behind. A young man sat beside the Squire in the carriage, and Mrs Dornell's consternation could scarcely be concealed when, abruptly entering with his companion, the Squire announced him as his friend Phelipson of Elm-Cranlynch.

Dornell passed on to Betty in the background and tenderly kissed her. 'Sting your mother's conscience, my maid!' he whispered. 'Sting her conscience by pretending you are struck with Phelipson, and would ha' loved him, as your old father's choice, much more than him she has forced upon 'ee.'

The simple-souled speaker fondly imagined that it was entirely in obedience to this direction that Betty's eyes stole interested glances at the frank and impulsive Phelipson that day at dinner, and he laughed grimly within himself to see how this joke of his, as he imagined it to be, was disturbing the peace of mind of the lady of the house. 'Now Sue sees what a mistake she has made!' said he.

Mrs Dornell was verily greatly alarmed, and as soon as she could speak a word with him alone she upbraided him. 'You ought not to have brought him here. O Thomas, how could you be so thoughtless! Lord, don't you see, dear, that what is done cannot be undone, and how all this foolery jeopardizes her happiness with her husband? Until you interfered, and spoke in her hearing about this Phelipson, she was as patient and as willing as a lamb, and looked forward to Mr Reynard's return with real pleasure. Since her visit to Falls-Park she has been monstrous close-mouthed and busy with her own thoughts. What mischief will you do? How will it end?'

'Own, then, that my man was best suited to her. I only brought him to convince you.'

'Yes, yes; I do admit it. But O! do take him back again at once! Don't keep him here! I fear she is even attracted by him already.'

'Nonsense, Sue. 'Tis only a little trick to tease 'ee!'

Nevertheless her motherly eye was not so likely to be deceived as his, and if Betty were really only playing at being love-struck that day, she played at it with the perfection of a Rosalind, and would have deceived the best professors into a belief that it was no counterfeit. The Squire, having obtained his victory, was quite ready to take back the too attractive youth, and early in the afternoon they set out on their return journey.

A silent figure who rode behind them was as interested as Dornell in that day's experiment. It was the staunch Tupcombe, who, with his eyes on the Squire's and young Phelipson's backs, thought how well the latter would have suited Betty, and how greatly the former had changed for the worse during these last two or three years. He cursed his mistress as the cause of the change.

After this memorable visit to prove his point, the lives of the Dornell couple flowed on quietly enough for the space of a twelvemonth, the Squire for the most part remaining at Falls, and Betty passing and repassing between them now and then, once or twice alarming her mother by not driving home from her father's house till midnight.

The repose of King's-Hintock was broken by the arrival of a special messenger. Squire Dornell had had an access of gout so violent as to be serious. He wished to see Betty again: why had she not come for so long?

Mrs Dornell was extremely reluctant to take Betty in that direction too frequently; but the girl was so anxious to go, her interests latterly seeming to be so entirely bound up in Falls-Park, and its neighbourhood, that there was nothing to be done but to let her set out and accompany her mother.

Squire Dornell had been impatiently awaiting her arrival. They found him very ill and irritable. It had been his habit to take powerful medicines to drive away his enemy, and they had failed in their effect on this occasion.

The presence of his daughter, as usual, calmed him much, even while, as usual, too, it saddened him; for he could never forget that she had disposed of herself for life in opposition to his wishes, though she had secretly assured him that she would never have consented had she been as old as she was now.

As on a former occasion, his wife wished to speak to him alone about the girl's future, the time now drawing nigh at which Reynard was expected to come and claim her. He would have done so already, but he had been put off by the earnest request of the young woman herself, which accorded with that of her parents, on the score of her youth. Reynard had deferentially submitted to their wishes in this respect, the understanding between them having been that he would not visit her before she was eighteen, except by the mutual consent of all parties. But this could not go on much longer, and there was no doubt, from the tenor of his last letter, that he would soon take possession of her whether or no.

To be out of the sound of this delicate discussion Betty was accordingly sent downstairs, and they soon saw her walking away into the shrubberies, looking very pretty in her sweeping green gown, and flapping broad-brimmed hat overhung with a feather.

On returning to the subject, Mrs Dornell found her husband's reluctance to reply in the affirmative to Reynard's letter to be as great as ever.

'She is three months short of eighteen!' he exclaimed. ''Tis too soon. I won't hear of it! If I have to keep him off sword in hand, he shall not have her yet.'

'But, my dear Thomas,' she expostulated, 'consider if anything should happen to you or to me, how much better it would be that she should be settled in her home with him!'

'I say it is too soon!' he argued, the veins of his forehead beginning to swell. 'If he gets her this side o' Candlemas I'll challenge en – I'll take my oath on't! I'll be back to King's-Hintock in two or three days, and I'll not lose sight of her day or night!'

She feared to agitate him further, and gave way, assuring him, in obedience to his demand, that if Reynard should write again before he got back, to fix a time for joining Betty, she would put the letter in her husband's hands, and he should do as he chose. This was all that required discussion privately, and Mrs Dornell went to call in Betty, hoping that she had not heard her father's loud tones.

She had certainly not done so this time. Mrs Dornell followed the path along which she had seen Betty wandering, but went a considerable distance without perceiving anything of her. The Squire's wife then turned round to proceed to the other side of the house by a short cut across the grass, when to her surprise and consternation, she beheld the object of her search sitting on the horizontal bough of a cedar, beside her being a young man, whose arm was round her waist. He moved a little, and she recognized him as young Phelipson.

Alas, then, she was right. The so-called counterfeit love was real. What Mrs Dornell called her husband at that moment, for his folly in originally throwing the young people together, it is not necessary to mention. She decided in a moment not to let the lovers know that she had seen them. She accordingly retreated, reached the front of the house by another route, and called at the top of her voice from a window, 'Betty!'

For the first time since her strategic marriage of the child, Susan Dornell doubted the wisdom of that step. Her husband had, as it were, been assisted by destiny to make his objection, originally trivial, a valid one. She saw the outlines of trouble in the future. Why had Dornell interfered? Why had he insisted upon producing his man? This, then, accounted for Betty's pleading for postponement whenever the subject of her husband's return was broached; this accounted for her attachment to Falls-Park. Possibly this very meeting that she had witnessed had been arranged by letter.

Perhaps the girl's thoughts would never have strayed for a moment if her father had not filled her head with ideas of repugnance to her early union, on the ground that she had been coerced into it before she knew her own mind; and she might have rushed to meet her husband with open arms on the appointed day.

Betty at length appeared in the distance in answer to the call, and came up pale, but looking innocent of having seen a living soul. Mrs Dornell groaned in spirit at such duplicity in the child of her bosom. This was the simple creature for whose development into womanhood they had all been so tenderly waiting – a forward minx, old enough not only to have a lover, but to conceal his existence as adroitly as any woman of the world! Bitterly did the Squire's lady regret that Stephen Reynard had not been allowed to come to claim her at the time he first proposed.

The two sat beside each other almost in silence on their journey back to King's-Hintock. Such words as were spoken came mainly from Betty, and their formality indicated how much her mind and heart were occupied with other things.

Mrs Dornell was far too astute a mother to openly attack Betty on the matter. That would be only fanning flame. The indispensable course seemed to her to be that of keeping the treacherous girl under lock and key till her husband came to take her off her mother's hands. That he would disregard Dornell's opposition, and come soon, was her devout wish.

It seemed, therefore, a fortunate coincidence that on her arrival at King's-Hintock a letter from Reynard was put into Mrs Dornell's hands.

It was addressed to both her and her husband, and courteously informed them that the writer had landed at Bristol, and proposed to come on to King's-Hintock in a few days, at last to meet and carry off his darling Betty, if she and her parents saw no objection.

Betty had also received a letter of the same tenor. Her mother had only to look at her face to see how the girl received the information. She was as pale as a sheet.

'You must do your best to welcome him this time, my dear Betty,' her mother said gently.

'But – but – I—'

'You are a woman now,' added her mother severely, 'and these postponements must come to an end.'

'But my father – O, I am sure he will not allow this! I am not ready. If he could only wait a year longer – if he could only wait a few months longer! O, I wish – I wish my dear father were here! I will send to him instantly.' She broke off abruptly, and falling upon her mother's neck, burst into tears, saying, 'O my mother, have mercy upon me – I do not love this man, my husband!'

The agonized appeal went too straight to Mrs Dornell's heart for her to hear it unmoved. Yet, things having come to this pass, what could she do? She was distracted, and for a moment was on Betty's side. Her original thought had been to write an affirmative reply to Reynard, allow him to come on to King's-Hintock, and keep her husband in ignorance of the whole proceeding till he should arrive from Falls on some fine day after his recovery, and find everything settled, and Reynard and Betty living together in harmony. But the events of the day, and her daughter's sudden outburst of feeling, had overthrown this intention. Betty was sure to do as she had threatened, and communicate instantly with her father, possibly attempt to fly to him. Moreover, Reynard's letter was addressed to Mr Dornell and herself conjointly, and she could not in conscience keep it from her husband.

'I will send the letter on to your father speedily,' she replied soothingly. 'He shall act entirely as he chooses, and you know that will not be in opposition to your wishes. He would ruin you rather than thwart you. I only hope he may be well enough to bear the agitation of this news. Do you agree to this?'

Poor Betty agreed, on condition that she should actually witness the despatch of the letter. Her mother had no objection to offer to this; but as soon as the horseman had cantered down the drive towards the highway, Mrs Dornell's sympathy with Betty's recalcitration began to die out. The girl's secret affection for young Phelipson could not possibly be condoned. Betty might communicate with him, might even try to reach him. Ruin lay that way. Stephen Reynard must be speedily installed in his proper place by Betty's side.

She sat down and penned a private letter to Reynard, which threw light upon her plan.

> 'It is Necessary that I should now tell you,' she said, 'what I have never Mentioned before – indeed I may have signified the Contrary – that her Father's Objection to your joining her has not as yet been overcome. As I personally Wish to delay you no longer – am indeed as anxious for your Arrival as you can be yourself, having the good of my Daughter at Heart – no course is left open to me but to assist your Cause without my Husband's Knowledge. He, I am sorry to say, is at present ill at Falls-Park, but I felt it my Duty to forward him your Letter. He will therefore be like to reply with a peremptory Command to you to go back again, for some Months, whence you came, till the Time he originally stipulated has expir'd. My Advice is, if you get such a Letter, to take no Notice of it, but to come on hither as you had proposed, letting me know the Day and Hour (after dark, if possible) at which we may expect you. Dear Betty is with me, and I warrant ye that she shall be in the House when you arrive.'

Mrs Dornell, having sent away this epistle unsuspected of anybody, next took steps to prevent her daughter leaving the Court, avoiding if possible to excite the girl's suspicions that she was under restraint. But, as if by divination, Betty had seemed to read the husband's approach in the aspect of her mother's face.

'He is coming!' exclaimed the maiden.

'Not for a week,' her mother assured her.

'He is then – for certain?'

'Well, yes.'

Betty hastily retired to her room, and would not be seen.

To lock her up, and hand over the key to Reynard when he should appear in the hall, was a plan charming in its simplicity, till her mother found, on trying the door of the girl's chamber softly, that Betty had already locked and bolted it on the inside, and had given directions to have her meals served where she was, by leaving them on a dumb-waiter outside the door.

Thereupon Mrs Dornell noiselessly sat down in her boudoir, which, as well as her bed-chamber, was a passage-room to the girl's apartment, and she resolved not to vacate her post night or day till her daughter's husband should appear, to which end she too arranged to breakfast, dine, and sup on the spot. It was impossible now that Betty should escape without her knowledge, even if she had wished, there being no other door to the chamber, except one admitting to a small inner dressing-room inaccessible by any second way.

But it was plain that the young girl had no thought of escape. Her ideas ran rather in the direction of intrenchment: she was prepared to stand a siege, but scorned flight. This, at any rate, rendered her secure. As to how Reynard would contrive a meeting with her coy daughter while in such a defensive humour, that, thought her mother, must be left to his own ingenuity to discover.

Betty had looked so wild and pale at the announcement of her husband's approaching visit that Mrs Dornell, somewhat uneasy, could not leave her to herself. She peeped through the keyhole an hour later. Betty lay on the sofa, staring listlessly at the ceiling.

'You are looking ill, child,' cried her mother. 'You've not taken the air lately. Come with me for a drive.'

Betty made no objection. Soon they drove through the park towards the village, the daughter still in the strained, strung-up silence that had fallen upon her. They left the park to return by another route, and on the open road passed a cottage.

Betty's eye fell upon the cottage-window. Within it she saw a young girl about her own age, whom she knew by sight, sitting in a chair and propped by a pillow. The girl's face was covered with scales, which glistened in the sun. She was a convalescent from smallpox – a disease whose prevalence at that period was a terror of which we at present can hardly form a conception.

An idea suddenly energized Betty's apathetic features. She glanced at her mother; Mrs Dornell had been looking in the opposite direction. Betty said that she wished to go back to the cottage for a moment to speak to a girl in whom she took an interest. Mrs Dornell appeared suspicious, but observing that the cottage had no back door, and that Betty could not escape without being seen, she allowed the carriage to be stopped. Betty ran back and entered the cottage, emerging again in about a minute, and resuming her seat in the carriage. As they drove on she fixed her eyes upon her mother and said, 'There, I have done it now!' Her pale face was stormy, and her eyes full of waiting tears.

'What have you done?' said Mrs Dornell.

'Nanny Priddle is sick of the smallpox, and I saw her at the window, and I went in and kissed her, so that I might take it; and now I shall have it, and *he* won't be able to come near me!'

'Wicked girl!' cries her mother. 'O, what am I to do! What – bring a distemper on yourself, and usurp the sacred prerogative of God, because you can't palate the man you've wedded!'

The alarmed woman gave orders to drive home as rapidly as possible, and on arriving, Betty, who was by this time also somewhat frightened at her own enormity, was put into a bath, and fumigated, and treated in every way that could be thought of to ward off the dreadful malady that in a rash moment she had tried to acquire.

There was now a double reason for isolating the rebellious daughter and wife in her own chamber, and there she accordingly remained for the rest of the day and the days that followed; till no ill results seemed likely to arise from her wilfulness.

Meanwhile the first letter from Reynard, announcing to Mrs Dornell and her husband jointly that he was coming in a few days, had sped on its way to Falls-Park. It was directed under cover to Tupcombe, the confidential servant, with instructions not to put it into his master's hands till he had been refreshed by a good long sleep. Tupcombe much regretted this commission, letters sent in this way always disturbing the Squire; but guessing that it would be infinitely worse in the end to withhold the news than to reveal it, he chose his time, which was early the next morning, and delivered the missive.

The utmost effect that Mrs Dornell had anticipated from the message was a peremptory order from her husband to Reynard to hold aloof a few months longer. What the Squire really did was to declare that he would go himself and confront Reynard at Bristol, and have it out with him there by word of mouth.

'But, master,' said Tupcombe, 'you can't. You cannot get out of bed.'

'You leave the room, Tupcombe, and don't say "can't" before me! Have Jerry saddled in an hour.'

The long-tried Tupcombe thought his employer demented, so utterly helpless was his appearance just then, and he went out reluctantly. No sooner was he gone than the Squire, with great difficulty, stretched himself over to a cabinet by the bedside, unlocked it, and took out a small bottle. It contained a gout specific, against whose use he had been repeatedly warned by his regular physician, but whose warning he now cast to the winds.

He took a double dose, and waited half an hour. It seemed to produce no effect. He then poured out a treble dose, swallowed it, leant back upon his pillow, and waited. The miracle he anticipated had been worked at last. It seemed as though the second draught had not only operated with its own strength, but had kindled into power the latent forces of the first. He put away the bottle, and rang up Tupcombe.

Less than an hour later one of the housemaids, who of course was quite aware that the Squire's illness was serious, was surprised to hear a bold and decided step descending the stairs from the direction of Mr Dornell's room, accompanied by the humming of a tune. She knew that the doctor had not paid a visit that morning, and that it was too heavy to be the valet or any other man-servant. Looking up, she saw Squire Dornell fully dressed, descending toward her in his drab caped riding-coat and boots, with the swinging easy movement of his prime. Her face expressed her amazement.

'What the devil beest looking at?' said the Squire. 'Did you never see a man walk out of his house before, wench?'

Resuming his humming – which was of a defiant sort – he proceeded to the library, rang the bell, asked if the horses were ready, and directed them to be brought round. Ten minutes later he rode away in the direction of Bristol, Tupcombe behind him, trembling at what these movements might portend.

They rode on over the airy uplands and through the monotonous straight lanes at an equal pace. The distance traversed might have been about fifteen miles when Tupcombe could perceive that the Squire was getting tired – as weary as he would have been after riding three times the distance ten years before. However, they reached Bristol without any mishap, and put up at the Squire's accustomed inn. Dornell almost immediately proceeded on foot to the inn which Reynard had given as his address, it being now about four o'clock.

Reynard had already dined – for people dined early then – and he was staying indoors. He had already received Mrs Dornell's reply to his letter; but before acting upon her advice and starting for King's-Hintock he made up his mind to wait another day, that Betty's father might at least have time to write to him if so minded. The returned traveller much desired to obtain the Squire's assent, as well as his wife's, to the proposed visit to his bride, that nothing might seem harsh or forced in his method of taking his position as one of the family. But though he anticipated some sort of objection from his father-in-law, in consequence of Mrs Dornell's warning, he was surprised at the announcement of the Squire in person.

Stephen Reynard formed the completest of possible contrasts to Dornell as they stood confronting each other in the best parlour of the Bristol tavern. The Squire, hot-tempered, gouty, impulsive, generous, reckless; the younger man, pale, tall, sedate, self-possessed – a man of the world, fully bearing out at least one couplet in his epitaph, still extant in King's-Hintock church, which places in the inventory of his good qualities

Engaging Manners, cultivated mind,
Adorn'd by Letters, and in Courts refin'd.

He was at this time about five-and-thirty, though careful living and an even, unemotional temperament caused him to look much younger than his years.

Squire Dornell plunged into his errand without much ceremony or preface.

'I am your humble servant, sir,' he said. 'I have read your letter writ to my wife and myself, and considered that the best way to answer it would be to do so in person.'

'I am vastly honoured by your visit, sir,' said Mr Stephen Reynard, bowing.

'Well, what's done can't be undone,' said Dornell, 'though it was mighty early, and was no doing of mine. She's your wife; and there's an end on't. But in brief, sir, she's too young for you to claim yet; we mustn't reckon by years; we must reckon by nature. She's still a girl; 'tis onpolite of 'ee to come yet; next year will be full soon enough for you to take her to you.'

Now, courteous as Reynard could be, he was a little obstinate when his resolution had once been formed. She had been promised him by her eighteenth birthday at latest – sooner if she were in robust health. Her mother had fixed the time on her own judgment, without a word of interference on his part. He had been hanging about foreign courts till he was weary. Betty was now a woman, if she would ever be one, and there was not, in his mind, the shadow of an excuse for putting him off longer. Therefore, fortified as he was by the support of her mother, he blandly but firmly told the Squire that he had been willing to waive his rights, out of deference to her parents, to any reasonable extent, but must now, in justice to himself and her, insist on maintaining them. He therefore, since she had not come to meet him, should proceed to King's-Hintock in a few days to fetch her.

This announcement, in spite of the urbanity with which it was delivered, set Dornell in a passion.

'O dammy, sir; you talk about rights, you do, after stealing her away, a mere child, against my will and knowledge! If we'd begged and prayed 'ee to take her, you could say no more.'

'Upon my honour, your charge is quite baseless, sir,' said his son-in-law. 'You must know by this time – or if you do not, it has been a monstrous cruel injustice to me that I should have been allowed to remain in your mind with such a stain upon my character – you must know that I used no seductiveness or temptation of any kind. Her mother assented; she assented. I took them at their word. That you was really opposed to the marriage was not known to me till afterwards.'

Dornell professed to believe not a word of it. 'You shan't have her till she's dree sixes full – no maid ought to be married till she's dree sixes! – and my daughter shan't be treated out of nater!' So he stormed on till Tupcombe, who had been alarmedly listening in the next room, entered suddenly, declaring to Reynard that his master's life was in danger if the interview were prolonged, he being subject to apoplectic strokes at these crises. Reynard immediately said that he would be the last to wish to injure Squire Dornell, and left the room, and as soon as the Squire had recovered breath and equanimity, he went out of the inn, leaning on the arm of Tupcombe.

Tupcombe was for sleeping in Bristol that night, but Dornell, whose energy seemed as invincible as it was sudden, insisted upon mounting and getting back as far as Falls-Park, to continue the journey to King's-Hintock the following day. At five they started, and took the southern road towards the Mendip Hills. The evening was dry and windy, and, excepting that the sun did not shine, strongly reminded Tupcombe of the evening of that March month, nearly five years earlier, when news had been brought to King's-Hintock Court of the child Betty's marriage in London – news which had produced upon Dornell such a marked effect for the worse ever since, and indirectly upon the household of which he was the head. Before that time the winters were lively at Falls-Park, as well as at King's-Hintock, although the Squire had ceased to make it his regular residence. Hunting-guests and shooting-guests came and went, and open house was kept. Tupcombe disliked the clever courtier who had put a stop to this by taking away from the Squire the only treasure he valued.

It grew darker with their progress along the lanes, and Tupcombe discovered from Mr Dornell's manner of riding that his strength was giving way; and spurring his own horse close alongside, he asked him how he felt.

'Oh, bad; damn bad, Tupcombe! I can hardly keep my seat. I shall never be any better, I fear! Have we passed Three-Man-Gibbet yet?'

'Not yet by a long ways, sir.'

'I wish we had. I can hardly hold on.' The Squire could not repress a groan now and then, and Tupcombe knew he was in great pain. 'I wish I was underground – that's the place for such fools as I! I'd gladly be there if it were not for Mistress Betty. He's coming on to King's-Hintock tomorrow – he won't put it off any longer; he'll set out and reach there tomorrow night, without stopping at Falls; and he'll take her unawares, and I want to be there before him.'

'I hope you may be well enough to do it, sir. But really—'

'I *must*, Tupcombe! You don't know what my trouble is; it is not so much that she is married to this man without my agreeing – for, after all, there's nothing to say against him, so far as I know; but that she don't take to him at all, seems to fear him – in fact, cares nothing about him; and if he comes forcing himself into the house upon her, why, 'twill be rank cruelty. Would to the Lord something would happen to prevent him!'

How they reached home that night Tupcombe hardly knew. The Squire was in such pain that he was obliged to recline upon his horse, and Tupcombe was afraid every moment lest he would fall into the road. But they did reach home at last, and Mr Dornell was instantly assisted to bed.

Next morning it was obvious that he could not possibly go to King's-Hintock for several days at least, and there on the bed he lay, cursing his inability to proceed on an errand so personal and so delicate that no emissary could perform it. What he wished to do was to ascertain from Betty's own lips if her aversion to Reynard was so strong that his presence would be positively distasteful to her. Were that the case, he would have borne her away bodily on the saddle behind him.

But all that was hindered now, and he repeated a hundred times in Tupcombe's hearing, and in that of the nurse and other servants, 'I wish to God something would happen to him!'

This sentiment, reiterated by the Squire as he tossed in the agony induced by the powerful drugs of the day before, entered sharply into the soul of Tupcombe and of all who were attached to the house of Dornell, as distinct from the house of his wife at King's-Hintock. Tupcombe, who was an excitable man, was hardly less disquieted by the thought of Reynard's return than the Squire himself was. As the morning drew on, and the afternoon advanced at which Reynard would in all probability be passing near Falls on his way to the Court, the Squire's feelings became acuter, and the responsive Tupcombe could hardly bear to come near him. Having left him in the hands of the doctor, the former went out upon the lawn, for he could hardly breathe in the contagion of excitement caught from the employer who had virtually made him his confidant. He had lived with the Dornells from his boyhood, had been born under the shadow of their walls; his whole life was annexed and welded to the life of the family in a degree which has no counterpart in these latter days.

He was summoned indoors, and learnt that it had been decided to send for Mrs Dornell: her husband was in great danger. There were two or three who could have acted as messenger, but Dornell wished Tupcombe to go, the reason showing itself when, Tupcombe being ready to start, Squire Dornell summoned him to his chamber and leaned down so that he could whisper in his ear:

'Put Peggy along smart, Tupcombe, and get there before him, you know – before him. This is the day he fixed. He has not passed Falls Cross-roads yet. If you can do that you will be able to get Betty to come – d'ye see? – after her mother has started; whom my illness will hinder waiting for him. Bring her by the lower road – he'll go by the upper. Your business is to make 'em miss each other – d'ye see? – but that's a thing I couldn't write down.'

Five minutes after, Tupcombe was astride the horse and on his way – the way he had followed so many times since his master, a florid young countryman, had first gone wooing to King's-Hintock Court. As soon as he had crossed the hills in the immediate neighbourhood of the manor, the road lay over a plain, where it ran in long straight stretches for several miles. In the best of times, when all had been gay in the united houses, that part of the road had seemed tedious. It was gloomy in the extreme now that he pursued it, at night and alone, on such an errand.

He rode and brooded. If the Squire were to die, he, Tupcombe, would be alone in the world and friendless, for he was no favourite with Mrs Dornell; and to find himself baffled, after all, in what he had set his mind on, would probably kill the Squire. Thinking thus, Tupcombe stopped his horse every now and then, and listened for the coming husband. The time was drawing on to the moment when Reynard might be expected to pass along this very route. He had watched the road well during the afternoon, and had inquired of the tavern-keepers as he came up to each, and he was convinced that the premature descent of the stranger-husband upon his young mistress had not been made by this highway as yet.

Besides the girl's mother, Tupcombe was the only member of the household who suspected Betty's tender feelings towards young Phelipson, so unhappily generated on her return from school; and he could therefore imagine, even better than her fond father, what would be her emotions on the sudden announcement of Reynard's advent that evening at King's-Hintock Court.

So he rode and rode, desponding and hopeful by turns. He felt assured that, unless in the unfortunate event of the almost immediate arrival of her son-in-law at his own heels, Mrs Dornell would not be able to hinder Betty from following to her father's bedside.

It was about nine o'clock that, having put twenty miles of country behind him, he turned in at the lodge-gate nearest to Ivell and King's-

Hintock village, and pursued the long north drive – itself much like a turnpike road – which led thence through the park to the Court. Though there were so many trees in King's-Hintock park, few bordered the carriage roadway; he could see it stretching ahead in the pale night light like an unrolled deal shaving. Presently the irregular frontage of the house came in view, of great extent, but low, except where it rose into the outlines of a broad square tower.

As Tupcombe approached he rode aside upon the grass, to make sure, if possible, that he was the first comer, before letting his presence be known. The Court was dark and sleepy, in no respect as if a bridegroom were about to arrive.

While pausing he distinctly heard the tread of a horse upon the track behind him, and for a moment despaired of arriving in time: here, surely, was Reynard! Pulling up closer to the densest tree at hand he waited, and found he had retreated nothing too soon, for the second rider avoided the gravel also, and passed quite close to him. In the profile he recognized young Phelipson.

Before Tupcombe could think what to do, Phelipson had gone on; but not to the door of the house. Swerving to the left, he passed round to the east angle, where, as Tupcombe knew, were situated Betty's apartments. Dismounting, Tupcombe left the horse tethered to a hanging bough, and followed behind.

Suddenly his eye caught sight of an object which explained the position immediately. It was a ladder stretching from beneath the trees, which there came pretty close to the house, up to a first-floor window – one which lighted Miss Betty's rooms. Yes, it was Betty's chamber; he knew every room in the house well.

The young horseman who had passed him, having evidently left his steed somewhere under the trees also, was perceptible at the top of the ladder, immediately outside Betty's window. While Tupcombe watched, a cloaked female figure stepped timidly over the sill, and the two cautiously descended, one before the other, the young man's arms enclosing the young woman between his grasp of the ladder, so that she could not fall. As soon as they reached the bottom, young Phelipson quickly removed the ladder and hid it under the bushes. The pair disappeared; till, in a few minutes, Tupcombe could discern a horse emerging from a remoter part of the umbrage. The horse carried double, the girl being on a pillion behind her lover.

Tupcombe hardly knew what to do or think; yet, though this was not exactly the kind of flight that had been intended, she had certainly escaped. He went back to his own animal, and rode round to the servants' door, where he delivered the letter for Mrs Dornell. To leave a verbal message for Betty was now impossible.

The Court servants desired him to stay over the night, but he would not do so, desiring to get back to the Squire as soon as possible and tell what he had seen. Whether he ought not to have intercepted the young people, and carried off Betty himself to her father, he did not know. However, it was too late to think of that now, and without wetting his lips or swallowing a crumb, Tupcombe turned his back upon King's-Hintock Court.

It was not till he had advanced a considerable distance on his way homeward that, halting under the lantern of a roadside inn while the horse was watered, there came a traveller from the opposite direction in a hired coach; the lantern lit the stranger's face as he passed along and dropped into the shade. Tupcombe exulted for the moment, though he could hardly have justified his exultation. The belated traveller was Reynard; and another had stepped in before him.

You may now be willing to know of the fortunes of Miss Betty. Left much to herself through the intervening days, she had ample time to brood over her desperate attempt at the stratagem of infection – thwarted, apparently, by her mother's promptitude. In what other way to gain time she could not think. Thus drew on the day and the hour of the evening on which her husband was expected to announce himself.

At some period after dark, when she could not tell, a tap at the window, twice and thrice repeated, became audible. It caused her to start up, for the only visitant in her mind was the one whose advances she had so feared as to risk health and life to repel them. She crept to the window, and heard a whisper without.

'It is I – Charley,' said the voice.

Betty's face fired with excitement. She had latterly begun to doubt her admirer's staunchness, fancying his love to be going off in mere attentions which neither committed him nor herself very deeply. She opened the window, saying in a joyous whisper, 'O Charley; I thought you had deserted me quite!'

He assured her he had not done that, and that he had a horse in waiting, if she would ride off with him. 'You must come quickly,' he said; 'for Reynard's on the way!'

To throw a cloak round herself was the work of a moment, and assuring herself that her door was locked against a surprise, she climbed over the window-sill and descended with him as we have seen.

Her mother meanwhile, having received Tupcombe's note, found the news of her husband's illness so serious as to displace her thoughts of the coming son-in-law, and she hastened to tell her daughter of the Squire's dangerous condition, thinking it might be desirable to take her to her father's bedside. On trying the door of the girl's room, she found it still locked. Mrs Dornell called, but there was no answer. Full of misgivings, she privately fetched the old house-steward and bade him burst open the door – an order by no means easy to execute, the joinery of the Court being massively constructed. However, the lock sprang open at last, and she entered Betty's chamber only to find the window unfastened and the bird flown.

For a moment Mrs Dornell was staggered. Then it occurred to her that Betty might have privately obtained from Tupcombe the news of her father's serious illness, and, fearing she might be kept back to meet her husband, have gone off with that obstinate and biassed servitor to Falls-Park. The more she thought it over the more probable did the supposition appear; and binding her own head-man to secrecy as to Betty's movements, whether as she conjectured, or otherwise, Mrs Dornell herself prepared to set out.

She had no suspicion how grievously her husband's malady had been aggravated by his ride to Bristol, and thought more of Betty's affairs than of her own. That Betty's husband should arrive by some other road tonight, and find neither wife nor mother-in-law to receive him, and no explanation of their absence, was possible; but never forgetting chances, Mrs Dornell as she journeyed kept her eyes fixed upon the highway on the off-side, where, before she had reached the town of Ivell, the hired coach containing Stephen Reynard flashed into the lamp-light of her own carriage.

Mrs Dornell's coachman pulled up, in obedience to a direction she had given him at starting; the other coach was hailed, a few words passed, and Reynard alighted and came to Mrs Dornell's carriage-window.

'Come inside,' says she. 'I want to speak privately to you. Why are you so late?'

'One hindrance and another,' says he. 'I meant to be at the Court by eight at latest. My gratitude for your letter. I hope—'

'You must not try to see Betty yet,' said she. 'There be far other and newer reasons against your seeing her now than there were when I wrote.'

The circumstances were such that Mrs Dornell could not possibly conceal them entirely; nothing short of knowing some of the facts would prevent his blindly acting in a manner which might be fatal to the future. Moreover, there are times when deeper intriguers than Mrs Dornell feel that they must let out a few truths, if only in self-indulgence. So she told so much of recent surprises as that Betty's heart had been attracted by another image than his, and that his insisting on visiting her now might drive the girl to desperation. 'Betty has, in fact, rushed off to her father to avoid you,' she said. 'But if you wait she will soon forget this young man, and you will have nothing to fear.'

As a woman and a mother she could go no further, and Betty's desperate attempt to infect herself the week before as a means of repelling him, together with the alarming possibility that, after all, she had not gone to her father, but to her lover, was not revealed.

'Well,' sighed the diplomatist, in a tone unexpectedly quiet, 'such things have been known before. After all, she may prefer me to him some day, when she reflects how very differently I might have acted than I am going to act towards her. But I'll say no more about that now. I can have a bed at your house for tonight?'

'Tonight, certainly. And you leave tomorrow morning early?' She spoke anxiously, for on no account did she wish him to make further discoveries. 'My husband is so woefully ill,' she continued, 'that my absence and Betty's on your arrival is naturally accounted for.'

He promised to leave early, and to write to her soon. 'And when I think the time is ripe,' he said, 'I'll write to her. I may have something to tell her that will bring her to graciousness.'

It was about one o'clock in the morning when Mrs Dornell reached Falls-Park. A double blow awaited her there. Betty had not arrived; her flight had been elsewhither; and her stricken mother divined with whom. She ascended to the bedside of her husband, where to her concern she found that the physician had given up all hope. The Squire was sinking, and his extreme weakness had almost changed his character, except in the particular that his old obstinacy sustained him in a refusal to see a clergyman. He shed tears at the least word, and sobbed at the sight of his wife. He asked for Betty, and it was with a heavy heart that Mrs Dornell told him that the girl had not accompanied her.

'He is not keeping her away?'

'No, no. He is going back – he is not coming to her for some time.'

'Then what is detaining her – cruel, neglectful maid!'

'No, no, Thomas; she is— She could not come.'

'How's that?'

Somehow the solemnity of these last moments of his gave him inquisitorial power, and the too cold wife could not conceal from him the flight which had taken place from King's-Hintock that night.

To her amazement, the effect upon him was electrical.

'What – Betty – a trump after all? Hurrah! She's her father's own maid! She's game! She knew he was her father's own choice! She vowed that my man should win! Well done, Bet! – haw! haw! Hurrah!'

He had raised himself in bed by starts as he spoke, and now fell back exhausted. He never uttered another word, and died before the dawn. People said there had not been such an ungenteel death in a good county family for years.

Now I will go back to the time of Betty's riding off on the pillion behind her lover. They left the park by an obscure gate to the east, and presently found themselves in the lonely and solitary length of the old Roman road now called Long-Ash Lane.

By this time they were rather alarmed at their own performance, for they were both young and inexperienced. Hence they proceeded almost in silence till they came to a mean roadside inn which was not yet closed; when Betty, who had held on to him with much misgivings all this while, felt dreadfully unwell, and said she thought she would like to get down.

They accordingly dismounted from the jaded animal that had brought them, and were shown into a small dark parlour, where they stood side by side awkwardly, like the fugitives they were. A light was brought, and when they were left alone Betty threw off the cloak which had enveloped her. No sooner did young Phelipson see her face than he uttered an alarmed exclamation.

'Why, Lord, Lord, you are sickening for the smallpox!' he cried.

'O – I forgot!' faltered Betty. And then she informed him that, on hearing of her husband's approach the week before, in a desperate attempt to keep him from her side, she had tried to imbibe the infection – an act which till this moment she had supposed to have been ineffectual, imagining her feverishness to be the result of her excitement.

The effect of this discovery upon young Phelipson was overwhelming. Better-seasoned men than he would not have been proof against it, and he was only a little over her own age. 'And you've been holding on to me!' he said. 'And suppose you get worse, and we both have it, what shall we do? Won't you be a fright in a month or two, poor, poor Betty!'

In his horror he attempted to laugh, but the laugh ended in a weakly giggle. She was more woman than girl by this time, and realized his feeling.

'What – in trying to keep off him, I keep off you?' she said miserably. 'Do you hate me because I am going to be ugly and ill?'

'O no, no!' he said soothingly. 'But I – I am thinking if it is quite right for us to do this. You see, dear Betty, if you was not married it would be different. You are not in honour married to him, we've often said; still you are his by law, and you can't be mine whilst he's alive. And with this terrible sickness coming on, perhaps you had better let me take you back, and – climb in at the window again.'

'Is *this* your love?' said Betty reproachfully. 'O, if you was sickening for the plague itself, and going to be as ugly as the Ooser in the church-vestry, I wouldn't—'

'No, no, you mistake, upon my soul!'

But Betty with a swollen heart had rewrapped herself and gone out of the door. The horse was still standing there. She mounted by the help of the upping-stock, and when he had followed her she said, 'Do not come near me, Charley; but please lead the horse, so that if you've not caught anything already you'll not catch it going back. After all, what keeps off you may keep off him. Now onwards.'

He did not resist her command, and back they went by the way they had come, Betty shedding bitter tears at the retribution she had already brought upon herself; for though she had reproached Phelipson, she was staunch enough not to blame him in her secret heart for showing that his love was only skin-deep. The horse was stopped in the plantation, and they walked silently to the lawn, reaching the bushes wherein the ladder still lay.

'Will you put it up for me?' she asked mournfully.

He re-erected the ladder without a word; but when she approached to ascend he said, 'Good-bye, Betty!'

'Good-bye!' said she; and involuntarily turned her face towards his. He hung back from imprinting the expected kiss: at which Betty started as if she had received a poignant wound. She moved away so suddenly that he hardly had time to follow her up the ladder to prevent her falling.

'Tell your mother to get the doctor at once!' he said anxiously.

She stepped in without looking behind; he descended, withdrew the ladder, and went away.

Alone in her chamber, Betty flung herself upon her face on the bed, and burst into shaking sobs. Yet she would not admit to herself that her lover's conduct was unreasonable; only that her rash act of the previous week had been wrong. No one had heard her enter, and she was too worn out, in body and mind, to think or care about medical aid. In an hour or so she felt yet more unwell, positively ill; and nobody coming to her at the usual bedtime, she looked towards the door. Marks of the lock having been forced were visible, and this made her chary of summoning a servant. She opened the door cautiously and sallied forth downstairs.

In the dining-parlour, as it was called, the now sick and sorry Betty was startled to see at that late hour not her mother, but a man sitting, calmly finishing his supper. There was no servant in the room. He turned, and she recognized her husband.

'Where's my mamma?' she demanded without preface.

'Gone to your father's. Is that—' He stopped, aghast.

'Yes, sir. This spotted object is your wife! I've done it because I don't want you to come near me!'

He was sixteen years her senior; old enough to be compassionate. 'My poor child, you must get to bed directly! Don't be afraid of me – I'll carry you upstairs, and send for a doctor instantly.'

'Ah, you don't know what I am!' she cried. 'I had a lover once; but now he's gone! 'Twasn't I who deserted him. He has deserted me; because I am ill he wouldn't kiss me, though I wanted him to!'

'Wouldn't he? Then he was a very poor slack-twisted sort of fellow. Betty, *I've* never kissed you since you stood beside me as my little wife, barely thirteen years old! May I kiss you now?'

Though Betty by no means desired his kisses, she had enough of the spirit of Cunigonde in Schiller's ballad to test his daring. 'If you have courage to venture, yes, sir!' said she. 'But you may die for it, mind!'

He came up to her and imprinted a deliberate kiss full upon her mouth, saying, 'May many others follow!'

She shook her head, and hastily withdrew, though secretly pleased at his hardihood. The excitement had supported her for the few minutes she had passed in his presence, and she could hardly drag herself back to her room. Her husband summoned the servants, and, sending them to her assistance, went off himself for a doctor.

The next morning Reynard waited at the Court till he had learnt from the medical man that Betty's attack promised to be a very light one – or, as it was expressed, 'very fine'; and in taking his leave sent up a note to her:

> Now I must be Gone. I promised your Mother I would not see You yet, and she may be anger'd if she finds me here. Promise to see me as Soon as you are well?

He was of all men then living one of the best able to cope with such an untimely situation as this. A contriving, sagacious, gentle-mannered man, a philosopher who saw that the only constant attribute of life is change, he held that, as long as she lives, there is nothing finite in the most impassioned attitude a woman may take up. In twelve months his girl-wife's recent infatuation might be as distasteful to her mind as it was now to his own. In a few years her very flesh would change – so said the scientific; – her spirit, so much more ephemeral, was capable of changing in one. Betty was his, and it became a mere question of means how to effect that change.

During the day Mrs Dornell, having closed her husband's eyes, returned to the Court. She was truly relieved to find Betty there, even though on a bed of sickness. The disease ran its course, and in due time Betty became convalescent, without having suffered deeply for her rashness, one little pit beneath her ear, and one beneath her chin, being all the marks she retained.

The Squire's body was not brought back to King's-Hintock. Where he was born, and where he had lived before wedding his Sue, there he had wished to be buried. No sooner had she lost him than Mrs Dornell, like certain other wives, though she had never shown any great affection for him while he lived, awoke suddenly to his many virtues, and zealously embraced his opinion about delaying Betty's union with her husband, which she had formerly combated strenuously. 'Poor man! how right he was, and how wrong was I!' Eighteen was certainly the lowest age at which Mr Reynard should claim her child – nay, it was too low! Far too low!

So desirous was she of honouring her lamented husband's sentiments in this respect, that she wrote to her son-in-law suggesting that, partly on account of Betty's sorrow for her father's loss, and out of consideration for his known wishes for delay, Betty should not be taken from her till her nineteenth birthday.

However much or little Stephen Reynard might have been to blame in his marriage, the patient man now almost deserved to be pitied. First Betty's skittishness; now her mother's remorseful *volte-face*: it was enough to exasperate anybody; and he wrote to the widow in a tone which led to a little coolness between those hitherto firm friends. However, knowing that he had a wife not to claim but to win, and that young Phelipson had been packed off to sea by his parents, Stephen was complaisant to a degree, returning to London, and holding quite aloof from Betty and her mother, who remained for the present in the country. In town he had a mild visitation of the distemper he had taken from Betty, and in writing to her he took care not to dwell upon its mildness. It was. now that Betty began to pity him for what she had inflicted upon him by the kiss, and her correspondence acquired a distinct flavour of kindness thenceforward.

Owing to his rebuffs, Reynard had grown to be truly in love with Betty in his mild, placid, durable way – in that way which perhaps, upon the whole, tends most generally to the woman's comfort under the institution of marriage, if not particularly to her ecstasy. Mrs Dornell's exaggeration of her husband's wish for delay in their living together was inconvenient, but he would not openly infringe it. He wrote tenderly to Betty, and soon announced that he had a little surprise in store for her. The secret was that the King had been graciously pleased to inform him privately, through a relation, that His Majesty was about to offer him a Barony. Would she like the title to be Ivell? Moreover, he had a reason for knowing that in a few years the dignity would be raised to that of an Earl, for which creation he thought the title of Wessex would be eminently suitable, considering the position of much of their property. As Lady Ivell, therefore, and future Countess of Wessex, he should beg leave to offer her his heart a third time.

He did not add, as he might have added, how greatly the consideration of the enormous estates at King's-Hintock and elsewhere which Betty would inherit, and her children after her, had conduced to this desirable honour.

Wheter the impending titles had really an effect upon Betty's regard for him I cannot state, for she was one of those close characters who never let their minds be known upon anything. That such honour was absolutely unexpected by her from such a quarter is, however, certain; and she could not deny that Stephen had shown her kindness, forbearance, even magnanimity; had forgiven her for an errant passion which he might with some reason have denounced, notwithstanding her cruel position as a child entrapped into marriage ere able to understand its bearings.

Her mother, in her grief and remorse for the loveless life she had led with her rough, though open-hearted, husband, made now a creed of his merest whim; and continued to insist that, out of respect to his known desire, her son-in-law should not reside with Betty till the girl's father had been dead a year at least, at which time the girl would still be under nineteen. Letters must suffice for Stephen till then.

'It is rather long for him to wait,' Betty hesitatingly said one day.

'What!' said her mother. 'From *you*? not to respect your dear dead father—'

'Of course it is quite proper,' said Betty hastily. 'I don't gainsay it. I was but thinking that – that—'

In the long slow months of the stipulated interval her mother tended and trained Betty carefully for her duties. Fully awake now to the many virtues of her dear departed one, she, among other acts of pious devotion to his memory, rebuilt the church of King's-Hintock village, and established valuable charities in all the villages of that name, as far as to Little-Hintock, several miles eastward.

In superintending these works, particularly that of the church-building, her daughter Betty was her constant companion, and the incidents of their execution were doubtless not without a soothing effect upon the young creature's heart. She had sprung from girl to woman by a sudden bound, and few would have recognized in the thoughtful face of Betty now the same person who, the year before, had seemed to have absolutely no idea whatever of responsibility, moral or other. Time passed thus till the Squire had been nearly a year in his vault; and Mrs Dornell was duly asked by letter by the patient Reynard if she were willing for him to come soon. He did not wish to take Betty away if her mother's sense of loneliness would be too great, but would willingly live at Kings-Hintock a while with them.

Before the widow had replied to this communication, she one day happened to observe Betty walking on the south terrace in the full sunlight, without hat or mantle, and was struck by her child's figure. Mrs Dornell called her in, and said suddenly: 'Have you seen your husband since the time of your poor father's death?'

'Well – yes, mamma,' says Betty, colouring.

'What – against my wishes and those of the dear deceased! I am shocked at your disobedience!'

'But my father said eighteen, ma'am, and you made it much longer—'

'Why, of course – out of consideration for you! When have ye seen him?'

'Well,' stammered Betty, 'in the course of his letters to me he said that I belonged to him, and if nobody knew that we met it would make no difference. And that I need not hurt your feelings by telling you.'

'Well?'

'So I went to Casterbridge that time you went to London about five months ago—'

'And met him there? When did you come back?'

'Dear mamma, it grew very late, and he said it was safer not to go back till next day, as the roads were bad; and as you were away from home—'

'I don't want to hear any more! This is your respect for your father's memory,' groaned the widow. 'When did you meet him again?'

'Oh – not for more than a fortnight.'

'A fortnight! How many times have ye seen him altogether?'

'I'm sure, mamma, I've not seen him altogether a dozen times – I mean quite alone, and not reckoning—'

'A dozen! And eighteen and a half years old barely!'

'Twice we met by accident,' pleaded Betty. 'Once at Abbot's-Cernel in the ruined chamber over the gate-house, and another time at the Red Lion, Melchester.'

'O thou deceitful girl!' cried Mrs Dornell. 'An *accident* took you to the

Red Lion tavern whilst I was staying at the White Hart! I remember – I wondered what could have happened, and then you came in at twelve o'clock at night, and said you'd been to see the cathedral by the light o' the moon!'

'My ever-honoured mamma, so I had! I only went to the Red Lion with him afterwards.'

'O Betty, Betty! That my child should have deceived me even in my widowed days!'

'But, my dearest mamma, you made me marry him!' says Betty with spirit, 'and of course I've to obey him more than you now!'

Mrs Dornell sighed. 'All I have to say is, that you'd better get your husband to join you as soon as possible,' she remarked. 'To go on playing the maiden like this – I'm ashamed to see you!'

She wrote instantly to Stephen Reynard: 'I wash my hands of the whole matter as between you two; though I should advise you to *openly* join each other as soon as you can – if you wish to avoid scandal.'

He came, though not till the promised title had been granted, and he could call Betty archly 'My Lady'.

People said in after years that she and her husband were very happy. However that may be, they had a numerous family; and she became in due course first Countess of Wessex, as he had foretold.

The little figured frock in which she had been married to him at the tender age of thirteen was carefully preserved among the relics at King's-Hintock Court, where it may still be seen by the curious – a yellowing, pathetic testimony to the small count taken of the happiness of an innocent child in the social strategy of those days, which might have led, but providentially did not lead, to great unhappiness.

When the Earl died Betty wrote him an epitaph, in which she described him as the best of husbands, fathers, and friends, and called herself his disconsolate widow.

Such is woman; or rather (not to give offence by so sweeping an assertion), such was Betty Dornell.

It was at a meeting of one of the Wessex Field and Antiquarian Clubs that the foregoing story, partly told, partly read from a manuscript, was made to do duty for the regulation papers on deformed butterflies, fossil ox-horns, prehistoric dung-mixens and such-like, that usually occupied the more serious attention of the members.

This Club was of an inclusive and intersocial character; to a degree, indeed, remarkable for the part of England in which it had its being – dear, delightful Wessex, whose statuesque dynasties are even now only just beginning to feel the shaking of the new and strange spirit without, like that which entered the lonely valley of Ezekiel's vision and made the dry bones move: where the honest squires, tradesmen, parsons, clerks, and people still praise the Lord with one voice for His best of all possible worlds.

The present meeting, which was to extend over two days, had opened its proceedings at the museum of the town whose buildings and environs were to be visited by the members. Lunch had ended and the afternoon excursion had been about to be undertaken, when the rain came down in an obstinate spatter, which revealed no sign of cessation. As the members waited they grew chilly, although it was only autumn, and a fire was lighted, which threw a cheerful shine upon the varnished skulls, urns, penates, tesserae, costumes, coats of mail, weapons; and missals, animated the fossilized ichthyosaurus and iguanodon; while the dead eyes of the stuffed birds – those never-absent familiars in such collections, though murdered to extinction out of doors – flashed as they had flashed to the rising sun above the neighbouring moors on the fatal morning when the trigger was pulled which ended their little flight. It was then that the historian produced his manuscript, which he had prepared, he said, with a view to publication. His delivery of the story having concluded as aforesaid, the speaker expressed his hope that the constraint of the weather, and the paucity of more scientific papers, would excuse any inappropriateness in his subject.

Several members observed that a storm-bound club could not presume to be selective, and they were all very much obliged to him for such a curious chapter from the domestic histories of the county.

The President looked gloomily from the window at the descending rain, and broke a short silence by saying that though the Club had met, there seemed little probability of its being able to visit the objects of interest set down among the *agenda*.

The Treasurer observed that they had at least a roof over their heads; and they had also a second day before them.

A sentimental member, leaning back in his chair, declared that he was in no hurry to go out, and that nothing would please him so much as another county story, with or without manuscript.

The Colonel added that the subject should be a lady, like the former, to which a gentleman known as the Spark said 'Hear, hear!'

Though these had spoken in jest, a rural dean who was present observed blandly that there was no lack of materials. Many, indeed, were the legends and traditions of gentle and noble dames, renowned in times past in that part of England, whose actions and passions were now, but for men's memories, buried under the brief inscription on a tomb or an entry of dates in a dry pedigree.

Another member, an old surgeon, a somewhat grim though sociable personage, was quite of the speaker's opinion, and felt fully sure that the memory of the reverend gentleman must abound with such curious tales of fair dames, of their loves and hates, their joys and their misfortunes, their beauty and their fate.

The parson, a trifle confused, retorted that their friend the surgeon, the son of a surgeon, seemed to him, as a man who had seen much and heard more during the long course of his own and his father's practice, the member of all others most likely to be acquainted with such lore.

The bookworm, the Colonel, the historian, the Vice-president, the churchwarden, the two curates, the gentleman-tradesman, the sentimental member, the crimson maltster, the quiet gentleman, the man of family, the Spark, and several others, quite agreed, and begged that he would recall something of the kind. The old surgeon said that, though a meeting of the South-Wessex Field and Antiquarian Club was the last place at which he should have expected to be called upon in this way, he had no objection; and the parson said he would come next. The surgeon then reflected, and decided to relate the history of a lady named Barbara, who lived towards the end of the last century, apologizing for his tale as being perhaps a little too professional. The crimson maltster winked to the Spark at hearing the nature of the apology, and the surgeon began.

DAME THE SECOND
BARBARA OF THE HOUSE OF GREBE

BY THE OLD SURGEON

It was apparently an idea, rather than a passion, that inspired Lord Uplandtowers' resolve to win her. Nobody ever knew when he formed it, or whence he got his assurance of success in the face of her manifest dislike of him. Possibly not until after that first important act of her life which I shall presently mention. His matured and cynical doggedness at the age of nineteen, when impulse mostly rules calculation, was remarkable, and might have owed its existence as much to his succession to the earldom and its accompanying local honours in childhood, as to the family character; an elevation which jerked him into maturity, so to speak, without his having known adolescence. He had only reached his twelfth year when his father, the fourth Earl, died, after a course of the Bath waters.

Nevertheless, the family character had a great deal to do with it. Determination was hereditary in the bearers of that escutcheon; sometimes for good, sometimes for evil.

The seats of the two families were about ten miles apart, the way between them lying along the now old, then new, turnpike-road connecting Havenpool and Warborne with the city of Melchester; a road which, though only a branch from what was known as the Great Western Highway, is probably, even at present, as it has been for the last hundred years, one of the finest examples of a macadamized turnpike-track that can be found in England.

The mansion of the Earl, as well as that of his neighbour, Barbara's father, stood back about a mile from the highway, with which each was connected by an ordinary drive and lodge. It was along this particular highway that the young Earl drove on a certain evening at Christmastide some twenty years before the end of the last century, to attend a ball at Chene Manor, the home of Barbara, and her parents Sir John and Lady Grebe. Sir John's was a baronetcy created a few years before the breaking out of the Civil War, and his lands were even more extensive than those of Lord Uplandtowers himself, comprising this Manor of Chene, another on the coast near, half the Hundred of Cockdene, and well-enclosed lands in several other parishes, notably Warborne and those contiguous. At this time Barbara was barely seventeen, and the ball is the first occasion on which we have any tradition of Lord Uplandtowers attempting tender relations with her; it was early enough, God knows.

An intimate friend – one of the Drenkhards – is said to have dined with him that day, and Lord Uplandtowers had, for a wonder, communciated to his guest the secret design of his heart.

'You'll never get her – sure; you'll never get her!' this friend had said at parting. 'She's not drawn to your lordship by love: and as for thought of a good match, why, there's no more calculation in her than in a bird.'

'We'll see,' said Lord Uplandtowers impassively.

He no doubt thought of his friend's forecast as he travelled along the highway in his chariot; but the sculptural repose of his profile against the vanishing daylight on his right hand would have shown his friend that the Earl's equanimity was undisturbed. He reached the solitary wayside tavern called Lornton Inn – the rendezvous of many a daring poacher for operations in the adjoining forest; and he might have observed, if he had taken the trouble, a strange post-chaise standing in the halting-space before the inn. He duly sped past it, and half-an-hour after through the little town of Warborne. Onward, a mile further, was the house of his entertainer.

At this date it was an imposing edifice – or, rather, congeries of edifices – as extensive as the residence of the Earl himself, though far less regular. One wing showed extreme antiquity, having huge chimneys, whose substructures projected from the external walls like towers; and a kitchen of vast dimensions, in which (it was said) breakfasts had been cooked for John of Gaunt. Whilst he was yet in the forecourt he could hear the rhythm of French horns and clarionets, the favourite instruments of those days at such entertainments.

Entering the long parlour, in which the dance had just been opened by Lady Grebe with a minuet – it being now seven o'clock, according to the tradition – he was received with a welcome befitting his rank, and looked round for Barbara. She was not dancing, and seemed to be preoccupied – almost, indeed, as though she had been waiting for him. Barbara at this time was a good and pretty girl, who never spoke ill of anyone, and hated other pretty women the very least possible. She did not refuse him for the country-dance which followed, and soon after was his partner in a second.

The evening wore on, and the horns and clarionets tootled merrily. Barbara evinced towards her lover neither distinct preference nor aversion; but old eyes would have seen that she pondered something. However, after supper she pleaded a headache, and disappeared. To pass the time of her absence, Lord Uplandtowers went into a little room adjoining the long gallery, where some elderly ones were sitting by the fire, – for he had a phlegmatic dislike of dancing for its own sake, – and, lifting the window-curtains, he looked out of the window into the park and wood, dark now as a cavern. Some of the guests appeared to be leaving even so soon as this, two lights showing themselves as turning away from the door and sinking to nothing in the distance.

His hostess put her head into the room to look for partners for the ladies, and Lord Uplandtowers came out. Lady Grebe informed him that Barbara had not returned to the ball-room: she had gone to bed in sheer necessity.

'She has been so excited over the ball all day,' her mother continued, 'that I feared she would be worn out early. . . But sure, Lord Uplandtowers, you won't be leaving yet?'

He said that it was near twelve o'clock, and that some had already left.

'I protest nobody has gone yet,' said Lady Grebe.

To humour her he stayed till midnight, and then set out. He had made no progress in his suit; but he had assured himself that Barbara gave no other guest the preference, and nearly everybody in the neighbourhood was there.

''Tis only a matter of time' said the calm young philosopher.

The next morning he lay till near ten o'clock, and he had only just come out upon the head of the staircase when he heard hoofs upon the gravel without; in a few moments the door had been opened, and Sir John Grebe met him in the hall, as he set foot on the lowest stair.

'My lord – where's Barbara – my daughter?'

Even the Earl of Uplandtowers could not repress amazement. 'What's the matter, my dear Sir John?' says he.

The news was startling, indeed. From the Baronet's disjointed explanation Lord Uplandtowers gathered that after his own and the other guests' departure Sir John and Lady Grebe had gone to rest without seeing any more of Barbara; it being understood by them that she had retired to bed when she sent word to say that she could not join the dancers again. Before then she had told her maid that she would dispense with her services for this night; and there was evidence to show that the young lady had never laid down at all, the bed remaining unpressed. Circumstances seemed to prove that the deceitful girl had feigned indisposition to get an excuse for leaving the ball-room, and that she had left the house within ten minutes, presumably during the first dance after supper.

'I saw her go,' said Lord Uplandtowers.

'The devil you did!' says Sir John.

'Yes.' And he mentioned the retreating carriage-lights, and how he was assured by Lady Grebe that no guest had departed.

'Surely that was it!' said the father. 'But she's not gone alone, d'ye know!'

'Ah – who is the young man?'

'I can on'y guess. My worst fear is my most likely guess. I'll say no more. I thought – yet I would not believe – it possible that you was the sinner. Would that you had been! But 'tis t'other, 'tis t'other, by Heaven! I must e'en up and after 'em!'

'Whom do you suspect?'

Sir John would not give a name, and, stultified rather than agitated, Lord Uplandtowers accompanied him back to Chene. He again asked upon whom were the Baronet's suspicions directed; and the impulsive Sir John was no match for the insistence of Uplandtowers.

He said at length, 'I fear 'tis Edmond Willowes.'

'Who's he?'

'A young fellow of Shottsford-Forum – a widow-woman's son,' the other told him, and explained that Willowes's father, or grandfather, was the last of the old glass-painters in that place, where (as you may know) the art lingered on when it had died out in every other part of England.

'By God, that's bad – mighty bad!' said Lord Uplandtowers, throwing himself back in the chaise in frigid despair.

They despatched emissaries in all directions; one by the Melchester Road, another by Shottsford-Forum, another coastwards.

But the lovers had a ten-hours' start; and it was apparent that sound judgment had been exercised in choosing as their time of flight the particular night when the movements of a strange carriage would not be noticed, either in the park or on the neighbouring highway, owing to the general press of vehicles. The chaise which had been seen waiting at Lornton Inn was, no doubt, the one they had escaped in; and the pair of heads which had planned so cleverly thus far had probably contrived marriage ere now.

The fears of her parents were realized. A letter sent by special messenger from Barbara, on the evening of that day, briefly informed them that her lover and herself were on the way to London, and before this communication reached her home they would be united as husband and wife. She had taken this extreme step because she loved her dear Edmond as she could love no other man, and because she had seen closing round her the doom of marriage with Lord Uplandtowers, unless she put that threatened fate out of possibility by doing as she had done. She had well considered the step beforehand, and was prepared to live like any other country-townsman's wife if her father repudiated her for her action.

'Damn her!' said Lord Uplandtowers, as he drove homeward that night. 'Damn her for a fool!' – which shows the kind of love he bore her.

Well; Sir John had already started in pursuit of them as a matter of duty, driving like a wild man to Melchester, and thence by the direct highway to the capital. But he soon saw that he was acting to no purpose; and by and by, discovering that the marriage had actually taken place, he forbore all attempts to unearth them in the City, and returned and sat down with his lady to digest the event as best they could.

To proceed against this Willowes for the abduction of our heiress was, possibly, in their power; yet, when they considered the now unalterable facts, they refrained from violent retribution. Some six weeks passed, during which time Barbara's parents, though they keenly felt her loss, held no communication with the truant, either for reproach or condonation. They continued to think of the disgrace she had brought upon herself; for, though the young man was an honest fellow, and the son of an honest father, the latter had died so early, and his widow had had such struggles to maintain herself, that the son was very imperfectly educated. Moreover, his blood was, as far as they knew, of no distinction whatever, whilst hers, through her mother, was compounded of the best juices of ancient baronial distillation, containing tinctures of Maundeville, and Mohun, and Syward, and Peverell, and Culliford, and Talbot, and Plantagenet, and York, and Lancaster, and God knows what besides, which it was a thousand pities to throw away.

The father and mother sat by the fireplace that was spanned by the four-centred arch bearing the family shields on its haunches, and groaned aloud – the lady more than Sir John.

'To think this should have come upon us in our old age!' said he.

'Speak for yourself!' she snapped through her sobs, 'I am only one-and-forty! . . . Why didn't ye ride faster and overtake 'em!'

In the meantime the young married lovers, caring no more about their blood than about ditch-water, were intensely happy – happy, that is, in the descending scale which, as we all know, Heaven in its wisdom has ordained for such rash cases; that is to say, the first week they were in the seventh heaven, the second in the sixth, the third week temperate, the fourth reflective, and so on; a lover's heart after possession being comparable to the earth in its geologic stages, as described to us sometimes by our worthy President; first a hot coal, then a warm one, then a cooling cinder, then chilly – the simile shall be pursued no further.

The long and the short of it was that one day a letter, sealed with their daughter's own little seal, came into Sir John and Lady Grebe's hands; and, on opening it, they found it to contain an appeal from the young couple to Sir John to forgive them for what they had done, and they would fall on their naked knees and be most dutiful children for evermore.

Then Sir John and his lady sat down again by the fireplace with the four-centred arch, and consulted, and re-read the letter. Sir John Grebe, if the truth must be told, loved his daughter's happiness far more, poor man, than he loved his name and lineage; he recalled to his mind all her little ways, gave vent to a sigh; and, by this time acclimatized to the idea of the marriage, said that what was done could not be undone, and that he supposed they must not be too harsh with her. Perhaps Barbara and her husband were in actual need; and how could they let their only child starve?

A slight consolation had come to them in an unexpected manner. They had been credibly informed that an ancestor of plebeian Willowes was once honoured with intermarriage with a scion of the aristocracy who had gone to the dogs. In short, such is the foolishness of distinguished parents, and sometimes of others also, that they wrote that very day to the address Barbara had given them, informing her that she might return home and bring her husband with her; they would not object to see him, would not reproach her, and would endeavour to welcome both, and to discuss with them what could best be arranged for their future.

In three or four days a rather shabby post-chaise drew up at the door of Chene Manor-house, at sound of which the tender-hearted baronet and his wife ran out as if to welcome a prince and princess of the blood. They were overjoyed to see their spoilt child return safe and sound – though she was only Mrs Willowes, wife of Edmond Willowes of nowhere. Barbara burst into penitential tears and both husband and wife were contrite enough, as well they might be, considering that they had not a guinea to call their own.

When the four had calmed themselves, and not a word of chiding had been uttered to the pair, they discussed the position soberly, young Willowes sitting in the background with great modesty till invited forward by Lady Grebe in no frigid tone.

'How handsome he is!' she said to herself. 'I don't wonder at Barbara's craze for him.'

He was, indeed, one of the handsomest men who ever set his lips on a maid's. A blue coat, murrey waistcoast, and breeches of drab set off a figure that could scarcely be surpassed. He had large dark eyes, anxious now, as they glanced from Barbara to her parents and tenderly back again to her; observing whom, even now in her trepidation, one could see why the *sang froid* of Lord Uplandtowers had been raised to more than lukewarmness. Her fair young face (according to the tale handed down by old women) looked out from under a gray conical hat, trimmed with white ostrich-feathers, and her little toes peeped from a buff petticoat worn under a puce gown. Her features were not regular: they were almost infantine, as you may see from miniatures in possession of the family, her mouth showing much sensitiveness, and one could be sure that her faults would not lie on the side of bad temper unless for urgent reasons.

Well, they discussed their state as became them, and the desire of the young couple to gain the goodwill of those upon whom they were literally dependent for everything induced them to agree to any temporizing measure that was not too irksome. Therefore, having been nearly two months united, they did not oppose Sir John's proposal that he should furnish Edmond Willlowes with funds sufficient for him to travel a year on the Continent in the company of a tutor, the young man undertaking to lend himself with the utmost diligence to the tutor's instructions, till he became polished outwardly and inwardly to the degree required in the husband of such a lady as Barbara. He was to apply himself to the study of languages, manners, history, society, ruins and everything else that came under his eyes, till he should return to take his place without blushing by Barbara's side.

'And by that time,' said worthy Sir John, 'I'll get my little place out at Yewsholt ready for you and Barbara to occupy on your return. The house is small and out of the way; but it will do for a young couple for a while.'

'If 'twere no bigger than a summer-house it would do!' says Barbara.

'If 'twere no bigger than a sedan-chair!' says Willowes. 'And the more lonely the better.'

'We can put up with the loneliness,' said Barbara, with less zest. 'Some friends will come, no doubt.'

All this being laid down, a travelled tutor was called in – a man of many gifts and great experience, – and on a fine morning away tutor and pupil went. A great reason urged against Barbara accompanying her youthful husband was that his attentions to her would naturally be such as to prevent his zealously applying every hour of his time to learning and seeing – an argument of wise prescience, and unanswerable. Regular days for letter-writing were fixed, Barbara and her Edmond exchanged their last kisses at the door, and the chaise swept under the archway into the drive.

He wrote to her from Le Havre, as soon as he reached that port, which was not for seven days, on account of adverse winds; he wrote from

Rouen, and from Paris; described to her his sight of the King and Court at Versailles, and the wonderful marble-work and mirrors in that palace; wrote next from Lyons; then, after a comparatively long interval, from Turin, narrating his fearful adventures in crossing Mont Cenis on mules, and how he was overtaken with a terrific snowstorm, which had well-nigh been the end of him, and his tutor, and his guides. Then he wrote glowingly of Italy; and Barbara could see the development of her husband's mind reflected in his letters month by month; and she much admired the forethought of her father in suggesting this education for Edmond. Yet she sighed sometimes – her husband being no longer in evidence to fortify her in her choice of him – and timidly dreaded what mortifications might be in store for her by reason of this *mésalliance*. She went out very little; for on the one or two occasions on which she had shown herself to former friends she noticed a distinct difference in their manner, as though they should say, 'Ah, my happy swain's wife; you're caught!'

Edmond's letters were as affectionate as ever; even more affectionate, after a while, than hers were to him. Barbara observed this growing coolness in herself; and like a good and honest lady was horrified and grieved, since her only wish was to act faithfully and uprightly. It troubled her so much that she prayed for a warmer heart, and at last wrote to her husband to beg him now that he was in the land of Art, to send her his portrait, ever so small, that she might look at it all day and every day, and never for a moment forget his features.

Willowes was nothing loth, and replied that he would do more than she wished: he had made friends with a sculptor in Pisa, who was much interested in him and his history; and he had commissioned this artist to make a bust of himself in marble, which when finished he would send her. What Barbara had wanted was something immediate; but she expressed no objection to the delay; and in his next communication Edmond told her that the sculptor, of his own choice, had decided to extend the bust to a full-length statue, so anxious was he to get a specimen of his skill introduced to the notice of the English aristocracy. It was progressing well, and rapidly.

Meanwhile, Barbara's attention began to be occupied at home with Yewsholt Lodge, the house that her kind-hearted father was preparing for her residence when her husband returned. It was a small place on the plan of a large one – a cottage built in the form of a mansion, having a central hall with a wooden gallery running round it, and rooms no bigger than closets to support this introduction. It stood on a slope so solitary, and surrounded by trees so dense, that the birds who inhabited the boughs sang at strange hours, as if they hardly could distinguish night from day.

During the progress of repairs at this bower Barbara frequently visited it. Though so secluded by the dense growth, it was near the high road, and one day while looking over the fence she saw Lord Uplandtowers riding past. He saluted her courteously, yet with mechanical stiffness, and did not halt. Barbara went home, and continued to pray that she might never cease to love her husband. After that she sickened, and did not come out of doors again for a long time.

The year of education had extended to fourteen months, and the house was in order for Edmond's return to take up his abode there with Barbara, when, instead of the accustomed letter for her, came one to Sir John Grebe in the handwriting of the said tutor, informing him of a terrible catastrophe that had occurred to them at Venice. Mr Willowes and himself had attended the theatre one night during the Carnival of the preceding week, to witness the Italian comedy, when, owing to the carelessness of one of the candle-snuffers, the theatre had caught fire, and been burnt to the ground. Few persons had lost their lives, owing to the super-human exertions of some of the audience in getting out the senseless sufferers; and, among them all, he who had risked his own life the most heroically was Mr Willowes. In re-entering for the fifth time to save his fellow-creatures some fiery beams had fallen upon him, and he had been given up for lost. He was, however, by the blessing of Providence, recovered, with the life still in him, though he was fearfully burnt; and by almost a miracle he seemed likely to survive, his constitution being wondrously sound. He was, of course, unable to write, but he was receiving the attention of several skilful surgeons. Further report would be made by the next mail or by private hand.

The tutor said nothing in detail of poor Willowes's sufferings, but as soon as the news was broken to Barbara she realized how intense they must have been, and her immediate instinct was to rush to his side, though, on consideration, the journey seemed impossible to her. Her health was by no means what it had been, and to post across Europe at that season of the year, or to traverse the Bay of Biscay in a sailing-craft, was an undertaking that would hardly be justified by the result. But she was anxious to go till, on reading to the end of the letter, her husband's tutor was found to hint very strongly against such a step if it should be contemplated, this being also the opinion of the surgeons. And though Willowes's comrade refrained from giving his reasons, they disclosed themselves plainly enough in the sequel.

The truth was that the worst of the wounds resulting from the fire had occurred to his head and face – that handsome face which had won her heart from her, – and both the tutor and the surgeons knew that for a sensitive young woman to see him before his wounds had healed would cause more misery to her by the shock than happiness to him by her ministrations.

Lady Grebe blurted out what Sir John and Barbara had thought, but had had too much delicacy to express.

'Sure, 'tis mighty hard for you, poor Barbara, that the one little gift he had to justify your rash choice of him – his wonderful good looks – should be taken away like this, to leave 'ee no excuse at all for your conduct in the world's eyes. . . Well, I wish you'd married t'other – that do I!' And the lady sighed.

'He'll soon get right again,' said her father soothingly.

Such remarks as the above were not often made; but they were frequent enough to cause Barbara an uneasy sense of self-stultification. She determined to hear them no longer; and the house at Yewsholt being ready and furnished, she withdrew thither with her maids, where for the first time she could feel mistress of a home that would be hers and her husband's exclusively, when he came.

After long weeks Willowes had recovered sufficiently to be able to write himself, and slowly and tenderly he enlightened her upon the full extent of his injuries. It is a mercy, he said, that he had not lost his sight entirely; but he was thankful to say that he still retained full vision in one eye, though the other was dark for ever. The sparing manner in which he meted out particulars of his condition told Barbara how appalling had been his experience. He was grateful for her assurance that nothing could change her; but feared she did not fully realize that he was so sadly disfigured as to make it doubtful if she would recognize him. However, in spite of all, his heart was as true to her as it ever had been.

Barbara saw from his anxiety how much lay behind. She replied that she submitted to the decrees of Fate, and would welcome him in any shape as soon as he could come. She told him of the pretty retreat in which she had taken up her abode, pending their joint occupation of it, and did not reveal how much she had sighed over the information that all his good looks were gone. Still less did she say that she felt a certain strangeness in awaiting him, the weeks they had lived together having been so short by comparsion with the length of his absence.

Slowly drew on the time when Willowes found himself well enough to come home. He landed at Southampton, and posted thence towards Yewsholt. Barbara arranged to go out to meet him as far as Lornton Inn – the spot between the Forest and the Chase at which he had waited for night on the evening of their elopement. Thither she drove at the appointed hour in a little pony-chaise, presented her by her father on her birthday for her especial use in her new house; which vehicle she sent back on arriving at the inn, the plan agreed upon being that she should perform the return journey with her husband in his hired coach.

There was not much accommodation for a lady at this wayside tavern; but, as it was a fine evening in early summer, she did not mind – walking about outside, and straining her eyes along the highway for the expected one. But each cloud of dust that enlarged in the distance and drew near was found to disclose a conveyance other than his post-chaise. Barbara remained till the appointment was two hours passed, and then began to fear that owing to some adverse wind in the Channel he was not coming that night.

While waiting she was conscious of a curious trepidation that was not entirely solicitude, and did not amount to dread; her tense state of incertitude bordered both on disappointment and on relief. She had lived six or seven weeks with an imperfectly educated yet handsome husband whom now she had not seen for seventeen months, and who was so changed physically by an accident that she was assured she would hardly know him. Can we wonder at her compound state of mind?

But her immediate difficulty was to get away from Lornton Inn, for her situation was becoming embarrassing. Like too many of Barbara's actions, this drive had been undertaken without much reflection. Expecting to wait no more than a few minutes for her husband in his post-chaise, and to enter it with him, she had not hesitated to isolate herself by sending back her own little vehicle. She now found that, being so well known in this neighbourhood, her excursion to meet her long-absent husband was exciting great interest. She was conscious that more eyes were watching her from the inn-windows than met her own gaze. Barbara had decided to get home by hiring whatever kind of conveyance the tavern afforded, when, straining her eyes for the last time over the now darkening highway, she perceived yet another dust cloud drawing near. She paused; a chariot ascended to the inn, and would have passed had not its occupant caught sight of her standing expectantly. The horses were checked on the instant.

'You here – and alone, my dear Mrs Willowes?' said Lord Uplandtowers, whose carriage it was.

She explained what had brought her into this lonely situation; and, as he was going in the direction of her own home, she accepted his offer of a seat beside him. Their conversation was embarrassed and fragmentary at first; but when they had driven a mile or two she was surprised to find herself talking earnestly and warmly to him: her impulsiveness was in truth but the natural consequence of her late existence – a somewhat desolate one by reason of the strange marriage she had made; and there is no more indiscreet mood than that of a woman surprised into talk who has long been imposing upon herself a policy of reserve. Therefore her ingenuous heart rose with a bound into her throat when, in response to his leading questions, or rather hints, she allowed her troubles to leak out of her. Lord Uplandtowers took her quite to her own door, although he had driven three miles out of his way to do so; and in handing her down she heard from him a whisper of stern reproach: 'It need not have been thus if you had listened to me!'

She made no reply, and went indoors. There, as the evening wore away, she regretted more and more that she had been so friendly with Lord Uplandtowers. But he had launched himself upon her so unexpectedly: if she had only foreseen the meeting with him, what a careful line of conduct she would have marked out! Barbara broke into a perspiration of disquiet when she thought of her unreserve, and, in self-chastisement, resolved to sit up till midnight on the bare chance of Edmond's return; directing that supper should be laid for him, improbable as his arrival till the morrow was.

The hours went past, and there was dead silence in and round about Yewsholt Lodge, except for the soughing of the trees; till, when it was near upon midnight, she heard the noise of hoofs and wheels approaching the door. Knowing that it could only be her husband, Barbara instantly went into the hall to meet him. Yet she stood there not without a sensation of faintness, so many were the changes since their parting! And owing to her casual encounter with Lord Uplandtowers, his voice and image still remained with her, excluding Edmond, her husband, from the inner circle of her impressions.

But she went to the door, and the next moment a figure stepped inside, of which she knew the outline, but little besides. Her husband was attired in a flapping black cloak and slouched hat, appearing altogether as a foreigner, and not as the young English burgess who had left her side. When he came forward into the light of the lamp, she perceived with surprise, and almost with fright, that he wore a mask. At first she had not noticed this – there being nothing in its colour which would lead a casual observer to think he was looking on anything but a real countenance.

He must have seen her start of dismay at the unexpectedness of his appearance, for he said hastily: 'I did not mean to come in to you like this – I thought you would have been in bed. How good you are, dear

Barbara!' He put his arm round her, but he did not attempt to kiss her.

'O Edmund – it *is* you? – it must be?' she said, with clasped hands, for though his figure and movement were almost enough to prove it and the tones were not unlike the old tones, the enunciation was so altered as to seem that of a stranger.

'I am covered like this to hide myself from the curious eyes of the inn-servants and others,' he said, in a low voice. 'I will send back the carriage and join you in a moment.'

'You are quite alone?'

'Quite. My companion stopped at Southampton.'

The wheels of the post-chaise rolled away as she entered the dining-room, where the supper was spread; and presently he rejoined her there. He had removed his cloak and hat, but the mask was still retained; and she could now see that it was of special make, of some flexible material like silk, coloured so as to represent flesh; it joined naturally to the front hair, and was otherwise cleverly executed.

'Barbara – you look ill,' he said, removing his glove, and taking her hand.

'Yes – I have been ill,' said she.

'Is this pretty little house ours?'

'O – yes.' She was hardly conscious of her words, for the hand he had ungloved in order to take hers was contorted, and had one or two of its fingers missing; while through the mask she discerned the twinkle of one eye only.

'I would give anything to kiss you, dearest, now at this moment!' he continued, with mournful passionateness. 'But I cannot – in this guise. The servants are abed, I suppose?'

'Yes,' said she. 'But I can call them? You will have some supper?'

He said he would have some, but that it was not necessary to call anybody at that hour. Thereupon they approached the table, and sat down, facing each other.

Despite Barbara's scared state of mind, it was forced upon her notice that her husband trembled, as if he feared the impression he was producing, or was about to produce, as much as, or more than, she. He drew nearer, and took her hand again.

'I had this mask made at Venice,' he began, in evident embarrassment. 'My darling Barbara – my dearest wife – do you think you – will mind when I take it off? You will not dislike me – will you?'

'O Edmond, of course I shall not mind,' said she. 'What has happened to you is our misfortune; but I am prepared for it.'

'Are you sure you are prepared?'

'O yes! You are my husband.'

'You really feel quite confident that nothing external can affect you?' he said again, in a voice rendered uncertain by his agitation.

'I think I am – quite,' she answered faintly.

He bent his head. 'I hope, I hope you are,' he whispered.

In the pause which followed, the ticking of the clock in the hall seemed to grow loud; and he turned a little aside to remove the mask. She breathlessly awaited the operation, which was one of some tediousness, watching him one moment, averting her face the next; and when it was done she shut her eyes at the dreadful spectacle that was revealed. A quick spasm of horror had passed through her; but though she quailed she forced herself to regard him anew, repressing the cry that would naturally have escaped from her ashy lips. Unable to look at him longer, Barbara sank down on the floor beside her chair, covering her eyes.

'You cannot look at me!' he groaned in a hopeless way. 'I am too terrible an object even for you to bear! I knew it; yet I hoped against it. O, this is a bitter fate – curse the skill of those Venetian surgeons who saved me alive! . . . Look up, Barbara,' he continued beseechingly; 'view me completely; say you loathe me, if you do loathe me, and settle the case between us for ever!'

His unhappy wife pulled herself together for a desperate strain. He was her Edmond; he had done her no wrong; he had suffered. A momentary devotion to him helped her, and lifting her eyes as bidden she regarded this human remnant, this *écorché*, a second time. But the sight was too much. She again involuntarily looked aside and shuddered.

'Do you think you can get used to this?' he said. 'Yes or no! Can you bear such a thing of the charnel-house near you? Judge for yourself, Barbara. Your Adonis, your matchless man, has come to this!'

The poor lady stood beside him motionless, save for the restlessness of her eyes. All her natural sentiments of affection and pity were driven clean out of her by a sort of panic; she had just the same sense of dismay and fearfulness that she would have had in the presence of an apparition. She could nohow fancy this to be her chosen one – the man she had loved; he was metamorphosed to a specimen of another species. 'I do not loathe you,' she said with trembling. 'But I am so horrified – so overcome! Let me recover myself. Will you sup now? And while you do so may I go to my room to – regain my old feeling for you? I will try, if I may leave you awhile? Yes, I will try!'

Without waiting for an answer from him, and keeping her gaze carefully averted, the frightened woman crept to the door and out of the room. She heard him sit down to the table, as if to begin supper; though, Heaven knows, his appetite was slight enough after a reception which had confirmed his worst surmises. When Barbara had ascended the stairs and arrived in her chamber she sank down, and buried her face in the coverlet of the bed.

Thus she remained for some time. The bed-chamber was over the dining-room, and presently as she knelt Barbara heard Willowes thrust back his chair, and rise to go into the hall. In five minutes that figure would probably come up the stairs and confront her again; it, – this new and terrible form, that was not her husband's. In the loneliness of this night, with neither maid nor friend beside her, she lost all self- control, and at the first sound of his footstep on the stairs, without so much as flinging a cloak round her, she flew from the room, ran along the gallery to the back staircase, which she descended, and, unlocking the back door, let herself out. She scarcely was aware what she had done till she found herself in the greenhouse, crouching on a flower-stand.

Here she remained, her great timid eyes strained through the glass upon the garden without, and her skirts gathered up, in fear of the field-mice which sometimes came there. Every moment she dreaded to hear footsteps which she ought by law to have longed for, and a voice that should have been as music to her soul. But Edmond Willowes came not that way. The nights were getting short at this season, and soon the dawn appeared, and the first rays of the sun. By daylight she had less fear than in the dark. She thought she could meet him, and accustom herself to the spectacle.

So the much-tried young woman unfastened the door of the hot-house, and went back by the way she had emerged a few hours ago. Her poor husband was probably in bed and asleep, his journey having been long; and she made as little noise as possible in her entry. The house was just as she had left it, and she looked about in the hall for his cloak and hat, but she could not see them; nor did she perceive the small trunk which had been all that he brought with him, his heavier baggage having been left at Southampton for the road-waggon. She summoned courage to mount the stairs; the bedroom-door was open as she had left it. She fearfully peeped round; the bed had not been pressed. Perhaps he had lain down on the dining-room sofa. She descended and entered; he was not there. On the table beside his unsoiled plate lay a note, hastily written on the leaf of a pocket-book. It was something like this:–

MY EVER-BELOVED WIFE, – The effect that my forbidding appearance has produced upon you was one which I foresaw as quite possible. I hoped against it, but foolishly so. I was aware that no *human* love could survive such a catastrophe. I confess I thought yours *divine*; but, after so long an absence, there could not be left sufficient warmth to overcome the too natural first aversion. It was an experiment, and it has failed. I do not blame you; perhaps, even, it is better so. Good-bye. I leave England for one year. You will see me again at the expiration of that time, if I live. Then I will ascertain your true feeling; and, if it be against me, go away for ever.

E.W.

On recovering from her surprise, Barbara's remorse was such that she felt herself absolutely unforgivable. She should have regarded him as an afflicted being, and not have been this slave to mere eyesight, like a child. To follow him and entreat him to return was her first thought. But on making inquiries she found that nobody had seen him: he had silently disappeared.

More than this, to undo the scene of last night was impossible. Her terror had been too plain, and he was a man unlikely to be coaxed back by her efforts to do her duty. She went and confessed to her parents all that had occurred; which, indeed, soon became known to more persons than those of her own family.

The year passed, and he did not return; and it was doubted if he were alive. Barbara's contrition for her unconquerable repugnance was now such that she longed to build a church-aisle, or erect a monument, and devote herself to deeds of charity for the remainder of her days. To that end she made inquiry of the excellent parson under whom she sat on Sundays, at a vertical distance of a dozen feet. But he could only adjust his wig and tap his snuff-box; for such was the lukewarm state of religion in those days, that not an aisle, steeple, porch, east window, Ten-Commandment board, lion-and-unicorn, or brass candlestick, was required anywhere at all in the neighbourhood as a votive offering from a distracted soul – the last century contrasting greatly in this respect with the happy times in which we live, when urgent appeals for contributions to such objects pour in by every morning's post, and nearly all churches have been made to look like new pennies. As the poor lady could not ease her conscience this way, she determined at least to be charitable, and soon had the satisfaction of finding her porch thronged every morning by the raggedest, idlest, most drunken, hypocritical, and worthless tramps in Christendom.

But human hearts are as prone to change as the leaves of the creeper on the wall, and in the course of time, hearing nothing of her husband,

Barbara could sit unmoved whilst her mother and friends said in her hearing, 'Well, what has happened is for the best.' She began to think so herself, for even now she could not summon up that lopped and mutilated form without a shiver, though whenever her mind flew back to her early wedded days, and the man who had stood beside her then, a thrill of tenderness moved her, which if quickened by his living presence might have become strong. She was young and inexperienced, and had hardly on his late return grown out of the capricious fancies of girlhood.

But he did not come again, and when she thought of his word that he would return once more, if living, and how unlikely he was to break his word, she gave him up for dead. So did her parents; so also did another person – that man of silence, of irresistible incisiveness, of still countenance, who was as awake as seven sentinels when he seemed to be as sound asleep as the figures on his family monument. Lord Uplandtowers, though not yet thirty, had chuckled like a caustic fogey of threescore when he heard of Barbara's terror and flight at her husband's return, and of the latter's prompt departure. He felt pretty sure, however, that Willowes, despite his hurt feelings, would have reappeared to claim his bright-eyed property if he had been alive at the end of the twelve months.

As there was no husband to live with her, Barbara had relinquished the house prepared for them by her father, and taken up her abode anew at Chene Manor, as in the days of her girlhood. By degrees the episode with Edmond Willowes seemed but a fevered dream, and as the months grew to years Lord Uplandtowers' friendship with the people at Chene – which had somewhat cooled after Barbara's elopement – revived considerably, and he again became a frequent visitor there. He could not make the most trivial alteration or improvement at Knollingwood Hall, where he lived, without riding off to consult with his friend Sir John at Chene; and thus putting himself frequently under her eyes, Barbara grew accustomed to him, and talked to him as freely as to a brother. She even began to look up to him as a person of authority, judgment, and prudence; and though his severity on the bench towards poachers, smugglers, and turnip-stealers was matter of common notoriety, she trusted that much of what was said might be misrepresentation.

Thus they lived on till her husband's absence had stretched to years, and there could be no longer any doubt of his death. A passionless manner of renewing his addresses seemed no longer out of place in Lord Uplandtowers. Barbara did not love him, but hers was essentially one of those sweet-pea or with-wind natures which require a twig of stouter fibre than its own to hang upon and bloom. Now, too, she was older, and admitted to herself that a man whose ancestor had run scores of Saracens through and through in fighting for the site of the Holy Sepulchre was a more desirable husband, socially considered, than one who could only claim with certainty to know that his father and grandfather were respectable burgesses.

Sir John took occasion to inform her that she might legally consider herself a widow; and, in brief, Lord Uplandtowers carried his point with her, and she married him, though he could never get her to own that she loved him as she had loved Willowes. In my childhood I knew an old lady whose mother saw the wedding, and she said that when Lord and Lady Uplandtowers drove away from her father's house in the evening it was in a coach-and-four, and that my lady was dressed in green and silver, and wore the gayest hat and feather that ever were seen; though whether it was that the green did not suit her complexion, or otherwise, the Countess looked pale, and the reverse of blooming. After their marriage her husband took her to London, and she saw the gaieties of a season there; then they returned to Knollingwood Hall, and thus a year passed away.

Before their marriage her husband had seemed to care but little about her inability to love him passionately. 'Only let me win you,' he had said, 'and I will submit to all that.' But now her lack of warmth seemed to irritate him, and he conducted himself towards her with a resentfulness which led to her passing many hours with him in painful silence. The heir-presumptive to the title was a remote relative, whom Lord Uplandtowers did not exclude from the dislike he entertained towards many persons and things besides, and he had set his mind upon a lineal successor. He blamed her much that there was no promise of this, and asked her what she was good for.

On a particular day in her gloomy life a letter, addressed to her as Mrs Willowes, reached Lady Uplandtowers from an unexpected quarter. A sculptor in Pisa, knowing nothing of her second marriage, informed her that the long-delayed life-size statue of Mr Willowes, which, when her husband left that city, he had been directed to retain till it was sent for, was still in his studio. As his commission had not wholly been paid, and the statue was taking up room he could ill spare, he should be glad to have the debt cleared off, and directions where to forward the figure. Arriving at a time when the Countess was beginning to have little secrets (of a harmless kind, it is true) from her husband, by reason of their growing estrangement, she replied to this letter without saying a word to Lord Uplandtowers, sending off the balance that was owing to the sculptor, and telling him to despatch the statue to her without delay.

It was some weeks before it arrived at Knollingwood Hall, and, by a singular coincidence, during the interval she received the first absolutely conclusive tidings of her Edmond's death. It had taken place years before, in a foreign land, about six months after their parting, and had been induced by the sufferings he had already undergone, coupled with much depression of spirit, which had caused him to succumb to a slight ailment. The news was sent her in a brief and formal letter from some relative of Willowes's in another part of England.

Her grief took the form of passionate pity for his misfortunes, and of reproach to herself for never having been able to conquer her aversion to his latter image by recollection of what Nature had originally made him. The sad spectacle that had gone from earth had never been her Edmond at all to her. O that she could have met him as he was at first! Thus Barbara thought. It was only a few days later that a waggon with two horses, containing an immense packing-case, was seen at breakfast-time both by Barbara and her husband to drive round to the back of the house, and by-and-by they were informed that a case labelled 'Sculpture' had arrived for her ladyship.

'What can that be?' said Lord Uplandtowers.

'It is the statue of poor Edmond, which belongs to me, but has never been sent till now,' she answered.

'Where are you going to put it?' asked he.

'I have not decided,' said the Countess. 'Anywhere, so that it will not annoy you.'

'Oh, it won't annoy me,' says he.

When it had been unpacked in a back room of the house, they went to examine it. The statue was a full-length figure, in the purest Carrara marble, representing Edmond Willowes in all his original beauty, as he had stood at parting from her when about to set out on his travels; a specimen of manhood almost perfect in every line and contour. The work had been carried out with absolute fidelity.

'Phoebus-Apollo, sure,' said the Earl of Uplandtowers, who had never seen Willowes, real or represented, till now.

Barbara did not hear him. She was standing in a sort of trance before the first husband, as if she had no consciousness of the other husband at her side. The mutilated features of Willowes had disappeared from her mind's eye; this perfect being was really the man she had loved, and not that later pitiable figure; in whom tenderness and truth should have seen this image always, but had not done so.

It was not till Lord Uplandtowers said roughly, 'Are you going to stay here all the morning worshipping him?' that she roused herself.

Her husband had not till now the least suspicion that Edmond Willowes originally looked thus, and he thought how deep would have been his jealousy years ago if Willowes had been known to him. Returning to the Hall in the afternoon he found his wife in the gallery, whither the statue had been brought.

She was lost in reverie before it, just as in the morning.

'What are you doing?' he asked.

She started and turned. 'I am looking at my husb— my statue, to see if it is well done,' she stammered. 'Why should I not?'

'There's no reason why,' he said. 'What are you going to do with the monstrous thing? It can't stand here for ever.'

'I don't wish it,' she said. 'I'll find a place.'

In her boudoir there was a deep recess, and while the Earl was absent from home for a few days in the following week, she hired joiners from the village, who under her directions enclosed the recess with a panelled door. Into the tabernacle thus formed she had the statue placed, fastening the door with a lock, the key of which she kept in her pocket.

When her husband returned he missed the statue from the gallery, and, concluding that it had been put away out of deference to his feelings, made no remark. Yet at moments he noticed something on his lady's face which he had never noticed there before. He could not construe it; it was a sort of silent ecstasy, a reserved beatification. What had become of the statue he could not divine, and growing more and more curious, looked about here and there for it till, thinking of her private room, he went towards that spot. After knocking he heard the shutting of a door, and the click of a key; but when he entered his wife was sitting at work, on what was in those days called knotting. Lord Uplandtowers' eye fell upon the newly-painted door where the recess had formerly been.

'You have been carpentering in my absence then, Barbara,' he said carelessly.

'Yes, Uplandtowers.'

'Why did you go putting up such a tasteless enclosure as that – spoiling the handsome arch of the alcove?'

'I wanted more closet-room; and I thought that as this was my own apartment—'

'Of course,' he returned. Lord Uplandtowers knew now where the statue of young Willowes was.

One night, or rather in the smallest hours of the morning, he missed the Countess from his side. Not being a man of nervous imaginings he fell asleep again before he had much considered the matter, and the next morning had forgotten the incident. But a few nights later the same circumstances occurred. This time he fully roused himself; but before he had moved to search for her she returned to the chamber in her dressing-gown, carrying a candle, which she extinguished as she approached, deeming him asleep. He could discover from her breathing that she was strangely moved; but not on this occasion either did he reveal that he had seen her. Presently, when she had laid down, affecting to wake, he asked her some trivial questions. 'Yes, *Edmond*,' she replied absently.

Lord Uplandtowers became convinced that she was in the habit of leaving the chamber in this queer way more frequently than he had observed, and he determined to watch. The next midnight he feigned deep sleep, and shortly after perceived her stealthily rise and let herself out of the room in the dark. He slipped on some clothing and followed. At the further end of the corridor, where the clash of flint and steel would be out of the hearing of one in the bed-chamber, she struck a light. He stepped aside into an empty room till she had lit a taper and had passed on to her boudoir. In a minute or two he followed. Arrived at the door of the boudoir, he beheld the door of the private recess open, and Barbara within it, standing with her arms clasped tightly round the neck of her Edmond, and her mouth on his. The shawl which she had thrown round her nightclothes had slipped from her shoulders, and her long white robe and pale face lent her the blanched appearance of a second statue embracing the first. Between her kisses, she apostrophized it in a low murmur of infantine tenderness:

'My only love – how could I be so cruel to you, my perfect one – so good and true – I am ever faithful to you, despite my seeming infidelity! I always think of you – dream of you – during the long hours of the day, and in the night-watches! O Edmond, I am always yours!' Such words as these, intermingled with sobs, and streaming tears, and dishevelled hair, testified to an intensity of feeling in his wife which Lord Uplandtowers had not dreamed of her possessing.

'Ha, ha!' says he to himself. 'This is where we evaporate – this is where my hopes of a successor in the title dissolve – ha! ha! This must be seen to, verily!'

Lord Uplandtowers was a subtle man when once he set himself to strategy; though in the present instance he never thought of the simple stratagem of constant tenderness. Nor did he enter the room and surprise his wife as a blunderer would have done, but went back to his chamber as silently as he had left it. When the Countess returned thither, shaken by spent sobs and sighs, he appeared to be soundly sleeping as usual. The next day he began his countermoves by making inquiries as to the whereabouts of the tutor who had travelled with his wife's first husband; this gentleman, he found, was now master of a grammar-school at no great distance from Knollingwood. At the first convenient moment Lord Uplandtowers went thither and obtained an interview with the said gentleman. The schoolmaster was much gratified by a visit from such an influential neighbour, and was ready to communicate anything that his lordship desired to know.

After some general conversation on the school and its progress, the visitor observed that he believed the schoolmaster had once travelled a good deal with the unfortunate Mr Willowes, and had been with him on the occasion of his accident. He, Lord Uplandtowers, was interested in knowing what had really happened at that time, and had often thought of inquiring. And then the Earl not only heard by word of mouth as much as he wished to know, but, their chat becoming more intimate, the schoolmaster drew upon paper a sketch of the disfigured head, explaining with bated breath various details in the representation.

'It was very strange and terrible!' said Lord Uplandtowers, taking the sketch in his hand. 'Neither nose nor ears, nor lips scarcely!'

A poor man in the town nearest to Knollingwood Hall, who combined the art of sign-painting with ingenious mechanical occupations, was sent for by Lord Uplandtowers to come to the Hall on a day in that week when the Countess had gone on a short visit to her parents. His employer made the man understand that the business in which his assistance was demanded was to be considered private, and money insured the observance of this request. The lock of the cupboard was picked, and the ingenious mechanic and painter, assisted by the schoolmaster's sketch, which Lord Uplandtowers had put in his pocket, set to work upon the god-like countenance of the statue under my lord's direction. What the fire had maimed in the original the chisel maimed in the copy. It was a fiendish disfigurement, ruthlessly carried out, and was rendered still more shocking by being tinted to the hues of life, as life had been after the wreck.

Six hours after, when the workman was gone, Lord Uplandtowers looked upon the result, and smiled grimly, and said:

'A statue should represent a man as he appeared in life, and that's as he appeared. Ha! ha! But 'tis done to good purpose, and not idly.'

He locked the door of the closet with a skeleton key, and went his way to fetch the Countess home.

That night she slept, but he kept awake. According to the tale, she murmured soft words in her dream; and he knew that the tender converse of her imaginings was held with one whom he had supplanted but in name. At the end of her dream the Countess of Uplandtowers awoke and arose, and then the enactment of former nights was repeated. Her husband remained still and listened. Two strokes sounded from the clock in the pediment without, when, leaving the chamber-door ajar, she passed along the corridor to the other end, where, as usual, she obtained a light. So deep was the silence that he could even from his bed hear her softly blowing the tinder to a glow after striking the steel. She moved on into the boudoir, and he heard, or fancied he heard, the turning of the key in the closet-door. The next moment there came from that direction a loud and prolonged shriek, which resounded to the furthest corners of the house. It was repeated, and there was the noise of a heavy fall.

Lord Uplandtowers sprang out of bed. He hastened along the dark corridor to the door of the boudoir, which stood ajar, and, by the light of the candle within, saw his poor young Countess lying in a heap in her nightdress on the floor of the closet. When he reached her side he found that she had fainted, much to the relief of his fears that matters were worse. He quickly shut up and locked in the hated image which had done the mischief, and lifted his wife in his arms, where in a few instants she opened her eyes. Pressing her face to his without saying a word, he carried her back to her room, endeavouring as he went to disperse her terrors by a laugh in her ear, oddly compounded of causticity, predilection, and brutality.

'Ho – ho – ho!' says he. 'Frightened, dear one, hey? What a baby 'tis! Only a joke, sure, Barbara – a splendid joke! But a baby should not go to closets at midnight to look for the ghost of the dear departed! If it do it must expect to be terrified at his aspect – ho – ho – ho!'

When she was in her bed-chamber, and had quite come to herself, though her nerves were still much shaken, he spoke to her more sternly. 'Now, my lady, answer me: do you love him – eh?'

'No – no!' she faltered, shuddering, with her expanded eyes fixed on her husband. 'He is too terrible – no, no!'

'You are sure?'

'Quite sure!' replied the poor broken-spirited Countess.

But her natural elasticity asserted itself. Next morning he again inquired of her: 'Do you love him now?' She quailed under his gaze, but did not reply.

'That means that you do still, by God!' he continued.

'It means that I will not tell an untruth, and do not wish to incense my lord,' she answered, with dignity.

'Then suppose we go and have another look at him?' As he spoke, he suddenly took her by the wrist, and turned as if to lead her towards the ghastly closet.

'No – no! O – no!' she cried, and her desperate wriggle out of his hand revealed that the fright of the night had left more impression upon her delicate soul than superficially appeared.

'Another dose or two, and she will be cured,' he said to himself.

It was now so generally known that the Earl and Countess were not in accord, that he took no great trouble to disguise his deeds in relation to this matter. During the day he ordered four men with ropes and rollers to attend him in the boudoir. When they arrived, the closet was open, and the upper part of the statue tied up in canvas. He had it taken to the sleeping-chamber. What followed is more or less matter of conjecture. The story, as told to me, goes on to say that, when Lady Uplandtowers retired with him that night, she saw facing the foot of the heavy oak four-poster, a tall dark wardrobe, which had not stood there before; but she did not ask what its presence meant.

'I have had a little whim,' he explained when they were in the dark.

'Have you?' says she.

'To erect a little shrine, as it may be called.'

'A little shrine?'

'Yes; to one whom we both equally adore – eh? I'll show you what it contains.'

He pulled a cord which hung covered by the bed-curtains, and the doors of the wardrobe slowly opened, disclosing that the shelves within had been removed throughout, and the interior adapted to receive the ghastly figure, which stood there as it had stood in the boudoir, but with a wax candle burning on each side of it to throw the cropped and distorted features in relief. She clutched him, uttered a low scream, and buried her head in the bedclothes. 'O, take it away – please take it away!' she implored.

'All in good time; namely, when you love me best,' he returned calmly. 'You don't quite yet – eh?'

'I don't know – I think – O Uplandtowers, have mercy – I cannot bear it – O, in pity, take it away!'

'Nonsense; one gets accustomed to anything. Take another gaze.'

In short, he allowed the doors to remain unclosed at the foot of the bed, and the wax-tapers burning; and such was the strange fascination of the grisly exhibition that a morid curiosity took possession of the Countess as she lay, and, at his repeated request, she did again look out from the coverlet, shuddered, hid her eyes, and looked again, all the while begging him to take it away, or it would drive her out of her senses. But he would not do so yet, and the wardrobe was not locked till dawn.

The scene was repeated the next night. Firm in enforcing his ferocious correctives, he continued the treatment till the nerves of the poor lady were quivering in agony under the virtuous tortures inflicted by her lord, to bring her truant heart back to faithfulness.

The third night, when the scene had opened as usual, and she lay staring with immense wild eyes at the horrid fascination, on a sudden she gave an unnatural laugh; she laughed more and more, staring at the image, till she literally shrieked with laughter: then there was silence, and he found her to have become insensible. He thought she had fainted, but soon saw that the event was worse: she was in an epileptic fit. He started up, dismayed by the sense that, like many other subtle personages, he had been too exacting for his own interests. Such love as he was capable of, though rather a selfish gloating than a cherishing solicitude, was fanned into life on the instant. He closed the wardrobe with the pulley, clasped her in his arms, took her gently to the window, and did all he could to restore her.

It was a long time before the Countess came to herself, and when she did so, a considerable change seemed to have taken place in her emotions. She flung her arms around him, and with gasps of fear abjectly kissed him many times, at last bursting into tears. She had never wept in this scene before.

'You'll take it away, dearest – you will!' she begged plaintively.

'If you love me.'

'I do – oh, I do!'

'And hate him, and his memory?'

'Yes – yes!'

'Thoroughly?'

'I cannot endure recollection of him!' cried the poor Countess slavishly. 'It fills me with shame – how could I ever be so depraved! I'll never behave badly again, Uplandtowers; and you will never put the hated statue again before my eyes?'

He felt that he could promise with perfect safety. 'Never,' said he.

'And then I'll love you,' she returned eagerly, as if dreading lest the scourge should be applied anew. 'And I'll never, never dream of thinking a single thought that seems like faithlessness to my marriage vow.'

The strange thing now was that the fictitious love wrung from her by terror took on, through mere habit of enactment, a certain quality of reality. A servile mood of attachment to the Earl became distinctly visible in her contemporaneously with an actual dislike for her late husband's memory. The mood of attachment grew and continued when the statue was removed. A permanent revulsion was operant in her, which intensified as time wore on. How fright could have effected such a change of idiosyncrasy learned physicians alone can say; but I believe such cases of reactionary instinct are not unknown.

The upshot was that the cure became so permanent as to be itself a new disease. She clung to him so tightly that she would not willingly be out of his sight for a moment. She would have no sitting-room apart from his, though she could not help starting when he entered suddenly to her. Her eyes were wellnigh always fixed upon him. If he drove out, she wished to go with him; his slightest civilities to other women made her frantically jealous; till at length her very fidelity became a burden to him, absorbing his time, and curtailing his liberty, and causing him to curse and swear. If he ever spoke sharply to her now, she did not revenge herself by flying off to a mental world of her own; all that affection for another, which had provided her with a resource, was now a cold black cinder.

From that time the life of this scared and enervated lady – whose existence might have been developed to so much higher purpose but for the ignoble ambition of her parents and the conventions of the time – was one of obsequious amativeness towards a perverse and cruel man. Little personal events came to her in quick succession – half a dozen, eight, nine, ten such events, – in brief, she bore him no less than eleven children in the nine following years, but half of them came prematurely into the world, or died a few days old; only one, a girl, attained to maturity; she in after years became the wife of the Honourable Mr Beltonleigh, who was created Lord d'Almaine, as may be remembered.

There was no living son and heir. At length, completely worn out in mind and body, Lady Uplandtowers was taken abroad by her husband, to try the effect of a more genial climate upon her wasted frame. But nothing availed to strengthen her, and she died at Florence, a few months after her arrival in Italy.

Contrary to expectation, the Earl of Uplandtowers did not marry again. Such affection as existed in him – strange, hard, brutal as it was – seemed untransferable, and the title, as is known, passed at his death to his nephew. Perhaps it may not be so generally known that, during the enlargement of the Hall for the sixth Earl, while digging in the grounds for the new foundations, the broken fragments of a marble statue were unearthed. They were submitted to various antiquaries, who said that, so far as the damaged pieces would allow them to form an opinion, the statue seemed to be that of a mutilated Roman satyr; or, if not, an allegorical figure of Death. Only one or two old inhabitants guessed whose statue those fragments had composed.

I should have added that, shortly after the death of the Countess, an excellent sermon was preached by the Dean of Melchester, the subject of which, though names were not mentioned, was unquestionably suggested by the aforesaid events. He dwelt upon the folly of indulgence in sensuous love for a handsome form merely; and showed that the only rational and virtuous growths of that affection were those based upon intrinsic worth. In the case of the tender but somewhat shallow lady whose life I have related, there is no doubt that an infatuation for the person of young Willowes was the chief feeling that induced her to marry him; which was the more deplorable in that his beauty, by all tradition, was the least of his recommendations, every report bearing out the inference that he must have been a man of steadfast nature, bright intelligence, and promising life.

The company thanked the old surgeon for his story, which the rural dean declared to be a far more striking one than anything he could hope to tell. An elderly member of the Club, who was mostly called the Bookworm, said that a woman's natural instinct of fidelity would, indeed, send back her heart to a man after his death in a truly wonderful manner sometimes – if anything occurred to put before her forcibly the original affection between them, and his original aspect in her eyes, – whatever his inferiority may have been, social or otherwise; and then general conversation ensued upon the power that a woman has of seeing the actual in the representation, the reality in the dream – a power which (according to the sentimental member) men have no faculty of equalling.

The rural dean thought that such cases as that related by the surgeon were rather an illustration of passion electrified back to life than of a latent, true affection. The story had suggested that he should try to recount to them one which he had used to hear in his youth, and which afforded an instance of the latter and better kind of feeling, his heroine being also a lady who had married beneath her, though he feared his narrative would be of a much slighter kind than the surgeon's. The Club begged him to proceed, and the parson began.

DAME THE THIRD
THE MARCHIONESS OF STONEHENGE

BY THE RURAL DEAN

I would have you know, then, that a great many years ago there lived in a classical mansion with which I used to be familiar, standing not a hundred miles from the city of Melchester, a lady whose personal charms were so rare and unparalleled that she was courted, flattered, and spoilt by almost all the young noblemen and gentlemen in that part of Wessex. For a time these attentions pleased her well. But as, in the words of good Robert South (whose sermons might be read much more than they are), the most passionate lover of sport, if tied to follow his hawks and hounds every day of his life, would find the pursuit the greatest torment and calamity, and would fly to the mines and galleys for his recreation, so did this lofty and beautiful lady after a while become satiated with the constant iteration of what she had in its novelty enjoyed; and by an almost natural revulsion turned her regards absolutely netherward, socially speaking. She perversely and passionately centred her affection on quite a plain-looking young man of humble birth and no position at all; though it is true that he was gentle and delicate in nature, of good address, and guileless heart. In short, he was the parish-clerk's son, acting as assistant to the land-steward of her father the Earl of Avon, with the hope of becoming some day a land-steward himself. It should be said that perhaps the Lady Caroline (as she was called) was a little stimulated in this passion by the discovery that a young girl of the village already loved the young man fondly, and that he had paid some attentions to her, though merely of a casual and good-natured kind.

Since his occupation brought him frequently to the manor-house and its environs, Lady Caroline could make ample opportunities of seeing and speaking to him. She had, in Chaucer's phrase, 'all the craft of fine loving' at her fingers' ends, and the young man, being of a readily-kindling heart, was quick to notice the tenderness in her eyes and voice. He could not at first believe in his good fortune, having no understanding of her weariness of more artificial men; but a time comes when the stupidest sees in an eye the glance of his other half; and it came to him, who was quite the reverse of dull. As he gained confidence accidental encounters led to encounters by design; till at length when they were alone together there was no reserve on the matter. They whispered tender words as other lovers do, and were as devoted a pair as ever was seen. But not a ray or symptom of this attachment was allowed to show itself to the outer world.

Now, as she became less and less scrupulous towards him under the influence of her affection, and he became more and more reverential under the influence of his, and they looked the situation in the face together, their condition seemed intolerable in its hopelessness. That she could ever ask to be allowed to marry him, or could hold her tongue and quietly renounce him, was equally beyond conception. They resolved upon a third course, possessing neither of the disadvantages of these two: to wed secretly, and live on in outward appearance the same as before. In this they differed from the lovers of my friend's story.

Not a soul in the parental mansion guessed, when Lady Caroline came coolly into the hall one day after a visit to her aunt, that, during the visit, her lover and herself had found an opportunity of uniting themselves till death should part them. Yet such was the fact; the young woman who rode fine horses, and drove in pony-chaises, and was saluted deferentially by every one, and the young man who trudged about, and directed the tree-felling, and the laying out of fish-ponds in the park, were husband and wife.

As they had planned, so they acted to the letter for the space of a month and more, clandestinely meeting when and where they best could do so; both being supremely happy and content. To be sure, towards the latter part of that month, when the first wild warmth of her love had gone off, the Lady Caroline sometimes wondered within herself how she, who might have chosen a peer of the realm, baronet, knight; or, if serious-minded, a bishop or judge of the more gallant sort who prefer young wives, could have brought herself to do a thing so rash as to make this marriage; particularly when, in their private meetings, she perceived that though her young husband was full of ideas, and fairly well read, they had not a single social experience in common. It was his custom to visit her after nightfall, in her own house, when he could find no opportunity for an interview elsewhere; and to further this course she would contrive to leave unfastened a window on the ground-floor overlooking the lawn, by entering which a back staircase was accessible; so that he could climb up to her apartments, and gain audience of his lady when the house was still.

One dark midnight, when he had not been able to see her during the day, he made use of this secret method, as he had done many times before;

and when they had remained in company about an hour he declared that it was time for him to descend.

He would have stayed longer but that the interview had been a somewhat painful one. What she had said to him that night had much excited and angered him, for it had revealed a change in her; cold reason had come to his lofty wife; she was beginning to have more anxiety about her own position and prospects than ardour for him. Whether from the agitation of this perception or not, he was seized with a spasm; he gasped, rose, and in moving towards the window for air he uttered in a short thick whisper, 'O, my heart!'

With his hand upon his chest he sank down to the floor before he had gone another step. By the time that she had relighted the candle, which had been extinguished in case any eye in the opposite grounds should witness his egress, she found that his poor heart had ceased to beat; and there rushed upon her mind what his cottage-friends had once told her, that he was liable to attacks of heart-failure, one of which, the doctor had informed them, might some day carry him off.

Accustomed as she was to doctoring the other parishioners, nothing that she could effect upon him in that kind made any difference whatever; and his stillness, and the increasing coldness of his feet and hands, disclosed too surely to the affrighted young woman that her husband was dead indeed. For more than an hour, however, she did not abandon her efforts to restore him; when she fully realized the fact that he was a corpse she bent over his body, distracted and bewildered as to what step she next should take.

Her first feelings had undoubtedly been those of passionate grief at the loss of him; her second thoughts were concern at her own position as the daughter of an earl. 'O, why, why, my unfortunate husband, did you die in my chamber at this hour!' she said piteously to the corpse. 'Why not have died in your own cottage if you would die! Then nobody would ever have known of our imprudent union, and no syllable would have been breathed of how I mismated myself for love of you!'

The clock in the courtyard striking the solitary hour of one aroused Lady Caroline from the stupor into which she had fallen, and she stood. up, and went towards the door. To awaken and tell her mother seemed her only way out of this terrible situation; yet when she put her hand on the key to unlock it she withdrew herself again. It would be impossible to call even her mother's assistance without risking a revelation to all the world through the servants; while if she could remove the body unassisted to a distance she might avert suspicion of their union even now. This thought of immunity from the social consequences of her rash act, of renewed freedom, was indubitably a relief to her, for, as has been said, the constraint and riskiness of her position had begun to tell upon the Lady Caroline's nerves.

She braced herself for the effort, and hastily dressed herself, and then dressed him. Tying his dead hands together with a handkerchief, she laid his arms round her shoulders, and bore him to the landing and down the narrow stairs. Reaching the bottom by the window, she let his body slide slowly over the sill till it lay on the ground without. She then climbed over the window-sill herself, and, leaving the sash open, dragged him on the lawn with a rustle not louder than the rustle of a broom. There she took a securer hold, and plunged with him under the trees, still dragging him by his tied hands.

Away from the precincts of the house she could apply herself more vigorously to her task, which was a heavy one enough for her, robust as she was; and the exertion and fright she had already undergone began to tell upon her by the time she reached the corner of a beech-plantation which intervened between the manor-house and the village. Here she was so nearly exhausted that she feared she might have to leave him on the spot. But she plodded on after a while, and keeping upon the grass at every opportunity she stood at last opposite the poor young man's garden-gate, where he lived with his father, the parish-clerk. How she accomplished the end of her task Lady Caroline never quite knew; but, to avoid leaving traces in the road, she carried him bodily across the gravel, and laid him down at the door. Perfectly aware of his ways of coming and going, she searched behind the shutter for the cottage door-key, which she placed in his cold hand. Then she kissed his face for the last time, and with silent little sobs bade him farewell.

Lady Caroline retraced her steps, and reached the mansion without hindrance; and to her great relief found the window open just as she had left it. When she had climbed in she listened attentively, fastened the window behind her, and ascending the stairs noiselessly to her room, set everything in order, and returned to bed.

The next morning it was speedily echoed around that the amiable and gentle young villager had been found dead outside his father's door, which he had apparently been in the act of unlocking when he fell. The circumstances were sufficiently exceptional to justify an inquest, at which syncope from heart-disease was ascertained to be beyond doubt the explanation of his death, and no more was said about the matter then. But, after the funeral, it was rumoured that some man who had been returning late from a distant horse-fair had seen in the gloom of night a person, apparently a woman, dragging a heavy body of some sort towards the cottage-gate, which, by the light of after events, would seem to have been the corpse of the young fellow. His clothes were thereupon examined more particularly than at first, with the result that marks of friction were visible upon them here and there, precisely resembling such as would be left by dragging on the ground.

Our beautiful and ingenious Lady Caroline was now in great consternation; and began to think that, after all, it might have been better to honestly confess the truth. But having reached this stage without discovery or suspicion, she determined to make another effort towards concealment; and a bright idea struck her as a means of securing it. I think I mentioned that, before she cast eyes on the unfortunate steward's clerk, he had been the beloved of a certain village damsel, the woodman's daughter, his neighbour, to whom he had paid some attentions; and possibly he was beloved of her still. At any rate, the Lady Caroline's influence on the estates of her father being considerable, she resolved to seek an interview with the young girl in furtherance of her plan to save her reputation, about which she was now exceedingly anxious; for by this time, the fit being over, she began to be ashamed of her mad passion for her late husband, and almost wished she had never seen him.

In the course of her parish-visiting she lighted on the young girl without much difficulty, and found her looking pale and sad, and wearing a simple black gown, which she had put on out of respect for the young man's memory, whom she had tenderly loved, though he had not loved her.

'Ah, you have lost your lover, Milly,' said Lady Caroline.

The young woman could not repress her tears. 'My lady, he was not quite my lover,' she said. 'But I was his – and now he is dead I don't care to live any more!'

'Can you keep a secret about him?' asks the lady; 'one in which his honour is involved – which is known to me alone, but should be known to you?'

The girl readily promised, and, indeed, could be safely trusted on such a subject, so deep was her affection for the youth she mourned.

'Then meet me at his grave tonight, half-an-hour after sunset, and I will tell it to you,' says the other.

In the dusk of that spring evening the two shadowy figures of the young women converged upon the assistant-steward's newly-turfed mound; and at that solemn place and hour, which she had chosen on purpose, the one of birth and beauty unfolded her tale: how she had loved him and married him secretly; how he had died in her chamber; and how, to keep her secret, she had dragged him to his own door.

'Married him, my lady!' said the rustic maiden, starting back.

'I have said so,' replied Lady Caroline. 'But it was a mad thing, and a mistaken course. He ought to have married you. You, Milly, were peculiarly his. But you lost him.'

'Yes,' said the poor girl; 'and for that they laughed at me. "Ha – ha, you mid love him, Milly," they said; "but he will not love you!"'

'Victory over such unkind jeerers would be sweet,' said Lady Caroline. 'You lost him in life; but you may have him in death *as if* you had had him in life; and so turn the tables upon them.'

'How?' said the breathless girl.

The young lady then unfolded her plan, which was that Milly should go forward and declare that the young man had contracted a secret marriage (as he truly had done); that it was with her, Milly, his sweetheart; that he had been visiting her in her cottage on the evening of his death; when, on finding he was a corpse, she had carried him to his house to prevent discovery by her parents, and that she had meant to keep the whole matter a secret till the rumours afloat had forced it from her.

'And how shall I prove this?' said the woodman's daughter, amazed at the boldness of the proposal.

'Quite sufficiently. You can say, if necessary, that you were married to him at the church of St Something, in Bath City, in my name, as the first that occurred to you, to escape detection. That was where he married me. I will support you in this.'

'O – I don't quite like—'

'If you will do so,' said the lady peremptorily, 'I will always be your father's friend and yours; if not, it will be otherwise. And I will give you my wedding-ring, which you shall wear as yours.'

'Have you worn it, my lady?'

'Only at night.'

There was not much choice in the matter, and Milly consented. Then this noble lady took from her bosom the ring she had never been able openly to exhibit, and, grasping the young girl's hand, slipped it upon her finger as she stood upon her lover's grave.

Milly shivered, and bowed her head, saying, 'I feel as if I had become a corpse's bride!'

But from that moment the maiden was heart and soul in the substitution. A blissful repose came over her spirit. It seemed to her that she had secured in death him whom in life she had vainly idolized; and she was almost content. After that the lady handed over to the young man's new wife all the little mementoes and trinkets he had given herself, even to a brooch containing his hair.

The next day the girl made her so-called confession, which the simple mourning she had already worn, without stating for whom, seemed to bear out; and soon the story of the little romance spread through the village and country-side, almost as far as Melchester. It was a curious psychological fact that, having once made the avowal, Milly seemed possessed with a spirit of ecstasy at her position. With the liberal sum of money supplied to her by Lady Caroline she now purchased the garb of a widow, and duly appeared at church in her weeds, her simple face looking so sweet against its margin of crape that she was almost envied her state by the other village-girls of her age. And when a woman's sorrow for her beloved can maim her young life so obviously as it had done Milly's there was, in truth, little subterfuge in the case. Her explanation tallied so well with the details of her lover's latter movements – those strange absences and sudden returnings, which had occasionally puzzled his friends – that nobody supposed for a moment that the second actor in these secret nuptials was other than she. The actual and whole truth would indeed have seemed a preposterous assertion beside this plausible one, by reason of the lofty demeanour of the Lady Caroline and the unassuming habits of the late villager. There being no inheritance in question, not a soul took the trouble to go to the city church, forty miiles off, and search the registers for marriage signatures bearing out so humble a romance.

In a short time Milly caused a decent tombstone to be erected over her nominal husband's grave, whereon appeared the statement that it was placed there by his heartbroken widow, which, considering that the payment for it came from Lady Caroline and the grief from Milly, was as truthful as such inscriptions usually are, and only required pluralizing to render it yet more nearly so.

The impressionable and complaisant Milly, in her character of widow, took delight in going to his grave every day, and indulging in sorrow which was a positive luxury to her. She placed fresh flowers on his grave, and so keen was her emotional imaginativeness that she almost believed herself to have been his wife indeed as she walked to and fro in her garb of woe. One afternoon, Milly being busily engaged in this labour of love at the grave, Lady Caroline passed outside the churchyard wall with some of her visiting friends, who, seeing Milly there, watched her actions with interest, remarked upon the pathos of the scene, and upon the intense affection the young man must have felt for such a tender creature as Milly. A strange light, as of pain, shot from the Lady Caroline's eye, as if for the fiirst time she begrudged to the young girl the position she had been at such pains to transfer to her; it showed that a slumbering affection for her husband still had life in Lady Caroline, obscured and stifled as it was by social considerations.

An end was put to this smooth arrangement by the sudden appearance in the churchyard one day of the Lady Caroline, when Milly had come there on her usual errand of laying flowers. Lady Caroline had been anxiously awaiting her behind the chancel, and her countenance was pale and agitated.

'Milly!' she said, 'come here! I don't know how to say to you what I am going to say. I am half dead!'

'I am sorry for your ladyship,' says Milly, wondering.

'Give me that ring!' says the lady, snatching at the girl's left hand.

Milly drew it quickly away.

'I tell you give it to me!' repeated Caroline, almost fiercely. 'O – but you don't know why? I am in a grief and a trouble I did not expect!' And Lady Caroline whispered a few words to the girl.

'O my lady!' said the thunderstruck Milly. 'What *will* you do?'

'You must say that your statement was a wicked lie, an invention, a scandal, a deadly sin – that I told you to make it to screen me! That it was I whom he married at Bath. In short, we must tell the truth, or I am ruined – body, mind, and reputation – for ever!'

But there is a limit to the flexibility of gentle-souled women. Milly by this time had so grown to the idea of being one flesh with this young man, of having the right to bear his name as she bore it; had so thoroughly come to regard him as her husband, to dream of him as her husband, to speak of him as her husband, that she could not relinquish him at a moment's peremptory notice.

'No, no,' she said desperately, 'I cannot, I will not give him up! Your ladyship took him away from me alive, and gave him back to me only when he was dead. Now I will keep him! I am truly his widow. More truly than you, my lady! for I love him and mourn for him, and call myself by his dear name, and your ladyship does neither!'

'I *do* love him!' cries Lady Caroline with flashing eyes, 'and I cling to him, and won't let him go to such as you! How can I, when he is the father of this poor child that's coming to me? I must have him back again! Milly, Milly, can't you pity and understand me, perverse girl that you are, and the miserable plight that I am in? O, this precipitancy – it is the ruin of women! Why did I not consider, and wait! Come, give me back all that I have given you, and assure me you will support me in confessing the truth!'

'Never, never!' persisted Milly, with woe-begone passionateness. 'Look at this headstone! Look at my gown and bonnet of crape – this ring: listen to the name they call me by! My character is worth as much to me as yours is to you! After declaring my Love mine, myself his, taking his name, making his death my own particular sorrow, how can I say it was not so? No such dishonour for me! I will outswear you, my lady; and I shall be believed. My story is so much the more likely that yours will be thought false. But, O please, my lady, do not drive me to this! In pity let me keep him!'

The poor nominal widow exhibited such anguish at a proposal which would have been truly a bitter humiliation to her, that Lady Caroline was warmed to pity in spite of her own condition.

'Yes, I see your position,' she answered. 'But think of mine! What can I do? Without your support it would seem an invention to save me from disgrace; even if I produced the register, the love of scandal in the world is such that the multitude would slur over the fact, say it was a fabrication, and believe your story. I do not know who were the witnesses, or the name of the church, or anything!'

In a few minutes these two poor young women felt, as so many in a strait have felt before, that union was their greatest strength, even now; and they consulted calmly together. The result of their deliberations was that Milly went home as usual, and Lady Caroline also, the latter confessing that very night to the Countess her mother of the marriage, and to nobody else in the world. And, some time after, Lady Caroline and her mother went away to London, where a little later still they were joined by Milly, who was supposed to have left the village to proceed to a watering-place in the North for the benefit of her health, at the expense of the ladies of the Manor, who had been much interested in her state of lonely and defenceless widowhood.

Early the next year the ostensible widow Milly came home with an infant in her arms, the family at the Manor House having meanwhile gone abroad. They did not return from their tour till the autumn ensuing, by which time Milly and the child had again departed from the cottage of her father the woodman, Milly having attained to the dignity of dwelling in a cottage of her own, many miles to the eastward of her native village; a comfortable little allowance had moreover been settled on her and the child for life, through the instrumentality of Lady Caroline and her mother.

Two or three years passed away, and the Lady Caroline married a nobleman – the Marquis of Stonehenge – considerably her senior, who had wooed her long and phlegmatically. He was not rich, but she led a placid life with him for many years, though there was no child of the marriage. Meanwhile Milly's boy, as the youngster was called, and as Milly herself considered him, grew up, and throve wonderfully, and loved her as she deserved to be loved for her devotion to him, in whom she every day traced more distinctly the lineaments of the man who had won her girlsih heart, and kept it even in the tomb.

She educated him as well as she could with the limited means at her disposal, for the allowance had never been increased, Lady Caroline, or the Marchioness of Stonehenge as she now was, seeming by degrees to care little what had become of them. Milly became extremely ambitious on the boy's account; she pinched herself almost of necessaries to send him to the Grammar School in the town to which they retired, and at twenty he enlisted in a cavalry regiment, joining it with a deliberate intent of making the Army his profession, and not in a freak of idleness. His exceptional attainments, his manly bearing, his steady conduct, speedily won him promotion, which was furthered by the serious war in which this country was at that time engaged. On his return to England after the peace he had risen to the rank of riding-master, and was soon after advanced another stage, and made quartermaster, though still a young man.

His mother – his corporeal mother, that is, the Marchioness of Stonehenge – heard tidings of this unaided progress; it reawakened her maternal instncts, and filled her with pride. She became keenly interested in her successful soldier-son; and as she grew older much wished to see him again, particularly when, the Marquis dying, she was left a solitary and childless widow. Whether or not she would have gone to him of her own impulse I cannot say; but one day, when she was driving in an open carriage in the outskirts of a neighbouring town, the troops lying at the barracks hard by passed her in marching order. She eyed them narrowly, and in the finest of the horsemen recognized her son from his likeness to her first husband.

This sight of him doubly intensified the motherly emotions which had lain dormant in her for so many years, and she wildly asked herself how she could so have neglected him? Had she possessed the true courage of affection she would have owned to her first marriage, and have reared him as her own! What would it have mattered if she had never obtained this precious coronet of pearls and gold leaves, by comparison with the gain of having the love and protection of such a noble and worthy son? These and other sad reflections cut the gloomy and solitary lady to the heart; and she repented of her pride in disclaiming her first husband more bitterly than she had ever repented of her infatuation in marrying him.

Her yearning was so strong that at length it seemed to her that she could not live without announcing herself to him as his mother. Come what might, she would do it: late as it was, she would have him away from that woman whom she began to hate with the fierceness of a deserted heart for having taken her place as the mother of her only child. She felt confidently enough that her son would only too gladly exchange a cottage-mother for one who was a peeress of the realm. Being now, in her widowhood, free to come and go as she chose, without question from anybody, Lady Stonehenge started next day for the little town where Milly yet lived, still in her robes of sable for the lost lover of her youth.

'He is *my* son,' said the Marchioness, as soon as she was alone in the cottage with Milly. 'You must give him back to me, now that I am in a position in which I can defy the world's opinion. I suppose he comes to see you continually?'

'Every month since he returned from the war, my lady. And sometimes he stays two or three days, and takes me about seeing sights everywhere!' She spoke with quiet triumph.

'Well, you will have to give him up,' said the Marchioness calmly. 'It shall not be the worse for you – you may see him when you choose. I am going to avow my first marriage, and have him with me.'

'You forget that there are two to be reckoned with, my lady. Not only me, but himself.'

'That can be arranged. You don't suppose that he wouldn't—' but not wishing to insult Milly by comparing their positions, she said, 'He is my own flesh and blood, not yours.'

'Flesh and blood's nothing!' said Milly, flashing with as much scorn as a cottager could show to a peeress, which, in this case, was not so little as may be supposed. 'But I will agree to put it to him, and let him settle it for himself.'

'That's all I require,' said Lady Stonehenge. 'You must ask him to come, and I will meet him here.'

The soldier was written to, and the meeting took place. He was not so much astonished at the disclosure of his parentage as Lady Stonehenge had been led to expect, having known for years that there was a little mystery about his birth. His manner towards the Marchioness, though respectful, was less warm than she could have hoped. The alternatives as to his choice of a mother were put before him. His answer amazed and stupefied her.

'No, my lady,' said the quartermaster. 'Thank you much, but I prefer to let things be as they have been. My father's name is mine in any case. You see, my lady, you cared little for me when I was weak and helpless; why should I come to you now I am strong? She, dear devoted soul [pointing to Milly], tended me from my birth, watched over me, nursed me when I was ill, and deprived herself of many a little comfort to push me on. I cannot love another mother as I love her. She *is* my mother, and I will always be her son!' As he spoke he put his manly arm around Milly's neck, and kissed her with the tenderest affection.

The agony of the poor Marchioness was pitiable. 'You kill me!' she said, between her shaking sobs. 'Cannot you – love – me – too?'

'No, my lady. If I must say it, you were once ashamed of my poor father, who was a sincere and honest man; therefore, I am now ashamed of you.'

Nothing would move him; and the suffering woman at last gasped, 'Cannot – O, cannot you give one kiss to me – as you did to her? It is not much – it is all I ask – all!'

'Certainly,' he replied.

He kissed her, but with a difference – quite coldly; and the painful scene came to an end. That day was the beginning of death to the unfortunate Marchioness of Stonehenge. It is in the perverseness of her human heart that his denial of her should add fuel to the fire of her craving for his love. How long afterwards she lived I do not know with any exactness, but it was no great length of time. That anguish that is sharper than a serpent's tooth wore her out soon. Utterly reckless of the world, its ways, and its opinions, she allowed her story to become known; and when the welcome end supervened (which, I grieve to say, she refused to lighten by the consolations of religion), a broken heart was the truest phrase in which to sum up its cause.

The rural dean having concluded, some observations upon his tale were made in due course. The sentimental member said that Lady Caroline's history afforded a sad instance of how an honest human affection will become shamefaced and mean under the frost of class-division and social prejudices. She probably deserved some pity; though her offspring, before he grew up to man's estate, had deserved more. There was no pathos like the pathos of childhood, when a child found itself in a world where it was not wanted, and could not understand the reason why. A tale by the speaker, further illustrating the same subject, though with different results from the last, naturally followed.

DAME THE FOURTH
LADY MOTTISFONT

BY THE SENTIMENTAL MEMBER

Of all the romantic towns in Wessex, Wintoncester is probably the most convenient for meditative people to live in; since there you have a cathedral with a nave so long that it affords space in which to walk and summon your remoter moods without continually turning on your heel, or seeming to do more than take an afternoon stroll under cover from the rain or sun. In an uninterrupted course of nearly three hundred steps eastward, and again nearly three hundred steps westward amid those magnificent tombs, you can, for instance, compare in the most leisurely way the dry dustiness which ultimately pervades the persons of kings and bishops with the damper dustiness that is usually the final shape of commoners, curates, and others who take their last rest out of doors. Then, if you are in love, you can, by sauntering in the chapels and behind the episcopal chantries with the bright-eyed one, so steep and mellow your ecstasy in the solemnities around, that it will assume a rarer and finer tincture, ever more grateful to the understanding, if not to the senses, than that form of the emotion which arises from such companionship in spots where all is life, and growth, and fecundity.

It was in this solemn place, whither they had withdrawn from the sight of relatives on one cold day in March, that Sir Ashley Mottisfont asked in marriage, as his second wife, Philippa, the gentle daughter of plain Squire Okehall. Her life had been an obscure one thus far; while Sir Ashley, though not a rich man, had a certain distinction about him; so that everybody thought what a convenient, elevating, and, in a word, blessed match it would be for such a supernumerary as she. Nobody thought so more than the amiable girl herself. She had been smitten with such affection for him that, when she walked the cathedral aisles at his side on the before-mentioned day, she did not know that her feet touched hard pavement; it seemed to her rather that she was floating in space. Philippa was an ecstatic, heart-thumping maiden, and could not understand how she had deserved to have sent to her such an illustrious lover, such a travelled personage, such a handsome man.

When he put the question, it was in no clumsy language, such as the ordinary bucolic country landlords were wont to use on like quivering occasions, but as elegantly as if he had been taught it in Enfield's *Speaker*. Yet he hesitated a little – for he had something to add.

'My pretty Philippa,' he said (she was not very pretty by the way), 'I have, you must know, a little girl dependent upon me: a little waif I found one day in a patch of wild oats [such was this worthy baronet's humour] when I was riding home: a little nameless creature, whom I wish to take care of till she is old enough to take care of herself, and to educate in a plain way. She is only fifteen months old, and is at present in the hands of a kind villager's wife in my parish. Will you object to give some attention to the little thing in her helplessness?'

It need hardly be said that our innocent young lady, loving him so deeply and joyfully as she did, replied that she would do all she could for the nameless child; and, shortly afterwards, the pair were married in the same cathedral that had echoed the whispers of his declaration, the officiating minister being the Bishop himself, a venerable and experienced man, so well accomplished in uniting people who had a mind for that sort of experiment, that the couple, with some sense of surprise, found themselves one while they were still vaguely gazing at each other as two independent beings.

After this operation they went home to Deansleigh Park, and made a beginning of living happily ever after. Lady Mottisfont, true to her promise, was always running down to the village during the following weeks to see the baby whom her husband had so mysteriously lighted on during his ride home – concerning which interesting discovery she had her own opinion; but being so extremely amiable and affectionate that she could have loved stocks and stones if there had been no living creatures to love, she uttered none of her thoughts. The little thing, who had been christened Dorothy, took to Lady Mottisfont as if the baronet's young wife had been her mother; and at length Philippa grew so fond of the child that she ventured to ask her husband if she might have Dorothy in her own home, and bring her up carefully, just as if she were her own. To this he answered that, though remarks might be made thereon, he had no objection; a fact which was obvious, Sir Ashley seeming rather pleased than otherwise with the proposal.

After this they lived quietly and uneventfully for two or three years at Sir Ashley Mottisfont's residence in that part of England, with as near an approach to bliss as the climate of this country allows. The child had been a godsend to Philippa, for there seemed no great probability of her having one of her own: and she wisely regarded the possession of Dorothy as a special kindness of Providence, and did not worry her mind at all as to Dorothy's possible origin. Being a tender and impulsive creature, she loved her husband without criticism, exhaustively and religiously, and the child not much otherwise. She watched the little foundling as if she had been her own by nature, and Dorothy became a great solace to her when her husband was absent on pleasure or business; and when he came home he looked pleased to see how the two had won each other's hearts. Sir Ashley would kiss his wife, and his wife would kiss little Dorothy, and little Dorothy would kiss Sir Ashley, and after this triangular burst of affection Lady Mottisfont would say, 'Dear me – I forgot she is not mine!'

'What does it matter?' her husband would reply. 'Providence is foreknowing. He has sent this one because he is not intending to send us one by any other channel.'

Their life was of the simplest. Since his travels the baronet had taken to sporting and farming; while Philippa was a pattern of domesticity. Their pleasures were all local. They retired early to rest, and rose with the cart-horses and whistling waggoners. They knew the names of every bird and tree not exceptionally uncommon, and could foretell the weather almost as well as anxious farmers and old people with corns.

One day Sir Ashley Mottisfont received a letter, which he read, and musingly laid down on the table without remark.

'What is it, dearest?' asked his wife, glancing at the sheet.

'Oh, it is from an old lawyer at Bath whom I used to know. He reminds me of something I said to him four or five years ago – some little time before we were married – about Dorothy.'

'What about her?'

'It was a casual remark I made to him, when I thought you might not take kindly to her, that if he knew a lady who was anxious to adopt a child, and could insure a good home to Dorothy, he was to let me know.'

'But that was when you had nobody to take care of her,' she said quickly. 'How absurd of him to write now! Does he know you are married? He must, surely.'

'O yes!'

He handed her the letter. The solicitor stated that a widow lady of. position, who did not at present wish her name to be disclosed, had lately become a client of his while taking the waters, and had mentioned to him that she would like a little girl to bring up as her own, if she could be certain of finding one of good and pleasing disposition; and, the better to insure this, she would not wish the child to be too young for judging her qualities. He had remembered Sir Ashley's observation to him a long while ago, and therefore brought the matter before him. It would be an excellent home for the little girl – of that he was positive – if she had not already found such a home.

'But it is absurd of the man to write so long after!' said Lady Mottisfont, with a lumpiness about the back of her throat as she thought how much Dorothy had become to her. 'I suppose it was when you first – found her – that you told him this?'

'Exactly – it was then.'

He fell into thought, and neither Sir Ashley nor Lady Mottisfont took the trouble to answer the lawyer's letter; and so the matter ended for the time.

One day at dinner, on their return from a short absence in town, whither they had gone to see what the world was doing, hear what it was saying, and to make themselves generally fashionable after rusticating for so long – on this occasion, I say, they learnt from some friend who had joined them at dinner that Fernell Hall – the manorial house of the estate next their own, which had been offered on lease by reason of the impecuniosity of its owner – had been taken for a term by a widow lady, an Italian Contessa, whose name I will not mention for certain reasons which may by and by appear. Lady Mottisfont expressed her surprise and interest at the probability of having such a neighbour. 'Though, if I had been born in Italy, I think I should have liked to remain there,' she said.

'She is not Italian, though her husband was,' said Sir Ashley.

'O; you have heard about her before now?'

'Yes; they were talking of her at Grey's the other evening. She is English.' And then, as her husband said no more about the lady, the friend who was dining with them told Lady Mottisfont that the Countess's father had speculated largely in East-India Stock, in which immense fortunes were being made at that time: through this his daughter had found herself enormously wealthy at his death, which had occurred only a few weeks after the death of her husband. It was supposed that the marriage of an enterprising English speculator's daughter to a poor foreign nobleman had been matter of arrangement merely. As soon as the Countess's widowhood was a little further advanced she would, no doubt, be the mark of all the schemers who came near her, for she was still quite young. But at present she seemed to desire quiet, and avoided society and town.

Some weeks after this time Sir Ashley Mottisfont sat looking fixedly at his lady for many moments. He said:

'It might have been better for Dorothy if the Countess had taken her. She is so wealthy in comparison with ourselves, and could have ushered the girl into the great world more effectually than we ever shall be able to do.'

'The Contessa take Dorothy?' said Lady Mottisfont with a start. 'What – was she the lady who wished to adopt her?'

'Yes; she was staying at Bath when Lawyer Gayton wrote to me.'

'But how do you know all this, Ashley?'

He showed a little hesitation. 'Oh, I've seen her,' he says. 'You know, she drives to the meet sometimes, though she does not ride; and she has informed me that she was the lady who inquired of Gayton.'

'You have talked to her as well as seen her, then?'

'O yes, several times; everybody has.'

'Why didn't you tell me?' says his lady. 'I had quite forgotten to call upon her. I'll go tomorrow, or soon. . . But I can't think, Ashley, how you can say that it might have been better for Dorothy to have gone to her; she is so much our own now that I cannot admit any such conjectures as those, even in jest.' Her eyes reproached him so eloquently that Sir Ashley Mottisfont did not answer.

Lady Mottisfont did not hunt any more than the Anglo-Italian Countess did; indeed, she had become so absorbed in household matters and in Dorothy's well-being that she had no mind to waste a minute on mere enjoyments. As she had said, to talk coolly of what might have been the best destination in days past for a child to whom they had become so attached seemed quite barbarous, and she could not understand how her husband should consider the point so abstractedly; for, as will probably have been guessed, Lady Mottisfont long before this time, if she had not done so at the very beginning, divined Sir Ashley's true relation to Dorothy. But the baronet's wife was so discreetly meek and mild that she never told him of her surmise, and took what Heaven had sent her without cavil, her generosity in this respect having been bountifully rewarded by the new life she found in her love for the little girl.

Her husband recurred to the same uncomfortable subject, when, a few days later, they were speaking of travelling abroad. he said that it was almost a pity, if they thought of going, that they had not fallen in with the Countess's wish. That lady had told him that she had met Dorothy walking with her nurse, and that she had never seen a child she liked so well.

'What – she covets her still? How impertinent of the woman!' said Lady Mottisfont.

'She seems to do so. . . You see, dearest Philippa, the advantage to Dorothy would have been that the Countess would have adopted her legally, and have made her as her own daughter; while we have not done that – we are only bringing up and educating a poor child in charity.'

'But I'll adopt her fully – make her mine legally!' cried his wife in an anxious voice. 'How is it to be done?'

'H'm.' He did not inform her, but fell into thought; and, for reasons of her own, his lady was restless and uneasy.

The very next day Lady Mottisfont drove to Fernell Hall to pay the neglected call upon her neighbour. The Countess was at home, and received her graciously. But poor Lady Mottisfont's heart died within her as soon as she set eyes on her new acquaintance. Such wonderful beauty, of the fully-developed kind, had never confronted her before inside the lines of a human face. She seemed to shine with every light and grace that woman can possess. Her finished Continental manners, her expanded mind, her ready wit, composed a study that made the other poor lady sick; for she, and latterly Sir Ashley himself, were rather rural in manners, and she felt abashed by new sounds and ideas from without. She hardly knew three words in any language but her own, while this divine creature, though truly English, had, apparently, whatever she wanted in the Italian and French tongues to suit every impression; which was considered a great improvement to speech in those days, and, indeed, is by many considered as such in these.

'How very strange it was about the little girl!' the Contessa said to Lady Mottisfont, in her gay tones. 'I mean, that the child the lawyer recommended should, just before that, have been adopted by you, who are now my neighbour. How is she getting on? I must come and see her.'

'Do you still want her?' asks Lady Mottisfont suspiciously.

'O, I should like to have her!'

'But you can't! She's mine!' said the other greedily.

A drooping manner appeared in the Countess from that moment.

Lady Mottisfont, too, was in a wretched mood all the way home that day. The Countess was so charming in every way that she had charmed her gentle ladyship; how should it be possible that she had failed to charm Sir Ashley? Moreover, she had awakened a strange thought in Philippa's mind. As soon as she reached home she rushed to the nursery, and there, seizing Dorothy, frantically, kissed her; then, holding her at arm's length, she gazed with a piercing inquisitiveness into the girl's lineaments. She sighed deeply, abandoned the wondering Dorothy, and hastened away.

She had seen there not only her husband's traits, which she had often beheld before, but others, of the shade, shape, and expression which characterized those of her new neighbour.

Then this poor lady perceived the whole perturbing sequence of things, and asked herself how she could have been such a walking piece of simplicity as not to have thought of this before. But she did not stay long upbraiding herself for her shortsightedness, so overwhelmed was she with misery at the spectacle of herself as an intruder between these. To be sure she could not have foreseen such a conjuncture; but that did not lessen her grief. The woman who had been both her husband's bliss and his backsliding had reappeared free when he was no longer so, and she evidently was dying to claim her own in the person of Dorothy, who had meanwhile grown to be, to Lady Mottisfont, almost the only source of each day's happiness, supplying her with something to watch over, inspiring her with the sense of maternity, and so largely reflecting her husband's nature as almost to deceive her into the pleasant belief that the girl reflected her own also.

If there was a single direction in which this devoted and virtuous lady erred, it was in the direction of over-submissiveness. When all is said and done, and the truth told, men seldom show much self-sacrifice in their conduct as lords and masters to helpless women bound to them for life, and perhaps (though I say it with all uncertainty) if she had blazed up in his face like a furze-faggot, directly he came home, she might have helped herself a little. But God knows whether this is a true supposition; at any rate she did no such thing, and waited and prayed that she might never do despite to him who, she was bound to admit, had always been tender and courteous towards her; and hoped that little Dorothy might never be taken away.

By degrees the two households became friendly, and very seldom did a week pass without their seeing something of each other. Try as she might, and dangerous as she assumed the acquaintanceship to be, Lady Mottisfont could detect no fault or flaw in her new friend. It was obvious that Dorothy had been the magnet which had drawn the Contessa hither, and not Sir Ashley. Such beauty, united with such understanding and brightness, Philippa had never before known in one of her own sex, and she tried to think (whether she succeeded I do not know) that she did not mind the propinquity; since a woman so rich, so fair, and with such a command of suitors, could not desire to wreck the happiness of so inoffensive a person as herself.

The season drew on when it was the custom for families of distinction to go off to The Bath, and Sir Ashley Mottisfont persuaded his wife to accompany him thither with Dorothy. Everybody of any note was there this year. From their own part of England came many that they knew; among the rest, Lord and Lady Purbeck, the Earl and Countess of Wessex, Sir John Grebe, the Drenkhards, Lady Stourvale, the old Duke of Hamptonshire, the Bishop of Melchester, the Dean of Exonbury, and other lesser lights of Court, pulpit and field. Thither also came the fair

Contessa, whom, as soon as Philippa saw how much she was sought after by young men, she could not conscientiously suspect of renewed designs upon Sir Ashley.

But the Countess had finer opportunities than ever with Dorothy; for Lady Mottisfont was often indisposed, and even at other times could not honestly hinder an intercourse which gave bright ideas to the child. Dorothy welcomed her new acquaintance with a strange and instinctive readiness that intimated the wonderful subtlety of the threads which bind flesh and flesh together.

At last the crisis came: it was precipitated by an accident. Dorothy and her nurse had gone out one day for an airing, leaving Lady Mottisfont alone indoors. While she sat gloomily thinking that in all likelihood the Countess would contrive to meet the child somewhere, and exchange a few tender words with her, Sir Ashley Mottisfont rushed in and informed her that Dorothy had just had the narrowest possible escape from death. Some workmen were undermining a house to pull it down for rebuilding, when, without warning, the front wall inclined slowly outwards for its fall, the nurse and child passing beneath it at the same moment. The fall was temporarily arrested by the scaffolding, while in the meantime the Countess had witnessed their imminent danger from the other side of the street. Springing across, she snatched Dorothy from under the wall, and pulled the nurse after her, the middle of the way being barely reached before they were enveloped in the dense dust of the descending mass, though not a stone touched them.

'Where is Dorothy?' says the excited Lady Mottisfont.

'She has her – she won't let her go for a time—'

'Has her? But she's *mine* – she's mine!' cries Lady Mottisfont.

Then her quick and tender eyes perceived that her husband had almost forgotten her intrusive existence in comtemplating the oneness of Dorothy's, the Countess's, and his own: he was in a dream of exaltation which recognized nothing necessary to his well-being outside that welded circle of three lives.

Dorothy was at length brought home; she was much fascinated by the Countess, and saw nothing tragic, but rather all that was truly delightful, in what had happened. In the evening, when the excitement was over, and Dorothy was put to bed, Sir Ashley said, 'She has saved Dorothy, and I have been asking myself what I can do for her as a slight acknowledgment of her heroism. Surely we ought to let her have Dorothy to bring up, since she still desires to do it? It would be so much to Dorothy's advantage. We ought to look at it in that light, and not selfishly.'

Philippa seized his hand. 'Ashley, Ashley! You don't mean it – that I must lose my pretty darling – the only one I have?' She met his gaze with her piteous mouth and wet eyes so painfully strained, that he turned away his face.

The next morning, before Dorothy was awake, Lady Mottisfont stole to the girl's bedside, and sat regarding her. When Dorothy opened her eyes, she fixed them for a long time upon Philippa's features.

'Mamma – you are not so pretty as the Contessa, are you?' she said at length.

'I am not, Dorothy.'

'Why are you not, mamma?'

'Dorothy – where would you rather live, always; with me, or with her?'

The little girl looked troubled. 'I am sorry, mamma; I don't mean to be unkind; but I would rather live with her; I mean, if I might without trouble, and you did not mind, and it could be just the same to us all, you know.'

'Has she ever asked you the same question?'

'Never, mamma.'

There lay the sting of it: the Countess seemed the soul of honour and fairness in this matter, test her as she might. That afternoon Lady Mottisfont went to her husband with singular firmness upon her gentle face.

'Ashley, we have been married nearly five years, and I have never challenged you with what I know perfectly well – the parentage of Dorothy.'

'Never have you, Philippa dear. Though I have seen that you knew from the first.'

'From the first as to her father, not as to her mother. Her I did not know for some time; but I know now.'

'Ah! you have discovered that too?' says he, without much surprise.

'Could I help it? Very well, that being so, I have thought it over; and I have spoken to Dorothy. I agree to her going. I can do no less than grant to the Countess her wish, after her kindness to my – your – her – child.'

Then this self-sacrificing woman went hastily away that he might not see that her heart was bursting; and thereupon, before they left the city, Dorothy changed her mother and her home. After this, the Countess went away to London for a while, taking Dorothy with her; and the baronet and his wife returned to their lonely place at Deansleigh Park without her.

To renounce Dorothy in the bustle of Bath was a different thing from living without her in this quiet home. One evening Sir Ashley missed his wife from the supper-table; her manner had been so pensive and woeful of late that he immediately became alarmed. He said nothing, but looked about outside the house narrowly, and discerned her form in the park, where recently she had been accustomed to walk alone. In its lower levels there was a pool fed by a trickling brook, and he reached this spot in time to hear a splash. Running forward, he dimly perceived her light gown floating in the water. To pull her out was the work of a few instants, and bearing her indoors to her room, he undressed her, nobody in the house knowing of the incident but himself. She had not been immersed long enough to lose her senses, and soon recovered. She owned that she had done it because the Contessa had taken away her child, as she persisted in calling Dorothy. Her husband spoke sternly to her, and impressed upon her the weakness of giving way thus, when all that had happened was for the best. She took his reproof meekly, and admitted her fault.

After that she became more resigned, but he often caught her in tears over some doll, shoe, or ribbon of Dorothy's, and decided to take her to the North of England for change of air and scene. This was not without its beneficial effect, corporeally no less than mentally, as later events showed, but she still evinced a preternatural sharpness of ear at the most casual mention of the child. When they reached home, the Countess and Dorothy were still absent from the neighbouring Fernell Hall, but in a month or two they returned, and a little later Sir Ashley Mottisfont came into his wife's room full of news.

'Well – would you think it, Philippa! After being so desperate, too, about getting Dorothy to be with her!'

'Ah – what?'

'Our neighbour, the Countess, is going to be married again! It is to somebody she has met in London.'

Lady Mottisfont was much surprised; she had never dreamt of such an event. The conflict for the possession of Dorothy's person had obscured the possibility of it; yet what more likely, the Countess being still under thirty, and so good-looking?

'What is of still more interest to us, or to you,' continued her husband, 'is a kind offer she has made. She is willing that you should have Dorothy back again. Seeing what a grief the loss of her has been to you, she will try to do without her.'

'It is not for that; it is not to oblige me,' said Lady Mottisfont quickly. 'One can see well enough what it is for!'

'Well, never mind; beggars mustn't be choosers. The reason or motive is nothing to us, so that you obtain your desire.'

'I am not a beggar any longer,' said Lady Mottisfont, with proud mystery.

'What do you mean by that?'

Lady Mottisfont hesitated. However, it was only too plain that she did not now jump at a restitution of one for whom some months before she had been breaking her heart.

The explanation of this change of mood became apparent some little time farther on. Lady Mottisfont, after five years of wedded life, was expecting to become a mother, and the aspect of many things was greatly altered in her view. Among the more important changes was that of no longer feeling Dorothy to be absolutely indispensable to her existence.

Meanwhile, in view of her coming marriage, the Countess decided to abandon the remainder of her term at Fernell Hall, and return to her pretty little house in town. But she could not do this quite so quickly as she had expected, and half a year or more elapsed before she finally quitted the neighbourhood, the interval being passed in alternations between the country and London. Prior to her last departure she had an interview with Sir Ashley Mottisfont, and it occurred three days after his wife had presented him with a son and heir.

'I wanted to speak to you,' said the Countess, looking him luminously in the face, 'about the dear foundling I have adopted temporarily, and thought to have adopted permanently. But my marriage makes it too risky!'

'I thought it might be that,' he answered, regarding her steadfastly back again, and observing two tears come slowly into her eyes as she heard her own voice describe Dorothy in those words.

'Don't criticize me,' she said hastily; and recovering herself, went on. 'If Lady Mottisfont could take her back again, as I suggested, it would be better for me, and certainly no worse for Dorothy. To every one but ourselves she is but a child I have taken a fancy to, and Lady Mottisfont coveted her so much, and was very reluctant to let her go. . . I am sure she will adopt her again?' she added anxiously.

'I will sound her afresh,' said the baronet. 'You leave Dorothy behind for the present?'

'Yes; although I go away, I do not give up the house for another month.'

He did not speak to his wife about the proposal till some few days later, when Lady Mottisfont had nearly recovered, and news of the Countess's marriage in London had just reached them. He had no sooner mentioned Dorothy's name than Lady Mottisfont showed symptoms of disquietude.

'I have not acquired any dislike of Dorothy,' she said, 'but I feel that there is one nearer to me now. Dorothy chose the alternative of going to the Countess, you must remember, when I put it to her as between the Countess and myself.'

'But, my dear Philippa, how can you argue thus about a child, and that child our Dorothy?'

'Not *ours*,' said his wife, pointing to the cot. 'Ours is here.'

'What, then, Philippa,' he said, surprised, 'you won't have her back after nearly dying of grief at the loss of her?'

'I cannot argue, dear Ashley. I should prefer not to have the responsibility of Dorothy again. Her place is filled now.'

Her husband sighed, and went out of the chamber. There had been a previous arrangement that Dorothy should be brought to the house on a visit that day, but instead of taking her up to his wife, he did not inform Lady Mottisfont of the child's presence. He entertained her himself as well as he could, and accompanied her into the park, where they had a ramble together. Presently he sat down on the root of an elm and took her upon his knee.

'Between this husband and this baby, little Dorothy, you who had two homes are left out in the cold,' he said.

'Can't I go to London with my pretty mamma?' said Dorothy, perceiving from his manner that there was a hitch somewhere.

'I am afraid not, my child. She only took you to live with her because she was lonely, you know.'

'Then can't I stay at Deansleigh Park with my other mamma and you?'

'I am afraid that cannot be done either,' said he sadly. 'We have a baby in the house now.' He closed the reply by stooping down and kissing her, there being a tear in his eye.

'Then nobody wants me!' said Dorothy pathetically.

'O yes, somebody wants you,' he assured her. 'Where would you like to live besides?'

Dorothy's experiences being rather limited, she mentioned the only other place in the world that she was acquainted with, the cottage of the villager who had taken care of her before Lady Mottisfont had removed her to the Manor House.

'Yes; that's where you'll be best off, and most independent,' he answered. 'And I'll come to see you, my dear girl, and bring you pretty things; and perhaps you'll be just as happy there.'

Nevertheless, when the change came, and Dorothy was handed over to the kind cottage-woman, the poor child missed the luxurious roominess of Fernell Hall and Deansleigh; and for a long time her little feet, which had been accustomed to carpets and oak floors, suffered from the cold of the stone flags on which it was now her lot to live and to play; while chilblains came upon her fingers with washing at the pump. But thicker shoes with nails in them somewhat remedied the cold feet, and her complaints and tears on this and other scores diminished to silence as she became inured anew to the hardships of the farm-cottage, and she grew up robust if not handsome. She was never altogether lost sight of by Sir Ashley, though she was deprived of the systematic education which had been devised and begun for her by Lady Mottisfont, as well as by her real mother, the enthusiastic Countess. The latter soon had other Dorothys to think of, who occupied her time and affection as fully as Lady Mottisfont's were occupied by her precious boy. In the course of time the doubly-desired and doubly-rejected Dorothy married, I believe, a respectable road-contractor – the same, if I mistake not, who repaired and improved the old highway running from Wintoncester south-westerly through the New Forest – and in the heart of this worthy man of business the poor girl found the nest which had been denied her by her own flesh and blood of higher degree.

Several of the listeners wished to hear another story from the sentimental member after this, but he said that he could recall nothing else at the moment, and that it seemed to him as if his friend on the other side of the fireplace had something to say from the look of his face.

The member alluded to was a respectable churchwarden, with a sly chink to one eyelid – possibly the result of an accident – and a regular attendant at the Club meetings. He replied that his looks had been mainly caused by his interest in the two ladies of the last story, apparently women of strong motherly instincts, even though they were not genuinely staunch in their tenderness. The tale had brought to his mind an instance of a firmer affection of that sort on the paternal side, in a nature otherwise culpable. As for telling the story, his manner was much against him, he feared; but he would do his best, if they wished.

Here the President interposed with a suggestion that as it was getting late in the afternoon it would be as well to adjourn to their respective inns and lodgings for dinner, after which those who cared to do so could return and resume these curious domestic traditions for the remainder of the evening, which might otherwise prove irksome enough. The curator had told him that the room was at their service. The churchwarden, who was beginning to feel hungry himself, readily acquiesced, and the Club separated for an hour and a half. Then the faithful ones began to drop in again – among whom were not the President; neither came the rural dean, nor the two curates, though the Colonel, and the man of family, cigars in mouth, were good enough to return, having found their hotel dreary. The museum had no regular means of illumination, and a solitary candle, less powerful than the rays of the fire, was placed on the table; also bottles and glasses, provided by some thoughtful member. The chink-eyed church-warden, now thoroughly primed, proceeded to relate in his own terms what was in substance as follows, while many of his listeners smoked.

PART SECOND
After Dinner

DAME THE FIFTH
THE LADY ICENWAY

BY THE CHURCHWARDEN

In the reign of His Most Excellent Majesty King George the Third, Defender of the Faith and of the American Colonies, there lived in 'a faire maner-place' (so Leland called it in his day, as I have been told), in one o' the greenest bits of woodland between Bristol and the city of Exonbury, a young lady who resembled some aforesaid ones in having many talents and exceeding great beauty. With these gifts she combined a somewhat imperious temper and arbitrary mind, though her experience of the world was not actually so large as her conclusive manner would have led the stranger to suppose. Being an orphan she resided with her uncle, who, though he was fairly considerate as to her welfare, left her pretty much to herself.

Now it chanced that when this lovely young lady was about nineteen, she (being a fearless horsewoman) was riding, with only a young lad as an attendant, in one o' the woods near her uncle's house, and, in trotting along her horse stumbled over the root of a felled tree. She slipped to the ground, not seriously hurt, and was assisted home by a gentleman who came in view at the moment of her mishap. It turned out that this gentleman, a total stranger to her, was on a visit at the house of a neighbouring landowner. He was of Dutch extraction, and occasionally came to England on business or pleasure from his plantations in Guiana, on the north coast of South America, where he usually resided.

On this account he was naturally but little known in Wessex, and was but a slight acquaintance of the gentleman at whose mansion he was a guest. However, the friendship between him and the Heymeres – as the uncle and niece were named – warmed and warmed by degrees, there being but few folk o' note in the vicinity at that time, which made a newcomer, if he were at all sociable and of good credit, always sure of a welcome. A tender feeling (as it is called by the romantic) sprang up between the two young people, which ripened into intimacy. Anderling, the foreign gentleman, was of an amorous temperament; and, though he endeavoured to conceal his feeling, it could be seen that Miss Maria

Heymere had impressed him rather more deeply than would be represented by a scratch upon a stone. He seemed absolutely unable to free himself from her fascination; and his inability to do so, much as he tried – evidently thinking he had not the ghost of a chance with her – gave her the pleasure of power; though she more than sympathized when she overheard him heaving his deep-drawn sighs – privately to himself, as he supposed.

After prolonging his visit by every conceivable excuse in his power, he summoned courage, and offered her his hand and his heart. Being in no way disinclined to him, though not so fervid as he, and her uncle making no objection to the match, she consented to share his fate, for better or otherwise, in the distant colony where, as he assured her, his rice, and coffee, and maize, and timber, produced him ample means – a statement which was borne out by his friend, her uncle's neighbour. In short, a day for their marriage was fixed, earlier in the engagement than is usual or desirable between comparative strangers, by reason of the necessity he was under of returning to look after his properties.

The wedding took place, and Maria left her uncle's mansion with her husband, going in the first place to London, and about a fortnight after sailing with him across the great ocean for their distant home – which, however, he assured her, should not be her home for long, it being his intention to dispose of his interests in this part of the world as soon as the war was over, and he could do so advantageously; when they could come to Europe, and reside in some favourite capital.

As they advanced on the slow voyage she observed that he grew more and more constrained; and, by the time they had drawn near the Line, he was quite depressed, just as he had been before proposing to her. A day or two before landing at Paramaribo he embraced her in a very tearful and passionate manner, and said he wished to make a confession. It had been his misfortune, he said, to marry at Quebec in early life a woman whose reputation proved to be in every way bad and scandalous. The discovery had nearly killed him; but he had ultimately separated from her, and had never seen her since. He had hoped and prayed she might be dead; but recently in London, when they were starting on this journey, he had discovered that she was still alive. At first he had decided to keep this dark intelligence from her beloved ears; but he had felt that he could not do it. All he hoped was that such a condition of things would make no difference in her feelings for him, as it need make no difference in the course of their lives.

Thereupon the spirit of this proud and masterful lady showed itself in violent turmoil, like the raging of a nor'-west thunderstorm – as well it might, God knows. But she was of too stout a nature to be broken down by his revelation, as many ladies of my acquaintance would have been – so far from home, and right under the tropical blaze o' the sun. Of the two, indeed, he was the more wretched and shattered in spirit, for he loved her deeply, and (there being a foreign twist in his make) had been tempted to this crime by her exceeding beauty, against which he had struggled day and night, till he had no further resistance left in him. It was she who came first to a decision as to what should be done – whether a wise one I do not attempt to judge.

'I put it to you,' says she, when many useless self-reproaches and protestations on his part had been uttered – 'I put it to you whether, if any manliness is left in you, you ought not to do exactly what I consider the best thing for me in this strait to which you have reduced me?'

He promised to do anything in the whole world. She then requested him to allow her to return, and announce him as having died of malignant ague immediately on their arrival at Paramaribo; that she should consequently appear in weeds as his widow in her native place; that he would never molest her, or come again to that part of the world during the whole course of his life – a good reason for which would be that the legal consequences might be serious.

He readily acquiesced in this, as he would have acquiesced in anything for the restitution of one he adored so deeply – even to the yielding of life itself. To put her in an immediate state of independence he gave her, in bonds and jewels, a considerable sum (for his worldly means had been in no way exaggerated); and by the next ship she sailed again for England, having travelled no further to Paramaribo. At parting he declared it to be his intention to turn all his landed possessions into personal property, and to be a wanderer on the face of the earth in remorse for his conduct towards her.

Maria duly arrived in England, and immediately on landing apprised her uncle of her return, duly appearing at his house in the garb of a widow. She was commiserated by all the neighbours as soon as her story was told; but only to her uncle did she reveal the real state of affairs, and her reason for concealing it. For, though she had been innocent of wrong, Maria's pride was of that grain which could not brook the least appearance of having been fooled, or deluded, or nonplussed in her worldly aims.

For some time she led a quiet life with her relative, and in due course a son was born to her. She was much respected for her dignity and reserve, and the portable wealth which her temporary husband had made over to her enabled her to live in comfort in a wing of the mansion, without assistance from her uncle at all. But, knowing that she was not what she seemed to be, her life was an uneasy one, and she often said to herself: 'Suppose his continued existence should become known here, and people should discern the pride of my motive in hiding my humiliation? It would be worse than if I had been frank at first, which I should have been but for the credit of this child.'

Such grave reflections as these occupied her with increasing force; and during their continuance she encountered a worthy man of noble birth and title – Lord Icenway his name – whose seat was beyond Wintoncester, quite at t'other end of Wessex. He being anxious to pay his addresses to her, Maria willingly accepted them, though he was a plain man, older than herself; for she discerned in a second marriage a method of fortifying her position against mortifying discoveries. In a few months their union took place, and Maria lifted her head as Lady Icenway, and left with her husband and child for his home as aforesaid, where she was quite unknown.

A justification, or a condemnation, of her step (according as you view it) was seen when, not long after, she received a note from her former husband Anderling. It was a hasty and tender epistle, and perhaps it was fortunate that it arrived during the temporary absence of Lord Icenway. His worthless wife, said Anderling, had just died in Quebec; he had gone there to ascertain particulars, and had seen the unfortunate woman buried. He now was hastening to England to repair the wrong he had done his Maria. He asked her to meet him at Southampton, his port of arrival; which she need be in no fear of doing, as he had changed his name, and was almost absolutely unknown in Europe. He would remarry her immediately, and live with her in any part of the Continent, as they had originally intended, where, for the great love he still bore her, he would devote himself to her service for the rest of his days.

Lady Icenway, self-possessed as it was her nature to be, was yet much disturbed at this news, and set off to meet him, unattended, as soon as she heard that the ship was in sight. As soon as they stood face to face she found that she still possessed all her old influence over him, though his power to fascinate her had quite departed. In his sorrow for his offence against her he had become a man of strict religious habits, self-denying as a lenten saint, though formerly he had been a free and joyous liver. Having first got him to swear to make her any amends she should choose (which he was imagining must be by a true marriage), she informed him that she had already wedded another husband, an excellent man of ancient family and possessions, who had given her a title, in which she much rejoiced.

At this the countenance of the poor foreign gentleman became cold as clay, and his heart withered within him; for as it had been her beauty and bearing which had led him to sin to obtain her, so, now that her beauty was in fuller bloom, and her manner more haughty by her success, did he feel her fascination to be almost more than he could bear. Nevertheless, having sworn his word, he undertook to obey her commands, which were simply a renewal of her old request – that he would depart for some foreign country, and never reveal his existence to her friends, or husband, or any person in England; never trouble her more, seeing how great a harm it would do her in the high position which she at present occupied.

He bowed his head. 'And the child – our child?' he said.

'He is well,' says she. 'Quite well.'

With this the unhappy gentleman departed, much sadder in his heart than on his voyage to England; for it had never occurred to him that a woman who rated her honour so highly as Maria had done, and who was the mother of a child of his, would have adopted such means as this for the restoration of that honour, and at so surprisingly early a date. He had fully calculated on making her his wife in law and truth, and on living in cheerful unity with her and his offspring, for whom he felt a deep and growing tenderness, though he had never once seen the child.

The lady returned to her mansion beyond Wintoncester, and told nothing of the interview to her noble husband, who had fortunately gone that day to do a little cocking and ratting out by Weydon Priors, and knew nothing of her movements. She had dismissed her poor Anderling peremptorily enough; yet she would often after this look in the face of the child of her so-called widowhood, to discover what and how many traits of his father were to be seen in his lineaments. For this she had ample opportunity during the following autumn and winter months, her husband being a matter-of-fact nobleman, who spent the greater part of his time in field-sports and agriculture.

One winter day, when he had started for a meet of the hounds a long way from the house – it being his custom to hunt three or four times a week at this season of the year – she had walked into the sunshine upon the terrace before the windows, where there fell at her feet some little white object that had come over a boundary wall hard by. It proved to be a tiny note wrapped round a stone. Lady Icenway opened it and read it, and immediately (no doubt, with a stern fixture of her queenly countenance) walked hastily along the terrace, and through the door into the shrubbery, whence the note had come. The man who had first married her stood under the bushes before her. It was plain from his appearance that something had gone wrong with him.

'You notice a change in me, my best-beloved,' he said. 'Yes, Maria – I have lost all the wealth I once possessed – mainly by reckless gambling in the Continental hells to which you banished me. But one thing in the world remains to me – the child – and it is for him that I have intruded here. Don't fear me, darling! I shall not inconvenience you long; I love you too well! But I think of the boy day and night – I cannot help it – I cannot keep my feeling for him down; and I long to see him, and speak a word to him once in my lifetime!'

'But your oath?' says she. 'You promised never to reveal by word or sign—'

'I will reveal nothing. Only let me see the child. I know what I have sworn to you, cruel mistress, and I respect my oath. Otherwise I might have seen him by some subterfuge. But I preferred the frank course of asking your permission.'

She demurred, with the haughty severity which had grown part of her character, and which her elevation to the rank of a peeress had rather intensified than diminished. She said that she would consider, and would give him an answer the day after the next, at the same hour and place, when her husband would again be absent with his pack of hounds.

The gentleman waited patiently. Lady Icenway, who had now no conscious love left for him, well considered the matter, and felt that it would be advisable not to push to extremes a man of so passionate a heart. On the day and hour she met him as she had promised to do.

'You shall see him,' she said, 'of course on the strict condition that you do not reveal yourself, and hence, though you see him, he must not see you, or your manner might betray you and me. I will lull him into a nap in the afternoon, and then I will come to you here, and fetch you indoors by a private way.'

The unfortunate father, whose misdemeanour had recoiled upon his own head in a way he could not have foreseen, promised to adhere to her instructions, and waited in the shrubberies till the moment when she should call him. This she duly did about three o'clock that day, leading him in by a garden door, and upstairs to the nursery where the child lay. He was in his little cot, breathing calmly, his arm thrown over his head, and his silken curls crushed into the pillow. His father, now almost to be pitied, bent over him, and a tear from his eye wetted the coverlet.

She held up a warning finger as he lowered his mouth to the lips of the boy.

'But O, why not?' implored he.

'Very well, then,' said she, relenting. 'But as gently as possible.'

He kissed the child without waking him, turned, gave him a last look, and followed her out of the chamber, when she conducted him off the premises by the way he had come.

But this remedy for his sadness of heart at being a stranger to his own son had the effect of intensifying the malady; for while originally, not knowing or having ever seen the boy, he had loved him vaguely and imaginatively only, he now became attached to him in flesh and bone, as any parent might; and the feeling that he could at best only see his child at the rarest and most cursory moments, if at all, drove him into a state of distraction which threatened to overthrow his promise to the boy's mother to keep out of his sight. But such was his chivalrous respect for Lady Icenway, and his regret at having ever deceived her, that he schooled his poor heart into submission. Owing to his loneliness, all the fervour of which he was capable – and that was much – flowed now in the channel of parental and marital love – for a child who did not know him, and a woman who had ceased to love him.

At length this singular punishment became such a torture to the poor foreigner that he resolved to lessen it at all hazards, compatible with punctilious care for the name of the lady his former wife, to whom his attachment seemed to increase in proportion to her punitive treatment of him. At one time of his life he had taken great interest in tulip-culture, as well as gardening in general; and since the ruin of his fortunes, and his arrival in England, he had made of his knowledge a precarious income in the hot-houses of nurserymen and others. With the new idea in his head he applied himself zealously to the business, till he acquired in a few months great skill in horticulture. Waiting till the noble lord, his lady's husband, had room for an under-gardener of a general sort, he offered himself for the place, and was engaged immediately by reason of his civility and intelligence before Lady Icenway knew anything of the matter. Much therefore did he surprise her when she found him in the conservatories of her mansion a week or two after his arrival. The punishment of instant dismissal, with which at first she haughtily threatened him, my lady thought fit, on reflection, not to enforce. While he served her thus she knew he would not harm her by a word, while, if he were expelled, chagrin might induce him to reveal in a moment of exasperation what kind treatment would assist him to conceal.

So he was allowed to remain on the premises, and had for his residence a little cottage by the garden-wall which had been the domicile of some of his predecessors in the same occupation. Here he lived absolutely alone, and spent much of his leisure in reading, but the greater part in watching the windows and lawns of his lady's house for glimpses of the form of the child. It was for that child's sake that he abandoned the tenets of the

Roman Catholic Church in which he had been reared, and became the most regular attendant at the services in the parish place of worship hard by, where, sitting behind the pew of my lady, my lord, and my lord's stepson, the gardener could pensively study the traits and movements of the youngster at only a few feet distance, without suspicion or hindrance.

He filled his post for more than two years with a pleasure to himself which, though mournful, was soothing, his lady never forgiving him, or allowing him to be anything more than 'the gardener' to her child, though once or twice the boy said, 'That gardener's eyes are so sad! Why does he look so sadly at me?' He sunned himself in her scornfulness as if it were love, and his ears drank in her curt monosyllables as though they were rhapsodies of endearment. Strangely enough, the coldness with which she treated her foreigner began to be the conduct of Lord Icenway towards herself. It was a matter of great anxiety to him that there should be a lineal successor to the barony, yet no sign of that successor had as yet appeared. One day he complained to her quite roughly of his fate. 'All will go to that dolt of a cousin!' he cried. 'I'd sooner see my name and place at the bottom of the sea!'

The lady soothed him and fell into thought, and did not recriminate. But one day, soon after, she went down to the cottage of the gardener to inquire how he was getting on, for he had been ailing of late, though, as was supposed, not seriously. Though she often visited the poor, she had never entered her under-gardener's home before, and was much surprised – even grieved and dismayed – to find that he was too ill to rise from his bed. She went back to her mansion and returned with some delicate soup, that she might have a reason for seeing him.

His condition was so feeble and alarming, and his face so thin, that it quite shocked her softening heart, and gazing upon him she said, 'You must get well – you must! *There's a reason.* I have been hard with you hitherto – I know it. I will not be so again.'

The sick and dying man – for he was dying indeed – took her hand and pressed it to his lips. 'Too late, my darling, too late!' he murmured.

'But you *must not* die! O, you must not!' she said. And on an impulse she bent down and whispered some words to him, blushing as she had blushed in her maiden days.

He replied by a faint wan smile. 'Ah – why did you not say so sooner? Time was . . . but that's past!' he said. 'I must die!'

And die he did, a few days later, as the sun was going down behind the garden-wall. Her harshness seemed to come trebly home to her then, and she remorsefully exclaimed against herself in secret and alone. Her one desire now was to erect some tribute to his memory without its being recognized as her handiwork. In the completion of this scheme there arrived a few months later a handsome stained-glass window for the church; and when it was unpacked and in course of erection Lord Icenway strolled into the building with his wife.

'"*Erected to his memory by his grieving widow,*"' he said, reading the legend on the glass. 'I didn't know that he had a wife; I've never seen her.'

'O yes, you must have, Icenway; only you forget,' replied his lady blandly. 'But she didn't live with him, and was never seen visiting him, because there were differences between them; which, as is usually the case, makes her all the more sorry now.'

'And go ruining herself by this expensive ruby-and-azure glass-design.'

'She is not poor, they say.'

As Lord Icenway grew older he became crustier and crustier, and whenever he set eyes on his wife's boy by her other husband he would burst out morosely, saying,

''Tis a very odd thing, my lady, that you could oblige your first husband, and couldn't oblige me.'

'Ah! if I had only thought of it sooner!' she murmured.

'What?' said he.

'Nothing, dearest,' replied Lady Icenway.

The Colonel was the first to comment upon the churchwarden's tale, by saying that the fate of the poor fellow was rather a hard one.

The gentleman-tradesman could not see that his fate was at all too hard for him. He was legally nothing to her, and he had served her shamefully. If he had been really her husband it would have stood differently.

The Bookworm remarked that Lord Icenway seemed to have been a very unsuspicious man, with which view a fat member with a crimson face agreed. It was true his wife was a very close-mouthed personage, which made a difference. If she had spoken out recklessly her lord might have been suspicious enough, as in the case of that lady who lived at Stapleford Park in their great-grandfathers' time. Though there, to be sure, considerations arose which made her husband view matters with much philosophy.

A few of the members doubted the possibility of this in such cases.

The crimson man, who was a retired maltster of comfortable means, *ventru*, and short in stature, cleared his throat, blew off his superfluous breath, and proceeded to give the instance before alluded to of such possibility, first apologizing for his heroine's lack of a title, it never having been his good fortune to know many of the nobility. To his style of narrative the following is only an approximation.

DAME THE SIXTH
SQUIRE PETRICK'S LADY

BY THE CRIMSON MALTSTER

Folk who are at all acquainted with the traditions of Stapleford Park will not need to be told that in the middle of the last century it was owned by that trump of mortgagees, Timothy Petrick, whose skill in gaining possession of fair estates by granting sums of money on their title-deeds has seldom if ever been equalled in our part of England. Timothy was a lawyer by profession, and agent to several noblemen, by which means his special line of business became opened to him by a sort of revelation. It is said that a relative of his, a very deep thinker, who afterwards had the misfortune to be transported for life for mistaken notions on the signing of a will, taught him considerable legal lore, which he creditably resolved never to throw away for the benefit of other people, but to reserve it entirely for his own.

However, I have nothing in particular to say about his early and active days, but rather of the time when, an old man, he had become the owner of vast estates by the means I have signified – among them the great manor of Stapleford, on which he lived, in the splendid old mansion now pulled down; likewise estates at Marlott, estates near Sherton Abbas, nearly all the borough of Millpool, and many properties near Ivell. Indeed, I can't call to mind half his landed possessions, and I don't know that it matters much at this time of day, seeing that he's been dead and gone many years. It is said that when he bought an estate he would not decide to pay the price till he had walked over every single acre with his own two feet, and prodded the soil at every point with his own spud, to test its quality, which, if we regard the extent of his properties, must have been a stiff business for him.

At the time I am speaking of he was a man over eighty, and his son was dead; but he had two grandsons, the elder of whom, his namesake, was married, and was shortly expecting issue. Just then the grandfather was taken ill, for death, as it seemed, considering his age. By his will the old man had created an entail (as I believe the lawyers call it), devising the whole of the estates to his elder grandson and his issue male, failing which, to his younger grandson and his issue male, failing which, to remoter relatives, who need not be mentioned now.

While old Timothy Petrick was lying ill, his elder grandson's wife, Annetta, gave birth to her expected child, who, as fortune would have it, was a son. Timothy, her husband, though sprung of a scheming family, was no great schemer himself; he was the single one of the Petricks then living whose heart had ever been greatly moved by sentiments which did not run in the groove of ambition; and on this account he had not married well, as the saying is; his wife having been the daughter of a family of no better beginnings than his own; that is to say, her father was a country townsman of the professional class. But she was a very pretty woman, by all accounts, and her husband had seen, courted, and married her in a high tide of infatuation, after a very short acquaintance, and with very little knowledge of her heart's history. He had never found reason to regret his choice as yet, and his anxiety for her recovery was great.

She was supposed to be out of danger, and herself and the child progressing well, when there was a change for the worse, and she sank so rapidly that she was soon given over. When she felt that she was about to leave him, Annetta sent for her husband, and, on his speedy entry and assurance that they were alone, she made him solemnly vow to give the child every care in any circumstances that might arise, if it should please Heaven to take her. This, of course, he readily promised. Then, after some hesitation, she told him that she could not die with a falsehood upon her soul, and dire deceit in her life; she must make a terrible confession to him before her lips were sealed for ever. She thereupon related an incident concerning the baby's parentage, which was not as he supposed.

Timothy Petrick, though a quick-feeling man, was not of a sort to show nerves outwardly; and he bore himself as heroically as he possibly could do in this trying moment of his life. That same night his wife died; and while she lay dead, and before her funeral, he hastened to the bedside of his sick grandfather, and revealed to him all that had happened: the baby's birth, his wife's confession, and her death, beseeching the aged man, as he loved him, to bestir himself now, at the eleventh hour, and alter his will so as to dish the intruder. Old Timothy, seeing matters in the same light as his grandson, required no urging against allowing anything to stand in the way of legitimate inheritance; he executed another will, limiting the entail to Timothy his grandson, for life, and his male heirs thereafter to be born; after them to his other grandson Edward, and Edward's heirs. Thus the newly-born infant, who had been the centre of so many hopes, was cut off, and scorned as none of the elect.

The old mortgagee lived but a short time after this, the excitement of the discovery having told upon him considerably, and he was gathered to his fathers like the most charitable man in his neighbourhood. Both wife and grandparent being buried, Timothy settled down to his usual life as well as he was able, mentally satisfied that he had by prompt action defeated the consequences of such dire domestic treachery as had been shown towards him, and resolving to marry a second time as soon as he could satisfy himself in the choice of a wife.

But men do not always know themselves. The embittered state of Timothy Petrick's mind bred in him by degrees such a hatred and mistrust of womankind that, though several specimens of high attractiveness came under his eyes, he could not bring himself to the point of proposing marriage. He dreaded to take up the position of husband a second time, discerning a trap in every petticoat, and a Slough of Despond in possible heirs. 'What has happened once, when all seemed so fair, may happen again,' he said to himself. 'I'll risk my name no more.' So he abstained from marriage, and overcame his wish for a lineal descendant to follow him in the ownership of Stapleford.

Timothy had scarcely noticed the unfortunate child that his wife had borne, after arranging for a meagre fulfilment of his promise to her to take care of the boy, by having him brought up in his house. Occasionally, remembering this promise, he went and glanced at the child, saw that he was doing well, gave a few special directions, and again went his solitary way. Thus he and the child lived on in the Stapleford mansion-house till two or three years had passed by. One day he was walking in the garden, and by some accident left his snuff-box on a bench. When he came back to find it he saw the little boy standing there; he had escaped his nurse, and was making a plaything of the box, in spite of the convulsive sneezings which the game brought in its train. Then the man with the encrusted heart became interested in the little fellow's persistence in his play under such discomforts; he looked in the child's face, saw there his wife's countenance, though he did not see his own, and fell into thought on the piteousness of childhood – particularly of despised and rejected childhood, like this before him.

From that hour, try as he would to counteract the feeling, the human necessity to love something or other got the better of what he had called his wisdom, and shaped itself in a tender anxiety for the youngster Rupert. The name had been given him by his dying mother when, at her request, the child was baptized in her chamber, lest he should not survive for public baptism; and her husband had never thought of it as a name of any significance till, about this time, he learnt by accident that it was the name of the young Marquis of Christminster, son of the Duke of Southwesterland, for whom Annetta had cherished warm feelings before her marriage. Recollecting some wandering phrases in his wife's last words, which he had not understood at the time, he perceived at last that this was the person to whom she had alluded when affording him a clue to little Rupert's history.

He would sit in silence for hours with the child, being no great speaker at the best of times; but the boy, on his part, was too ready with his tongue for any break in discourse to arise because Timothy Petrick had nothing to say. After idling away his mornings in this manner, Petrick would go to his own rom and swear in long loud whispers, and walk up and down, calling himself the most ridiculous dolt that ever lived, and declaring that he would never go near the little fellow again; to which resolve he would adhere for the space perhaps of a day. Such cases are happily not new to human nature, but there never was a case in which a man more completely befooled his former self than in his.

As the child grew up, Timothy's attachment to him grew deeper, till Rupert became almost the sole object for which he lived. There had been enough of the family ambition latent in him for Timothy Petrick to feel a little envy when, some time before this date, his brother Edward had been accepted by the Honourable Harriet Mountclere, daughter of the second Viscount of that name and title; but having discovered, as I have before stated, the paternity of his boy Rupert to lurk in even a higher stratum of society, those envious feelings speedily dispersed. Indeed, the more he reflected thereon, after his brother's aristocratic marriage, the more content did he become. His late wife took softer outline in his memory, as he thought of the lofty taste she had displayed, though only a plain burgher's daughter, and the justification for his weakness in loving the child – the justification that he had longed for – was afforded now in the knowledge that the boy was by nature, if not by name, a representative of one of the noblest houses in England.

'She was a woman of grand instincts, after all,' he said to himself proudly. 'To fix her choice upon the immediate successor in that ducal line – it was finely conceived! Had he been of low blood like myself or my relations she would scarce have deserved the harsh measure that I have dealt out to her and her offspring. How much less, then, when such grovelling tastes were furthest from her soul! The man Annetta loved was noble, and my boy is noble in spite of me.'

The afterclap was inevitable, and it soon came. 'So far,' he reasoned, 'from cutting off this child from inheritance of my estates, as I have done, I should have rejoiced in the possession of him! He is of blue-stock on one side at least, whilst in the ordinary run of affairs he would have been a commoner to the bone.'

Being a man, whatever his faults, of good old beliefs in the divinity of kings and those about 'em, the more he overhauled the case in this light, the more strongly did his poor wife's conduct in improving the blood and breed of the Petrick family win his heart. He considered what ugly, idle, hard-drinking scamps many of his own relations had been; the miserable scriveners, usurers, and pawnbrokers that he had numbered among his forefathers, and the probability that some of their bad qualities would have come out in a merely corporeal child of his loins, to give him sorrow in his old age, turn his black hairs gray, his gray hairs white, cut down every stick of timber, and Heaven knows what all, had he not, or rather his good wife, like a skilful gardener, given attention to the art of grafting, and changed the sort; till at length this right-minded man fell down on his knees every night and morning and thanked God that he was not as other meanly descended fathers in such matters.

It was in the peculiar disposition of the Petrick family that the satisfaction which ultimately settled in Timothy's breast found nourishment. The Petricks had adored the nobility, and plucked them at the same time. That excellent man Izaak Walton's feelings about fish were much akin to those of old Timothy Petrick, and of his descendants in a lesser degree, concerning the landed aristocracy. To torture and to love simultaneously is a proceeding strange to reason, but possible to practice, as these instances show.

Hence, when Timothy's brother Edward said slightingly one day that Timothy's son was well enough, but that he had nothing but shops and offices in his backward historical perspective, while his own children, should he have any, would be far different, in possessing such a mother as the Honourable Harriet, Timothy felt a bound of triumph within him at the power he possessed of contradicting that statement if he chose.

So much was he interested in his boy in this new aspect that he now began to read up chronicles of the illustrious house ennobled as the Dukes of Southwesterland, from their very beginning in the glories of the Restoration of the blessed Charles till the year of his own time. He mentally noted their gifts from royalty, grants of lands, purchases, intermarriages, plantings and buildings; more particularly their political and military achievements, which had been great, and their performances in art and letters, which had been by no means contemptible. He studied prints of the portraits of that family, and then, like a chemist watching a crystallization, began to examine young Rupert's face for the unfolding of those historic curves and shades that the painters Vandyke and Lely had perpetuated on canvas.

When the boy reached the most fascinating age of childhood, and his shouts of laughter ran through Stapleford House from end to end, the remorse that oppressed Timothy Petrick knew no bounds. Of all people in the world this Rupert was one on whom he could have wished the estates to devolve; yet Rupert, by Timothy's own desperate strategy at the time of his birth, had been ousted from all inheritance of them; and, since he did not mean to remarry, the manors would pass to his brother and his brother's children, who would be nothing to him, and whose boasted pedigree on one side would be nothing to his Rupert's after all.

Had he only left the first will of his grandfather alone!

His mind ran on the wills continually, both of which were in existence, and the first, the cancelled one, in his own possession. Night after night, when the servants were all abed, and the click of safety locks sounded as loud as a crash, he looked at that first will, and wished it had been the second and not the first.

The crisis came at last. One night, after having enjoyed the boy's company for hours, he could no longer bear that his beloved Rupert of the aristocratic blood should be dispossessed; and he committed the felonious deed of altering the date of the earlier will to a fortnight later, which made its execution appear subsequent to the date of the second will already proved. He then boldly propounded the first will as the second.

His brother Edward submitted to what appeared to be not only incontestable fact, but a far more likely disposition of old Timothy's property; for, like many others, he had been much surprised at the limitations defined in the other will, having no clue to their cause. He joined his brother Timothy in setting aside the hitherto accepted document, and matters went on in their usual course, there being no dispositions in the substituted will differing from those in the other, except such as related to a future which had not yet arrived.

The years moved on. Rupert had not yet revealed the anxiously expected historic lineaments which should foreshadow the political abilities of the ducal family aforesaid, when it happened on a certain day that Timothy Petrick made the acquaintance of a well-known physician of Budmouth, who had been the medical adviser and friend of the late Mrs Petrick's family for many years; though after Annetta's marriage, and consequent removal to Stapleford, he had seen no more of her, the neighbouring practitioner who attended the Petricks having then become her doctor as a matter of course. Timothy was impressed by the insight and knowledge disclosed in the conversation of the Budmouth physician, and the acquaintance ripening to intimacy, the physician alluded to a form of hallucination to which Annetta's mother and grandmother had been subject – that of believing in certain dreams as realities. He delicately inquired if Timothy had ever noticed anything of the sort in his wife during her lifetime; he, the physician, had fancied that he discerned germs of the same peculiarity in Annetta when he attended her in her girlhood. One explanation begat another, till the dumbfoundered Timothy Petrick was persuaded in his own mind that Annetta's confession to him had been based on a delusion.

'You look down in the mouth?' said the doctor, pausing.

'A bit unmanned. 'Tis unexpected-like,' sighed Timothy.

But he could hardly believe it possible; and, thinking it best to be frank with the doctor, told him the whole story which, till now, he had never related to living man, save his dying grandfather. To his surprise, the physician informed him that such a form of delusion was precisely what he would have expected from Annetta's antecedents at such a physical crisis in her life.

Petrick prosecuted his inquiries elsewhere; and the upshot of his labours was, briefly, that a comparison of dates and places showed irrefutably that his poor wife's assertion could not possibly have foundation in fact. The young Marquis of her tender passion – a highly moral and bright-minded nobleman – had gone abroad the year before Annetta's marriage, and had not returned till after her death. The young girl's love for him had been a delicate ideal dream – no more.

Timothy went home, and the boy ran out to meet him; whereupon a strangely dismal feeling of discontent took possession of his soul. After all, then, there was nothing but plebeian blood in the veins of the heir to his name and estates; he was not to be succeeded by a noble-natured line. To be sure, Rupert was his son physically; but that glory and halo he believed him to have inherited from the ages, outshining that of his brother's children, had departed from Rupert's brow for ever; he could no longer read history in the boy's face, and centuries of domination in his eyes.

His manner towards his son grew colder and colder from that day forward; and it was with bitterness of heart that he discerned the characteristic features of the Petricks unfolding themselves by degrees. Instead of the elegant knife-edged nose, so typical of the Dukes of Southwesterland, there began to appear on his face the broad nostril and hollow bridge of his grandfather Timothy. No illustrious line of politicians was promised a continuator in that graying blue eye, for it was acquiring the expression of the orb of a particularly objectionable cousin of his own; and, instead of the mouth-curves which had thrilled

Parliamentary audiences in speeches now bound in calf in every well-ordered library, there was the bull-lip of that very uncle of his who had had the misfortune with the signature of a gentleman's will, and had been transported for life in consequence.

To think how he himself, too, had sinned in this same matter of a will for this mere fleshly reproduction of a wretched old uncle whose very name he wished to forget! The boy's Christian name, even, was an imposture and an irony, for it implied hereditary force and brilliancy to which he plainly would never attain. The consolation of real sonship was always left him certainly; but he could not help groaning to himself, 'Why cannot a son be one's own and somebody else's likewise!'

The Marquis was shortly afterwards in the neighbourhood of Stapleford, and Timothy Petrick met him, and eyed his noble countenance admiringly. The next day, when Petrick was in his study, somebody knocked at the door.

'Who's there?'

'Rupert.'

'I'll Rupert thee, you young impostor! Say, only a poor commonplace Petrick!' his father grunted. 'Why didn't you have a voice like the Marquis's I saw yesterday?' he continued, as the lad came in. 'Why haven't you his looks, and a way of commanding, as if you'd done it for centuries – hey?'

'Why? How can you expect it, father, when I'm not related to him?'

'Ugh! Then you ought to be!' growled his father.

As the narrator paused, the surgeon, the Colonel, the historian, the Spark, and others exclaimed that such subtle and instructive psychological studies as this (now that psychology was so much in demand) were precisely the tales they desired, as members of a scientific club, and begged the master-maltster to tell another curious mental delusion.

The maltster shook his head, and feared he was not genteel enough to tell another story with a sufficiently moral tone in it to suit the club; he would prefer to leave the next to a better man.

The Colonel had fallen into reflection. True it was, he observed, that the more dreamy and impulsive nature of woman engendered within her erratic fancies, which often started her on strange tracks, only to abandon them in sharp revulsion at the dictates of her common sense – sometimes with ludicrous effect. Events which had caused a lady's action to set in a particular direction might continue to enforce the same line of conduct, while she, like a mangle, would start on a sudden in a contrary course, and end where she began.

The Vice-President laughed, and applauded the Colonel, adding that there surely lurked a story somewhere behind that sentiment, if he were not much mistaken.

The Colonel fixed his face to a good narrative pose, and went on without further preamble.

DAME THE SEVENTH
ANNA, LADY BAXBY

BY THE COLONEL

It was in the time of the great Civil War – if I should not rather, as a loyal subject, call it, with Clarendon, the Great Rebellion. It was, I say, at that unhappy period of our history that, towards the autumn of a particular year, the Parliament forces sat down before Sherton Castle with over seven thousand foot and four pieces of cannon. The Castle, as we all know, was in that century owned and occupied by one of the Earls of Severn, and garrisoned for his assistance by a certain noble Marquis who commanded the King's troops in these parts. The said Earl, as well as the young Lord Baxby, his eldest son, were away from home just now, raising forces for the King elsewhere. But there were present in the Castle, when the besiegers arrived before it, the son's fair wife Lady Baxby, and her servants, together with some friends and near relatives of her husband; and the defence was so good and well-considered that they anticipated no great danger.

The Parliamentary forces were also commanded by a noble lord – for the nobility were by no means, at this stage of the war, all on the King's side – and it had been observed during his approach in the night-time, and in the morning when the reconnoitring took place, that he appeared sad and much depressed. The truth was that, by a strange freak of destiny, it had come to pass that the stronghold he was set to reduce was the home of his own sister, whom he had tenderly loved during her maidenhood, and whom he loved now, in spite of the estrangement which had resulted from hostilities with her husband's family. He believed, too, that, notwithstanding this cruel division, she still was sincerely attached to him.

His hesitation to point his ordnance at the walls was inexplicable to those who were strangers to his family history. He remained in the field on the north side of the Castle (called by his name to this day because of his encampment there) till it occurred to him to send a messenger to his sister Anna with a letter, in which he earnestly requester her, as she valued her life, to steal out of the place by the little gate to the south, and make away in that direction to the residence of some friends.

Shortly after he saw, to his great surprise, coming from the front of the Castle walls a lady on horseback, with a single attendant. She rode straight forward into the field, and up the slope to where his army and tents were spread. It was not till she got quite near that he discerned her to be his sister Anna; and much was he alarmed that she should have run such risk as to sally out in the face of his forces without knowledge of their proceedings, when at any moment their first discharge might have burst forth, to her own destruction in such exposure. She dismounted before she was quite close to him, and he saw that her familiar face, though pale, was not at all tearful, as it would have been in their younger days. Indeed, if the particulars as handed down are to be believed, he was in a more tearful state than she, in his anxiety about her. He called her into his tent, out of the gaze of those around; for though many of the soldiers were honest and serious-minded men, he could not bear that she who had been his dear companion in childhood should be exposed to curious observation in this her great grief.

When they were alone in the tent he clasped her in his arms, for he had not seen her since those happier days when, at the commencement of the war, her husband and himself had been of the same mind about the arbitrary conduct of the King, and had little dreamt that they would not go to extremes together. She was the calmer of the two, it is said, and was the first to speak connectedly.

'William, I have come to you,' said she, 'but not to save myself as you suppose. Why, O, why do you persist in supporting this disloyal cause, and grieving us so?'

'Say not that,' he replied hastily. 'If truth hides at the bottom of a well, why should you suppose justice to be in high places? I am for the right at any price. Anna, leave the Castle; you are my sister; come away, my dear, and save thy life!'

'Never!' says she. 'Do you plan to carry out this attack, and level the Castle indeed?'

'Most certainly I do,' says he. 'What meaneth this army around us if not so?'

'Then you will find the bones of your sister buried in the ruins you cause!' said she. And without another word she turned and left him.

'Anna – abide with me!' he entreated. 'Blood is thicker than water, and what is there in common between you and your husband now?'

But she shook her head and would not hear him; and hastening out, mounted her horse, and returned towards the Castle as she had come. Ay, many's the time when I have been riding to hounds across that field that I have thought of that scene!

When she had quite gone down the field, and over the intervening ground, and round the bastion, so that he could no longer even see the tip of her mare's white tail, he was much more deeply moved by emotions concerning her and her welfare than he had been while she was before him. He wildly reproached himself that he had not detained her by force for her own good, so that, come what might, she would be under his protection and not under that of her husband, whose impulsive nature rendered him too open to instantaneous impressions and sudden changes of plan; he was now acting in this cause and now in that, and lacked the cool judgment necessary for the protection of a woman in these troubled times. Her brother thought of her words again and again, and sighed, and even considered if a sister were not of more value than a principle, and if he would not have acted more naturally in throwing in his lot with hers.

The delay of the besiegers in attacking the Castle was said to be entirely owing to this distraction on the part of their leader, who remained on the spot attempting some indecisive operations, and parleying with the Marquis then in command, with far inferior forces, within the Castle. It never occurred to him that in the meantime the young Lady Baxby, his sister, was in much the same mood as himself. Her brother's familiar voice and eyes, much worn and fatigued by keeping the field, and by family distractions on account of this unhappy feud, rose upon her vision all the afternoon, and as day waned she grew more and more Parliamentarian in her principles, though the only arguments which had addressed themselves to her were those of family ties.

Her husband, General Lord Baxby, had been expected to return all the day from his excursion into the east of the country, a message having been sent to him informing him of what had happened at home; and in the evening he arrived with reinforcements in unexpected numbers. Her brother retreated before these to a hill near Ivell, four or five miles off, to afford the men and himself some repose. Lord Baxby duly placed his forces, and there was no longer any immediate danger. By this time Lady Baxby's feelings were more Parliamentarian than ever, and in her fancy the fagged countenance of her brother, beaten back by her husband, seemed to reproach her for heartlessnes. When her husband entered her apartment, ruddy and boisterous, and full of hope, she received him but sadly; and upon his casually uttering some slighting words about her brother's withdrawal, which seemed to convey an imputation upon his courage, she resented them, and retorted that he, Lord Baxby himself, had been against the Court-party at first, where it would be much more to his credit if he were at present, and showing her brother's consistency of opinion, instead of supporting the lying policy of the King (as she called it) for the sake of a barren principle of loyalty, which was but an empty expression when a King was not at one with his people. The dissension grew bitter between them, reaching to little less than a hot quarrel, both being quick-tempered souls.

Lord Baxby was weary with his long day's march and other excitements, and soon retired to bed. His lady followed some time after. Her husband slept profoundly, but not so she; she sat brooding by the window-slit, and lifting the curtain looked forth upon the hills without.

In the silence between the footfalls of the sentinels she could hear faint sounds of her brother's camp on the distant hills, where the soldiery had hardly settled as yet into their bivouac since their evening's retreat. The first frosts of autumn had touched the grass, and shrivelled the more delicate leaves of the creepers; and she thought of William sleeping on the chilly ground, under the strain of these hardships. Tears flooded her eyes as she returned to her husband's imputations upon his courage, as if there could be any doubt of Lord William's courage after what he had done in the past days.

Lord Baxby's long and reposeful breathings in his comfortable bed vexed her now, and she came to a determination on an impulse. Hastily lighting a taper, she wrote on a scrap of paper: '*Blood is thicker than water, dear William – I will come*'; and with this in her hand, she went to the door of the room, and out upon the stairs; on second thoughts turning back for a moment, to put on her husband's hat and cloak – not the one he was daily wearing – that if seen in the twilight she might at a casual glance appear as some lad or hanger-on of one of the household women; thus accoutred she descended a flight of circular stairs, at the bottom of which was a door opening upon the terrace towards the west, in the direction of her brother's position. Her object was to slip out without the sentry seeing her, get to the stables, arouse one of the varlets, and send him ahead of her along the highway with the note to warn her brother of her approach to throw in her lot with his.

She was still in the shadow of the wall on the west terrace, waiting for the sentinel to be quite out of the way, when her ears were greeted by a voice, saying, from the adjoining shade –

'Here I be!'

The tones were the tones of a woman. Lady Baxby made no reply, and stood close to the wall.

'My Lord Baxby,' the voice continued; and she could recognize in it the local accent of some girl from the little town of Sherton, close at hand. 'I be tired of waiting, my dear Lord Baxby! I was afeared you would never come!'

Lady Baxby flushed hot to her toes.

'How the wench loves him!' she said to herself, reasoning from the tones of the voice, which were plaintive and sweet and tender as a bird's. She changed from the home-hating truant to the strategic wife in one moment.

'Hist!' she said.

'My lord, you told me ten o'clock, and 'tis near twelve now,' continues the other. 'How could ye keep me waiting so if you love me as you said? I should have stuck to my lover in the Parliament troops if it had not been for thee, my dear lord!'

There was not the least doubt that Lady Baxby had been mistaken for her husband by this intriguing damsel. Here was a pretty underhand business! Here were sly manoeuvrings! Here was faithlessness! Here was a precious assignation surprised in the midst! Her wicked husband, whom till this very moment she had ever deemed the soul of good faith – how could he!

Lady Baxby precipitately retreated to the door in the turret, closed it, locked it, and ascended one round of the staircase, where there was a loophole. 'I am not coming! I, Lord Baxby, despise 'ee and all your wanton tribe!' she hissed through the opening; and then crept upstairs as firmly rooted in Royalist principles as any man in the Castle.

Her husband still slept the sleep of the weary, well-fed, and well-drunken, if not of the virtuous; and Lady Baxby quickly disrobed herself without assistance – being, indeed, supposed by her woman to have retired to rest long ago. Before lying down she noiselessly locked the door and placed the key under her pillow. More than that, she got a staylace, and, creeping up to her lord, in great stealth tied the lace in a tight knot to one of his long locks of hair, attaching the other end of the lace to the bedpost; for, being tired herself now, she feared she might sleep heavily; and, if her husband should wake, this would be a delicate hint that she had discovered all.

It is added that, to make assurance trebly sure, her gentle ladyship, when she had lain down to rest, held her lord's hand in her own during the whole of the night. But this is old-wives' gossip, and not corroborated. What Lord Baxby thought and said when he awoke the next morning, and found himself so strangely tethered, is likewise only matter of conjecture; though there is no reason to suppose that his rage was great. The extent of his culpability as regards the intrigue was this much: that, while halting at a cross-road near Sherton that day, he had flirted with a pretty young woman, who seemed nothing loth, and had invited her to the castle terrace after dark – an invitation which he quite forgot on his arrival home.

The subsequent relations of Lord and Lady Baxby were not again greatly embittered by quarrels, so far as is known; though the husband's conduct in later life was occasionally eccentric, and the vicissitudes of his public career culminated in long exile. The siege of the Castle was not regularly undertaken till two or three years later than the time I have been describing, when Lady Baxby and all the women therein, except the wife of the then Governor, had been removed to safe distance. That memorable siege of fifteen days by Fairfax, and the surrender of the old place on an August evening, is matter of history, and need not be told by me.

The Man of Family spoke approvingly across to the Colonel when the Club had done smiling, declaring that the story was an absolutely faithful page of history, as he had good reason to know, his own people having been engaged in that well-known scrimmage. He asked if the Colonel had ever heard the equally well-authenticated, though less martial tale of a certain Lady Penelope, who lived in the same century, and not a score of miles from the same place?

The Colonel had not heard it, nor had anybody except the local historian; and the inquirer was induced to proceed forthwith.

DAME THE EIGHTH
THE LADY PENELOPE

BY THE MAN OF FAMILY

In going out of Casterbridge by the low-lying road which eventually conducts to the town of Ivell, you see on the right hand an ivied manor-house, flanked by battlemented towers, and more than usually distinguished by the size of its many mullioned windows. Though still of good capacity, the building is somewhat reduced from its original grand proportions; it has, moreover, been shorn of the fair estate which once appertained to its lord, with the exception of a few acres of park-land immediately around the mansion. This was formerly the seat of the ancient and knightly family of the Drenghards, or Drenkhards, now extinct in the male line, whose name, according to the local chronicles, was interpreted to mean *Strenuus Miles, vel Potator,* though certain members of the family were averse to the latter signification, and a duel was fought by one of them on that account, as is well known. With this, however, we are not now concerned.

In the early part of the reign of the first King James there was visiting near this place of the Drenghards a lady of noble family and extraordinary beauty. She was of the purest descent; ah, there's seldom such blood nowadays as hers! She possessed no great wealth, it was said, but was sufficiently endowed. Her beauty was so perfect, and her manner so entrancing, that suitors seemed to spring out of the ground wherever she went, a sufficient cause of anxiety to the Countess her mother, her only living parent. Of these there were three in particular, whom neither her mother's complaints of prematurity, nor the ready raillery of the maiden herself, could effectually put off. The said gallants were a certain Sir John Gale, a Sir William Hervy, and the well-known Sir George Drenghard, one of the Drenghard family before-mentioned. They had, curiously enough, all been equally honoured with the distinction of knighthood, and their schemes for seeing her were manifold, each fearing that one of the others would steal a march over himself. Not content with calling, on every imaginable excuse, at the house of the relative with whom she sojourned, they intercepted her in rides and in walks; and if any one of them chanced to surprise another in the act of paying her marked attentions, the encounter often ended in an altercation of great violence. So heated and impassioned, indeed, would they become, that the lady hardly felt herself safe in their company at such times, notwithstanding that she was a brave and buxom damsel, not easily put out, and with a daring spirit of humour in her composition, if not of coquetry.

At one of these altercations, which had place in her relative's grounds, and was unusually bitter, threatening to result in a duel, she found it necessary to assert herself. Turning haughtily upon the pair of disputants, she declared that whichever should be the first to break the peace between them, no matter what the provocation, that man should never be admitted to her presence again; and thus would she effectually stultify the aggressor by making the promotion of a quarrel a distinct bar to its object.

While the two knights were wearing rather a crestfallen appearance at her reprimand, the third, never far off, came upon the scene, and she repeater her caveat to him also. Seeing, then, how great was the concern of all at her peremptory mood, the lady's manner softened, and she said with a roguish smile –

'Have patience, have patience, you foolish men! Only bide your time quietly, and, in faith, I will marry you all in turn!'

They laughed heartily at this sally, all three together, as though they were the best of friends; at which she blushed, and showed some embarrassment, not having realized that her arch jest would have sounded so strange when uttered. The meeting which resulted thus, however, had its good effect in checking the bitterness of their rivalry; and they repeated her speech to their relatives and acquaintance with a hilarious frequency and publicity that the lady little divined, or she might have blushed and felt more embarrassment still.

In the course of time the position resolved itself, and the beauteous Lady Penelope (as she was called) made up her mind; her choice being the eldest of the three knights, Sir George Drenghard, owner of the mansion aforesaid, which thereupon became her home; and her husband being a pleasant man, and his family, though not so noble, of as good repute as her own, all things seemed to show that she had reckoned wisely in honouring him with her preference.

But what may lie behind the sill and silent veil of the future none can foretell. In the course of a few months the husband of her choice died of his convivialities (as if, indeed, to bear out his name), and the Lady Penelope was left alone as mistress of his house. By this time she had apparently quite forgotten her careless declaration to her lovers collectively; but the lovers themselves had not forgotten it; and, as she would now be free to take a second one of them, Sir John Gale appeared at her door as early in her widowhood as it was proper and seemly to do so.

She gave him little encouragement; for, of the two remaining, her best beloved was Sir William, of whom, if the truth must be told, she had often thought during her short married life. But he had not yet reappeared. Her heart began to be so much with him now that she contrived to convey to him, by indirect hints through his friends, that she would not be displeased by a renewal of his former attentions. Sir William, however, misapprehended her gentle signalling, and from excellent, though mistaken motives of delicacy, delayed to intrude himself upon her for a long time. Meanwhile Sir John, now created a baronet, was unremitting, and she began to grow somewhat piqued at the backwardness of him she secretly desired to be forward.

'Never mind,' her friends said jestingly to her (knowing of her humorous remark, as everybody did, that she would marry them all three if they would have patience) – 'never mind; why hesitate upon the order of them? Take 'em as they come.'

This vexed her still more, and regretting deeply, as she had often done, that such a careless speech should ever have passed her lips, she fairly broke down under Sir John's importunity, and accepted his hand. They were married on a fine spring morning, about the very time at which the unfortunate Sir William discovered her preference for him, and was beginning to hasten home from a foreign court to declare his unaltered devotion to her. On his arrival in England he learnt the sad truth.

If Sir William suffered at her precipitancy under what she had deemed his neglect, the Lady Penelope herself suffered more. She had not long been the wife of Sir John Gale before he showed a disposition to retaliate upon her for the trouble and delay she had put him to in winning her. With increasing frequency he would tell her that, as far as he could perceive, she was an article not worth such labour as he had bestowed in obtaining it, and such snubbings as he had taken from his rivals on the same account. These and other cruel things he repeated till he made the lady weep sorely, and wellnigh broke her spirit, though she had formerly been such a mettlesome dame. By degrees it became perceptible to all her friends that her life was a very unhappy one; and the fate of the fair woman seemed yet the harder in that it was her own stately mansion, left to her sole use by her first husband, which her second had entered into and was enjoying, his being but a mean and meagre erection.

But such is the flippancy of friends that when she met them, and secretly confided her grief to their ears, they would say cheerily, 'Lord, never mind, my dear; there's a third to come yet!' – at which maladroit remark she would show much indignation, and tell them they should know better than to trifle on so solemn a theme. Yet that the poor lady would have been only too happy to be the wife of the third, instead of Sir John whom she had taken, was painfully obvious, and much she was blamed for her foolish choice by some people. Sir William, however, had returned to foreign cities on learning the news of her marriage, and had never been heard of since.

Two or three years of suffering were passed by Lady Penelope as the despised and chidden wife of this man Sir John, amid regrets that she had so greatly mistaken him, and sighs for one whom she thought never to see again, till it chanced that her husband fell sick of some slight ailment. One day after this, when she was sitting in his room, looking from the window upon the expanse in front, she beheld, approaching the house on foot, a form she seemed to know well. Lady Penelope withdrew silently from the sickroom, and descended to the hall, whence, through the doorway, she saw entering between the two round towers which at that time flanked the gateway, Sir William Hervy, as she had surmised, but looking thin and travel-worn. She advanced into the courtyard to meet him.

'I was passing through Casterbridge,' he said, with faltering deference, 'and I walked out to ask after your ladyship's health. I felt that I could do not less; and, of course, to pay my respects to your good husband, my heretofore acquaintance. . . But O, Penelope, th'st look sick and sorry!'

'I am heartsick, that's all,' said she.

They could see in each other an emotion which neither wished to express, and they stood thus a long time with tears in their eyes.

'He does not treat 'ee well, I hear,' said Sir William in a low voice. 'May God in Heaven forgive him; but it is asking a great deal!'

'Hush, hush!' said she hastily.

'Nay, but I will speak what I may honestly say,' he answered. 'I am not under your roof, and my tongue is free. Why didst not wait for me, Penelope, or send to me a more overt letter? I would have travelled night and day to come!'

'Too late, William; you must not ask it,' said she, endeavouring to quiet him as in old times. 'My husband just now is unwell. He will grow better in a day or two, maybe. You must call again and see him before you leave Casterbridge.'

As she said this their eyes met. Each was thinking of her lightsome words about taking the three men in turn; each thought that two-thirds of that promise had been fulfilled. But as if it were unpleasant to her that this recollection should have arisen, she spoke again quickly: 'Come again in a day or two, when my husband will be well enough to see you.'

Sir William departed without entering the house, and she returned to Sir John's chamber. He, rising from his pillow, said, 'To whom hast been talking, wife, in th' courtyard? I heard voices there.'

She hesitated, and he repeated the question more impatiently.

'I do not wish to tell you now,' said she.

'But I will know!' said he.

Then she answered, 'Sir William Hervy.'

'By God, I thought as much!' cried Sir John, drops of perspiration standing on his white face. 'A sulking villain! A sick man's ears are keen, my lady. I heard that they were lover-like tones, and he called 'ee by your Christian name. These be your intrigues, my lady, when I am off my legs a while!'

'On my honour,' cried she, 'you do me a wrong. I swear I did not know of his coming!'

'Swear as you will,' said Sir John, 'I don't believe 'ee.' And with this he taunted her, and worked himself into a greater passion which much increased his illness. His lady sat still, brooding. There was that upon her face which had seldom been there since her marriage; and she seemed to think anew of what she had so lightly said in the days of her freedom, when her three lovers were one and all coveting her hand. 'I began at the wrong end of them,' she murmured. 'My God – that did I!'

'What?' said he.

'A trifle,' said she. 'I spoke to myself only.'

It was somewhat strange that after this day, while she went about the house with even a sadder face than usual, her churlish husband grew worse; and what was more, to the surprise of all, though to the regret of few, he died a fortnight later. Sir William had not called upon him as he had promised, having received a private communication from Lady Penelope, frankly informing him that to do so would be inadvisable, by reason of her husband's temper.

Now when Sir John was gone, and his remains carried to his family burying-place in another part of England, the lady began in due time to wonder whither Sir William had betaken himself. But she had been cured of precipitancy (if ever woman were), and was prepared to wait her whole lifetime a widow if the said Sir William should not reappear. Her life was now passed mostly within the walls, or in promenading between the pleasaunce and the bowling-green; and she very seldom went even so far as the high road which then gave entrance from the north, though it has now, and for many years, been diverted to the south side. Her patience was rewarded (if love be in any case a reward); for one day, many months after her second husband's death, a messenger arrived at her gate with the intelligence that Sir William Hervy was again in Casterbridge, and would be glad to know if it were her pleasure that he should wait upon her.

It need hardly be said that permission was joyfully granted, and within two hours her lover stood before her, a more thoughtful man than formerly, but in all essential respects the same man, generous, modest to diffidence, and sincere. The reserve which womanly decorum threw over her manner was but too obviously artificial, and when he said, 'The ways of Providence are strange,' and added after a moment, 'and merciful likewise,' she could not conceal her agitation, and burst into tears upon his neck.

'But this is too soon,' she said, starting back.

'But no,' said he. 'You are eleven months gone in widowhood, and it is not as if Sir John had been a good husband to you.'

His visits grew pretty frequent now, as may well be guessed, and in a month or two he began to urge her to an early union. But she counselled a little longer delay.

'Why?' said he. 'Surely I have waited long! Life is short; we are getting older every day, and I am the last of the three.'

'Yes,' said the lady frankly. 'And that is why I would not have you hasten. Our marriage may seem so strange to everybody, after my unlucky remark on that occasion we know so well, and which so many others know likewise, thanks to talebearers.'

On this representation he conceded a little space, for the sake of her good name. But the destined day of their marriage at last arrived, and it was a gay time for the villagers and all concerned, and the bells in the parish church rang from noon till night. Thus at last she was united to the man who had loved her the most tenderly of them all, who but for his reticence might perhaps have been the first to win her. Often did he say to himself, 'How wondrous that her words should have been fulfilled! Many a truth hath been spoken in jest, but never a more remarkable one!' The noble lady herself preferred not to dwell on the coincidence, a certain shyness, if not shame, crossing her fair face at any allusion thereto.

But people will have their say, sensitive souls or none, and their sayings on this third occasion took a singular shape. 'Surely,' they whispered, 'there is something more than chance in this. . . The death of the first was possibly natural; but what of the death of the second, who ill-used her, and whom, loving the third so desperately, she must have wished out of the way?'

Then they pieced together sundry trivial incidents of Sir John's illness, and dwelt upon the indubitable truth that he had grown worse after her lover's unexpected visit; till a very sinister theory was built up as to the hand she may have had in Sir John's premature demise. But nothing of this suspicion was said openly, for she was a lady of noble birth – nobler, indeed, than either of her husbands – and what people suspected they feared to express in formal accusation.

The mansion that she occupied had been left to her for so long a time as she should choose to reside in it, and, having a regard for the spot, she had coaxed Sir William to remain there. But in the end it was unfortunate; for one day, when in the full tide of his happiness, he was walking among the willows near the gardens, where he overheard a conversation between some basketmakers who were cutting the osiers for their use. In this fatal dialogue the suspicions of the neighbouring townsfolk were revealed to him for the first time.

'A cupboard close to his bed, and the key in her pocket. Ah!' said one.

'And a blue phial therein – h'm!' said another.

'And spurge-laurel leaves among the hearth-ashes. Oh-oh!' said a third.

On his return home Sir William seemed to have aged years. But he said nothing; indeed, it was a thing impossible. And from that hour a ghastly estrangement began. She could not understand it, and simply waited. One day he said, however, 'I must go abroad.'

'Why?' said she. 'William, have I offended you?'

'No,' said he; 'but I must go.'

She could coax little more out of him, and in itself there was nothing unnatural in his departure, for he had been a wanderer from his youth. In a few days he started off, apparently quite another man than he who had rushed to her side so devotedly a few months before.

It is not known when, or how, the rumours, which were so thick in the atmosphere around her, actually reached the Lady Penelope's ears, but that they did reach her there is no doubt. It was impossible that they should not; the district teemed with them; they rustled in the air like night-birds of evil omen. Then a reason for her husband's departure occurred to her appalled mind, and a loss of health became quickly apparent. She dwindled thin in the face, and the veins in her temples could all be distinctly traced. An inner fire seemed to be withering her away. Her rings fell off her fingers, and her arms hung like the flails of the threshers, though they had till lately been so round and so elastic. She wrote to her husband repeatedly, begging him to return to her; but he, being in extreme and wretched doubt, moreover, knowing nothing of her ill-health, and never suspecting that the rumours had reached her also, deemed absence best, and postponed his return a while, giving various good reasons for his delay.

At length, however, when the Lady Penelope had given birth to a still-born child, her mother, the Countess, addressed a letter to Sir William, requesting him to come back to her if he wished to see her alive; since she was wasting away of some mysterious disease, which seemed to be rather mental than physical. It was evident that his mother-in-law knew nothing of the secret, for she lived at a distance; but Sir William promptly hastened home, and stood beside the bed of his now dying wife.

'Believe me, William,' she said when they were alone, 'I am innocent – innocent!'

'Of what?' said he. 'Heaven forbid that I should accuse you of anything!'

'But you do accuse me – silently!' she gasped. 'I could not write thereon – and ask you to hear me. It was too much, too degrading. But would that I had been less proud! They suspect me of poisoning him, William! But, O my dear husband, I am innocent of that wicked crime! He died naturally. I loved you – too soon; but that was all!'

Nothing availed to save her. The worm had gnawed too far into her heart before Sir William's return for anything to be remedial now; and in a few weeks she breathed her last. After her death the people spoke louder, and her conduct became a subject of public discussion. A little later on, the physician who had attended the late Sir John heard the rumour, and came down from the place near London to which he latterly had retired, with the express purpose of calling upon Sir William Hervy, now staying in Casterbridge.

He stated that, at the request of a relative of Sir John's, who wished to be assured on the matter by reason of its suddenness, he had, with the assistance of a surgeon, made a private examination of Sir John's body immediately after his decease, and found that it had resulted from purely natural causes. Nobody at this time had breathed a suspicion of foul play, and therefore nothing was said which might afterwards have established her innocence.

It being thus placed beyond doubt that this beautiful and noble lady had been done to death by a vile scandal that was wholly unfounded, her husband was stung with a dreadful remorse at the share he had taken in her misfortunes, and left the country anew, this time never to return alive. He survived her but a few years, and his body was brought home and buried beside his wife's under the tomb which is still visible in the parish church. Until lately there was a good portrait of her, in weeds for her first husband, with a cross in her hand, at the ancestral seat of her family, where she was much pitied, as she deserved to be. Yet there were some severe enough to say – and these not unjust persons in other respects –

that though unquestionably innocent of the crime imputed to her, she had shown an unseemly wantonness in contracting three marriages in such rapid succession; that the untrue suspicion might have been ordered by Providence (who often works indirectly) as a punishment for her self-indulgence. Upon that point I have no opinion to offer.

The reverend the Vice-President, however, the tale being ended, offered as his opinion that her fate ought to be quite clearly recognized as a chastisement. So thought the churchwarden, and also the quiet gentleman sitting near. The latter knew many other instances in point, one of which could be narrated in a few words.

DAME THE NINTH
THE DUCHESS OF HAMPTONSHIRE

BY THE QUIET GENTLEMAN

Some fifty years ago the then Duke of Hamptonshire, fifth of that title, was incontestably the head man in his county, and particularly in the neighbourhood of Batton. He came of the ancient and loyal family of Saxelbye, which, before its ennoblement, had numbered many knightly and ecclesiastical celebrities in its male line. It would have occupied a painstaking county historian a whole afternoon to take rubbings of the numerous effigies and heraldic devices graven to their memory on the brasses, tablets, and altar-tombs in the aisle of the parish church. The Duke himself, however, was a man little attracted by ancient chronicles in stone and metal, even when they concerned his own beginnings. He allowed his mind to linger by preference on the many graceless and unedifying pleasures which his position placed at his command. He could on occasion close the mouths of his dependants by a good bomb-like oath, and he argued doggedly with the parson on the virtues of cock-fighting and baiting the bull.

This nobleman's personal appearance was somewhat impressive. His complexion was that of the copper-beech tree. His frame was stalwart, though slightly stooping. His mouth was large, and he carried an unpolished sapling as his walking-stick, except when he carried a spud for cutting up any thistle he encountered on his walks. His castle stood in the midst of a park, surrounded by dusky elms, except to the southward; and when the moon shone out, the gleaming stone façade, backed by heavy boughs, was visible from the distant high road as a white spot on the surface of darkness. Though called a castle, the building was little fortified, and had been erected with greater eye to internal convenience than those crannied places of defence to which the name strictly appertains. It was a castellated mansion as regular as a chessboard on its ground-plan, ornamented with make-believe bastions and machicolations, behind which were stacks of battlemented chimneys. On still mornings, at the fire-lighting hour, when ghostly housemaids stalk the corridors, and thin streaks of light through the shutter-chinks lend startling winks and smiles to ancestors on canvas, twelve or fifteen thin stems of blue smoke sprouted upwards from these chimney-tops, and spread into a flat canopy on high. Around the site stretched ten thousand acres of good, fat, unimpeachable soil, plentiful in glades and lawns wherever visible from the castle-windows, and merging in homely arable where screened from the too curious eye by ingeniously-contrived plantations.

Some way behind the owner of all this came the second man in the parish, the rector, the Honourable and Reverend Mr Oldbourne, a widower, over stiff and stern for a clergyman, whose severe white neck-cloth, well-kept gray hair, and right-lined face betokened none of those sympathetic traits whereon depends so much of a parson's power to do good among his fellow-creatures. The last, far-removed man of the series – altogether the Neptune of these local primaries – was the curate, Mr Alwyn Hill. He was a handsome young deacon with curly hair, dreamy eyes – so dreamy that to look long into them was like ascending and floating among summer clouds – a complexion as fresh as a flower, and a chin absolutely beardless. Though his age was about twenty-five, he looked not much over nineteen.

The rector had a daughter called Emmeline, of so sweet and simple a nature that her beauty was discovered, measured, and inventoried by almost everybody in that part of the country before it was suspected by herself to exist. She had been bred in comparative solitude; a rencounter with men troubled and confused her. Whenever a strange visitor came to her father's house she slipped into the orchard and remained till he was gone, ridiculing her weakness in apostrophes, but unable to overcome it. Her virtues lay in no resistant force of character, but in a natural inappetency for evil things, which to her were as unmeaning as joints of flesh to a herbivorous creature. Her charms of person, manner, and mind, had been clear for some time to the Antinous in orders, and no less so to the Duke, who, though scandalously ignorant of dainty phrases, ever showing a clumsy manner towards the gentler sex, and, in short, not at all a lady's man, took fire to a degree that was wellnigh terrible at sudden sight of Emmeline, a short time after she was turned seventeen.

It occurred one afternoon at the corner of a shrubbery between the castle and the rectory, where the Duke was standing to watch the heaving of a mole, when the fair girl brushed past at a distance of a few yards, in the full light of the sun, and without hat or bonnet. The Duke went home like a man who had seen a spirit. He ascended to the picture-gallery of his castle, and there passed some time in staring at the bygone beauties of his line as if he had never before considered what an important part those specimens of womankind had played in the evolution of the Saxelbye race. He dined alone, drank rather freely, and declared to himself that Emmeline Oldbourne must be his.

Meanwhile there had unfortunately arisen between the curate and this girl some sweet and secret understanding. Particulars of the attachment remained unknown then and always, but it was plainly not approved of by her father. His procedure was cold, hard, and inexorable. Soon the curate disappeared from the parish, almost suddenly, after bitter and hard words had been heard to pass between him and the rector one evening in the garden, intermingled with which, like the cries of the dying in the din of battle, were the beseeching sobs of a woman. Not long after this it was announced that a marriage between the Duke and Miss Oldbourne was to be solemnized at a surprisingly early date.

The wedding-day came and passed; and she was a Duchess. Nobody seemed to think of the ousted man during the day, or else those who thought of him concealed their meditations. Some of the less subservient ones were disposed to speak in a jocular manner of the august husband and wife, others to make correct and pretty speeches about them, according as their sex and nature dictated. But in the evening, the ringers in the belfry, with whom Alwyn had been a favourite, eased their minds a little concerning the gentle young man, and the possible regrets of the woman he had loved.

'Don't you see something wrong in it all?' said the third bell as he wiped his face. 'I know well enough where she would have liked to stable her horses tonight, when they have done their journey.'

'That is, you would know if you could tell where young Mr Hill is living, which is known to none in the parish.'

'Except to the lady that this ring o' grandsire triples is in honour of.'

Yet these friendly cottagers were at this time far from suspecting the real dimensions of Emmeline's misery, nor was it clear even to those who came into much closer communion with her than they, so well had she concealed her heart-sickness. But bride and bridegroom had not long been home at the castle when the young wife's unhappiness became plainly enough perceptible. Her maids and men said that she was in the habit of turning to the wainscot and shedding stupid scalding tears at a time when a right-minded lady would have been overhauling her wardrobe. She prayed earnestly in the great church-pew, where she sat lonely and insignificant as a mouse in a cell, instead of counting her rings, falling asleep, or amusing herself in silent laughter at the queer old people in the congregation, as previous beauties of the family had done in their time. She seemed to care no more for eating and drinking out of crystal and silver than from a service of earthen vessels. Her head was, in truth, full of something else; and that such was the case was only too obvious to the Duke, her husband. At first he would only taunt her for her folly in thinking of that milk-and-water parson; but as time went on his charges took a more positive shape. He would not believe her assurance that she had in no way communicated with her former lover, nor he with her, since their parting in the presence of her father. This led to some strange scenes between them which need not be detailed; their result was soon to take a catastrophic shape.

One dark quiet evening, about two months after the marriage, a man entered the gate admitting from the highway to the park and avenue which ran up to the house. He arrived within two hundred yards of the walls, when he left the gravelled drive and drew near to the castle by a roundabout path leading into a shrubbery. Here he stood still. In a few minutes the strokes of the castle-clock resounded, and then a female figure entered the same secluded nook from an opposite direction. There the two indistinct persons leapt together like a pair of dewdrops on a leaf; and then they stood apart, facing each other, the woman looking down.

'Emmeline, you begged me to come, and here I am, Heaven forgive me!' said the man hoarsely.

'You are going to emigrate, Alwyn,' she said in broken accents. 'I have heard of it; you sail from Plymouth in three days in the *Western Glory*?'

'Yes. I can live in England no longer. Life is as death to me here,' says he.

'My life is even worse – worse than death. Death would not have driven me to this extremity. Listen, Alwyn – I have sent for you to beg to go with you, or at least to be near you – to do anything so that it be not to stay here.'

'To go away with me?' he said in a startled tone.

'Yes, yes – or under your direction, or by your help in some way! Don't be horrifed at me – you must bear with me whilst I implore it. Nothing short of cruelty would have driven me to this. I could have borne my doom in silence had I been left unmolested; but he tortures me, and I shall soon be in the grave if I cannot escape.'

To his shocked inquiry how her husband tortured her, the Duchess said that it was by jealousy. 'He tries to wring admissions from me concerning you,' she said, 'and will not believe that I have not communicated with you since my engagement to him was settled by my father, and I was forced to agree to it.'

The poor curate said that this was the heaviest news of all. 'He has not personally ill-used you?' he asked.

'Yes,' she whispered.

'What has he done?'

She looked fearfully around, and said, sobbing: 'In trying to make me confess to what I have never done, he adopts plans I dare not describe for terrifying me into a weak state, so that I may own to anything! I resolved to write to you, as I had no other friend.' She added, with dreary irony, 'I thought I would give him some ground for his suspicion, so as not to disgrace his judgment.'

'Do you really mean, Emmeline,' he tremblingly inquired, 'that you – that you want to fly with me?'

'Can you think that I would act otherwise than in earnest at such a time as this?'

He was silent for a minute or more. 'You must not go with me,' he said.

'Why?'

'It would be sin.'

'It *cannot* be sin, for I have never wanted to commit sin in my life; and it isn't likely I would begin now, when I pray every day to die and be sent to Heaven out of my misery!'

'But it is wrong, Emmeline, all the same.'

'Is it wrong to run away from the fire that scorches you?'

'It would look wrong, at any rate, in this case.'

'Alwyn, Alwyn, take me, I beseech you!' she burst out. 'It is not right in general, I know, but it is such an exceptional instance, this. Why has such a severe strain been put upon me? I was doing no harm, injuring no one, helping many people, and expecting happiness; yet trouble came. Can it be that God holds me in derision? I had no supporter – I gave way; and now my life is a burden and a shame to me. . . O, if you only knew how much to me this request to you is – how my life is wrapped up in it, you could not deny me!'

'This is almost beyond endurance – Heaven support us,' he groaned. 'Emmy, you are the Duchess of Hamptonshire, the Duke of Hamptonshire's wife; you must not go with me!'

'And am I then refused? – O, am I refused?' she cried frantically. 'Alwyn, Alwyn, do you say it indeed to me?'

'Yes, I do, dear, tender heart! I do most sadly say it. You must not go. Forgive me, for there is no alternative but refusal. Though I die, though you die, we must not fly together. It is forbidden in God's law. Good-bye, for always and ever!'

He tore himself away, hastened from the shrubbery, and vanished among the trees.

Three days after this meeting and farewell, Alwyn, his soft, handsome features stamped with a haggard hardness that ten years of ordinary wear and tear in the world could scarcely have produced, sailed from Plymouth on a drizzling morning, in the passenger-ship *Western Glory*. When the land had faded behind him he mechanically endeavoured to school himself into a stoical frame of mind. His attempt, backed up by the strong moral staying power that had enabled him to resist the passionate temptation to which Emmeline, in her reckless trustfulness, had exposed him, was rewarded by a certain kind of success, though the murmuring stretch of waters whereon he gazed day after day too often seemed to be articulating to him in tones of her well-remembered voice.

He framed on his journey rules of conduct for reducing to mild proportions the feverish regrets which would occasionally arise and agitate him, when he indulged in visions of what might have been had he not hearkened to the whispers of conscience. He fixed his thoughts for so many hours a day on philosophical passages in the volumes he had brought with him, allowing himself now and then a few minutes' thought of Emmeline, with the strict yet reluctant niggardliness of an ailing epicure proportioning the rank drinks that cause his malady. The voyage was marked by the usual incidents of a sailing-passage in those days – a storm, a calm, a man overboard, a birth, and a funeral – the latter sad event being one in which he, as the only clergyman on board, officiated, reading the service ordained for the purpose. The ship duly arrived at Boston early in the month following, and thence he proceeded to Providence to seek out a distant relative.

After a short stay at Providence he returned again to Boston, and by applying himself to a serious occupation made good progress in shaking off the dreary melancholy which enveloped him even now. Distracted and weakened in his beliefs by his recent experiences, he decided that he could not for a time worthily fill the office of a minister of religion, and applied for the mastership of a school. Some introductions, given him before starting, were useful now, and he soon became known as a respectable scholar and gentleman to the trustees of one of the colleges. This ultimately led to his retirement from the school and installation in the college as Professor of rhetoric and oratory.

Here and thus he lived on, exerting himself solely because of a conscientious determination to do his duty. He passed his winter evenings in turning sonnets and elegies, often giving his thoughts voice in 'Lines to an Unfortunate Lady', while his summer leisure at the same hour would be spent in watching the lengthening shadows from his window, and fancifully comparing them with the shades of his own life. If he walked, he mentally inquired which was the eastern quarter of the landscape, and thought of two thousand miles of water that way, and of what was beyond it. In a word he was at all spare times dreaming of her who was only a memory to him, and would probably never be more.

Nine years passed by, and under their wear and tear Alwyn Hill's face lost a great many of the attractive characteristics which had formerly distinguished it. He was kind to his pupils and affable to all who came in contact with him; but the kernel of his life, his secret, was kept as snugly shut up as though he had been dumb. In talking to his acquaintances of England and his life there, he omitted the episode of Batton Castle and Emmeline as if it had no existence in his calendar at all. Though of towering importance to himself, it had filled but a short and small fragment of time, and ephemeral season which would have been wellnigh imperceptible, even to him, at this distance, but for the incident it enshrined.

One day, at this date, when cursorily glancing over an old English newspaper, he observed a paragraph which, short as it was, contained for him whole tomes of thrilling information – rung with more passion-stirring rhythm than the collected cantos of all the poets. It was an announcement of the death of the Duke of Hamptonshire, leaving behind him a widow, but no children.

The current of Alwyn's thoughts now completely changed. On looking again at the newspaper he found it to be one that was sent him long ago, and had been carelessly thrown aside. But for an accidental overhauling of the waste journals in his study he might not have known of the event for years. At this moment of reading the Duke had already been dead seven months. Alwyn could now no longer bind himself down to machine-made synecdoche, antithesis, and climax, being full of spontaneous specimens of all these rhetorical forms, which he dared not utter. Who shall wonder that his mind luxuriated in dreams of a sweet possibility just laid open for the first time these many years? for Emmeline was to him now as ever the one dear thing in all the world. The issue of his silent romancing was that he resolved to return to her at the very earliest moment.

But he could not abandon his professional work on the instant. He did not get really quite free from engagements till four months later; but, though suffering throes of impatience continually, he said to himself every day: 'If she has continued to love me nine years she will love me ten; she will think the more tenderly of me when her present hours of solitude shall have done their proper work; old times will revive with the cessation of her recent experience, and every day will favour my return.'

The enforced interval soon passed, and he duly arrived in England, reaching the village of Batton on a certain winter day between twelve and thirteen months subsequent to the time of the Duke's death.

It was evening; yet such was Alwyn's impatience that he could not forbear taking, this very night, one look at the castle which Emmeline had entered as unhappy mistress ten years before. He threaded the park trees, gazed in passing at well-known outlines which rose against the dim sky, and was soon interested in observing that lively country-people, in parties of two and three, were walking before and behind him up the interlaced avenue to the castle gateway. Knowing himself to be safe from recognition, Alwyn inquired of one of these pedestrians what was going on.

'Her Grace gives her tenantry a ball tonight, to keep up the old custom of the Duke and his father before him, which she does not wish to change.'

'Indeed. Has she lived here entirely alone since the Duke's death?'

'Quite alone. But though she doesn't receive company herself, she likes the village people to enjoy themselves, and often has 'em here.'

'Kind-hearted, as always!' thought Alwyn.

On reaching the castle he found that the great gates at the tradesmen's entrance were thrown back against the wall as if they were never to be closed again; that the passages and rooms in that wing were brilliantly lighted up, some of the numerous candles guttering down over the green leaves which decorated them, and upon the silk dresses of the happy farmers' wives as they passed beneath, each on her husband's arm. Alwyn found no difficulty in marching in along with the rest, the castle being Liberty Hall tonight. He stood unobserved in a corner of the large apartment where dancing was about to being.

'Her Grace, though hardly out of mourning, will be sure to come down and lead off the dance with neighbour Bates,' said one.

'Who is neighbour Bates?' asked Alwyn.

'An old man she respects much – the oldest of her tenant-farmers. He was seventy-eight his last birthday.'

'Ah, to be sure!' said Alwyn, at his ease. 'I remember.'

The dancers formed in line, and waited. A door opened at the further end of the hall, and a lady in black silk came forth. She bowed, smiled, and proceeded to the top of the dance.

'Who is that lady?' said Alwyn, in a puzzled tone. 'I thought you told me that the Duchess of Hamptonshire—'

'That is the Duchess,' said his informant.

'But there is another?'

'No; there is no other.'

'But she is not the Duchess of Hamptonshire – who used to—' Alwyn's tongue stuck to his mouth, he could get no farther.

'What's the matter?' said his acquaintance. Alwyn had retired, and was supporting himself against the wall.

The wretched Alwyn murmured something about a stitch in his side from walking. Then the music struck up, the dance went on, and his neighbour became so interested in watching the movements of this strange Duchess through its mazes as to forget Alwyn for a while.

It gave him an opportunity to brace himself up. He was a man who had suffered, and he could suffer again. 'How came that person to be your Duchess?' he asked in a firm, distinct voice, when he had attained complete self-command. 'Where is her other Grace of Hamptonshire? There certainly was another. I know it.'

'Oh, the previous one! Yes, yes. She ran away years and years ago with the young curate. Mr Hill was the young man's name, if I recollect.'

'No! She never did. What do you mean by that?' he said.

'Yes, she certainly ran away. She met the curate in the shrubbery about a couple of months after her marriage with the Duke. There were folks who saw the meeting and heard some words of their talk. They arranged to go, and she sailed from Plymouth with him a day or two afterward.'

'That's not true.'

'Then 'tis the queerest lie ever told by man. Her father believed and knew to his dying day that she went with him; and so did the Duke, and everybody about here. Ay, there was a fine upset about it at the time. The Duke traced her to Plymouth.'

'Traced her to Plymouth?'

'He traced her to Plymouth, and set on his spies; and they found that she went to the shipping-office, and inquired if Mr Alwyn Hill had entered his name as passenger by the *Western Glory*; and when she found that he had, she booked herself for the same ship, but not in her real name. When the vessel had sailed a letter reached the Duke from her, telling him what she had done. She never came back here again. His Grace lived by himself a number of years, and married this lady only twelve months before he died.'

Alwyn was in a state of indescribable bewilderment. But, unmanned as he was, he called the next day on the, to him, spurious Duchess of Hamptonshire. At first she was alarmed at his statement, then cold, then she was won over by his condition to give confidence for confidence. She showed him a letter which had been found among the papers of the late Duke, corroborating what Alwyn's informant had detailed. It was from Emmeline, bearing the postmarked date at which the *Western Glory* sailed, and briefly stated that she had emigrated by that ship to America.

Alwyn applied himself body and mind to unravel the remainder of the mystery. The story repeated to him was always the same: 'She ran away with the curate.' A strangely circumstantial piece of intelligence was added to this when he had pushed his inquiries a little further. There was given him the name of a waterman at Plymouth, who had come forward at the time that she was missed and sought for by her husband, and had stated that he put her on board the *Western Glory* at dusk one evening before that vessel sailed.

After several days of search about the alleys and quays of Plymouth Barbican, during which these impossible words, 'She ran off with the curate,' became branded on his brain, Alwyn found this important waterman. He was positive as to the truth of his story, still remembering the incident well, and he described in detail the lady's dress, as he had long ago described it to her husband, which description corresponded in every particular with the dress worn by Emmeline on the evening of their parting.

Before proceeding to the other side of the Atlantic to continue his inquiries there, the puzzled and distracted Alwyn set himself to ascertain the address of Captain Wheeler, who had commanded the *Western Glory* in the year of Alwyn's voyage out, and immediately wrote a letter to him on the subject.

The only circumstances which the sailor could recollect or discover from his papers in connection with such a story were, that a woman bearing the name which Alwyn had mentioned as fictitious certainly did come aboard for a voyage he made about that time; that she took a common berth among the poorest emigrants; that she died on the voyage out, at about five days' sail from Plymouth; that she seemed a lady in manners and education. Why she had not applied for a first-class passage, why she had no trunks, they could not guess, for though she had little money in her pocket she had that about her which would have fetched it. 'We buried her at sea,' continued the captain. 'A young parson, one of the cabin-passengers, read the burial-service over her, I remember well.'

The whole scene and proceedings darted upon Alwyn's recollection in a moment. It was a fine breezy morning on that long-past voyage out, and he had been told that they were running at the rate of a hundred and odd miles a day. The news went round that one of the poor young women in the other part of the vessel was ill of fever, and delirious. The tidings caused no little alarm among all the passengers, for the sanitary conditions of the ship were anything but satisfactory. Shortly after this the doctor announced that she had died. Then Alwyn had learnt that she was laid out for burial in great haste, because of the danger that would have been incurred by delay. And next the funeral scene rose before him, and the prominent part that he had taken in that solemn ceremony. The captain had come to him, requesting him to officiate, as there was no chaplain on board. This he had agreed to do; and as the sun went down with a blaze in his face he read amidst them all assembled: 'We therefore commit her body to the deep, to be turned into corruption, looking for the resurrection of the body when the sea shall give up her dead.'

The captain also forwarded the addresses of the ship's matron and of other persons who had been engaged on board at the date. To these Alwyn went in the course of time. A categorical description of the clothes of the dead truant, the colour of the hair, and other things, extinguished for ever all hope of a mistake in identity.

At last, then, the course of events had become clear. On that unhappy evening when he left Emmeline in the shrubbery, forbidding her to follow him because it would be a sin, she must have disobeyed. She must have followed at his heels silently through the darkness, like a poor pet animal that will not be driven back. She could have accumulated nothing for the journey more than she might have carried in her hand; and thus poorly provided she must have embarked. Her intention had doubtless been to make her presence on board known to him as soon as she could muster courage to do so.

Thus the ten years' chapter of Alwyn Hill's romance wound itself up under his eyes. That the poor young woman in the steerage had been the young Duchess of Hamptonshire was never publicly disclosed. Hill had no longer any reason for remaining in England, and soon after left its shores with no intention to return. Previous to his departure he confided his story to an old friend from his native town – grandfather of the person who now relates it to you.

A few members, including the Bookworm, seemed to be impressed by the quiet gentleman's tale; but the member we have called the Spark – who, by the way, was getting somewhat tinged with the light of other days, and owned to eight-and-thirty – walked daintily about the room instead of sitting down by the fire with the majority, and said that for his part he preferred something more lively than the last story – something in which such long-separated lovers were ultimately united. He also liked stories that were more modern in their date of action than those he had heard today.

Members immediately requested him to give them a specimen, to which the Spark replied that he didn't mind, as far as that went. And though the Vice-President, the Man of Family, the Colonel, and others, looked at their watches, and said they must soon retire to their respective quarters in the hotel adjoining, they all decided to sit out the Spark's story.

DAME THE TENTH
THE HONOURABLE LAURA

BY THE SPARK

It was a cold and gloomy Christmas Eve. The mass of cloud overhead was almost impervious to such daylight as still lingered; the snow lay several inches deep upon the ground, and the slanting downfall which still went on threatened to considerably increase its thickness before the morning. The Prospect Hotel, a building standing near the wild north coast of Lower Wessex, looked so lonely and so useless at such a time as this that a passing wayfarer would have been left to forget summer possibilities, and to wonder at the commercial courage which could invest capital, on the basis of the popular taste for the picturesque, in a country subject to such dreary phases. That the district was alive with visitors in August seemed but a dim tradition in weather so totally opposed to all that tempts mankind from home. However, there the hotel stood immovable; and the cliffs, creeks, and headlands which were the primary attractions of the spot, rising in full view on the opposite side of the valley, were now but stern angular outlines, while the townlet in front was tinged over with a grimy dirtiness rather than the pearly gray that in summer lent such beauty to its appearance.

Within the hotel commanding this outlook the landlord walked idly about with his hands in his pockets, not in the least expectant of a visitor, and yet unable to settle down to any occupation which should compensate in some degree for the losses that winter idleness entailed on his regular profession. So little, indeed, was anybody expected, that the coffee-room waiter – a genteel boy, whose plated buttons in summer were as close together upon the front of his short jacket as peas in a pod – now appeared in the back yard, metamorphosed into the unrecognizable shape of a rough country lad in corduroys and hobnailed boots, sweeping the snow away, and talking the local dialect in all its purity, quite oblivious of the new polite accent he had learned in the hot weather from the well-behaved visitors. The front door was closed, and, as if to express still more fully the sealed and chrysalis state of the establishment, a sand-bag was placed at the bottom to keep out the insidious snowdrift, the wind setting in directly from that quarter.

The landlord, entering his own parlour, walked to the large fire which it was absolutely necessary to keep up for his comfort, no such blaze burning in the coffee-room or elsewhere, and after giving it a stir returned to a table in the lobby, whereon lay the visitor's book – now closed and pushed back against the wall. He carelessly opened it; not a name had been entered there since the 19th of the previous November, and that was only the name of a man who had arrived on a tricycle, who, indeed, had not been asked to enter at all.

While he was engaged thus the evening grew darker; but before it was as yet too dark to distinguish objects upon the road winding round the back of the cliffs, the landlord perceived a black spot on the distant white, which speedily enlarged itself and drew near. The probabilities were that this vehicle – for a vehicle of some sort it seemed to be – would pass by and pursue its way to the nearest railway-town as others had done. But, contrary to the landlord's expectation, as he stood conning it through the yet unshuttered windows, the solitary object, on reaching the corner, turned into the hotel-front, and drove up to the door.

It was a conveyance particularly unsuited to such a season and weather, being nothing more substantial than an open basket-carriage drawn by a single horse. Within sat two persons, of different sexes, as could soon be discerned, in spite of their muffled attire. The man held the reins, and the lady had got some shelter from the storm by clinging close to his side. The landlord rang the hostler's bell to attract the attention of the stable-man, for the approach of the visitors had been deadened to noiselessness by the snow, and when the hostler had come to the horse's head the gentleman and lady alighted, the landlord meeting them in the hall.

The male stranger was a foreign-looking individual of about eight-and-twenty. He was close-shaven, excepting a moustache, his features being good, and even handsome. The lady, who stood timidly behind him, seemed to be much younger – possibly not more than eighteen, though it was difficult to judge either of her age or appearance in her present wrappings.

The gentleman expressed his wish to stay till the morning, explaining somewhat unnecessarily, considering that the house was an inn, that they had been unexpectedly benighted on their drive. Such a welcome being given them as landlords can give in dull times, the latter ordered fires in the drawing- and coffee-rooms, and went to the boy in the yard, who soon scrubbed himself up, dragged his disused jacket from its box, polished the buttons with his sleeve, and appeared civilized in the hall. The lady was shown into a room where she could take off her snow-damped garments, which she sent down to be dried, her companion, meanwhile, putting a couple of sovereigns on the table, as if anxious to make everything smooth and comfortable at starting, and requesting that a private sitting-room might be got ready. The landlord assured him that the best upstairs parlour – usually public – should be kept private this evening, and sent the maid to light the candles. Dinner was prepared for them, and, at the gentleman's desire, served in the same apartment; where, the young lady having joined him, they were left to the rest and refreshment they seemed to need.

That something was peculiar in the relations of the pair had more than once struck the landlord, though wherein that peculiarity lay it was hard to decide. But that his guest was one who paid his way readily had been proved by his conduct, and dismissing conjectures he turned to practical affairs.

About nine o'clock he re-entered the hall, and, everything being done for the day, again walked up and down, occasionally gazing through the glass door at the prospect without, to ascertain how the weather was progressing. Contrary to prognostication, snow had ceased falling, and, with the rising of the moon, the sky had partially cleared, light fleeces of cloud drifting across the silvery disk. There was every sign that a frost was going to set in later on. For these reasons the distant rising road was even more distinct now between its high banks than it had been in the declining daylight. Not a track or rut broke the virgin surface of the white mantle that lay along it, all marks left by the lately arrived travellers having been speedily obliterated by the flakes falling at the time.

And now the landlord beheld by the light of the moon a sight very similar to that he had seen by the light of day. Again a black spot was advancing down the road that margined the coast. He was in a moment or two enabled to perceive that the present vehicle moved onward at a more headlong pace than the little carriage which had preceded it; next, that it was a brougham drawn by two powerful horses; next, that this carriage, like the former one, was bound for the hotel-door. This desirable feature of resemblance caused the landlord once more to withdraw the sand-bag. and advance into the porch.

An old gentleman was the first to alight. He was followed by a young one, and both unhesitatingly came forward.

'Has a young lady, less than nineteen years of age, recently arrived here in the company of a man some years her senior?' asked the old gentleman, in haste. 'A man cleanly shaven for the most part, having the appearance of an opera-singer, and calling himself Signor Smittozzi?'

'We have had arrivals lately,' said the landlord, in the tone of having had twenty at least – not caring to acknowledge the attenuated state of business that afflicted Prospect Hotel in winter.

'And among them can your memory recall two persons such as those I describe? – the man a sort of baritone?'

'There certainly is or was a young couple staying in the hotel; but I could not pronounce on the compass of the gentleman's voice.'

'No, no; of course not. I am quite bewildered. They arrived in a basket-carriage, altogether badly provided?'

'They came in a carriage, I believe, as most of our visitors do.'

'Yes, yes. I must see them at once. Pardon my want of ceremony, and show us in to where they are.'

'But, sir, you forget. Suppose the lady and gentleman I mean are not the lady and gentleman you mean? It would be awkward to allow you to rush in upon them just now while they are at dinner, and might cause me to lose their future patronage.'

'True, true. They may not be the same persons. My anxiety, I perceive, makes me rash in my assumptions!'

'Upon the whole, I think they must be the same, Uncle Quantock,' said the young man, who had not till now spoken. And turning to the landlord: 'You possibly have not such a large assemblage of visitors here, on this somewhat forbidding evening, that you quite forget how this couple arrived, and what the lady wore?' His tone of addressing the landlord had in it a quiet frigidity that was not without irony.

'Ah! what she wore; that's it, James. What did she wear?'

'I don't usually take stock of my guests' clothing,' replied the landlord drily, for the ready money of the first arrival had decidedly biassed him in favour of that gentleman's cause. 'You can certainly see some of it if you want to,' he added carelessly, 'for it is drying by the kitchen fire.'

Before the words were half out of his mouth the old gentleman had exclaimed, 'Ah!' and precipitated himself along what seemed to be the passage to the kitchen; but as this turned out to be only the entrance to a dark china-closet he hastily emerged again, after a collision with the inn-crockery had told him of his mistake.

'I beg your pardon, I'm sure; but it you only knew my feelings (which I cannot at present explain), you would make allowances. Anything I have broken I will willingly pay for.'

'Don't mention it, sir,' said the landlord. And showing the way, they adjourned to the kitchen without further parley. The eldest of the party instantly seized the lady's cloak, that hung upon a clothes-horse, exclaiming: 'Ah! yes, James, it is hers. I knew we were on their track.'

'Yes, it is hers,' answered the nephew quietly, for he was much less excited than his companion.

'Show us their room at once,' said the uncle.

'William, have the lady and gentleman in the front sitting-room finished dining?'

'Yes, sir, long ago,' said the hundred plated buttons.

'Then show up these gentlemen to them at once. You stay here tonight, gentlemen, I presume? Shall the horses be taken out?'

'Feed the horses and wash their mouths. Whether we stay or not depends upon circumstances,' said the placid younger man, as he followed his uncle and the waiter to the staircase.

'I think, Nephew James,' said the former, as he paused with his foot on the first step – 'I think we had better not be announced, but take them by surprise. She may go throwing herself out of the window, or do some equally desperate thing!'

'Yes, certainly, we'll enter unannounced.' And he called back the lad who preceded them.

'I cannot sufficiently thank you, James, for so effectually aiding me in this pursuit!' exclaimed the old gentleman, taking the other by the hand. 'My increasing infirmities would have hindered my overtaking her tonight, had it not been for your timely aid.'

'I am only too happy, uncle, to have been of service to you in this or any other matter. I only wish I could have accompanied you on a pleasanter journey. However, it is advisable to go up to them at once, or they may hear us.' And they softly ascended the stairs.

On the door being opened a room too large to be comfortable was disclosed, lit by the best branch-candlesticks of the hotel, before the fire of which apartment the truant couple were sitting, very innocently looking over the hotel scrap-book and the album containing views of the neighbourhood. No sooner had the old man entered than the young lady – who now showed herself to be quite as young as described, and remarkably prepossessing as to features – perceptibly turned pale. When the nephew entered she turned still paler, as if she were going to faint. The young man described as an opera-singer rose with grim civility, and placed chairs for his visitors.

'Caught you, thank God!' said the old gentleman breathlessly.

'Yes, worse luck, my lord!' murmured Signor Smittozzi, in native London-English, that distinguished Italian having, in fact, first seen the light as the baby of Mr and Mrs Smith in the vicinity of the City Road. 'She would have been mine tomorrow. And I think that under the peculiar circumstances it would be wiser – considering how soon the breath of scandal will tarnish a lady's fame – to let her be mine tomorrow, just the same.'

'Never!' said the old man. 'Here is a lady under age, without experience – child-like in her maiden innocence and virtue – whom you have plied by your vile arts, till this morning at dawn—'

'Lord Quantock, were I not bound to respect your gray hairs—'

'Till this morning at dawn you tempted her away from her father's roof. What blame can attach to her conduct that will not, on a full explanation of the matter, be readily passed over in her and thrown entirely on you? Laura, you return at once with me. I should not have arrived, after all, early enough to deliver you, if it had not been for the disinterestedness of your cousin, Captain Northbrook, who, on my discovering your flight this morning, offered with a promptitude for which I can never sufficiently thank him, to accompany me on my journey, as the only male relative I have near me. Come, do you hear? Put on your things; we are off at once.'

'I don't want to go!' pouted the young lady.

'I daresay you don't,' replied her father drily. 'But children never know what's best for them. So come along, and trust to my opinion.'

Laura was silent, and did not move, the opera gentleman looked helplessly into the fire, and the lady's cousin sitting meditatively calm, as the single one of the four whose position enabled him to survey the whole escapade with the cool criticism of a comparative outsider.

'I say to you, Laura, as the father of a daughter under age, that you instantly come with me. What? Would you compel me to use physical force to reclaim you?'

'I don't want to return!' again declared Laura.

'It is your duty to return nevertheless, and at once, I inform you.'

'I don't want to!'

'Now, dear Laura, this is what I say: return with me and your Cousin James quietly, like a good and repentant girl, and nothing will be said. Nobody knows what has happened yet, and if we start at once, we shall be home before it is light tomorrow morning. Come.'

'I am not obliged to come at your bidding, father, and I would rather not!'

Now James, the cousin, during this dialogue might have been observed to grow somewhat restless, and even impatient. More than once he had parted his lips to speak, but second thoughts each time held him back. The moment had come, however, when he could keep silence no longer.

'Come, madam!' he spoke out, 'this farce with your father has, in my opinion, gone on long enough. Just make no more ado, and step downstairs with us.'

She gave herself an intractable little twist, and did not reply.

'By the Lord Harry, Laura, I won't stand this!' he said angrily. 'Come, get on your things before I come and compel you. There is a kind of compulsion to which this talk is child's play. Come, madam – instantly, I say!'

The old nobleman turned to his nephew and said mildly: 'Leave me to insist, James. It doesn't become you. I can speak to her sharply enough, if I choose.'

James, however, did not heed his uncle, and went on to the troublesome young woman: 'You say you don't want to come, indeed! A pretty story to tell me, that! Come, march out of the room at once, and leave that hulking fellow for me to deal with afterward. Get on quickly – come!' and he advanced toward her as if to pull her by the hand.

'Nay, nay,' expostulated Laura's father, much surprised at his nephew's sudden demeanour. 'You take too much upon yourself. Leave her to me.'

'I won't leave her to you any longer!'

'You have no right, James, to address either me or her in this way; so just hold your tongue. Come, my dear.'

'I have every right!' insisted James.

'How do you make that out?'

'I have the right of a husband.'

'Whose husband?'

'Hers.'

'What?'

'She's my wife.'

'James!'

'Well, to cut a long story short, I may say that she secretly married me, in spite of your lordship's prohibition, about three months ago. And I must add that, though she cooled down rather quickly, everything went on smoothly enough between us for some time; in spite of the awkwardness of meeting only by stealth. We were only waiting for a convenient moment to break the news to you when this idle Adonis turned up, and after poisoning her mind against me, brought her into this disgrace.'

Here the operatic luminary, who had sat in rather an abstracted and nerveless attitude till the cousin made his declaration, fired up and cried: 'I declare before Heaven that till this moment I never knew she was a wife! I found her in her father's house an unhappy girl – unhappy, as I believe, because of the loneliness and dreariness of that establishment, and the want of society, and for nothing else whatever. What this statement about her being your wife means I am quite at a loss to understand. Are you indeed married to him, Laura?'

Laura nodded from within her tearful handkerchief. 'It was because of my anomalous position in being privately married to him,' she sobbed, 'that I was unhappy at home – and – and I didn't like him so well as I did at first – and I wished I could get out of the mess I was in! And then I saw you a few times, and when you said, "We'll run off," I thought I saw a way out of it all, and then I agreed to come with you-oo-oo!'

'Well! well! well! And is this true?' murmured the bewildered old nobleman, staring from James to Laura, and from Laura to James, as if he fancied they might be figments of the imagination. 'Is this, then, James, the secret of your kindness to your old uncle in helping him to find his daughter? Good Heavens! What further depths of duplicity are there left for a man to learn!'

'I have married her, Uncle Quantock, as I said,' answered James coolly. 'The deed is done, and can't be undone by talking here.'

'Where were you married?'

'At St Mary's, Toneborough.'

'When?'

'On the 29th of September, during the time she was visiting there.'

'Who married you?'

'I don't know. One of the curates – we were quite strangers to the place. So, instead of my assisting you to recover her, you may as well assist me.'

'Never! never!' said Lord Quantock. 'Madam, and sir, I beg to tell you that I wash my hands of the whole affair. If you are man and wife, as it seems you are, get reconciled as best you may. I have no more to say or do with either of you. I leave you, Laura, in the hands of your husband, and much joy may you bring him; though the situation, I own, is not encouraging.'

Saying this, the indignant speaker pushed back his chair against the table with such force that the candlesticks rocked on their bases, and left the room.

Laura's wet eyes roved from one of the young men to the other, who now stood glaring face to face, and, being much frightened at their aspect, slipped out of the room after her father. Him, however, she could hear going out of the front door, and, not knowing where to take shelter, she crept into the darkness of an adjoining bedroom, and there awaited events with a palpitating heart.

Meanwhile the two men remaining in the sitting-room drew nearer to each other, and the opera-singer broke the silence by saying, 'How could you insult me in the way you did, calling me a fellow, and accusing me of poisoning her mind toward you, when you knew very well I was as ignorant of your relation to her as an unborn babe?'

'O yes, you were quite ignorant; I can believe that readily,' sneered Laura's husband.

'I here call Heaven to witness that I never knew!'

'Recitativo – the rhythm excellent, and the tone well sustained. Is it likely that any man could win the confidence of a young fool her age, and not get that out of her? Preposterous! Tell it to the most improved new pit-stalls.'

'Captain Northbrook, your insinuations are as despicable as your wretched person!' cried the baritone, losing all patience. And springing forward he slapped the captain in the face with the palm of his hand.

Northbrook flinched but slightly, and calmly using his handkerchief to learn if his nose was bleeding, said, 'I quite expected this insult, so I came prepared.' And he drew forth from a black valise which he carried in his hand a small case of pistols.

The baritone started at the unexpected sight, but recovering from his surprise said, 'Very well, as you will,' though perhaps his tone showed a slight want of confidence.

'Now,' continued the husband, quite confidingly, 'we want no parade, no nonsense, you know. Therefore we'll dispense with seconds?'

The Signor slightly nodded.

'Do you know this part of the country well?' Cousin James went on, in the same cool and still manner. 'If you don't, I do. Quite at the bottom of the rocks out there, just beyond the stream which falls over them to the shore, is a smooth sandy space, not so much shut in as to be out of the moonlight; and the way down to it from this side is over steps cut in the cliff; and we can find our way down without trouble. We – we two – will find our way down; but only one of us will find his way up, you understand?'

'Quite.'

'Then suppose we start; the sooner it is over the better. We can order supper before we go out – supper for two, for though we are three at present—'

'Three?'

'Yes; you and I and she—'

'O yes.'

'– we shall be only two by-and-by; so that, as I say, we will order supper for two; for the lady and *a* gentleman. Whichever comes back alive will tap at her door, and call her in to share the repast with him – she's not off the premises. But we must not alarm her now; and above all things we must not let the inn-people see us go out; it would look so odd for two to go out, and only one come in. Ha! ha!'

'Ha! ha! exactly.'

'Are you ready?'

'Oh – quite.'

'Then I'll lead the way.'

He went softly to the door and downstairs, ordering supper to be ready in an hour, as he had said; then making a feint of returning to the room again he beckoned to the singer, and together they slipped out of the house by a side door.

The sky was now quite clear, and the wheelmarks of the brougham which had borne away Laura's father, Lord Quantock, remained distinctly visible. Soon the verge of the down was reached, the captain leading the way, and the baritone following silently, casting furtive glances at his companion, and beyond him at the scene ahead. In due course they arrived at the chasm in the cliff which formed the waterfall. The outlook here was wild and picturesque in the extreme, and fully justified the many praises, paintings, and photographic views to which the spot had given birth. What in summer was charmingly green and gray, was now rendered weird and fantastic by the snow.

From their feet the cascade plunged downward almost vertically to a depth of eighty or a hundred feet before finally losing itself in the sand, and though the stream was but small, its impact upon jutting rocks in its descent divided it into a hundred spirts and splashes that sent up a mist into the upper air. A few marginal drippings had been frozen into icicles, but the centre flowed on unimpeded.

The operatic artist looked down as he halted, but his thoughts were plainly not of the beauty of the scene. His companion with the pistols was immediately in front of him, and there was no handrail on the side of the path toward the chasm. Obeying a quick impulse, he stretched out his arm, and with a superhuman thrust sent Laura's husband reeling over. A whirling human shape, diminishing downward in the moon's rays further and further toward invisibility, a smack-smack upon the projecting ledges of rock – at first louder and heavier than that of the brook, and then scarcely to be distinguished from it – then a cessation, then the splashing of the stream as before, and the accompanying murmur of the sea, were all the incidents that disturbed the customary flow of the lofty waterfall.

The singer waited in a fixed attitude for a few minutes, then turning, he rapidly retraced his steps over the intervening upland toward the road, and in less than a quarter of an hour was at the door of the hotel. Slipping quietly in as the clock struck ten, he said to the landlord, over the bar hatchway –

'The bill as soon as you can let me have it, including charges for the supper that was ordered, though we cannot stay to eat it, I am sorry to say.' He added with forced gaiety, 'The lady's father and cousin have thought better of intercepting the marriage, and after quarrelling with each other have gone home independently.'

'Well done, sir!' said the landlord, who still sided with this customer in preference to those who had given trouble and barely paid for baiting the horses. '"Love will find out the way!" as the saying is. Wish you joy, sir!'

Signor Smittozzi went upstairs, and on entering the sitting-room found that Laura had crept out from the dark adjoining chamber in his absence. She looked up at him with eyes red from weeping, and with symptoms of alarm.

'What is it? – where is he?' she said apprehensively.

'Captain Northbrook has gone back. He says he will have no more to do with you.'

'And I am quite abandoned by them! – and they'll forget me, and nobody care about me any more!' She began to cry afresh.

'But it is the luckiest thing that could have happened. All is just as it was before they came disturbing us. But, Laura, you ought to have told me about that private marriage, though it is all the same now; it will be dissolved, of course. You are a wid— virtually a widow.'

'It is no use to reproach me for what is past. What am I to do now?'

'We go at once to Cliff-Martin. The horse has rested thoroughly these last three hours, and he will have no difficulty in doing an additional half-dozen miles. We shall be there before twelve, and there are late taverns in the place, no doubt. There we'll sell both horse and carriage tomorrow morning; and go by the coach to Downstaple. Once in the train we are safe.'

'I agree to anything,' she said listlessly.

In about ten minutes the horse was put in, the bill paid, the lady's dried wraps put about her, and the journey resumed.

When about a mile on their way they saw a glimmering light in advance of them. 'I wonder what that is?' said the baritone, whose manner had latterly become nervous, every sound and sight causing him to turn his head.

'It is only a turnpike,' said she. 'That light is the lamp kept burning over the door.'

'Of course, of course, dearest. How stupid I am!'

On reaching the gate, they perceived that a man on foot had approached it, apparently by some more direct path than the roadway they pursued, and was, at the moment they drew up, standing in conversation with the gatekeeper.

'It is quite impossible that he could fall over the cliff by accident or the will of God on such a light night as this,' the pedestrian was saying. 'These two children I tell you of saw two men go along the path toward the waterfall, and ten minutes later only one of 'em came back, walking fast, like a man who wanted to get out of the way because he had done something queer. There is no manner of doubt that he pushed the other man over, and, mark me, it will soon cause a hue and cry for that man.'

The candle shone in the face of the Signor and showed that there had arisen upon it a film of ghastliness. Laura, glancing toward him for a few moments, observed it, till, the gatekeeper having mechanically swung open the gate, her companion drove through, and they were soon again enveloped in the white silence.

Her conductor had said to Laura, just before, that he meant to inquire the way at this turnpike; but he had certainly not done so.

As soon as they had gone a little further the omission, intentional or not, began to cause them some trouble. Beyond the secluded district which they now traversed ran the more frequented road, where progress would be easy, the snow being probably already beaten there to some extent by traffic; but they had not yet reached it, and having no one to guide them their journey began to appear less feasible than it had done before starting. When the little lane which they had entered ascended another hill, and seemed to wind round in a direction contrary to the expected route to Cliff-Martin, the question grew serious. Ever since overhearing the conversation at the turnpike, Laura had maintained a perfect silence, and had even shrunk somewhat away from the side of her lover.

'Why don't you talk, Laura,' he said with forced buoyancy, 'and suggest the way we should go?'

'O yes, I will,' she responded, a curious fearfulness being audible in her voice.

After this she uttered a few occasional sentences which seemed to persuade him that she suspected nothing. At last he drew rein, and the weary horse stood still.

'We are in a fix,' he said.

She answered eagerly: 'I'll hold the reins while you run forward to the top of the ridge, and see if the road takes a favourable turn beyond. It would give the horse a few minutes' rest, and if you find out no change in the direction, we will retrace this lane, and take the other turning.'

The expedient seemed a good one in the circumstances, especially when recommended by the singular eagerness of her voice; and placing the reins in her hands – a quite unnecessary precaution, considering the state of their hack – he stepped out and went forward through the snow till she could see no more of him.

No sooner was he gone than Laura, with a rapidity which contrasted strangely with her previous stillness, made fast the reins to the corner of the phaeton, and slipping out on the opposite side, ran back with all her might down the hill, till, coming to an opening in the fence, she scrambled through it, and plunged into the copse which bordered this portion of the lane. Here she stood in hiding under one of the large bushes, clinging so closely to its umbrage as to seem but a portion of its mass, and listening intently for the faintest sound of pursuit. But nothing disturbed the stillness save the occasional slipping of gathered snow from the boughs, or the rustle of some wild animal over the crisp flake-bespattered herbage. At length, apparently convinced that her former companion was either unable to find her, or not anxious to do so in the present strange state of affairs, she crept out from the bushes, and in less than an hour found herself again approaching the door of the Prospect Hotel.

As she drew near, Laura could see that, far from being wrapped in darkness, as she might have expected, there were ample signs that all the tenants were on the alert, lights moving about the open space in front. Satisfaction was expressed in her face when she discerned that no reappearance of her baritone and his pony-carriage was causing this sensation; but it speedily gave way to grief and dismay when she saw by the lights the form of a man borne on a stretcher by two others into the porch of the hotel.

'I have caused all this,' she murmured between her quivering lips. 'He has murdered him!' Running forward to the door, she hastily asked of the first person she met if the man on the stretcher was dead.

'No, miss,' said the labourer addressed, eyeing her up and down as an unexpected apparition. 'He is still alive, they say, but not sensible. He either fell or was pushed over the waterfall; 'tis thoughted he was pushed. He is the gentleman who came here just now with the old lord, and went out afterward (as is thoughted) with a stranger who had come a little earlier. Anyhow, that's as I had it.'

Laura entered the house, and acknowledging without the least reserve that she was the injured man's wife, had soon installed herself as head nurse by the bed on which he lay. When the two surgeons who had been sent for arrived, she learnt from them that his wounds were so severe as to leave but a slender hope of recovery, it being little short of miraculous that he was not killed on the spot, which his enemy had evidently reckoned to be the case. She knew who that enemy was, and shuddered.

Laura watched all night, but her husband knew nothing of her presence. During the next day he slightly recognized her, and in the evening was able to speak. He informed the surgeons that, as was surmised, he had been pushed over the cascade by Signor Smittozzi; but he communicated nothing to her who nursed him, not even replying to her remarks; he nodded courteously at any act of attention she rendered, and that was all.

In a day or two it was declared that everything favoured his recovery, notwithstanding the severity of his injuries. Full search was made for Smittozzi, but as yet there was no intelligence of his whereabouts, though the repentant Laura communicated all she knew. As far as could be judged, he had come back to the carriage after searching out the way, and finding the young lady missing, had looked about for her till he was tired; then had driven on to Cliff-Martin, sold the horse and carriage next morning, and disappeared, probably by one of the departing coaches which ran thence to the nearest station, the only difference from his original programme being that he had gone alone.

During the days and weeks of that long and tedious recovery Laura watched by her husband's bedside with a zeal and assiduity which would have considerably extenuated any fault save one of such magnitude as hers. That her husband did not forgive her was soon obvious. Nothing that she could do in the way of smoothing pillows, easing his position, shifting bandages, or administering draughts, could win from him more than a few measured words of thankfulness, such as he would probably have uttered to any other woman on earth who had performed these particular services for him.

'Dear, dear James,' she said one day, bending her face upon the bed in an excess of emotion. 'How you have suffered! It has been too cruel. I am more glad you are getting better than I can say. I have prayed for it – and I am sorry for what I have done; I am innocent of the worst, and – I hope you will not think me so very bad, James!'

'O no. On the contrary, I shall think you very good – as a nurse,' he answered, the caustic severity of his tone being apparent through its weakness.

Laura let fall two or three silent tears, and said no more that day.

Somehow or other Signor Smittozzi seemed to be making good his escape. It transpired that he had not taken a passage in either of the suspected coaches, though he had certainly got out of the county; altogether, the chance of finding him was problematical.

Not only did Captain Northbrook survive his injuries, but it soon appeared that in the course of a few weeks he would find himself little if any the worse for the catastrophe. It could also be seen that Laura, while secretly hoping for her husband's forgiveness for a piece of folly of which she saw the enormity more clearly every day, was in great doubt as to what her future relations with him would be. Moreover, to add to the complication, whilst she, as a runaway wife, was unforgiven by her husband, she and her husband, as a runaway couple, were unforgiven by her father, who had never once communicated with either of them since his departure from the inn. But her immediate anxiety was to win the pardon of her husband, who possibly might be bearing in mind, as he lay upon his couch, the familiar words of Brabantio, 'She has decieved her father, and may thee'.

Matters went on thus till Captain Northbrook was able to walk about. He then removed with his wife to quiet apartments on the south coast, and here his recovery was rapid. Walking up the cliffs one day, supporting him by her arm as usual, she said to him, simply, 'James, if I go on as I am going now, and always attend to your smallest want, and never think of anything but devotion to you, will you – try to like me a little?'

'It is a thing I must carefully consider,' he said, with the same gloomy dryness which characterized all his words to her now. 'When I have considered, I will tell you.'

He did not tell her that evening, though she lingered long at her routine work of making his bedroom comfortable, putting the light so that it would not shine into his eyes, seeing him fall asleep, and then retiring noiselessly to her own chamber. When they met in the morning at breakfast, and she had asked him as usual how he had passed the night, she added timidly, in the silence which followed his reply, 'Have you considered?'

'No, I have not considered sufficiently to give you an answer.'

Laura sighed, but to no purpose; and the day wore on with intense heaviness to her, and the customary modicum of strength gained to him.

The next morning she put the same question, and looked up despairingly in his face, as though her whole life hung upon his reply.

'Yes, I have considered,' he said.

'Ah!'

'We must part.'

'O James!'

'I cannot forgive you; no man would. Enough is settled upon you to keep you in comfort, whatever your father may do. I shall sell out, and disappear from this hemisphere.'

'You have absolutely decided?' she asked miserably. 'I have nobody now to c-c-care for—'

'I have absolutely decided,' he shortly returned. 'We had better part here. You will go back to your father. There is no reason why I should accompany you, since my presence would only stand in the way of the forgiveness he will probably grant you if you appear before him alone. We will say farewell to each other in three days from this time. I have calculated on being ready to go on that day.'

Bowed down with trouble she withdrew to her room, and the three days were passed by her husband in writing letters and attending to other business-matters, saying hardly a word to her the while. The morning of departure came; but before the horses had been put in to take the severed twain in different directions, out of sight of each other, possibly for ever, the postman arrived with the morning letters.

There was one for the captain; none for her – there were never any for her. However, on this occasion something was enclosed for her in his, which he handed her. She read it and looked up helpless.

'My dear father – is dead!' she said. In a few moments she added, in a whisper, 'I must go to the Manor to bury him. . . Will you go with me, James?'

He musingly looked out of the window. 'I suppose it is an awkward and melancholy undertaking for a woman alone,' he said coldly. 'Well, well – my poor uncle! – Yes, I'll go with you, and see you through the business.'

So they went off together instead of asunder, as planned. It is unnecessary to record the details of the journey, or of the sad week which followed it at her father's house. Lord Quantock's seat was a fine old mansion standing in its own park, and there were plenty of opportunities for husband and wife either to avoid each other, or to get reconciled if they were so minded, which one of them was at least. Captain Northbrook was not present at the reading of the will. She came to him afterward, and found him packing up his papers, intending to start next morning, now that he had seen her through the turmoil occasioned by her father's death.

'He has left me everything that he could!' she said to her husband. 'James, will you forgive me now, and stay?'

'I cannot stay.'

'Why not?'

'I cannot stay,' he repeated.

'But why?'

'I don't like you.'

He acted up to his word. When she came downstairs the next morning she was told that he had gone.

Laura bore her double bereavement as best she could. The vast mansion in which she had hitherto lived, with all its historic contents, had gone to her father's successor in the title; but her own was no unhandsome one. Around lay the undulating park, studded with trees a dozen times her own age; beyond it, the wood; beyond the wood, the farms. All this fair and quiet scene was hers. She nevertheless remained a lonely, repentant, depressed being, who would have given the greater part of everything she possessed to ensure the presence and affection of that husband whose very austerity and phlegm – qualities that had formerly led to the alienation between them – seemed now to be adorable features in his character.

She hoped and hoped again, but all to no purpose. Captain Northbrook did not alter his mind and return. He was quite a different sort of man from one who altered his mind; that she was at last despairingly forced to admit. And then she left off hoping, and settled down to a mechanical routine of existence which in some measure dulled her grief, but at the expense of all her natural animation and the sprightly wilfulness which had once charmed those who knew her, though it was perhaps all the while a factor in the production of her unhappiness.

To say that her beauty quiet departed as the years rolled on would be to overstate the truth. Time is not a merciful master, as we all know, and he was not likely to act exceptionally in the case of a woman who had mental troubles to bear in addition to the ordinary weight of years. Be this as it may, eleven other winters came and went, and Laura Northbrook remained the lonely mistress of house and lands without once hearing of her husband. Every probability seemed to favour the assumption that he had died in some foreign land; and offers for her hand were not few as the probability verged on certainty with the long lapse of time. But the idea of remarriage seemed never to have entered her head for a moment. Whether she continued to hope even now for his return could not be distinctly ascertained; at all events she lived a life unmodified in the slightest degree from that of the first six months of his absence.

This twelfth year of Laura's loneliness, and the thirtieth of her life drew on apace, and the season approached that had seen the unhappy adventure for which she so long had suffered. Christmas promised to be rather wet than cold, and the trees on the outskirts of Laura's estate dripped monotonously from day to day upon the turnpike-road which bordered them. On an afternoon in this week between three and four o'clock a hired fly might have been seen driving along the highway at this point, and on reaching the top of the hill it stopped. A gentleman of middle age alighted from the vehicle.

'You need drive no further,' he said to the coachman. 'The rain seems to have nearly ceased. I'll stroll a little way, and return on foot to the inn by dinner-time.'

The flyman touched his hat, turned the horse, and drove back as directed. When he was out of sight the gentleman walked on, but he had not gone far before the rain again came down pitilessly, though of this the pedestrian took little heed, going leisurely onward till he reached Laura's park gate, which he passed through. The clouds were thick and the days were short, so that by the time he stood in front of the mansion it was dark. In addition to this his appearance, which on alighting from the carriage had been untarnished, partook now of the character of a drenched wayfarer not too well blessed with this world's goods. He halted for no more than a moment at the front entrance, and going round to the servants' quarter, as if he had a preconceived purpose in so doing, there rang the bell. When a page came to him he inquired if they would kindly allow him to dry himself by the kitchen fire.

The page retired, and after a murmured colloquy returned with the cook, who informed the wet and muddy man that though it was not her custom to admit strangers, she should have no particular objection to his drying himself, the night being so damp and gloomy. Therefore the wayfarer entered and sat down by the fire.

'The owner of this house is a very rich gentleman, no doubt?' he asked, as he watched the meat turning on the spit.

''Tis not a gentleman, but a lady,' said the cook.

'A widow, I presume?'

'A sort of widow. Poor soul, her husband is gone abroad, and has never been heard of for many years.'

'She sees plenty of company, no doubt, to make up for his absence?'

'No, indeed – hardly a soul. Service here is as bad as being in a nunnery.'

In short, the wayfarer, who had at first been so coldly received, contrived by his frank and engaging manner to draw the ladies of the kitchen into a most confidential conversation, in which Laura's history was minutely detailed, from the day of her husband's departure to the present. The salient feature in all their discourse was her unflagging devotion to his memory.

Having apparently learned all that he wanted to know – among other things that she was at this moment, as always, alone – the traveller said he was quite dry; and thanking the servants for their kindness, departed as he had come. On emerging into the darkness he did not, however, go down the avenue by which he had arrived. He simply walked round to the front door. There he rang, and the door was opened to him by a man-servant whom he had not seen during his sojourn at the other end of the house.

In answer to the servant's inquiry for his name, he said ceremoniously, 'Will you tell the Honourable Mrs Northbrook that the man she nursed many years ago, after a frightful accident, has called to thank her?'

The footman retreated, and it was rather a long time before any further signs of attention were apparent. Then he was shown into the drawing-room, and the door closed behind him.

On the couch was Laura, trembling and pale. She parted her lips and held out her hands to him, but could not speak. But he did not require speech, and in a moment they were in each other's arms.

Strange news circulated through that mansion and the neighbouring town on the next and following days. But the world has a way of getting used to things, and the intelligence of the return of the Honourable Mrs Northbrook's long-absent husband was soon received with comparative calm.

A few days more brought Christmas, and the forlorn home of Laura Northbrook blazed from basement to attic with light and cheerfulness. Not that the house was overcrowded with visitors, but many were present, and the apathy of a dozen years came at length to an end. The animation which set in thus at the close of the old year did not diminish on the arrival of the new; and by the time its twelve months had likewise run the course of its predecessors, a son had been added to the dwindled line of the Northbrook family.

At the conclusion of this narrative the Spark was thanked, with a manner of some surprise, for nobody had credited him with a taste for tale-telling. Though it had been resolved that this story should be the last, a few of the weather-bound listeners were for sitting on into the small hours over their pipes and glasses, and raking up yet more episodes of family history. But the majority murmured reasons for soon getting to their lodgings.

It was quite dark without, except in the immediate neighbourhood of the feeble street-lamps, and before a few shop-windows which had been hardily kept open in spite of the obvious unlikelihood of any chance customer traversing the muddy thoroughfares at that hour.

By one, by two, and by three the benighted members of the Field-Club rose from their seats, shook hands, made appointments, and dropped away to their respective quarters, free or hired, hoping for a fair morrow. It would probably be not until the next summer meeting, months away in the future, that the easy intercourse which now existed between them all would repeat itself. The crimson maltster, for instance, knew that on the following market-day his friends the President, the Rural Dean, and the Bookworm would pass him in the street, if they met him, with the barest nod of civility, the President and the Colonel for social reasons, the Bookworm for intellectual reasons, and the Rural Dean for moral ones, the latter being a staunch teetotaller, dead against John Barleycorn. The sentimental member knew that when, on his rambles, he met his friend the Bookworm with a pocket-copy of something or other under his nose, the latter would not love his companionship as he had done today; and the President, the aristocrat, and the farmer knew that affairs political, sporting, domestic, or agricultural would exclude for a long time all rumination on the characters of dames gone to dust for scores of years, however beautiful and noble they may have been in their day.

The last member at length departed, the attendant at the museum lowered the fire, the curator locked up the rooms, and soon there was only a single pirouetting flame on the top of a single coal to make the bones of the ichthyosaurus seem to leap, the stuffed birds to wink, and to draw a smile from the varnished skulls of Vespasian's soldiery.

LIFE'S LITTLE IRONIES

PREFATORY NOTE TO 'LIFE'S LITTLE IRONIES'

Of the following collection the first story, 'An Imaginative Woman', originally stood in *Wessex Tales*, but was brought into this volume as being more nearly its place, turning as it does upon a trick of Nature, so to speak, a physical possibility that may attach to a wife of vivid imaginings, as is well known to medical practitioners and other observers of such manifestations.

The two stories named 'A Tradition of Eighteen Hundred and Four' and 'The Melancholy Hussar of the German Legion', which were formerly printed in this series, were also transferred to *Wessex Tales*, where they more naturally belong.

The present narratives and sketches, though separately published at various antecedent dates, were first collected and issued in a volume in 1894.

T.H.

MAY 1912

AN IMAGINATIVE WOMAN

When William Marchmill had finished his inquiries for lodgings at the well-known watering-place of Solentsea in Upper Wessex, he returned to the hotel to find his wife. She, with the children, had rambled along the shore, and Marchmill followed in the direction indicated by the military-looking hall-porter.

'By Jove, how far you've gone! I am quite out of breath,' Marchmill said, rather impatiently, when he came up with his wife, who was reading as she walked, the three children being considerably further ahead with the nurse.

Mrs Marchmill started out of the reverie into which the book had thrown her. 'Yes,' she said, 'you've been such a long time. I was tired of staying in that dreary hotel. But I am sorry if you have wanted me, Will.'

'Well, I have had trouble to suit myself. When you see the airy and comfortable rooms heard of, you find they are stuffy and uncomfortable. Will you come and see if what I've fixed on will do? There is not much room, I am afraid; but I can light on nothing better. The town is rather full.'

The pair left the children and nurse to continue their ramble, and went back together.

In age well-balanced, in personal appearance fairly matched, and in domestic requirements conformable, in temper this couple differed, though even here they did not often clash, he being equable, if not lymphatic, and she decidedly nervous and sanguine. It was to their tastes and fancies, those smallest, greatest particulars, that no common denominator could be applied. Marchmill considered his wife's likes and inclinations somewhat silly; she considered his sordid and material. The husband's business was that of a gunmaker in a thriving city northwards, and his soul was in that business always; the lady was best characterized by that superannuated phrase of elegance 'a votary of the muse'. An impressionable, palpitating creature was Ella, shrinking humanely from detailed knowledge of her husband's trade whenever she reflected that everything he manufactured had for its purpose the destruction of life. She could only recover her equanimity by assuring herself that some, at least, of his weapons were sooner or later used for the extermination of horrid vermin and animals almost as cruel to their inferiors in species as human beings were to theirs.

She had never antecedently regarded this occupation of his as any objection to having him for a husband. Indeed, the necessity of getting life-leased at all cost, a cardinal virtue which all good mothers teach, kept her from thinking of it at all till she had closed with William, had passed the honeymoon, and reached the reflecting stage. Then, like a person who has stumbled upon some object in the dark, she wondered what she had got; mentally walked round it, estimated it; whether it were rare or common; contained gold, silver, or lead; were a clog or a pedestal, everything to her or nothing.

She came to some vague conclusions, and since then had kept her heart alive by pitying her proprietor's obtuseness and want of refinement, pitying herself, and letting off her delicate and ethereal emotions in imaginative occupations, day-dreams, and night-sighs, which perhaps would not much have disturbed William if he had known of them.

Her figure was small, elegant, and slight in build, tripping, or rather bounding, in movement. She was dark-eyed, and had that marvellously bright and liquid sparkle in each pupil which characterizes persons of Ella's cast of soul, and is too often a cause of heartache to the possessor's male friends, ultimately sometimes to herself. Her husband was a tall, long-featured man, with a brown beard; he had a pondering regard; and was, it must be added, usually kind and tolerant to her. He spoke in squarely shaped sentences, and was supremely satisfied with a condition of sublunary things which made weapons a necessity.

Husband and wife walked till they had reached the house they were in search of, which stood in a terrace facing the sea, and was fronted by a small garden of wind-proof and salt-proof evergreens, stone steps leading up to the porch. It had its number in the row, but, being rather larger than the rest, was in addition sedulously distinguished as Coburg House by its landlady, though everybody else called it 'Thirteen, New Parade'. The spot was bright and lively now; but in winter it became necessary to place sandbags against the door, and to stuff up the keyhole against the wind and rain, which had worn the paint so thin that the priming and knotting showed through.

The householder, who had been watching for the gentleman's return, met them in the passage, and showed the rooms. She informed them that she was a professional man's widow, left in needy circumstances by the rather sudden death of her husband, and she spoke anxiously of the conveniences of the establishment.

Mrs Marchmill said that she liked the situation and the house; but, it being small, there would not be accommodation enough, unless she could have all the rooms.

The landlady mused with an air of disappointment. She wanted the visitors to be her tenants very badly, she said, with obvious honesty. But unfortunately two of the rooms were occupied permanently by a bachelor gentleman. He did not pay season prices, it was true; but as he kept on his apartments all the year round, and was an extremely nice and interesting young man, who gave no trouble, she did not like to turn him out for a month's 'let', even at a high figure. 'Perhaps, however,' she added, 'he might offer to go for a time.'

They would not hear of this, and went back to the hotel, intending to proceed to the agent's to inquire further. Hardly had they sat down to tea when the landlady called. Her gentleman, she said, had been so obliging as to offer to give up his rooms for three or four weeks rather than drive the new-comers away.

'It is very kind, but we won't inconvenience him in that way,' said the Marchmills.

'O, it won't inconvenience him, I assure you!' said the landlady eloquently. 'You see, he's a different sort of young man from most – dreamy, solitary, rather melancholy – and he cares more to be here when the south-westerly gales are beating against the door, and the sea washes over the Parade, and there's not a soul in the place, than he does now in the season. He'd just as soon be where, in fact, he's going temporarily, to a little cottage on the Island opposite, for a change.' She hoped therefore that they would come.

The Marchmill family accordingly took possession of the house next day, and it seemed to suit them very well. After luncheon Mr Marchmill strolled out towards the pier, and Mrs Marchmill, having despatched the children to their outdoor amusements on the sands, settled herself in more completely, examining this and that article, and testing the reflecting powers of the mirror in the wardrobe door.

In the small back sitting-room which had been the young bachelor's, she found furniture of a more personal nature than in the rest. Shabby books, of correct rather than rare editions, were piled up in a queerly reserved manner in corners, as if the previous occupant had not conceived the possibility that any incoming person of the season's bringing could care to look inside them. The landlady hovered on the threshold to rectify anything that Mrs Marchmill might not find to her satisfaction.

'I'll make this my own little room,' said the latter, 'because the books are here. By the way, the person who has left seems to have a good many. He won't mind my reading some of them, Mrs Hooper, I hope?'

'O dear no, ma'am. Yes, he has a good many. You see, he is in the literary line himself somewhat. He is a poet – yes, really a poet – and he has a little income of his own, which is enough to write verses on, but not enough for cutting a figure, even if he cared to.'

'A poet! Oh, I did not know that.'

Mrs Marchmill opened one of the books, and saw the owner's name written on the title-page. 'Dear me!' she continued; 'I know his name very well – Robert Trewe – of course I do; and his writings! And it is *his* rooms we have taken, and *him* we have turned out of his home?'

Ella Marchmill, sitting down alone a few mintues later, thought with interested surprise of Robert Trewe. Her own latter history will best explain that interest. Herself the only daughter of a struggling man of letters, she had during the last year or two taken to writing poems, in an endeavour to find a congenial channel in which to let flow her painfully embayed emotions, whose former limpidity and sparkle seemed departing in the stagnation caused by the routine of a practical household and the gloom of bearing children to a commonplace father. These poems, subscribed with a masculine pseudonym, had appeared in various obscure magazines, and in two cases in rather prominent ones. In the second of the latter the page which bore her effusion at the bottom, in smallish print, bore at the top, in large print, a few verses on the same subject by this very man, Robert Trewe. Both of them had, in fact, been struck by a tragic incident reported in the daily papers, and had used it simultaneously as an inspiration, the editor remarking in a note upon the coincidence, and that the excellence of both poems prompted him to give them together.

After that event Ella, otherwise 'John Ivy', had watched with much attention the appearance anywhere in print of verse bearing the signature of Robert Trewe, who, with a man's unsusceptibility on the question of sex, had never once thought of passing himself off as a woman. To be sure, Mrs Marchmill had satisfied herself with a sort of reason for doing the contrary in her case; since nobody might believe in her inspiration if they found that the sentiments came from a pushing tradesman's wife, from the mother of three children by a matter-of-fact small-arms manufacturer.

Trewe's verse contrasted with that of the rank and file of recent minor poets in being impassioned rather than ingenious, luxuriant rather than finished. Neither *symboliste* nor *décadent*, he was a pessimist in so far as that character applies to a man who looks at the worst contingencies as well as the best in the human condition. Being little attracted by excellences of form and rhythm apart from content, he sometimes, when feeling outran his artistic speed, perpetrated sonnets in the loosely rhymed Elizabethan fashion, which every right-minded reviewer said he ought not to have done.

With sad and hopeless envy Ella Marchmill had often and often scanned the rival poet's work, so much stronger as it always was than her own feeble lines. She had imitated him, and her inability to touch his level would send her into fits of despondency. Months passed away thus, till she observed from the publishers' list that Trewe had collected his fugitive pieces into a volume, which was duly issued, and was much or little praised according to chance, and had a sale quite sufficient to pay for the printing.

This step onward had suggested to 'John Ivy' the idea of collecting her pieces also, or at any rate of making up a book of her rhymes by adding many in manuscript to the few that had seen the light, for she had been able to get no great number into print. A ruinous charge was made for costs of publication; a few reviews noticed her poor little volume; but nobody talked of it, nobody bought it, and it fell dead in a fortnight – if it had ever been alive.

The author's thoughts were diverted to another groove just then by the discovery that she was going to have a third child, and the collapse of her poetical venture had perhaps less effect upon her mind than it might have done if she had been domestically unoccupied. Her husband had paid the publisher's bill with the doctor's, and there it all had ended for the time. But, though less than a poet of her century, Ella was more than a mere multiplier of her kind, and latterly she had begun to feel the old afflatus once more. And now by an odd conjunction she found herself in the rooms of Robert Trewe.

She thoughtfully rose from her chair and searched the apartment with the interest of a fellow-tradesman. Yes, the volume of his own verse was among the rest. Though quite familiar with its contents, she read it here as if it spoke aloud to her, then called up Mrs Hooper, the landlady, for some trivial service, and inquired again about the young man.

'Well, I'm sure you'd be interested in him, ma'am, if you could see him, only he's so shy that I don't suppose you will.' Mrs Hooper seemed nothing loth to minister to her tenant's curiosity about her predecessor. 'Lived here long? Yes, nearly two years. He keeps on his rooms even when he's not here: the soft air of this place suits his chest, and he likes to be able to come back at any time. He is mostly writing or reading, and doesn't see many people, though, for the matter of that, he is such a good, kind young fellow that folks would only be too glad to be friendly with him if they knew him. You don't meet kind-hearted people every day.'

'Ah, he's kind-hearted . . . and good.'

'Yes; he'll oblige me in anything if I ask him. "Mr Trewe," I say to him sometimes, "you are rather out of spirits." "Well, I am, Mrs Hooper," he'll say, "though I don't know how you should find it out." "Why not take a little change?" I ask. Then in a day or two he'll say that he will take a trip to Paris, or Norway, or somewhere; and I assure you he comes back all the better for it.'

'Ah, indeed! His is a sensitive nature, no doubt.'

'Yes. Still he's odd in some things. Once when he had finished a poem of his composition late at night he walked up and down the room rehearsing it; and the floors being so thin – jerry-built houses, you know, though I say it myself – he kept me awake up above him till I wished him further . . . But we get on very well.'

This was but the beginning of a series of conversations about the rising poet as the days went on. On one of these occasions Mrs Hooper drew Ella's attention to what she had not noticed before: minute scribblings in pencil on the wall-paper behind the curtains at the head of the bed.

'O! let me look,' said Mrs Marchmill, unable to conceal a rush of tender curiosity as she bent her pretty face close to the wall.

'These,' said Mrs Hooper, with the manner of a woman who knew things, 'are the very beginnings and first thoughts of his verses. He has tried to rub most of them out, but you can read them still. My belief is that he wakes up in the night, you know, with some rhyme in his head, and jots it down there on the wall lest he should forget it by the morning. Some of these very lines you see here I have seen afterwards in print in the magazines. Some are newer; indeed, I have not seen that one before. It must have been done only a few days ago.'

'O yes! . . . '

Ella Marchmill flushed without knowing why, and suddenly wished her companion would go away, now that the information was imparted. An indescribable consciousness of personal interest rather than literary made her anxious to read the inscription alone; and she accordingly waited till she could do so, with a sense that a great store of emotion would be enjoyed in the act.

Perhaps because the sea was choppy outside the Island, Ella's husband found it much pleasanter to go sailing and steaming about without his wife, who was a good sailor, than with her. He did not disdain to go thus alone on board the steamboats of the cheap-trippers, where there was dancing by moonlight, and where the couples would come suddenly down with a lurch into each other's arms; for, as he blandly told her, the company was too mixed for him to take her amid such scenes. Thus, while this thriving manufacturer got a great deal of change and sea-air out of his sojourn here, the life, external at least, of Ella was monotonous enough, and mainly consisted in passing a certain number of hours each day in bathing and walking up and down a stretch of shore. But the poetic impulse having again waxed strong, she was possessed by an inner flame which left her hardly conscious of what was proceeding around her.

She had read till she knew by heart Trewe's last little volume of verses, and spent a great deal of time in vainly attempting to rival some of them, till, in her failure, she burst into tears. The personal element in the magnetic attraction exercised by this circumambient, unapproachable master of hers was so much stronger than the intellectual and abstract that she could not understand it. To be sure, she was surrounded noon and night by his customary environment, which literally whispered of him to her at every moment; but he was a man she had never seen, and that all that moved her was the instinct to specialize a waiting emotion on the first fit thing that came to hand did not, of course, suggest itself to Ella.

In the natural way of passion under the too practical conditions which civilization has devised for its fruition, her husband's love for her had not survived, except in the form of fitful friendship, any more than, or even so much as, her own for him; and, being a woman of very living ardours, that required sustenance of some sort, they were beginning to feed on this chancing material, which was, indeed, of a quality far better than chance usually offers.

One day the children had been playing hide-and-seek in a closet, whence, in their excitement, they pulled out some clothing. Mrs Hooper explained that it belonged to Mr Trewe, and hung it up in the closet again. Possessed of her fantasy, Ella went later in the afternoon, when nobody was in that part of the house, opened the closet, unhitched one of the articles, a mackintosh, and put it on, with the waterproof cap belonging to it.

'The mantle of Elijah!' she said. 'Would it might inspire me to rival him, glorious genius that he is!'

Her eyes always grew wet when she thought like that, and she turned to look at herself in the glass. *His* heart had beat inside that coat, and *his* brain had worked under that hat at levels of thought she would never reach. The consciousness of her weakness beside him made her feel quite sick. Before she had got the things off her the door opened, and her husbnd entered the room.

'What the devil—'

She blushed, and removed them.

'I found them in the closet here,' she said, 'and put them on in a freak. What have I else to do? You are always away!'

'Always away? Well . . . '

That evening she had a further talk with the landlady, who might herself have nourished a half-tender regard for the poet, so ready was she to discourse ardently about him.

'You are interested in Mr Trewe, I know, ma'am,' she said; 'and he has just sent to say that he is going to call tomorrow afternoon to look up some books of his that he wants, if I'll be in, and he may select them from your room?'

'O yes!'

'You could very well meet Mr Trewe then, if you'd like to be in the way!'

She promised with secret delight, and went to bed musing of him.

Next morning her husband observed: 'I've been thinking of what you said, Ell: that I have gone about a good deal and left you without much to amuse you. Perhaps it's true. Today, as there's not much sea, I'll take you with me on board the yacht.'

For the first time in her experience of such an offer Ella was not glad. But she accepted it for the moment. The time for setting out drew near, and she went to get ready. She stood reflecting. The longing to see the poet she was now distinctly in love with overpowered all other considerations.

'I don't want to go,' she said to herself. 'I can't bear to be away! And I won't go.'

She told her husband that she had changed her mind about wishing to sail. He was indifferent, and went his way.

For the rest of the day the house was quiet, the children having gone out upon the sands. The blinds waved in the sunshine to the soft, steady stroke of the sea beyond the wall; and the notes of the Green Silesian band, a troop of foreign gentlemen hired for the season, had drawn almost all the residents and promenaders away from the vicinity of Coburg House. A knock was audible at the door.

Mrs Marchmill did not hear any servant go to answer it, and she became impatient. The books were in the room where she sat; but nobody came up. She rang the bell.

'There is some person waiting at the door,' she said.

'O no, ma'am! He's gone long ago. I answered it,' the servant replied, and Mrs Hooper came in herself.

'So disappointing!' she said. 'Mr Trewe not coming after all!'

'But I heard him knock, I fancy!'

'No; that was somebody inquiring for lodgings who came to the wrong house. I forgot to tell you that Mr Trewe sent a note just before lunch to say I needn't get any tea for him, as he should not require the books, and wouldn't come to select them.'

Ella was miserable, and for a long time could not even re-read his mournful ballad on 'Severed Lives', so aching was her erratic little heart, and so tearful her eyes. When the children came in with wet stockings, and ran up to her to tell her of their adventures, she could not feel that she cared about them half as much as usual.

'Mrs Hooper, have you a photograph of – the gentleman who lived here?' She was getting to be curiously shy in mentioning his name.

'Why, yes. It's in the ornamental frame on the mantelpiece in your own bedroom, ma'am.'

'No; the Royal Duke and Duchess are in that.'

'Yes, so they are; but he's behind them. He belongs rightly to that frame, which I bought on purpose; but as he went away he said: "Cover me up from those strangers that are coming, for God's sake. I don't want them staring at me, and I am sure they won't want me staring at them." So I slipped in the Duke and Duchess temporarily in front of him, as they had no frame, and royalties are more suitable for letting furnished than a private young man. If you take 'em out you'll see him under. Lord, ma'am, he wouldn't mind if he knew it! He didn't think the next tenant would be such an attractive lady as you, or he wouldn't have thought of hiding himself, perhaps.'

'Is he handsome?' she asked timidly.

'*I* call him so. Some, perhaps, wouldn't.'

'Should I?' she asked, with eagerness.

'I think you would, though some would say he's more striking than handsome; a large-eyed, thoughtful fellow, you know, with a very electric flash in his eye when he looks round quickly, such as you'd expect a poet to be who doesn't get his living by it.'

'How old is he?'

'Several years older than yourself, ma'am; about thirty-one or two, I think.'

Ella was, as a matter of fact, a few months over thirty herself; but she did not look nearly so much. Though so immature in nature, she was entering on that tract of life in which emotional women begin to suspect that last love may be stronger than first love; and she would soon, alas! enter on the still more melancholy tract when at least the vainer ones of her sex shrink from receiving a male visitor otherwise than with their backs to the window or the blinds half down. She reflected on Mrs Hooper's remark, and said no more about age.

Just then a telegram was brought up. It came from her husband, who had gone down the Channel as far as Budmouth with his friends in the yacht, and would not be able to get back till next day.

After her light dinner Ella idled about the shore with the children till dusk, thinking of the yet uncovered photograph in her room, with a serene sense of something ecstatic to come. For, with the subtle luxuriousness of fancy in which this young woman was an adept, on learning that her husand was to be absent that night she had refrained from incontinently rushing upstairs and opening the picture-frame, preferring to reserve the inspection till she could be alone, and a more romantic tinge be imparted to the occasion by silence, candles, solemn sea and stars outside, than was afforded by the garish afternoon sunlight.

The children had been sent to bed and Ella soon followed, though it was not yet ten o'clock. To gratify her passionate curiosity she now made her preparations, first getting rid of superfluous garments and putting on her dressing-gown, then arranging a chair in front of the table and reading several pages of Trewe's tenderest utterances. Next she fetched the portrait-frame to the light, opened the back, took out the likeness, and set it up before her.

It was a striking countenance to look upon. The poet wore a luxuriant black moustache and imperial, and a slouched hat which shaded the forehead. The large dark eyes described by the landlady showed an unlimited capacity for misery; they looked out from beneath well-shaped brows as if they were reading the universe in the microcosm of the confronter's face, and were not altogether overjoyed at what the spectacle portended.

Ella murmured in the lowest, richest, tenderest tone: 'And it's *you* who've so cruelly eclipsed me these many times!'

As she gazed long at the portrait she fell into thought, till her eyes filled with tears, and she touched the cardboard with her lips. Then she laughed with a nervous lightness, and wiped her eyes.

She thought how wicked she was, a woman having a husband and three children, to let her mind stray to a stranger in this unconscionable manner. No, he was not a stranger! She knew his thoughts and feelings as well as she knew her own; they were, in fact, the self-same thoughts and feelings as hers, which her husband distinctly lacked; perhaps luckily for himself considering that he had to provide for family expenses.

'He's nearer my real self, he's more intimate with the real me than Will is, after all, even though I've never seen him,' she said.

She laid his book and picture on the table at the bedside, and when she was reclining on the pillow she re-read those of Robert Trewe's verses which she had marked from time to time as most touching and true. Putting these aside she set up the photograph on its edge upon the coverlet, and contemplated it as she lay. Then she scanned again by the light of the candle the half-obliterated pencillings on the wall-paper beside her head. There they were – phrases, couplets, *bouts-rimés*, beginnings and middles of lines, ideas in the rough, like Shelley's scraps, and the least of them so intense, so sweet, so palpitating, that it seemed as if his very breath, warm and loving, fanned her cheeks from those walls, walls that had surrounded his head times and times as they surrounded her own now. He must often have put up his hand so – with the pencil in it. Yes, the writing was sideways, as it would be if executed by one who extended his arm thus.

These inscribed shapes of the poet's world,

> Forms more real than living man,
> Nurslings of immortality,

were, no doubt, the thoughts and spirit-strivings which had come to him in the dead of night, when he could let himself go and have no fear of the frost of criticism. No doubt they had often been written up hastily by the light of the moon, the rays of the lamp, in the blue-grey dawn, in full daylight perhaps never. And now her hair was dragging where his arm had lain when he secured the fugitive fancies; she was sleeping on a poet's lips, immersed in the very essence of him, permeated by his spirit as by an ether.

While she was dreaming the minutes away thus, a footstep came upon the stairs, and in a moment she heard her husband's heavy step on the landing immediately without.

'Ell, where are you?'

What possessed her she could not have described, but, with an instinctive objection to let her husband know what she had been doing, she slipped the photgraph under the pillow just as he flung open the door with the air of a man who had dined not badly.

'O, I beg pardon,' said William Marchmill. 'Have you a headache? I am afraid I have disturbed you.'

'No, I've not got a headache,' said she. 'How is it you've come?'

'Well, we found we could get back in very good time after all, and I didn't want to make another day of it, because of going somewhere else tomorrow.'

'Shall I come down again?'

'O no. I'm as tired as a dog. I've had a good feed, and I shall turn in straight off. I want to get out at six o'clock tomorrow if I can. . . I shan't disturb you by my getting up; it will be long before you are awake.' And he came forward into the room.

While her eyes followed his movements, Ella softly pushed the photograph further out of sight.

'Sure you're not ill?' he asked, bending over her.

'No, only wicked!'

'Never mind that.' And he stooped and kissed her. 'I wanted to be with you tonight.'

Next morning Marchmill was called at six o'clock; and in waking and yawning she heard him muttering to himself: 'What the deuce is this that's been crackling under me so?' Imagining her asleep he searched round him and withdrew something. Through her half-opened eyes she perceived it to be Mr Trewe.

'Well, I'm damned!' her husband exclaimed.

'What, dear?' said she.

'Oh, you are awake? Ha! ha!'

'What *do* you mean?'

'Some bloke's photograph – a friend of our landlady's, I suppose. I wonder how it came here; whisked off the mantelpiece by accident perhaps when they were making the bed.'

'I was looking at it yesterday, and it must have dropped in then.'

'O, he's a friend of yours? Bless his picturesque heart!'

Ella's loyalty to the object of her admiration could not endure to hear him ridiculed. 'He's a clever man!' she said, with a tremor in her gentle voice which she herself felt to be absurdly uncalled for. 'He is a rising poet – the gentleman who occupied two of these rooms before we came, though I've never seen him.'

'How do you know, if you've never seen him?'

'Mrs Hooper told me when she showed me the photograph.'

'O, well, I must up and be off. I shall be home rather early. Sorry I can't take you today, dear. Mind the children don't go getting drowned.'

That day Mrs Marchmill inquired if Mr Trewe were likely to call at any other time.

'Yes,' said Mrs Hooper. 'He's coming this day week to stay with a friend near here till you leave. He'll be sure to call.'

Marchmill did return quite early in the afternoon; and, opening some letters which had arrived in his absence, declared suddenly that he and his family would have to leave a week earlier than they had expected to do – in short, in three days.

'Surely we can stay a week longer?' she pleaded. 'I like it here.'

'I don't. It is getting rather slow.'

'Then you might leave me and the children!'

'How perverse you are, Ell! What's the use? And have to come to fetch you! No: we'll all return together; and we'll make out our time in North Wales or Brighton a little later on. Besides, you've three days longer yet.'

It seemed to be her doom not to meet the man for whose rival talent she had a despairing admiration, and to whose person she was now absolutely attached. Yet she determined to make a last effort; and having gathered from her landlady that Trewe was living in a lonely spot not far from the fashionable town on the Island opposite, she crossed over in the packet from the neighbouring pier the following afternoon.

What a useless journey it was! Ella knew but vaguely where the house stood, and when she fancied she had found it, and ventured to inquire of a pedestrian if he lived there, the answer returned by the man was that he did not know. And if he did live there, how could she call upon him? Some women might have the assurance to do it, but she had not. How crazy he would think her. She might have asked him to call upon her, perhaps; but she had not the courage for that, either. She lingered mournfully about the picturesque seaside eminence till it was time to return to the town and enter the steamer for recrossing, reaching home for dinner without having been greatly missed.

At the last moment, unexpectedly enough, her husband said that he should have no objection to letting her and the children stay on till the end of the week, since she wished to do so, if she felt herself able to get home without him. She concealed the pleasure this extension of time gave her; and Marchmill went off the next morning alone.

But the week passed, and Trewe did not call.

On Saturday morning the remaining members of the Marchmill family departed from the place which had been productive of so much fervour in her. The dreary, dreary train; the sun shining in moted beams upon the hot cushions; the dusty permanent way; the mean rows of wire – these things were her accompaniment: while out of the window the deep blue sea-levels disappeared from her gaze, and with them her poet's home. Heavy-hearted, she tried to read, and wept instead.

Mr Marchmill was in a thriving way of business, and he and his family lived in a large new house, which stood in rather extensive grounds a few miles outside the midland city wherein he carried on his trade. Ella's life was lonely here, as the suburban life is apt to be, particularly at certain seasons; and she had ample time to indulge her taste for lyric and elegiac composition. She had hardly got back when she encountered a piece by Robert Trewe in the new number of her favourite magazine, which must have been written almost immediately before her visit to Solentsea, for it contained the very couplet she had seen pencilled on the wall-paper by the bed, and Mrs Hooper had declared to be recent. Ella could resist no longer, but seizing a pen impulsively, wrote to him as a brother-poet, using the name of John Ivy, congratulating him in her letter on his triumphant executions in metre and rhythm of thoughts that moved his soul, as compared with her own brow-beaten efforts in the same pathetic trade.

To this address there came a response in a few days, little as she had dared to hope for it – a civil and brief note, in which the young poet stated that, though he was not well acquainted with Mr Ivy's verse, he recalled the name as being one he had seen attached to some very promising pieces; that he was glad to gain Mr Ivy's acquaintance by letter, and should certainly look with much interest for his productions in the future.

There must have been something juvenile or timid in her own epistle, as one ostensibly coming from a man, she declared to herself; for Trewe quite adopted the tone of an elder and superior in this reply. But what did it matter? He had replied; he had written to her with his own hand from that very room she knew so well, for he was now back again in his quarters.

The correspondence thus begun was continued for two months or more, Ella Marchmill sending him from time to time some that she considered to be the best of her pieces, which he very kindly accepted, though he did not say he sedulously read them, nor did he send her any of his own in return. Ella would have been more hurt at this than she was if she had not known that Trewe laboured under the impression that she was one of his own sex.

Yet the situation was unsatisfactory. A flattering little voice told her that, were he only to see her, matters would be otherwise. No doubt she would have helped on this by making a frank confession of womanhood, to begin with, if something had not happened, to her delight, to render it unnecessary. A friend of her husband's, the editor of the most important newspaper in their city and county, who was dining with them one day, observed during their conversation about the poet that his (the editor's) brother the landscape-painter was a friend of Mr Trewe's, and that the two men were at that very moment in Wales together.

Ella was slightly acquainted with the editor's brother. The next morning down she sat and wrote, inviting him to stay at her house for a short time on his way back, and requesting him to bring with him, if practicable, his companion Mr Trewe, whose acquaintance she was anxious to make. The answer arrived after some few days. Her correspondent and his friend Trewe would have much satisfaction in accepting her invitation on their way southward, which would be on such and such a day in the following week.

Ella was blithe and buoyant. Her scheme had succeeded; her beloved though as yet unseen one was coming. 'Behold, he standeth behind our wall; he looked forth at the windows, showing himself through the lattice,' she thought ecstatically. 'And, lo, the winter is past, the rain is over and gone, the flowers appear on the earth, the time of the singing of birds is come, and the voice of the turtle is heard in our land.'

But it was necessary to consider the details of lodging and feeding him. This she did most solicitously, and awaited the pregnant day and hour.

It was about five in the afternoon when she heard a ring at the door and the editor's brother's voice in the hall. Poetess as she was, or as she thought herself, she had not been too sublime that day to dress with infinite trouble in a fashionable robe of rich material, having a faint resemblance to the *chiton* of the Greeks, a style just then in vogue among ladies of an artistic and romantic turn, which had been obtained by Ella of her Bond Street dressmaker when she was last in London. Her visitor entered the drawing-room. She looked towards his rear; nobody else came through the door. Where, in the name of the God of Love, was Robert Trewe?

'O, I'm sorry,' said the painter, after their introductory words had been spoken. 'Trewe is a curious fellow, you know, Mrs Marchmill. He said he'd come; then he said he couldn't. He's rather dusty. We've been doing a few miles with knapsacks, you know; and he wanted to get on home.'

'He – he's not coming?'

'He's not; and he asked me to make his apologies.'

'When did you p-p-part from him?' she asked, her nether lip starting off quivering so much that it was like a *tremolo*-stop opened in her speech. She longed to run away from this dreadful bore and cry her eyes out.

'Just now, in the turnpike road yonder there.'

'What! he has actually gone past my gates?'

'Yes. When we got to them – handsome gates they are, too, the finest bit of modern wrought-iron work I have seen – when we came to them we stopped, talking there a little while, and then he wished me good-bye and went on. The truth is, he's a little bit depressed just now, and doesn't want to see anybody. He's a very good fellow, and a warm friend, but a little uncertain and gloomy sometimes; he thinks too much of things. His poetry is rather too erotic and passionate, you know, for some tastes; and he has just come in for a terrible slating from the —— *Review* that was published yesterday; he saw a copy of it at the station by accident. Perhaps you've read it?'

'No.'

'So much the better. O, it is not worth thinking of; just one of those articles written to order, to please the narrow-minded set of subscribers upon whom the circulation depends. But he's upset by it. He says it is the misrepresentation that hurts him so; that, though he can stand a fair attack, he can't stand lies that he's powerless to refute and stop from spreading. That's just Trewe's weak point. He lives so much by himself that these things affect him much more than they would if he were in the bustle of fashionable or commercial life. So he wouldn't come here, making the excuse that it all looked so new and monied – if you'll pardon—'

'But – he must have known – there was sympathy here! Has he never said anything about getting letters from this address?'

'Yes, yes, he has, from John Ivy – perhaps a relative of yours, he thought, visiting here at the time?'

'Did he – like Ivy, did he say?'

'Well, I don't know that he took any great interest in Ivy.'

'Or in his poems?'

'Or in his poems – so far as I know, that is.'

Robert Trewe took no interest in her house, in her poems, or in their writer. As soon as she could get away she went into the nursery and tried to let off her emotion by unnecessarily kissing the children, till she had a sudden sense of disgust at being reminded how plain-looking they were, like their father.

The obtuse and single-minded landscape-painter never once perceived from her conversation that it was only Trewe she wanted, and not himself. He made the best of his visit, seeming to enjoy the society of Ella's husband, who also took a great fancy to him, and showed him everywhere about the neighbourhood, neither of them noticing Ella's mood.

The painter had been gone only a day or two when, while sitting upstairs alone one morning, she glanced over the London paper just arrived, and read the following paragraph:

SUICIDE OF A POET

Mr Robert Trewe, who has been favourably known for some years as one of our rising lyrists, committed suicide at his lodgings at Solentsea on Saturday evening last by shooting himself in the right temple with a revolver. Readers

> hardly need to be reminded that Mr Trewe has recently attracted the attention of a much wider public than had hitherto known him, by his new volume of verse, mostly of an impassioned kind, entitled 'Lyrics to a Woman Unknown', which has been already favourably noticed in these pages for the extraordinary gamut of feeling it traverses, and which has been made the subject of a severe, if not ferocious, criticism in the —— *Review*. It is supposed, though not certainly known, that the article may have partially conduced to the sad act, as a copy of the review in question was found on his writing-table; and he has been observed to be in a somewhat depressed state of mind since the critique appeared.

Then came the report of the inquest, at which the following letter was read, it having been addressed to a friend at a distance:

> DEAR——, Before these lines reach your hands I shall be delivered from the inconveniences of seeing, hearing, and knowing more of the things around me. I will not trouble you by giving my reasons for the step I have taken, though I can assure you they were sound and logical. Perhaps had I been blessed with a mother, or a sister, or a female friend of another sort tenderly devoted to me, I might have thought it worth while to continue my present existence. I have long dreamt of such an unattainable creature, as you know; and she, this undiscoverable, elusive one, inspired my last volume; the imaginary woman alone, for, in spite of what has been said in some quarters, there is no real woman behind the title. She has continued to the last unrevealed, unmet, unwon. I think it desirable to mention this in order that no blame may attach to any real woman as having been the cause of my decease by cruel or cavalier treatment of me. Tell my landlady that I am sorry to have caused her this unpleasantness; but my occupancy of the rooms will soon be forgotten. There are ample funds in my name at the bank to pay all expenses.
>
> R.T.

Ella sat for a while as if stunned, then rushed into the adjoining chamber and flung herself upon her face on the bed.

Her grief and distraction shook her to pieces; and she lay in this frenzy of sorrow for more than an hour. Broken words came every now and then from her quivering lips: 'O, if he had only known of me – known of me – me! . . . O, if I had only once met him – only once; and put my hand upon his hot forehead – kissed him – let him know how I loved him – that I would have suffered shame and scorn, would have lived and died, for him! Perhaps it would have saved his dear life! . . . But no – it was not allowed! God is a jealous God; and that happiness was not for him and me!'

All possibilities were over; the meeting was stultified. Yet it was almost visible to her in her fantasy even now, though it could never be substantiated:

> The hour which might have been, yet might not be,
> Which man's and woman's heart conceived and bore,
> Yet whereof life was barren.

She wrote to the landlady at Solentsea in the third person, in as subdued a style as she could command, enclosing a postal order for a sovereign, and informing Mrs Hooper that Mrs Marchmill had seen in the papers the sad account of the poet's death, and having been, as Mrs Hooper was aware, much interested in Mr Trewe during her stay at Coburg House, she would be obliged if Mrs Hooper could obtain a small portion of his hair before his coffin was closed down, and send it her as a memorial of him, as also the photograph that was in the frame.

By the return-post a letter arrived containing what had been requested. Ella wept over the portrait and secured it in her private drawer; the lock of hair she tied with white ribbon and put in her bosom, whence she drew it and kissed it every now and then in some unobserved nook.

'What's the matter?' said her husband, looking up from his newspaper on one of these occasions. 'Crying over something? A lock of hair? Whose is it?'

'He's dead!' she murmured.

'Who?'

'I don't want to tell you, Will, just now, unless you insist!' she said, a sob hanging heavy in her voice.

'O, all right.'

'Do you mind my refusing? I will tell you some day.'

'It doesn't matter in the least, of course.'

He walked away whistling a few bars of no tune in particular; and when he had got down to his factory in the city the subject came into Marchmill's head again.

He, too, was aware that a suicide had taken place recently at the house they had occupied at Solentsea. Having seen the volume of poems in his wife's hand of late, and heard fragments of the landlady's conversation about Trewe when they were her tenants, he all at once said to himself, 'Why of course it's he! . . . How the devil did she get to know him? What sly animals women are!'

Then he placidly dismissed the matter, and went on with his daily affairs. By this time Ella at home had come to a determination. Mrs Hooper, in sending the hair and photograph, had informed her of the day of the funeral; and as the morning and noon wore on an overpowering wish to know where they were laying him took possession of the sympathetic woman. Caring very little now what her husband or anyone else might think of her eccentricities, she wrote Marchmill a brief note, stating that she was called away for the afternoon and evening, but would return on the following morning. This she left on his desk, and having given the same information to the servants, went out of the house on foot.

When Mr Marchmill reached home early in the afternoon the servants looked anxious. The nurse took him privately aside, and hinted that her mistress's sadness during the past few days had been such that she feared she had gone out to drown herself. Marchmill reflected. Upon the whole he thought that she had not done that. Without saying whither he was bound he also started off, telling them not to sit up for him. He drove to the railway-station, and took a ticket for Solentsea.

It was dark when he reached the place, though he had come by a fast train, and he knew that if his wife had preceded him thither it could only have been by a slower train, arriving not a great while before his own. The season at Solentsea was now past: the parade was gloomy, and the flys were few and cheap. He asked the way to the Cemetery, and soon reached it. The gate was locked, but the keeper let him in, declaring, however, that there was nobody within the precincts. Although it was not late, the autumnal darkness had now become intense; and he found some difficulty in keeping to the serpentine path which led to the quarter where, as the man had told him, the one or two interments for the day had taken place. He stepped upon the grass, and, stumbling over some pegs, stooped now and then to discern if possible a figure against the sky. He could see none; but lighting on a spot where the soil was trodden, beheld a crouching object beside a newly-made grave. She heard him, and sprang up.

'Ell, how silly this is!' he said indignantly. 'Running away from home – I never heard such a thing! Of course I am not jealous of this unfortunate man; but it is too ridiculous that you, a married woman with three children and a fourth coming, should go losing your head like this over a dead lover! . . . Do you know you were locked in? You might not have been able to get out all night.'

She did not answer.

'I hope it didn't go far between you and him, for your own sake.'

'Don't insult me, Will.'

'Mind, I won't have any more of this sort of thing; do you hear?'

'Very well,' she said.

He drew her arm within his own, and conducted her out of the

Cemetery. It was impossible to get back that night; and not wishing to be recognized in their present sorry condition he took her to a miserable little coffee-house close to the station, whence they departed early in the morning, travelling almost without speaking, under the sense that it was one of those dreary situations occurring in married life which words could not mend, and reaching their own door at noon.

The months passed, and neither of the twain ever ventured to start a conversation upon this episode. Ella seemed to be only too frequently in a sad and listless mood, which might almost have been called pining. The time was approaching when she would have to undergo the stress of childbirth for a fourth time, and that apparently did not tend to raise her spirits.

'I don't think I shall get over it this time!' she said one day.

'Pooh! what childish foreboding! Why shouldn't it be as well now as ever?'

She shook her head. 'I feel almost sure I am going to die; and I should be glad, if it were not for Nelly, and Frank, and Tiny.'

'And me!'

'You'll soon find somebody to fill my place,' she murmured, with a sad smile. 'And you'll have a perfect right to; I assure you of that.'

'Ell, you are not thinking still about that – poetical friend of yours?'

She neither admitted nor denied the charge. 'I am not going to get over my illness this time,' she reiterated. 'Something tells me I shan't.'

This view of things was rather a bad beginning, as it usually is; and, in fact six weeks later, in the month of May, she was lying in her room, pulseless and bloodless, with hardly strength enough left to follow up one feeble breath with another, the infant for whose unnecessary life she was slowly parting with her own being fat and well. Just before her death she spoke to Marchmill softly:

'Will, I want to confess to you the entire circumstances of that – about you know what – that time we visited Solentsea. I can't tell what possessed me – how I could forget you so, my husband! But I had got into a morbid state: I thought you had been unkind; that you had neglected me; that you weren't up to my intellectual level, while he was, and far above it. I wanted a fuller appreciator, perhaps, rather than another lover—'

She could get no further then for very exhaustion; and she went off in sudden collapse a few hours later, without having said anything more to her husband on the subject of her love for the poet. William Marchmill, in truth, like most husbands of several years' standing, was little disturbed by retrospective jealousies, and had not shown the least anxiety to press her for confessions concerning a man dead and gone beyond any power of inconveniencing him more.

But when she had been buried a couple of years it chanced one day that, in turning over some forgotten papers that he wished to destroy before his second wife entered the house, he lighted on a lock of hair in an envelope, with the photograph of the deceased poet, a date being written on the back in his late wife's hand. It was that of the time they spent at Solentsea.

Marchmill looked long and musingly at the hair and portrait, for something struck him. Fetching the little boy who had been the death of his mother, now a noisy toddler, he took him on his knee, held the lock of hair against the child's head, and set up the photograph on the table behind, so that he could closely compare the features each countenance presented. By a known but inexplicable trick of Nature there were undoubtedly strong traces of resemblance to the man Ella had never seen; the dreamy and peculiar expression of the poet's face sat, as the transmitted idea, upon the child's, and the hair was of the same hue.

'I'm damned if I didn't think so!' murmured Marchmill. 'Then she *did* play me false with that fellow at the lodgings! Let me see: the dates – the second week in August . . . the third week in May. . . Yes. . . yes. . . Get away, you poor little brat! You are nothing to me!'

1893

THE SON'S VETO

I

To the eyes of a man viewing it from behind the nut-brown hair was a wonder and a mystery. Under the black beaver hat surmounted by its tuft of black feathers, the long locks, braided and twisted and coiled like the rushes of a basket, composed a rare, if somewhat barbaric, example of ingenious art. One could understand such weavings and coilings being wrought to last intact for a year or even a calendar month; but that they should be all demolished regularly at bedtime, after a single day of permanence, seemed a reckless waste of successful fabrication.

And she had done it all herself, poor thing. She had no maid and it was almost the only accomplishment she could boast of. Hence the unstinted pains.

She was a young invalid lady – not so very much of an invalid – sitting in a wheeled chair, which had been pulled up in the front part of a green enclosure, close to a bandstand where a concert was going on, during a warm June afternoon. It had place in one of the minor parks or private gardens that are to be found in the suburbs of London, and was the effort of a local association to raise money for some charity. There are worlds within worlds in the great city, and though nobody outside the immediate district had ever heard of the charity, or the band, or the garden, the enclosure was filled with an interested audience sufficiently informed on all these.

As the strains proceeded many of the listeners observed the chaired lady, whose back hair, by reason of her prominent position, so challenged inspection. Her face was not easily discernible, but the aforesaid cunning tress-weavings, the white ear and poll, and the curve of a cheek which was neither flaccid nor sallow, were signals that led to the expectation of good beauty in front. Such expectations are not infrequently disappointed as soon as the disclosure comes; and in the present case, when the lady, by a turn of the head, at length revealed herself, she was not so handsome as the people behind her had supposed, and even hoped – they did not know why.

For one thing (alas! the commonness of this complaint), she was less young than they had fancied her to be. Yet attractive her face unquestionably was, and not at all sickly. The revelation of its details came each time she turned to talk to a boy of twelve or thirteen who stood beside her, and the shape of whose hat and jacket implied that he belonged to a well-known public school. The immediate bystanders could hear that he called her 'Mother'.

When the end of the recital was reached, and the audience withdrew, many chose to find their way out by passing at her elbow. Almost all turned their heads to take a full and near look at the interesting woman, who remained stationary in the chair till the way should be clear enough for her to be wheeled out without obstruction. As if she expected their glances, and did not mind gratifying their curiosity, she met the eyes of several of her observers by lifting her own, showing these to be soft, brown, and affectionate orbs, a little plaintive in their regard.

She was conducted out of the gardens, and passed along the pavement till she disappeared from view, the schoolboy walking beside her. To inquiries made by some persons who watched her away, the answer came that she was the second wife of the incumbent of a neighbouring parish, and that she was lame. She was generally believed to be a woman with a story – an innocent one, but a story of some sort or other.

In conversing with her on their way home the boy who walked at her elbow said that he hoped his father had not missed them.

'He have been so comfortable these last few hours that I am sure he cannot have missed us,' she replied.

'*Has*, dear mother – not *have*!' exclaimed the public-school boy, with an impatient fastidiousness that was almost harsh. 'Surely you know that by this time!'

His mother hastily adopted the correction, and did not resent his making it, or retaliate, as she might well have done, by bidding him to wipe that crumby mouth of his, whose condition had been caused by surreptitious attempts to eat a piece of cake without taking it out of the pocket wherein it lay concealed. After this the pretty woman and the boy went onward in silence.

That question of grammar bore upon her history, and she fell into reverie, of a somewhat sad kind to all appearance. It might have been assumed that she was wondering if she had done wisely in shaping her life as she had shaped it, to bring out such a result as this.

In a remote nook in North Wessex, forty miles from London, near the thriving county-town of Aldbrickham, there stood a pretty village with its church and parsonage, which she knew well enough, but her son had never seen. It was her native village, Gaymead, and the first event bearing upon her present situation had occurred at that place when she was only a girl of nineteen.

How well she remembered it, that first act in her little tragi-comedy, the death of her reverend husband's first wife. It happened on a spring evening, and she who now and for many years had filled that first wife's place was then parlour-maid in the parson's house.

When everything had been done that could be done, and the death was announced, she had gone out in the dusk to visit her parents, who were living in the same village, to tell them the sad news. As she opened the white swing-gate and looked towards the trees which rose westward, shutting out the pale light of the evening sky, she discerned, without much surprise, the figure of a man standing in the hedge, though she roguishly exclaimed as a matter of form, 'O, Sam, how you frightened me!'

He was a young gardener of her aquaintance. She told him the particulars of the late event, and they stood silent, these two young people, in that elevated, calmly philosophic mind which is engendered when a tragedy has happened close at hand, and has not happened to the philosophers themselves. But it had its bearing upon their relations.

'And will you stay on now at the Vicarage, just the same?' asked he.

She had hardly thought of that. 'O yes – I suppose!' she said. 'Everything will be just as usual, I imagine?'

He walked beside her towards her mother's. Presently his arm stole round her waist. She gently removed it; but he placed it there again, and she yielded the point. 'You see, dear Sophy, you don't know that you'll stay on; you may want a home, and I shall be ready to offer one someday, though I may not be ready just yet.'

'Why, Sam, how can you be so fast! I've never even said I liked 'ee; and it is all your own doing, coming after me!'

'Still, it is nonsense to say I am not to have a try at you like the rest.' He stooped to kiss her a farewell, for they had reached her mother's door.

'No, Sam; you shan't!' she cried, putting her hand over his mouth. 'You ought to be more serious on such a night as this.' And she bade him adieu without allowing him to kiss her or to come indoors.

The vicar just left a widower was at this time a man about forty years of age, of good family, and childless. He had led a secluded existence in this college living, partly because there were no resident landowners; and his loss now intensified his habit of withdrawal from outward observation. He was seen still less than heretofore, kept himself still less in time with the rhythm and racket of the movements called progress in the world without. For many months after his wife's decease the economy of his household remained as before; the cook, the housemaid, the parlour-maid, and the man out-of-doors performed their duties or left them undone, just as Nature prompted them – the vicar knew not which. It was then represented to him that his servants seemed to have nothing to do in his small family of one. He was stuck with the truth of this representation, and decided to cut down his establishment. But he was forestalled by Sophy, the parlour-maid, who said one evening that she wished to leave him.

'And why?' said the parson.

'Sam Hobson has asked me to marry him, sir.'

'Well – do you want to marry?'

'Not much. But it would be a home for me. And we have heard that one of us will have to leave.'

A day or two after she said: 'I don't want to leave just yet, sir, if you don't wish it. Sam and I have quarrelled.'

He looked up at her. He had hardly ever observed her before, though he had been frequently conscious of her soft presence in the room. What a kitten-like, flexuous, tender creature she was! She was the only one of the servants with whom he came into immediate and continuous relation. What should he do if Sophy were gone?

Sophy did not go, but one of the others did, and things went on quietly again.

When Mr Twycott, the vicar, was ill, Sophy brought up his meals to him, and she had no sooner left the room one day than he heard a noise on the stairs. She had slipped down with the tray, and so twisted her foot that she could not stand. The village surgeon was called in; the vicar got better, but Sophy was incapacitated for a long time; and she was informed that she must never again walk much or engage in any occupation which required her to stand long on her feet. As soon as she was comparatively well she spoke to him alone. Since she was forbidden to walk and bustle about, and, indeed, could not do so, it became her duty to leave. She could very well work at something sitting down, and she had an aunt a seamstress.

The parson had been very greatly moved by what she had suffered on his account, and he exclaimed, 'No, Sophy; lame or not lame, I cannot let you go. You must never leave me again!'

He came close to her, and, though she could never exactly tell how it happened, she became conscious of his lips upon her cheek. He then asked her to marry him. Sophy did not exactly love him, but she had a respect for him which almost amounted to veneration. Even if she had wished to get away from him she hardly cared refuse a personage so reverend and august in her eyes, and she assented forthwith to be his wife.

Thus it happened that one fine morning, when the doors of the church were naturally open for ventilation, and the singing birds fluttered in and alighted on the tie-beams of the roof, there was a marriage-service at the communion-rails, which hardly a soul knew of. The parson and a neighbouring curate had entered at one door, and Sophy at another, followed by two necessary persons, whereupon in a short time there emerged a newly-made husband and wife.

Mr Twycott knew perfectly well that he had committed social suicide by this step, despite Sophy's spotless character, and he had taken his measures accordingly. An exchange of livings had been arranged with an acquaintance who was incumbent of a church in the south of London, and as soon as possible the couple removed thither, abandoning their pretty country home, with trees and shrubs and glebe, for a narrow, dusty house in a long, straight street, and their fine peal of bells for the wretchedest one-tongued clangour that ever tortured mortal ears. It was all on her account. They were, however, away from every one who had known her former position; and also under less observation from without that they would have had to put up with in any country parish.

Sophy the woman was as charming a partner as a man could possess, though Sophy the lady had her deficiencies. She showed a natural aptitude for little domestic refinements, so far as related to things and manners; but in what is called culture she was less intuitive. She had now been married more than fourteen years, and her husband had taken much trouble with her education; but she still held confused ideas on the use of 'was' and 'were', which did not beget a respect for her among the few acquaintances she made. Her great grief in this relation was that her only child, on whose education no expense had been and would be spared, was now old enough to perceive these deficiencies in his mother, and not only to see them but to feel irritated at their existence.

Thus she lived on in the city, and wasted hours in braiding her beautiful hair, till her once apple cheeks waned to pink of the very faintest. Her foot had never regained its natural strength after the accident, and she was mostly obliged to avoid walking altogether. Her husband had grown to like London for its freedom and its domestic privacy; but he was twenty years his Sophy's senior, and had latterly been seized with a serious illness. On this day, however, he had seemed to be well enough to justify her accompanying her son Randolph to the concert.

2

The next time we get a glimpse of her is when she appears in the mournful attire of a widow.

Mr Twycott had never rallied, and now lay in a well-parked cemetery to the south of the great city, where, if all the dead it contained had stood erect and alive, not one would have known him or recognized his name. The boy had dutifully followed him to the grave, and was now again at school.

Throughout these changes Sophy had been treated like the child she was in nature though not in years. She was left with no control over anything that had been her husband's beyond her modest personal income. In his anxiety lest her inexperience should be overreached he had safe-guarded with trustees all he possibly could. The completion of the boy's course at the public school, to be followed in due time by Oxford and ordination, had been all previsioned and arranged, and she really had nothing to occupy her in the world but to eat and drink, and make a business of indolence, and go on weaving and coiling the nut-brown hair, merely keeping a home open for the son whenever he came to her during vacations.

Foreseeing his probable decease long years before her, her husband in his lifetime had purchased for her use a semi-detached villa in the same long, straight road whereon the church and parsonage faced, which was to be hers as long as she chose to live in it. Here she now resided, looking out upon the fragment of lawn in front, and through the railings at the ever-flowing traffic; or, bending forward over the window-sill on the first floor, stretching her eyes far up and down the vista of sooty trees, hazy air, and drab house-façades, along which echoed the noises common to a suburban main thoroughfare.

Somehow, her boy, with his aristocratic school-knowledge, his grammars, and his aversions, was losing those wide infantine sympathies, extending as far as to the sun and moon themselves, with which he, like other children, had been born, and which his mother, a child of nature herself, had loved in him; he was reducing their compass to a population of a few thousand wealthy and titled people, the mere veneer of a thousand million or so of others who did not interest him at all. He drifted further and further away from her. Sophy's *milieu* being a suburb of minor tradesmen and under-clerks, and her almost only companions the two servants of her own house, it was not surprising that after her husband's death she soon lost the little artificial tastes she had acquired from him, and became – in her son's eyes – a mother whose mistakes and origin it was his painful lot as a gentleman to blush for. As yet he was far from being man enough – if he ever would be – to rate these sins of hers at their true infinitesimal value beside the yearning fondness that welled up and remained penned in her heart till it should be more fully accepted by him, or by some other person or thing. If he had lived at home with her he would have had all of it; but he seemed to require so very little in present circumstances, and it remained stored.

Her life became insupportably dreary; she could not take walks, and had no interest in going for drives, or, indeed, in travelling anywhere. Nearly two years passed without an event, and still she looked on that suburban road, thinking of the village in which she had been born, and whither she would have gone back – O how gladly! – even to work in the fields.

Taking no exercise she often could not sleep, and would rise in the night or early morning to look out upon the then vacant thoroughfare, where the lamps stood like sentinels waiting for some procession to go by. An approximation to such a procession was indeed made early every morning about one o'clock, when the country vehicles passed up with loads of vegetables for Covent Garden market. She often saw them creeping along at this silent and dusky hour – waggon after waggon, bearing green bastions of cabbages nodding to their fall, yet never falling, walls of baskets enclosing masses of beans and peas, pyramids of snow-white turnips, swaying howdahs of mixed produce – creeping along behind aged night-horses, who seemed ever patiently wondering between their hollow coughs why they had always to work at that still hour when all other sentient creatures were privileged to rest. Wrapped in a cloak it was soothing to watch and sympathize with them when depression and nervousness hindered sleep, and to see how the fresh green-stuff brightened to life as it came opposite the lamp, and how the sweating animals steamed and shone with their miles of travel.

They had an interest, almost a charm, for Sophy, these semi-rural people and vehicles moving in an urban atmosphere, leading a life quite distinct from that of the daytime toilers on the same road. One morning a man who accompanied a waggonload of potatoes gazed rather hard at the house-fronts as he passed, and with a curious emotion she thought his form was familiar to her. She looked out for him again. His being an old-fashioned conveyance, with a yellow front, it was easily recognizable, and on the third night after she saw it a second time. The man alongside was, as she had fancied, Sam Hobson, formerly gardener at Gaymead, who would at one time have married her.

She had occasionally thought of him, and wondered if life in a cottage with him would not have been a happier lot than the life she had accepted. She had not thought of him passionately, but her now dismal situation lent an interest to his resurrection – a tender interest which it is impossible to exaggerate. She went back to bed, and began thinking. When did these market-gardeners, who travelled up to town so regularly at one or two in the morning, come back? She dimly recollected seeing their empty waggons, hardly noticeable amid the ordinary day-traffic, passing down at some hour before noon.

It was only April, but that morning, after breakfast, she had the window opened, and sat looking out, the feeble sun shining full upon her. She affected to sew, but her eyes never left the street. Between ten and eleven the desired waggon, now unladen reappeared on its return journey. But Sam was not looking round him then, and drove on in a reverie.

'Sam!' cried she.

Turning with a start, his face lighted up. He called to him a little boy to hold the horse, alighted, and came and stood under the window.

'I can't come down easily, Sam, or I would!' she said. 'Did you know I lived here?'

'Well, Mrs Twycott, I knew you lived along here somewhere. I have often looked out for 'ee.'

He briefly explained his own presence on the scene. He had long since given up his gardening in the village near Aldbrickham, and was now manager at a market-gardener's on the south side of London, it being part of his duty to go up to Covent Garden with waggon-loads of produce two or three times a week. In answer to her curious inquiry, he admitted that he had come to this particular district because he had seen in the Aldbrickham paper, a year or two before, the announcement of the death in south London of the aforetime vicar of Gaymead, which had revived an interest in her dwelling-place that he could not extinguish, leading him to hover about the locality till his present post had been secured.

They spoke of their native village in dear old North Wessex, the spots in which they had played together as children. She tried to feel that she was a dignified personage now, that she must not be too confidential with Sam. But she could not keep it up, and the tears hanging in her eyes were indicated in her voice.

'You are not happy, Mrs Twycott, I'm afraid?' he said.

'O, of course not! I lost my husband only the year before last.'

'Ah! I meant in another way. You'd like to be home again?'

'This is my home – for life. The house belongs to me. But I understand—' She let it out then. 'Yes, Sam. I long for home – *our* home! I *should* like to be there, and never leave it, and die there.' But she remembered herself. 'That's only a momentary feeling. I have a son, you know, a dear boy. He's at school now.'

'Somewhere handy, I suppose? I see there's lots on 'em along this road.'

'O no! Not in one of these wretched holes! At a public school – one of the most distinguished in England.'

'Chok' it all! of course! I forget, ma'am, that you've been a lady for so many years.'

'No, I am not a lady,' she said sadly. 'I never shall be. But he's a gentleman, and that – makes it – O how difficult for me!'

3

The acquaintance thus oddly reopened proceeded apace. She often looked out to get a few words with him, by night or by day. Her sorrow was that she could not accompany her one old friend on foot a little way, and talk more freely than she could do while he paused before the house. One night, at the beginning of June, when she was again on the watch after an absence of some days from the window, he entered the gate and said softly, 'Now, wouldn't some air do you good? I've only half a load this morning. Why not ride up to Covent Garden with me? There's a nice seat on the cabbages, where I've spread a sack. You can be home again in a cab before anybody is up.'

She refused at first, and then, trembling with excitement, hastily finished her dressing, and wrapped herself up in cloak and veil, afterwards sidling downstairs by the aid of the handrail, in a way she could adopt on an emergency. When she had opened the door she found Sam on the step, and he lifted her bodily on his strong arm across the little forecourt into his vehicle. Not a soul was visible or audible in the infinite length of the straight, flat highway, with its ever-waiting lamps converging to points in each direction. The air was fresh as country air at this hour, and the stars shone, except to the north-eastward, where there was a whitish light – the dawn. Sam carefully placed her in the seat and drove on.

They talked as they had talked in old days, Sam pulling himself up now and then, when he thought himself too familiar. More than once she said with misgiving that she wondered if she ought to have indulged in the freak. 'But I am so lonely in my house,' she added, 'and this makes me so happy!'

'You must come again, dear Mrs Twycott. There is no time o' day for taking the air like this.'

It grew lighter and lighter. The sparrows became busy in the streets, and the city waxed denser around them. When they approached the river it was day, and on the bridge they beheld the full blaze of morning sunlight in the drection of St Paul's, the river glistening towards it, and not a craft stirring.

Near Covent Garden he put her into a cab, and they parted, looking into each other's faces like the very old friends they were. She reached home without adventure, limped to the door, and let herself in with her latch-key unseen.

The air and Sam's presence had revived her: her cheeks were quite pink – almost beautiful. She had something to live for in addition to her son. A woman of pure instincts, she knew there had been nothing really wrong in the journey, but supposed it conventionally to be very wrong indeed.

Soon, however, she gave way to the temptation of going with him again, and on this occasion their conversation was distinctly tender, and Sam said he never should forget her, notwithstanding that she had served him rather badly at one time. After much hesitation he told her of a plan it was in his power to carry out, and one he should like to take in hand, since he did not care for London work: it was to set up as a master greengrocer down at Aldbrickham, the county-town of their native place. He knew of an opening – a shop kept by aged people who wished to retire.

'And why don't you do it, then, Sam?' she asked with a slight heartsinking.

'Because I'm not sure if – you'd join me. I know you wouldn't, couldn't! Such a lady as ye've been so long, you couldn't be a wife to a man like me.'

'I hardly suppose I could!' she assented, also frightened at the idea.

'If you could', he said eagerly, 'you'd on'y have to sit in the back parlour and look through the glass partition when I was away sometimes – just to keep an eye on things. The lameness wouldn't hinder that. . . I'd keep you as genteel as ever I could, dear Sophy – if I might think of it!' he pleaded.

'Sam, I'll be frank,' she said, putting her hand on his. 'If it were only myself I would do it, and gladly, though everything I possess would be lost to me by marrying again.'

'I don't mind that! It's more independent.'

'That's good of you, dear, dear Sam. But there's something else. I have a son. . . I almost fancy when I am miserable sometimes that he is not really mine, but one I hold in trust for my late husband. He seems to belong so little to me personally, so entirely to his dead father. He is so much educated and I so little that I do not feel dignified enough to be his mother. . . Well, he would have to be told.'

'Yes. Unquestionably.' Sam saw her thought and her fear. 'Still, you can do as you like, Sophy – Mrs Twycott,' he added. 'It is not you who are the child, but he.'

'Ah, you don't know! Sam, if I could, I would marry you, some day. But you must wait a while, and let me think.'

It was enough for him, and he was blithe at their parting. Not so she. To tell Randolph seemed impossible. She could wait till he had gone up to Oxford, when what she did would affect his life but little. But would he ever tolerate the idea? And if not, could she defy him?'

She had not told him a word when the yearly cricket-match came on at Lord's between the public schools, though Sam had already gone back to Aldbrickham. Mrs Twycott felt stronger than usual: she went to the match with Randolph, and was able to leave her chair and walk about occasionally. The bright idea occurred to her that she could casually broach the subject while moving round among the spectators, when the boy's spirits were high with interest in the game, and he would weigh domestic matters as feathers in the scale beside the day's victory. They promenaded under the lurid July sun, this pair, so wide apart, yet so near, and Sophy saw the large proportion of boys like her own, in their broad white collars and dwarf hats, and all around the rows of great coaches under which was jumbled the *débris* of luxurious luncheons: bones, pie-crusts, champagne-bottles, glasses, plates, napkins, and the family silver; while on the coaches sat the proud fathers and mothers; but never a poor mother like her. If Randolph had not appertained to these, had not centred all his interests in them, had not cared exclusively for the class they belonged to, how happy would things have been! A great huzza at some small performance with the bat burst from the multitude of relatives, and Randolph jumped wildly into the air to see what had happened. Sophy fetched up the sentence that had been already shaped; but she could not get it out. The occasion was, perhaps, an inopportune one. The contrast between her story and the display of fashion to which Randolph had grown to regard himself as akin would be fatal. She awaited a better time.

It was on an evening when they were alone in their plain suburban residence, where life was not blue but brown, that she ultimately broke silence, qualifying her announcement of a probable second marriage by assuring him that it would not take place for a long time to come, when he would be living quite independently of her.

The boy thought the idea a very reasonable one, and asked if she had chosen anybody. She hesitated; and he seemed to have a misgiving. He hoped his stepfather would be a gentleman, he said.

'Not what you call a gentleman,' she answered timidly. 'He'll be much as I was before I knew your father'; and by degrees she acquainted him with the whole. The youth's face remained fixed for a moment; then he flushed, leant on the table, and burst into passionate tears.

His mother went up to him, kissed all of his face that she could get at, and patted his back as if he were still the baby he once had been, crying herself the while. When he had somewhat recovered from his paroxysm he went hastily to his own room and fastened the door.

Parleyings were attempted through the keyhole, outside which she waited and listened. It was long before he would reply, and when he did it was to say sternly at her from within: 'I am ashamed of you! It will ruin me! A miserable bore! a churl! a clown! It will degrade me in the eyes of all the gentlemen of England!'

'Say no more – perhaps I am wrong! I will struggle against it!' she cried miserably.

Before Randolph left her that summer a letter arrived from Sam to inform her that he had been unexpectedly fortunate in obtaining the shop. He was in possession; it was the largest in the town, combining fruit with vegetables, and he thought it would form a home worthy even of her some day. Might he not run up to town to see her?

She met him by stealth, and said he must still wait for her final answer. The autumn dragged on, and when Randolph was home at Christmas for the holiday she broached the matter again. But the young gentleman was inexorable.

It was dropped for months; renewed again; abandoned under his repugnance; again attempted; and thus the gentle creature reasoned and pleaded till four or five long years had passed. Then the faithful Sam revived his suit with some peremptoriness. Sophy's son, now an undergraduate, was down from Oxford one Easter, when she again opened the subject. As soon as he was ordained, she argued, he would have a home of his own, wherein she, with her bad grammar and her ignorance, would be an encumbrance to him. Better obliterate her as much as possible.

He showed a more manly anger now, but would not agree. She on her side was more persistent, and he had doubts whether she could be trusted in his absence. But by indignation and contempt for her taste he completely maintained his ascendency; and finally taking her before a little cross and altar that he had erected in his bedroom for his private devotions, there bade her kneel, and swear that she would not wed Samuel Hobson without his consent. 'I owe this to my father!' he said.

The poor woman swore, thinking he would soften as soon as he was ordained and in full swing of clerical work. But he did not. His education had by this time sufficiently ousted his humanity to keep him quite firm; though his mother might have led an idyllic life with her faithful fruiterer and greengrocer, and nobody have been anything the worse in the world.

Her lameness became more confirmed as time went on, and she seldom or never left the house in the long southern thoroughfare, where she seemed to be pining her heart away. 'Why mayn't I say to Sam that I'll marry him? Why mayn't I?' she would murmur plaintively to herself when nobody was near.

Some four years after this date a middle-aged man was standing at the door of the largest fruiterer's shop in Aldbrickham. He was the proprietor, but today, instead of his usual business attire, he wore a neat suit of black; and his window was partly shuttered. From the railway-station a funeral procession was seen approaching: it passed his door and went out of the town towards the village of Gaymead. The man, whose eyes were wet, held his hat in his hand as the vehicles moved by; while from the mourning-coach a young smooth-shaven priest in a high waistcoat looked black as a cloud at the shopkeeper standing there.

DECEMBER 1891

FOR CONSCIENCE' SAKE

I

Whether the utilitarian or the intuitive theory of the moral sense be upheld it is beyond question that there are a few subtle-souled persons with whom the absolute gratuitousness of an act of reparation is an inducement to perform it; while exhortation as to its necessity would breed excuses for leaving it undone. The case of Mr Millborne and Mrs Frankland particularly illustrated this, and perhaps something more.

There were few figures better known to the local crossing-sweeper than Mr Millborne's in his daily comings and goings along a familiar and quiet London street, where he lived inside the door marked eleven, though not as householder. In age he was fifty at least, and his habits were as regular as those of a person can be who has no occupation but the study of how to keep himself employed. He turned almost always to the right on getting to the end of the street, then he went onward down Bond Street to his club, whence he returned by precisely the same course about six o'clock, on foot; or, if he went to dine, later on in a cab. He was known to be a man of some means, though apparently not wealthy. Being a bachelor he seemed to prefer his present mode of living as a lodger in Mrs Towney's best rooms, with the use of furniture which he had bought ten times over in rent during his tenancy, to having a house of his own.

None among his acquaintance tried to know him well, for his manner and moods did not excite curiosity or deep friendship. He was not a man who seemed to have anything on his mind, anything to conceal, anything to impart. From his casual remarks it was generally understood that he was country-born, a native of some place in Wessex; that he had come to London as a young man in a banking-house, and had risen to a post of responsibility; when, by the death of his father, who had been fortunate in his investments, the son succeeded to an income which led him to retire from a business life somewhat early.

One evening, when he had been unwell for several days, Doctor Bindon came in, after dinner, from the adjoining medical quarter, and smoked with him over the fire. The patient's ailment was not such as to require much thought, and they talked together on indifferent subjects.

'I am a lonely man, Bindon – a lonely man,' Millborne took occasion to say, shaking his head gloomily. 'You don't know such loneliness as mine. . . And the older I get the more I am dissatisfied with myself. And today I have been, through an accident, more than usually haunted by what, above all other events of my life, causes that dissatisfaction – the recollection of an unfulfilled promise made twenty years ago. In ordinary affairs I have always been considered a man of my word; and perhaps it is on that account that a particular vow I once made, and did not keep, comes back to me with a magnitude out of all proportion (I daresay) to its real gravity, especially at this time of day. You know the discomfort caused at night by the half-sleeping sense that a door or window has been left unfastened, or in the day by the remembrance of unanswered letters. So does that promise haunt me from time to time, and has done today particularly.'

There was a pause, and they smoked on. Millborne's eyes, though fixed on the fire, were really regarding attentively a town in the west of England.

'Yes,' he continued, 'I have never quite forgotten it, though during the busy years of my life it was shelved and buried under the pressure of my pursuits. And, as I say, today in particular, an incident in the law-report of a somewhat similar kind has brought it back again vividly. However, what it was I can tell you in a few words, though no doubt you, as a man of the world, will smile at the thinness of my skin when you hear it. . . I came up to town at one-and-twenty, from Toneborough, in Outer Wessex, where I was born, and here, before I left, I had won the heart of a young woman of my own age. I promised her marriage, took advantage of my promise, and – am a bachelor.'

'The old story.'

The other nodded.

'I left the place, and thought at the time I had done a very clever thing in getting so easily out of an entanglement. But I have lived long enough for that promise to return to bother me – to be honest, not altogether as a pricking of the conscience, but as a dissatisfaction with myself as a specimen of the heap of flesh called humanity. If I were to ask you to lend me fifty pounds, which I would repay you next midsummer, and I did not repay you, I should consider myself a shabby sort of fellow, especially if you wanted the money badly. Yet I promised that girl just as distinctly; and then coolly broke my word, as if doing so were rather smart conduct than a mean action, for which the poor victim herself, encumbered with a child, and not I, had really to pay the penalty, in spite of certain pecuniary aid that was given. . . There, that's the retrospective trouble that I am always unearthing; and you may hardly believe that though so many years have elapsed, and it is all gone by and done with, and she must be getting on for an old woman now, as I am for an old man, it really often destroys my sense of self-respect still.'

'O, I can understand it. All depends upon the temperament. Thousands of men would have forgotten all about it; so would you, perhaps, if you had married and had a family. Did she ever marry?'

'I don't think so. O no – she never did. She left Toneborough, and later on appeared under another name at Exonbury, in the next county, where she was not known. It is very seldom that I go down into that part of the country, but in passing through Exonbury, on one occasion, I learnt that she was quite a settled resident there, as a teacher of music, or something of the kind. That much I casually heard when I was there two or three years ago. But I have never set eyes on her since our original acquaintance, and should not know her if I met her.'

'Did the child live?' asked the doctor.

'For several years, certainly,' replied his friend. 'I cannot say if she is living now. It was a little girl. She might be married by this time as far as years go.'

'And the mother – was she a decent, worthy young woman?'

'O yes; a sensible, quiet girl, neither attractive nor unattractive to the ordinary observer; simply commonplace. Her position at the time of our acquaintance was not so good as mine. My father was a solicitor, as I think I have told you. She was a young girl in a music-shop; and it was represented to me that it would be beneath my position to marry her. Hence the result.'

'Well, all I can say is that after twenty years it is probably too late to think of mending such a matter. It has doubtless by this time mended itself. You had better dismiss it from your mind as an evil past your control. Of course, if mother and daughter are alive, or either, you might settle something upon them if you were inclined, and had it to spare.'

'Well, I haven't much to spare, and I have relations in narrow circumstances – perhaps narrower than theirs. But that is not the point. Were I ever so rich I feel I could not rectify the past by money. I did not promise to enrich her. On the contrary, I told her it would probably be dire poverty for both of us. But I did promise to make her my wife.'

'Then find her and do it,' said the doctor jocularly as he rose to leave.

'Ah, Bindon! That, of course, is the obvious jest. But I haven't the slightest desire for marriage; I am quite content to live as I have lived. I am a bachelor by nature, and instinct, and habit, and everything. Besides, though I respect her still (for she was not an atom to blame), I haven't any shadow of love for her. In my mind she exists as one of those women you think well of, but find uninteresting. It would be purely with the idea of putting wrong right that I should hunt her up, and propose to do it off-hand.'

You don't think of it seriously?' said his surprised friend.

'I sometimes think that I would, if it were practicable; simply, as I say, to recover my sense of being a man of honour.'

'I wish you luck in the enterprise,' said Doctor Bindon. 'You'll soon be out of that chair, and then you can put your impulse to the test. But – after twenty years of silence – I should say, don't!'

2

The doctor's advice remained counterpoised, in Millborne's mind, by the aforesaid mood of seriousness and sense of principle, approximating often to religious sentiment, which had been evolving itself in his breast for months, and even years.

The feeling, however, had no immediate effect upon Mr Millborne's actions. He soon got over his trifling illness, and was vexed with himself for having, in a moment of impulse, confided such a case of conscience to anybody.

But the force which had prompted it, though latent, remained with him and ultimately grew stronger. The upshot was that about four months after the date of his illness and disclosure, Millborne found himself on a mild spring morning at Paddington Station, in a train that was starting for the west. His many intermittent thoughts on his broken promise from time to time, in those hours when loneliness brought him face to face with his own personality, had at last resulted in this course.

The decisive stimulus had been given when, a day or two earlier, on looking into a Post-Office Directory, he learnt that the woman he had not met for twenty years was still living on at Exonbury under the name she had assumed when, a year or two after her disappearance from her native town and his, she had returned from abroad as a young widow with a child, and taken up her residence at the former city. Her condition was apparently but little changed, and her daughter seemed to be with her, their names standing in the directory as 'Mrs Leonora Frankland and Miss Frankland, Teachers of Music and Dancing.'

Mr Millborne reached Exonbury in the afternoon, and his first business, before even taking his luggage into the town, was to find the house occupied by the teachers. Standing in a central and open place it was not difficult to discover, a well-burnished brass door-plate bearing their names prominently. He hesitated to enter without further knowledge, and ultimately took lodgings over a toy-shop opposite, securing a sitting-room which faced a similar drawing- or sitting-room at the Franklands', where the dancing lessons were given. Installed here he was enabled to make indirectly, and without suspicion, inquiries and observations on the character of the ladies over the way, which he did with much deliberateness.

He learnt that the widow, Mrs Frankland, with her one daughter, Frances, was of cheerful and excellent repute, energetic and painstaking with her pupils, of whom she had a good many, and in whose tuition her daughter assisted her. She was quite a recognized townswoman, and though the dancing branch of her profession was perhaps a trifle worldly, she was really a serious-minded lady who, being obliged to live by what she knew how to teach, balanced matters by lending a hand at charitable bazaars, assisting at sacred concerts, and giving musical recitations in aid of funds for bewildering happy savages, and other such enthusiasms of this enlightened country. Her daughter was one of the foremost of the bevy of young women who decorated the churches at Easter and Christmas, was organist in one of those edifices, and had subscribed to the testimonial of a silver broth-basin that was presented to the Reverend Mr Walker as a token of gratitude for his faithful and arduous intonations of six months as sub-precentor in the Cathedral. Altogether mother and daughter appeared to be a typical and innocent pair among the genteel citizens of Exonbury.

As a natural and simple way of advertising their profession they allowed the windows of the music-room to be a little open so that you had the pleasure of hearing all along the street at any hour between surnrise and sunset fragmentary gems of classical music as interpreted by the young people of twelve or fourteen who took lessons there. But it was said that Mrs Frankland made most of her income by letting out pianos on hire, and by selling them as agent for the makers.

The report pleased Millborne; it was highly creditable, and far better than he had hoped. He was curious to get a view of the two women who led such blameless lives.

He had not long to wait to get a glimpse of Leonora. It was when she was standing on her own doorstep, opening her parasol, on the morning after his arrival. She was thin, though not gaunt, with greying hair; and a good, well-wearing, thoughtful face had taken the place of the one which had temporarily attracted him in the days of his nonage. She wore black, and it became her in her character of widow. The daughter next appeared; she was a smoothed and rounded copy of her mother, with the same decision in her mien that Leonora had, and a bounding gait in which he traced a faint resemblance to his own at her age.

For the first time he absolutely made up his mind to call on them. But his antecedent step was to send Leonora a note the next morning, stating his proposal to visit her, and suggesting the evening as the time, because she seemed to be so greatly occupied in her professional capacity during the day. He purposely worded his note in such a form as not to require an answer from her which would be possibly awkward to write.

No answer came. Naturally he should not have been surprised at this; and yet he felt a little checked, even though she had only refrained from volunteering a reply that was not demanded.

At eight, the hour fixed by himself, he crossed over and was passively admitted by the servant. Mrs Frankland, as she called herself, received him in the large music-and-dancing room on the first-floor front, and not in any private little parlour as he had expected. This cast a distressingly business-like colour over their first meeting after so many years of severance. The woman he had wronged stood before him, well dressed, even to his metropolitan eyes, and her manner as she came up to him was dignified even to hardness. She certainly was not glad to see him. But what could he expect after a neglect of twenty years!

'How do you do, Mr Millborne?' she said cheerfully, as to any chance caller. 'I am obliged to receive you here because my daughter has a friend downstairs.'

'Your daughter – and mine.'

'Ah – yes, yes,' she replied hastily, as if the addition had escaped her memory. 'But perhaps the less said about that the better, in fairness to me. You will consider me a widow, please.'

'Certainly, Leonora . . . ' He could not get on, her manner was so cold and indifferent. The expected scene of sad reproach, subdued to delicacy by the run of years, was absent altogether. He was obliged to come to the point without preamble.

'You are quite free, Leonora – I mean as to marriage? There is nobody who has your promise, or—'

'O yes; quite free, Mr Millborne,' she said, somewhat surprised.

'Then I will tell you why I have come. Twenty years ago I promised to make you my wife; and I am here to fulfil that promise. Heaven forgive my tardiness!'

Her surprise was increased, but she was not agitated. She seemed to become gloomy, disapproving. 'I – fear I could not entertain such an idea at this time of life,' she said after a moment or two. 'It would complicate matters too greatly. I have a very fair income, and require no help of any sort. I have no wish to marry. . . What could have induced you to come on such an errand now? It seems quite extraordinary, if I may say so?'

'It must – I daresay it does, Millborne replied vaguely, 'and I must tell you that impulse – I mean in the sense of passion – has little to do with it. I wish to marry you, Leonora; I much desire to marry you. But it is an affair of conscience, a case of fulfilment. I promised you, and it was dishonourable of me to go away. I want to remove that sense of dishonour before I die. No doubt we might get to love each other as warmly as we did in old times?'

She dubiously shook her head. 'I appreciate your motives, Mr Millborne; but you must consider my position; and you will see that, short of the personal wish to marry, which I don't feel, there is no reason why I should change my state even though by so doing I should ease your conscience. My position in this town is a respected one; I have built it up by my own hard labours, and, in short, I don't wish to alter it. My daughter, too, is just on the verge of an engagement to be married, to a young man who will make her an excellent husband. It will be in every way a desirable match for her. He is downstairs now.'

'Does she know – anything about me?'

'O no, no; God forbid! Her father is dead and buried to her. So that, you see, things are going on smoothly, and I don't want to disturb their progress.'

He nodded. 'Very well,' he said, and rose to go. At the door, however, he came back again.

'Still, Leonora,' he urged, 'I have come on purpose; and I don't see what disturbance would be caused. You would simply marry an old friend. Won't you reconsider? It is no more than right that we should be united, remembering the girl.'

She shook her head, and patted with her foot nervously.

'Well, I won't detain you,' he added. 'I shall not be leaving Exonbury yet. You will allow me to see you again?'

'Yes; I don't mind,' she said reluctantly.

The obstacles he had encountered, though they did not reanimate his dead passion for Leonora, did certainly make it appear indispensable to his peace of mind to overcome her coldness. He called frequently. The first meeting with the daughter was a trying ordeal, though he did not feel drawn towards her as he had expected to be; she did not excite his sympathies. Her mother confided to Frances the errand of 'her old friend', which was viewed by the daughter with strong disfavour. His desire being thus uncongenial to both, for a long time Millborne made not the least impression upon Mrs Frankland. His attentions pestered her rather than pleased her. He was surprised at her firmness, and it was only when he hinted at moral reasons for their union that she was ever shaken. 'Strictly speaking,' he would say, 'we ought, as honest persons, to marry; and that's the truth of it, Leonora.'

'I have looked at it in that light,' she said quickly. 'It struck me at the very first. But I don't see the force of the argument. I totally deny that after this interval of time I am bound to marry you for honour's sake. I would have married you, as you know well enough, at the proper time. But what is the use of remedies now?'

They were standing at the window. A scantly-whiskered young man, in clerical attire, called at the door below. Leonora flushed with interest.

'Who is he?' said Mr Millborne.

'My Frances's lover. I am so sorry – she is not at home! Ah! they have told him where she is, and he has gone to find her. . . I hope that suit will prosper, at any rate!'

'Why shouldn't it?'

'Well, he cannot marry yet; and Frances sees but little of him now he has left Exonbury. He was formerly doing duty here, but now he is curate of St John's, Ivell, fifty miles up the line. There is a tacit agreement between them, but – there have been friends of his who object, because of our vocation. However, he sees the absurdity of such an objection as that, and is not influenced by it.'

'Your marriage with me would help the match, instead of hindering it, as you have said.'

'Do you think it would?'

'It certainly would, by taking you out of this business altogether.'

By chance he had found the way to move her somewhat, and he followed it up. This view was imparted to Mrs Frankland's daughter, and it led her to soften her opposition. Millborne, who had given up his lodging in Exonbury, journeyed to and fro regularly, till at last he overcame her negations, and she expressed a reluctant assent.

They were married at the nearest church; and the goodwill – whatever that was – of the music-and-dancing connection was sold to a successor only too ready to jump into the place, the Millbornes having decided to live in London.

3

Millborne was a householder in his old district, though not in his old street, and Mrs Millborne and their daughter had turned themselves into

Londoners. Frances was well reconciled to the removal by her lover's satisfaction at the change. It suited him better to travel from Ivell a hundred miles to see her in London, where he frequently had other engagements, than fifty in the opposite direction where nothing but herself required his presence. So here they were, furnished up to the attics, in one of the small but popular streets of the West district, in a house whose front, till lately of the complexion of a chimney-sweep, had been scraped to show to the surprised wayfarer the bright yellow and red brick that had lain lurking beneath the soot of fifty years.

The social life that the two women had derived from the alliance was considerable; but when the exhilaration which accompanies a first residence in London, the sensation of standing on a pivot of the world, had passed, their lives promised to get somewhat duller than when, at despised Exonbury, they had enjoyed a nodding acquaintance with three-fourths of the town. Mr Millborne did not criticize his wife; he could not. Whatever defects of hardness and acidity his original treatment and the lapse of years might have developed in her, his sense of a realized idea, of a re-established self-satisfaction, was always thrown into the scale on her side, and outweighed all objections.

It was about a month after their settlement in town that the household decided to spend a week at a watering-place in the Isle of Wight, and while there the Reverend Percival Cope (the young curate aforesaid) came to see them, Frances in particular. No formal engagement of the young pair had been announced as yet, but it was clear that their mutual understanding could not end in anything but marriage without grievous disappointment to one of the parties at least. Not that Frances was sentimental. She was rather of the imperious sort, indeed; and, to say all, the young girl had not fulfilled her father's expectation of her. But he hoped and worked for her welfare as sincerely as any father could do.

Mr Cope was introduced to the new head of the family, and stayed with them in the Island two or three days. On the last day of his visit they decided to venture on a two hours' sail in one of the small yachts which lay there for hire. The trip had not progressed far before all, except the curate, found that sailing in a breeze did not quite agree with them; but as he seemed to enjoy the experience, the other three bore their conditions as well as they could without grimace or complaint, till the young man, observing their discomfort, gave immediate directions to tack about. On the way back to port they sat silent, facing each other.

Nausea in such circumstances, like midnight watching, fatigue, trouble, fright, has this marked effect upon the countenance, that it often brings out strongly the divergences of the individual from the norm of his race, accentuating superficial peculiarities to radical distinctions. Unexpected physiognomies will uncover themselves at these times in well-known faces; the aspect becomes invested with the spectral presence of entombed and forgotten ancestors; and family lineaments of special or exclusive cast, which in ordinary moments are masked by a stereotyped expression and mien, start up with crude insistence to the view.

Frances, sitting beside her mother's husband, with Mr Cope opposite, was naturally enough much regarded by the curate during the tedious sail home; at first with sympathetic smiles. Then, as the middle-aged father and his child grew each gray-faced, as the pretty blush of Frances disintegrated into spotty stains, and the soft rotundities of her features diverged from their familiar and reposeful beauty into elemental lines, Cope was gradually struck with the resemblance between a pair in their discomfort who in their ease presented nothing to the eye in common. Mr Millborne and Frances in their indisposition were strangely, startlingly alike.

The inexplicable fact absorbed Cope's attention quite. He forgot to smile at Frances, to hold her hand; and when they touched the shore he remained sitting for some moments like a man in a trance.

As they went homeward, and recovered their complexions and contours, the similarities one by one disappeared, and Frances and Mr Millborne were again masked by the commonplace differences of sex and age. It was as if, during the voyage, a mysterious veil had been lifted, temporarily revealing a strange pantomime of the past.

During the evening he said to her casually: 'Is your step-father a cousin of your mother, dear Frances?'

'O no,' said she. 'There is no relationship. He was only an old friend of hers. Why did you suppose such a thing?'

He did not explain, and the next morning started to resume his duties at Ivell.

Cope was an honest young fellow, and shrewd withal. At home in his quiet rooms in St Peter's Street, Ivell, he pondered long and unpleasantly on the revelations of the cruise. The tale it told was distinct enough, and for the first time his position was an uncomfortable one. He had met the Franklands at Exonbury as parishioners, had been attracted by Frances, and had floated thus far into an engagement which was indefinite only because of his inability to marry just yet. The Franklands' past had apparently contained mysteries, and it did not coincide with his judgment to marry into a family whose mystery was of the sort suggested. So he sat and sighed, between his reluctance to lose Frances and his natural dislike of forming a connection with people whose antecedents would not bear the strictest investigation.

A passionate lover of the old-fashioned sort might possibly never have halted to weigh these doubts; but though he was in the Church Cope's affections were fastidious – distinctly tempered with the alloys of the century's decadence. He delayed writing to Frances for some while, simply because he could not tune himself up to enthusiasm when worried by suspicion of such a kind.

Meanwhile the Millbornes had returned to London, and Frances was growing anxious. In talking to her mother of Cope she had innocently alluded to his curious inquiry if her mother and her step-father were connected by any tie of cousinship. Mrs Millborne made her repeat the words. Frances did so, and watched with inquisitive eyes their effect upon her elder, which was a distinct one.

'What is there so startling in his inquiry then? Frances asked. 'Can it have anything to do with his not writing to me?'

Her mother flinched, but did not inform her, and Frances also was now drawn within the atmosphere of suspicion. That night when standing by chance outside the chamber of her parents she heard for the first time their voices engaged in a sharp altercation.

The apple of discord had, indeed, been dropped into the house of the Millbornes. The scene within the chamber-door was Mrs Millborne standing before her dressing-table, looking across to her husband in the dressing-room adjoining, where he was sitting down, his eyes fixed on the floor.

'Why did you come and disturb my life a second time?' she harshly asked. 'Why did you pester me with your conscience, till I was driven to accept you to get rid of your importunity? Frances and I were doing well: the one desire of my life was that she should marry that good young man. And now the match is broken off by your cruel interference! Why did you show yourself in my world again, and raise this scandal upon my hard-won respectability – won by such weary years of labour as none will ever know!' She bent her face upon the table and wept passionately.

There was no reply from Mr Millborne, Frances lay awake nearly all that night, and when at breakfast-time the next morning still no letter appeared from Mr Cope, she entreated her mother to go to Ivell and see if the young man were ill.

Mrs Millborne went, returning the same day. Frances, anxious and haggard, met her at the station.

Was all well? Her mother could not say it was; though he was not ill.

One thing she had found out, that it was a mistake to hunt up a man when his inclinations were to hold aloof. Returning with her mother in the cab Frances insisted upon knowing what the mystery was which plainly had alienated her lover. The precise words which had been spoken at the interview with him that day at Ivell Mrs Millborne could not be induced to repeat; but thus far she admitted, that the estrangement was fundamentally owing to Mr Millborne having sought her out and married her.

'And why did he seek you out – and why were you obliged to marry him?' asked the distressed girl. Then the evidences pieced themselves together in her acute mind, and, her colour gradually rising, she asked her mother if what they pointed to was indeed the fact. Her mother admitted that it was.

A flush of mortification succeeded to the flush of shame upon the young woman's face. How could a scrupulously correct clergyman and lover like Mr Cope ask her to be his wife after this discovery of her irregular birth? She covered her eyes with her hands in a silent despair.

In the presence of Mr Millborne they at first suppressed their anguish. But by and by their feelings got the better of them, and when he was asleep in his chair after dinner Mrs Millborne's irritation broke out. The embittered Frances joined her in reproaching the man who had come as the spectre to their intended feast of Hymen, and turned its promise to ghastly failure.

'Why were you so weak, mother, as to admit such an enemy to your house – one so obviously your evil genius – much less accept him as a husband, after so long? If you had only told me all, I could have advised you better! But I suppose I have no right to reproach him, bitter as I feel, and even though he has blighted my life for ever!'

'Frances, I did hold out; I saw it was a mistake to have any more to say to a man who had been such an unmitigated curse to me! But he would not listen; he kept on about his conscience and mine, till I was bewildered, and said Yes! . . . Bringing us away from a quiet town where we were known and respected – what an ill-considered thing it was! O the content of those days! We had society there, people in our own position, who did not expect more of us than we expected of them. Here, where there is so much, there is nothing! He said London society was so bright and brilliant that it would be like a new world. It may be to those who are in it; but what is that to us two lonely women; we only see it flashing past! . . . O the fool, the fool that I was!'

Now Millborne was not so soundly asleep as to prevent his hearing these animadversions that were almost execrations, and many more of the same sort. As there was no peace for him at home, he went again to his club, where, since his reunion with Leonora, he had seldom if ever been seen. But the shadow of the troubles in his household interfered with his comfort here also: he could not, as formerly, settle down into his favourite chair with the evening paper, reposeful in the celibate's sense that where he was his world's centre had its fixture. His world was now an ellipse, with a dual centrality, of which his own was not the major.

The young curate of Ivell still held aloof, tantalizing Frances by his elusiveness. Plainly he was waiting upon events. Millborne bore the reproaches of his wife and daughter almost in silence; but by degrees he grew meditative, as if revolving a new idea. The bitter cry about blighting their existence at length became so impassioned that one day Millborne calmly proposed to return again to the country; not necessarily to Exonbury, but, if they were willing, to a little old manor-house which he had found was to be let, standing a mile from Mr Cope's town of Ivell.

They were surprised, and, despite their view of him as the bringer of ill, were disposed to accede. 'Though I suppose,' said Mrs Millborne to him, 'it will end in Mr Cope's asking you flatly about the past, and your being compelled to tell him; which may dash all my hopes for Frances. She gets more and more like you every day, particularly when she is in a bad temper. People will see you together, and notice it; and I don't know what may come of it!'

'I don't think they will see us together,' he said; but he entered into no argument when she insisted otherwise. The removal was eventually resolved on; the town-house was disposed of, and again came the invasion by furniture-men and vans, till all the movables and servants were whisked away. He sent his wife and daugther to an hotel while this was going on, taking two or three journeys himelf to Ivell to superintend the refixing, and the improvement of the grounds. When all was done he returned to them in town.

The house was ready for their reception, he told them, and there only remained the journey. He accompanied them and their personal luggage to the station only, having, he said, to remain in town a short time on business with his lawyer. They went, dubious and discontented; for the much-loved Cope had made no sign.

'If we were going down to live here alone,' said Mrs Millborne to her daughter in the train; 'and there was no intrusive tell-tale presence! . . . But let it be!'

The house was a lovely little place in a grove of elms, and they liked it much. The first person to call upon them as new residents was Mr Cope. He was delighted to find that they had come so near, and (though he did not say this) meant to live in such excellent style. He had not, however, resumed the manner of a lover.

'Your father spoils all!' murmured Mrs Millborne.

But three days later she received a letter from her husband, which caused her no small degree of astonishment. It was written from Boulogne.

It began with a long explanation of settlements on his property, in which he had been engaged since their departure. The chief feature in the business was that Mrs Millborne found herself the absolute mistress of a comfortable sum in personal estate, and Frances of a life-interest in a larger sum, the principal to be afterwards divided amongst her children if she had any. The remainder of his letter ran as hereunder:

> I have learnt that there are some derelictions of duty which cannot be blotted out by tardy accomplishment. Our evil actions do not remain isolated in the past, waiting only to be reversed: like locomotive plants they spread and re-root till to destroy the original stem has no material effects in killing them. I made a mistake in searching you out; I admit it; whatever the remedy may be in a such cases it is not marriage and the best thing for you and me is that you do not see me more. You had better not seek me, for you will not be likely to find me: you are well provided for, and we may do ourselves more harm than good by meeting again.
>
> F.M.

Millborne, in short, disappeared from that day forward. But a searching inquiry would have revealed that, soon after the Millbornes went to Ivell, an Englishman, who did not give the name of Millborne, took up his residence in Brussels; a man who might have been recognized by Mrs Millborne if she had met him. One afternoon in the ensuing summer, when this gentleman was looking over the English papers, he saw the announcement of Miss Frances Frankland's marriage. She had become the Reverend Mrs Cope.'

'Thank God!' said the gentleman.

But his momentary satisfaction was far from being happiness. As he formerly had been weighted with a sad conscience, so now he was burdened with the heavy thought which oppressed Antigone, that by honourable observance of a rite he had obtained for himself the reward of dishonourable laxity. Occasionally he had to be helped to his lodgings by his servant from the *Cercle* he frequented, through having imbibed a little too much liquor to be able to take care of himself. But he was harmless, and even when he had been drinking said little.

MARCH 1891

A TRAGEDY OF TWO AMBITIONS

I

The shouts of the village-boys came in at the window, accompanied by broken laughter from loungers at the inn-door; but the brothers Halborough worked on.

They were sitting in a bedroom of the master-millwright's house, engaged in the untutored reading of Greek and Latin. It was no tale of Homeric blows and knocks, Argonautic voyaging, or Theban family woe that inflamed their imaginations and spurred them onward. They were plodding away at the Greek Testament, immersed in a chapter of the idiomatic and difficult Epistle to the Hebrews.

The Dog-day sun in its decline reached the low ceiling with slanting sides, and the shadows of the great goat's-willow swayed and interchanged upon the walls like a spectral army manoeuvring. The open casement which admitted the remoter sounds now brought the voice of some one close at hand. It was their sister, a pretty girl of fourteen, who stood in the court below.

'I can see the tops of your heads! What's the use of staying up there? I like you not to go out with the street-boys; but do come and play with me!'

They treated her as an inadequate interlocutor, and put her off with some slight word. She went away disappointed. Presently there was a dull noise of heavy footsteps at the side of the house, and one of the brothers sat up. 'I fancy I hear him coming,' he murmured, his eyes on the window.

A man in the light drab clothes of an old-fashioned country tradesman approached from round the corner, reeling as he came. The elder son, flushed with anger, rose from his books, and descended the stairs. The younger sat on, till, after the lapse of a few minutes, his brother re-entered the room.

'Did Rosa see him?'

'No.'

'Nor anybody?'

'No.'

'What have you done with him?'

'He's in the straw-shed. I got him in with some trouble, and he has fallen asleep. I thought this would be the explanation of his absence! No stones dressed for Miller Kench, the great wheel of the saw-mills waiting for new float-boards, even the poor folk not able to get their waggons wheeled.'

'What *is* the use of poring over this!' said the younger, shutting up Donnegan's *Lexicon* with a slap. 'O if we had only been able to keep mother's nine hundred pounds, what we could have done!'

'How well she had estimated the sum necessary! Four hundred and fifty each, she thought. And I have no doubt that we could have done it on that, with care.'

This loss of the nine hundred pounds was the sharp thorn of their crown. It was a sum which their mother had amassed with great exertion and self-denial, by adding to a chance legacy such other small amounts as she could lay hands on from time to time; and she had intended with the hoard to indulge the dear wish of her heart – that of sending her sons, Joshua and Cornelius, to one of the Universities, having been informed that from four hundred to four hundred and fifty each might carry them through their terms with such great economy as she knew she could trust them to practise. But she had died a year or two before this time, worn out by too keen a strain towards these ends; and the money, coming unreservedly into the hands of their father, had been nearly dissipated. With its exhaustion went all opportunity and hope of a university degree for the sons.

'It drives me mad when I think of it,' said Joshua, the elder. 'And here we work and work in our own bungling way, and the utmost we can hope for is a term of years as national schoolmasters, and possible admission to a theological college, and ordination as despised licentiates.'

The anger of the elder was reflected as simple sadness in the face of the other. 'We can preach the Gospel as well without a hood on our surplices as with one,' he said with feeble consolation.

'Preach the Gospel – true,' said Joshua with a slight pursing of mouth. 'But we can't rise!'

'Let us make the best of it, and grind on.'

The other was silent, and they drearily bent over their books again.

The cause of all this gloom, the millwright Halborough, now snoring in the shed, had been a thriving master-machinist, notwithstanding his free and careless disposition, till a taste for a more than adequate quantity of strong liquor took hold of him; since when his habits had interfered with his business sadly. Already millers went elsewhere for their gear, and only one set of hands was now kept going, though there were formerly two. Already he found a difficulty in meeting his men at the week's end, and though they had been reduced in number there was barely enough work to do for those who remained.

The sun dropped lower and vanished, the shouts of the village children ceased to resound, darkness cloaked the students' bedroom, and all the scene outwardly breathed peace. None knew of the fevered youthful ambitions that throbbed in two breasts within the quiet creeper-covered walls of the millwright's house.

In a few months the brothers left the village of their birth to enter themselves as students in a training college for schoolmasters; first having placed their young sister Rosa under as efficient a tuition at a fashionable watering-place as the means at their disposal could command.

2

A man in semi-clerical dress was walking along the road which led from the railway-station into a provincial town. As he walked he read persistently, only looking up once now and then to see that he was keeping on the foot-track and to avoid other passengers. At those moments, whoever had known the former students at the millwright's would have perceived that one of them, Joshua Halborough, was the peripatetic reader here.

What had been simple force in the youth's face was energized judgment in the man's. His character was gradually writing itself out in his countenance. That he was watching his own career with deeper and deeper interest, that he continually 'heard his days before him', and cared to hear little else, might have been hazarded from what was seen there. His ambitions were, in truth, passionate, yet controlled; so that the germs of many more plans than ever blossomed to maturity had place in him; and forward visions were kept purposely in twilight, to avoid distraction.

Events so far had been encouraging. Shortly after assuming the mastership of his first school he had obtained an introduction to the Bishop of a diocese far from his native county, who had looked upon him as a promising young man and taken him in hand. He was now in the second year of his residence at the theological college of the cathedral-town, and would soon be presented for ordination.

He entered the town, turned into a back street, and then into a yard, keeping his book before him till he set foot under the arch of the latter place. Round the arch was written 'National School', and the stonework of the jambs was worn away as nothing but boys and the waves of ocean will wear it. He was soon amid the sing-song accents of the scholars.

His brother Cornelius, who was the schoolmaster here, laid down the pointer with which he was directing attention to the Capes of Europe and came forward.

'That's his brother Jos!' whispered one of the sixth-standard boys. 'He's going to a be a pa'son. He's now at college.'

'Corney is going to be one, too, when he's saved enough money,' said another.

After greeting his brother, whom he had not seen for several months, the junior began to explain his system of teaching geography.

But Halborough the elder took no interest in the subject. 'How about your own studies?' he asked. 'Did you get the books I sent?'

Cornelius had received them, and he related what he was doing.

'Mind you work in the morning. What time do you get up?'

The younger replied: 'Half-past five.'

'Half-past four is not a minute too soon this time of the year. There is no time like the morning for construing. I don't know why, but when I feel even too dreary to read a novel I can translate – there is something mechanical about it I suppose. Now, Cornelius, you are rather behind-hand, and have some heavy reading before you if you mean to get out of this next Christmas.'

'I am afraid I have.'

'We must soon sound the Bishop. I am sure you will get a title without difficulty when he has heard all. The sub-dean, the principal of my college, says that the best plan will be for you to come there when his lordship is present at an examination, and he'll get you a personal interview with him. Mind you make a good impression upon him. I found in my case that that was everything, and doctrine almost nothing. You'll do for a deacon, Corney, if not for a priest.'

The younger remained thoughtful. 'Have you heard from Rosa lately?' he asked; 'I had a letter this morning.'

'Yes. The little minx writes rather too often. She is homesick – though Brussels must be an attractive place enough. But she must make the most of her time over there. I thought a year would be enough for her, after that high-class school at Sandbourne, but I have decided to give her two, and make a good job of it, expensive as the establishment is.'

Their two rather harsh faces had softened directly they began to speak of their sister, whom they loved more ambitiously than they loved themselves.

'But where is the money to come from, Joshua?'

'I have already got it.' He looked round, and finding that some boys were near withdrew a few steps. 'I have borrowed it at five per cent from the farmer who used to occupy the farm next our field. You remember him.'

'But about paying him?'

'I shall pay him by degrees out of my stipend. No, Cornelius, it was no use to do the thing by halves. She promises to be a most attractive, not to say beautiful, girl. I have seen that for years; and if her face is not her fortune, her face and her brains together will be, if I observe and contrive aright. That she should be, every inch of her, an accomplished and refined woman, was indispensable for the fulfilment of her destiny, and for moving onwards and upwards with us; and she'll do it, you will see. I'd half starve myself rather than take her away from that school now.'

They looked round the school they were in. To Cornelius it was natural and familiar enough, but to Joshua, with his limited human sympathies, who had just dropped in from a superior sort of place, the sight jarred unpleasantly, as being that of something he had left behind. 'I shall be glad when you are out of this,' he said, 'and in your pulpit, and well through your first sermon.'

'You may as well say inducted into my fat living, while you are about it.'

'Ah, well – don't think lightly of the Church. There's a fine work for any man of energy in the Church, as you'll find,' he said fervidly. 'Torrents of infidelity to be stemmed, new views of old subjects to be expounded, truths in spirit to be substituted for truths in the letter . . . ' He lapsed into reverie with the vision of his career, persuading himself that it was ardour for Christianity which spurred him on, and not pride of place. He had shouldered a body of doctrine, and was prepared to defend it tooth and nail, solely for the honour and glory that warriors win.

'If the Church is elastic, and stretches to the shape of the time, she'll last, I suppose,' said Cornelius. 'If not— Only think, I bought a copy of Paley's *Evidences*, best edition, broad margins, excellent preservation, at a bookstall the other day for – ninepence; and I thought that at this rate Christianity must be in rather a bad way.'

'No, no!' said the other almost angrily. 'It only shows that such defences are no longer necessary. Men's eyes can see the truth without extraneous assistance. Besides, we are in for Christianity, and must stick to her whether or no. I am just now going right through Pusey's *Library of the Fathers*.'

'You'll be a bishop, Joshua, before you have done!'

'Ah!' said the other bitterly, shaking his head. 'Perhaps I might have been – I might have been! But where is my D.D. or LL.D.; and how be a bishop without that kind of appendage? Archbishop Tillotson was the son of a Sowerby clothier, but he was sent to Clare College. To hail Oxford or Cambridge as *alma mater* is not for me – for us! My God! when I think of what we should have been – what fair promise has been blighted by that cursed, worthless—'

'Hush, hush! . . . But I feel it, too, as much as you. I have seen it more forcibly lately. You would have obtained your degree long before this time – possibly fellowship – and I should have been on my way to mine.'

'Don't talk of it,' said the other. 'We must do the best we can.'

They looked out of the window sadly, through the dusty panes, so high up that only the sky was visible. By degrees the haunting trouble loomed again, and Cornelius broke the silence with a whisper: 'He has called on me!'

The living pulses died on Joshua's face, which grew arid as a clinker. 'When was that?' he asked quickly.

'Last week.'

'How did he get here – so many miles?'

'Came by railway. He came to ask for money.'

'Ah!'

'He says he will call on you.'

Joshua replied resignedly. The theme of their conversation spoilt his buoyancy for that afternoon. He returned in the evening, Cornelius accompanying him to the station; but he did not read in the train which took him back to the Fountall Theological College, as he had done on the way out. That ineradicable trouble still remained as a squalid spot in the expanse of his life. He sat with the other students in the cathedral choir next day; and the recollection of the trouble obscured the purple splendour thrown by the panes upon the floor.

It was afternoon. All was as still in the close as a cathedral-green can be between the Sunday services, and the incessant cawing of the rooks was the only sound. Joshua Halborough had finished his ascetic lunch, and had gone into the library, where he stood for a few moments looking out of the large window facing the green. He saw walking slowly across it a man in a fustian coat and a battered white hat with a much-ruffled nap, having upon his arm a tall gipsy-woman wearing long brass earrings. The man was staring quizzically at the west front of the cathedral, and Halborough recognized in him the form and features of his father. Who the woman was he knew not. Almost as soon as Joshua became conscious of these things, the sub-dean, who was also the principal of the college, and of whom the young man stood in more awe than of the bishop himself, emerged from the gate and entered a path across the close. The pair met the dignitary, and to Joshua's horror his father turned and addressed the sub-dean.

What passed between them he could not tell. But as he stood in a cold sweat he saw his father place his hand familiarly on the sub-dean's shoulder; the shrinking response of the latter, and his quick withdrawal, told his feeling. The woman seemed to say nothing, but when the sub-dean had passed by they came on towards the college gate.

Halborough flew along the corridor and out at a side door, so as to intercept them before they could reach the front entrance, for which they were making. He caught them behind a clump of laurel.

'By Jerry, here's the very chap! Well, you're a fine fellow, Jos, never to send your father as much as a twist o' baccy on such an occasion, and to leave him to travel all these miles to find 'ee out!'

'First, who is this?' said Joshua Halborough with pale dignity, waving his hand towards the buxom woman with the great earrings.

'Dammy, the mis'ess! Your step-mother! Didn't you know I'd married? She helped me home from market one night, and we came to terms, and struck the bargain. Didn't we, Selinar?'

'Oi, by the great Lord an' we did!' simpered the lady.

'Well, what sort of a place is this you are living in?' asked the millwright. 'A kind of house-of-correction apparently?'

Joshua listened abstractedly, his features set to resignation. Sick at heart he was going to ask them if they were in want of any necessary, any meal, when his father cut him short by saying, 'Why, we've called to ask ye to come round and take pot-luck with us at the Cock-and-Bottle, where we've put up for the day, on our way to see mis'ess's friends at Binegar Fair, where they'll be lying under canvas for a night or two. As for the victuals at the Cock I can't testify to 'em at all; but for the drink, they've the rarest drop of Old Tom that I've tasted for many a year.'

'Thanks; but I am a teetotaller; and I have lunched,' said Joshua, who could fully believe his father's testimony to the gin, from the odour of his breath. 'You see we have to observe regular habits here; and I couldn't be seen at the Cock-and-Bottle just now.'

'O dammy, then don't come, your reverence. Perhaps you won't mind standing treat for those who can be seen there?'

'Not a penny,' said the younger firmly. 'You've had enough already.'

'Thank you for nothing. By the bye, who was that spindle-legged, shoe-buckled parson feller we met by now? He seemed to think we should poison him!'

Joshua remarked coldly that it was the principal of his college, guardedly inquiring, 'Did you tell him whom you were come to see?'

His father did not reply. He and his strapping gipsy wife – if she were his wife – stayed no longer, and disappeared in the direction of the High Street. Joshua Halborough went back to the library. Determined as was his nature, he wept hot tears upon the books, and was immeasurably more wretched that afternoon than the unwelcome millwright. In the evening he sat down and wrote a letter to his brother, in which, after stating what had happened, and expatiating upon this new disgrace in the gipsy wife, he propounded a plan for raising money sufficient to induce the couple to emigrate to Canada. 'It is our only chance,' he said. 'The case as it stands is maddening. For a successful painter, sculptor, musician, author, who takes society by storm, it is no drawback, it is sometimes even a romantic recommendation, to hail from outcasts and profligates. But for a clergyman of the Church of England! Cornelius, it is fatal! To succeed in the Church, people must believe in you, first of all, as a gentleman, secondly as a man of means, thirdly as a scholar, fourthly as a preacher, fifthly, perhaps, as a Christian – but always first as a gentleman, with all their heart and soul and strength. I would have faced the fact of being a small machinist's son, and have taken my chance, if he'd been in any sense respectable and decent. The essence of Christianity is humility, and by the help of God I would have brazened it out. But this terrible vagabondage and disreputable connection! If he does not accept my terms and leave the country, it will extinguish us and kill me. For how can we live, and relinquish our high aim, and bring down our dear sister Rosa to the level of a gipsy's step-daughter?'

3

There was excitement in the parish of Narrobourne one day. The congregation had just come out from morning service, and the whole conversation was of the new curate, Mr Halborough, who had officiated for the first time, in the absence of the rector.

Never before had the feeling of the villagers approached a level which could be called excitement on such a matter as this. The droning which had been the rule in that quiet old place for a century seemed ended at last. They repeated the text to each other as a refrain: 'O Lord, be thou my helper!' Not within living memory till today had the subject of the sermon formed the topic of conversation from the church door to the churchyard gate, to the exclusion of personal remarks on those who had been present, and on the week's news in general.

The thrilling periods of the preacher hung about their minds all that day. The parish being steeped in indifferentism, it happened that when the youths and maidens, middle-aged and old people, who had attended church that morning, recurred as by a fascination to what Halborough had said, they did so more or less indirectly, and even with the subterfuge of a light laugh that was not real, so great was their shyness under the novelty of their sensations.

What was more curious than that these unconventional villagers should have been excited by a preacher of a new school for forty years of familiarity with the old hand who had had charge of their souls, was the effect of Halborough's address upon the occupants of the manor-house pew, including the owner of the estate. These thought they knew how to discount the mere sensational sermon, how to minimize flash oratory to its bare proportions; but they had yielded like the rest of the assembly to the charm of the newcomer.

Mr Fellmer, the landowner, was a young widower, whose mother, still in the prime of life, had returned to her old position in the family mansion since the death of her son's wife in the year after her marriage, at the birth of a fragile little girl. From the date of his loss to the present time, Fellmer had led an inactive existence in the seclusion of the parish; a lack of motive seemed to leave him listless. He had gladly reinstated his mother in the gloomy house, and his main occupation now lay in stewarding his estate, which was not large. Mrs Fellmer, who had sat beside him under Halborough this morning, was a cheerful, straightforward woman, who did her marketing and her alms-giving in person, was fond of old-fashioned flowers, and walked about the village on very wet days visiting the parishioners. These, the only two great ones of Narrobourne, were impressed by Joshua's eloquence as much as the cottagers.

Halborough had been briefly introduced to them on his arrival some days before, and, their interest being kindled, they waited a few moments till he came out of the vestry, to walk down the churchyard-path with him. Mrs Fellmer spoke warmly of the sermon, of the good fortune of the parish in his advent, and hoped he had found comfortable quarters.

Halborough, faintly flushing, said that he had obtained very fair lodgings in the roomy house of a farmer, whom he named.

She feared he would find it very lonely, especially in the evenings, and hoped they would see a good deal of him. When would he dine with them? Could he not come that day – it must be so dull for him the first Sunday evening in country lodgings?

Halborough replied that it would give him much pleasure, but that he feared he must decline. 'I am not altogether alone,' he said. 'My sister, who has just returned from Brussels, and who felt, as you do, that I should be rather dismal by myself, has accompanied me hither to stay a few days till she has put my rooms in order and set me going. She was too fatigued to come to church, and is waiting for me now at the farm.'

'O, but bring your sister – that will be still better! I shall be delighted to know her. How I wish I had been aware! Do tell her, please, that we had no idea of her presence.'

Halborough assured Mrs Fellmer that he would certainly bear the message; but as to her coming he was not so sure. The real truth was, however, that the matter would be decided by him, Rosa having an almost filial respect for his wishes. But he was uncertain as to the state of her wardrobe, and had determined that she should not enter the manor-house at a disadvantage that evening, when there would probably be plenty of opportunities in the future of her doing so becomingly.

He walked to the farm in long strides. This, then, was the outcome of his first morning's work as curate here. Things had gone fairly well with him. He had been ordained; he was in a comfortable parish, where he would exercise almost sole supervision, the rector being infirm. He had made a deep impression at starting, and the absence of a hood seemed to have done him no harm. Moreover, by considerable persuasion and payment, his father and the dark woman had been shipped off to Canada, where they were not likely to interfere greatly with his interests.

Rosa came out to meet him. 'Ah! you should have gone to church like a good girl,' he said.

'Yes – I wished I had afterwards. But I do so hate church as a rule that even your preaching was underestimated in my mind. It was too bad of me!'

The girl who spoke thus playfully was fair, tall, and sylph-like, in a muslin dress, and with just the coquettish *désinvolture* which an English girl brings home from abroad, and loses again after a few months of native life. Joshua was the reverse of playful; the world was too important a concern for him to indulge in light moods. He told her in decided, practical phraseology of the invitation.

'Now, Rosa, we must go – that's settled – if you've a dress that can be made fit to wear all on the hop like this. You didn't, of course, think of bringing an evening dress to such an out-of-the-way place?'

But Rosa had come from the wrong city to be caught napping in those matters. 'Yes, I did,' said she. 'One never knows what may turn up.'

'Well done! Then off we go at seven.'

The evening drew on, and at dusk they started on foot, Rosa pulling up the edge of her skirt under her cloak out of the way of the dews, so that it formed a great windbag all round her, and carrying her satin shoes under her arm. Joshua would not let her wait till she got indoors before changing them, as she proposed, but insisted on her performing that operation under a tree, so that they might enter as if they had not walked. He was nervously formal about such trifles, while Rosa took the whole proceeding – walk, dressing, dinner, and all – as a pastime. To Joshua it was a serious step in life.

A more unexpected kind of person for a curate's sister was never presented at a dinner. The surprise of Mrs Fellmer was unconcealed. She had looked forward to a Dorcas, or Martha, or Rhoda at the outside, and a shade of misgiving crossed her face. It was possible that, had the young lady accompanied her brother to church, there would have been no dining at Narrobourne House that day.

Not so with the young widower, her son. He resembled a sleeper who had awaked in a summer noon expecting to find it only dawn. He could scarcely help stretching his arms and yawning in their faces, so strong was his sense of being suddenly aroused to an unforeseen thing. When they had sat down to table he at first talked to Rosa somewhat with the air of a ruler in the land; but the woman lurking in the acquaintance soon brought him to his level, and the girl from Brussels saw him looking at her mouth, her hands, her contour, as if he could not quite comprehend how they got created: then he dropped into the more satisfactory stage which discerns no particulars.

He talked but little; she said much. The homeliness of the Fellmers, to her view, though they were regarded with such awe down here, quite disembarrassed her. The squire had become so unpractised, had dropped so far into the shade during the last year or so of his life, that he had almost forgotten what the world contained till this evening reminded him. His mother, after her first moments of doubt, appeared to think that he must be left to his own guidance, and gave her attention to Joshua.

With all his foresight and doggedness of aim, the result of that dinner exceeded Halborough's expectations. In weaving his ambitions he had viewed his sister Rosa as a slight, bright thing to be helped into notice by his abilities; but it now began to dawn upon him that the physical gifts of Nature to her might do more for them both than Nature's intellectual gifts to himself. While he was patiently boring the tunnel Rosa seemed about to fly over the mountain.

He wrote the next day to his brother, now occupying his own old rooms in the theological college, telling him exultingly of the unanticipated *début* of Rosa at the manor-house. The next post brought him a reply of congratulation, dashed with the counter-acting intelligence that his father did not like Canada – that his gipsy wife had deserted him, which made him feel so dreary that he thought of returning home.

In his recent satisfaction at his own successes Joshua Halborough had well-nigh forgotten his chronic trouble – latterly screened by distance. But it now returned upon him; he saw more in this brief announcement than his brother seemed to see. It was the cloud no bigger than a man's hand.

4

The following December, a day or two before Christmas, Mrs Fellmer and her son were walking up and down the broad gravel path which bordered the east front of the house. Till within the last half-hour the morning had been a drizzling one, and they had just emerged for a short turn before luncheon.

'You see, dear mother,' the son was saying, 'it is the peculiarity of my position which makes her appear to me in such a desirable light. When you consider how I have been crippled at starting, how my life has been maimed; that I feel anything like publicity distasteful, that I have no political ambition, and that my chief aim and hope lie in the education of the little thing Annie has left me, you must see how desirable a wife like Miss Halborough would be, to prevent my becoming a mere vegetable.'

'If you adore her, I suppose you must have her!' replied his mother with dry indirectness. 'But you'll find that she will not be content to live on here as you do, giving her whole mind to a young child.'

'That's just where we differ. Her very disqualification, that of being a nobody, as you call it, is her recommendation in my eyes. Her lack of influential connections limits her ambition. From what I know of her, a life in this place is all that she would wish for. She would never care to go outside the park-gates if it were necessary to stay within.'

'Being in love with her, Albert, and meaning to marry her, you invent your practical reasons to make the case respectable. Well, do as you will; I have no authority over you, so why should you consult me? You mean to propose on this very occasion, no doubt. Don't you, now?'

'By no means, I am merely revolving the idea in my mind. If on further acquaintance she turns out to be as good as she has hitherto seemed – well, I shall see. Admit, now, that you like her.'

'I readily admit it. She is very captivating at first sight. But as a step-mother to your child! You seem mighty anxious, Albert, to get rid of me!'

'Not at all. And I am not so reckless as you think. I don't make up my mind in a hurry. But the thought having occurred to me, I mention it to you at once, mother. If you dislike it, say so.'

'I don't say anything. I will try to make the best of it if you are determined. When does she come?'

'Tomorrow.'

All this time there were great preparations in train at the curate's, who was now a householder. Rosa, whose two or three weeks' stay on two occasions earlier in the year had so affected the squire, was coming again, and at the same time her younger brother Cornelius, to make up a family party. Rosa, who journeyed from the Midlands, could not arrive till late in the evening, but Cornelius was to get there in the afternoon, Joshua going out to meet him in his walk across the fields from the railway.

Everything being ready in Joshua's modest abode he started on his way, his heart buoyant and thankful, if ever it was in his life. He was of such good report himself that his brother's path into holy orders promised to be unexpectedly easy; and he longed to compare experiences with him, even though there was on hand a more exciting matter still. From his youth he had held that, in old-fashioned country places, the Church conferred social prestige up to a certain point at a cheaper price than any other profession or pursuit; and events seemed to be proving him right.

He had walked about half-an-hour when he saw Cornelius coming along the path; and in a few minutes the two brothers met. The experiences of Cornelius had been less immediately interesting than those of Joshua, but his personal position was satisfactory, and there was nothing to account for the singularly subdued manner that he exhibited, which at first Joshua set down to the fatigue of over-study; and he proceeded to the subject of Rosa's arrival in the evening, and the probable consequences of this her third visit. 'Before next Easter she'll be his wife, my boy,' said Joshua with grave exultation.

Cornelius shook his head. 'She comes too late!' he returned.

'What do you mean?'

'Look here.' He produced the Fountall paper, and placed his finger on a paragraph, which Joshua read. It appeared under the report of Petty Sessions, and was a commonplace case of disorderly conduct, in which a man was sent to prison for seven days for breaking windows in that town.

'Well?' said Joshua.

'It happened during an evening that I was in the street; and the offender is our father.'

'Not – how – I sent him more money on his promising to stay in Canada?'

'He is home, safe enough.' Cornelius in the same gloomy tone gave the remainder of his information. He had witnessed the scene, unobserved of his father, and had heard him say that he was on his way to see his daughter, who was going to marry a rich gentleman. The only good fortune attending the untoward incident was that the millwright's name had been printed as Joshua Alborough.

'Beaten! We are to be beaten on the eve of our expected victory!' said the elder brother. 'How did he guess that Rosa was likely to marry? Good Heaven! Cornelius, you seem doomed to bring bad news always, do you not?'

'I do,' said Cornelius. 'Poor Rosa!'

It was almost in tears, so great was their heart-sickness and shame, that the brothers walked the remainder of the way to Joshua's dwelling. In the evening they set out to meet Rosa, bringing her to the village in a fly; and when she had come into the house, and was sitting down with them, they almost forgot their secret anxiety in contemplating her, who knew nothing about it.

Next day the Fellmers came, and the two or three days after that were a lively time. That the squire was yielding to his impulses – making up his mind – there could be no doubt. On Sunday Cornelius read the service, and Joshua preached. Mrs Fellmer was quite maternal towards Rosa, and it appeared that she had decided to welcome the inevitable with a good grace. The pretty girl was to spend yet another afternoon with the elder lady, superintending some parish treat at the house in observance of Christmas, and afterwards to stay on to dinner, her brothers to fetch her in the evening. They were also invited to dine, but they could not accept owing to an engagement.

The engagement was of a sombre sort. They were going to meet their father, who would that day be released from Fountall Gaol, and try to persuade him to keep away from Narrobourne. Every exertion was to be made to get him back to Canada, to his old home in the Midlands – anywhere, so that he would not impinge disastrously upon their courses, and blast their sister's prospects of the auspicious marriage which was just then hanging in the balance.

As soon as Rosa had been fetched away by her friends at the manor-house her brothers started on their expedition, without waiting for dinner or tea. Cornelius, to whom the millwright always addressed his letters when he wrote any, drew from his pocket and re-read as he walked the curt note which had led to this journey being undertaken; it was despatched by their father the night before, immediately upon his liberation, and stated that he was setting out for Narrobourne at the moment of writing; that having no money he would be obliged to walk all the way; that he calculated on passing through the intervening town of Ivell about six on the following day, where he should sup at the Castle

Inn, and where he hoped they would meet him with a carriage-and-pair, or some other such conveyance, that he might not disgrace them by arriving like a tramp.

'That sounds as if he gave a thought to our position,' said Cornelius.

Joshua knew the satire that lurked in the paternal words, and said nothing. Silence prevailed during the greater part of their journey. The lamps were lighted in Ivell when they entered the streets, and Cornelius, who was quite unknown in this neighbourhood, and who, moreover, was not in clerical attire, decided that he should be the one to call at the Castle Inn. Here, in answer to his inquiry under the darkness of the archway, they told him that such a man as he had described left the house about a quarter of an hour earlier, after making a meal in the kitchen-settle. He was rather the worse for liquor.

'Then,' said Joshua, when Cornelius joined him outside with this intelligence, 'we must have met and passed him! And now that I think of it, we did meet someone who was unsteady in his gait, under the trees on the other side of Hendford Hill, where it was too dark to see him.'

They rapidly retraced their steps; but for a long stretch of the way home could discern nobody. When, however, they had gone about three-quarters of the distance, they became conscious of an irregular footfall in front of them, and could see a whitish figure in the gloom. They followed dubiously. The figure met another wayfarer – the single one that had been encountered on this lonely road – and they distinctly heard him ask the way to Narrobourne. The stranger replied – what was quite true – that the nearest way was by turning in at the stile by the next bridge, and following the footpath which branched thence across the meadows.

When the brothers reached the stile they also entered the path, but did not overtake the subject of their worry till they had crossed two or three meads, and the lights from Narrobourne manor-house were visible before them through the trees. Their father was no longer walking; he was seated against the wet bank of an adjoining hedge. Observing their forms he shouted, 'I'm going to Narrobourne; who may you be?'

They went up to him, and revealed themselves, reminding him of the plan which he had himself proposed in his note, that they should meet him at Ivell.

'By Jerry, I'd forgot it!' he said. 'Well, what do you want me to do?' His tone was distinctly quarrelsome.

A long conversation followed, which became embittered at the first hint from them that he should not come to the village. The millwright drew a quart bottle from his pocket, and challenged them to drink if they meant friendly and called themselves men. Neither of the two had touched alcohol for years, but for once they thought it best to accept, so as not to needlessly provoke him.

'What's in it?' said Joshua.

'A drop of weak gin-and-water. It won't hurt 'ee. Drink from the bottle.' Joshua did so, and his father pushed up the bottom of the vessel so as to make him swallow a good deal in spite of himself. It went down into his stomach like molten lead.

'Ha, ha, that's right!' said old Halborough. 'But 'twas raw spirit – ha, ha!'

'Why should you take me in so?' said Joshua, losing his self-command, try as he would to keep calm.

'Because you took me in, my lad, in banishing me to that cursed country under pretence that it was for my good. You were a pair of hypocrites to say so. It was done to get rid of me – no more nor less. But, by Jerry, I'm a match for ye now! I'll spoil your souls for preaching. My daughter is going to be married to the squire here. I've heard the news – I saw it in a paper!'

'It is premature—'

'I know it is true; and I'm her father, and I shall give her away, or there'll be a hell of a row, I can assure 'ee! Is that where the gennleman lives?'

Joshua Halborough writhed in impotent despair. Fellmer had not yet positively declared himself, his mother was hardly won round; a scene with their father in the parish would demolish as fair a palace of hopes as was ever builded. The millwright rose. 'If that's where the squire lives I'm going to call. Just arrived from Canady with her fortune – ha, ha! I wish no harm to the gennleman, and the gennleman will wish no harm to me. But I like to take my place in the family, and stand upon my rights, and lower people's pride!'

'You've succeeded already! Where's that woman you took with you—'

'Woman! She was my wife as lawful as the Constitution – a sight more lawful than your mother was till some time after you were born!'

Joshua had for many years before heard whispers that his father had cajoled his mother in their early acquaintance, and had made somewhat tardy amends; but never from his father's lips till now. It was the last stroke, and he could not bear it. He sank back against the hedge. 'It is over!' he said. 'He ruins us all!'

The millwright moved on, waving his stick triumphantly, and the two brothers stood still. They could see his drab figure stalking along the path, and over his head the lights from the conservatory of Narrobourne House, inside which Albert Fellmer might possibly be sitting with Rosa at that moment, holding her hand, and asking her to share his home with him.

The staggering whity-brown form, advancing to put a blot on all this, had been diminishing in the shade; and now suddenly disappeared beside a weir. There was the noise of a flounce in the water.

'He has fallen in!' said Cornelius, starting forward to run for the place at which his father had vanished.

Joshua, awaking from the stupefied reverie into which he had sunk, rushed to the other's side before he had taken ten steps. 'Stop, stop, what are you thinking of?' he whispered hoarsely, grasping Cornelius's arm.

'Pulling him out!'

'Yes, yes – so am I. But – wait a moment—'

'But, Joshua!'

'Her life and happiness, you know – Cornelius – and your reputation and mine – and our chance of rising together, all three—'

He clutched his brother's arm to the bone; and as they stood breathless the splashing and floundering in the weir continued; over it they saw the hopeful lights from the manor-house conservatory winking through the trees as their bare branches waved to and fro. In their pause there had been time to save him twice over.

The floundering and splashing grew weaker and they could hear gurgling words: 'Help – I'm drownded! Rosie – Rosie!'

'We'll go – we *must* save him. O Joshua!'

'Yes, yes! we must!'

Still they did not move, but waited, holding each other, each thinking the same thought. Weights of lead seemed to be affixed to their feet, which would no longer obey their wills. The mead became silent. Over it they fancied they could see figures moving in the conservatory. The air up there seemed to emit gentle kisses.

Cornelius started forward at last, and Joshua almost simultaneously. Two or three minutes brought them to the brink of the stream. At first they could see nothing in the water, though it was not so deep nor the night so dark but that their father's light kerseymere coat would have been visible if he had lain at the bottom. Joshua looked this way and that.

'He has drifted into the culvert,' he said.

Below the foot-bridge of the weir the stream suddenly narrowed to half its width, to pass under a barrel arch or culvert constructed for waggons to cross into the middle of the mead in haymaking time. It being at present the season of high water the arch was full to the crown, against which the ripples clucked every now and then. At this point he had just caught sight of a pale object slipping under. In a moment it was gone.

They went to the lower end, but nothing emerged. For a long time they tried at both ends to effect some communication with the interior, but to no purpose.

'We ought to have come sooner!' said the conscience-stricken Cornelius, when they were quite exhausted, and dripping wet.

'I suppose we ought,' replied Joshua heavily. He perceived his father's walking-stick on the bank; hastily picking it up he stuck it into the mud among the sedge. Then they went on.

'Shall we – say anything about this accident?' whispered Cornelius as they approached the door of Joshua's house.

'What's the use? It can do no good. We must wait until he is found.'

They went indoors and changed their clothes; after which they started for the manor-house, reaching it about ten o'clock. Beside their sister there were only three guests; an adjoining landowner and his wife, and the infirm old rector.

Rosa, although she had parted from them so recently, grasped their hands in an ecstatic, brimming, joyful manner, as if she had not seen them for years. 'You look pale,' she said.

The brothers answered that they had had a long walk, and were somewhat tired. Everybody in the room seemed charged full with some sort of interesting knowledge: the squire's neighbour and neighbour's wife looked wisely around; and Fellmer himself played the part of host with a preoccupied bearing which approached fervour. They left at eleven, not accepting the carriage offered, the distance being so short and the roads dry. The squire came rather further into the dark with them than he need have done, and wished Rosa good-night in a mysterious manner, slightly apart from the rest.

When they were walking along Joshua said, with a desperate attempt at joviality, 'Rosa, what's going on?'

'O, I—' she began between a gasp and a bound. 'He—'

'Never mind – if it disturbs you.'

She was so excited that she could not speak connectedly at first, the practised air which she had brought home with her having disappeared. Calming herself she added, 'I am not disturbed, and nothing has happened. Only he said he wanted to ask me *something*, some day; and I said never mind that now. He hasn't asked yet, and is coming to speak to you about it. He would have done so tonight, only I asked him not to be in a hurry. But he will come tomorrow, I am sure!'

5

It was summer-time, six months later, and mowers and haymakers were at work in the meads. The manor-house, being opposite them, frequently formed a peg for conversation during these operations; and the doings of the squire, and the squire's young wife, the curate's sister – who was at present the admired of most of them, and the interest of all – met with their due amount of criticism.

Rosa was happy, if ever woman could be said to be so. She had not learnt the fate of her father, and sometimes wondered – perhaps with a sense of relief – why he did not write to her from his supposed home in Canada. Her brother Joshua had been presented to a living in a small town, shortly after her marriage, and Cornelius had thereupon succeeded to the vacant curacy of Narrobourne.

These two had awaited in deep suspense the discovery of their father's body; and yet the discovery had not been made. Every day they expected a man or a boy to run up from the meads with the intelligence; but he had never come. Days had accumulated to weeks and months; the wedding had come and gone: Joshua had tolled and read himself in at his new parish; and never a shout of amazement over the millwright's remains.

But now, in June, when they were mowing the meads, the hatches had to be drawn and the water let out of its channels for the convenience of the mowers. It was thus that the discovery was made. A man, stooping low with his scythe, caught a view of the culvert lengthwise, and saw something entangled in the recently bared weeds of its bed. A day or two after there was an inquest; but the body was unrecognizable. Fish and flood had been busy with the millwright; he had no watch or marked article which could be identified; and a verdict of the accidental drowning of a person unknown settled the matter.

As the body was found in Narrobourne parish, there it had to be buried. Cornelius wrote to Joshua, begging him to come and read the service, or to send some one; he himself could not do it. Rather than let in a stranger Joshua came, and silently scanned the coroner's order handed him by the undertaker:

'I, Henry Giles, Coroner for the Mid-Division of Outer Wessex, do hereby order the burial of the body now shown to the Inquest Jury as the body of an Adult Male Person Unknown . . .' etc.

Joshua Halborough got through the service in some way, and rejoined his brother Cornelius at his house. Neither accepted an invitation to lunch at their sister's; they wished to discuss parish matters together. In the afternoon she came down, though they had already called on her, and had not expected to see her again. Her bright eyes, brown hair, flowery bonnet, lemon-coloured gloves, and flush beauty, were like an irradiation into the apartment, which they in their gloom could hardly bear.

'I forgot to tell you,' she said, 'of a curious thing which happened to me a month or two before my marriage – something which I have thought may have had a connection with the accident to the poor man you have buried today. It was on that evening I was at the manor-house waiting for you to fetch me; I was in the winter-garden with Albert, and we were silent together, when we fancied we heard a cry in the distant meadow. We opened the door, and while Albert ran to fetch his hat, leaving me standing there, the cry was repeated, and my excited senses made me think I heard my own name. When Albert came back all was silent, and we decided that it was only a drunken shout, and not a cry for help. We both forgot the incident, and it never has occurred to me till since the funeral today that it might have been this stranger's cry. The name of course was only fancy, or he might have had a wife or child with a name something like mine, poor man!'

When she was gone the brothers were silent till Cornelius said, 'Now mark this, Joshua. Sooner or later she'll know.'

'How?'

'From one of us. Do you think human hearts are iron-cased safes, that you suppose we can keep this secret for ever?'

'Yes, I think they are, sometimes,' said Joshua.

'No. It will out. We shall tell.'

'What, and ruin her – kill her? Disgrace her children, and pull down the whole auspicious house of Fellmer abut our ears? No! May I – drown where he was drowned before I do it! Never, never. Surely you can say the same, Cornelius!'

Cornelius seemed fortified, and no more was said. For a long time after that day he did not see Joshua, and before the next year was out a son and heir was born to the Fellmers. The villagers rang the three bells every evening for a week and more, and were made merry by Mr Fellmer's ale; and when the christening came on Joshua paid Narrobourne another visit.

Among all the people who assembled on that day the brother clergymen were the least interested. Their minds were haunted by a spirit in kerseymere. In the evening they walked together in the fields.

'She's all right,' said Joshua. 'But here are you doing journey-work, Cornelius, and likely to continue at it till the end of the day, as far as I can see. I, too, with my petty living – what am I after all? . . . To tell the truth, the church is a poor forlorn hope for people without influence, particularly when their enthusiasm begins to flag. A social regenerator has a better chance outside, where he is unhampered by dogma and tradition. As for me, I would rather have gone on mending mills, with my crust of bread and liberty.'

Almost automatically they had bent their steps along the margin of the river; they now paused. They were standing on the brink of the well-known weir. There were the hatches, there was the culvert; they could see the pebbly bed of the stream through the pellucid water. The notes of the church-bells were audible, still jangled by the enthusiastic villagers.

'Why, see – it was there I hid his walking-stick!' said Joshua, looking towards the sedge. The next moment, during a passing breeze, something flashed white on the spot to which the attention of Cornelius was drawn.

From the sedge rose a straight little silver-poplar, and it was the leaves of this sapling which caused the flicker of whiteness.

'His walking-stick has grown!' Joshua added. 'It was a rough one – cut from the hedge, I remember.'

At every puff of wind the tree turned white till they could not bear to look at it; and they walked away.

'I see him every night,' Cornelius murmured . . . 'Ah, we read our *Hebrews* to little account, Jos! *Υπέμεινε σταυρὸν, αι'χύνηζ καταψρονήοαζ.* To have *endured* the cross, *despising* the shame – there lay greatness! But now I often feel that I should like to put an end to trouble here in this selfsame spot.'

'I have thought of it myself,' said Joshua.

'Perhaps we shall, some day,' murmured his brother.

'Perhaps,' said Joshua moodily.

With that contingency to consider in the silence of their nights and days they bent their steps homewards.

DECEMBER 1888

ON THE WESTERN CIRCUIT

I

The man who played the disturbing part in the two quiet feminine lives hereunder depicted – no great man, in any sense, by the way – first had knowledge of them on an October evening, in the city of Melchester. He had been standing in the Close, vainly endeavouring to gain amid the darkness a glimpse of the most homogeneous pile of mediaeval architecture in England, which towered and tapered from the damp and level sward in front of him. While he stood the presence of the Cathedral walls was revealed rather by the ear than by the eyes; he could not see them, but they reflected sharply a roar of sound which entered the Close by a street leading from the city square, and, falling upon the building, was flung back upon him.

He postponed till the morrow his attempt to examine the deserted edifice, and turned his attention to the noise. It was compounded of steam barrel-organs, the clanging of gongs, the ringing of hand-bells, the clack of rattles, and the undistinguishable shouts of men. A lurid light hung in the air in the direction of the tumult. Thitherward he went, passing under the arched gateway, along a straight street, and into the square.

He might have searched Europe over for a greater contrast between juxtaposed scenes. The spectacle was that of the eighth chasm of the Inferno as to colour and flame, and, as to mirth, a development of the Homeric heaven. A smoky glare, of the complexion of brass-filings, ascended from the fiery tongues of innumerable naphtha lamps affixed to booths, stalls, and other temporary erections which crowded the spacious market-square. In front of this irradiation scores of human figures, more or less in profile, were darting athwart and across, up, down, and around, like gnats against a sunset.

Their motions were so rhythmical that they seemed to be moved by machinery. And it presently appeared that they were moved by machinery indeed; the figures being those of the patrons of swings, see-saws, flying-leaps, above all of the three steam round-abouts which occupied the centre of the position. It was from the latter that the din of steam-organs came.

Throbbing humanity in full light was, on second thoughts, better than architecture in the dark. The young man, lighting a short pipe, and putting his hat on one side and one hand in his pocket, to throw himself into harmony with his new environment, drew near to the largest and most patronized of the steam circuses, as the roundabouts were called by their owners. This was one of brilliant finish, and it was now in full revolution. The musical instrument around which and to whose tones the riders revolved, directed its trumpet-mouths of brass upon the young man, and the long plate-glass mirrors set at angles, which revolved with the machine, flashed the gyrating personages and hobby-horses kaleidoscopically into his eyes.

It could now be seen that he was unlike the majority of the crowd. A gentlemanly young fellow, one of the species found in large towns only, and London particularly, built on delicate lines, well, though not fashionably dressed, he appeared to belong to the professional class; he had nothing square or practical about his look, much that was curvilinear and sensuous. Indeed some would have called him a man not altogether typical of the middle-class male of a century wherein sordid ambition is the master-passion that seems to be taking the time-honoured place of love.

The revolving figures passed before his eyes with an unexpected and quiet grace in a throng whose natural movements did not suggest gracefulness or quietude as a rule. By some contrivance there was imparted to each of the hobby-horses a motion which was really the triumph and perfection of roundabout inventiveness – a galloping rise and fall, so timed that, of each pair of steeds, one was on the spring while the other was on the pitch. The riders were quite fascinated by these equine undulations in this most delightful holiday-game of our times. There were riders as young as six, and as old as sixty years, with every age between. At first it was difficult to catch a personality, but by and by the observer's eyes centred on the prettiest girl out of the several pretty ones revolving.

It was not that one with the light frock and light hat whom he had been at first attracted by; no, it was the one with the black cape, gray skirt, light gloves and – no, not even she, but the one behind her; she with the crimson skirt, dark jacket, brown hat and brown gloves. Unmistakably that was the prettiest girl.

Having finally selected her, this idle spectator studied her as well as he was able during each of her brief transits across his visual field. She was absolutely unconscious of everything save the act of riding: her features were rapt in an ecstatic dreaminess; for the moment she did not know her age or her history or her lineaments, much less her troubles. He himself was full of vague latter-day glooms and popular melancholies, and it was a refreshing sensation to behold this young thing then and there, absolutely as happy as if she were in a Paradise.

Dreading the moment when the inexorable stoker, grimily lurking behind the glittering rococo-work, should decide that this set of riders had had their pennyworth, and bring the whole concern of steam-engine, horses, mirrors, trumpets, drums, cymbals, and such-like to pause and silence, he waited for her every reappearance, glancing indifferently over the intervening forms, including the two plainer girls, the old woman and child, the two youngsters, the newly-married couple, the old man with a clay pipe, the sparkish youth with a ring, the young ladies in the charriot, the pair of journeyman-carpenters, and others, till his select country beauty followed on again in her place. He had never seen a fairer product of nature, and at each round she made a deeper mark in his sentiments. The stoppage then came, and the sighs of the riders were audible.

He moved round to the place at which he reckoned she would alight; but she retained her seat. The empty saddles began to refill, and she plainly was deciding to have another turn. The young man drew up to the side of her steed, and pleasantly asked her if she had enjoyed her ride.

'O yes!' she said with dancing eyes. 'It has been quite unlike anything I have ever felt in my life before!'

It was not difficult to fall into conversation with her. Unreserved – too unreserved – by nature, she was not experienced enough to be reserved by art, and after a little coaxing she answered his remarks readily. She had come to live in Melchseter from a village on the Great Plain, and this was the first time that she had ever seen a steam-circus; she could not understand how such wonderful machines were made. She had come to the city on the invitation of Mrs Harnham, who had taken her into her household to train her as a servant, if she showed any aptitude. Mrs Harnham was a young lady who before she married had been Miss Edith White, living in the country near the speaker's cottage; she was now very kind to her through knowing her in childhood so well. She was even taking the trouble to educate her. Mrs Harnham was the only friend she had in the world, and being without children had wished to have her near her in preference to anybody else, though she had only lately come; allowed her to do almost as she liked, and to have a holiday whenever she asked for it. The husband of this kind young lady was a rich wine-merchant of the town, but Mrs Harnham did not care much about him. In the daytime you could see the house from where they were talking. She, the speaker, liked Melchester better than the lonely country, and she was going to have a new hat for next Sunday that was to cost fifteen and ninepence.

Then she inquired of her acquaintance where he lived, and he told her in London, that ancient and smoky city, where everybody lived who lived at all, and die because they could not live there. He came into Wessex two or three times a year for professional reasons; he had arrived from Wintoncester yesterday, and was going on into the next county in a day or two. For one thing he did like the country better than the town, and it was because it contained such girls as herself.

Then the pleasure-machine started again, and, to the light-hearted girl, the figure of the handsome young man, the market-square with its lights and crowd, the houses beyond, and the world at large, began moving round as before, countermoving in the revolving mirrors on her right hand, she being as it were the fixed point in an undulating, dazzling, lurid universe, in which loomed forward most prominently of all the form of her late interlocutor. Each time that she approached the half of her orbit that lay nearest him they gazed at each other with smiles, and with that unmistakable expression which means so little at the moment, yet so often leads up to passion, heartache, union, disunion, devotion, over-population, drudgery, content, resignation, despair.

When the horses slowed anew he stepped to her side and proposed another heat. 'Hang the expense for once,' he said. 'I'll pay!'

She laughed till the tears came.

'Why do you laugh, dear?' said he.

'Because – you are so genteel that you must have plenty of money, and only say that for fun!' she returned.

'Ha-ha!' laughed the young man in unison, and gallantly producing his money she was enabled to whirl on again.

As he stood smiling there in the motley crowd, with his pipe in his hand, and clad in the rough pea-jacket and wideawake that he had put on for his stroll, who would have supposed him to be Charles Bradford Raye, Esquire, stuff-gownsman, educated at Wintoncester, called to the Bar at Lincoln's Inn, now going the Western Circuit, merely detained in Melchester by a small arbitration after his brethren had moved on to the next county-town?

2

The square was overlooked from its remoter corner by the house of which the young girl had spoken, a dignified residence of considerable size, having several windows on each floor. Inside one of these, on the first floor, the apartment being a large drawing-room, sat a lady, in appearance from twenty-eight to thirty years of age. The blinds were still undrawn, and the lady was absently surveying the weird scene without, her cheek resting on her hand. The room was unlit from within, but enough of the glare from the market-place entered it to reveal the lady's face. She was what is called an interesting creature rather than a handsome woman; dark-eyed, thoughtful, and with sensitive lips.

A man sauntered into the room from behind and came forward.

'O, Edith, I didn't see you,' he said. 'Why are you sitting here in the dark?'

'I am looking at the fair,' replied the lady in a languid voice.

'Oh? Horrid nuisance every year! I wish it could be put a stop to.'

'I like it.'

'H'm. There's no accounting for taste.'

For a moment he gazed from the window with her, for politeness' sake, and then went out again.

In a few minutes she rang.

'Hasn't Anna come in?' asked Mrs Harnham.

'No, m'm.'

She ought to be in by this time. I meant her to go for ten minutes only.'

'Shall I go and look for her, m'm?' said the housemaid alertly.

'No. It is not necessary: she is a good girl and will come soon.'

However, when the servant had gone Mrs Harnham arose, went up to her room, cloaked and bonneted herself, and proceeded downstairs, where she found her husband.

'I want to see the fair,' she said; 'and I am going to look for Anna. I have made myself responsible for her, and must see she comes to no harm. She ought to be indoors. Will you come with me?'

'Oh, she's all right. I saw her on one of those whirligig things, talking to her young man as I came in. But I'll go if you wish, though I'd rather go a hundred miles the other way.'

'Then please do so. I shall come to no harm alone.'

She left the house and entered the crowd which thronged the market-place, where she soon discovered Anna, seated on the revolving horse. As soon as it stopped Mrs Harnham advanced and said severely, 'Anna, how can you be such a wild girl? You were only to be out for ten minutes.'

Anna looked blank, and the young man, who had dropped into the background, came to help her alight.

'Please don't blame her,' he said politely. 'It is my fault that she has stayed. She looked so graceful on the horse that I induced her to go round again. I assure you that she has been quite safe.'

'In that case I'll leave her in your hands,' said Mrs Harnham, turning to retrace her steps.

But this for the moment it was not so easy to do. Something had attracted the crowd to a spot in their rear, and the wine-merchant's wife, caught by its sway, found herself pressed against Anna's acquaintance without power to move away. Their faces were within a few inches of each other, his breath fanned her cheek as well as Anna's. They could do no other than smile at the accident; but neither spoke, and each waited passively. Mrs Harnham then felt a man's hand clasping her fingers, and from the look of consciousness on the young fellow's face she knew the hand to be his: she also knew that from the position of the girl he had no other thought than that the imprisoned hand was Anna's. What prompted her to refrain from undeceiving him she could hardly tell. Not content with holding the hand, he playfully slipped two of his fingers inside her glove, against her palm. Thus matters continued till the pressure lessened; but several minutes passed before the crowd thinned sufficiently to allow Mrs Harnham to withdraw.

'How did they get to know each other, I wonder?' she mused as she retreated. 'Anna is really very forward – and he very wicked and nice.'

She was so gently stirred wtih the stranger's manner and voice, with the tenderness of his idle touch, that instead of re-entering the house she turned back again and observed the pair from a screened nook. Really she argued (being little less impulsive than Anna herself) it was very excusable in Anna to encourage him, however she might have contrived to make his acquaintance; he was so gentlemanly, so fascinating, had such beautiful eyes. The thought that he was several years her junior produced a reasonless sigh.

At length the couple turned from the roundabout towards the door of Mrs Harnham's house, and the young man could be heard saying that he would accompany her home. Anna, then, had found a lover, apparently a very devoted one. Mrs Harnham was quite interested in him. When they drew near the door of the wine-merchant's house, a comparatively deserted spot by this time, they stood invisible for a little while in the shadow of a wall, where they separated, Anna going on to the entrance, and her acquaintance returning across the square.

'Anna,' said Mrs Harnham, coming up. 'I've been looking at you! That young man kissed you at parting, I am almost sure.'

'Well,' stammered Anna; 'he said, if I didn't mind – it would do me no harm, and – and – him a great deal of good!'

'Ah, I thought so! and he was a stranger till tonight?'

'Yes, ma'am.'

'Yet I warrant you told him your name and everything about yourself?'

'He asked me.'

'But he didn't tell you his?'

'Yes, ma'am, he did!' cried Anna victoriously. 'It is Charles Bradford, of London.'

'Well, if he's respectable, of course I've nothing to say against your knowing him,' remarked her mistress, prepossessed, in spite of general principles, in the young man's favour. 'But I must reconsider all that, if he attempts to renew your acquaintance. A country-bred girl like you, who has never lived in Melchester till this month, who had hardly ever seen a black-coated man till you came here, to be so sharp as to capture a young Londoner like him!'

'I didn't capture him. I didn't do anything,' said Anna, in confusion.

When she was indoors and alone Mrs Harnham thought what a well-bred and chivalrous young man Anna's companion had seemed. There had been a magic in his wooing touch of her hand; and she wondered how he had come to be attracted by the girl.

The next morning the emotional Edith Harnham went to the usual week-day service in Melchester cathedral. In crossing the Close through the fog she again perceived him who had interested her the previous evening, gazing up thoughtfully at the high-piled architecture of the nave: and as soon as she had taken her seat he entered and sat down in a stall opposite hers.

He did not particularly heed her; but Mrs Harnham was continually occupying her eyes with him, and wondered more than ever what had attracted him in her unfledged maid-servant. The mistress was almost as unaccustomed as the maiden herself to the end-of-the-age young man, or she might have wondered less. Raye, having looked about him a while, left abruptly, without regard to the service that was proceeding; and Mrs Harnham – lonely, impressionable creature that she was – took no further interest in praising the Lord. She wished she had married a London man who knew the subtleties of love-making as they were evidently known to him who had mistakenly caressed her hand.

3

The calendar at Melchester had been light, occupying the court only a few hours; and the assizes at Casterbridge, the next county-town on the Western Circuit, having no business for Raye, he had not gone thither. At the next town after that they did not open till the following Monday, trials to begin on Tuesday morning. In the natural order of things Raye would have arrived at the latter place on Monday afternoon; but it was not till the middle of Wednesday that his gown and gray wig, curled in tiers, in the best fashion of Assyrian bas-reliefs, were seen blowing and bobbing behind him as he hastily walked up the High Street from his lodgings. But though he entered the assize building there was nothing for him to do, and sitting at the blue baize table in the well of the court, he mended pens with a mind far away from the case in progress. Thoughts of unpremeditated conduct, of which a week earlier he would not have believed himself capable, threw him into a mood of dissatisfied depression.

He had contrived to see again the pretty rural maiden Anna, the day after the fair, had walked out of the city with her to the earthworks of Old Melchester, and feeling a violent fancy for her, had remained in Melchester all Sunday, Monday, and Tuesday; by persuasion obtaining walks and meeting with the girl six or seven times during the interval; had in brief won her, body and soul.

He supposed it must have been owing to the seclusion in which he had lived of late in town that he had given way so unrestrainedly to a passion for an artless creature whose inexperience had, from the first, led her to place herself unreservedly in his hands. Much he deplored trifling with her feelings for the sake of a passing desire; and he could only hope that she might not live to suffer on his account.

She had begged him to come to her again; entreated him; wept. He had promised that he would do so, and he meant to carry out that promise. He could not desert her now. Awkward as such unintentional connections were, the interspace of a hundred miles – which to a girl of her limited capabilities was like a thousand – would effectually hinder this summer fancy from greatly encumbering his life; while thought of her simple love might do him the negative good of keeping him from idle pleasures in town when he wished to work hard. His circuit journeys would take him to Melchester three or four times a year; and then he could always see her.

The pseudonym, or rather partial name, that he had given her as his before knowing how far the acquaintance was going to carry him, had been spoken on the spur of the moment, without any ulterior intention whatever. He had not afterwards disturbed Anna's error, but on leaving her he had felt bound to give her an address at a stationer's not far from his chambers, at which she might write to him under the initials 'C.B.'

In due time Raye returned to his London abode, having called at Melchester on his way and spent a few additional hours with his fascinating child of nature. In town he lived monotonously every day. Often he and his rooms were enclosed by a tawny fog from all the world besides, and when he lighted the gas to read or write by, his situation seemed so unnatural that he would look into the fire and think of that trusting girl at Melchester again and again. Often, oppressed by absurd fondness for her, he would enter the dim religious nave of the Law Courts by the north door, elbow other juniors habited like himself, and like him unretained; edge himself into this or that crowded court where a sensational case was going on, just as if he were in it, though the police officers at the door knew as well as he knew himself that he had no more concern with the business in hand than the patient idlers at the gallery-door outside, who had waited to enter since eight in the morning because, like him, they belonged to the classes that live on expectation. But he would do these things to no purpose, and think how greatly the characters in such scenes contrasted with the pink and breezy Anna.

An unexpected feature in that peasant maiden's conduct was that she had not as yet written to him, though he had told her she might do so if she wished. Surely a young creature had never before been so reticent in such circumstances. At length he sent her a brief line, postively requesting her to write. There was no answer by the return post, but the day after a letter in a neat feminine hand, and bearing the Melchester post-mark, was handed to him by the stationer.

The fact alone of its arrival was sufficient to satisfy his imaginative sentiment. He was not anxious to open the epistle, and in truth did not begin to read it for nearly half-an-hour, anticipating readily its terms of passionate retrospect and tender adjuration. When at last he turned his feet to the fireplace and unfolded the sheet, he was surprised and pleased to find that neither extravagance nor vulgarity was there. It was the most charming little missive he had ever received from woman. To be sure the language was simple and the ideas were slight; but it was so self-possessed; so purely that of a young girl who felt her womanhood to be enough for her dignity that he read it through twice. Four sides were filled, and a few lines written across, after the fashion of former days; the paper, too, was common, and not of the latest shade and surface. But what of those things? He had received letters from women who were fairly called ladies, but never so sensible, so human a letter as this. He could not single out any one sentence and say it was at all remarkable or clever; the *ensemble* of the letter it was which won him; and beyond the one request that he would write or come to her again soon there was nothing to show her sense of a claim upon him.

To write again and develop a correspondence was the last thing Raye would have preconceived as his conduct in such a situation; yet he did send a short, encouraging line or two, signed with his pseudonym, in which he asked for another letter, and cheeringly promised that he would try to see her again on some near day, and would never forget how much they had been to each other during their short acquaintance.

4

To return now to the moment at which Anna, at Melchester, had received Raye's letter.

It had been put into her own hand by the postman on his morning rounds. She flushed down to her neck on receipt of it, and turned it over and over. 'It is mine?' she said.

'Why, yes, can't you see it is?' said the postman, smiling as he guessed the nature of the document and the cause of the confusion.

'O yes, of course!' replied Anna, looking at the letter, forcedly tittering, and blushing still more.

Her look of embarrassment did not leave her with the postman's departure. She opened the envelope, kissed its contents, put away the letter in her pocket, and remained musing till her eyes filled with tears.

A few minutes later she carried up a cup of tea to Mrs Harnham in her bed-chamber. Anna's mistress looked at her, and said: 'How dismal you seem this morning, Anna. What's the matter?'

'I'm not dismal. I'm glad; only I—' She stopped to stifle a sob.

'Well?'

'I've got a letter – and what good is it to me, if I can't read a word in it!'

'Why, I'll read it, child, if necessary.'

'But this is from somebody – I don't want anybody to read it but myself!' Anna murmured.

'I shall not tell anybody. Is it from that young man?'

'I think so.' Anna slowly produced the letter, saying: 'Then will you read it to me, ma'am?'

This was the secret of Anna's embarrassment and flutterings. She could neither read nor write. She had grown up under the care of an aunt by marriage at one of the lonely hamlets on the great Mid-Wessex Plain where, even in days of national education, there had been no school within a distance of two miles. Her aunt was an ignorant woman; there had been nobody to investigate Anna's circumstances, nobody to care about her learning the rudiments; though, as often in such cases, she had been well fed and clothed and not unkindly treated. Since she had come to live at Melchester with Mrs Harnham, the latter, who took a kindly interest in the girl, had taught her to speak correctly, in which accomplishment Anna showed considerable readiness, as is not unusual with the illiterate; and soon became quite fluent in the use of her mistress's phraseology. Mrs Harnham also insisted upon her getting a spelling and copy book, and beginning to practise in these. Anna was slower in this branch of her education, and meanwhile here was the letter.

Edith Harnham's large dark eyes expressed some interest in the contents, though, in her character of mere interpreter, she threw into her tone as much as she could of mechanical passiveness. She read the short epistle on to its concluding sentence, which idly requested Anna to send him a tender answer.

'Now – you'll do it for me, won't you, dear mistress?' said Anna eagerly. 'And you'll do it as well as ever you can, please? Because I couldn't bear him to think I am not able to do it myself. I should sink into the earth with shame if he knew that!'

From some words in the letter Mrs Harnham was led to ask questions, and the answers she received confirmed her suspicions. Deep concern filled Edith's heart at perceiving how the girl had committed her happiness to the issue of this new-sprung attachment. She blamed herself for not interfering in a flirtation which had resulted so seriously for the poor little creature in her charge; though at the time of seeing the pair together she had a feeling that it was hardly within her province to nip young affection in the bud. However, what was done could not be undone, and it behoved her now, as Anna's only protector, to help her as much as she could. To Anna's eager request that she, Mrs Harnham, should compose and write the answer to this young London man's letter, she felt bound to accede, to keep alive his attachment to the girl if possible; though in other circumstances she might have suggested the cook as an amanuensis.

A tender reply was thereupon concocted, and set down in Edith Harnham's hand. This letter it had been which Raye had received and delighted in. Written in the presence of Anna it certainly was, and on Anna's humble note-paper, and in a measure indited by the young girl; but the life, the spirit, the individuality, were Edith Harnham's.

'Won't you at least put your name yourself?' she said. 'You can manage to write that by this time?'

'No, no,' said Anna, shrinking back. 'I should do it so bad. He'd be ashamed of me, and never see me again!'

The note, so prettily requesting another from him, had, as we have seen, power enough in its pages to bring one. He declared it to be such a pleasure to hear from her that she must write every week. The same process of manufacture was accordingly repeated by Anna and her mistress, and continued for several weeks in succession; each letter being penned and suggested by Edith, the girl standing by; the answer read and commented on by Edith, Anna standing by and listening again.

Late on a winter evening, after the dispatch of the sixth letter, Mrs Harnham was sitting alone by the remains of her fire. Her husband had retired to bed, and she had fallen into that fixity of musing which takes no count of hour or temperature. The state of mind had been brought about in Edith by a strange thing which she had done that day. For the first time since Raye's visit Anna had gone to stay over a night or two with her cottage friends on the Plain, and in her absence had arrived, out of its time, a letter from Raye. To this Edith had replied on her own responsibility, from the depths of her own heart, without waiting for her maid's collaboration. The luxury of writing to him what would be known to no consciousness but his was great, and she had indulged herself therein.

Why was it a luxury?

Edith Harnham led a lonely life. Influenced by the belief of the British parent that a bad marriage with its aversions is better than free womanhood with its interests, dignity, and leisure, she had consented to marry the elderly wine-merchant as a *pis aller*, at the age of seven-and-twenty – some three years before this date – to find afterwards that she had made a mistake. That contract had left her still a woman whose deeper nature had never been stirred.

She was now clearly realizing that she had become possessed to the bottom of her soul with the image of a man to whom she was hardly so much as a name. From the first he had attracted her by his looks and voice; by his tender touch; and, with these as generators, the writing of letter after letter and the reading of their soft answers had insensibly developed on her side an emotion which fanned his; till there had resulted a magnetic reciprocity between the correspondents, notwithstanding that one of them wrote in a character not her own. That he had been able to seduce another woman in two days was his crowning though unrecognized fascination for her as the she-animal.

They were her own impassioned and pent-up ideas – lowered to monosyllabic phraseology in order to keep up the disguise – that Edith put into letters signed with another name, much to the shallow Anna's delight, who, unassisted, could not for the world have conceived such pretty fancies for winning him, even had she been able to write them. Edith found that it was these, her own foisted-in sentiments, to which the young barrister mainly responded. The few sentences occasionally added from Anna's own lips made apparently no impression upon him.

The letter-writing in her absence Anna never discovered; but on her return the next morning she declared she wished to see her lover about something at once, and begged Mrs Harnham to ask him to come.

There was a strange anxiety in her manner which did not escape Mrs Harnham, and ultimately resolved itself into a flood of tears. Sinking down at Edith's knees, she made confession that the result of her relations with her lover it would soon become necessary to disclose.

Edith Harnham was generous enough to be very far from inclined to cast Anna adrift at this conjuncture. No true woman ever is so inclined from her own personal point of view, however prompt she may be in taking such steps to safeguard those dear to her. Although she had written to Raye so short a time previously, she instantly penned another Anna-note hinting clearly though delicately the state of affairs.

Raye replied by a hasty line to say how much he was concerned at her news: he felt that he must run down to see her almost immediately.

But a week later the girl came to her mistress's room with another note, which on being read informed her that after all he could not find time for the journey. Anna was broken with grief; but by Mrs Harnham's counsel strictly refrained from hurling at him the reproaches and bitterness customary from young women so situated. One thing was imperative: to keep the young man's romantic interest in her alive. Rather therefore did Edith, in the name of her *protégée*, request him on no account to be distressed about the looming event, and not to inconvenience himself to hasten down. She desired above everything to be no weight upon him in his career, no clog upon his high activities. She had wished him to know what had befallen: he was to dismiss it again from his mind. Only he must write tenderly as ever, and when he should come again on the spring circuit it would be soon enough to discuss what had better be done.

It may well be supposed that Anna's own feelings had not been quite in accord with these generous expressions; but the mistress's judgment had ruled, and Anna had acquiesced. 'All I want is that *niceness* you can so well put into your letters, my dear, dear mistress, and that I can't for the life o' me make up out of my own head; though I mean the same thing and feel it exactly when you've written it down!'

When the letter had been sent off, and Edith Harnham was left alone, she bowed herself on the back of her chair and wept.

'I wish his child was mine – I wish it was!' she murmured. 'Yet how can I say such a wicked thing!'

5

The letter moved Raye considerably when it reached him. The intelligence itself had affected him less than her unexpected manner of treating him in relation to it. The absence of any word of reproach, the devotion to his interests, the self-sacrifice apparent in every line, all made up a nobility of character that he had never dreamt of finding in womankind.

'God forgive me!' he said tremulously 'I have been a wicked wretch. I did not know she was such a treasure as this!'

He reassured her instantly – declaring that he would not of course desert her, that he would provide a home for her somewhere. Meanwhile she was to stay where she was as long as her mistress would allow her.

But a misfortune supervened in this direction. Whether an inkling of Anna's circumstances reached the knowledge of Mrs Harnham's husband or not cannot be said, but the girl was compelled, in spite of Edith's entreaties, to leave the house. By her own choice she decided to go back for a while to the cottage on the Plain. This arrangement led to a consultation as to how the correspondence should be carried on; and in the girl's inability to continue personally what had been begun in her name, and in the difficulty of their acting in concert as heretofore, she requested Mrs Harnham – the only well-to-do friend she had in the world – to receive the letters and reply to them off-hand, sending them on afterwards to herself on the Plain, where she might at least get some neighbour to read them to her, if a trustworthy one could be met with. Anna and her box then departed for the Plain.

Thus it befell that Edith Harnham found herself in the strange position of having to correspond, under no supervision by the real woman, with a man not her husband, in terms which were virtually those of a wife, concerning a corporeal condition that was not Edith's at all; the man being one for whom, mainly through the sympathies involved in playing this part, she secretly cherished a predilection, subtle and imaginative truly, but strong and absorbing. She opened each letter, read it as if intended for herself, and replied from the promptings of her own heart and no other.

Throughout this correspondence, carried on in the girl's absence, the high-strung Edith Harnham lived in the ecstasy of fancy; the vicarious intimacy engendered such a flow of passionateness as was never exceeded. For conscience' sake Edith at first sent on each of his letters to Anna, and even rough copies of her replies; but later on these so-called copies were much abridged, and many letters on both sides were not sent on at all.

Though sensuous, and, superficially at least, infested with the self-indulgent vices of artificial society, there was a substratum of honesty and fairness in Raye's character. He had really a tender regard for the country girl, and it grew more tender than ever when he found her apparently capable of expressing the deepest sensibilities in the simplest words. He meditated, he wavered, and finally resolved to consult his sister, a maiden lady much older than himself, of lively sympathies and good intent. In making this confidence he showed her some of the letters.

'She seems fairly educated,' Miss Raye observed. 'And bright in ideas. She expresses herself with a taste that must be innate.'

'Yes. She writes very prettily, doesn't she, thanks to these elementary schools?'

'One is drawn out towards her, in spite of one's self, poor thing.'

The upshot of the discussion was that though he had not been directly advised to do it, Raye wrote, in his real name, what he would never have decided to write on his own responsibility; namely, that he could not live without her, and would come down in the spring and shelve her looming difficulty by marrying her.

This bold acceptance of the situation was made known to Anna by Mrs Harnham driving out immediately to the cottage on the Plain. Anna jumped for joy like a little child. And poor, crude directions for answering appropriately were given to Edith Harnham, who on her return to the city carried them out with warm intensifications.

'O!' she groaned, as she threw down the pen. 'Anna – poor good little fool – hasn't intelligence enough to appreciate him! How should she? While I – don't bear his child!'

It was now February. The correspondence had continued altogether for four months, and the next letter from Raye contained incidentally a statement of his position and prospects. He said that in offering to wed her he had, at first, contemplated the step of retiring from a profession which hitherto had brought him very slight emolument, and which, to speak plainly, he had thought might be difficult of practice after his union with her. But the unexpected mines of brightness and warmth that her letters had disclosed to be lurking in her sweet nature had led him to abandon that somewhat sad prospect. He felt sure that, with her powers of development, after a little private training in the social forms of London under his supervision, and a little help from a governess if necessary, she would make as good a professional man's wife as could be desired, even if he should rise to the woolsack. Many a Lord Chancellor's wife had been less intuitively a lady than she had shown herself to be in her lines to him.

'O – poor fellow, poor fellow!' mourned Edith Harnham.

Her distress now raged as high as her infatuation. It was she who had wrought him to this pitch – to a marriage which meant his ruin; yet she could not, in mercy to her maid, do anything to hinder his plan. Anna was coming to Melchester that week, but she could hardly show the girl this last reply from the young man; it told too much of the second individuality that had usurped the place of the first.

Anna came, and her mistress took her into her own room for privacy. Anna began by saying with some anxiety that she was glad the wedding was so near.

'O, Anna!' replied Mrs Harnham. 'I think we must tell him all – that I have been doing your writing for you? – lest he should not know it till after you become his wife, and it might lead to dissension and recriminations—'

'O, mis'ess, dear mis'ess – please don't tell him now!' cried Anna in distress. 'If you were to do it perhaps he would not marry me; and what should I do then? It would be terrible what would come to me! And I am getting on with my writing, too. I have brought with me the copybook you were so good as to give me, and I practise every day, and though it is so, so hard, I shall do it well at last, I believe, if I keep on trying.'

Edith looked at the copybook. The copies had been set by herself, and such progress as the girl had made was in the way of grotesque facsimile of her mistress's hand. But even if Edith's flowing caligraphy were reproduced the inspiration would be another thing.

'You do it so beautifully,' continued Anna, 'and say all that I want to say so much better than I could say it, that I do hope you won't leave me in the lurch just now!'

'Very well,' replied the other. 'But I – but I thought I ought not to go on!'

'Why?'

Her strong desire to confide her sentiments led Edith to answer truly:

'Because of its effect upon me.'

'But it *can't* have any!'

'Why, child?'

'Because you are married already!' said Anna with lucid simplicity.

'Of course it can't,' said her mistress hastily; yet glad, despite her conscience, that two or three oupourings still remained to her. 'But you must concentrate your attention on writing your name as I write it here.'

6

Soon Raye wrote about the wedding. Having decided to make the best of what he feared was a piece of romantic folly, he had acquired more zest for the grand experiment. He wished the ceremony to be in London, for greater privacy. Edith Harnham would have preferred it at Melchester;

Anna was passive. His reasoning prevailed, and Mrs Harnham threw herself with mournful zeal into the preparations for Anna's departure. In a last desperate feeling that she must at every hazard be in at the death of her dream, and see once again the man who by a species of telepathy had exercised such an influence on her, she offered to go up with Anna and be with her through the ceremony – 'to see the end of her', as her mistress put it with forced gaiety; an offer which the girl gratefully accepted; for she had no other friend capable of playing the part of companion and witness, in the presence of a gentlemanly bridegroom, in such a way as not to hasten an opinion that he had mde an irremediable social blunder.

It was a muddy morning in March when Raye alighted from a four-wheel cab at the door of a registry-office in the S.W. district of London, and carefully handed down Anna and her companion Mrs Harnham. Anna looked attractive in the somewhat fashionable clothes which Mrs Harnham had helped her to buy, though not quite so attractive as, an innocent child, she had appeared in her country gown on the back of the wooden horse at Melchester Fair.

Mrs Harnham had come up this morning by an early train, and a young man – a friend of Raye's – having met them at the door, all four entered the registry-office together. Till an hour before this time Raye had never known the wine-merchant's wife, except at that first casual encounter, and in the flutter of the performance before them he had little opportunity for more than a brief acquaintance. The contract of marriage at a registry is soon got through; but somehow, during its progress, Raye discovered a strange and secret gravitation between himself and Anna's friend.

The formalities of the wedding – or rather ratification of a previous union – being concluded, the four went in one cab to Raye's lodgings, newly taken in a new suburb in preference to a house, the rent of which he could ill afford just then. Here Anna cut the little cake which Raye had bought at a pastrycook's on his way home from Lincoln's Inn the night before. But she did not do much besides. Raye's friend was obliged to depart almost immediately, and when he had left the only ones virtually present were Edith and Raye, who exchanged ideas with much animation. The conversation was indeed their only, Anna being as a domestic animal who humbly heard but understood not. Raye seemed startled in awakening to this fact, and began to feel dissatisfied with her inadequacy.

At last, more disappointed than he cared to own, he said, 'Mrs Harnham, my darling is so flurried that she doesn't know what she is doing or saying. I see that after this event a little quietude will be necessary before she gives tongue to that tender philosophy which she used to treat me to in her letters.'

They had planned to start early that afternon for Knollsea, to spend the few opening days of their married life there, and as the hour for departure was drawing near Raye asked his wife if she would go to the writing-desk in the next room and scribble a little note to his sister, who had been unable to attend through indisposition, informing her that the ceremony was over, thanking her for her little present, and hoping to know her well now that she was the writer's sister as well as Charles's.

'Say it in the pretty poetical way you know so well how to adopt,' he added, 'for I want you particularly to win her, and both of you to be dear friends.'

Anna looked uneasy, but departed to her task, Raye remaining to talk to their guest. Anna was a long while absent, and her husband suddenly rose and went to her.

He found her still bending over the writing-table, with tears brimming up in her eyes; and he looked down upon the sheet of note-paper with some interest, to discover with what tact she had expressed her goodwill in the delicate circumstances. To his surprise she had progressed but few lines, in the characters and spelling of a child of eight, and with the ideas of a goose.

'Anna,' he said, staring; 'what's this?'

'It only means – that I can't do it any better!' she answered, through her tears.

'Eh? Nonsense!'

'I can't!' she insisted, with miserable, sobbing hardihood. 'I – I – didn't write those letters, Charles! I only told *her* what to write! And not always that! But I am learning, O so fast, my dear, dear husband! And you'll forgive me, won't you, for not telling you before?' She slid to her knees, abjectly clasped his waist and laid her face against him.

He stood a few moments, raised her, abruptly turned, and shut the door upon her, rejoining Edith in the drawing-room. She saw that something untoward had been discovered, and their eyes remained fixed on each other.

'Do I guess rightly?' he asked, with wan quietude. '*You* were her scribe through all this?'

'It was necessary,' said Edith.

'Did she dictate every word you ever wrote to me?'

'Not every word.'

'In fact, very little?'

'Very little.'

'You wrote a great part of those pages every week from your own conception, though in her name!'

'Yes.'

'Perhaps you wrote many of the letters when you were alone, without communication with her?'

'I did.'

He turned to the bookcase, and leant with his hand over his face; and Edith, seeing his distress, became white as a sheet.

'You have deceived me – ruined me!' he murmured.

'O, don't say it!' she cried in her anguish, jumping up and putting her hand on his shoulder. 'I can't bear that!'

'Delighting me deceptively! Why did you do it – *why* did you!'

'I began doing it in kindness to her! How could I do otherwise than try to save such a simple girl from misery? But I admit that I continued it for pleasure to myself.'

Raye looked up. 'Why did it give you pleasure?' he asked.

'I must not tell,' she said.

He continued to regard her, and saw that her lips suddenly began to quiver under his scrutiny, and her eyes to fill and droop. She started aside, and said that she must go to the station to catch the return train: could a cab be called immediately?

But Raye went up to her, and took her unresisting hand. 'Well, to think of such a thing as this!' he said. 'Why, you and I are friends – lovers – devoted lovers – by correspondence!'

'Yes; I suppose.'

'More.'

'More?'

'Plainly more. It is no use blinking that. Legally I have married her – God help us both! – in soul and spirit I have married you, and no other woman in the world!'

'Hush!'

'But I will not hush! Why should you try to disguise the full truth, when you have already owned half of it? Yes, it is between you and me that the bond is – not between me and her! Now I'll say no more. But, O my cruel one, I think I have one claim upon you!'

She did not say what, and he drew her towards him, and bent over her. 'If it was all pure invention in those letters,' he said emphatically, 'give me your cheek only. If you meant what you said, let it be lips. It is for the first and last time, remember!'

She put up her mouth, and he kissed her long. 'You forgive me?' she said, crying.

'Yes.'

'But you are ruined!'

'What matter!' he said, shrugging his shoulders. 'It serves me right!'

She withdrew, wiped her eyes, entered and bade good-bye to Anna, who had not expected her to go so soon, and was still wrestling with the letter. Raye followed Edith downstairs, and in three minutes she was in a hansom driving to the Waterloo station.

He went back to his wife. 'Never mind the letter, Anna, today,' he said gently. 'Put on your things. We, too, must be off shortly.'

The simple girl, upheld by the sense that she was indeed married, showed her delight at finding that he was as kind as ever after the disclosure. She did not know that before his eyes he beheld as it were a galley, in which he, the fastidious urban, was chained to work for the remainder of his life, with her, the unlettered peasant, chained to his side.

Edith travelled back to Melchester that day with a face that showed the very stupor of grief, her lips still tingling from the desperate pressure of his kiss. The end of her impassioned dream had come. When at dusk she reached the Melchester station her husband was there to meet her, but in his perfunctoriness and her preoccupation they did not see each other, and she went out of the station alone.

She walked mechanically homewards without calling a fly. Entering, she could not bear the silence of the house, and went up in the dark to where Anna had slept, where she remained thinking awhile. She then returned to the drawing-room, and not knowing what she did, crouched down upon the floor.

'I have ruined him!' she kept repeating. 'I have ruined him; because I would not deal treacherously towards her!'

In the course of half an hour a figure opened the door of the apartment.

'Ah – who's that?' she said, starting up, for it was dark.

'Your husband – who should it be?' said the worthy merchant.

'Ah – my husband! – I forgot I had a husband!' She whispered to herself.

'I missed you at the station,' he continued. 'Did you see Anna safely tied up? I hope so, for 'twas time.'

'Yes – Anna is married.'

Simultaneously with Edith's journey home Anna and her husband were sitting at the opposite windows of a second-class carriage which sped along to Knollsea. In his hand was a pocket-book full of creased sheets closely written over. Unfolding them one after another he read them in silence, and sighed.

'What are you doing, dear Charles?' she said timidly from the other window, and drew nearer to him as if he were a god.

'Reading over all those sweet letters to me signed "Anna",' he replied with dreary resignation.

AUTUMN 1891

TO PLEASE HIS WIFE

I

The interior of St James's Church, in Havenpool Town, was slowly darkening under the close clouds of a winter afternoon. It was Sunday: service had just ended, the face of the parson in the pulpit was buried in his hands, and the congregation, with a cheerful sigh of release, were rising from their knees to depart.

For the moment the stillness was so complete that the surging of the sea could be heard outside the harbour-bar. Then it was broken by the footsteps of the clerk going towards the west door to open it in the usual manner for the exit of the assembly. Before, however, he had reached the doorway, the latch was lifted from without, and the dark figure of a man in a sailor's garb appeared against the light.

The clerk stepped aside, the sailor closed the door gently behind him, and advanced up the nave till he stood at the chancel-step. The parson looked up from the private little prayer which, after so many for the parish, he quite fairly took for himself, rose to his feet, and stared at the intruder.

'I beg your pardon, sir,' said the sailor, addressing the minister in a voice distinctly audible to all the congregation. 'I have come here to offer thanks for my narrow escape from shipwreck. I am given to understand that it is a proper thing to do, if you have no objection?'

The parson, after a moment's pause, said hesitatingly, 'I have no objection; certainly. It is usual to mention any such wish before service, so that the proper words may be used in the General Thanksgiving. But, if you wish, we can read from the form for use after a storm at sea.'

'Ay, sure; I ain't particular,' said the sailor.

The clerk thereupon directed the sailor to the page in the prayer-book where the collect of thanksgiving would be found, and the rector began reading it, the sailor kneeling where he stood, and repeating it after him word by word in a distinct voice. The people, who had remained agape and motionless at the proceeding, mechanically knelt down likewise; but they continued to regard the isolated form of the sailor who, in the precise middle of the chancel-step, remained fixed on his knees, facing the east, his hat beside him, his hands joined, and he quite unconscious of his appearance in their regard.

When the thanksgiving had come to an end he rose; the people rose also; and all went out of church together. As soon as the sailor emerged, so that the remaining daylight fell upon his face, old inhabitants began to recognize him as no other than Shadrach Jolliffe, a young man who had not been seen at Havenpool for several years. A son of the town, his parents had died when he was quite young, on which account he had early gone to sea, in the Newfoundland trade.

He talked with this and that townsman as he walked, informing them that, since leaving his native place years before, he had become captain and owner of a small coasting-ketch, which had providentially been saved from the gale as well as himself. Presently he drew near to two girls who were going out of the churchyard in front of him; they had been sitting in the nave at his entry, and had watched his doings with deep interest, afterwards discussing him as they moved out of church together. One was a slight and gentle creature; the other a tall, large-framed, deliberative girl. Captain Jolliffe regarded the loose curls of their hair, their backs and shoulders, down to their heels, for some time.

'Who may them two maids be?' he whispered to his neighbour.

'The little one is Emily Hanning; the tall one Joanna Phippard.'

'Ah! I recollect 'em now, to be sure.'

He advanced to their elbow, and genially stole a gaze at them.

'Emily, you don't know me?' said the sailor, turning his beaming brown eyes on her.

'I think I do, Mr Jolliffe,' said Emily shyly.

The other girl looked straight at him with her dark eyes.

'The face of Miss Joanna I don't call to mind so well,' he continued. 'But I know her beginnings and kindred.'

They walked and talked together, Jolliffe narrating particulars of his late narrow escape, till they reached the corner of Sloop Lane, in which Emily Hanning dwelt, when, with a nod and smile, she left them. Soon the sailor parted also from Joanna, and, having no especial errand or appointment, turned back towards Emily's house. She lived with her father, who called himself an accountant, the daughter, however, keeping a little stationery-shop as a supplemental provision for the gaps of his somewhat uncertain business. On entering Joliffe found father and daughter about to begin tea.

'O, I didn't know it was tea-time,' he said. 'Ay, I'll have a cup with much pleasure.'

He remained to tea and long afterwards, telling more tales of his seafaring life. Several neighbours called to listen, and were asked to come in. Somehow Emily Hanning lost her heart to the sailor that Sunday night, and in the course of a week or two there was a tender understanding between them.

One moonlight evening in the next month Shadrach was ascending out of the town by the long straight road eastward, to an elevated suburb where the more fashionable houses stood – if anything near this ancient port could be called fashionable – when he saw a figure before him whom, from her manner of glancing back, he took to be Emily. But, on coming up, he found she was Joanna Phippard. He gave a gallant greeting, and walked beside her.

'Go along,' she said, 'or Emily will be jealous!'

He seemed not to like the suggestion, and remained.

What was said and what was done on that walk never could be clearly recollected by Shadrach; but in some way or other Joanna contrived to wean him away from her gentler and younger rival. From that week onwards, Jolliffe was seen more and more in the wake of Joanna Phippard and less in the company of Emily, and it was soon rumoured about the quay that old Jolliffe's son, who had come home from sea, was going to be married to the former young woman, to the great disappointment of the latter.

Just after this report had gone about, Joanna dressed herself for a walk one morning, and started for Emily's house in the little cross-street. Intelligence of the deep sorrow of her friend on account of the loss of Shadrach had reached her ears also, and her conscience reproached her for winning him away.

Joanna was not altogether satisfied with the sailor. She liked his attentions, and she coveted the dignity of matrimony; but she had never been deeply in love with Jolliffe. For one thing, she was ambitious, and socially his position was hardly so good as her own, and there was always the chance of an attractive woman mating considerably above her. It had long been in her mind that she would not strongly object to give him back again to Emily if her friend felt so very badly about him. To this end she had written a letter of renunciation to Shadrach, which letter she carried in her hand, intending to send it if personal observation of Emily convinced her that her friend was suffering.

Joanna entered Sloop Lane and stepped down into the stationery shop, which was below the pavement level. Emily's father was never at home at this hour of the day, and it seemed as though Emily were not at home either, for the visitor could make nobody hear. Customers came so seldom hither that a five minutes' absence of the proprietor counted for little. Joanna waited in the little shop, where Emily had tastefully set out – as women can – articles in themselves of slight value, so as to obscure the meagreness of the stock-in-trade; till she saw a figure pausing without the window apparently absorbed in the contemplation of the sixpenny books, packets of paper, and prints hung on a string. It was Captain Shadrach Jolliffe, peering in to ascertain if Emily were there alone. Moved by an impulse of reluctance to meet him in a spot which breathed of Emily, Joanna slipped through the door that communicated with the parlour at the back. She had frequently done so before, for in her friendship with Emily she had the freedom of the house without ceremony.

Jolliffe entered the shop. Through the thin blind which screened the glass partition she could see that he was disappointed at not finding Emily there. He was about to go out again, when Emily's form darkened the doorway, hastening home from some errand. At sight of Jolliffe she started back as if she would have gone out again.

'Don't run away, Emily; don't! said he. 'What can make 'ee afraid?'

'I'm not afraid, Captain Jolliffe. Only – only I saw you all of a sudden, and – it made me jump!' Her voice showed that her heart had jumped even more than the rest of her.

'I just called as I was passing,' he said.

'For some paper?' She hastened behind the counter.

'No, no, Emily; why do you get behind there? Why not stay by me? You seem to hate me.'

'I don't hate you. How can I?'

'Then come out, so that we can talk like Christians.'

Emily obeyed with a fitful laugh, till she stood again beside him in the open part of the shop.

'There's a dear,' he said.

'You mustn't say that, Captain Jolliffe; because the words belong to somebody else.'

'Ah! I know what you mean. But, Emily, upon my life I didn't know till this morning that you cared one bit about me, or I should not have done as I have done. I have the best of feelings for Joanna, but I know that from the beginning she hasn't cared for me more than in a friendly way; and I see now the one I ought to have asked to be my wife. You know, Emily, when a man comes home from sea after a long voyage he's as blind as a bat – he can't see who's who in women. They are all alike to him, beautiful creatures, and he takes the first that comes easy, without thinking if she loves him, or if he might not soon love another better than her. From the first I inclined to you most, but you were so backward and shy that I thought you didn't want me to bother 'ee, and so I went to Joanna.'

'Don't say any more, Mr Jolliffe, don't!' said she, choking. 'You are going to marry Joanna next month, and it is wrong to – to—'

'O, Emily, my darling!' he cried, and clasped her little figure in his arms before she was aware.

Joanna, behind the curtain, turned pale, tried to withdraw her eyes, but could not.

'It is only you I love as a man ought to love the woman he is going to marry; and I know this from what Joanna has said, that she will willingly let me off! She wants to marry higher, I know, and only said "Yes" to me out of kindness. A fine, tall girl like her isn't the sort for a plain sailor's wife; you be the best suited for that.'

He kissed her and kissed her again, her flexible form quivering in the agitation of his embrace.

'I wonder – are you sure – Joanna is going to break off with you? O, are you sure? Because—'

'I know she would not wish to make us miserable. She will release me.'

'O, I hope – I hope she will! Don't stay any longer, Captain Jolliffe!'

He lingered, however, till a customer came for a penny stick of sealing-wax, and then he withdrew.

Green envy had overspread Joanna at the scene. She looked about for a way of escape. To get out without Emily's knowledge of her visit was indispensable. She crept from the parlour into the passage, and thence to the back door of the house, where she let herself noiselessly into the street.

The sight of that caress had reversed all her resolutions. She could not let Shadrach go. Reaching home she burnt the letter, and told her mother that if Captain Jolliffe called she was too unwell to see him.

Shadrach, however, did not call. He sent her a note expressing in simple language the state of his feelings; and asked to be allowed to take advantage of the hints she had given him that her affection, too, was little more than friendly, by cancelling the engagement.

Looking out upon the harbour and the island beyond he waited and waited in his lodgings for an answer that did not come. The suspense grew to be so intolerable that after dark he went up the High Street. He could not resist calling at Joanna's to learn his fate.

Her mother said her daughter was too unwell to see him, and to his questioning admitted that it was in consequence of a letter received from himself, which had distressed her deeply.

'You know what it was about, perhaps, Mrs Phippard?' he said.

Mrs Phippard owned that she did, adding that it put them in a very painful position. Thereupon Shadrach, fearing that he had been guilty of an enormity, explained that if his letter had pained Joanna it must be owing to a misunderstanding, since he had thought it would be a relief to her. If otherwise, he would hold himself bound by his word, and she was to think of the letter as never having been written.

Next morning he received an oral message from the young woman, asking him to fetch her home from a meeting that evening. This he did, and while walking from the Town Hall to her door, with her hand in his arm, she said:

'It is all the same as before between us, isn't it, Shadrach? Your letter was sent in mistake?'

'It is all the same as before,' he answered, 'if you say it must be.'

'I wish it to be,' she murmured, with hard lineaments, as she thought of Emily.

Shadrach was a religious and scrupulous man, who respected his word as his life. Shortly afterwards the wedding took place, Jolliffe having conveyed to Emily as gently as possible the error he had fallen into when estimating Joanna's mood as one of indifference.

2

A month after the marriage Joanna's mother died, and the couple were obliged to turn their attention to very practical matters. Now that she was left without a parent, Joanna could not bear the notion of her husband going to sea again, but the question was, What could he do at home? They finally decided to take on a small grocer's shop in High Street, the goodwill and stock of which were waiting to be disposed of at that time. Shadrach knew nothing of shopkeeping, and Joanna very little, but they hoped to learn.

To the management of this grocery business they now devoted all their energies, and continued to conduct it for many succeeding years, without great success. Two sons were born to them, whom their mother loved to idolatry, although she had never passionately loved her husband; and she lavished upon them all her forethought and care. But the shop did not thrive, and the large dreams she had entertained of her sons' education and career became attenuated in the face of realities. Their schooling was of the plainest, but, being by the sea, they grew alert in all such nautical arts and enterprises as were attractive to their age.

The great interest of the Jolliffes' married life, outside their own immediate household, had lain in the marriage of Emily. By one of those odd chances which lead those that lurk in unexpected corners to be discovered, while the obvious are passed by, the gentle girl had been seen and loved by a thriving merchant of the town, a widower, some years older than herself, though still in the prime of life. At first Emily had declared that she never, never could marry anyone; but Mr Lester had quietly persevered, and had at last won her reluctant assent. Two children also were the fruits of this union, and, as they grew and prospered, Emily declared that she had never supposed that she could live to be so happy.

The worthy merchant's home, one of those large, substantial brick mansions frequently jammed up in old-fashioned towns, faced directly on the High Street, nearly opposite to the grocery shop of the Jolliffes, and it now became the pain of Joanna to behold the woman whose place she had usurped out of pure covetousness, looking down from her position of comparative wealth upon the humble shop-window with its dusty sugar-loaves, heaps of raisins, and canisters of tea, over which it was her own lot to preside. The business having so dwindled, Joanna was obliged to serve in the shop herself, and it galled and mortified her that Emily Lester, sitting in her large drawing-room over the way, could witness her own dancings up and down behind the counter at the beck and call of wretched twopenny customers, whose patronage she was driven to welcome gladly; persons to whom she was compelled to be civil in the street, while Emily was bounding along with her children and her governess, and conversing with the genteelest people of the town and neighbourhood. This was what she had gained by not letting Shadrach Jolliffe, whom she had so faintly loved, carry his affection elsewhere.

Shadrach was a good and honest man, and he had been faithful to her in heart and in deed. Time had clipped the wings of his love for Emily in his devotion to the mother of his boys; he had quite lived down that impulsive earlier fancy, and Emily had become in his regard nothing more than a friend. It was the same with Emily's feelings for him. Possibly, had she found the least cause for jealousy, Joanna would almost have been better satisfied. It was in the absolute acquiescence of Emily and Shadrach in the results she herself had contrived that her discontent found nourishment.

Shadrach was not endowed with the narrow shrewdness necessary for developing a retail business in the face of many competitors. Did a customer inquire if the grocer could really recommend the wondrous substitute for eggs which a persevering bagman had forced into his stock, he would answer that 'when you did not put eggs into a pudding it was difficult to taste them there'; and when he was asked if his 'real Mocha coffee' was real Mocha, he would say grimly, 'as understood in small shops'. The way to wealth was not by this route.

One summer day, when the big brick house opposite was reflecting the oppressive sun's heat into the shop, and nobody was present but husband and wife, Joanna looked across at Emily's door, where a wealthy visitor's carriage had drawn up. Traces of patronage had been visible in Emily's manner of late.

'Shadrach, the truth is, you are not a business-man,' his wife sadly murmured. 'You were not brought up to shopkeeping, and it is impossible for a man to make a fortune at an occupation he has jumped into, as you did in this.'

Jolliffe agreed with her, in this as in everything else. 'Not that I care a rope's end about making a fortune,' he said cheerfully. 'I am happy enough, and we can rub on somehow.'

She looked again at the great house through the screen of bottled pickles.

'Rub on – yes,' she said bitterly. 'But see how well off Emmy Lester is, who used to be so poor! Her boys will go to College, no doubt; and think of yours – obliged to go to the Parish School!'

Shadrach's thoughts had flown to Emily.

'Nobody,' he said good-humouredly, 'ever did Emily a better turn than you did, Joanna, when you warned her off me and put an end to that little simpering nonsense between us, so as to leave it in her power to say "Aye" to Lester when he came along.'

This almost maddened her.

'Don't speak of bygones!' she implored, in stern sadness. 'But think, for the boys' and my sake, if not for your own, what are we to do to get richer?'

'Well,' he said, becoming serious, 'to tell the truth, I have always felt myself unfit for this business, though I've never liked to say so. I seem to want more room for sprawling; a more open space to strike out in than here among friends and neighbours. I could get rich as well as any man, if I tried my own way.'

'I wish you would! What is your way?'

'To go to sea again.'

She had been the very one to keep him at home, hating the semi-widowed existence of sailor's wives. But her ambition checked her instincts, now, and she said:

'Do you think success really lies that way?'

'I am sure it lies in no other.'

'Do you want to go, Shadrach?'

'Not for the pleasure of it, I can tell 'ee. There's no such pleasure at sea, Joanna, as I can find in my back parlour here. To speak honest, I have no love for the brine. I never had much. But if it comes to a question of a fortune for you and the lads, it is another thing. That's the only way to it for one born and bred a seafarer as I.'

'Would it take long to earn?'

'Well, that depends; perhaps not.'

The next morning Shadrach pulled from a chest of drawers the nautical jacket he had worn during the first months of his return, brushed out the moths, donned it, and walked down to the quay. The port still did a fair business in the Newfoundland trade, though not so much as formerly.

It was not long after this that he invested all he possessed in purchasing a part-ownership in a brig, of which he was appointed captain. A few months were passed in coast-trading, during which interval Shadrach wore off the land-rust that had accumulated upon him in his grocery phase; and in the spring the brig sailed for Newfoundland.

Joanna lived on at home with her sons, who were now growing up into strong lads, and occupying themselves in various ways about the harbour and quay.

'Never mind, let them work a little,' their fond mother said to herself. 'Our necessities compel it now, but when Shadrach comes home they will be only seventeen and eighteen, and they shall be removed from the port, and their education thoroughly taken in hand by a tutor; and with the money they'll have they will perhaps be as near to gentlemen as Emmy Lester's precious two, with their algebra and their Latin!'

The date for Shadrach's return drew near and arrived, and he did not appear. Joanna was assured that there was no cause for anxiety, sailing-ships being so uncertain in their coming; which assurance proved to be well grounded, for late one wet evening, about a month after the calculated time, the ship was announced as at hand, and presently the slip-slop step of Shadrach as the sailor sounded in the passage, and he entered. The boys had gone out and had missed him, and Joanna was sitting alone.

As soon as the first emotion of reunion between the couple had passed, Jolliffe explained the delay as owing to a small speculative contract, which had produced good results.

'I was determined not to disappoint 'ee,' he said; 'and I think you'll own that I haven't!'

With this he pulled out an enormous canvas bag, full and rotound as the money-bag of the giant whom Jack slew, untied it, and shook the contents out into her lap as she sat in her low chair by the fire. A mass of sovereigns and guineas (there were guineas on the earth in those days) fell into her lap with a sudden thud, weighing down her gown to the floor.

'There!' said Shadrach complacently. 'I told 'ee, dear, I'd do it; and have I done it or no?'

Somehow her face, after the first excitement of possession, did not retain its glory.

'It is a lot of gold, indeed,' she said. 'And – is this *all*?'

'All? Why, dear Joanna, do you know you can count to three hundred in that heap? It is a fortune!'

'Yes – yes. A fortune – judged by sea; but judged by land—'

However, she banished considerations of the money for the nonce. Soon the boys came in, and next Sunday Shadrach returned thanks to God – this time by the more ordinary channel of the italics in the General Thanksgiving. But a few days after, when the question of investing the money arose, he remarked that she did not seem so satisfied as he had hoped.

'Well, you see, Shadrach,' she answered, '*we* count by hundreds; *they* count by thousands' (nodding towards the other side of the street). 'They have set up a carriage and pair since you left.'

'O, have they?'

'My dear Shadrach, you don't know how the world moves. However, we'll do the best we can with it. But they are rich, and we are poor still!'

The greater part of a year was desultorily spent. She moved sadly about the house and shop, and the boys were still occupying themselves in and around the harbour.

'Joanna,' he said, one day, 'I see by your movements that it is not enough.'

'It is not enough,' said she. 'My boys will have to live by steering the ships that the Lesters own; and I was once above her!'

Jolliffe was not an argumentative man, and he only murmured that he thought he would make another voyage. He meditated for several days, and coming home from the quay one afternoon said suddenly:

'I could do it for 'ee, dear, in one more trip, for certain, if – if—'

'Do what, Shadrach?'

'Enable 'ee to count by thousands instead of hundreds.'

'If what?'

'If I might take the boys.'

She turned pale.

'Don't say that, Shadrach,' she answered hastily.

'Why?'

'I don't like to hear it! There's danger at sea. I want them to be something genteel, and no danger to them. I couldn't let them risk their lives at sea. O, I couldn't ever, ever!'

'Very well, dear, it shan't be done.'

Next day, after a silence, she asked a question:

'If they were to go with you it would make a great deal of difference, I suppose, to the profit?'

''Twould treble what I should get from the venture single-handed. Under my eye they would be as good as two more of myself.'

Later on she said: 'Tell me more about this.'

'Well, the boys are almost as clever as master-mariners in handling a craft, upon my life! There isn't a more cranky place in the Northern Seas than about the sandbanks of this harbour, and they've practised here from their infancy. And they are so steady. I couldn't get their steadiness and their trustworthiness in half a dozen men twice their age.'

'And is it *very* dangerous at sea; now, too, there are rumours of war?' she asked uneasily.

'O, well, there be risks. Still . . .'

The idea grew and magnified, and the mother's heart was crushed and stifled by it. Emmy was growing *too* patronizing; it could not be borne. Shadrach's wife could not help nagging him about their comparative poverty. The young men, amiable as their father, when spoken to on the subject of a voyage of enterprise, were quite willing to embark; and though they, like their father, had no great love for the sea, they became quite enthusiastic when the proposal was detailed.

Everything now hung upon their mother's assent. She withheld it long, but at last gave the word: the young men might accompany their father. Shadrach was unusually cheerful about it: Heaven had preserved him hitherto, and he had uttered his thanks. God would not forsake those who were faithful to him.

All that the Jolliffes possessed in the world was put into the enterprise. The grocery stock was pared down to the least that possibly could afford a bare sustenance to Joanna during the absence, which was to last through the usual 'New-f'nland spell'. How she would endure the weary time she hardly knew, for the boys had been with her formerly; but she nerved herself for the trial.

The ship was laden with boots and shoes, ready-made clothing, fishing-tackle, butter, cheese, cordage, sailcloth, and many other commodities; and was to bring back oil, furs, skins, fish, cranberries, and what else came to hand. But much speculative trading to other ports was to be undertaken between the voyages out and homeward, and thereby much money made.

3

The brig sailed on a Monday morning in spring; but Joanna did not witness its departure. She could not bear the sight that she had been the means of bringing about. Knowing this, her husband told her overnight that they were to sail some time before noon next day; hence when, awakening at five the next morning, she heard them bustling about downstairs, she did not hasten to descend, but lay trying to nerve herself for the parting, imagining they would leave about nine, as her husband had done on his previous voyage. When she did descend she beheld words chalked upon the sloping face of the bureau; but no husband or sons. In the hastily-scrawled lines Shadrach said they had gone off thus not to pain her by a leave-taking; and the sons had chalked under his words: 'Good-bye, mother!'

She rushed to the quay, and looked down the harbour towards the blue rim of the sea, but she could only see the masts and bulging sails of the *Joanna*; no human figures. ''Tis I have sent them!' she said wildly, and burst into tears. In the house the chalked 'Good-bye' nearly broke her heart. But when she had re-entered the front room, and looked across at Emily's, a gleam of triumph lit her thin face at her anticipated release from the thraldom of subservience.

To do Emily Lester justice, her assumption of superiority was mainly a figment of Joanna's brain. That the circumstances of the merchant's wife were more luxurious than Joanna's, the former could not conceal; though whenever the two met, which was not very often now, Emily endeavoured to subdue the difference by every means in her power.

The first summer lapsed away; and Joanna meagrely maintained herself by the shop, which now consisted of little more than a window and a counter. Emily, was in truth, her only large customer; and Mrs Lester's kindly readiness to buy anything and everything without questioning the quality had a sting of bitterness in it, for it was the uncritical attitude of a patron, and almost of a donor. The long dreary winter moved on; the face of the bureau had been turned to the wall to protect the chalked words of farewell, for Joanna could never bring herself to rub them out; and she often glanced at them with wet eyes. Emily's handsome boys came home for the Christmas holidays; the University was talked of for them; and still Joanna subsisted as it were with held breath, like a person submerged. Only one summer more, and the 'spell' would end. Towards the close of the time Emily called on her quondam friend. She had heard that Joanna began to feel anxious; she had received no letter from husband or sons for some months. Emily's silks rustled arrogantly when, in response to

Joanna's almost dumb invitation, she squeezed through the opening of the counter and into the parlour behind the shop.

'*You* are all success, and *I* am all the other way!' said Joanna.

'But why do you think so?' said Emily. 'They are to bring back a fortune, I hear.'

'Ah! will they come? The doubt is more than a woman can bear. All three in one ship – think of that! And I have not heard of them for months!'

'But the time is not up. You should not meet misfortune half-way.'

'Nothing will repay me for the grief of their absence!'

'Then why did you let them go? You were doing fairly well.'

'I *made* them go!' she said, turning vehemently upon Emily. 'And I'll tell you why! I could not bear that we should be only muddling on, and you so rich and thriving! Now I have told you, and you may hate me if you will!'

'I shall never hate you, Joanna.'

And she proved the truth of her words afterwards. The end of the autumn came, and the brig should have been in port; but nothing like the *Joanna* appeared in the channel between the sands. It was now really time to be uneasy. Joanna Jolliffe sat by the fire, and every gust of wind caused her a cold thrill. She had always feared and detested the sea; to her it was a treacherous, restless, slimy creature, glorying in the griefs of women. 'Still,' she said, 'they *must* come!'

She recalled to her mind that Shadrach had said before starting that if they returned safe and sound, with success crowning their enterprise, he would go as he had gone after his shipwreck, and kneel with his sons in the church, and offer sincere thanks for their deliverance. She went to church regularly morning and afternoon, and sat in the most forward pew, nearest the chancel-step. Her eyes were mostly fixed on that step, where Shadrach had knelt in the bloom of his young manhood: she knew to an inch the spot which his knees had pressed twenty winters before; his outline as he had knelt, his hat on the step beside him. God was good. Surely her husband must kneel there again: a son on each side as he had said; George just here, Jim just there. By long watching the spot as she worshipped became as if she saw the three returned ones there kneeling; the two slim outlines of her boys, the more bulky form between them; their hands clasped, their heads shaped against the eastern wall. The fancy grew almost to an hallucination; she could never turn her worn eyes to the step without seeing them there.

Nevertheless they did not come. Heaven was merciful, but it was not yet pleased to relieve her soul. This was her purgation for the sin of making them the slaves of her ambition. But it became more than purgation soon, and her mood approached despair. Months had passed since the brig had been due, but it had not returned.

Joanna was always hearing or seeing evidences of their arrival. When on the hill behind the port, whence a view of the open Channel could be obtained, she felt sure that a little speck on the horizon, breaking the eternally level waste of waters southward, was the truck of the *Joanna's* mainmast. Or when indoors, a shout or excitement of any kind at the corner of the Town Cellar, where the High Street joined the Quay, caused her to spring to her feet and cry: ''Tis they!'

But it was not. The visionary forms knelt every Sunday afternoon on the chancel-step, but not the real. Her shop had, as it were, eaten itself hollow. In the apathy which had resulted from her loneliness and grief she had ceased to take in the smallest supplies, and thus had sent away her last customer.

In this strait Emily Lester tried by every means in her power to aid the afflicted woman; but she met with constant repulses.

'I don't like you! I can't bear to see you!' Joanna would whisper hoarsely when Emily came to her and made advances.

'But I want to help and soothe you, Joanna,' Emily would say.

'You are a lady, with a rich husband and fine sons! What can you want with a bereaved crone like me!'

'Joanna, I want this: I want you to come and live in my house, and not stay alone in this dismal place any longer.'

'And suppose they come and don't find me at home? You wish to separate me and mine! No, I'll stay here. I don't like you, and I can't thank you, whatever kindness you do me!'

However, as time went on Joanna could not afford to pay the rent of the shop and house without an income. She was assured that all hope of the return of Shadrach and his sons was vain, and she reluctantly consented to accept the asylum of the Lesters' house. Here she was allotted a room of her own on the second floor, and went and came as she chose, without contact with the family. Her hair greyed and whitened, deep lines channelled her forehead, and her form grew gaunt and stooping. But she still expected the lost ones, and when she met Emily on the staircase she would say morosely: 'I know why you've got me here! They'll come, and be disappointed at not finding me at home, and perhaps go away again; and then you'll be revenged for my taking Shadrach away from 'ee!'

Emily Lester bore these reproaches from the grief-stricken soul. She was sure – all the people of Havenpool were sure – that Shadrach and his sons had gone to the bottom. For years the vessel had been given up as lost. Nevertheless, when awakened at night by any noise, Joanna would rise from bed and glance at the shop opposite by the light from the flickering lamp, to make sure it was not they.

It was a damp and dark December night, six years after the departure of the brig *Joanna*. The wind was from the sea, and brought up a fishy mist which mopped the face like moist flannel. Joanna had prayed her usual prayer for the absent ones with more fervour and confidence than she had felt for months, and had fallen asleep about eleven. It must have been between one and two when she suddenly started up. She had certainly heard steps in the street, and the voices of Shadrach and her sons calling at the door of the grocery shop. She sprang out of bed, and, hardly knowing what clothing she dragged on herself, hastened down Emily's large and carpeted staircase, put the candle on the hall-table, unfastened the bolts and chain, and stepped into the street. The mist, blowing up the street from the Quay, hindered her seeing the shop, although it was so near; but she had crossed to it in a moment. How was it? Nobody stood there. The wretched woman walked wildly up and down with her bare feet – there was not a soul. She returned and knocked with all her might at the door which had once been her own – they might have been admitted for the night, unwilling to disturb her till the morning. It was not till several minutes had elapsed that the young man who now kept the shop looked out of an upper-window, and saw the skeleton of something human standing below half-dressed.

'Has anybody come?' asked the form.

'O, Mrs Jolliffe, I didn't know it was you,' said the young man kindly, for he was aware how her baseless expectations moved her.

'No; nobody has come.'

JUNE 1891

THE FIDDLER OF THE REELS

'Talking of Exhibitions, World's Fairs, and what not,' said the old gentleman, 'I would not go round the corner to see a dozen of them nowadays. The only exhibition that ever made, or ever will make, any impression upon my imagination was the first of the series, the parent of them all, and now a thing of old times – the Great Exhibition of 1851, in Hyde Park, London. None of the younger generation can realize the sense of novelty it produced in us who were then in our prime. A noun substantive went so far as to become an adjective in honour of the occasion. It was "exhibition" hat, "exhibition" razor-strop, "exhibition" watch; nay, even "exhibition" weather, "exhibition" spirits, sweethearts, babies, wives – for the time.

'For South Wessex, the year formed in many ways an extraordinary chronological frontier or transit-line, at which there occurred what one might call a precipice in Time. As in a geological "fault", we had presented to us a sudden bringing of ancient and modern into absolute contact, such as probably in no other single year since the Conquest was ever witnessed in this part of the country.'

These observations led us onward to talk of the different personages, gentle and simple, who lived and moved within our narrow and peaceful horizon at that time; and of three people in particular, whose queer little history was oddly touched at points by the Exhibition, more concerned with it than that of anybody else who dwelt in those outlying shades of the world, Stickleford, Mellstock, and Egdon. First in prominence among these three came Wat Ollamoor – if that were his real name – whom the seniors in our party had known well.

He was a woman's man, they said, – supremely so – externally little else. To men he was not attractive; perhaps a little repulsive at times. Musician, dandy, and company-man in practice; veterinary surgeon in theory, he lodged awhile in Mellstock village, coming from nobody knew where; though some said his first appearance in this neighbourhood had been as fiddle-player in a show at Greenhill Fair.

Many a worthy villager envied him his power over unsophisticated maidenhood – a power which seemed sometimes to have a touch of the weird and wizardly in it. Personally he was not ill-favoured, though rather un-English, his complexion being a rich olive, his rank hair dark and rather clammy – made still clammier by secret ointments, which, when he came fresh to a party, caused him to smell like 'boys'-love' (Southernwood) steeped in lamp-oil. On occasion he wore curls – a double row – running almost horizontally around his head. But as these were sometimes noticeably absent, it was concluded that they were not altogether of Nature's making. By girls whose love for him had turned to hatred he had been nicknamed 'Mop', from this abundance of hair, which was long enought to rest upon his shoulders; as time passed the name more and more prevailed.

His fiddling possibly had the most to do with the fascination he exercised, for, to speak fairly, it could claim for itself a most peculiar and personal quality, like that in a moving preacher. There were tones in it which bred the immediate conviction that indolence and averseness to systematic application were all that lay between 'Mop' and the career of a second Paganini.

While playing he invariably closed his eyes; using no notes, and, as it were, allowing the violin to wander on at will into the most plaintive passages ever heard by rustic man. There was a certain lingual character in the supplicatory expressions he produced, which would wellnigh have drawn an ache from the heart of a gate-post. He could make any child in the parish, who was at all sensitive to music, burst into tears in a few minutes by simply fiddling one of the old dance-tunes he almost entirely affected – country jigs, reels, and 'Favourite Quick Steps' of the last century – some mutilated remains of which even now reappear as nameless phantoms in new quadrilles and gallops, where they are recognized only by the curious, or by such old-fashioned and far-between people as have been thrown with men like Wat Ollamoor in their early life.

His date was a little later than that of the old Mellstock quire-band which comprised the Dewys, Mail, and the rest – in fact, he did not rise above the horizon thereabout till those well-known musicians were disbanded as ecclesiastical funtionaries. In their honest love of thoroughness they despised the new man's style. Theophilus Dewy (Reuben the tranter's younger brother) used to say there was no 'plumness' in it – no bowing, no solidity – it was all fantastical. And probably this was true. Anyhow, Mop had, very obviously, never bowed a note of church-music from his birth; he never once sat in the gallery of

Mellstock Church where the others had tuned their venerable psalmody so many hundreds of times; had never, in all likelihood, entered a church at all. All were devil's tunes in his repertory. 'He could no more play the Wold Hundredth to his true time than he could play the brazen serpent,' the tranter would say. (The brazen serpent was supposed in Mellstock to be a musical instrument particularly hard to blow.)

Occasionally Mop could produce the aforesaid moving effect upon the souls of grown-up persons, especially young women of fragile and responsive organization. Such an one was Car'line Aspent. Though she was already engaged to be married before she met him, Car'line, of them all, was the most influenced by Mop Ollamoor's heart-stealing melodies, to her discomfort, nay, positive pain and ultimate injury. She was a pretty, invocating, weak-mouthed girl, whose chief defect as a companion with her sex was a tendency to peevishness now and then. At this time she was not a resident in Mellstock parish where Mop lodged, but lived some miles off at Stickleford, further down the river.

How and where she first made acquaintance with him and his fiddling is not truly known, but the story was that it either began or was developed on one spring evening, when, in passing through Lower Mellstock, she chanced to pause on the bridge near his house to rest herself, and languidly leaned over the parapet. Mop was standing on his door-step, as was his custom, spinning the insidious thread of semi- and demi-semiquavers from the E string of his fiddle for the benefit of passers-by, and laughing as the tears rolled down the cheeks of the little children hanging around him. Car'line pretended to be engrossed with the rippling of the stream under the arches, but in reality she was listening, as he knew. Presently the aching of the heart seized her simultaneously with a wild desire to glide airily in the mazes of an infinite dance. To shake off the fascination she resolved to go on, although it would be necessary to pass him as he played. On stealthily glancing ahead at the performer, she found to her relief that his eyes were closed in abandonment to instrumentation, and she strode on boldly. But when closer her step grew timid, her tread convulsed itself more and more accordantly with the time of the melody, till she very nearly danced along. Gaining another glance at him when immediately opposite, she saw that *one* of his eyes was open, quizzing her as he smiled at her emotional state. Her gait could not divest itself of its compelled capers till she had gone a long way past the house; and Car'line was unable to shake off the strange infatuation for hours.

After that day, whenever there was to be in the neighbourhood a dance to which she could get an invitation, and where Mop Ollamoor was to be the musician, Car'line contrived to be present, though it sometimes involved a walk of several miles; for he did not play so often in Stickleford as elsewhere.

The next evidences of his influence over her were singular enough, and it would require a neurologist to fully explain them. She would be sitting quietly, any evening after dark, in the house of her father, the parish clerk, which stood in the middle of Stickleford village street, this being the highroad between Lower Mellstock and Moreford, five miles eastward. Here, without a moment's warning, and in the midst of a general conversation between her father, sister, and the young man before alluded to, who devotedly wooed her in ignorance of her infatuation, she would start from her seat in the chimney-corner as if she had received a galvanic shock, and spring convulsively towards the ceiling; then she would burst into tears, and it was not till some half-hour had passed that she grew calm as usual. Her father, knowing her hysterical tendencies, was always excessively anxious about this trait in his youngest girl, and feared the attack to be a species of epileptic fit. Not so her sister Julia. Julia had found out what was the cause. At the moment before the jumping, only an exceptionally sensitive ear situated in the chimney-nook could have caught from down the flue the beat of a man's footstep along the highway without. But it was in that footfall, for which she had been waiting, that the origin of Car'line's involuntary springing lay. The pedestrian was Mop Ollamoor, as the girl well knew; but his business that way was not to visit her; he sought another woman whom he spoke of as his Intended, and who lived at Moreford, two miles further on. On one, and only one, occasion did it happen that Car'line could not control her utterance; it was when her sister alone chanced to be present. 'O – O – O –!' she cried. 'He's going to *her*, and not coming to *me*!'

To do the fiddler justice, he had not at first thought greatly of, or spoken much to, this girl of impressionable mould. But he had soon found out her secret, and could not resist a little by-play with her too easily hurt heart, as an interlude between his more serious lovemakings at Moreford. The two became well acquainted, though only by stealth, hardly a soul in Stickleford except her sister, and her lover Ned Hipcroft, being aware of the attachment. Her father disapproved of her coldness to Ned; her sister, too, hoped she might get over this nervous passion for a man of whom so little was known. The ultimate result was that Car'line's manly and simple wooer Edward found his suit becoming practically hopeless. He was a respectable mechanic, in a far sounder position than Mop the nominal horse-doctor; but when, before leaving her, Ned put his flat and final question, would she marry him, then and there, now or never, it was with little expectation of obtaining more than the negative she gave him. Though her father supported him and her sister supported him, he could not play the fiddle so as to draw your soul out of your body like a spider's thread, as Mop did, till you felt as limp as withywind and yearned for something to cling to. Indeed, Hipcroft had not the slightest ear for music; could not sing two notes in tune, much less play them.

The No he had expected and got from her, in spite of a preliminary encouragement, gave Ned a new start in life. It had been uttered in such a tone of sad entreaty that he resolved to persecute her no more; she should not even be distressed by a sight of his form in the distant perspective of the street and lane. He left the place, and his natural course was to London.

The railway to South Wessex was in process of construction, but it was not as yet opened for traffic; and Hipcroft reached the capital by a six days' trudge on foot, as many a better man had done before him. He was one of the last of the artisan class who used that now extinct method of travel to the great centres of labour, so customary then from time immemorial.

In London he lived and worked regularly at his trade. More fortunate than many, his disinterested willingness recommended him from the first. During the ensuing four years he was never out of employment. He neither advanced nor receded in the modern sense; he improved as a workman, but he did not shift one jot in social position. About his love for Car'line he maintained a rigid silence. No doubt he often thought of her; but being always occupied, and having no relations at Stickleford, he held no communication with that part of the country, and showed no desire to return. In his quiet lodging in Lambeth he moved about after working-hours with the facility of a woman, doing his own cooking, attending to his stocking-heels, and shaping himself by degrees to a lifelong bachelorhood. For this conduct one is bound to advance the canonical reason that time could not efface from his heart the image of little Car'line Aspent – and it may be in part true; but there was also the inference that his was a nature not greatly dependent upon the ministrations of the other sex for its comforts.

The fourth year of his residence as a mechanic in London was the year of the Hyde-Park Exhibition already mentioned, and at the construction of this huge glass-house, then unexampled in the world's history, he worked daily. It was an era of great hope and activity among the nations and industries. Though Hipcroft was, in his small way, a central man in the movement, he plodded on with his usual outward placidity. Yet for him, too, the year was destined to have its surprises, for when the bustle of getting the building ready for the opening day was past, the ceremonies had been witnessed, and people were flocking thither from all parts of the globe, he received a letter from Car'line. Till that day the silence of four years between himself and Stickleford had never been broken.

She informed her old lover, in an uncertain penmanship which suggested a trembling hand, of the trouble she had been put to in ascertaining his address, and then broached the subject which had prompted her to write. Four years ago, she said with the greatest delicacy of which she was capable, she had been so foolish as to refuse him. Her wilful wrong-headedness had since been a grief to her many times, and of late particularly. As for Mr Ollamoor, he had been absent almost as long as Ned – she did not know where. She would gladly marry Ned now if he were to ask her again, and be a tender little wife to him till her life's end.

A tide of warm feeling must have surged through Ned Hipcroft's frame on receipt of this news, if we may judge by the issue. Unquestionably he loved her still, even if not to the exclusion of every other happiness. This from his Car'line, she who had been dead to him these many years, alive to him again as of old, was in itself a pleasant, gratifying thing. Ned had grown so resigned to, or satisfied with, his lonely lot, that he probably would not have shown much jubilation at anything. Still, a certain ardour of preoccupation, after his first surprise, revealed how deeply her confession of faith in him had stirred him. Measured and methodical in his ways, he did not answer the letter that day, nor the next, nor the next. He was having a 'good think'. When he did answer it, there was a great deal of sound reasoning mixed in with the unmistakable tenderness of his reply; but the tenderness itself was sufficient to reveal that he was pleased with her straight-forward frankness; that the anchorage she had once obtained in his heart was renewable, if it had not been continuously firm.

He told her – and as he wrote his lips twitched humorously over the few gentle words of raillery he indited among the rest of his sentences – that it was all very well for her to come round at this time of day. Why wouldn't she have him when he wanted her? She had no doubt learned that he was not married, but suppose his affections had since been fixed on another? She ought to beg his pardon. Still, he was not the man to forget her. But considering how he had been used, and what he had suffered, she could not quite expect him to go down to Stickleford and fetch her. But if she would come to him, and say she was sorry, as was only fair; why, yes, he would marry her, knowing what a good little woman she was at the core. He added that the request for her to come to him was a less one to make than it would have been when he first left Stickleford, or even a few months ago; for the new railway into South Wessex was now open, and there had just begun to be run wonderfully contrived special trains, called excursion-trains, on account of the Great Exhibition; so that she could come up easily alone.

She said in her reply how good it was of him to treat her so generously, after her hot-and-cold treatment of him; that though she felt frightened at the magnitude of the journey, and was never as yet in a railway-train, having only seen one pass at a distance, she embraced his offer with all her heart; and would, indeed, own to him how sorry she was, and beg his pardon, and try to be a good wife always, and make up for lost time.

The remaining details of when and where were soon settled, Car'line informing him, for her ready identification in the crowd, that she would be wearing 'my new sprigged-laylock cotton gown', and Ned gaily responding that, having married her the morning after her arrival, he would make a day of it by taking her to the Exhibition. One early summer afternoon, accordingly, he came from his place of work, and hastened towards Waterloo Station to meet her. It was as wet and chilly as an English June day can occasionally be, but as he waited on the platform in the drizzle he glowed inwardly, and seemed to have something to live for again.

The 'excursion-train' – an absolutely new departure in the history of travel – was still a novelty on the Wessex line, and probably everywhere. Crowds of people had flocked to all the stations on the way up to witness the unwonted sight of so long a train's passage, even where they did not take advantage of the opportunity it offered. The seats for the humbler class of travellers in these early experiments in steam-locomotion, were open trucks, without any protection whatever from the wind and rain; and damp weather having set in with the afternoon, the unfortunate occupants of these vehicles were, on the train drawing up at the London terminus, found to be in a pitiable condition from their long journey; blue-faced, stiff-necked, sneezing, rain-beaten, chilled to the marrow, many of the men being hatless; in fact, they resembled people who had been out all night in an open boat on a rough sea, rather than inland excursionists for pleasure. The women had in some degree protected themselves by turning up the skirts of their gowns over their heads, but as by this arrangement they were additionally exposed about the hips, they were all more or less in a sorry plight.

In the bustle and crush of alighting forms of both sexes which followed the entry of the huge concatenation into the station, Ned Hipcroft soon discerned the slim little figure his eye was in search of, in the sprigged lilac, as described. She came up to him with a frightened smile – still pretty, though so damp, weather-beaten, and shivering from long exposure to the wind.

'O Ned!' she sputtered, 'I – I—' He clasped her in his arms and kissed her, whereupon she burst into a flood of tears.

'You are wet, my poor dear! I hope you'll not get cold,' he said. And surveying her and her multifarious surrounding packages, he noticed that by the hand she led a toddling child – a little girl of three or so – whose hood was as clammy and tender face as blue as those of the other travellers.

'Who is this – somebody you know?' asked Ned curiously.

'Yes, Ned. She's mine.'

'Yours?'

'Yes – my own.'

'Your own child?'

'Yes!'

'But who's the father?'

'The young man I had after you courted me.'

'Well – as God's in—'

'Ned, I didn't name it in my letter, because, you see, it would have been so hard to explain! I thought that when we met I could tell you how she happened to be born, so much better than in writing! I hope you'll excuse it this once, dear Ned, and not scold me, now I've come so many, many miles!'

'This means Mr Mop Ollamoor, I reckon!' said Hipcroft, gazing palely at them from the distance of the yard or two to which he had withdrawn with a start.

Car'line gasped. 'But he's been gone away for years!' she supplicated. 'And I never had a young man before! And I was so onlucky to be catched the first time he took advantage o' me, though some of the girls down there go on like anything!'

Ned remained in silence, pondering.

'You'll forgive me, dear Ned?' she added, beginning to sob outright. 'I haven't taken 'ee in after all, because – because you can pack us back again, if you want to; though 'tis hundreds o' miles, and so wet, and night a-coming on, and I with no money!'

'What the devil can I do!' Hipcroft groaned.

A more pitiable picture than the pair of helpless creatures presented was never seen on a rainy day, as they stood on the great, gaunt, puddled platform, a whiff of drizzle blowing under the roof upon them now and then; the pretty attire in which they had started from Stickleford in the early morning bemuddled and sodden, weariness on their faces, and fear of him in their eyes; for the child began to look as if she thought she too had done some wrong, remaining in an appalled silence till the tears rolled down her chubby cheeks.

'What's the matter, my little maid?' said Ned mechanically.

'I do want to go home!' she let out, in tones that told of a bursting heart. 'And my totties be cold, an' I shan't have no bread an' butter no more!'

'I don't know what to say to it all!' declared Ned, his own eye moist as he turned and walked a few steps with his head down; then regarded them again point-blank. From the child escaped troubled breaths and silently welling tears.

'Want some bread and butter, do 'ee?' he said, with factitious hardness.

'Ye-e-s!'

'Well, I dare say I can get 'ee a bit! Naturally, you must want some. And you, too, for that matter, Car'line.'

'I do feel a little hungered. But I can keep it off,' she murmured.

'Folk shouldn't do that,' he said gruffly. . . 'There, come along!' He caught up the child, as he added, 'You must bide here tonight, anyhow, I s'pose! What can you do otherwise? I'll get 'ee some tea and victuals; and as for this job, I'm sure I don't know what to say! This is the way out.'

They pursued their way, without speaking, to Ned's lodgings, which were not far off. There he dried them and made them comfortable, and prepared tea; they thankfully sat down. The ready-made household of which he suddenly found himself the head imparted a cosy aspect to his room, and a paternal one to himself. Presently he turned to the child and kissed her now blooming cheeks; and, looking wistfully at Car'line, kissed her also.

'I don't see how I can send you back all them miles,' he growled, 'now you've come all the way o' purpose to join me. But you must trust me, Car'line, and show you've real faith in me. Well, do you feel better now, my little woman?'

The child nodded beamingly, her mouth being otherwise occupied.

'I did trust you, Ned, in coming; and I shall always!'

Thus, without any definite agreement to forgive her, he tacitly acquiesced in the fate that Heaven had sent him; and on the day of their marriage (which was not quite so soon as he had expected it could be, on account of the time necessary for banns) he took her to the Exhibition when they came back from church, as he had promised. While standing near a large mirror in one of the courts devoted to furniture, Car'line started, for in the glass appeared the reflection of a form exactly resembling Mop Ollamoor's – so exactly, that it seemed impossible to believe anybody but that artist in person to be the original. On passing round the objects which hemmed in Ned, her, and the child from a direct view, no Mop was to be seen. Whether he were really in London or not at that time was never known; and Car'line always stoutly denied that her readiness to go and meet Ned in town arose from any rumour that Mop had also gone thither; which denial there was no reasonable ground for doubting.

And then the year glided away, and the Exhibition folded itself up and became a thing of the past. The park trees that had been enclosed for six months were again exposed to the winds and storms, and the sod grew green anew. Ned found that Car'line resolved herself into a very good wife and companion, though she had made herself what is called cheap to him; but in that she was like another domestic article, a cheap tea-pot, which often brews better tea than a dear one. One autumn Hipcroft found himself with but little work to do, and a prospect of less for the winter. Both being country born and bred, they fancied they would like to live again in their natural atmosphere. It was accordingly decided between them that they should leave the pent-up London lodging, and that Ned should seek out employment near his native place, his wife and her daughter staying with Car'line's father during the search for occupation and an abode of their own.

Tinglings of pride pervaded Car'line's spasmodic little frame as she journeyed down with Ned to the place she had left two or three years before, in silence and under a cloud. To return to where she had once been despised, a smiling London wife with a distinct London accent, was a triumph which the world did not witness every day.

The train did not stop at the petty roadside station that lay nearest to Stickleford, and the trio went on to Casterbridge. Ned thought it a good opportunity to make a few preliminary inquiries for employment at workshops in the borough where he had been known; and feeling cold from her journey, and it being dry underfoot and only dusk as yet, with a moon on the point of rising, Car'line and her little girl walked on towards Stickleford, leaving Ned to follow at a quicker pace, and pick her up at a certain half-way house, widely known as an inn.

The woman and child pursued the well-remembered way comfortably enough, though they were both becoming wearied. In the course of three miles they had passed Heedless-William's Pond, the familiar landmark by Bloom's End, and were drawing near the Quiet Woman, a lone roadside hostel on the lower verge of the Egdon Heath, since and for many years abolished. In stepping up towards it Car'line heard more voices within than had formerly been customary at such an hour, and she learned that an auction of fat stock had been held near the spot that afternoon. The child would be the better for a rest as well as herself, she thought, and she entered.

The guests and customers overflowed into the passage, and Car'line had no sooner crossed the threshold than a man whom she remembered by sight came forward with a glass and mug in his hands towards a friend leaning against the wall; but, seeing her, very gallantly offered her a drink of the liquor, which was gin-and-beer hot, pouring her out a tumblerful and saying, in a moment or two: 'Surely, 'tis little Car'line Aspent that was – down at Stickleford?'

She assented, and, though she did not exactly want this beverage, she drank it since it was offered, and her entertainer begged her to come in further and sit down. Once within the room she found that all the persons present were seated close against the walls, and there being a chair vacant she did the same. An explanation of their position occurred the next moment. In the opposite corner stood Mop, rosining his bow and looking just the same as ever. The company had cleared the middle of the room for dancing, and they were about to dance again. As she wore a veil to keep off the wind she did not think he had recognized her, or could possibly guess the identity of the child; and to her satisfied surprise she found that she could confront him quite calmly – mistress of herself in the dignity her London life had given her. Before she had quite emptied her glass the dance was called, the dancers formed in two lines, the music sounded, and the figure began.

Then matters changed for Car'line. A tremor quickened itself to life in her, and her hand so shook that she could hardly set down her glass. It was not the dance nor the dancers, but the notes of that old violin which thrilled the London wife, these having still all the witchery that she had so well known of yore, and under which she had used to lose her power of independent will. How it all came back! There was the fiddling figure against the wall; the large, oily, mop-like head of him, and beneath the mop the face with closed eyes.

After the first moments of paralyzed reverie the familiar tune in the familiar rendering made her laugh and shed tears simultaneously. Then a man at the bottom of the dance, whose partner had dropped away, stretched out his hand and beckoned to her to take the place. She did not want to dance; she entreated by signs to be left where she was, but she was entreating of the tune and its player rather than of the dancing man. The saltatory tendency which the fiddler and his cunning instrument had ever been able to start in her was seizing Car'line just as it had done in earlier years, possibly assisted by the gin-and-beer hot. Tired as she was she grasped her little girl by the hand, and plunging in at the bottom of the figure, whirled about with the rest. She found that her companions were mostly people of the neighbouring hamlets and farms – Bloom's End, Mellstock, Lewgate, and elsewhere; and by degrees she was recognized as she convulsively danced on, wishing that Mop would cease and let her heart rest from the aching he caused, and her feet also.

After long and many minutes the dance ended, when she was urged to fortify herself with more gin-and-beer; which she did, feeling very weak and overpowered with hysteric emotion. She refrained from unveiling, to keep Mop in ignorance of her presence, if possible. Several of the guests having left, Car'line hastily wiped her lips and also turned to go; but, according to the account of some who remained, at that very moment a five-handed reel was proposed, in which two or three begged her to join.

She declined on the plea of being tired and having to walk to Stickleford, when Mop began aggressively tweedling 'My Fancy-Lad', in D major, as the air to which the reel was to be footed. He must have recognized her, though she did not know it, for it was the strain of all seductive strains which she was least able to resist – the one he had played when she was leaning over the bridge at the date of their first acquaintance. Car'line stepped despairingly into the middle of the room with the other four.

Reels were resorted to hereabouts at this time by the more robust spirits, for the reduction of superfluous energy which the ordinary figure-dances were not powerful enough to exhaust. As everybody knows, or does not know, the five reelers stood in the form of a cross, the reel being performed by each line of three alternately, the persons who successively came to the middle place dancing in both directions. Car'line soon found herself in this place, the axis of the whole performance, and could not get out of it, the tune turning into the first part without giving her opportunity. And now she began to suspect that Mop did know her, and was doing this on purpose, though whenever she stole a glance at him his closed eyes betokened obliviousness to everything outside his own brain. She continued to wend her way through the figure of 8 that was formed by her course, the fiddler introducing into his notes the wild and agonizing sweetness of a living voice in one too highly wrought; its pathos running high and running low in endless variation, projecting through her nerves excruciating spasms, a sort of blissful torture. The room swam; the tune was endless; and in about a quarter of an hour the only other woman in the figure dropped out exhausted, and sank panting on a bench.

The reel instantly resolved itself into a four-handed one. Car'line would have given anything to leave off; but she had, or fancied she had, no power, while Mop played such tunes; and thus another ten minutes slipped by, a haze of dust now clouding the candles, the floor being of stone, sanded. Then another dancer fell out – one of the men – and went into the passage in a frantic search for liquor. To turn the figure into a three-handed reel was the work of a second, Mop modulating at the same time into 'The Fairy Dance', as better suited to the contracted movement, and no less one of those foods of love which, as manufactured by his bow, had always intoxicated her.

In a reel for three there was no rest whatever, and four or five minutes were enough to make her remaining two partners, now thoroughly blown, stamp their last bar, and, like their predecessors, limp off into the next room to get something to drink. Car'line, half-stifled inside her veil, was left dancing alone, the apartment now being empty of everybody save herself, Mop and their little girl.

She flung up the veil, and cast her eyes upon him, as if imploring him to withdraw himself and his acoustic magnetism from the atmosphere. Mop opened one of his own orbs, as though for the first time, fixed it peeringly upon her, and smiling dreamily, threw into his strains the reserve of expression which he could not afford to waste on a big and noisy dance. Crowds of little chromatic subtleties, capable of drawing tears from a statue, proceeded straightway from the ancient fiddle, as if it were dying of the emotion which had been pent up within it ever since its banishment from the Italian or German city where it first took shape and sound. There was that in the look of Mop's one dark eye which said: 'You cannot leave off, dear, whether you would or no!' and it bred in her a paroxysm of desperation that defied him to tire her down.

She thus continued to dance alone, defiantly as she thought, but in truth slavishly and abjectly, subject to every wave of the melody, and probed by the gimlet-like gaze of her fascinator's open eye; keeping up at the same time a feeble smile in his face, as a feint to signify it was still her own pleasure which led her on. A terrified embarrassment as to what she could say to him if she were to leave off, had its unrecognized share in keeping her going. The child, who was beginning to be distressed by the strange situation, came up and whimpered: 'Stop, mother, stop, and let's go home!' as she seized Car'line's hand.

Suddenly Car'line sank staggering to the floor, and rolling over on her face, prone she remained. Mop's fiddle thereupon emitted an elfin shriek of finality; stepping quickly down from the nine-gallon beer-cask which had formed his rostrum, he went to the little girl, who disconsolately bent over her mother.

The guests who had gone into the back room for liquor and change of air, hearing something unusual, trooped back hitherward, where they endeavoured to revive poor, weak Car'line by blowing her with the bellows and opening the window. Ned, her husband, who had been detained in Casterbridge, as aforesaid, came along the road at this juncture, and hearing excited voices through the open casement, and, to his great surprise, the mention of his wife's name, he entered amid the rest upon the scene. Car'line was now in convulsions, weeping violently, and for a long time nothing could be done with her. While he was sending for a cart to take her onward to Stickleford Hipcroft anxiously inquired how it had all happened; and then the assembly explained that a fiddler formerly known in the locality had lately visited his old haunts, and had taken upon himself without invitation to play that evening at the inn and raise a dance.

Ned demanded the fiddler's name, and they said Ollamoor.

'Ah!' exlaimed Ned, looking round him. 'Where is he, and where – where's my little girl?'

Ollamoor had disappeared, and so had the child. Hipcroft was in ordinary a quiet and tractable fellow, but a determination which was to be feared settled in his face now. 'Blast him!' he cried. 'I'll beat his skull in for'n, if I swing for it tomorrow!'

He had rushed to the poker which lay on the hearth, and hastened down the passage, the people following. Outside the house, on the other side of the highway, a mass of dark heath-land rose sullenly upward to its not easily accessible interior, a ravined plateau, whereon jutted into the sky, at the distance of a couple of miles, the fir-woods of Mistover backed by the Yalbury coppices – a place of Dantesque gloom at this hour, which would have afforded secure hiding for a battery of artillery, much less a man and a child.

Some other men plunged thitherward with him, and more went along the road. They were gone about twenty minutes altogether, returning without result to the inn. Ned sat down in the settle, and clasped his forehead with his hands.

'Well – what a fool the man is, and hev been all these years, if he thinks the child his, as a' do seem to!' they whispered. 'And everybody else knowing otherwise!'

'No, I don't think 'tis mine!' cried Ned hoarsely, as he looked up from his hands. 'But she *is* mine, all the same! Ha'n't I nussed her! Ha'n't I fed her and teached her? Ha'n't I played wi' her? O, little Carry – gone with that rogue – gone!'

'You ha'n't lost your mis'ess, anyhow,' they said to console him. 'She's throwed up the sperrits, and she is feeling better, and she's more to 'ee than a child that isn't yours.'

'She isn't! She's not so particular much to me, especially now she's lost the little maid! But Carry's the whole world to me!'

'Well, ver' like you'll find her tomorrow.'

'Ah – but shall I? Yet he *can't* hurt her – surely he can't! Well – how's Car'line now? I am ready. Is the cart here?'

She was lifted into the vehicle, and they sadly lumbered on toward Stickleford. Next day she was calmer; but the fits were still upon her; and her will seemed shattered. For the child she appeared to show singularly little anxiety, though Ned was nearly distracted by his passionate paternal love for a child not his own. It was nevertheless quite expected that the impish Mop would restore the lost one after a freak of a day or two; but time went on, and neither he nor she could be heard of, and Hipcroft murmured that perhaps he was exercising upon her some unholy musical charm, as he had done upon Car'line herself. Weeks passed, and still they could obtain no clue either to the fiddler's whereabouts or to the girl's; and how he could have induced her to go with him remained a mystery.

Then Ned, who had obtained only temporary employment in the neighbourhood, took a sudden hatred towards his native district, and a rumour reaching his ears through the police that a somewhat similar man and child had been seen at a fair near London, he playing a violin, she dancing on stilts, a new interest in the capital took possession of Hipcroft with an intensity which would scarcely allow him time to pack before returning thither. He did not, however, find the lost one, though he made it the entire business of his over-hours to stand about in by-streets in the hope of discovering her, and would start up in the night, saying, 'That rascal's torturing her to maintain him!' To which his wife would answer peevishly, 'Don't 'ee raft yourself so, Ned! You prevent my getting a bit o' rest! He won't hurt her!' and fall asleep again.

That Carry and her father had emigrated to America was the general opinion; Mop, no doubt, finding the girl a highly desirable companion when he had trained her to keep him by her earnings as a dancer. There, for that matter, they may be performing in some capacity now, though he must be an old scamp verging on three-score-and-ten, and she a woman of four-and-forty.

MAY 1893

A FEW CRUSTED CHARACTERS

Introduction – Tony Kytes, the Arch-Deceiver – This History of the Hardcomes – The Superstitious Man's Story – Andrey Satchel and the Parson and Clerk – Old Andrey's Experience as a Musician – Absent-Mindedness in a Parish Choir – The Winters and the Palmleys – Incident in the Life of Mr George Crookhill – Netty Sargent's Copyhold

INTRODUCTION

It is a Saturday afternoon of blue and yellow autumn-time, and the large scene is the High Street of a well-known market-town. A large carrier's van stands in the quadrangular fore-court of the White Hart Inn, upon the sides of its spacious tilt being painted, in weather-beaten letters: 'Burthen, Carrier to Longpuddle'. These vans, so numerous hereabout, are a respectable, if somewhat lumbering, class of conveyance, much resorted to by decent travellers not overstocked with money, the better among them roughly corresponding to the old French *diligences*.

The present one is timed to leave the town at four in the afternoon precisely, and it is now half-past three by the clock in the turret at the top of the street. In a few seconds errand-boys from the shops begin to arrive with packages, which they fling into the vehicle, and turn away whistling, and care for the packages no more. At twenty minutes to four an elderly woman places her basket upon the shafts, slowly mounts, takes up a seat inside, and folds her hands and her lips. She has secured her corner for the journey, though there is as yet no sign of a horse being put in, nor of a carrier. At the three-quarters, two other women arrive, in whom the first recognizes the postmistress of Upper Longpuddle and the registrar's wife, they recognizing her as the aged groceress of the same village. At five minutes to the hour there approach Mr Profitt, the schoolmaster, in a soft felt hat, and Christopher Twink, the master-thatcher; and as the hour strikes there rapidly drop in the parish clerk and his wife, the seedsman and his aged father, the registrar; also Mr Day, the world-ignored local landscape-painter, an elderly man who resides in his native place, and has never sold a picture outside it, though his pretensions to art have been nobly supported by his fellow-villagers, whose confidence in his genius has been as remarkable as the outer neglect of it, leading them to buy his paintings so extensively (at the price of a few shillings each, it is true) that every dwelling in the parish exhibits three or four of those admired productions on its walls.

Burthen, the carrier, is by this time seen bustling round the vehicle; the horses are put in, the proprietor arranges the reins and springs up into his seat as if he were used to it – which he is.

'Is everybody here?' he asks preparatorily over his shoulder to the passengers within.

As those who were not there did not reply in the negative the muster was assumed to be complete, and after a few hitches and hindrances the van with its human freight was got under way. It jogged on at an easy pace till it reached the bridge which formed the last outpost of the town. The carrier pulled up suddenly.

'Bless my soul!' he said, 'I've forgot the curate!'

All who could do so gazed from the little back-window of the van, but the curate was not in sight.

'Now I wonder where that there man is?' continued the carrier.

'Poor man, he ought to have a living at his time of life.'

'And he ought to be punctual,' said the carrier. '"Four o'clock sharp is my time for starting", I said to 'en. And he said, "I'll be there." Now he's not here; and as a serious old church-minister he ought to be as good as his word. Perhaps Mr Flaxton knows, being in the same line of life?' He turned to the parish clerk.

'I was talking an immense deal with him, that's true, half an hour ago,' replied that ecclesiastic, as one of whom it was no erroneous supposition that he should be on intimate terms with another of the cloth. 'But he didn't say he would be late.'

The discussion was cut off by the appearance round the corner of the van of rays from the curate's spectacles, followed hastily by his face and a few white whiskers, and the swinging tails of his long gaunt coat. Nobody reproached him, seeing how he was reproaching himself; and he entered breathlessly and took his seat.

'Now be we all here?' said the carrier again. They started a second time, and moved on till they were about three hundred yards out of the town, and had nearly reached the second bridge, behind which, as every native remembers, the road takes a turn, and travellers by this highway disappear finally from the view of gazing burghers.

'Well, as I'm alive!' cried the postmistress from the interior of the conveyance, peering through the little square back-window along the road townward.

'What?' said the carrier.

'A man hailing us!'

Another sudden stoppage. 'Somebody else?' the carrier asked.

'Ay, sure!' All waited silently, while those who could gaze out did so.

'Now, who can that be?' Burthen continued. 'I just put it to ye, neighbours, can any man keep time with such hindrances? Bain't we full a' ready? Who in the world can the man be?'

'He's a sort of gentleman,' said the schoolmaster, his position commanding the road more comfortably than that of his comrades.

The stranger, who had been holding up his umbrella to attract their notice, was walking forward leisurely enough, now that he found, by their stopping, that it had been secured. His clothes were decidedly not of a local cut, though it was difficult to point out any particular mark of difference. In his left hand he carried a small leather travelling-bag. As soon as he had overtaken the van he glanced at the inscription on its side, as if to assure himself that he had hailed the right conveyance, and asked if they had room.

The carrier replied that though they were pretty well laden he supposed they could carry one more, whereupon the stranger mounted, and took the seat cleared for him within. And then the horses made another move, this time for good, and swung along with their burden of fourteen souls all told.

'You bain't one of these parts, sir?' said the carrier. 'I could tell that as far as I could see 'ee.'

'Yes, I am one of these parts,' said the stranger.

'Oh? H'm.'

The silence which followed seemed to imply a doubt of the truth of the new-comer's assertion. 'I was speaking of Upper Longpuddle, more particular,' continued the carrier hardily, 'and I think I know most faces of that valley.'

'I was born at Longpuddle, and nursed at Longpuddle, and my father and grandfather before me,' said the passenger quietly.

'Why, to be sure,' said the aged groceress in the background, 'it isn't John Lackland's son – never – it can't be – he who went to foreign parts five-and-thirty years ago with his wife and family? Yet – what do I hear? – that's his father's voice!'

'That's the man,' replied the stranger. 'John Lackland was my father, and I am John Lackland's son. Five-and-thirty years ago, when I was a boy of eleven, my parents emigrated across the seas, taking me and my sister with them. Kyte's boy Tony was the one who drove us and our belongings to Casterbridge on the morning we left; and his was the last Longpuddle face I saw. We sailed the same week across the ocean, and there we've been ever since, and there I've left those I went with – all three.'

'Alive or dead?'

'Dead, he replied in a low voice. 'And I have come back to the old place, having nourished a thought – not a definite intention, but just a thought – that I should like to return here in a year or two, to spend the remainder of my days.'

'Married man, Mr Lackland?'

'No.'

'And have the world used 'ee well, sir – or rather John, knowing 'ee as a child? In these rich new countries that we hear of so much, you've got rich with the rest?'

'I am not very rich,' Mr Lackland said. 'Even in new countries, you know, there are failures. The race is not always to the swift, nor the battle to the strong; and even if it sometimes is, you may be neither swift nor strong. However, that's enough about me. Now, having answered your inquiries, you must answer mine; for being in London, I have come down here entirely to discover what Longpuddle is looking like, and who are living there. That was why I preferred a seat in your van to hiring a carriage for driving across.'

'Well, as for Longpuddle, we rub on there much as usual. Old figures have dropped out o' their frames, so to speak it, and new ones have been put in their places. You mentioned Tony Kytes as having been the one to drive your family and your goods to Casterbridge in his father's waggon when you left. Tony is, I believe, living still, but not at Longpuddle. He went away and settled at Lewgate, near Mellstock, after his marriage. Ah, Tony was a sort o' man!'

'His character had hardly come out when I knew him.'

'No. But 'twas well enough, as far as that goes – except as to women. I shall never forget his courting – never!'

The returned villager waited silently, and the carrier went on:

TONY KYTES, THE ARCH-DECEIVER

'I shall never forget Tony's face. 'Twas a little, round, firm, tight face, with a seam here and there left by the smallpox, but not enough to hurt his looks in a woman's eye, though he'd had it badish when he was a boy. So very serious looking and unsmiling 'a was, that young man, that it really seemed as if he couldn't laugh at all without great pain to his conscience.

He looked very hard at a small speck in your eye when talking to 'ee. And there was no more sign of a whisker or beard on Tony Kytes's face than on the palm of my hand. He used to sing "The Tailor's Breeches" with a religious manner, as if it were a hymn:

'"O the petticoats went off, and the breeches they went on!"

and all the rest of the scandalous stuff. He was quite the women's favourite, and in return for their likings he loved 'em in shoals.

'But in course of time Tony got fixed down to one in particular, Milly Richards, a nice, light, small, tender little thing; and it was soon said that they were engaged to be married. One Saturday he had been to market to do business for his father, and was driving home the waggon in the afternoon. When he reached the foot of the very hill we shall be going over in ten minutes who should he see waiting for him at the top but Unity Sallet, a handsome girl, one of the young women he'd been very tender towards before he'd got engaged to Milly.

'As soon as Tony came up to her she said, "My dear Tony, will you give me a lift home?"

'"That I will, darling," said Tony. "You don't suppose I could refuse 'ee?"

'She smiled a smile, and up she hopped, and on drove Tony.

'"Tony," she says, in a sort of tender chide, "why did ye desert me for that other one? In what is she better than I? I should have made 'ee a finer wife, and a more loving one, too. 'Tisn't girls that are so easily won at first that are the best. Think how long we've known each other – ever since we were children almost – now haven't we, Tony?"

'"Yes, that we have," says Tony, a-struck with the truth o't.

'"And you've never seen anything in me to complain of, have ye, Tony? Now tell the truth to me!"

'"I never have, upon my life," says Tony.

'"And – can you say I'm not pretty, Tony? Now look at me!"

'He let his eyes light upon her for a long while. "I really can't," says he. "In fact, I never knowed you was so pretty before!"

'"Prettier than she?"

'What Tony would have said to that nobody knows, for before he could speak, what should he see ahead, over the hedge past the turning, but a feather he knew well – the feather in Milly's hat – she to whom he had been thinking of putting the question as to giving out the banns that very week.

'"Unity," says he, as mild as he could, "here's Milly coming. Now I shall catch it mightly if she sees 'ee riding here with me; and if you get down she'll be turning the corner in a moment, and, seeing 'ee in the road, she'll know we've been coming on together. Now, dearest Unity, will ye, to avoid all unpleasantness, which I know ye can't bear any more than I, will ye lie down in the back part of the waggon, and let me cover you over with the tarpaulin till Milly has passed? It will all be done in a minute. Do! – and I'll think over what we've said, and perhaps I shall put a loving question to you after all, instead of to Milly. 'Tisn't true that it is all settled between her and me."

'Well, Unity Sallet agreed, and lay down at the back end of the waggon, and Tony covered her over, so that the waggon seemed to be empty but for the loose tarpaulin; and then he drove on to meet Milly.

'"My dear Tony!" cries Milly, looking up with a little pout at him as he came near. "How long you've been coming home! Just as if I didn't live at Upper Longpuddle at all! And I've come to meet you as you asked me to do, and to ride back with you, and talk over our future home – since you asked me, and I promised. But I shouldn't have come else, Mr Tony!"

'"Ay, my dear, I did ask 'ee – to be sure I did, now I think of it – but I had quite forgot it. To ride back with me, did you say, dear Milly?"

'"Well, of course! What can I do else? Surely you don't want me to walk, now I've come all this way?"

'"O no, no! I was thinking you might be going on to town to meet your mother. I saw her there – and she looked as if she might be expecting 'ee."

'"O no; she's just home. She came across the fields, and so got back before you."

'"Ah! I didn't know that," says Tony. And there was no help for it but to take her up beside him.

'They talked on very pleasantly, and looked at the trees, and beasts, and birds, and insects, and at the ploughmen at work in the fields, till presently who should they see looking out of the upper window of a house that stood beside the road they were following, but Hannah Jolliver, another young beauty of the place at that time, and the very first woman that Tony had fallen in love with – before Milly and before Unity, in fact – the one that he had almost arranged to marry instead of Milly. She was a much more dashing girl than Milly Richards, though he'd not thought much of her of late. The house Hannah was looking from was her aunt's.

'"My dear Milly – my coming wife, as I may call 'ee,' says Tony in his modest way, and not so loud that Unity could overhear, 'I see a young woman a-looking out of window, who I think may accost me. The fact is, Milly, she had a notion that I was wishing to marry her, and since she's discovered I've promised another, and a prettier than she, I'm rather afeared of her temper if she sees us together. Now, Milly, would you do me a favour – my coming wife, as I may say?"

'"Certainly, dearest Tony," says she.

'"Then would ye creep under the empty sack just here in the front of the waggon, and hide there out of sight till we've passed the house? She hasn't seen us yet. You see, we ought to live in peace and goodwill since 'tis almost Christmas, and 'twill prevent angry passions rising, which we always should do."

'"I don't mind, to oblige you, Tony," Milly said; and though she didn't care much about doing it, she crept under, and crouched down just behind the seat, Unity being snug at the other end. So they drove on till they got near the road-side cottage. Hannah had soon seen him coming, and waited at the window, looking down upon him. She tossed her head a little disdainful and smiled off-hand.

'"Well, aren't you going to be civil enough to ask me to ride home with you!' she says, seeing that he was for driving past with a nod and a smile.

'"Ah, to be sure! What was I thinking of?" said Tony, in a flutter. "But you seem as if you was staying at your aunt's?"

"No, I am not," she said. "Don't you see I have my bonnet and jacket on? I have only called to see her on my way home. How can you be so stupid, Tony?"

'"In that case – ah – of course you must come along wi' me," says Tony, feeling a dim sort of sweat rising up inside his clothes. And he reined in the horse, and waited till she'd come downstairs, and then helped her up beside him, her feet outside. He drove on again, his face as long as a face that was a round one by nature well could be.

'Hannah looked round sideways into his eyes. "This is nice, isn't it, Tony?" she says. "I like riding with you."

'Tony looked back into her eyes. "And I with you," he said after a while. In short, having considered her, he warmed up, and the more he looked at her the more he liked her, till he couldn't for the life on him think why he had ever said a word about marriage to Milly or Unity while Hannah Jolliver was in question. So they sat a little closer and closer, their feet upon the foot-board and their shoulders touching, and Tony thought over and over again how handsome Hannah was. He spoke tenderer and tenderer, and called her "dear Hannah" in a whisper at last.

'"You've settled it with Milly by this time, I suppose?" said she.

'"N-no, not exactly."

'"What? How low you talk, Tony."

'"Yes – I've a kind of hoarseness. I said, not exactly."

'"I suppose you mean to?"

'"Well, as to that—" His eyes rested on her face, and hers on his. He wondered how he could have been such a fool as not to follow up Hannah. "My sweet Hannah!" he bursts out, taking her hand, not being really able to help it, and forgetting Milly and Unity, and all the world besides. "Settled it? I don't think I have!"

'"Hark!" says Hannah.

'"What?" says Tony, letting go her hand.

'"Surely I heard a sort of little screaming squeak under those sacks? Why, you've been carrying corn, and there's mice in this waggon, I declare!" She began to haul up the tails of her gown.

'"O no, 'tis the axle," said Tony in an assuring way. "It do go like that sometimes in dry weather."

'"Perhaps it was. . . Well, now, to be quite honest, dear Tony, do you like her better than me? Because – because, although I've held off so independent, I'll own at last that I do like 'ee, Tony, to tell the truth; and I wouldn't say no if you asked me – you know what."

'Tony was so won over by this pretty offering mood of a girl who had been quite the reverse (Hannah had a backward way with her at times, if you can mind) that he just glanced behind, and then whispered very soft, "I haven't quite promised her, and I think I can get out of it, and ask you that question you speak of."

'"Throw over Milly? – all to marry me! How delightful!" broke out Hannah, quite loud, clapping her hands.

'At this there was a real squeak – an angry, spiteful squeak, and afterward a long moan, as if something had broke its heart, and a movement of the empty sacks.

'"Something's there!" said Hannah, starting up.

'"It's nothing really," says Tony in a soothing voice, and praying inwardly for a way out of this. "I wouldn't tell 'ee at first, because I wouldn't frighten 'ee. But, Hannah, I've really a couple of ferrets in a bag under there, for rabbiting, and they quarrel sometimes. I don't wish it knowed, as 'twould be called poaching. Oh, they can't get out, bless 'ee – you are quite safe! And – and – what a fine day it is, isn't it, Hannah, for this time of year? Be you going to market next Saturday? How is your aunt now?" And so on, says Tony, to keep her from talking any more about love in Milly's hearing.

'But he found his work cut out for him, and wondering again how he should get out of this ticklish business, he looked about for a chance. Nearing home he saw his father in a field not far off, holding up his hand as if he wished to speak to Tony.

'"Would you mind taking the reins a moment, Hannah," he said, much relieved, "while I go and find out what father wants?"

'She consented, and away he hastened into the field, only too glad to get breathing time. He found that his father was looking at him with rather a stern eye.

'"Come, come, Tony," said old Mr Kytes, as soon as his son was alongside him, "this won't do, you know."

'"What?" says Tony.

'"Why, if you mean to marry Milly Richards, do it, and there's an end o't. But don't go driving about the country with Jolliver's daughter and making a scandal. I won't have such things done."

'"I only asked her – that is, she asked me, to ride home."

'"She? Why, now, if it had been Milly, 'twould have been quite proper; but you and Hannah Jolliver going about by yourselves—"

'"Milly's there, too, father."

'"Milly? Where?"

'"Under the corn-sacks! Yes, the truth is, father, I've got rather into a nunnywatch, I'm afeared! Unity Sallet is there, too – yes, at the other end, under the tarpaulin. All three are in that waggon, and what to do with 'em I know no more than the dead! The best plan is, as I'm thinking, to speak out loud and plain to one of 'em before the rest, and that will settle it; not but what 'twill cause 'em to kick up a bit of a miff, for certain. Now which would you marry, father, if you was in my place?"

'"Whichever of 'em did *not* ask to ride with thee."

'"That was Milly, I'm bound to say, as she only mounted by my invitation. But Milly—"

'"Then stick to Milly, she's the best. . . But look at that!"

'His father pointed toward the waggon. "She can't hold that horse in. You shouldn't have left the reins in her hands. Run on and take the horse's head, or there'll be some accident to them maids!"

'Tony's horse, in fact, in spite of Hannah's tugging at the reins, had started on his way at a brisk walking pace, being very anxious to get back to the stable, for he had had a long day out. Without another word Tony rushed away from his father to overtake the horse.

'Now of all things that could have happened to wean him from Milly there was nothing so powerful as his father's recommending her. No; it could not be Milly, after all. Hannah must be the one, since he could not marry all three as he longed to do. This he thought while running after the waggon. But queer things were happening inside it.

'It was, of course, Milly who had screamed under the sack-bags, being obliged to let off her bitter rage and shame in that way at what Tony was saying, and never daring to show, for very pride and dread o' being laughed at, that she was in hiding. She became more and more restless, and in twisting herself about, what did she see but another woman's foot and white stocking close to her head. It quite frightened her, not knowing that Unity Sallet was in the waggon likewise. But after the fright was over she determined to get to the bottom of all this, and she crept and crept along the bed of the waggon, under the tarpaulin, like a snake, when lo and behold she came face to face with Unity.

'"Well, if this isn't disgraceful!" says Milly in a raging whisper to Unity.

'"'Tis," says Unity, "to see you hiding in a young man's waggon like this, and no great character belonging to either of ye!"

'"Mind what you are saying!" replied Milly, getting louder. "I am engaged to be married to him, and haven't I a right to be here? What right have you, I should like to know? What has he been promising you? A pretty lot of nonsense, I expect! But what Tony says to other women is all mere wind, and no concern to me!"

'"Don't you be too sure!" says Unity. "He's going to have Hannah, and not you, nor me either; I could hear that."

'Now at these strange voices sounding from under the cloth Hannah was thunderstruck a'most into a swound; and it was just at this time that the horse moved on. Hannah tugged away wildly, not knowing what she was doing; and as the quarrel rose louder and louder Hannah got so horrified that she let go the reins altogether. The horse went on at his own pace, and coming to the corner where we turn round to drop down the hill to Lower Longpuddle he turned too quick, the off wheels went up the bank, the waggon rose sideways till it was quite on edge upon the near axles, and out rolled the three maidens into the road in a heap. The horse looked round and stood still.

'When Tony came up, frightened and breathless, he was relieved enough to see that neither of his darlings was hurt, beyond a few scratches from the brambles of the hedge. But he was rather alarmed when he heard how they were going on at one another.

'"Don't ye quarrel, my dears – don't ye!" says he, taking off his hat out of respect to 'em. And then he would have kissed them all round, as fair and square as a man could, but they were in too much of a taking to let him, and screeched and sobbed till they was quite spent.

'"Now I'll speak out honest, because I ought to," says Tony, as soon as he could get heard. "And this is the truth," says he. "I've asked Hannah to be mine, and she is willing, and we are going to put up the banns next—"

'Tony had not noticed that Hannah's father was coming up behind, nor had he noticed that Hannah's face was beginning to bleed from the scratch of a bramble. Hannah had seen her father, and had run to him, crying worse than ever.

'"My daughter is *not* willing, sir!" says Mr Jolliver hot and strong. "Be you willing, Hannah? I ask ye to have spirit enough to refuse him, if yer virtue is left to 'ee and you run no risk?"

'"She's as sound as a bell for me, that I'll swear!" says Tony, flaring up. "And so's the others, come to that, though you may think it an onusual thing in me!"

'"I have spirit, and I do refuse him!" says Hannah, partly because her father was there, and partly, too, in a tantrum because of the discovery, and the scar that might be left on her face. "Little did I think when I was so soft with him just now that I was talking to such a false deceiver!"

'"What, you won't have me, Hannah?" says Tony, his jaw hanging down like a dead man's.

'"Never – I would sooner marry no – nobody at all!" she gasped out, though with her heart in her throat, for she would not have refused Tony if he had asked her quietly, and her father had not been there, and her face had not been scratched by the bramble. And having said that, away she walked upon her father's arm, thinking and hoping he would ask her again.

'Tony didn't know what to say next. Milly was sobbing her heart out; but as his father had strongly recommended her he couldn't feel inclined that way. So he turned to Unity.

'"Well, will you, Unity dear, be mine?" he says.

'"Take her leavings? Not I!" says Unity. "I'd scorn it!" And away walks Unity Sallet likewise, though she looked back when she'd gone some way, to see if he was following her.

'So there at last were left Milly and Tony by themselves, she crying in watery streams, and Tony looking like a tree struck by lightning.

'"Well, Milly," he says at last, going up to her, "it do seem as if fate had ordained that it should be you and I, or nobody. And what must be must be, I suppose. Hey, Milly?"

'"If you like, Tony. You didn't really mean what you said to them?"

'"Not a word of it!" declares Tony, bringing down his fist upon his palm.

'And then he kissed her, and put the waggon to rights, and they mounted together; and their banns were put up the very next Sunday. I was not able to go to their wedding, but it was a rare party they had, by all account. Everybody in Longpuddle was there almost; you among the rest, I think, Mr Flaxton?' The speaker turned to the parish clerk.

'I was,' said Mr Flaxton. 'And that party was the cause of a very curious change in some other people's affairs; I mean in Steve Hardcome's and his cousin James's.'

'Ah! the Hardcomes,' said the stranger. 'How familiar that name is to me! What of them?'

The clerk cleared his throat and began:

THE HISTORY OF THE HARDCOMES

'Yes, Tony's was the very best wedding-randy that ever I was at; and I've been at a good many, as you may suppose' – turning to the newly-arrived one – 'having, as a church-officer, the privilege to attend all christening, wedding, and funeral parties – such being our Wessex custom.

''Twas on a frosty night in Christmas week, and among the folk invited were the said Hardcomes o' Climmerston – Steve and James – first cousins, both of them small farmers, just entering into business on their own account. With them came, as a matter of course, their intended wives, two young women of the neighbourhood, both very pretty and sprightly maidens, and numbers of friends from Abbot's-Cernel, and Weatherbury, and Mellstock, and I don't know where – a regular houseful.

'The kitchen was cleared of furniture for dancing, and the old folk played at "Put" and "All-fours" in the parlour, though at last they gave that up to join in the dance. The top of the figure was by the large front window of the room, and there were so many couples that the lower part of the figure reached through the door at the back, and into the darkness of the out-house; in fact, you couldn't see the end of the row at all, and 'twas never known exactly how long that dance was, the lowest couples being lost among the faggots and brushwood in the outhouse.

'When we had danced a few hours, and the crowns of we taller men were swelling into lumps with bumping the beams of the ceiling, the first fiddler laid down his fiddle-bow, and said he should play no more, for he wished to dance. And in another hour the second fiddler laid down his, and said he wanted to dance, too; so there was only the third fiddler left, and he was a' old, veteran man, very weak in the wrist. However, he managed to keep up a faltering tweedle-dee; but there being no chair in the room, and his knees being as weak as his wrists, he was obliged to sit upon as much of the little corner-table as projected beyond the corner-cupboard fixed over it, which was not a very wide seat for a man advanced in years.

'Among those who danced most continually were the two engaged couples, as was natural to their situation. Each pair was very well matched, and very unlike the other. James Hardcome's intended was called Emily Darth, and both she and James were gentle, nice-minded, in-door people, fond of a quiet life. Steve and his chosen, named Olive Pawle, were different; they were of a more bustling nature, fond of racketing about and seeing what was going on in the world. The two couples had arranged to get married on the same day, and that not long thence; Tony's wedding being a sort of stimulant, as is often the case; I've noticed it professionally many times.

'They danced with such a will as only young people in that stage of courtship can dance; and it happened that as the evening wore on James had for his partner Stephen's plighted one, Olive, at the same time that Stephen was dancing with James's Emily. It was noticed that in spite o' the exchange the young men seemed to enjoy the dance no less than before. By and by they were treading another tune in the same changed order as we had noticed earlier, and though at first each one had held the other's mistress strictly at half-arm's length, lest there should be shown any objection to too close quarters by the lady's proper man, as time passed there was a little more closeness between 'em; and presently a little more closeness still.

'The later it got the more did each of the two cousins dance with the wrong young girl, and the tighter did he hold her to his side as he whirled her round; and, what was very remarkable, neither seemed to mind what the other was doing. The party began to draw towards its end, and I saw no more that night, being one of the first to leave, on account of my morning's business. But I learnt the rest of it from those that knew.

'After finishing a particularly warming dance with the changed partners, as I've mentioned, the two young men looked at one another, and in a moment or two went out into the porch together.

'"James," says Steve, "what were you thinking of when you were dancing with my Olive?"

'"Well," said James, "perhaps what you were thinking of when you were dancing with my Emily."

'"I was thinking," said Steve, with some hesitation, "that I wouldn't mind changing for good and all!"

'"It was what I was feeling likewise," said James.

'"I willingly agree to it, if you think we could manage it."

'"So do I. But what would the girls say?"

'"'Tis my belief," said Steve, "that they wouldn't particularly object. Your Emily clung as close to me as if she already belonged to me, dear girl."

'"And your Olive to me," says James. "I could feel her heart beating like a clock."

'Well, they agreed to put it to the girls when they were all four walking home together. And they did so. When they parted that night the exchange was decided on – all having been done under the hot excitement of that evening's dancing. Thus it happened that on the following Sunday morning, when the people were sitting in the church with mouths wide open to hear the names published as they had expected, there was no small amazement to hear them coupled the wrong way, as it seemed. The congregation whispered, and thought the parson had made a mistake; till they discovered that his reading of the names was verily the true way. As they had decided, so they were married, each one to the other's original property.

'Well, the two couples lived on for a year or two ordinarily enough, till the time came when these young people began to grow a little less warm to their respective spouses, as is the rule of married life; and the two cousins wondered more and more in their hearts what had made 'em so mad at the last moment to marry crosswise as they did, when they might have married straight, as was planned by Nature, and as they had fallen in love. 'Twas Tony's party that had done it, plain enough, and they half wished they had never gone there. James, being a quiet, fireside, perusing man, felt at times a wide gap between himself and Olive, his wife, who loved riding and driving and outdoor jaunts to a degree; while Steve, who was always knocking about hither and thither, had a very domestic wife, who worked samplers, and made hearthrugs, scarcely ever wished to cross the threshold, and only drove out with him to please him.

'However, they said very little about this mismating to any of their acquaintances, though sometimes Steve would look at James's wife, and sigh, and James would look at Steve's wife and do the same. Indeed, at last the two men were frank enough towards each other not to mind mentioning it quietly to themselves, in a long-faced, sorry-smiling, whimsical sort of way, and would shake their heads together over their foolishness in upsetting a well-considered choice on the strength of an hour's fancy in the whirl and wildness of a dance. Still, they were sensible and honest fellows enough, and did their best to make shift with their lot as they had arranged it, and not to repine at what could not now be altered or mended.

'So things remained till one fine summer day then went for their yearly little outing together, as they had made it their custom to do for a long while past. This year they chose Budmouth-Regis as the place to spend their holiday in; and off they went in their best clothes at nine o'clock in the morning.

'When they had reached Budmouth-Regis they walked two and two along the shore – their new boots going squeakity-squash upon the clammy velvet sands. I can seem to see 'em now! Then they looked at the ships in the harbour; and then went up to the Look-out; and then had dinner at an inn, and then again walked two and two, squeakity-squash, upon the velvet sands. As evening drew on they sat on one of the public seats upon the Esplanade, and listened to the band; and then they said, "What shall we do next?"

'"Of all things," said Olive (Mrs James Hardcome, that is), "I should like to row in the bay! We could listen to the music from the water as well as from here, and have the fun of rowing besides."

'"The very thing; so should I," says Stephen, his tastes being always like hers.'

Here the clerk turned to the curate.

'But you, sir, know the rest of the strange particulars of that strange evening of their lives better than anybody else, having had much of it from their own lips, which I had not; and perhaps you'll oblige the gentleman?'

'Certainly, if it is wished,' said the curate. And he took up the clerk's tale:

'Stephen's wife hated the sea, except from land, and couldn't bear the thought of going into a boat. James, too, disliked the water, and said that for his part he would much sooner stay on and listen to the band in the seat they occupied, though he did not wish to stand in his wife's way if she desired a row. The end of the discussion was that James and his cousin's wife Emily agreed to remain where they were sitting and enjoy the music, while they watched the other two hire a boat just beneath, and take their water-excursion of half an hour or so, till they should choose to come back and join the sitters on the Esplanade; when they would all start homeward together.

'Nothing could have pleased the other two restless ones better than this arrangement; and Emily and James watched them go down to the boatman below and choose one of the little yellow skiffs, and walk carefully out upon the little plank that was laid on trestles to enable them to get alongside the craft. They saw Stephen hand Olive in, and take his seat facing her; when they were settled they waved their hands to the couple watching them, and then Stephen took the pair of sculls and pulled off to the tune beat by the band, she steering through the other boats skimming about, for the sea was smooth as glass that evening, and pleasure-seekers were rowing everywhere.

'"How pretty they look moving on, don't they?" said Emily to James (as I've been assured). "They both enjoy it equally. In everything their likings are the same."

'"That's true," said James.

'"They would have made a handsome pair if they had married," said she.

'"Yes," said he. "'Tis a pity we should have parted 'em."

'"Don't talk of that, James," said she. "For better or for worse we decided to do as we did, and there's an end of it."

'They sat on after that without speaking, side by side, and the band played as before; the people strolled up and down; and Stephen and Olive shrank smaller and smaller as they shot straight out to sea. The two on shore used to relate how they saw Stephen stop rowing a moment, and take off his coat to get at his work better; but James's wife sat quite still in the stern, holding the tiller-ropes by which she steered the boat. When they had got very small indeed she turned her head to shore.

'"She is waving her handkerchief to us," said Stephen's wife, who thereupon pulled out her own, and waved it as a return signal.

'The boat's course had been a little awry while Mrs James neglected her steering to wave her handkerchief to her husband and Mrs Stephen; but now the light skiff went straight onward again, and they could soon see nothing more of the two figures it contained than Olive's light mantle and Stephen's white shirt-sleeves behind.

'The two on the shore talked on. "'Twas very curious – our changing partners at Tony Kytes's wedding," Emily declared. "Tony was of a fickle nature by all account, and it really seemed as if his character had infected us that night. Which of you two was it that first proposed not to marry as we were engaged?"

'"H'm – I can't remember at this moment," says James. "We talked it over, you know; and no sooner said than done."

'"'Twas the dancing," said she. "People get quite crazy sometimes in a dance."

'"They do," he owned.

'"James – do you think they care for one another still?" asks Mrs Stephen.

'James Hardcome mused and admitted that perhaps a little tender feeling might flicker up in their hearts for a moment now and then. "Still, nothing of any account," he said.

'"I sometimes think that Olive is in Steve's mind a good deal," murmurs Mrs Stephen; "particularly when she pleases his fancy by riding past our window at a gallop on one of the draught-horses... I never could do anything of that sort; I could never get over my fear of a horse."

'"And I am no horseman, though I pretend to be on her account," murmured James Hardcome. "But isn't it almost time for them to turn and sweep round to the shore, as the other boating folk have done? I wonder what Olive means by steering away straight to the horizon like that? She has hardly swerved from a direct line seaward since they started."

'"No doubt they are talking, and don't think of where they are going," suggests Stephen's wife.

'"Perhaps so," said James. "I didn't know Steve could row like that."

'"O yes," says she. "He often comes here on business, and generally has a pull round the bay."

'"I can hardly see the boat or them," says James again; "and it is getting dark."

'The heedless pair afloat now formed a mere speck in the films of the coming night, which thickened apace, till it completely swallowed up their distant shapes. They had disappeared while still following the same straight course away from the world of land-livers, as if they were intending to drop over the sea-edge into space, and never return to earth again.

'The two on the shore continued to sit on, punctually abiding by their agreement to remain on the same spot till the others returned. The Esplanade lamps were lit one by one, the bandsmen folded up their stands and departed, the yachts in the bay hung out their riding lights, and the little boats came back to shore one after another, their hirers walking on to the sands by the plank they had climbed to go afloat; but among these Stephen and Olive did not appear.

'"What a time they are!" said Emily. "I am getting quite chilly. I did not expect to have to sit so long in the evening air."

'Thereupon James Hardcome said that he did not require his overcoat, and insisted on lending it to her.

'He wrapped it round Emily's shoulders.

'"Thank you, James," she said. "How cold Olive must be in that thin jacket!"

'He said he was thinking so, too. "Well, they are sure to be quite close at hand by this time, though we can't see 'em. The boats are not all in yet. Some of the rowers are fond of paddling along the shore to finish out their hour of hiring."

'"Shall we walk by the edge of the water," said she, "to see if we can discover them?"

'He assented, reminding her that they must not lose sight of the seat, lest the belated pair should return and miss them, and be vexed that they had not kept the appointment.

'They walked a sentry-beat up and down the sands immediately opposite the seat; and still the others did not come. James Hardcome at last went to the boatman, thinking that after all his wife and cousin might have come in under shadow of the dusk without being perceived, and might have forgotten the appointment at the bench.

'"All in?" asked James.

'"All but one boat," said the lessor. "I can't think where that couple is keeping to. They might run foul of something or other in the dark."

'Again Stephen's wife and Olive's husband waited, with more and more anxiety. But no little yellow boat returned. Was it possible they could have landed further down the Esplanade?

'"It may have been done to escape paying," said the boat-owner. "But they didn't look like people who would do that."

'James Hardcome knew that he could found no hope on such a reason as that. But now, remembering what had been casually discussed between Steve and himself about their wives from time to time, he admitted for the first time the possibility that their old tenderness had been revived by their face-to-face position more strongly than either had anticipated at starting – the excursion having been so obviously undertaken for the pleasure of the performance only – and that they had landed at some steps he knew of further down towards the pier, to be longer alone together.

'Still he disliked to harbour the thought, and would not mention its existence to his companion. He merely said to her, "Let us walk further on."

'They did so, and lingered between the boat-stage and the pier till Stephen Hardcome's wife was uneasy, and was obliged to accept James's offered arm. Thus the night advanced. Emily was presently so worn out by fatigue that James felt it necessary to conduct her home; there was, too, a remote chance that the truants had landed in the harbour on the other side of the town, or elsewhere, and hastened home in some unexpected way, in the belief that their consorts would not have waited so long.

'However, he left a direction in the town that a look-out should be kept, though this was arranged privately, the bare possibility of an elopement being enough to make him reticent; and, full of misgivings, the two remaining ones hastened to catch the last train out of Budmouth-Regis; and when they got to Casterbridge drove back to Upper Longpuddle.'

'Along this very road as we do now,' remarked the parish clerk.

'To be sure – along this very road,' said the curate. 'However, Stephen and Olive were not at their homes; neither had entered the village since leaving it in the morning. Emily and James Hardcome went to their respective dwellings to snatch a hasty night's rest, and at daylight the next morning they drove again to Casterbridge and entered the Budmouth train, the line being just opened.

'Nothing had been heard of the couple there during this brief absence. In the course of a few hours some young men testified to having seen such a man and woman rowing in a frail hired craft, the head of the boat kept straight to sea; they had sat looking in each other's faces as if they were in a dream, with no consciousness of what they were doing, or whither they were steering. It was not till late that day that more tidings reached James's ears. The boat had been found drifting bottom upward a long way from land. In the evening the sea rose somewhat, and a cry spread through the town that two bodies were cast ashore in Lulwind Bay, several miles to the eastward. They were brought to Budmouth, and inspection revealed them to be the missing pair. It was said that they had been found tightly locked in each other's arms, his lips upon hers, their features still wrapt in the same calm and dream-like repose which had been observed in their demeanour as they had glided along.

'Neither James nor Emily questioned the original motives of the unfortunate man and woman in putting to sea. They were both above suspicion as to intention. Whatever their mutual feelings might have led them on to, underhand behaviour at starting was foreign to the nature of either. Conjecture pictured that they might have fallen into tender reverie while gazing each into a pair of eyes that had formerly flashed for him and her alone, and, unwilling to avow what their mutual sentiments were, they had done no more than continue thus, oblivious of time and space, till darkness suddenly overtook them far from land. But nothing was truly known. It had been their destiny to die thus. The two halves, intended by Nature to make the perfect whole, had failed in that result during their lives, though "in their death they were not divided". Their bodies were brought home, and buried on one day. I remember that, on looking round the churchyard while reading the service, I observed nearly all the parish at their funeral.'

'It was so, sir,' said the clerk.

'The remaining two,' continued the curate (whose voice had grown husky while relating the lovers' sad fate), 'were a more thoughtful and far-seeing, though less romantic, couple than the first. They were now mutually bereft of a companion, and found themselves by this accident in a position to fulfil their destiny according to Nature's plan and their own original and calmly-formed intention. James Hardcome took Emily to wife in the course of a year and a half; and the marriage proved in every respect a happy one. I solemnized the service, Hardcome having told me, when he came to give notice of the proposed wedding, the story of his first wife's loss almost word for word as I have told it to you.'

'And are they living in Longpuddle still?' asked the new-comer.

'O no, sir,' interposed the clerk. 'James has been dead these dozen years, and his mis'ess about six or seven. They had no children. William Privett used to be their odd man till he died.'

'Ah – William Privett! He dead, too? – dear me!' said the other. 'All passed away!'

'Yes, sir. William was much older than I. He'd ha' been over eighty if he had lived till now.'

'There was something very strange about William's death – very strange indeed!' sighed a melancholy man in the back of the van. It was the seedman's father, who had hitherto kept silence.

'And what might that have been?' asked Mr Lackland.

THE SUPERSTITIOUS MAN'S STORY

'William, as you may know, was a curious, silent man; you could feel when he came near 'ee; and if he was in the house or anywhere behind your back without your seeing him, there seemed to be something clammy in the air, as if a cellar door was opened close by your elbow. Well, one Sunday, at a time that William was in very good health to all appearance, the bell that was ringing for church went very heavy all of a sudden; the sexton, who told me o't, said he'd not known the bell go so heavy in his hand for years – and he feared it meant a death in the parish. That was on the Sunday, as I say. During the week after, it chanced that William's wife was staying up late one night to finish her ironing, she doing the washing for Mr and Mrs Hardcome. Her husband had finished his supper and gone to bed as usual some hour or two before. While she ironed she heard him coming downstairs; he stopped to put on his boots at the stair-foot, where he always left them, and then came on into the living-room where she was ironing, passing through it towards the door, this being the only way from the staircase to the outside of the house. No word was said on either side, William not being a man given to much speaking, and his wife being occupied with her work. He went out and closed the door behind him. As her husband had now and then gone out in this way at night before when unwell, or unable to sleep for want of a pipe, she took no particular notice, and continued at her ironing. This she finished shortly after, and as he had not come in she waited a while for him, putting away the irons and things, and preparing the table for his breakfast in the morning. Still he did not return, and supposing him not far off, and wanting to get to bed herself, tired as she was, she left the door unbarred and went to the stairs, after writing on the back of the door with chalk: *Mind and do the door* (because he was a forgetful man).

'To her great surprise, and I might say alarm, on reaching the foot of the stairs his boots were standing there as they always stood when he had gone to rest; going up to their chamber she found him in bed sleeping as sound as a rock. How he could have got back again without her seeing or hearing him was beyond her comprehension. It could only have been by passing behind her very quietly while she was bumping with the iron. But this notion did not satisfy her: it was surely impossible that she should not have seen him come in through a room so small. She could not unravel the mystery, and felt very queer and uncomfortable about it. However, she would not disturb him to question him then, and went to bed herself.

'He rose and left for his work very early the next morning, before she was awake, and she waited his return to breakfast with much anxiety for an explanation, for thinking over the matter by daylight made it seem only the more startling. When he came in to the meal he said, before she could put her question, "What's the meaning of them words chalked on the door?"

'She told him, and asked him about his going out the night before. William declared that he had never left the bedroom after entering it, having in fact undressed, lain down, and fallen asleep directly, never once waking till the clock struck five, and he rose up to go to his labour.

'Betty Privett was as certain in her own mind that he did go out as she was of her own existence, and was little less certain that he did not return. She felt too disturbed to argue with him, and let the subject drop as though she must have been mistaken. When she was walking down Longpuddle street later in the day she met Jim Weedle's daughter Nancy, and said, "Well, Nancy, you do look sleepy today!"

'"Yes, Mrs Privett," says Nancy. "Now don't tell anybody, but I don't mind letting you know what the reason o't is. Last night, being Old Midsummer Eve, some of us went to church porch, and didn't get home till near one."

'"Did ye?" says Mrs Privett. "Old Midsummer yesterday, was it? Faith I didn't think whe'r 'twas Midsummer or Michaelmas; I'd too much work to do."

'"Yes. And we were frightened enough, I can tell 'ee, by what we saw."

'"What did ye see?"

'(You may not remember, sir, having gone off to foreign parts so young, that on Midsummer Night it is believed hereabout that the faint shapes of all the folk in the parish who are going to be at death's door within the year can be seen entering the church. Those who get over their illness come out again after a while; those that are doomed to die do not return.)

'"What did you see?" asked William's wife.

'"Well," says Nancy, backwardly – "we needn't tell what we saw, or who we saw."

'"You saw my husband," says Betty Privett, in a quiet way.

'"Well, since you put it so," says Nancy, hanging fire, "we – thought we did see him; but it was darkish, and we was frightened, and of course it might not have been he."

'"Nancy, you needn't mind letting it out, though 'tis kept back in kindness. And he didn't come out of church again: I know it as well as you."

'Nancy did not answer yes or no to that, and no more was said. But three days after, William Privett was mowing with John Chiles in Mr Hardcome's meadow, and in the heat of the day they sat down to eat their bit o' nunch under a tree, and empty their flagon. Afterwards both of 'em fell asleep as they sat. John Chiles was the first to wake, and as he looked towards his fellow-mower he saw one of those great white miller's-souls as we call 'em – that is to say, a miller-moth – come from William's open mouth while he slept, and fly straight away. John thought it odd enough, as William had worked in a mill for several years when he was a boy. He then looked at the sun, and found by the place o't that they had slept a long while, and as William did not wake, John called him and said it was high time to begin work again. He took no notice, and then John went up and shook him, and found he was dead.

'Now on that very day old Philip Hookhorn was down at Longpuddle spring dipping up a pitcher of water; and as he turned away, who should he see coming down to the spring on the other side but William, looking very pale and odd. This surprised Philip Hookhorn very much, for years before that time William's little son – his only child – had been drowned in that spring while at play there, and this had so preyed upon William's mind that he'd never been seen near the spring afterwards, and had been known to go half a mile out of his way to avoid the place. On inquiry, it was found that William in body could not have stood by the spring, being in the mead two miles off; and it also came out that the time at which he was seen at the spring was the very time when he died.'

*

'A rather melancholy story,' observed the emigrant, after a minute's silence.

'Yes, yes. Well, we must take ups and downs together,' said the seedman's father.

'You don't know, Mr Lackland, I suppose, what a rum start that was between Andrey Satchel and Jane Vallens and the pa'son and clerk o' Scrimpton?' said the master-thatcher, a man with a spark of subdued liveliness in his eye, who had hitherto kept his attention mainly upon small objects a long way ahead, as he sat in front of the van with his feet outside. 'Theirs was a queerer experience of a pa'son and clerk than some folks get and may cheer 'ee up a little after this dampness that's been flung over yer soul.'

The returned one replied that he knew nothing of the history, and should be happy to hear it, quite recollecting the personality of the man Satchel.

'Ah, no; this Andrey Satchel is the son of the Satchel that you knew; this one has not been married more than two or three years, and 'twas at the time o' the wedding that the accident happened that I could tell 'ee of, or anybody else here, for that matter.'

'No, no; you must tell it, neighbour, if anybody,' said several; a request in which Mr Lackland joined, adding that the Satchel family was one he had known well before leaving home.

'I'll just mention, as you be a stranger,' whispered the carrier to Lackland, 'that Christopher's stories will bear pruning.'

The emigrant nodded.

'Well, I can soon tell it,' said the master-thatcher, schooling himself to a tone of actuality. 'Though as it has more to do with the pa'son and clerk than with Andrey himself, it ought to be told by a better churchman than I.

ANDREY SATCHEL AND THE PARSON AND CLERK

'It all arose, you must know, from Andrey being fond of a drop of drink at that time – though he's a sober enough man now by all account, so much the better for him. Jane, his bride, you see, was somewhat older than Andrey; how much older I don't pretend to say; she was not one of our parish, and the register alone may be able to tell that. But, at any rate, her being a little ahead of her young man in mortal years, coupled with other bodily circumstances owing to that young man –'

('Ah, poor thing!' sighed the women.)

'– made her very anxious to get the thing done before he changed his mind; and 'twas with a joyful countenance (they say) that she, with Andrey and his brother and sister-in-law, marched off to church one November morning as soon as 'twas day a'most to be made one with Andrey for the rest of her life. He had left our place long before it was light, and the folks that were up all waved their lanterns at him, and flung up their hats as he went.

'The church of her parish was a mile and more from where she lived, and, as it was a wonderful fine day for the time of year, the plan was that as soon as they were married they would make out a holiday by driving straight off to Port Bredy, to see the ships and the sea and the sojers, instead of coming back to a meal at the house of the distant relation she lived wi', and moping about there all the afternoon.

'Well, some folks noticed that Andrey walked with rather wambling steps to church that morning; the truth o't was that his nearest neighbour's child had been christened the day before, and Andrey, having stood godfather, had stayed all night keeping up the christening, for he had said to himself, "Not if I live to be a thousand shall I again be made a godfather one day, and a husband the next, and perhaps a father the next, and therefore I'll make the most of the blessing." So that when he started from home in the morning he had not been in bed at all. The result was, as I say, that when he and his bride-to-be walked up the church to get married, the pa'son (who was a very strict man inside the church, whatever he was outside) looked hard at Andrey, and said, very sharp:

'"How's this, my man? You are in liquor. And so early, too. I'm ashamed of you!"

'"Well, that's true, sir," says Andrey. "But I can walk straight enough for practical purposes. I can walk a chalk line," he says (meaning no offence), "as well as some other folk: and" – (getting hotter) – "I reckon that if you, Pa'son Billy Toogood, had kept up a christening all night so thoroughly as I have done, you wouldn't be able to stand at all; d— me if you would!"

'This answer made Pa'son Billy – as they used to call him – rather spitish, not to say hot, for he was a warm-tempered man if provoked, and he said, very decidedly: "Well, I cannot marry you in this state; and I will not! Go home and get sober!" And he slapped the book together like a rat-trap.

'Then the bride burst out crying as if her heart would break, for very fear that she would lose Andrey after all her hard work to get him, and begged and implored the pa'son to go on with the ceremony. But no.

'"I won't be a party to your solemnizing matrimony with a tipsy man," says Mr Toogood. "It is not right and decent. I am sorry for you, my young woman, seeing the condition you are in, but you'd better go home again. I wonder how you could think of bringing him here drunk like this!"

'"But if – if he don't come drunk he won't come at all, sir!" she says, through her sobs.

'"I can't help that," says the pa'son; and plead as she might, it did not move him. Then she tried him another way.

'"Well, then, if you'll go home, sir, and leave us here, and come back to the church in an hour or two, I'll undertake to say that he shall be as sober as a judge," she cries. "We'll bide here, with your permission; for if he once goes out of this here church unmarried, all Van Amburgh's horses won't drag him back again!"

'"Very well," says the parson. "I'll give you two hours, and then I'll return."

'"And please, sir, lock the door, so that we can't escape!" says she.

'"Yes," says the parson.

'"And let nobody know that we are here."

'The pa'son then took off his clane white surplice, and went away; and the others consulted upon the best means for keeping the matter a secret, which it was not a very hard thing to do, the place being so lonely, and the hour so early. The witnesses, Andrey's brother and brother's wife, neither one o' which cared about Andrey's marrying Jane, and had come rather against their will, said they couldn't wait two hours in that hole of a place, wishing to get home to Longpuddle before dinner-time. They were altogether so crusty that the clerk said there was no difficulty in their doing as they wished. They could go home as if their brother's wedding had actually taken place and the married couple had gone onward for their day's pleasure jaunt to Port Bredy as intended. He, the clerk, and any casual passer-by would act as witnesses when the pa'son came back.

'This was agreed to, and away Andrey's relations went, nothing loath, and the clerk shut the church door and prepared to lock in the couple. The bride went up and whispered to him, with her eyes a-streaming still.

'"My dear good clerk," she says, "if we bide here in the church, folk may see us through the windows, and find out what has happened; and 'twould cause such a talk and scandal that I never should get over it: and perhaps, too, dear Andrey might try to get out and leave me! Will ye lock us up in the tower, my dear good clerk?" she says. "I'll tole him in there if you will."

'The clerk had no objection to do this to oblige the poor young woman, and they toled Andrey into the tower, and the clerk locked 'em both up straightway, and then went home, to return at the end of the two hours.

'Pa'son Toogood had not been long in his house after leaving the church when he saw a gentleman in pink and top-boots ride past his windows, and with a sudden flash of heat he called to mind that the hounds met that day just on the edge of his parish. The pa'son was one who dearly loved sport, and much he longed to be there.

'In short, except o' Sundays and at tide-times in the week, Pa'son Billy was the life o' the hunt. 'Tis true that he was poor, and that he rode all of a heap, and that his black mare was rat-tailed and old, and his tops older, and all over of one colour, whitey-brown, and full o' cracks. But he'd been in at the death of three thousand foxes. And – being a bachelor man – every time he went to bed in summer he used to open the bed at bottom and crawl up head foremost, to mind en of the coming winter and the good sport he'd have, and the foxes going to earth. And whenever there was a christening at the Squire's, and he had dinner there afterwards, as he always did, he never failed to christen the chiel over again in a bottle of port wine.

'Now the clerk was the pa'son's groom and gardener and general manager, and had just got back to his work in the garden when he, too, saw the hunting man pass, and presently saw lots more of 'em, noblemen and gentry, and then he saw the hounds, the huntsman, Jim Treadhedge, the whipper-in, and I don't know who besides. The clerk loved going to cover as frantical as the pa'son, so much so that whenever he saw or heard the pack he could no more rule his feelings than if they were the winds of heaven. He might be bedding, or he might be sowing – all was forgot. So he throws down his spade and rushes in to the pa'son, who was by this time as frantical to go as he.

'"That there mare of yours, sir, do want exercise bad, very bad, this morning!" the clerk says, all of a tremble. "Don't ye think I'd better trot her round the downs for an hour, sir?"

'"To be sure, she does want exercise badly. I'll trot her round myself," says the pa'son.

'"Oh – you'll trot her yerself? Well, there's the cob, sir. Really that cob is getting oncontrollable through biding in a stable so long! If you wouldn't mind my putting on the saddle—"

'"Very well. Take him out, certainly," says the pa'son, never caring what the clerk did so long as he himself could get off immediately. So, scrambling into his riding-boots and breeches as quick as he could, he rode off towards the meet, intending to be back in an hour. No sooner was he gone than the clerk mounted the cob, and was off after him. When the pa'son got to the meet he found a lot of friends, and was as jolly as he could be; the hounds found a'most as soon as they threw off, and there was great excitement. So, forgetting that he had meant to go back at once, away rides the pa'son with the rest o' the hunt, all across the fallow ground that lies between Lippet Wood and Green's Copse; and as he galloped he looked behind for a moment, and there was the clerk close to his heels.

'"Ha, ha, clerk – you here?" he says.

'"Yes, sir, here be I," says t'other.

'"Fine exercise for the horses!"

'"Ay, sir – hee, hee!" says the clerk.

'So they went on and on, into Green's Copse, then across to Higher Jirton; then on across this very turnpike-road to Waterston Ridge, then away towards Yalbury Wood: up hill and down dale, like the very wind, the clerk close to the pa'son, and the pa'son not far from the hounds. Never was there a finer run knowed with that pack than they had that day; and neither pa'son nor clerk thought one word about the unmarried couple locked up in the church tower waiting to get j'ined.'

'"These hosses of yours, sir, will be much improved by this!" says the clerk as he rode along, just a neck behind the pa'son. "'Twas a happy thought of your reverent mind to bring 'em out today. Why, it may be frosty and slippery in a day or two, and then the poor things mid not be able to leave the stable for weeks."

'"They may not, they may not, it is true. A merciful man is merciful to his beast," says the pa'son.

'"Hee, hee!" says the clerk, glancing sly into the pa'son's eye.

'"Ha, ha!" says the pa'son, a-glancing back into the clerk's. "Halloo!" he shouts, as he sees the fox break cover at that moment.

'"Halloo!" cries the clerk. "There he goes! Why, dammy, there's two foxes—"

'"Hush, clerk, hush! Don't let me hear that word again! Remember our calling."

'"True, sir, true. But really, good sport do carry away a man so, that he's apt to forget his high persuasion!" And the next minute the corner of the clerk's eye shot again into the corner of the pa'son's, and the pa'son's back again to the clerk's. "Hee, hee!" said the clerk.

'"Ha, ha!" said Pa'son Toogood.

'"Ah, sir," says the clerk again, "this is better than crying Amen to your Ever-and-ever on a winter's morning!"

'"Yes, indeed, clerk! To everything there's a season," says Pa'son Toogood, quite pat, for he was a learned Christian man when he liked, and had chapter and ve'se at his tongue's end, as a pa'son should.

'At last, late in the day, the hunting came to an end by the fox running into a' old woman's cottage, under her table, and up the clock-case. The pa'son and clerk were among the first in at the death, their faces a-staring in at the old woman's winder, and the clock striking as he'd never been heard to strik' before. Then came the question of finding their way home.

'Neither the pa'son nor the clerk knowed how they were going to do this, for their beasts were wellnigh tired down to the ground. But they started back-along as well as they could, though they were so done up that they could only drag along at a' amble, and not much of that at a time.

'"We shall never, never get there!" groaned Mr Toogood, quite bowed down.

'"Never!" groans the clerk. "'Tis a judgment upon us for our iniquities!"

'"I fear it is," murmured the pa'son.

'Well, 'twas quite dark afore they entered the pa'sonage gate, having crept into the parish as quiet as if they'd stole a hammer, little wishing their congregation to know what they'd been up to all day long. And as they were so dog-tired, and so anxious about the horses, never once did they think of the unmarried people. As soon as ever the horses had been stabled and fed, and the pa'son and clerk had had a bit and a sup theirselves, they went to bed.

'Next morning when Pa'son Toogood was at breakfast, thinking of the glorious sport he'd had the day before, the clerk came in a hurry to the door and asked to see him.

'"It has just come into my mind, sir, that we've forgot all about the couple that we was to have married yesterday!"

'The half-chawed victuals dropped from the pa'son's mouth as if he'd been shot. "Bless my soul," says he, "so we have! How very awkward!"

'"It is, sir; very. Perhaps we've ruined the 'ooman!"

'"Ah – to be sure – I remember! She ought to have been married before."

'"If anything has happened to her up in that there tower, and no doctor or nuss –"'

('Ah – poor thing!' sighed the women.)

'"–'twill be a quarter-sessions matter for us, not to speak of the disgrace to the Church!"

'"Good God, clerk, don't drive me wild!" says the pa'son. "Why the hell didn't I marry 'em, drunk or sober!" (Pa'sons used to cuss in them days like plain honest men.) "Have you been to the church to see what happened to them, or inquired in the village?"

'"Not I, sir! It only came into my head a moment ago, and I always like to be second to you in church matters. You could have knocked me down with a sparrow's feather when I thought o't, sir; I assure 'ee you could!"

'Well, the pa'son jumped up from his breakfast, and together they went off to the church.

'"It is not at all likely that they are there now," says Mr Toogood, as they went; "and indeed I hope they are not. They be pretty sure to have escaped and gone home."

'However, they opened the church-hatch, entered the churchyard, and looking up at the tower there they seed a little small white face at the belfry-winder, and a little small hand waving. 'Twas the bride.

'"God my life, clerk," says Mr Toogood. "I don't know how to face 'em!" And he sank down upon a tombstone. "How I wish I hadn't been so cussed particular!"

'"Yes – 'twas a pity we didn't finish it when we'd begun," the clerk said. "Still, since the feelings of your holy priestcraft wouldn't let ye, the couple must put up with it."

'"True, clerk, true! Does she look as if anything premature had took place?"

'"I can't see her no lower down than her arm-pits, sir."

'Well – how do her face look?"

'"It do look mighty white!"

'"Well, we must know the worst! Dear me, how the small of my back do ache from that ride yesteday! . . . But to more godly business!"

'They went on into the church, and unlocked the tower stairs, and immediately poor Jane and Andrey busted out like starved mice from a cupboard, Andrey limp and sober enough now, and his bride pale and cold, but otherwise as usual.

'"What," says the pa'son with a great breath of relief, "you haven't been here ever since?"

'"Yes, we have, sir!" says the bride, sinking down upon a seat in her weakness. "Not a morsel, wet or dry, have we had since! It was impossible to get out without help, and here we've stayed!"

'"But why didn't you shout, good souls!" said the pa'son.

'"She wouldn't let me," says Andrey.

'"Because we were so ashamed at what had led to it," sobs Jane. "We felt that if it were noised abroad it would cling to us all our lives! Once or twice Andrey had a good mind to toll the bell, but then he said: 'No; I'll starve first. I won't bring disgrace on my name and yours, my dear.' And so we waited and waited, and walked round and round; but never did you come till now!"

'"To my regret!" says the pa'son. "Now, then, we will soon get it over."

'"I – I should like some victuals," said Andrey; "'twould gie me courage to do it, if it is only a crust o' bread and a' onion; for I am that leery that I can feel my stomach rubbing against my backbone."

'"I think we had better get it done," said the bride, a bit anxious in manner; "since we are all here convenient, too!"

'Andrey gave way about the victuals, and the clerk called in a second witness who wouldn't be likely to gossip about it, and soon the knot was tied, and the bride looked smiling and calm forthwith, and Andrey limper than ever.

'"Now," said Pa'son Toogood, "you two must come to my house, and have a good lining put to your insides before you go a step further."

'They were very glad of the offer, and went out of the churchyard by one path while the pa'son and clerk went out by the other, and so did not attract notice, it being still early. They entered the rectory as if they'd just come back from their trip to Port Bredy; and then they knocked in the victuals and drink till they could hold no more.

'It was a long while before the story of what they had gone through was known, but it was talked of in time, and they themselves laugh over it now; though what Jane got for her pains was no great bargain after all. 'Tis true she saved her name.'

'Was that the same Andrey who went to the squire's house as one of the Christmas fiddlers?' asked the seedsman.

'No, no,' replied Mr Profitt, the schoolmaster. 'It was his father did that. Ay, it was all owing to his being such a man for eating and drinking.' Finding that he had the ear of the audience, the schoolmaster continued without delay:

OLD ANDREY'S EXPERIENCE AS A MUSICIAN

'I was one of the quire-boys at that time, and we and the players were to appear at the manor-house as usual that Christmas week, to play and sing in the hall to the Squire's people and visitors (among 'em being the archdeacon, Lord and Lady Baxby, and I don't know who); afterwards going, as we always did, to have a good supper in the servants' hall. Andrew knew this was the custom, and meeting us when we were starting to go, he said to us: "Lord, how I should like to join in that meal of beef, and turkey, and plum-pudding, and ale, that you happy ones be going to just now! One more or less will make no difference to the Squire. I am too old to pass as a singing boy, and too bearded to pass as a singing girl; can ye lend me a fiddle, neighbours, that I may come with ye as a bandsman?"

'Well, we didn't like to be hard upon him, and lent him an old one, though Andrew knew no more of music than the Giant o' Cernel; and armed with the instrument he walked up to the Squire's house with the others of us at the time appointed, and went in boldly, his fiddle under his arm. He made himself as natural as he could in opening the music-books and moving the candles to the best points for throwing light upon the notes; and all went well till we had played and sung "While shepherds watch", and "Star, arise", and "Hark the glad sound". Then the Squire's mother, a tall gruff old lady, who was much interested in church music, said quite unexpectedly to Andrew: "My man, I see you don't play your instrument with the rest. How is that?"

'Every one of the quire was ready to sink into the earth with concern at the fix Andrew was in. We could see that he had fallen into a cold sweat, and how he would get out of it we did not know.

'"I've had a misfortune, mem," he says, bowing as meek as a child. "Coming along the road I fell down and broke my bow."

'"O, I am sorry to hear that" says she. "Can't it be mended?"

'"O no, mem," says Andrew. "'Twas broke all to splinters."

'"I'll see what I can do for you," says she.

'And then it seemed all over, and we played "Rejoice, ye drowsy mortals all", in D and two sharps. But no sooner had we got through it than she says to Andrew:

'"I've sent up into the attic, where we have some old musical instruments, and found a bow for you." And she hands the bow to poor wretched Andrew, who didn't even know which end to take hold of. "Now we shall have the full accompaniment," says she.

'Andrew's face looked as if it were made of rotten apple as he stood in the circle of players in front of his book; for if there was one person in the parish that everybody was afraid of, 'twas this hook-nosed old lady. However, by keeping a little behind the next man he managed to make pretence of beginning, sawing away with his bow without letting it touch the strings, so that it looked as if he were driving into the tune with heart and soul. 'Tis a question if he wouldn't have got through all right if one of the Squire's visitors (no other than the archdeacon) hadn't noticed that he held the fiddle upside down, the nut under his chin, and the tail-piece in his hand; and they began to crowd round him, thinking 'twas some new way of performing.

'This revealed everything; the Squire's mother had Andrew turned out of the house as a vile impostor, and there was great interruption to the harmony of the proceedings, the Squire declaring he should have notice to leave his cottage that day fortnight. However, when we got to the servants' hall there sat Andrew, who had been let in at the back door by the orders of the Squire's wife, after being turned out at the front by the orders of the Squire, and nothing more was heard about his leaving his cottage. But Andrew never performed in public as a musician after that night; and now he's dead and gone, poor man, as we all shall be!'

'I had quite forgotten the old choir, with their fiddles and bass-viols,' said the home-comer, musingly. 'Are they still going on the same as of old?'

'Bless the man!' said Christopher Twink, the master-thatcher; 'why, they've been done away with these twenty year. A young teetotaller plays the organ in church now, and plays it very well; though 'tis not quite such good music as in old times, because the organ is one of them that go with a winch, and the young teetotaller says he can't always throw the proper feeling into the tune without wellnigh working his arms off.'

'Why did they make the change, then?'

'Well, partly because of fashion, partly because the old musicians got into a sort of scrape. A terrible scrape, 'twas, too – wasn't it, John? I shall never forget it – never! They lost their character as officers of the church as complete as if they'd never had any character at all.'

'That was very bad for them.'

'Yes.' The master-thatcher attentively regarded past times as if they lay about a mile off, and went on:

ABSENT-MINDEDNESS IN A PARISH CHOIR

'It happened on Sunday after Christmas – the last Sunday ever they played in Longpuddle church gallery, as it turned out, though they didn't know it then. As you may know, sir, the players formed a very good band – almost as good as the Mellstock parish players that were led by the Dewys; and that's saying a great deal. There was Nicholas Puddingcome, the leader, with the first fiddle; there was Timothy Thomas, the bass-viol man; John Biles, the tenor fiddler, Dan'l Hornhead, with the serpent; Robert Dowdle, with the clarionet; and Mr Nicks, with the oboe – all sound and powerful musicians, and strong-winded men – they that blowed. For that reason they were very much in demand Christmas week for little reels and dancing parties: for they could turn a jig or a hornpipe out of hand as well as ever they could turn out a psalm, and perhaps better, not to speak irreverent. In short, one half-hour they could be playing a Christmas carol in the Squire's hall to the ladies and gentlemen, and drinking tay and coffee with 'em as modest as saints; and the next, at The Tinker's Arms, blazing away like wild horses with the "Dashing White Sergeant" to nine couple of dancers and more, and swallowing rum-and-cider hot as flame.

'Well, this Christmas they'd been out to one rattling randy after another every night, and had got next to no sleep at all. Then came the Sunday after Christmas, their fatal day. 'Twas so mortal cold that year that they could hardly sit in the gallery; for though the congregation down in the body of the church had a stove to keep off the frost, the players in the gallery had nothing at all. So Nicholas said at morning service, when 'twas freezing an inch an hour, "Please the Lord I won't stand this numbing weather no longer: this afternoon we'll have something in our insides to make us warm, if it cost a king's ransom."

'So he brought a gallon of hot brandy and beer, ready mixed, to church with him in the afternoon, and by keeping the jar well wrapped up in Timothy Thomas's bass-viol bag it kept drinkably warm till they wanted it, which was just a thimbleful in the Absolution, and another after the Creed, and the remainder at the beginning o' the sermon. When they'd had the last pull they felt quite comfortable and warm, and as the sermon went on – most unfortunately for 'em it was a long one that afternoon – they fell asleep, every man jack of 'em; and there they slept on as sound as rocks.

''Twas a very dark afternoon, and by the end of the sermon all you could see of the inside of the church were the pa'son's two candles alongside of him in the pulpit, and his spaking face behind 'em. The sermon being ended at last, the pa'son gie'd out the Evening Hymn. But no quire set about sounding up the tune, and the people began to turn their heads to learn the reason why, and then Levi Limpet, a boy who sat in the gallery, nudged Timothy and Nicholas, and said, "Begin! begin!"

'"Hey? what" says Nicholas, starting up; and the church being so dark and his head so muddled he thought he was at the party they had played at all the night before, and away he went, bow and fiddle, at "The Devil among the Tailors", the favourite jig of our neighbourhood at that time. The rest of the band, being in the same state of mind and nothing doubting, followed their leader with all their strength, according to custom. They poured out that there tune till the lower bass notes of "The Devil among the Tailors" made the cobwebs in the roof shiver like ghosts; then Nicholas, seeing nobody moved, shouted out as he scraped (in his usual commanding way at dances when the folk didn't know the figures), "Top couples cross hands! And when I make the fiddle squeak at the end, every man kiss his pardner under the mistletoe!"

'The boy Levi was so frightened that he bolted down the gallery stairs and out homeward like lightning. The pa'son's hair fairly stood on end when he heard the evil tune raging through the church, and thinking the quire had gone crazy he held up his hand and said: "Stop, stop, stop! Stop, stop! What's this?" But they didn't hear'n for the noise of their own playing, and the more he called the louder they played.

'Then the folks came out of their pews, wondering down to the ground, and saying: "What do they mean by such wickedness! We shall be consumed like Sodom and Gomorrah!"

'And the Squire, too, came out of his pew lined wi' green baize, where lots of lords and ladies visiting at the house were worshipping along with him, and went and stood in front of the gallery, and shook his fist in the musicians' faces, saying, "What! In this reverent edifice! What!"

'And at last they heard'n through their playing, and stopped.

'"Never such an insulting, disgraceful thing – never!" says the Squire, who couldn't rule his passion.

'"Never!" says the pa'son, who had come down and stood beside him.

'"Not if the Angels of Heaven," says the Squire (he was a wickedish man, the Squire was, though now for once he happened to be on the Lord's side) – "not if the Angels of Heaven come down," he says, "shall one of you villainous players ever sound a note in this church again; for the insult to me, and my family, and my visitors, and the pa'son, and God Almighty, that you've a-perpetrated this afternoon!"

'Then the unfortunate church band came to their senses, and remembered where they were; and 'twas a sight to see Nicholas Puddingcome and Timothy Thomas and John Biles creep down the gallery stairs with their fiddles under their arms, and poor Dan'l Hornhead with his serpent, and Robert Dowdle with his clarionet, all looking as little as ninepins; and out they went. The pa'son might have forgi'ed 'em when he learned the truth o't, but the Squire would not. That very week he sent for a barrel-organ that would play two-and-twenty new psalm-tunes, so exact and particular that, however sinful inclined you was, you could play nothing but psalm-tunes whatsomever. He had a really respectable man to turn the winch, as I said, and the old players played no more.'

'And, of course, my old acquaintance, the annuitant, Mrs Winter, who always seemed to have something on her mind, is dead and gone?' said the home-comer, after a long silence.

Nobody in the van seemed to recollect the name.

'O yes, she must be dead long since: she was seventy when I as a child knew her,' he added.

'I can recollect Mrs Winter very well, if nobody else can,' said the aged groceress. 'Yes, she's been dead these five-and-twenty year at least. You knew what it was upon her mind, sir, that gave her that hollow-eyed look, I suppose?'

'It had something to do with a son of hers, I think I once was told. But I was too young to know particulars.'

The groceress sighed as she conjured up a vision of days long past. 'Yes,' she murmured, 'it had all to do with a son.' Finding that the van was still in a listening mood, she spoke on:

THE WINTERS AND THE PALMLEYS

'To go back to the beginning – if one must – there were two women in the parish when I was a child, who were to a certain extent rivals in good looks. Never mind particulars, but in consequence of this they were at daggers-drawn, and they did not love each other any better when one of them tempted the other's lover away from her and married him. He was a young man of the name of Winter, and in due time they had a son.

'The other woman did not marry for many years: but when she was about thirty a quiet man named Palmley asked her to be his wife, and she accepted him. You don't mind when the Palmleys were Longpuddle folk, but I do well. She had a son also, who was, of course, nine or ten years younger than the son of the first. The child proved to be of rather weak intellect, though his mother loved him as the apple of her eye.

'This woman's husband died when the child was eight years old, and left his widow and boy in poverty. Her former rival, also a widow now, but fairly well provided for, offered for pity's sake to take the child as errand-boy, small as he was, her own son, Jack, being hard upon seventeen. Her poor neighbour could do no better than let the child go there. And to the richer woman's house little Palmley straightway went.

'Well, in some way or other – how, it was never exactly known – the thriving woman, Mrs Winter, sent the little boy with a message to the next village one December day, much against his will. It was getting dark, and the child prayed to be allowed not to go, because he would be afraid coming home. But the mistress insisted, more out of thoughtlessness than cruelty, and the child went. On his way back he had to pass through Yalbury Wood, and something came out from behind a tree and frightened him into fits. The child was quite ruined by it; he became quite a drivelling idiot, and soon afterward died.

'Then the other woman had nothing left to live for, and vowed vengeance against the rival who had first won away her lover, and now had been the cause of her bereavement. This last affliction was certainly not intended by her thriving acquaintance, though it must be owned that when it was done she seemed but little concerned. Whatever vengeance poor Mrs Palmley felt, she had no opportunity of carrying it out, and time might have softened her feelings into forgetfulness of her supposed wrongs as she dragged on her lonely life. So matters stood when, a year after the death of the child, Mrs Palmley's niece, who had been born and bred in the city of Exonbury, came to live with her.

'This young woman – Miss Harriet Palmley – was a proud and handsome girl, very well brought up, and more stylish and genteel than the people of our village, as was natural, considering where she came from. She regarded herself as much above Mrs Winter and her son in position as Mrs Winter and her son considered themselves above poor Mrs Palmley. But love is an unceremonious thing, and what in the world should happen but that young Jack Winter must fall woefully and wildly in love with Harriet Palmley almost as soon as he saw her.

'She, being better educated than he, and caring nothing for the village notion of his mother's superiority to her aunt, did not give him much encouragement. But Longpuddle being being no very large world, the two could not help seeing a good deal of each other while she was staying there, and, disdainful young woman as she was, she did seem to take a little pleasure in his attentions and advances.

'One day when they were picking apples together, he asked her to marry him. She had not expected anything so practical as that at so early a time, and was led by her surprise into a half-promise; at any rate, she did not absolutely refuse him, and accepted some little presents that he made her.

'But he saw that her view of him was rather as a simple village lad than as a young man to look up to, and he felt that he must do something bold to secure her. So he said one day, "I am going away, to try to get into a better position than I can get here." In two or three weeks he wished her good-bye, and went away to Monksbury, to superintend a farm, with a view to start as a farmer himself; and from there he wrote regularly to her, as if their marriage were an understood thing.

'Now Harriet liked the young man's presents and the admiration of his eyes; but on paper he was less attractive to her. Her mother had been a schoolmistress, and Harriet had besides a natural aptitude for pen-and-ink work, in days when to be a ready writer was not such a common thing as it is now, and when actual handwriting was valued as an accomplishment in itself. Jack Winter's performances in the shape of love-letters quite jarred her city nerves and her finer taste, and when she answered one of them, in the lovely running hand that she took such pride in, she very strictly and loftily bade him to practise with a pen and spelling-book if he wished to please her. Whether he listened to her request or not nobody knows, but his letters did not improve. He ventured to tell her in his clumsy way that if her heart were more warm towards him she would not be so nice about his handwriting and spelling; which indeed was true enough.

'Well, in Jack's absence the weak flame that had been set alight in Harriet's heart soon sank low, and at last went out altogether. He wrote and wrote, and begged and prayed her to give a reason for her coldness; and then she told him plainly that she was town born, and he was not sufficiently well educated to please her.

'Jack Winter's want of pen-and-ink training did not make him less thin-skinned than others; in fact, he was terribly tender and touchy about anything. This reason that she gave for finally throwing him over grieved him, shamed him, and mortified him more than can be told in these times, the pride of that day in being able to write with beautiful flourishes, and the sorrow at not being able to do so, raging so high. Jack replied to her with an angry note, and then she hit back with smart little stings, telling him how many words he had misspelt in his last letter, and declaring again that this alone was sufficient justification for any woman to put an end to an understanding with him. Her husband must be a better scholar.

'He bore her rejection of him in silence, but his suffering was sharp – all the sharper in being untold. She communicated with Jack no more; and as his reason for going out into the world had been only to provide a home worthy of her, he had no further object in planning such a home now that she was lost to him. He therefore gave up the farming occupation by which he had hoped to make himself a master-farmer, and left the spot to return to his mother.

'As soon as he got back to Longpuddle he found that Harriet had already looked wi' favour upon another lover. He was a young road-contractor, and Jack could not but admit that his rival was both in manners and scholarship much ahead of him. Indeed, a more sensible match for the beauty who had been dropped into the village by fate could hardly have been found than this man, who could offer her so much better a chance than Jack would have done, with his uncertain future and narrow abilities for grappling with the world. The fact was so clear to him that he could hardly blame her.

'One day by accident Jack saw on a scrap of paper the handwriting of Harriet's new beloved. It was flowing like a stream, well spelt, the work of a man accustomed to the ink-bottle and the dictionary, of a man already called in the parish a good scholar. And then it struck all of a sudden into Jack's mind what a contrast the letters of this young man must make to his own miserable old letters, and how ridiculous they must make his lines appear. He groaned and wished he had never written to her, and wondered if she had ever kept his poor performances. Possibly she had kept them, for women are in the habit of doing that, he thought, and whilst they were in her hands there was always a chance of his honest, stupid love-assurances to her being joked over by Harriet with her present lover, or by anybody who should accidentally uncover them.

'The nervous, moody young man could not bear the thought of it, and at length decided to ask her to return them, as was proper when engagements were broken off. He was some hours in framing, copying, and recopying the short note in which he made his request, and having finished it he sent it to her house. His messenger came back with the answer, by word of mouth, that Miss Palmley bade him say she should not part with what was hers, and wondered at his boldness in troubling her.

'Jack was much affronted at this, and determined to go for his letters himself. He chose a time when he knew she was at home, and knocked and went in without much ceremony; for though Harriet was so high and mighty, Jack had small respect for her aunt, Mrs Palmley, whose little child had been his boot-cleaner in earlier days. Harriet was in the room, this being the first time they had met since she had jilted him. He asked for his letters with a stern and bitter look at her.

'At first she said he might have them for all that she cared, and took them out of the bureau where she kept them. Then she glanced over the outside one of the packet, and suddenly altering her mind, she told him shortly that his request was a silly one, and slipped the letters into her aunt's work-box, which stood open on the table, locking it and saying with a bantering laugh that of course she thought it best to keep 'em, since they might be useful to produce as evidence that she had good cause for declining to marry him.

'He blazed up hot. "Give me those letters!" he said. They are mine!"

'"No, they are not," she replied; "they are mine."

'"Who'sever they are I want them back," says he. "I don't want to be made sport of for my penmanship: you've another young man now! He has your confidence, and you pour all your tales into his ear. You'll be showing them to him!"

'"Perhaps," said my lady Harriet, with calm coolness, like the heartless woman that she was.

'Her manner so maddened him that he made a step towards the work-box, but she snatched it up, locked it in the bureau, and turned upon him triumphant. For a moment he seemed to be going to wrench the key of the bureau out of her hand; but he stopped himself, and swung round upon his heel and went away.

'When he was out-of-doors alone, and it got night, he walked about restless, and stinging with the sense of being beaten at all points by her. He could not help fancying her telling her new lover or her acquaintances of this scene with himself, and laughing with them over those poor blotted, crooked lines of his that he had been so anxious to obtain. As the evening passed on he worked himself into a dogged resolution to have them back at any price, come what might.

'At the dead of night he came out of his mother's house by the back door, and creeping through the garden hedge went along the field adjoining till he reached the back of her aunt's dwelling. The moon struck bright and flat upon the walls, 'twas said, and every shiny leaf of the creepers was like a little looking-glass in the rays. From long acquaintance Jack knew the arrangement and position of everything in Mrs Palmley's house as well as in his own mother's. The back window close to him was a casement with little leaded squares, as it is to this day, and was, as now, one of two lighting the sitting-room. The other, being in front, was closed up with shutters, but this back one had not even a blind, and the moonlight as it streamed in showed every article of the furniture to him outside. To the right of the room is the fireplace, as you may remember; to the left was the bureau at that time; inside the bureau was Harriet's work-box, as he supposed (though it was really her aunt's), and inside the work-box were his letters. Well, he took out his pocket-knife, and without noise lifted the leading of one of the panes, so that he could take out the glass, and putting his hand through the hole he unfastened the casement, and climbed in through the opening. All the household – that is to say, Mrs Palmley, Harriet, and the little maidservant – were asleep. Jack went straight to the bureau, so he said, hoping it might have been unfastened again – it not being kept locked in ordinary – but Harriet had never unfastened it since she secured her letters there the day before. Jack told afterward how he thought of her asleep upstairs, caring nothing for him, and of the way she had made sport of him and of his letters; and having advanced so far, he was not to be hindered now. By forcing the large blade of his knife under the flap of the bureau, he burst the weak lock; within was the rosewood work-box just as she had placed it in her hurry to keep it from him. There being no time to spare for getting the letters out of it then, he took it under his arm, shut the bureau, and made the best of his way out of the house, latching the casement behind him, and refixing the pane of glass in its place.

'Winter found his way back to his mother's as he had come, and being dog-tired, crept upstairs to bed, hiding the box till he could destroy its contents. The next morning early he set about doing this, and carried it to the linhay at the back of his mother's dwelling. Here by the hearth he opened the box, and began burning one by one the letters that had cost him so much labour to write and shame to think of, meaning to return the box to Harriet, after repairing the slight damage he had caused it by opening it without a key, with a note – the last she would ever receive from him – telling her triumphantly that in refusing to return what he had asked for she had calculated too surely upon his submission to her whims.

'But on removing the last letter from the box he received a shock; for underneath it, at the very bottom, lay money – several golden guineas – "Doubtless Harriet's pocket-money," he said to himself; though it was not, but Mrs Palmley's. Before he had got over his qualms at the discovery he heard footsteps coming through the house-passage to where he was. In haste he pushed the box and what was in it under some brushwood which lay in the linhay; but Jack had been already seen. Two constables entered the out-house, and seized him as he knelt before the fireplace, securing the work-box and all it contained at the same moment. They had come to apprehend him on a charge of breaking into the dwelling-house of Mrs Palmley on the night preceding; and almost before the lad knew what had happened to him they were leading him along the lane that connects that end of the village with this turnpike-road, and along they marched him between 'em all the way to Casterbridge jail.

'Jack's act amounted to night burglary – though he had never thought of it – and burglary was felony, and a capital offence in those days. His figure had been seen by some one against the bright wall as he came away from Mrs Palmley's back window, and the box and money were found in his possession, while the evidence of the broken bureau-lock and tinkered window-pane was more than enough for circumstantial detail. Whether his protestation that he went only for his letters, which he believed to be wrongfully kept from him, would have availed him anything if supported by other evidence I do not know; but the one person who could have borne it out was Harriet, and she acted entirely under the sway of her aunt. That aunt was deadly towards Jack Winter. Mrs Palmley's time had come. Here was her revenge upon the woman who had first won away her lover, and next ruined and deprived her of her heart's treasure – her little son. When the assize week drew on, and Jack had to stand his trial, Harriet did not appear in the case at all, which was allowed to take its course, Mrs Palmley testifying to the general facts of the burglary. Whether Harriet would have come forward if Jack had appealed to her is not known; possibly she would have done it for pity's sake; but Jack was too proud to ask a single favour of a girl who had jilted him; and he let her alone. The trial was a short one, and the death sentence was passed.

'The day o' young Jack's execution was a cold dusty Saturday in March. He was so boyish and slim that they were obliged in mercy to hang him in the heaviest fetters kept in the jail, lest his heft should not break his neck, and they weighed so upon him that he could hardly drag himself up to the drop. At that time the gover'ment was not strict about burying the body of an executed person within the precincts of the prison, and at the earnest prayer of his poor mother his body was allowed to be brought home. All the parish waited at their cottage doors in the evening for its arrival: I remember how, as a very little girl, I stood by my mother's side. About eight o'clock, as we hearkened on our door-stones in the cold bright starlight, we could hear the faint crackle of a waggon from the direction of the turnpike-road. The noise was lost as the waggon dropped into a hollow, then it was plain again as it lumbered down the next long incline, and presently it entered Longpuddle. The coffin was laid in the belfry for the night, and the next day, Sunday, between the services, we buried him. A funeral sermon was preached the same afternoon, the text chosen being, "He was the only son of his mother, and she was a widow." . . . Yes, they were cruel times!

'As for Harriet, she and her lover were married in due time; but by all account her life was no jocund one. She and her goodman found that they could not live comfortably at Longpuddle, by reason of her connection with Jack's misfortunes, and they settled in a distant town, and were no more heard of by us; Mrs Palmley, too, found it advisable to join 'em shortly after. The dark-eyed, gaunt old Mrs Winter, remembered by the emigrant gentleman here, was, as you will have foreseen, the Mrs Winter of this story; and I can well call to mind how lonely she was, how afraid the children were of her, and how she kept herself as a stranger among us, though she lived so long.'

'Longpuddle has had her sad experiences as well as her sunny ones,' said Mr Lackland.

'Yes, yes. But I am thankful to say not many like that, though good and bad have lived among us.'

'There was Georgy Crookhill – he was one of the shady sort, as I have reason to know,' observed the registrar, with the manner of a man who would like to have his say also.

'I used to hear what he was as a boy at school.'

'Well, as he began so he went on. It never got so far as a hanging matter with him, to be sure; but he had some narrow escapes of penal servitude; and once it was a case of the biter bit.'

INCIDENT IN THE LIFE OF MR GEORGE CROOKHILL

'One day,' the registrar continued, 'Georgy was ambling out of Melchester on a miserable screw, the fair being just over, when he saw in front of him a fine-looking young farmer riding out of the town in the same direction. He was mounted on a good strong handsome animal, worth fifty guineas if worth a crown. When they were going up Bissett Hill, Georgy made it his business to overtake the young farmer. They passed the time o' day to one another; Georgy spoke of the state of the roads, and jogged alongside the well-mounted stranger in very friendly conversation. The farmer had not been inclined to say much to Georgy at first, but by degrees he grew quite affable, too – as friendly as Georgy was towards him. He told Crookhill that he had been doing business at the Melchester fair, and was going on as far as Shottsford-Forum that night, so as to reach Casterbridge market the next day. When they came to Woodyates Inn they stopped to bait their horses, and agreed to drink together; with this they got more friendly than ever, and on they went again. Before they had nearly reached Shottsford it came on to rain, and as they were now passing through the village of Trantridge, and it was quite dark, Georgy persuaded the young farmer to go no further that night; the rain would most likely give them a chill. For his part he had heard that the little inn here was comfortable, and he meant to stay. At last the young farmer agreed to put up there also; and they dismounted, and entered, and had a good supper together, and talked over their affairs like men who had known and proved each other a long time. When it was the hour for retiring they went upstairs to a double-bedded room which Georgy Crookhill had asked the landlord to let them share, so sociable were they.

'Before they fell asleep they talked across the room about one thing and another, running from this to that till the conversation turned upon disguises, and changing clothes for particular ends. The farmer told Georgy that he had often heard tales of people doing it; but Crookhill professed to be very ignorant of all such tricks; and soon the young farmer sank into slumber.

'Early in the morning, while the tall young farmer was still asleep (I tell you the story as 'twas told me), honest Georgy crept out of his bed by stealth, and dressed himself in the farmer's clothes, in the pockets of the said clothes being the farmer's money. Now though Georgy particularly wanted the farmer's nice clothes and nice horse, owing to a little transaction at the fair which made it desirable that he should not be too easily recognized, his desires had their bounds: he did not wish to take his young friend's money, at any rate more of it than was necessary for paying his bill. This he abstracted, and leaving the farmer's purse containing the rest on the bedroom table, went downstairs. The inn folks had not particularly noticed the faces of their customers, and the one or two who were up at this hour had no thought but that Georgy was the farmer; so when he had paid the bill very liberally, and said he must be off, no objection was made to his getting the farmer's horse saddled for himself; and he rode away upon it as if it were his own.

'About half an hour after, the young farmer awoke, and looking across the room saw that his friend Georgy had gone away in clothes which didn't belong to him, and had kindly left for himself the seedy ones worn by Georgy. At this he sat up in a deep thought for some time, instead of hastening to give an alarm. "The money, the money is gone," he said to himself, "and that's bad. But so are the clothes."

'He then looked upon the table and saw that the money, or most of it, had been left behind.

'"Ha, ha, ha!" he cried, and began to dance about the room. "Ha, ha, ha!" he said again, and made beautiful smiles to himself in the shaving-glass and in the brass candlestick; and then swung about his arms for all the world as if he were going through the sword exercise.

'When he had dressed himself in Georgy's clothes and gone downstairs, he did not seem to mind at all that they took him for the other; and even when he saw that he had been left a bad horse for a good one, he was not inclined to cry out. They told him his friend had paid the bill, at which he seemed much pleased, and without waiting for breakfast he mounted Georgy's horse and rode away likewise, choosing the nearest by-lane in preference to the highroad, without knowing that Georgy had chosen that by-lane also.

'He had not trotted more than two miles in the personal character of Georgy Crookhill when, suddenly rounding a bend that the lane made thereabout, he came upon a man struggling in the hands of two village constables. It was his friend Georgy, the borrower of his clothes and horse. But so far was the young farmer from showing any alacrity in rushing forward to claim his property that he would have turned the poor beast he rode into the wood adjoining, if he had not been already perceived. '"Help, help, help!" cried the constables. "Assistance in the name of the Crown!"

'The young farmer could do nothing but ride forward. "What's the matter?" he inquired, as coolly as he could.

'"A deserter – a deserter!" said they. "One who's to be tried by court-martial and shot without parley. He deserted from the Dragoons at Cheltenham some days ago, and was tracked; but the search-party can't find him anywhere, and we told 'em if we met him we'd hand him on to 'em forthwith. The day after he left the barracks the rascal met a respectable farmer and made him drunk at an inn, and told him what a fine soldier he would make, and coaxed him to change clothes, to see how well a military uniform would become him. This the simple farmer did; when our deserter said that for a joke he would leave the room and go to the landlady, to see if she would know him in that dress. He never came back, and Farmer Jollice found himself in soldier's clothes, the money in his pockets gone, and, when he got to the stable, his horse gone, too."

'"A scoundrel!" says the young man in Georgy's clothes. "And is this the wretched caitiff?" (pointing to Georgy).

'"No, no!" cries Georgy, as innocent as a babe of this matter of the soldier's desertion. "He's the man! He was wearing Farmer Jollice's suit o' clothes, and he slept in the same room wi' me, and brought up the subject of changing clothes, which put it into my head to dress myself in his suit before he was awake. He's got on mine!"

'"D'ye hear the villain?" groans the tall young man to the constables. "Trying to get out of his crime by charging the first innocent man with it that he sees! No, master soldier – that won't do!"

'"No, no! That won't do!" the constables chimed in. "To have the impudence to say such as that, when we caught him in the act almost! But, thank God, we've got the handcuffs on him at last."

'"We have, thank God," said the tall young man. "Well, I must move on. Good luck to ye with your prisoner!" And off he went, as fast as his poor jade would carry him.

The constables then, with Georgy handcuffed between 'em, and leading the horse, marched off in the other direction, towards the village where they had been accosted by the escort of soldiers sent to bring the deserter back, Georgy groaning: "I shall be shot, I shall be shot!" They had not gone more than a mile before they met them.

'"Hoi, there!" says the head constable.

'"Hoi, yerself!" says the corporal in charge.

'"We've got your man," says the constable.

'"Where?" says the corporal.

'"Here, between us," said the constable. "Only you don't recognize him out o' uniform."

'The corporal looked at Georgy hard enough; then shook his head and said he was not the absconder.

'"But the absconder changed clothes with Farmer Jollice, and took his horse; and this man has 'em, d'ye see!"

'" 'Tis not our man," said the soldiers. "He's a tall young fellow with a mole on his right cheek, and a military bearing, which this man decidedly has not."

'"I told the two officers of justice that 'twas the other!" pleaded Georgy. "But they wouldn't believe me."

'And so it became clear that the missing dragoon was the tall young farmer, and not Georgy Crookhill – a fact which Farmer Jollice himself corroborated when he arrived on the scene. As Georgy had only robbed the robber, his sentence was comparatively light. The deserter from the Dragoons was never traced: his double shift of clothing having been of the greatest advantage to him in getting off; though he left Georgy's horse behind him a few miles ahead, having found the poor creature more hindrance than aid.'

The man from abroad seemed to be less interested in the questionable characters of Longpuddle and their strange adventures than in the ordinary inhabitants and the ordinary events, though his local fellow-travellers preferred the former as subjects of discussion. He now for the first time asked concerning young persons of the opposite sex – or rather those who had been young when he left his native land. His informants, adhering to their own opinion that the remarkable was better worth telling than the ordinary, would not allow him to dwell upon the simple chronicles of those who had merely come and gone. They asked him if he remembered Netty Sargent.

'Netty Sargent – I do, just remember her. She was a young woman living with her uncle when I left, if my childish recollection may be trusted.'

'That was the maid. She was a oneyer, if you like, sir. Not any harm in her, you know, but up to everything. You ought to hear how she got the copyhold of her house extended. Oughtn't he, Mr Day?'

'He ought,' replied the world-ignored old painter.

'Tell him, Mr Day. Nobody can do it better than you, and you know the legal part better than some of us.'

Day apologized, and began:

NETTY SARGENT'S COPYHOLD

'She continued to live with her uncle, in the lonely house by the copse, just as at the time you knew her; a tall spry young woman. Ah, how well one can remember her black hair and dancing eyes at that time, and her sly way of screwing up her mouth when she meant to tease ye! Well, she was hardly out of short frocks before the chaps were after her, and by long and by late she was courted by a young man whom perhaps you did not know – Jasper Cliff was his name – and, though she might have had many a better fellow, he so greatly took her fancy that 'twas Jasper or nobody for her. He was a selfish customer, always thinking less of what he was going to do than of what he was going to gain by his doings. Jasper's eyes might have been fixed upon Netty, but his mind was upon her uncle's house; though he was fond of her in his way – I admit that.

'This house, built by her great-great-grandfather, with its garden and little field, was copyhold – granted upon lives in the old way, and had been so granted for generations. Her uncle's was the last life upon the property; so that at his death, if there was no admittance of new lives, it would all fall into the hands of the lord of the manor. But 'twas easy to admit – a slight "fine", as 'twas called, of a few pounds, was enough to entitle him to a new deed o' grant by the custom of the manor; and the lord could not hinder it.

'Now there could be no better provision for his niece and only relative than a sure house over her head, and Netty's uncle should have seen to the renewal in time, owing to the peculiar custom of forfeiture by the dropping of the last life before the new fine was paid; for the Squire was very anxious to get hold of the house and land; and every Sunday when the old man came into the church and passed the Squire's pew, the Squire would say, "A little weaker in his knees, a little crookeder in his back – and the re-admittance not applied for: ha! ha! I shall be able to make a complete clearing of that corner of the manor some day!"

''Twas extraordinary, now we look back upon it, that old Sargent should have been so dilatory; yet some people are like it; and he put off calling at the Squire's agent's office with the fine week after week, saying to himself, "I shall have more time next market-day than I have now." One unfortunate hindrance was that he didn't very well like Jasper Cliff, and as Jasper kept urging Netty, and Netty on that account kept urging her uncle, the old man was inclined to postpone the reliveing as long as he could, to spite the selfish young lover. At last old Mr Sargent fell ill, and then Jasper could bear it no longer: he produced the fine-money himself, and handed it to Netty, and spoke to her plainly.

'"You and your uncle ought to know better. You should press him more. There's the money. If you let the house and ground slip between ye, I won't marry; hang me if I will! For folks won't deserve a husband that can do such things."

'The worried girl took the money and went home, and told her uncle that it was no house no husband for her. Old Mr Sargent pooh-poohed the money, for the amount was not worth consideration, but he did now bestir himself, for he saw she was bent upon marrying Jasper, and he did not wish to make her unhappy, since she was so determined. It was much to the Squire's annoyance that he found Sargent had moved in the matter at last; but he could not gainsay it, and the documents were prepared (for on this manor the copyholders had writings with their holdings, though on some manors they had none). Old Sargent being now too feeble to go to the agent's house, the deed was to be brought to his house signed, and handed over as a receipt for the money; the counterpart to be signed by Sargent, and sent back to the Squire.

'The agent had promised to call on old Sargent for this purpose at five o'clock, and Netty put the money into her desk to have it close at hand. While doing this she heard a slight cry from her uncle, and turning round, saw that he had fallen forward in his chair. She went and lifted him, but he was unconscious; and unconscious he remained. Neither medicine nor stimulants would bring him to himself. She had been told that he might possibly go off in that way, and it seemed as if the end had come. Before she had started for the doctor his face and extremities grew quite cold and white, and she saw that help would be useless. He was stone-dead.

'Netty's situation rose upon her distracted mind in all its seriousness. The house, garden, and field were lost – by a few hours – and with them a home for herself and her lover. She would not think so meanly of Jasper as to suppose that he would adhere to the resolution declared in a moment of impatience; but she trembled, nevertheless. Why could not her uncle have lived a couple of hours longer, since he had lived so long? It was now past three o'clock; at five the agent was to call, and, if all had gone well, by ten minutes past five the house and holding would have been securely hers for her own and Jasper's lives, these being two of the three proposed to be added by paying the fine. How that wretched old Squire would rejoice at getting the little tenancy into his hands! He did not really require it, but constitutionally hated these tiny copyholds and leaseholds and freeholds, which made islands of independence in the fair, smooth ocean of his estates.

'Then an idea struck into the head of Netty how to accomplish her object in spite of her uncle's negligence. It was a dull December afternoon: and the first step in her scheme – so the story goes, and I see no reason to doubt it—'

''Tis true as the light,' affirmed Christopher Twink. 'I was just passing by.'

'The first step in her scheme was to fasten the outer door, to make sure of not being interrupted. Then she set to work by placing her uncle's small, heavy oak table before the fire; then she went to her uncle's corpse, sitting in the chair as he had died – a stuffed arm-chair, on casters, and rather high in the seat, so it was told me – and wheeled the chair, uncle and all, to the table, placing him with his back towards the window, in the attitude of bending over the said oak table, which I knew as a boy as well as I know any piece of furniture in my own house. On the table she laid the large family Bible open before him, and placed his forefinger on the page; and then she opened his eyelids a bit, and put on him his spectacles, so that from behind he appeared for all the world as if he were reading the Scriptures. Then she unfastened the door and sat down, and when it grew dark she lit a candle, and put it on the table beside her uncle's book.

'Folk may well guess how the time passed with her till the agent came, and how, when his knock sounded upon the door, she nearly started out of her skin – at least that's as it was told me. Netty promptly went to the door.

'"I am sorry, sir," she says, under her breath; "my uncle is not so well tonight, and I'm afraid he can't see you."

'"H'm! – that's a pretty tale," says the steward. "So I've come all this way about this trumpery little job for nothing!"

'"O no, sir – I hope not," says Netty. "I suppose the business of granting the new deed can be done just the same?"

'"Done? Certainly not. He must pay the renewal money, and sign the parchment in my presence."

'She looked dubious. "Uncle is dreadful nervous about law business," says she, "that, as you know, he's put it off and put if off for years; and now today really I've feared it would verily drive him out of his mind. His poor three teeth quite chattered when I said to him that you would be here soon with the parchment writing. He always was afraid of agents, and folks that come for rent, and such-like."

'"Poor old fellow – I'm sorry for him. Well, the thing can't be done unless I see him and witness his signature."

'"Suppose, sir, tht you see him sign, and he don't see you looking at him! I'd soothe his nerves by saying you weren't strict about the form of witnessing, and didn't wish to come in. So that it was done in your bare presence it would be sufficient, would it not? As he's such an old, shrinking, shivering man, it would be a great considerateness on your part if that would do."

'"In my bare presence would do, of course – that's all I come for. But how can I be a witness without his seeing me?"

'"Why, in this way, sir; if you'll oblige me by just stepping here." She conducted him a few yards to the left, till they were opposite the parlour window. The blind had been left up purposely, and the candle-light shone out upon the garden bushes. Within the agent could see, at the other end of the room, the back and side of the old man's head, and his shoulders and arm, sitting with the book and candle before him, and his spectacles on his nose, as she had placed him.

'"He's reading his Bible, as you see, sir," she says, quite in her meekest way.

'"Yes. I thought he was a careless sort of man in matters of religion?"

'"He always was fond of his Bible," Netty assured him. "Though I think he's nodding over it just at this moment. However, that's natural in an old man, and unwell. Now you could stand here and see him sign, couldn't you, sir, as he's such an invalid?"

'"Very well," said the agent, lighting a cigar. "You have ready by you the merely nominal sum you'll have to pay for the admittance, of course?"

'"Yes," said Netty. "I'll bring it out." She fetched the cash, wrapped in paper, and handed it to him, and when he had counted it the steward took from his breast pocket the precious parchments and gave one to her to be signed.

'"Uncle's hand is a little paralyzed," she said. "And what with his being half asleep, too, really I don't know what sort of a signature he'll be able to make."

'"Doesn't matter, so that he signs."

'"Might I hold his hand?"

'"Ay, hold his hand, my young woman – that will be near enough."

'Netty re-entered the house, and the agent continued smoking outside the window. Now came the ticklish part of Netty's performance. The steward saw her put the inkhorn – "horn", says I in my old-fashioned way – the inkstand, before her uncle, and touch his elbow as if to arouse him, and speak to him, and spread out the deed; when she had pointed to show him where to sign she dipped the pen and put it into his hand. To hold his hand she artfully stepped behind him, so that the agent could only see a little bit of his head, and the hand she held; but he saw the old man's hand trace his name on the document. As soon as 'twas done she came out to the steward with the parchment in her hand, and the steward signed as witness by the light from the parlour window. Then he gave her the deed signed by the Squire, and left; and next morning Netty told the neighbours that her uncle was dead in his bed.'

'She must have undressed him and put him there.'

'She must. O, that girl had a nerve, I can tell ye! Well, to cut a long story short, that's how she got back the house and field that were, strictly speaking, gone from her; and by getting them, got her a husband.

'Every virtue has its reward, they say. Netty had hers for her ingenious contrivance to gain Jasper. Two years after they were married he took to beating her – not hard, you know; just a smack or two, enough to set her in a temper, and let out to the neighbours what she had done to win him, and how she repented of her pains. When the old Squire was dead, and his son came into the property, this confession of hers began to be whispered about. But Netty was a pretty young woman, and the Squire's son was a pretty young man at that time, and wider-minded than his father, having no objection to little holdings; and he never took any proceedings against her.'

There was now a lull in the discourse, and soon the van descended the hill leading into the long straggling village. When the houses were reached the passengers dropped off one by one, each at his or her own door. Arrived at the inn, the returned emigrant secured a bed, and having eaten a light meal, sallied forth upon the scene he had known so well in his early days. Though flooded with the light of the rising moon, none of the objects wore the attractiveness in this their real presentation that had ever accompanied their images in the field of his imagination when he was more than two thousand miles removed from them. The peculiar charm attaching to an old village in an old country, as seen by the eyes of an absolute foreigner, was lowered in his case by magnified expectations from infantine memories. He walked on, looking at this chimney and that old wall, till he came to the churchyard, which he entered.

The head-stones, whitened by the moon, were easily decipherable; and now for the first time Lackland began to feel himself amid the village community that he had left behind him five-and-thirty years before. Here, beside the Sallets, the Darths, the Pawles, the Privetts, the Sargents, and others of whom he had just heard, were names he remembered even better than those: the Jickses, and the Crosses, and the Knights, and the Olds. Doubtless representatives of these families, or some of them, were yet among the living; but to him they would all be as strangers. Far from finding his heart ready-supplied with roots and tendrils here, he perceived that in returning to this spot it would be incumbent upon him to re-establish himself from the beginning, precisely as though he had never known the place, nor it him. Time had not condescended to wait his pleasure, nor local life his greeting.

The figure of Mr Lackland was seen at the inn, and in the village street, and in the fields and lanes about Upper Longpuddle, for a few days after his arrival, and then, ghost-like, it silently disappeared. He had told some of the villagers that his immediate purpose in coming had been fulfilled by a sight of the place, and by conversation with its inhabitants; but that his ulterior purpose – of coming to spend his latter days among them – would probably never be carried out. It is now a dozen or fifteen years since his visit was paid, and his face has not again been seen.

MARCH 1891

A CHANGED MAN
AND OTHER TALES

PREFATORY NOTE TO 'A CHANGED MAN' AND OTHER TALES

I reprint in this volume, for what they may be worth, a dozen minor novels that have been published in the periodical press at various dates in the past, in order to render them accessible to readers who desire to have them in the complete series issued by my publishers. For aid in reclaiming some of the narratives I express my thanks to the proprietors and editors of the newspapers and magazines in whose pages they first appeared.

T.H.

AUGUST 1913

A CHANGED MAN

I

The person who, next to the actors themselves, chanced to know most of their story, lived just below 'Top o' Town' (as the spot was called) in an old substantially-built house, distinguished among its neighbours by having an oriel window on the first floor, whence could be obtained a raking view of the High Street, west and east, the former including Laura's dwelling, the end of the Town Avenue hard by (in which were played the odd pranks hereafter to be mentioned), the Port-Bredy road rising westwards, and the turning that led to the cavalry barracks where the Captain was quartered. Looking eastward down the town from the same favoured gazebo, the long perspective of houses declined and dwindled till they merged in the highway across the moor. The white riband of road disappeared over Grey's Bridge a quarter of a mile off, to plunge into innumerable rustic windings, shy shades, and solitary undulations up hill and down dale for one hundred and twenty miles till it exhibited itself at Hyde Park Corner as a smooth bland surface in touch with a busy and fashionable world.

To the barracks aforesaid had recently arrived the —th Hussars, a regiment new to the locality. Almost before any acquaintance with its members had been made by the townspeople, a report spread that they were a 'crack' body of men, and had brought a splendid band. For some reason or other the town had not been used as the headquarters of cavalry for many years, the various troops stationed there having consisted of casual detachments only; so that it was with a sense of honour that everybody – even the small furniture-broker from whom the married troopers hired tables and chairs – received the news of their crack quality.

In those days the Hussar regiments still wore over the left shoulder that attractive attachment, or frilled half-coat, hanging loosely behind like the wounded wing of a bird, which was called the pelisse, though it was known among the troopers themselves as a 'sling-jacket'. It added amazingly to their picturesqueness in women's eyes, and, indeed, in the eyes of men also.

The burgher who lived in the house with the oriel window sat during a great many hours of the day in that projection, for he was an invalid, and time hung heavily on his hands unless he maintained a contant interest in proceedings without. Not more than a week after the arrival of the Hussars his ears were assailed by the shout of one schoolboy to another in the street below.

'Have 'ee heard this about the Hussars? They are haunted! Yes – a ghost troubles 'em; he has followed 'em about the world for years.'

A haunted regiment: that was a new idea for either invalid or stalwart. The listener in the oriel came to the conclusion that there were some lively characters among the —th Hussars.

He made Captain Maumbry's acquaintance in an informal manner at an afternoon tea to which he went in a wheeled chair – one of the very rare outings that the state of his health permitted. Maumbry showed himself to be a handsome man of twenty-eight or thirty, with an attractive hint of wickedness in his manner that was sure to make him adorable with good young women. The large dark eyes that lit his pale face expressed this wickedness strongly, though such was the adaptability of their rays that one could think they might have expressed sadness or seriousness just as readily, if he had had a mind for such.

An old and deaf lady who was present asked Captain Maumbry bluntly: 'What's this we hear about you? They say your regiment is haunted.'

The Captain's face assumed an aspect of grave, even sad, concern. 'Yes,' he replied, 'it is too true.'

Some younger ladies smiled till they saw how serious he looked, when they looked serious likewise.

'Really?' said the old lady.

'Yes. We naturally don't wish to say much about it.'

'No, no; of course not. But – how haunted?'

'Well; the – *thing*, as I'll call it, follows us. In country quarters or town, abroad or at home, it's just the same.'

'How do you account for it?'

'H'm.' Maumbry lowered his voice. 'Some crime committed by certain of our regiment in past years, we suppose.'

'Dear me. . . How very horrid, and singular!'

'But, as I said, we don't speak of it much.'

'No . . . no.'

When the Hussar was gone, a young lady, disclosing a long-suppressed interest, asked if the ghost had been seen by any of the town.

The lawyer's son, who always had the latest borough news, said that, though it was seldom seen by anyone but the Hussars themselves, more than one townsman and woman had already set eyes on it, to his or her terror. The phantom mostly appeared very late at night, under the dense trees of the town-avenue nearest the barracks. It was about ten feet high; its teeth chattered with a dry naked sound, as if they were those of a skeleton; and its hip-bones could be heard grating in their sockets.

During the darkest weeks of winter several timid persons were seriously frightened by the object answering to this cheerful description, and the police began to look into the matter. Whereupon the appearances grew less frequent, and some of the Boys of the regiment thankfully stated that they had not been so free from ghostly visitation for years as they had become since their arrival in Casterbridge.

This playing at ghosts was the most innocent of the amusements indulged in by the choice young spirits who inhabited the lichened, red-brick building at the top of the town bearing 'W.D.' and a broad arrow on its quoins. Far more serious escapades – levities relating to love, wine, cards, betting – were talked of, with no doubt more or less of exaggeration. That the Hussars, Captain Maumbry included, were the cause of bitter tears to several young women of the town and country is unquestionably true, despite the fact that the gaieties of the young men wore a more staring colour in this old-fashioned place than they would have done in a large and modern city.

2

Regularly once a week they rode out in marching order.

Returning up the town on one of these occasions, the romantic pelisse flapping behind each horseman's shoulder in the soft south-west wind, Captain Maumbry glanced up at the oriel. A mutual nod was exchanged between him and the person who sat there reading. The reader and a friend in the room with him followed the troop with their eyes all the way up the street, till, when the soldiers were opposite the house in which Laura lived, that young lady became discernible in the balcony.

'They are engaged to be married, I hear,' said the friend.

'Who – Maumbry and Laura? Never – so soon?'

'Yes.'

'He'll never marry. Several girls have been mentioned in connection with his name. I am sorry for Laura.'

'Oh, but you needn't be. They are excellently matched.'

'She's only one more.'

'She's one more, and more still. She has regularly caught him. She is a born player of the game of hearts, and she knew how to beat him in his own practices. If there is one woman in the town who has any chance of holding her own and marrying him, she is that woman.'

This was true, as it turned out. By natural proclivity Laura had from the first entered heart and soul into military romance as exhibited in the plots and characters of those living exponents of it who came under her notice. From her earliest young womanhood civilians, however promising, had no chance of winning her interest if the meanest warrior were within the horizon. It may be that the position of her uncle's house (which was her home) at the corner of West Street nearest the barracks, the daily passing of the troops, the constant blowing of trumpet-calls a furlong from her windows, coupled with the fact that she knew nothing of the inner realities of military life, and hence idealized it, had also helped her mind's original bias for thinking men-at-arms the only ones worthy of a woman's heart.

Captain Maumbry was a typical prize; one whom all surrounding maidens had coveted, ached for, angled for, wept for, had by her judicious management become subdued to her purpose; and in addition to the pleasure of marrying the man she loved, Laura had the joy of feeling herself hated by the mothers of all the marriageable girls of the neighbourhood.

The man in the oriel went to the wedding; not as a guest, for at this time he was but slightly acquainted with the parties; but mainly because the church was close to his house; partly, too, for a reason which moved many others to be spectators of the ceremony; a subconsciousness that, though the couple might be happy in their experiences, there was sufficient possibility of their being otherwise to colour the musings of an onlooker with a pleasing pathos of conjecture. He could on occasion do a pretty stroke of rhyming in those days, and he beguiled the time of waiting by pencilling on a blank page of his prayer-book a few lines which, though kept private then, may be given here:

AT A HASTY WEDDING

(Triolet)

If hours be years the twain are blest,
For now they solace swift desire
By lifelong ties that tether zest
If hours be years. The twain are blest
Do eastern suns slope never west,
Nor pallid ashes follow fire.
If hours be years the twain are blest,
For now they solace swift desire.

As if, however, to falsify all prophecies, the couple seemed to find in marriage the secret of perpetuating the intoxication of a courtship which, on Maumbry's side at least, had opened without serious intent. During the winter following they were the most popular pair in and about Casterbridge – nay, in South Wessex itself. No smart dinner in the country houses of the younger and gayer families within driving distance of the borough was complete without their lively presence; Mrs Maumbry was the blithest of the whirling figures at the county ball; and when followed that inevitable incident of garrison-town life, an amateur dramatic entertainment, it was just the same. The acting was for the benefit of such and such an excellent charity – nobody cared what, provided the play were played – and both Captain Maumbry and his wife were in the piece, having been in fact, by mutual consent, the originators of the performance. And so with laughter, and thoughtlessness, and movement, all went merrily. There was a little backwardness in the bill-paying of the couple; but in justice to them it must be added that sooner or later all owings were paid.

3

At the chapel-of-ease attended by the troops there arose above the edge of the pulpit one Sunday an unknown face. This was the face of a new curate. He placed upon the desk, not the familiar sermon book, but merely a Bible. The person who tells these things was not present at that service, but he soon learnt that the young curate was nothing less than a great surprise to his congregation; a mixed one always, for though the Hussars occupied the body of the building, its nooks and corners were crammed with civilians, whom, up to the present, even the least uncharitable would have described as being attracted thither less by the services than by the soldiery.

Now there arose a second reason for squeezing into an already overcrowded church. The persuasive and gentle eloquence of Mr Sainway operated like a charm upon those accustomed only to the higher and drier styles of preaching, and for a time the other churches of the town were thinned of their sitters.

At this point in the nineteenth century the sermon was the sole reason for churchgoing amongst a vast body of religious people. The liturgy was a formal preliminary, which, like the Royal proclamation in a court of assize, had to be got through before the real interest began; and on reaching home the question was simply: Who preached, and how did he handle his subject? Even had an archbishop officiated in the service proper nobody would have cared much about what was said or sung. People who had formerly attended in the morning only began to go in the evening, and even to the special addresses in the afternoon.

One day when Captain Maumbry entered his wife's drawing-room, filled with hired furniture, she thought he was somebody else, for he had not come upstairs humming the most catching air afloat in musical circles or in his usual careless way.

'What's the matter, Jack?' she said without looking up from a note she was writing.

'Well – not much, that I know.'

'O, but there is,' she murmured as she wrote.

'Why – this cursed new lath in a sheet – I mean the new parson! He wants us to stop the band-playing on Sunday afternoons.'

Laura looked up aghast.

'Why, it is the one thing that enables the few rational beings hereabouts to keep alive from Saturday to Monday!'

'He says all the town flock to the music and don't come to the service, and that the pieces played are profane, or mundane, or inane, or something – not what ought to be played on Sunday. Of course 'tis Lautmann who settles those things.'

Lautmann was the bandmaster.

The barrack-green on Sunday afternoons had, indeed, become the promenade of a great many townspeople cheerfully inclined, many even of those who attended in the morning at Mr Sainway's service; and little boys who ought to have been listening to the curate's afternoon lecture were too often seen rolling upon the grass and making faces behind the more dignified listeners.

Laura heard no more about the matter, however, for two or three weeks, when suddenly remembering it she asked her husband if any further objections had been raised.

'O – Mr Sainway. I forgot to tell you. I've made his acquaintance. He is not a bad sort of man.'

Laura asked if either Maumbry or some others of the officers did not give the presumptuous curate a good setting down for his interference.

'O well – we've forgotten that. He's a stunning preacher, they tell me.'

The acquaintance developed apparently, for the Captain said to her a little later on, 'There's a good deal in Sainway's argument about having no band on Sunday afternoons. After all, it is close to his church. But he doesn't press his objections unduly.'

'I am surprised to hear you defend him!'

'It was only a passing thought of mine. We naturally don't wish to offend the inhabitants of the town if they don't like it.'

'But they do.'

The invalid in the oriel never clearly gathered the details of progress in this conflict of lay and clerical opinion; but so it was that, to the disappointment of musicians, the grief of out-walking lovers, and the regret of the junior population of the town and country round, the band-playing on Sunday afternoons ceased in Casterbridge barrack-square.

By this time the Maumbrys had frequently listened to the preaching of the gentle if narrow-minded curate; for these light-natured, hit-or-miss, rackety people went to church like others for respectability's sake. None so orthodox as your unmitigated worldling. A more remarkable event was the sight to the man in the window of Captain Maumbry and Mr Sainway walking down the High Street in earnest conversation. On his mentioning this fact to a caller he was assured that it was a matter of common talk that they were always together.

The observer would soon have learnt this with his own eyes if he had not been told. They began to pass together nearly every day. Hitherto Mrs Maumbry, in fashionable walking clothes, had usually been her husband's companion; but this was less frequent now. The close and singular friendship between the two men went on for nearly a year, when Mr Sainway was presented to a living in a densely-populated town in the midland counties. He bade the parishioners of his old place a reluctant farewell and departed, the touching sermon he preached on the occasion being published by the local printer. Everybody was sorry to lose him; and it was with genuine grief that his Casterbridge congregation learnt later on that soon after his induction to his benefice, during some bitter weather, he had fallen seriously ill of inflammation of the lungs, of which he eventually died.

We now get below the surface of things. Of all who had known the dead curate, none grieved for him like the man who on his first arrival had called him a 'lath in a sheet'. Mrs Maumbry had never greatly sympathized with the impressive parson; indeed, she had been secretly glad that he had gone away to better himeslf. He had considerably diminished the pleasures of a woman by whom the joys of earth and good company had been appreciated to the full. Sorry for her husband in the loss of a friend who had been none of hers, she was yet quite unprepared for the sequel.

'There is something that I have wanted to tell you lately, dear,' he said one morning at breakfast with hesitation. 'Have you guessed what it is?'

She had guessed nothing.

'That I think of retiring from the army.'

'What!'

'I have thought more and more of Sainway since his death, and of what he used to say to me so earnestly. And I feel certain I shall be right in obeying a call within me to give up this fighting trade and enter the Church.'

'What – be a parson?'

'Yes.'

'But what should *I* do?'

'Be a parson's wife.'

'Never!' she affirmed.

'But how can you help it?'

'I'll run away rather!' she said vehemently.

'No, you mustn't,' Maumbry replied, in the tone he used when his mind was made up. 'You'll get accustomed to the idea, for I am constrained to carry it out, though it is against my worldly interest. I am forced on by a Hand outside me to tread in the steps of Sainway.'

'Jack,' she asked, with calm pallor and round eyes; 'do you mean to say seriously that you are arranging to be a curate instead of a soldier?'

'I might say a curate *is* a soldier – of the church militant; but I don't want to offend you with doctrine. I distinctly say, yes.'

Late one evening, a little time onward, he caught her sitting by the dim firelight in her room. She did not know he had entered; and he found her weeping. 'What are you crying about, poor dearest?' he said.

She started. 'Because of what you have told me!'

The Captain grew very unhappy; but he was undeterred.

In due time the town learnt, to its intense surprise, that Captain Maumbry had retired from the —th Hussars and gone to Fountall Theological College to prepare for the ministry.

4

'O, the pity of it! Such a dashing soldier – so popular – such an acquisition to the town – the soul of social life here! and now! . . . One should not speak ill of the dead, but that dreadful Mr Sainway – it was too cruel of him!'

This is a summary of what was said when Captain, now the Reverend, John Maumbry was enabled by circumstances to indulge his heart's desire of returning to the scene of his former exploits in the capacity of a minister of the Gospel. A low-lying district of the town, which at that date was crowded with impoverished cottagers, was crying for a curate, and Mr Maumbry generously offered himself as one willing to undertake labours that were certain to produce little result, and no thanks, credit, or emolument.

Let the truth be told about him as a clergyman; he proved to be anything but a brilliant success. Painstaking, single-minded, deeply in earnest as all could see, his delivery was laboured, his sermons were dull to listen to, and alas, too, too long. Even the dispassionate judges who sat by the hour in the bar-parlour of the White Hart – an inn standing at the dividing line between the poor quarter aforesaid and the fashionable quarter of Maumbry's former triumphs, and hence affording a position of strict impartiality – agreed in substance with the young ladies to the westward, though their views were somwhat more tersely expressed: 'Surely, God A'mighty spwiled a good sojer to make a bad pa'son when He shifted Cap'n Ma'mbry into a sarpless!'

The latter knew that such things were said, but he pursued his daily labours in and out of the hovels with serene unconcern.

It was about this time that the invalid in the oriel became more than a mere bowing acquaintance of Mrs Maumbry's. She had returned to the town with her husband, and was living with him in a little house in the centre of his circle of ministration, when by some means she became one of the invalid's visitors. After a general conversation while sitting in his room with a friend of both, an incident led up to the matter that still rankled deeply in her soul. Her face was now paler and thinner than it had been; even more attractive, her disappointments having inscribed themselves as meek thoughtfulness on a look that was once a little frivolous. The two ladies had called to be allowed to use the window for observing the departure of the Hussars, who were leaving for barracks much nearer to London.

The troopers turned the corner of Barrack Road into the top of High Street, headed by their band playing 'The girl I left behind me' (which was formerly always the tune for such times, though it is now nearly disused). They came and passed the oriel, where an officer or two, looking up and discovering Mrs Maumbry, saluted her, whose eyes filled with tears as the notes of the band waned away. Before the little group had recovered from that sense of the romantic which such spectacles impart, Mr Maumbry came along the pavement. He probably had bidden his former brethren-in-arms a farewell at the top of the street, for he walked from that direction in his rather shabby clerical clothes, and with a basket on his arm which seemed to hold some purchases he had been making for his poorer parishioners. Unlike the soldiers he went along quite unconscious of his appearance or of the scene around.

The contrast was too much for Laura. With lips that now quivered, she asked the invalid what he thought of the change that had come to her.

It was difficult to answer, and with a wilfulness that was too strong in her she repeated the question.

'Do you think,' she added, 'that a woman's husband has a right to do such thing, even if he does feel a certain call to it?'

Her listener sympathized too largely with both of them to be anything but unsatisfactory in his reply. Laura gazed longingly out of the window towards the thin dusty line of Hussars, now smalling towards the Mellstock Ridge. 'I,' she said, 'who should have been in their van on the way to London, am doomed to fester in a hole in Durnover Lane!'

Many events had passed and many rumours had been current concerning her before the invalid saw her again after her leave-taking that day.

5

Casterbridge had known many military and civil episodes; many happy times, and times less happy; and now came the time of her visitation. The scourge of cholera had been laid on the suffering country, and the low-lying purlieus of this ancient borough had more than their share of the infliction. Mixen Lane, in the Durnover quarter, and in Maumbry's parish, was where the blow fell most heavily. Yet there was a certain mercy in its choice of a date, for Maumbry was the man for such an hour.

The spread of the epidemic was so rapid that many left the town and took lodgings in the villages and farms. Mr Maumbry's house was close to the most infected street, and he himself was occupied morn, noon, and night in endeavours to stamp out the plague and in alleviating the sufferings of the victims. So, as a matter of ordinary precaution, he decided to isolate his wife somewhere away from him for a while.

She suggested a village by the sea, near Budmouth Regis, and lodgings were obtained for her at Creston, a spot divided from Casterbridge valley by a high ridge that gave it quite another atmosphere, though it lay no more than six miles off.

Thither she went. While she was rusticating in this place of safety, and her husband was slaving in the slums, she struck up an acquaintance with a lieutenant in the —st Foot, a Mr Vannicock, who was stationed with his regiment at the Budmouth infantry barracks. As Laura frequently sat on the shelving beach, watching each thin wave slide up to her, and hearing, without heeding, its gnaw at the pebbles in its retreat, he often took a walk that way.

The acquaintance grew and ripened. Her situation, her history, her beauty, her age – a year or two above his own – all tended to make an impression on the young man's heart, and a reckless flirtation was soon in blithe progress upon that lonely shore.

It was said by her detractors afterwards that she had chosen her lodging to be near this gentleman, but there is reason to believe that she had never seen him till her arrival there. Just now Casterbridge was so deeply occupied with its own sad affairs – a daily burying of the dead and destruction of contaminated clothes and bedding – that it had little inclination to promulgate such gossip as may have reached its ears on the pair. Nobody long considered Laura in the tragic cloud which overhung all.

Meanwhile, on the Budmouth side of the hill the very mood of men was in contrast. The visitation there had been slight and much earlier, and normal occupations and pastimes had been resumed. Mr Maumbry had arranged to see Laura twice a week in the open air, that she might run no risk from him; and, having heard nothing of the faint rumour, he met her as usual one dry and windy afternoon on the summit of the dividing hill, near where the high road from town to town crosses the old Ridgeway at right angles.

He waved his hand, and smiled as she approached, shouting to her: 'We will keep this wall between us, dear.' (Walls formed the field-fences here.) 'You mustn't be endangered. It won't be for long, with God's help!'

'I will do as you tell me, Jack. But you are running too much risk yourself, aren't you? I get little news of you; but I fancy you are.'

'Not more than others.'

Thus somewhat formally they talked, an insulating wind beating the wall between them like a mill-weir.

'But you wanted to ask me something?' he added.

'Yes. You know we are trying in Budmouth to raise some money for your sufferers; and the way we have thought of is by a dramatic performance. They want me to take part.'

His face saddened. 'I have known so much of that sort of thing, and all that accompanies it! I wish you had thought of some other way.'

She said lightly that she was afraid it was all settled. 'You object to my taking a part, then? Of course—'

He told her that he did not like to say he positively objected. He wished they had chosen an oratorio, or lecture, or anything more in keeping with the necessity it was to relieve.

'But,' said she impatiently, 'people won't come to oratorios or lectures! They will crowd to comedies and farces.'

'Well, I cannot dictate to Budmouth how it shall earn the money it is going to give us. Who is getting up this performance?'

'The boys of the —st.'

'Ah, yes; our old game!' replied Mr Maumbry. 'The grief of Casterbridge is the excuse for their frivolity. Candidly, dear Laura, I wish you wouldn't play in it. But I don't forbid you to. I leave the whole to your judgment.'

The interview ended, and they went their ways northward and southward. Time disclosed to all concerned that Mrs Maumbry played in the comedy as the heroine, the lover's part being taken by Mr Vannicock.

6

Thus was helped on an event which the conduct of the mutually-attracted ones had been generating for some time.

It is unnecessary to give details – the —st Foot left for Bristol, and this precipitated their action. After a week of hesitation she agreed to leave her home at Creston and meet Vannicock on the ridge hard by, and to accompany him to Bath, where he had secured lodgings for her, so that she would be only about a dozen miles from his quarters.

Accordingly, on the evening chosen, she laid on her dressing-table a note for her husband, running thus:

> DEAR JACK, – I am unable to endure this life any longer, and I have resolved to put an end to it. I told you I should run away if you persisted in being a cleryman, and now I am doing it. One cannot help one's nature. I have resolved to throw in my lot with Mr Vannicock, and I hope rather than expect you will forgive me. – L.

Then, with hardly a scrap of luggage, she went, ascending to the ridge in the dusk of early evening. Almost on the very spot where her husband had stood at their last tryst she beheld the outline of Vannicock, who had come all the way from Bristol to fetch her.

'I don't like meeting here – it is so unlucky!' she cried to him. 'For God's sake let us have a place of our own. Go back to the milestone, and I'll come on.'

He went back to the milestone that stands on the north slope of the ridge, where the old and new roads diverge, and she joined him there.

She was taciturn and sorrowful when he asked her why she would not meet him on the top. At last she inquired how they were going to travel.

He explained that he proposed to walk to Mellstock Hill, on the other side of Casterbridge, where a fly was waiting to take them by a cross-cut into the Ivell Road, and onward to that town. The Bristol railway was open to Ivell.

This plan they followed, and walked briskly through the dull gloom till they neared Casterbridge, which place they avoided by turning to the right at the Roman Amphitheatre and bearing round to Durnover Cross. Thence the way was solitary and open across the moor to the hill whereon the Ivell fly awaited them.

'I have noticed for some time,' she said, 'a lurid glare over the Durnover end of the town. It seems to come from somewhere about Mixen Lane.'

'The lamps,' he suggested.

'There's not a lamp as big as a rushlight in the whole lane. It is where the cholera is worst.'

By Standfast Corner, a little beyond the Cross, they suddenly obtained an end view of the lane. Large bonfires were burning in the middle of the way, with a view to purifying the air; and from the wretched tenements with which the lane was lined in those days persons were bringing out bedding and clothing. Some was thrown into the fires, the rest placed in wheel-barrows and wheeled into the moor directly in the track of the fugitives.

They followed on, and came up to where a vast copper was set in the open air. Here the linen was boiled and disinfected. By the light of the lanterns Laura discovered that her husband was standing by the copper, and that it was he who unloaded the barrow and immersed its contents. The night was so calm and muggy that the conversation by the copper reached her ears.

'Are there many more loads tonight?'

'There's the clothes o' they that died this afternoon, sir. But that might bide till tomorrow, for you must be tired out.'

'We'll do it at once, for I can't ask anybody else to undertake it. Overturn that load on the grass and fetch the rest.'

The man did so and went off with the barrow. Maumbry paused for a moment to wipe his face, and resumed his homely drudgery amid this squalid and reeking scene, pressing down and stirring the contents of the copper, with what looked like an old rolling-pin. The steam therefrom, laden with death, travelled in a low trail across the meadow.

Laura spoke suddenly: 'I won't go tonight after all. He is so tired, and I must help him. I didn't know things were as bad as this!'

Vannicock's arm dropped from her waist, where it had been resting as they walked. 'Will you leave?' she asked.

'I will if you say I must. But I'd rather help too.' There was no expostulation in his tone.

Laura had gone forward. 'Jack,' she said, 'I am come to help!'

The weary curate turned and held up the lantern. 'O – what, is it you, Laura?' he asked in surprise. 'Why did you come into this? You had better go back – the risk is great.'

'But I want to help you, Jack. Please let me help! I didn't come by myself – Mr Vannicock kept me company. He will make himself useful too, if he's not gone on. Mr Vannicock!'

The young lieutenant came forward reluctantly. Mr Maumbry spoke formally to him, adding as he resumed his labour, 'I thought the —st Foot had gone to Bristol.'

'We have. But I have run down again for a few things.'

The two newcomers began to assist, Vannicock placing on the ground the small bag containing Laura's toilet articles that he had been carrying. The barrow-man soon returned with another load, and all continued work for nearly a half-hour, when a coachman came out from the shadows to the north.

'Beg pardon, sir,' he whispered to Vannicock, 'but I've waited so long on Mellstock Hill that at last I drove down to the turnpike; and seeing the light here, I ran on to find out what had happened.'

Lieutenant Vannicock told him to wait a few minutes, and the last barrow-load was got through. Mr Maumbry stretched himself and breathed heavily, saying, 'There; we can do no more.'

As if from the relaxation of effort he seemed to be seized with violent pain. He pressed his hands to his sides and bent forward.

'Ah! I think it has got hold of me at last,' he said with difficulty. 'I must try to get home. Let Mr Vannicock take you back, Laura.'

He walked a few steps, they helping him, but was obliged to sink down on the grass.

'I am – afraid – you'll have to send for a hurdle, or shutter, or something,' he went on feebly, 'or try to get me into the barrow.'

But Vannicock had called to the driver of the fly, and they waited until it was brought on from the turnpike hard by. Mr Maumbry was placed therein. Laura entered with him, and they drove to his humble residence near the Cross, where he was got upstairs.

Vannicock stood outside by the empty fly a while, but Laura did not reappear. He thereupon entered the fly and told the driver to take him back to Ivell.

7

Mr Maumbry had over-exerted himself in the relief of the suffering poor, and fell a victim – one of the last – to the pestilence which had carried off so many. Two days later he lay in his coffin.

Laura was in the room below. A servant brought in some letters, and she glanced them over. One was the note from herself to Maumbry, informing him that she was unable to endure life with him any longer and was about to elope with Vannicock. Having read the letter she took it upstairs to where the dead man was, and slipped it into his coffin. The next day she buried him.

She was now free.

She shut up his house at Durnover Cross and returned to her lodgings at Creston. Soon she had a letter from Vannicock, and six weeks after her husband's death her lover came to see her.

'I forgot to give you back this – that night,' he said presently, handing her the little bag she had taken as her whole luggage when leaving.

Laura received it and absently shook it out. There fell upon the carpet her brush, comb, slippers, nightdress, and other simple necessaries for a journey. They had an intolerably ghastly look now, and she tried to cover them.

'I can now,' he said, 'ask you to belong to me legally – when a proper interval has gone – instead of as we meant.'

There was languor in his utterance, hinting at a possibility that it was perfunctorily made. Laura picked up her articles, answering that he certainly could so ask her – she was free. Yet not her expression either could be called an ardent response. Then she blinked more and more quickly and put her handkerchief to her face. She was weeping violently.

He did not move or try to comfort her in any way. What had come between them? No living person. They had been lovers. There was now no material obstacle whatever to their union. But there was the insistent shadow of that unconscious one; the thin figure of him, moving to and fro in front of the ghastly furnace in the gloom of Durnover Moor.

Yet Vannicock called upon Laura when he was in the neighbourhood, which was not often; but in two years, as if on purpose to further the marriage which everybody was expecting, the —st Foot returned to Budmouth Regis.

Thereupon the two could not help encountering each other at times. But whether because the obstacle had been the source of the love, or from a sense of error, and because Mrs Maumbry bore a less attractive look as a widow than before, their feelings seemed to decline from their former incandescence to a mere tepid civility. What domestic issues supervened in Vannicock's further story the man in the oriel never knew; but Mrs Maumbry lived and died a widow.

1900

THE WAITING SUPPER

I

Whoever had perceived the yeoman standing on Squire Everard's lawn in the dusk of that October evening fifty years ago, might have said at first sight that he was loitering there from idle curiosity. For a large five-light window of the manor-house in front of him was unshuttered and uncurtained, so that the illuminated room within could be scanned almost to its four corners. Obviously nobody was ever expected to be in this part of the grounds after nightfall.

The apartment thus swept by an eye from without was occupied by two persons; they were sitting over desert, the tablecloth having been removed in the old-fashioned way. The fruits were local, consisting of apples, pears, nuts, and such other products of the summer as might be presumed to grow on the estate. There was strong ale and rum on the table, and but little wine. Moreover, the appointments of the dining-room were simple and homely even for the date, betokening a countrified household of the smaller gentry, without much wealth or ambition – formerly a numerous class, but now in great part ousted by the territorial landlords.

One of the two sitters was a young lady in white muslin, who listened somewhat impatiently to the remarks of her companion, an elderly, rubicund personage, whom the merest stranger could have pronounced to be her father. The watcher evinced no signs of moving, and it became evident that affairs were not so simple as they first had seemed. The tall farmer was in fact no accidental spectator, and he stood by premeditation close to the trunk of a tree, so that had any traveller passed along the road without the park gate, or even round the law to the door, that person would scarce have noticed the other, notwithstanding that the gate was quite near at hand, and the park little larger than a paddock. There was still light enough in the western heaven to brighten faintly one side of the man's face, and to show against the trunk of the tree behind the admirable cut of his profile; also to reveal that the front of the manor-house, small though it seemed, was solidly built of stone in that never-to-be-surpassed style for the English country residence – the mullioned and transomed Elizabethan.

The lawn, although neglected, was still as level as a bowling-green – which indeed it might once have served for; and the blades of grass before the window were raked by the candle-shine, which stretched over them so far as to touch the yeoman's face in front.

Within the dining-room there were also, with one of the twain, the same signs of a hidden purpose that marked the farmer. The young lady's mind was straying as clearly into the shadows as that of the loiterer was fixed upon the room – nay, it could be said that she was quite conscious of his presence outside. Impatience caused her foot to beat silently on the carpet, and she more than once rose to leave the table. This proceeding was checked by her father, who would put his hand upon her shoulder and unceremoniously press her down into her chair, till he should have concluded his observations. Her replies were brief enough, and there was a factitiousness in her smiles of assent to his views. A small iron casement between two of the mullions was open, and some occasional words of the dialogue were audible without.

'As for drains – how can I put in drains? The pipes don't cost much, that's true; but the labour in sinking the trenches is ruination. And then the gates – they should be hung to stone posts, otherwise there's no keeping them up through harvest.' The Squire's voice was strongly toned with the local accent, so that he said 'draïns' and 'geäts' like the rustics on his estate.

The landscape without grew darker, and the young man's figure seemed to be absorbed into the trunk of the tree. The small stars filled in between the larger, the nebulae between the small stars, the trees quite lost their voice; and if there was still a sound, it was from the cascade of a stream which stretched along under the trees that bounded the lawn on its northern side.

At last the young girl did get to her feet and secure her retreat. 'I have something to do, papa,' she said. 'I shall not be in the drawing-room just yet.'

'Very well,' replied he. 'Then I won't hurry.' And closing the door behind her, he drew his decanters together and settled down in his chair.

Three minutes after that a woman's shape emerged from the drawing-room window, and passing through a wall-door to the entrance front, came across the grass. She kept well clear of the dining-room window, but enough of its light fell on her to show, escaping from the dark-hooded cloak that she wore, stray verges of the same light dress which had figured but recently at the dinner-table. The hood was contracted tight about her face with a drawing-string, making her countenance small and baby-like, and lovelier even than before.

Without hesitation she brushed across the grass to the tree under which the young man stood concealed. The moment she had reached him he enclosed her form with his arm. The meeting and embrace, though by no means formal, were yet not passionate; the whole proceeding was that of persons who had repeated the act so often as to be unconscious of its performance. She turned within his arm, and faced in the same direction with himself, which was towards the window; and thus they stood without speaking, the back of her head leaning against his shoulder. For a while each seemed to be thinking his and her diverse thoughts.

'You have kept me waiting a long time, dear Christine,' he said at last. 'I wanted to speak to you particularly, or I should not have stayed. How came you to be dining at this time o' night?'

'Father has been out all day, and dinner was put back till six. I know I have kept you; but, Nicholas, how can I help it sometimes, if I am not to run any risk? My poor father insists upon my listening to all he has to say; since my brother left he has had nobody else to listen to him; and tonight he was particularly tedious on his usual topics – draining, and tenant-farmers, and the village people. I must take daddy to London; he gets so narrow always staying here.'

'And what did you say to it all?'

'Well, I took the part of the tenant-farmers, of course, as the beloved of one should in duty do.' There followed a little break or gasp, implying a strangled sigh.

'You are sorry you have encouraged that beloving one?'

'O no, Nicholas. . . What is it you want to see me for particularly?'

'I know you *are* sorry, as time goes on, and everything is at a deadlock, with no prospect of change, and your rural swain loses his freshness! Only think, this secret understanding between us has lasted near three year, ever since you was a little over sixteen.'

'Yes; it has been a long time.'

'And I an untamed, uncultivated man, who has never seen London, and knows nothing about society at all.'

'Not uncultivated, dear Nicholas. Untravelled, socially unpractised, if you will,' she said, smiling. 'Well, I did sigh; but not because I regret being your promised one. What I do sometimes regret is that the scheme, which my meetings with you are but a part of, has not been carried out completely. You said, Nicholas, that if I consented to swear to keep faith with you, you would go away and travel, and see nations, and peoples, and cities, and take a professor with you, and study books and art, simultaneously with your study of men and manners; and then come back at the end of two years, when I should find that my father would by no means be indisposed to accept you as a son-in-law. You said your reason for wishing to get my promise before starting was that your mind would then be more at rest when you were far away, and so could give itself more completely to knowledge than if you went as my unaccepted lover only, fuming with anxiety as to how I should be when you came back. I saw how reasonable that was; and solemnly swore myself to you in consequence. But instead of going to see the world you stay on and on here to see me.'

'And you don't want me to see you?'

'Yes – no – it is not that. It is that I have latterly felt frightened at what I am doing when not in your actual presence. It seems so wicked not to tell my father that I have a lover close at hand, within touch and view of both of us; whereas if you were absent my conduct would not seem quite so treacherous. The realities would not stare at one so. You would be a pleasant dream to me, which I should be free to indulge in without reproach of my conscience; I should live in hopeful expectation of your returning fully qualified to boldly claim me of my father. There, I have been terribly frank, I know.'

He in his turn had lapsed into gloomy breathings now. 'I did plan it as you state,' he answered. 'I did mean to go away the moment I had your promise. But, dear Christine, I did not foresee two or three things. I did not know what a lot of pain it would cost to tear myself from you. And I did not know that my stingy uncle – heaven forgive me calling him so! – would so flatly refuse to advance me money for my purpose – the scheme of travelling with a first-rate tutor costing a formidable sum o' money. You have no idea what it would cost!'

'But I have said that I'll find the money.'

'Ah, there,' he returned, 'you have hit a sore palce. To speak truly, dear, I would rather stay unpolished a hundred years than take your money.'

'But why? Men continually use the money of the women they marry.'

'Yes; but not till afterwards. No man would like to touch your money at present, and I should feel very mean if I were to do so in present circumstances. That brings me to what I was going to propose. But no – upon the whole I will not propose it now.'

'Ah! I would guarantee expenses, and you won't let me! The money is my personal possession: it comes to me from my late grandfather, and not from my father at all.'

He laughed forcedly and pressed her hand. 'There are more reasons why I cannot tear myself away,' he added. 'What would become of my uncle's farming? Six hundred acres in this parish, and five hundred in the next – a constant traipsing from one farm to the other; he can't be in two places at once. Still, that might be got over if it were not for the other matters. Besides, dear, I still should be a little uneasy, even though I have your promise, lest somebody should snap you up away from me.'

'Ah, you should have thought of that before. Otherwise I have committed myself for nothing.'

'I should have thought of it,' he answered gravely. 'But I did not. There lies my fault, I admit it freely. Ah, if you would only commit yourself a little more, I might at least get over that difficulty! But I won't ask you. You have no idea how much you are to me still; you could not argue so coolly if you had. What properly belongs to you I hate the very sound of; it is you I care for. I wish you hadn't a farthing in the world but what I could earn for you!'

'I don't altogether wish that,' she murmured.

'I wish it, because it would have made what I was going to propose much easier to do than it is now. Indeed I will not propose it, although I came on purpose, after what you have said in your frankness.'

'Nonsense, Nic. Come, tell me. How can you be so touchy?'

'Look at this then, Christine dear.' He drew from his breast-pocket a sheet of paper and unfolded it, when it was observable that a seal dangled from the bottom.

'What is it?' She held the paper sideways, so that what there was of window-light fell on its surface. 'I can only read the Old English letters – why – our names! Surely it is not a marriage-licence?'

'It is.'

She trembled. 'O Nic! how could you do this – and without telling me!'

'Why should I have thought to tell you? You had not spoken "frankly" then as you have now. We have been all to each other more than these two years, and I thought I would propose that we marry privately, and that I then leave you on the instant. I would have taken my travelling-bag to church, and you would have gone home alone. I should not have started on my adventures in the brilliant manner of our original plan, but should have roughed it a little at first; my great gain would have been that the absolute possession of you would have enabled me to work with spirit and purpose, such as nothing else could do. But I dare not ask you now – so frank as you have been.'

She did not answer. The document he had produced gave such unexpected substantiality to the venture with which she had so long toyed as a vague dream merely, that she was, in truth, frightened a little. 'I – don't know about it!' she said.

'Perhaps not. Ah, my little lady, you are wearying of me!'

'No, Nic,' responded she, creeping closer. 'I am not. Upon my word, and truth, and honour, I am not, Nic.'

'A mere tiller of the soil, as I should be called,' he continued, without heeding her. 'And you – well, a daughter of one of the – I won't say oldest families, because that's absurd, all families are the same age – one of the longest chronicled families about here, whose name is actually the name of the place.'

'That's not much, I am sorry to say! My poor brother – but I won't speak of that. . . Well,' she murmured mischievously, after a pause, 'you certainly would not need to be uneasy if I were to do this that you want me to do. You would have me safe enough in your trap then; I couldn't get away!'

'That's just it!' he said vehemently. 'It *is* a trap – you feel it so, and that though you wouldn't be able to get away from me you might particularly wish to! Ah, if I had asked you two years ago you would have agreed instantly. But I thought I was bound to wait for the proposal to come from you as the superior!'

'Now you are angry, and take seriously what I meant purely in fun. You don't know me even yet! To show you that you have not been mistaken in me, I *do* propose to carry out this licence. I'll marry you, dear Nicholas, tomorrow morning.'

'Ah, Christine! I am afraid I have stung you on to this, so that I cannot—'

'No, no, no!' she hastily rejoined, and there was something in her tone which suggested that she had been put upon her mettle and would not flinch. 'Take me whilst I am in the humour. What church is the licence for?'

'That I've not looked to see – why, our parish church here, of course. Ah, then we cannot use it! We dare not be married here.'

'We do dare,' said she. 'And we will too, if you'll be there.'

'*If* I'll be there!'

They speedily came to an agreement that he should be in the church-porch at ten minutes to eight on the following morning, awaiting her; and that, immediately after the conclusion of the service which would make them one, Nicholas should set out on his long-deferred educational tour, towards the cost of which she was resolving to bring a substantial subscription with her to church. Then, slipping from him, she went indoors by the way she had come, and Nicholas bent his steps homewards.

2

Instead of leaving the spot by the gate, he flung himself over the fence, and pursued a direction towards the river under the trees. And it was now, in his lonely progress, that he showed for the first time outwardly that he was not altogether worthy of her. He wore long water-boots reaching above his knees, and, instead of making a circuit to find a bridge by which he might cross the Froom – the river aforesaid – he made straight for the point whence proceeded the low roar that was at this hour the only evidence of the stream's existence. He speedily stood on the verge of the waterfall which caused the noise, and stepping into the water at the top of the fall, waded through with the sure tread of one who knew every inch of his footing, even though the canopy of trees rendered the darkness almost absolute, and a false step would have precipitated him into the pool beneath. Soon reaching the boundary of the grounds, he continued in the same direct line to traverse the alluvial valley, full of brooks and tributaries to the main stream – in former times quite impassable, and impassable in winter, now. Sometimes he would cross a deep gully on a plank not wider than the hand; at another time he ploughed his way through beds of spear-grass, where at a few feet to the right or left he might have been sucked down into a morass. At last he reached firm land on the other side of this watery tract, and came to his house on the rise behind – Elsenford – an ordinary farmstead, from the back of which rose indistinct breathings, belchings, and snortings, the rattle of halters, and other familiar features of an agriculturist's home.

While Nicholas Long was packing his bag in an upper room of this dwelling, Miss Christian Everard sat at a desk in her own chamber at Froom-Everard manor-house, looking with pale fixed countenance at the candles.

'I ought – I must now!' she whispered to herself. 'I should not have begun it if I had not meant to carry it through! It runs in the blood of us, I suppose.' She alluded to a fact unknown to her lover, the clandestine marriage of an aunt under circumstances somewhat similar to the present. In a few minutes she had penned the following note:

October 13, 183–

DEAR MR BEALAND, – Can you make it convenient to yourself to meet me at the Church tomorrow morning at eight? I name the early hour because it would suit me better than later on in the day. You will find me in the chancel, if you can come. An answer yes or no by the bearer of this will be sufficient.

CHRISTINE EVERARD

She sent the note to the rector immediately, waiting at a small side-door of the house till she heard the servant's footsteps returning along the lane, when she went round and met him in the passage. The rector had taken the trouble to write a line, and answered that he would meet her with pleasure.

A dripping fog which ushered in the next morning was highly favourable to the scheme of the pair. At that time of the century Froom-Everard House had not been altered and enlarged; the public lane passed close under its walls; and there was a door opening directly from one of the old parlours – the south parlour, as it was called – into the lane which led to the village. Christine came out this way, and after following the lane for a short distance entered upon a path within a belt of plantation, by which the church could be reached privately. She even avoided the churchyard, walking along to a place where the turf without the low wall rose into a mound, enabling her to mount upon the coping and spring down inside. She crossed the wet graves, and so glided round to the door. He was there, with his bag in his hand. He kissed her with a sort of surprise, as if he had expected that at the last moment her heart would fail her.

Though it had not failed her, there was, nevertheless, no great ardour in Christine's bearing – merely the momentum of an antecedent impulse. They went up the aisle together, the bottle-green glass of the old lead quarries admitting but little light at that hour, and under such an atmosphere. They stood by the altar-rail in silence, Christine's skirt visibly quivering at each beat of her heart.

Presently a quick step ground upon the gravel, and Mr Bealand came round by the front. He was a quiet bachelor, courteous towards Christine, and not at first recognizing in Nicholas a neighbouring yeoman (for he lived aloofly in the next parish), advanced to her without revealing any surprise at her unusual request. But in truth he was surprised, the keen interest taken by many country young women at the present day in church decoration and festivals being then unknown.

'Good morning,' he said; and repeated the same words to Nicholas more mechanically.

'Good morning,' she replied gravely. 'Mr Bealand, I have a serious reason for asking you to meet me – us, I may say. We wish you to marry us.'

The rector's gaze hardened to fixity, rather between than upon either of them, and he neither moved nor replied for some time.

'Ah!' he said at last.

'And we are quite ready.'

'I had no idea—'

'It has been kept rather private,' she said calmly.

'Where are your witnesses?'

'They are outside in the meadow, sir. I can call them in a moment,' said Nicholas.

'Oh – I see it is – Mr Nicholas Long,' said Mr Bealand, and turning again to Christine, 'Does your father know of this?'

'Is it necessary that I should answer that question, Mr Bealand?'

'I am afraid it is – highly necessary.'

Christine began to look concerned.

'Where is the licence?' the rector asked; 'since there have been no banns.'

Nicholas produced it, Mr Bealand read it, an operation which occupied him several minutes – or at least he made it appear so; till Christine said impatiently, 'We are quite ready, Mr Bealand. Will you proceed? Mr Long has to take a journey of a great many miles today.'

'And you?'

'No. I remain.'

Mr Bealand assumed firmness. 'There is something wrong in this,' he said. 'I cannot marry you without your father's presence.'

'But have you a right to refuse us?' interposed Nicholas. 'I believe we are in a position to demand your fulfilment of our request.'

'No, you are not! Is Miss Everard of age? I think not. I think she is months from being so. Eh, Miss Everard?'

'Am I bound to tell that?'

'Certainly. At any rate you are bound to write it. Meanwhile I refuse to solemnize the service. And let me entreat you two young people to do nothing so rash as this, even if by going to some strange church, you may do so without discovery. The tragedy of marriage—'

'Tragedy?'

'Certainly. It is full of crises and catastrophes, and ends with the death of one of the actors. The tragedy of marriage, as I was saying, is one I shall not be a party to your beginning with such light hearts, and I shall feel bound to put your father on his guard, Miss Everard. Think better of it, I entreat you! Remember the proverb "Marry in haste and repent at leisure".'

Christine, spurred by opposition, almost stormed at him. Nicholas implored; but nothing would turn that obstinate rector. She sat down and reflected. By-and-by she confronted Mr Bealand.

'Our marriage is not to be this morning, I see,' she said. 'Now grant me one favour, and in return I'll promise you to do nothing rashly. Do not tell my father a word of what has happened here.'

'I agree – if you undertake not to elope.'

She looked at Nicholas, and he looked at her. 'Do you wish me to elope, Nic?' she asked.

'No,' he said.

So the compact was made, and they left the church singly, Nicholas remaining till the last, and closing the door. On his way home, carrying the well-packed bag which was just now to go no further, the two men who were mending water-carriers in the meadows approached the hedge, as if they had been on the alert all the time.

'You said you mid want us for zummat, sir?'

'All right – never mind,' he answered, through the hedge. 'I did not require you after all.'

3

At a manor not far away there lived a queer and primitive couple who had lately been blessed with a son and heir. The christening took place during the week under notice, and this had been followed by a feast to the parishioners. Christine's father, one of the same generation and kind, had been asked to drive over and assist in the entertainment, and Christine, as a matter of course, accompanied him.

When they reached Athelhall, as the house was called, they found the usually quiet nook a lively spectacle. Tables had been spread in the apartment which lent its name to the whole building – the hall proper – covered with a fine open-timbered roof, whose braces, purlins and rafters made a brown thicket of oak overhead. Here tenantry of all ages sat with their wives and families, and the servants were assisted in their ministrations by the sons and daughters of the owner's friends and neighbours. Christine lent a hand among the rest.

She was holding a plate in each hand towards a huge brown platter of baked rice-pudding, from which a footman was scooping a large spoonful, when a voice reached her ear over her shoulder: 'Allow me to hold them for you.'

Christine turned, and recognized in the speaker the nephew of the entertainer, a young man from London, whom she had already met on two or three occasions. She accepted the proffered help, and from that moment, whenever he passed her in their marchings to and fro during the remainder of the serving, he smiled acquaintance. When their work was done, he improved the few words into a conversation. He plainly had been attracted by her fairness.

Bellston was a self-assured young man, not particularly good-looking, with more colour in his skin than even Nicholas had. He had flushed a little in attracting her notice, though the flush had nothing of nervousness in it – the air with which it was accompanied making it curiously suggestive of a flush of anger; and even when he laughed it was difficult to banish that fancy.

The late autumn sunlight streamed in through the window panes upon the heads and shoulders of the venerable patriarchs of the hamlet, and upon the middle-aged, and upon the young; upon men and women who had played out, or were to play, tragedies or tragi-comedies in that nook of civilization not less great, essentially, than those which, enacted on more central arenas, fix the attention of the world. One of the party was a cousin of Nicholas Long's, who sat with her husband and children.

To make himself as locally harmonious as possible, Mr Bellston remarked to his companion on the scene –

'It does one's heart good,' he said, 'to see these simple peasants enjoying themselves.'

'O Mr Bellston!' exclaimed Christine; 'don't be too sure about that word "simple"! You little think what they see and meditate! Their reasonings and emotions are as complicated as ours.'

She spoke with a vehemence which would have been hardly present in her words but for her own relation to Nicholas. The sense of that produced in her a nameless depression thenceforward. The young man, however, still followed her up.

'I am glad to hear you say it,' he returned warmly. 'I was merely attuning myself to your mood, as I thought. The real truth is that I know more of the Parthians, and Medes, and dwellers in Mesopotamia – almost of any people, indeed – than of the English rustics. Travel and exploration are my profession, not the study of the British peasantry.'

Travel. There was sufficient coincidence between his declaration and the course she had urged upon her lover, to lend Bellston's account of himself a certain interest in Christine's ears. He might perhaps be able to tell her something that would be useful to Nicholas, if their dream were carried out. A door opened from the hall into the garden, and she somehow found herself outside, chatting with Mr Bellston on this topic, till she thought that upon the whole she liked the young man. The garden being his uncle's, he took her round it with an air of proprietorship; and they went on amongst the Michaelmas daisies and chrysanthemums, and through a door to the fruit-garden. A green-house was open, and he went in and cut her a bunch of grapes.

'How daring of you! They are your uncle's.'

'O, he don't mind – I do anything here. A rough old buffer, isn't he?'

She was thinking of her Nic, and felt that, by comparison with her present acquaintance, the farmer more than held his own as a fine and intelligent fellow; but the harmony with her own existence in little things, which she found here, imparted an alien tinge to Nicholas just now. The latter, idealized by moonlight, or a thousand miles of distance, was altogether a more romantic object for a woman's dream than this smart new-lacquered man; but in the sun of afternoon, and amid a surrounding company, Mr Bellston was a very tolerable companion.

When they re-entered the hall, Bellston entreated her to come with him up a spiral stair in the thickness of the wall, leading to a passage and gallery whence they could look down upon the scene below. The people had finished their feast, the newly-christened baby had been exhibited, and a few words having been spoken to them they began, amid a racketing of forms, to make for the greensward without, Nicholas's cousin and cousin's husband and cousin's children among the rest. While they were filing out, a voice was heard calling –

'Hullo! – here, Jim; where are you?' said Bellston's uncle. The young man descended, Christine following at leisure.

'Now will ye be a good fellow,' the Squire continued, 'and set them going outside in some dance or other that they know? I'm dog-tired, and I want to have a vew words with Mr Everard before we join 'em – hey, Everard? They are shy till somebody starts 'em; afterwards they'll keep gwine brisk enough.'

'Ay, that they wool,' said Squire Everard.

They followed to the lawn; and here it proved that James Bellston was as shy, or rather as averse, as any of the tenantry themselves, to acting the part of fugleman. Only the parish people had been at the feast, but outlying neighbours had now strolled in for a dance.

'They want "Speed the Plough",' said Bellston, coming up breathless. 'It must be a country dance, I suppose? Now, Miss Everard, do have pity upon me. I am supposed to lead off; but really know no more about speeding the plough than a child just born! Would you take one of the villagers? – just to start them, my uncle says. Suppose you take that handsome young farmer over there – I don't know his name, but I dare say you do – and I'll come on with one of the dairyman's daughters as a second couple.'

Christine turned in the direction signified, and changed colour – though in the shade nobody noticed it. 'Oh, yes – I know him,' she said coolly. 'He is from near our own place – Mr Nicholas Long.'

'That's capital – then you can easily make him stand as first couple with you. Now I must pick up mine.'

'I – I think I'll dance with you, Mr Bellston,' she said with some trepidation. 'Because, you see,' she explained eagerly, 'I know the figure and you don't – so that I can help you; while Nicholas Long, I know, is familiar with the figure, and that will make two couples who know it – which is necessary at least.'

Bellston showed his gratification by one of his angry-pleasant flushes – he had hardly dared to ask for what she proffered freely; and having requested Nicholas to take the dairyman's daughter, led Christine to her place, Long promptly stepping up second with his charge. There were grim silent depths in Nic's character; a small deedy spark in his eye, as it caught Christine's, was all that showed his consciousness of her. Then the fiddlers began – the celebrated Mellstock fiddlers who, given free stripping, could play from sunset to dawn without turning a hair. The couples wheeled and swung, Nicholas taking Christine's hand in the course of business with the figure, when she waited for him to give it a little squeeze; but he did not.

Christine had the greatest difficulty in steering her partner through the maze, on account of his self-will, and when at last they reached the bottom of the long line, she was breathless with her hard labour. Resting here, she watched Nic and his lady; and, though she had decidedly cooled off in these later months, began to admire him anew. Nobody knew these dances like him, after all, or could do anything of this sort so well. His performance with the dairyman's daughter so won upon her, that when 'Speed the Plough' was over she contrived to speak to him.

'Nic, you are to dance with me next time.'

He said he would, and presently asked her in a formal public manner, lifting his hat gallantly. She showed a little backwardness, which he quite understood, and allowed him to lead her to the top, a row of enormous length appearing below them as if by magic as soon as they had taken their places. Truly the Squire was right when he said that they only wanted starting.

'What is it to be?' whispered Nicholas.

She turned to the band. '"The Honeymoon",' she said.

And then they trod the delightful last-century measure of that name, which if it had ever been danced better, was never danced with more zest. The perfect responsiveness which their tender acquaintance threw into the motions of Nicholas and his partner lent to their gyrations the fine adjustment of two interacting parts of a single machine. The excitement of the movement carried Christine back to the time – when she and Nic had been incipient lovers only; and it made her forget the carking anxieties, the vision of social breakers ahead, that had begun to take the gilding off her position now. Nicholas, on his part, had never ceased to be a lover; no personal worries had as yet made him conscious of any staleness, flatness, or unprofitableness in his admiration of Christine.

'Not quite so wildly, Nic,' she whispered. 'I don't object personally; but they'll notice us. How came you here?'

'I heard that you had driven over; and I set out – on purpose for this.'

'What – you have walked?'

'Yes. If I had waited for one of uncle's horses I should have been too late.'

'Five miles here and five back – ten miles on foot – merely to dance!'

'With you. What made you think of this old "Honeymoon" thing?'

'O! it came into my head when I saw you, as what would have been a reality with us if you had not been stupid about that licence, and had got it for a distant church.'

'Shall we try again?'

'No – I don't know. I'll think it over.'

The villagers admired their grace and skill, as the dancers themselves perceived; but they did not know what accompanied that admiration in one spot, at least.

'People who wonder they can foot it so featly together should know what some others think,' a waterman was saying to his neighbour. 'Then their wonder would be less.'

His comrade asked for information.

'Well – really I hardly believe it – but 'tis said they be man and wife. Yes, sure – went to church and did the job a'most afore 'twas light one morning. But mind, not a word of this; for 'twould be the loss of a winter's work to me if I had spread such a report and it were not true.'

When the dance had ended she rejoined her own section of the company. Her father and Mr Bellston the elder had now come out from the house, and were smoking in the background. Presently she found that her father was at her elbow.

'Christine, don't dance too often with young Long – as a mere matter of prudence, I mean, as volk might think it odd, he being one of our own neighbouring farmers. I should not mention this to 'ee if he were an ordinary young fellow; but being superior to the rest it behoves you to be careful.'

'Exactly, papa,' said Christine.

But the revived sense that she was deceiving him threw a damp over her spirits. 'But, after all,' she said to herself, 'he is a young man of Elsenford, handsome, able, and the soul of honour; and I am a young woman of the adjoining parish, who have been constantly thrown into communication with him. Is it not, by Nature's rule, the most proper thing in the world that I should marry him, and is it not an absurd conventional regulation which says that such a union would be wrong?'

It may be concluded that the strenth of Christine's large-minded argument was rather an evidence of weakness than of strength in the passion it concerned, which had required neither argument nor reasoning of any kind for its maintenance when full and flush in its early days.

When driving home in the dark with her father she sank into pensive silence. She was thinking of Nicholas having to trudge on foot all those miles back after his exertions on the sward. Mr Everard, arousing himself from a nap, said suddenly, 'I have something to mention to 'ee, by George – so I have, Chris! You probably know what it is?'

She expressed ignorance, wondering if her father had discovered anything of her secret.

'Well, according to *him* you know it. But I will tell 'ee. Perhaps you noticed young Jim Bellston walking me off down the lawn with him? – whether or no, we walked together a good while; and he informed me that he wanted to pay his addresses to 'ee. I naturally said that it depended upon yourself; and he replied that you were willing enough; you had given him particular encouragement – showing your preference for him by specially choosing him for your partner – hey? "In that case," says I, "go on and conquer – settle it with her – I have no objection." The poor fellow was very grateful, and in short, there we left the matter. He'll propose tomorrow.'

She saw now to her dismay what James Bellston had read as encouragement. 'He has mistaken me altogether,' she said. 'I had no idea of such a thing.'

'What, you won't have him?'

'Indeed, I cannot!'

'Chrissy,' said Mr Everard with emphasis, 'there's *noo*body whom I should so like you to marry as that young man. He's a thoroughly clever fellow, and fairly well provided for. He's travelled all over the temperate zone; but he says that directly he marries he's going to give up all that, and be a regular stay-at-home. You would be nowhere safer than in his hands.'

'It is true,' she answered. 'He *is* a highly desirable match, and I *should* be well provided for, and probably very safe in his hands.'

'Then don't be skittish, and stand-to.'

She had spoken from her conscience and understanding, and not to please her father. As a reflecting woman she believed that such a marriage would be a wise one. In great things Nicholas was closest to her nature; in little things Bellston seemed immeasurably nearer than Nic; and life was made up of little things.

Altogether the firmament looked black for Nicholas Long, notwithstanding her half-hour's ardour for him when she saw him dancing with the dairyman's daughter. Most great passions, movements, and beliefs – individual and national – burst during their decline into a temporary irradiation, which rivals their original splendour; and then they speedily become extinct. Perhaps the dance had given the last flare-up to Christine's love. It seemed to have improvidently consumed for its immediate purpose all her ardour forwards, so that for the future there was nothing left but frigidity.

Nicholas had certainly been very foolish about that licence!

4

This laxity of emotional tone was further increased by an incident, when, two days later, she kept an appointment with Nicholas in the Sallows. The Sallows was an extension of the shrubberies and plantations along the banks of the Froom, accessible from the lawn of Froom-Everard House only, except by wading through the river at the waterfall or elsewhere. Near the brink was a thicket of box in which a trunk lay prostrate; this had been once or twice their trysting-place, though it was by no means a safe one; and it was here she sat awaiting him now.

The noise of the stream muffled any sound of footsteps, and it was before she was aware of his approach that she looked up and saw him wading across at the top of the waterfall.

Noontide lights and dwarfed shadows always banished the romantic aspect of her love for Nicholas. Moreover, something new had occurred to disturb her; and if ever she had regretted giving way to a tenderness for him – which perhaps she had not done with any distinctness – she regretted it now. Yet in the bottom of their hearts those two were excellently paired, the very twin halves of a perfect whole; and their love was pure. But at this hour surfaces showed garishly, and obscured the depths. Probably her regret appeared in her face.

He walked up to her without speaking, the water running from his boots; and, taking one of her hands in each of his own, looked narrowly into her eyes.

'Have you thought it over?'

'What?'

'Whether we shall try again; you remember saying you would at the dance?'

'Oh, I had forgotten that!'

'You are sorry we tried at all!' he said accusingly.

'I am not so sorry for the fact as for the rumours,' she said.

'Ah! rumours?'

'They say we are already married.'

'Who?'

'I cannot tell exactly. I heard some whispering to that effect. Somebody in the village told one of the servants, I believe. This man said that he was crossing the churchyard early on that unfortunate foggy morning, and heard voices in the chancel, and peeped through the window as well as the dim panes would let him; and there he saw you and me and Mr Bealand, and so on; but thinking his surmises would be dangerous knowledge, he hastened on. And so the story got afloat. Then your aunt, too—'

'Good Lord! – what has she done?'

'The story was told her, and she said, proudly, "O yes, it is true enough. I have seen the licence. But it is not to be known yet."'

'Seen the licence? How the—'

'Accidentally, I believe, when your coat was hanging somewhere.'

The information, coupled with the infelicitous word 'proudly', caused Nicholas to flush with mortification. He knew that it was in his aunt's nature to make a brag of that sort; but worse than the brags was the fact that this was the first occasion on which Christine had deigned to show her consciousness that such a marriage would be a source of pride to his relatives – the only two he had in the world.

'You are sorry, then, even to be thought my wife, much less to be it.' He dropped her hand, which fell lifelessly.

'It is not sorry exactly, dear Nic. But I feel uncomfortable and vexed, that after screwing up my courage, my fidelity, to the point of going to church, you should have so muddled – managed the matter that it has ended in neither one thing nor the other. How can I meet acquaintances, when I don't know what they are thinking of me?'

'Then, dear Christine, let us mend the muddle. I'll go away for a few days and get another licence, and you can come to me.'

She shrank from this perceptibly. 'I cannot screw myself up to it a second time,' she said. 'I am sure I cannot! Besides, I promised Mr Bealand. And yet how can I continue to see you after such a rumour? We shall be watched now, for certain.'

'Then don't see me.'

'I fear I must not for the present. Altogether—'

'What?'

'I am very depressed.'

These views were not very inspiriting to Nicholas, as he construed them. It may indeed have been possible that he construed them wrongly, and should have insisted upon her making the rumour true. Unfortunately, too, he had come to her in a hurry through brambles and briars, water and weed, and the shaggy wildness which hung about his appearance at this fine and correct time of day lent an impracticability to the look of him.

'You blame me – you repent your courses – you repent that you ever, ever owned anything to me!'

'No, Nicholas, I do not repent that,' she returned gently, though with firmness. 'But I think that you ought not to have got that licence without asking me first; and I also think that you ought to have known how it would be if you lived on here in your present position, and made no effort to better it. I can bear whatever comes, for social ruin is not personal ruin or even personal disgrace. But as a sensible, new-risen poet says, whom I have been reading this morning:

> The world and its ways have a certain worth:
> And to press a point while these oppose
> Were simple policy. Better wait.

As soon as you had got my promise, Nic, you should have gone away – yes – and made a name, and come back to claim me. That was my silly girlish dream about my hero.'

'Perhaps I can do as much yet! And would you have indeed liked better to live away from me for family reasons, than to run a risk in seeing me for affection's sake? O what a cold heart it has grown! If I had been a prince, and you a dairymaid, I'd have stood by you in the face of the world!'

She shook her head. 'Ah – you don't know what society is – you don't know.'

'Perhaps not. Who was that strange gentleman of about seven-and-twenty I saw at Mr Bellston's christening feast?'

'Oh – that was his nephew James. Now he is a man who has seen an unusual extent of the world of his age. He is a great traveller, you know.'

'Indeed.'

'In fact an explorer. He is very entertaining.'

'No doubt.'

Nicholas received no shock of jealousy from her announcement. He knew her so well that he could see she was not in the least in love with

Bellston. But he asked if Bellston were going to continue his explorations.

'Not if he settles in life. Otherwise he will, I suppose.'

'Perhaps I could be a great explorer, too, if I tried.'

'You could, I am sure.'

They sat apart, and not together; each looking afar off at vague objects, and not in each other's eyes. Thus the sad autumn afternoon waned, while the waterfall hissed sarcastically of the inevitableness of the unpleasant. Very different this from the time when they had first met there.

The nook was most picturesque; but it looked horridly common and stupid now. Their sentiment had set a colour hardly less visible than a material one on surrounding objects, as sentiment must where life is but thought. Nicholas was as devoted as ever to the fair Christine; but unhappily he too had moods and humours, and the division between them was not closed.

She had no sooner got indoors and sat down to her work-table than her fathered entered the drawing-room. She handed him his newspaper; he took it without a word, went and stood on the hearthrug, and flung the paper on the floor.

'Christine, what's the meaning of this terrible story? I was just on my way to look at the register.'

She looked at him without speech.

'You have married – Nicholas Long?'

'No, father.'

'No? Can you say no in the face of such facts as I have been put in possession of?'

'Yes.'

'But – the note you wrote to the rector – and the going to church?'

She briefly explained that their attempt had failed.

'Ah! Then this is what that dancing meant, was it? By—, it makes me—. How long has this been going on, may I ask?'

'This what?'

'What, indeed! Why, making him your beau. Now listen to me. All's well that ends well; from this day, madam, this moment, he is to be nothing more to you. You are not to see him. Cut him adrift instantly! I only wish his volk were on my farm – out they should go, or I would know the reason why. However, you are to write him a letter to this effect at once.'

'How can I cut him adrift?'

'Why not? You must, my good maid!'

'Well, though I have not actually married him, I have solemnly sworn to be his wife when he comes home from abroad to claim me. It would be gross perjury not to fulfil my promise. Besides, no woman can go to church with a man to deliberately solemnize matrimony, and refuse him afterwards, if he does nothing wrong meanwhile.'

The uttered sound of her strong conviction seemed to kindle in Christine a livelier perception of all its bearings than she had known while it had lain unformulated in her mind. For when she had done speaking she fell down on her knees before her father, covered her face, and said, 'Please, please forgive me, papa! How *could* I do it without letting you know! I don't know, I don't know!'

When she looked up she found that, in the turmoil of his mind, her father was moving about the room. 'You are within an ace of ruining yourself, ruining me, ruining us all!' he said. 'You are nearly as bad as your brother, begad!'

'Perhaps I am – yes – perhaps I am!'

'That I should father such a harum-scarum brood!'

'It is very bad; but Nicholas—'

'He's a scoundrel!'

'He is *not* a scoundrel!' cried she, turning quickly. 'He's as good and worthy as you or I, or anybody bearing our name, or any nobleman in the kingdom, if you come to that! Only – only' – she could not continue the argument on those lines. 'Now, father, listen!' she sobbed: 'if you taunt me I'll go off and join him at his farm this very day, and marry him to-morrow, that's what I'll do!'

'I don't taant ye!'

'I wish to avoid unseemliness as much as you.'

She went away. When she came back a quarter of an hour later, thinking to find the room empty, he was standing there as before, never having apparently moved. His manner had quite changed. He seemed to take a resigned and entirely different view of circumstances.

'Christine, here's a paragraph in the paper hinting at a secret wedding, and I'm blazed if it don't point to you. Well, since this was to happen, I'll bear it, and not complain. All volk have crosses, and this is one of mine. Well, this is what I've got to say – I feel that you must carry out this attempt at marrying Nicholas Long. Faith, you must! The rumour will become a scandal if you don't – that's my view. I have tried to look at the brightest side of the case. Nicholas Long is a young man superior to most of his class, and fairly presentable. And he's not poor – at least his uncle is not. I believe the old muddler could buy me up any day. However, a farmer's wife you must be, as far as I can see. As you've made your bed, so ye must lie. Parents propose, and ungrateful children dispose. You shall marry him, and immediately.'

Christine hardly knew what to make of this. 'He is quite willing to wait, and so am I. We can wait for two or three years, and then he will be as worthy as—'

'You must marry him. And the sooner the better, if 'tis to be done at all. . . And yet I did wish you could have been Jim Bellston's wife. I did wish it! But no.'

'I, too, wished it and do still, in one sense,' she returned gently. His moderation had won her out of her defiant mood, and she was willing to reason with him.

'You do?' he said, surprised.

'I see that in a worldly sense my conduct with Mr Long may be considered a mistake.'

'H'm – I am glad to hear that – after my death you may see it more clearly still; and you won't have long to wait, to my reckoning.'

She fell into bitter repentance, and kissed him in her anguish. 'Don't say that!' she cried. 'Tell me what to do?'

'If you'll leave me for an hour or two I'll think. Drive to the market and back – the carriage is at the door – and I'll try to collect my senses. Dinner can be put back till you return.'

In a few minutes she was dressed, and the carriage bore her up the hill which divided the village and manor from the market-town.

5

A quarter of an hour brought her into the High Street, and for want of a more important errand she called at the harness-maker's for a dog-collar that she required.

It happened to be market-day, and Nicholas, having postponed the engagements which called him thither to keep the appointment with her in the Sallows, rushed off at the end of the afternoon to attend to them as well as he could. Arriving thus in a great hurry on account of the lateness of the hour, he still retained the wild, amphibious appearance which had marked him when he came up from the meadows to her side – an exceptional condition of things which had scarcely ever before occurred. When she crossed the pavement from the shop door, the shopman bowing and escorting her to the carriage, Nicholas chanced to be standing at the road-waggon office, talking to the master of the waggons. There were a good many people about, and those near paused and looked at her transit, in the full stroke of the level October sun, which went under the brims of their hats, and pierced through their button-holes. From the group she heard murmured the words: 'Mrs Nicholas Long'.

The unexpected remark, not without distinct satire in its tone, took her so greatly by surprise that she was confounded. Nicholas was by this time nearer, though coming against the sun he had not yet perceived her. Influenced by her father's lecture, she felt angry with him for being there and causing this awkwardness. Her notice of him was therefore slight, supercilious perhaps, slurred over; and her vexation at his presence showed distinctly in her face as she sat down in her seat. Instead of catching his waiting eye, she positively turned her head away.

A moment after she was sorry she had treated him so; but he was gone.

Reaching home she found on her dressing-table a note from her father. The statement was brief:

> I have considered and am of the same opinion. You must marry him. He can leave home at once and travel as proposed. I have written to him to this effect. I don't want any victuals, so don't wait dinner for me.

Nicholas was the wrong kind of man to be blind to his Christine's mortification, though he did not know its entire cause. He had lately foreseen something of this sort as possible.

'It serves me right,' he thought, as he trotted homeward. 'It was absurd – wicked of me to lead her on so. The sacrifice would have been too great – too cruel!' And yet, though he thus took her part, he flushed with indignation every time he said to himself, 'She is ashamed of me!'

On the ridge which overlooked Froom-Everard he met a neighbour of his – a stock-dealer – in his gig, and they drew rein and exchanged a few words. A part of the dealer's conversation had much meaning for Nicholas.

'I've had occasion to call on Squire Everard,' the former said; 'but he couldn't see me on account of being quite knocked up at some bad news he has heard.'

Nicholas rode on past Froom-Everard to Elsenford Farm, pondering. He had new and startling matter for thought as soon as he got there. The Squire's note had arrived. At first he could not credit its import; then he saw further, took in the tone of the letter, saw the writer's contempt behind the words, and understood that the letter was written as by a man hemmed into a corner. Christine was defiantly – insultingly – hurled at his head. He was accepted because he was so despised.

And yet with what respect he had treated her and hers! Now he was reminded of what an agricultural friend had said years ago, seeing the eyes of Nicholas fixed on Christine as on an angel when she passed: 'Better a little fire to warm 'ee than a great one to burn 'ee. No good can come of throwing your heart there.' He went into the mead, sat down, and asked himself four questions:

1. How could she live near her acquaintance as his wife, even in his absence, without suffering martyrdom from the stings of their contempt?

2. Would not this entail total estrangement between Christine and her family also, and her own consequent misery?

3. Must not such isolation extinguish her affection for him?

4. Supposing that her father rigged them out as colonists and sent them off to America, was not the effect of such exile upon one of her gentle nurture likely to be as the last?

In short, whatever they should embark in together would be cruelty to her, and his death would be a relief. It would, indeed, in one aspect be a relief to her now, if she were so ashamed of him as she had appeared to be that day. Were he dead, this little episode with him would fade away like a dream.

Mr Everard was a good-hearted man at bottom, but to take his enraged offer seriously was impossible. Obviously it was hotly made in his first bitterness at what he had heard. The least thing that he could do would be to go away and never trouble her more. To travel and learn and come back in two years, as mapped out in their first sanguine scheme, required a staunch heart on her side, if the necessary expenditure of time and money were to be afterwards justified; and it were folly to calculate on that when he had seen today that her heart was failing her already. To travel and disappear and not be heard of for many years would be a far more independent stroke, and it would leave her entirely unfettered. Perhaps he might rival in this kind the accomplished Mr Bellston, of whose journeyings he had heard so much.

He sat and sat, and the fog rose out of the river, enveloping him like a fleece; first his feet and knees, then his arms and body, and finally submerging his head. When he had come to a decision he went up again into the homestead. He would be independent, if he died for it, and he would free Christine. Exile was the only course. The first step was to inform his uncle of his determination.

Two days later Nicholas was on the same spot in the mead, at almost the same hour of eve. But there was no fog now; a blusterous autumn wind had ousted the still, golden days and misty nights; and he was going, full of purpose, in the opposite direction. When he had last entered the mead he was an inhabitant of the Froom valley; in forty-eight hours he had severed himself from that spot as completely as if he had never belonged to it. All that appertained to him in the Froom valley now was circumscribed by the portmanteau in his hand.

In making his preparations for departure he had unconsciously held a faint, foolish hope that she would communicate with him and make up their estrangement in some soft womanly way. But she had given no signal, and it was too evident to him that her latest mood had grown to be her fixed one, proving how well-founded had been his impulse to set her free.

He entered the Sallows, found his way in the dark to the garden-door of the house, slipped under it a note to tell her of his departure, and explaining its true reason to be a consciousness of her growing feeling that he was an encumbrance and a humiliation. Of the direction of his journey and of the date of his return he said nothing.

His course now took him into the high road, which he pursued for some miles in a north-easterly direction, still spinning the thread of sad inferences, and asking himself why he should ever return. At daybreak he stood on the hill above Shottsford-Forum, and awaited a coach which passed about this time along that highway towards Melchester and London.

6

Some fifteen years after the date of the foregoing incidents, a man who had dwelt in far countries, and viewed many cities, arrived at Roy-Town, a roadside hamlet on the old western turnpike road, not five miles from Froom-Everard, and put up at the Buck's Head, an isolated inn at that spot. He was still barely of middle age, but it could be seen that a haze of gray was settling upon the locks of his hair, and that his face had lost colour and curve, as if by exposure to bleaching climates and strange atmospheres, or from ailments incidental thereto. He seemed to observe little around him, by reason of the intrusion of his musings upon the scene. In truth Nicholas Long was just now the creature of old hopes and fears consequent upon his arrival – this man who once had not cared if his name were blotted out from that district. The evening light showed wistful lines which he could not smooth away by the worldling's gloss of nonchalance that he had learnt to fling over his face.

The Buck's Head was a somewhat unusual place for a man of this sort to choose as a house of sojourn in preference to some Casterbridge inn four miles further on. Before he left home it had been a lively old tavern at which High-flyers, and Heralds, and Tally-hoes had changed horses on their stages up and down the country; but now the house was rather cavernous and chilly, the stable-roofs were hollow-backed, the landlord was asthmatic, and the traffic gone.

He arrived in the afternoon, and when he had sent back the fly and was having a nondescript meal, he put a question to the waiting-maid with a mien of indifference.

'Squire Everard, of Froom-Everard Manor, has been dead some years, I believe?'

She replied in the affirmative.

'And are any of the family left there still?'

'O no, bless you, sir! They sold the place years ago – Squire Everard's son did – and went away. I've never heard where they went to. They came quite to nothing.'

'Never heard anything of the young lady – the Squire's daughter?'

'No. You see 'twas before I came to these parts.'

When the waitress left the room, Nicholas pushed aside his plate and gazed out of the window. He was not going over into the Froom valley altogether on Christine's account, but she had greatly animated his motive in coming that way. Anyhow he would push on there now that he was so near, and not ask questions here where he was liable to be wrongly informed. The fundamental inquiry he had not ventured to make – whether Christine had married before the family went away. He had abstained because of an absurd dread of extinguishing hopeful surmise. That the Everards had left their old home was bad enough intelligence for one day.

Rising from the table he put on his hat and went out, ascending towards the upland which divided this district from his native vale. The first familiar feature that met his eye was a little spot on the distant sky – a clump of trees standing on a barrow which surmounted a yet more remote upland – a point where, in his childhood, he had believed people could stand and see America. He reached the further verge of the plateau on which he had entered. Ah, there was the valley – a greenish-gray stretch of colour – still looking placid and serene, as though it had not much missed him. If Christine was no longer there, why should he pause over it this evening? His uncle and aunt were dead, and tomorrow would be soon enough to inquire for remoter relatives. Thus, disinclined to go further, he turned to retrace his way to the inn.

In the backward path he now perceived the figure of a woman, who had been walking at a distance behind him; and as she drew nearer he began to be startled. Surely, despite the variations introduced into that figure by changing years, its ground-lines were those of Christine?

Nicholas had been sentimental enough to write to Christine immediately on landing at Southampton a day or two before this, addressing his letter at a venture to the old house, and merely telling her that he planned to reach the Roy-Town inn on the present afternoon. The news of the scattering of the Everards had dissipated his hope of hearing of her; but here she was.

So they met – there, alone, on the open down by a pond, just as if the meeting had been carefully arranged.

She threw up her veil. She was still beautiful, though the years had touched her; a little more matronly – much more homely. Or was it only that he was much less homely now – a man of the world – the sense of homeliness being relative? Her face had grown to be pre-eminently of the sort that would be called interesting. Her habiliments were of a demure and sober cast, though she was one who had used to dress so airily and so gaily. Years had laid on a few shadows too in this.

'I received your letter,' she said, when the momentary embarrassment of their first approach had passed. 'And I thought I would walk across the hills today, as it was fine. I have just called at the inn, and they told me you were out. I was now on my way homeward.'

He hardly listened to this, though he intently gazed at her. 'Christine,' he said, 'One word. Are you free?'

'I – I am in a certain sense,' she replied, colouring.

The announcement had a magical effect. The intervening time between past and present closed up for him, and moved by an impulse which he had combated for fifteen years, he seized her two hands and drew her towards him.

She started back, and became almost a mere acquaintance. 'I have to tell you,' she gasped, 'that I have – been married.'

Nicholas's rose-coloured dream was immediately toned down to a grayish tinge.

'I did not marry till many years after you had left,' she continued in the humble tones of one confessing to a crime. 'Oh Nic,' she cried reproachfully, 'how could you stay away so long?'

'Whom did you marry?'

'Mr Bellston.'

'I – ought to have expected it.' He was going to add, 'And is he dead?' but he checked himself. Her dress unmistakably suggested widowhood; and she had said she was free.

'I must now hasten home,' said she. 'I felt that, considering my shortcomings at our parting so many years ago, I owed you the initiative now.'

'There is some of your generosity in that. I'll walk with you, if I may. Where are you living, Christine?'

'In the same house, but not on the old conditions. I have part of it on lease; the farmer now tenanting the premises found the whole more than he wanted, and the owner allowed me to keep what rooms I chose. I am poor now, you know, Nicholas, and almost friendless. My brother sold the Froom-Everard estate when it came to him, and the person who bought it turned our home into a farmhouse. Till my father's death my husband and I lived in the manor-house with him, so that I have never lived away from the spot.'

She was poor. That, and the change of name, sufficiently accounted for the inn-servant's ignorance of her continued existence within the walls of her old home.

It was growing dusk, and he still walked with her. A woman's head arose from the declivity before them, and as she drew nearer, Christine asked him to go back. 'This is the wife of the farmer who shares the house,' she said. 'She is accustomed to come out and meet me whenever I walk far and am benighted. I am obliged to walk everywhere now.'

The farmer's wife, seeing that Christine was not alone, paused in her advance, and Nicholas said, 'Dear Christine, if you are obliged to do these things, I am not, and what wealth I can command you may command likewise. They say rolling stones gather no moss; but they gather dross sometimes. I was one of the pioneers of the gold-fields, you know, and made a sufficient fortune there for my wants. What is more, I kept it. When I had done this I was coming home, but hearing of my uncle's death I changed my plan, travelled, speculated, and increased my fortune. Now, before we part; you remember you stood with me at the altar once, and therefore I speak with less preparation than I should otherwise use. Before we part then I ask, shall another again intrude between us? Or shall we complete the union we began?'

She trembled – just as she had done at that very minute of standing with him in the church, to which he had recalled her mind. 'I will not enter into that now, dear Nicholas,' she replied. 'There will be more to talk of and consider first – more to explain, which it would have spoiled this meeting to have entered into now.'

'Yes, yes; but—'

'Further than the brief answer I gave, Nic, don't press me tonight. I still have the old affection for you, or I should not have sought you. Let that suffice for the moment.'

'Very well, dear one. And when shall I call to see you?'

'I will write and fix an hour. I will tell you everything of my history then.'

And thus they parted, Nicholas feeling that he had not come here fruitlessly. When she and her companion were out of sight he retraced his steps to Roy-Town, where he made himself as comfortable as he could in the deserted old inn of his boyhood's days. He missed her companionship this evening more than he had done at any time during the whole fifteen years; and it was as though instead of separation there had been constant communion with her throughout that period. The tones of her voice had stirred his heart in a nook which had lain stagnant ever since he last heard them. They recalled the woman to whom he had once lifted his eyes as to a goddess. Her announcement that she had been another's came as a little shock to him, and he did not now lift his eyes to her in precisely the same way as he had lifted them at first. But he forgave her for marrying Bellston; what could he expect after fifteen years?

He slept at Roy-Town that night, and in the morning there was a short note from her, repeating more emphatically her statement of the previous evening – that she wished to inform him clearly of her circumstances, and to calmly consider with him the position in which she was placed. Would he call upon her on Sunday afternoon, when she was sure to be alone?

'Nic,' she wrote on, 'what a cosmopolite, you are! I expected to find my old yeoman still; but I was quite awed in the presence of such a citizen of the world. Did I seem rusty and unpractised? Ah – you seemed so once to me!'

Tender playful words; the old Christine was in them. She said Sunday afternoon, and it was now only Saturday morning. He wished she had said today; that short revival of her image had vitalized to sudden heat feelings that had almost been stilled. Whatever she might have to explain as to her position – and it was awkwardly narrowed, no doubt – he could not give her up. Miss Everard or Mrs Bellston, what mattered it? – she was the same Christine.

He did not go outside the inn all Saturday. He had no wish to see or do anything but to await the coming interview. So he smoked, and read the local newspaper of the previous week, and stowed himself in the chimney-corner. In the evening he felt that he could remain indoors no longer, and the moon being near the full, he started from the inn on foot in the same direction as that of yesterday, with the view of contemplating the old village and its precincts, and hovering round her house under the cloak of night.

With a stout stick in his hand he climbed over the five miles of upland in a comparatively short space of time. Nicholas had seen many strange lands and trodden many strange ways since he last walked that path, but as he trudged he seemed wonderfully like his old self, and had not the slightest difficulty in finding the way. In descending to the meads the streams perplexed him a little, some of the old foot-bridges having been removed; but he ultimately got across the larger water-courses, and pushed on to the village, avoiding her residence for the moment, lest she should encounter him, and think he had not respected the time of her appointment.

He found his way to the churchyard, and first ascertained where lay the two relations he had left alive at his departure; then he observed the gravestones of other inhabitants with whom he had been well acquainted, till by degrees he seemed to be in the society of all the elder Froom-Everard population, as he had known the place. Side by side as they had lived in his day here were they now. They had moved house in mass.

But no tomb of Mr Bellston was visible, though, as he had lived at the manor-house, it would have been natural to find it here. In truth Nicholas was more anxious to discover that than anything, being curious to know how long he had been dead. Seeing from the glimmer of a light in the church that somebody was there cleaning for Sunday he entered, and looked round upon the walls as well as he could. But there was no monument to her husband, though one had been erected to the Squire.

Nicholas addressed the young man who was sweeping. 'I don't see any monument or tomb to the late Mr Bellston?'

'O no, sir; you won't see that,' said the young man drily.

'Why, pray?'

'Because he's not buried here. He's not Christian-buried anywhere, as far as we know. In short, perhaps he's not buried at all; and between ourselves, perhaps he's alive.'

Nicholas sank an inch shorter. 'Ah,' he answered.

'Then you don't know the peculiar cirumstances, sir?'

'I am a stranger here – as to late years.'

'Mr Bellston was a traveller – an explorer – it was his calling; you may have heard his name as such?'

'I remember.' Nicholas recalled the fact that this very bent of Mr Bellston's was the incentive to his own roaming.

'Well, when he married he came and lived here with his wife and his wife's father, and said he would travel no more. But after a time he got weary of biding quiet here, and weary of her – he was not a good husband to the young lady by any means – and he betook himself again to his old trick of roving – with her money. Away he went, quite out of the realm of human foot, into the bowels of Asia, and never was heard of more. He was murdered, it is said, but nobody knows; though as that was nine years ago he's dead enough in principle, if not in corporation. His widow lives quite humble, for between her husband and her brother she's left in very lean pasturage.'

Nicholas went back to the Buck's Head without hovering round her dwelling. This then was the explanation which she had wanted to make. Not dead, but missing. How could he have expected that the first fair promise of happiness held out to him would remain untarnished? She had said that she was free; and legally she was free, no doubt. Moreover, from her tone and manner he felt himself justified in concluding that she would be willing to run the risk of a union with him, in the improbability of her husband's existence. Even if that husband lived, his return was not a likely event, to judge from his character. A man who could spend her money on his own personal adventures would not be anxious to disturb her poverty after such a lapse of time.

Well, the prospect was not so unclouded as it had seemed. But could he, even now, give up Christine?

7

Two months more brought the year nearly to a close, and found Nicholas Long tenant of a spacious house in the market-town nearest to Froom-Everard. A man of means, genial character, and a bachelor, he was an object of great interest to his neighbours, and to his neighbours' wives and daughters. But he took little note of this, and had made it his business to go twice a week, no matter what the weather, to the now farmhouse at Froom-Everard, a wing of which had been retained as the refuge of Christine. He always walked, to give no trouble in putting up a horse to a housekeeper whose staff was limited.

The two had put their heads together on the situation, had gone to a solicitor, had balanced possibilities, and had resolved to make the plunge of matrimony. 'Nothing venture, nothing have,' Christine had said, with some of her old audacity.

With almost gratuitous honesty they had let their intentions be widely known. Christine, it is true, had rather shrunk from publicity at first; but Nicholas argued that their boldness in this respect would have good results. With his friends he held that there was not the slightest probability of her being other than a widow, and a challenge to the missing man now, followed by no response, would stultify any unpleasant remarks which might be thrown at her after their union. To this end a paragraph was inserted in the Wessex papers, announcing that their marriage was proposed to be celebrated on such and such a day in December.

His periodic walks along the south side of the valley to visit her were among the happiest experiences of his life. The yellow leaves falling around him in the foreground, the well-watered meads on the left hand, and the woman he loved awaiting him at the back of the scene, promised a future of much serenity, as far as human judgment could foresee. On arriving, he would sit with her in the 'parlour' of the wing she retained, her general sitting-room, where the only relics of her early surroundings were an old clock from the other end of the house, and her own piano. Before it was quite dark they would stand, hand in hand, looking out of the window across the flat turf to the dark clump of trees which hid further view from their eyes.

'Do you wish you were still mistress here, dear?' he once said.

'Not at all,' said she cheerfully. 'I have a good enough room, and a good enough fire, and a good enough friend. Besides, my latter days as mistress of the house were not happy ones, and they spoilt the place for me. It was a punishment for my faithlessness. Nic, you do forgive me? Really you do?'

The twenty-third of December, the eve of the wedding-day, had arrived at last in the train of such uneventful ones as these. Nicholas had arranged to visit her that day a little later than usual, and see that everything was ready with her for the morrow's event and her removal to his house; for he had begun to look after her domestic affairs, and to lighten as much as possible the duties of her house-keeping.

He was to come to an early supper, which she had arranged to take the place of a wedding-breakfast next day – the latter not being feasible in her present situation. An hour or so after dark the wife of the farmer who lived in the other part of the house entered Christine's parlour to lay the cloth.

'What with getting the ham skinned, and the black-puddings hotted up,' she said, 'it will take me all my time before he's here, if I begin this minute.'

'I'll lay the table myself,' said Christine, jumping up. 'Do you attend to the cooking.'

'Thank you, ma'am. And perhaps 'tis no matter, seeing that it is the last night you'll have to do such work. I knew this sort of life wouldn't last long for 'ee, being born to better things.'

'It has lasted rather long, Mrs Wake. And if he had not found me out it would have lasted all my days.'

'But he did find you out.'

'He did. And I'll lay the cloth immediately.'

Mrs Wake went back to the kitchen, and Christine began to bustle about. She greatly enjoyed preparing this table for Nicholas and herself with her own hands. She took artistic pleasure in adjusting each article to its position, as if half-an-inch in error were a point of high importance. Finally she placed the two candles where they were to stand, and sat down by the fire.

Mrs Wake re-entered and regarded the effect. 'Why not have another candle or two, ma'am?' she said. ''Twould make it livelier. Say four.'

'Very well,' said Christine, and four candles were lighted. 'Really,' she added, surveying them, 'I have been now so long accustomed to little economies that they look quite extravagant.'

'Ah, you'll soon think nothing of forty in his grand new house! Shall I bring in supper directly he comes, ma'am?'

'No, not for half-an-hour; and, Mrs Wake, you and Betsy are busy in the kitchen, I know; so when he knocks don't disturb yourselves; I can let him in.'

She was again left alone, and, as it still wanted some time to Nicholas's appointment, she stood by the fire, looking at herself in the glass over the mantel. Reflectively raising a lock of her hair just above her temple she uncovered a small scar. That scar had a history. The terrible temper of her late husband – those sudden moods of irascibility which had made even his friendly excitements look like anger – had once caused him to set that mark upon her with a bezel of a ring he wore. He declared that the whole thing was an accident. She was a woman and kept her own opinion.

Christine then turned her back to the glass and scanned the table and the candles, shining one at each corner like types of the four Evangelists, and thought they looked too assuming – too confident. She glanced up at the clock, which stood also in this room, there not being space enough for it in the passage. It was nearly seven, and she expected Nicholas at half-past. She liked the company of this venerable article in her lonely life: its tickings and whizzings were a sort of conversation. It now began to strike the hour. At the end something grated slightly. Then, without any warning, the clock slowly inclined forward and fell at full length upon the floor.

The crash brought the farmer's wife rushing into the room. Christine had wellnigh sprung out of her shoes. Mrs Wake's enquiry what had happened was answered by the evidence of her own eyes.

'How did it occur?' she said.

'I cannot say; it was not firmly fixed, I suppose. Dear me, how sorry I am! My dear father's hall-clock! And now I suppose it is ruined.'

Assisted by Mrs Wake, she lifted the clock. Every inch of glass was, of course, shattered, but very little harm besides appeared to be done. They propped it up temporarily, though it would not go again.

Christine had soon recovered her composure, but she saw that Mrs

Wake was gloomy. 'What does it mean, Mrs Wake?' she said. 'Is it ominous?'

'It is a sign of a violent death in the family.'

'Don't talk of it. I don't believe such things; and don't mention it to Mr Long when he comes. *He*'s not in the family yet, you know.'

'O no, it cannot refer to him,' said Mrs Wake musingly.

'Some remote cousin, perhaps,' observed Christine, no less willing to humour her than to get rid of a shapeless dread which the incident had caused in her own mind. 'And – supper is almost ready, Mrs Wake?'

'In three-quarters of an hour.'

Mrs Wake left the room, and Christine sat on. Though it still wanted fifteen minutes to the hour at which Nicholas had promised to be there, she began to grow impatient. After the accustomed ticking the dead silence was oppressive. But she had not to wait so long as she had expected; steps were heard approaching the door, and there was a knock.

Christine was already there to open it. The entrance had no lamp, but it was not particularly dark out of doors. She could see the outline of a man, and cried cheerfully, 'You are early; it is very good of you.'

'I beg pardon. It is not Mr Bellston himself – only a messenger with his bag and greatcoat. But he will be here soon.'

The voice was not the voice of Nicholas, and the intelligence was strange. 'I – I don't understand. Mr Bellston?' she faintly replied.

'Yes, ma'am. A gentleman – a stranger to me – gave me these things at Casterbridge station to bring on here, and told me to say that Mr Bellston had arrived there, and is detained for half-an-hour, but will be here in the course of the evening.'

She sank into a chair. The porter put a small battered portmanteau on the floor, the coat on a chair, and looking into the room at the spread table said, 'If you are disappointed, ma'am, that your husband (as I s'pose he is) is not come, I can assure you he'll soon be here. He's stopped to get a shave, to my thinking, seeing he wanted it. What he said was that I could tell you he had heard the news in Ireland, and would have come sooner, his hand being forced; but was hindered crossing by the weather, having took passage in a sailing vessel. What news he meant he didn't say.'

'Ah, yes,' she faltered. It was plain that the man knew nothing of her intended re-marriage.

Mechanically rising and giving him a shilling, she answered to his 'good-night', and he withdrew, the beat of his footsteps lessening in the distance. She was alone; but in what a solitude.

Christine stood in the middle of the hall, just as the man had left her, in the gloomy silence of the stopped clock within the adjoining room, till she aroused herself, and turning to the portmanteau and greatcoat brought them to the light of the candles, and examined them. The portmanteau bore painted upon it the initials 'J.B.' in white letters – the well-known initials of her husband.

She examined the greatcoat. In the breast-pocket was an empty spirit flash, which she firmly fancied she recognized as the one she had filled many times for him when he was living at home with her.

She turned desultorily hither and thither, until she heard another tread without, and there came a second knocking at the door. She did not respond to it; and Nicholas – for it was he – thinking that he was not heard by reason of a concentration on tomorrow's proceedings, opened the door softly, and came on to the door of her room, which stood unclosed, just as it had been left by the Casterbridge porter.

Nicholas uttered a blithe greeting, cast his eye round the parlour, which with its tall candles, blazing fire, snow-white cloth, and prettily-spread table, formed a cheerful spectacle enough for a man who had been walking in the dark for an hour.

'My bride – almost, at last!' he cried, encircling her with his arms.

Instead of responding, her figure became limp, frigid, heavy; her head fell back, and he found that she had fainted.

It was natural, he thought. She had had many little worrying matters to attend to, and but slight assistance. He ought to have seen more effectually to her affairs; the closeness of the event had over-excited her. Nicholas kissed her unconscious face – more than once, little thinking what news it was that had changed its aspect. Loth to call Mrs Wake, he carried Christine to a couch and laid her down. This had the effect of reviving her. Nicholas bent and whispered in her ear, 'Lie quiet, dearest, no hurry; and dream, dream, dream of happy days. It is only I. You will soon be better.' He held her by the hand.

'No, no, no!' she said, with a stare. 'O, how can this be?'

Nicholas was alarmed and perplexed, but the disclosure was not long delayed. When she had sat up, and by degrees made the stunning event known to him, he stood as if transfixed.

'Ah – is it so?' said he. Then, becoming quite meek, 'And why was he so cruel as to – delay his return till now?'

She dutifully recited the explanation her husband had given her through the messenger; but her mechanical manner of telling it showed how much she doubted its truth. It was too unlikely that his arrival at such a dramatic moment should not be a contrived surprise, quite of a piece with his previous dealings towards her.

'But perhaps it may be true – and he may have become kind now – not as he used to be,' she faltered. 'Yes, perhaps, Nicholas, he is an altered man – we'll hope he is. I suppose I ought not to have listened to my legal advisers, and assumed his death so surely! Anyhow, I am roughly received back into – the right way!'

Nicholas burst out bitterly: 'O what too, too honest fools we were! – to so court daylight upon our intention by putting that announcement in the papers! Why could we not have married privately, and gone away, so that he would never have known what had become of you, even if he had returned? Christine, he has done it to. . . But I'll say no more. Of course we – might fly now.'

'No, no; we might not,' she said hastily.

'Very well. But this is hard to bear! "When I looked for good then evil came unto me, and when I waited for light there came darkness." So once said a sorely tried man in the land of Uz, and so say I now! . . . I wonder if he is almost here at this moment?'

She told him she supposed Bellston was approaching by the path across the fields, having sent on his greatcoat, which he would not want walking.

'And is this meal laid for him, or for me?'

'It was laid for you.'

'And it will be eaten by him?'

'Yes.'

'Christine, are you *sure* that he is come, or have you been sleeping over the fire and dreaming it?'

She pointed anew to the portmanteau with the initials 'J.B.', and to the coat beside it.

'Well, good-bye – good-bye! Curse that parson for not marrying us fifteen years ago!'

It is unnecessary to dwell further upon that parting. There are scenes wherein the words spoken do not even approximate to the level of the mental communion between the actors. Suffice it to say that part they did, and quickly; and Nicholas, more dead than alive, went out of the house homewards.

Why had he ever come back? During his absence he had not cared for Christine as he cared now. If he had been younger he might have felt tempted to descend into the meads instead of keeping along their edge. The Froom was down there, and he knew of quiet pools in that stream to which death would come easily. But he was too old to put an end to himself for such a reason as love; and another thought, too, kept him from seriously contemplating any desperate act. His affection for her was strongly protective, and in the event of her requiring a friend's support in future troubles there was none but himself left in the world to afford it. So he walked on.

Meanwhile Christine had resigned herself to circumstances. A resolve to continue worthy of her history and of her family lent her heroism and dignity. She called Mrs Wake, and explained to that worthy woman as much of what had occurred as she deemed necessary. Mrs Wake was too amazed to reply; she retreated slowly, her lips parted; till at the door she said with a dry mouth, 'And the beautiful supper, ma'am?'

'Serve it when he comes.'

'When Mr Bellston – yes, ma'am, I will.' She still stood gazing, as if she could hardly take in the order.

'That will do, Mrs Wake. I am much obliged to you for all your kindness.' And Christine was left alone again, and then she wept.

She sat down and waited. That awful silence of the stopped clock began anew, but she did not mind it now. She was listening for a footfall in a state of mental tensity which almost took away from her the power of motion. It seemed to her that the natural interval for her husband's journey thither must have expired; but she was not sure, and waited on.

Mrs Wake again came in. 'You have not rung for supper—'

'He is not yet come, Mrs Wake. If you want to go to bed, bring in the supper and set it on the table. It will be nearly as good cold. Leave the door unbarred.'

Mrs Wake did as was suggested, made up the fire, and went away. Shortly afterwards Christine heard her retire to her chamber. But Christine still sat on, and still her husband postponed his entry.

She aroused herself once or twice to freshen the fire, but was ignorant how the night was going. Her watch was upstairs, and she did not make the effort to go up to consult it. In her seat she continued; and still the supper waited, and still he did not come.

At length she was so nearly persuaded that the arrival of his things must have been a dream after all, that she again went over to them, felt them, and examined them. His they unquestionably were; and their forwarding by the porter had been quite natural. She sighed and sat down again.

Presently she fell into a doze, and when she again became conscious she found that the four candles had burned into their sockets and gone out. The fire still emitted a feeble shine. Christine did not take the trouble to get more candles, but stirred the fire and sat on.

After a long period she heard a creaking of the chamber floor and stairs at the other end of the house, and knew that the farmer's family were getting up. By-and-by Mrs Wake entered the room, candle in hand, bouncing open the door in her morning manner, obviously without any expectation of finding a person there.

'Lord-a-mercy! What, sitting here again, ma'am?'

'Yes, I am sitting here still.'

'You've been there ever since last night?'

'Yes.'

'Then—'

'He's not come.'

'Well, he won't come at this time o' morning,' said the farmer's wife. 'Do 'ee get on to bed, ma'am. You must be shrammed to death!'

It occurred to Christine now that possibly her husband had thought better of obtruding himself upon her company within an hour of revealing his existence to her, and decided to pay a more formal visit next day. She therefore adopted Mrs Wake's suggestion and retired.

8

Nicholas had gone straight home, neither speaking to nor seeing a soul. From that hour a change seemed to come over him. He had ever possessed a full share of self-consciousness; he had been readily piqued, had shown an unusual dread of being personally obtrusive. But now his sense of self, as an individual provoking opinion, appeared to leave him. When, therefore, after a day or two of seclusion, he came forth again, and the few acquaintances he had formed in the town condoled with him on what had happened, and pitied his haggard looks, he did not shrink from their regard as he would have done formerly, but took their sympathy as it would have been accepted by a child.

It reached his ears that Bellston had not appeared on the evening of his arrival at any hotel in the town or neighbourhood, or entered his wife's house at all. 'That's a part of his cruelty,' thought Nicholas. And when two or three days had passed, and still no account came to him of Bellston having joined her, he ventured to set out for Froom-Everard.

Christine was so shaken that she was obliged to receive him as she lay on a sofa, beside the square table which was to have borne their evening feast. She fixed her eyes wistfully upon him, and smiled a sad smile.

'He has not come?' said Nicholas under his breath.

'He has not.'

Then Nicholas sat beside her, and they talked on general topics merely like saddened old friends. But they could not keep away the subject of Bellston, their voices dropping as it forced its way in. Christine, no less than Nicholas, knowing her husband's character, inferred that, having stopped her game, as he would have phrased it, he was taking things leisurely, and, finding nothing very attractive in her limited mode of living, was meaning to return to her only when he had nothing better to do.

The bolt which laid low their hopes had struck so recently that they could hardly look each other in the face when speaking that day. But when a week or two had passed, and all the horizon still remained as vacant of Bellston as before, Nicholas and she could talk of the event with calm wonderment. Why had he come, to go again like this?

And then there set a period of resigned surmise, during which

So like so very like, was day to day,

that to tell of one of them is to tell of all. Nicholas would arrive between three and four in the afternoon, a faint trepidation influencing his walk as he neared her door. He would knock; she would always reply in person, having watched for him from the window. Then he would whisper –

'He has not come?'

'He has not,' she would say.

Nicholas would enter then, and she being ready bonneted, they would walk into the Sallows together as far as to the spot which they had frequently made their place of appointment in their youthful days. A plank bridge, which Bellston had caused to be thrown over the stream during his residence with her in the manor-house, was now again removed, and all was just the same as in Nicholas's time, when he had been accustomed to wade across on the edge of the cascade and come up to her like a merman from the deep. Here on the felled trunk, which still lay rotting in its old place, they would now sit, gazing at the descending sheet of water, with its never-ending sarcastic hiss at their baffled attempts to make themselves one flesh. Returning to the house they would sit down together to tea, after which, and the confidential chat that accompanied it, he walked home by the declining light. This proceeding became as periodic as an astronomical recurrence. Twice a week he came – all through that winter, all through the spring following, through the summer, through the autumn, the next winter, the next year, and the next, till an appreciable span of human life had passed by. Bellston still tarried.

Years and years Nick walked that way, at this interval of three days, from his house in the neighbouring town; and in every instance the aforesaid order of things was customary; and still on his arrival the form of words went on –

'He has not come?'

'He has not.'

So they grew older. The dim shape of that third one stood continually between them; they could not displace it; neither, on the other hand, could it effectually part them. They were in close communion, yet not indissolubly united; lovers, yet never growing cured of love. By the time that the fifth year of Nic's visiting had arrived, on about the five-hundredth occasion of his presence at her tea-table, he noticed that the bleaching process which had begun upon his own locks was also spreading to hers. He told her so, and they laughed. Yet she was in good health: a condition of suspense, which would have half-killed a man, had been endured by her without complaint, and even with composure.

One day, when these years of abeyance had numbered seven, they had strolled as usual as far as the waterfall, whose faint roar formed a sort of calling voice sufficient in the circumstances to direct their listlessness. Pausing there, he looked up at her face and said, 'Why should we not try again, Christine? We are legally at liberty to do so now. Nothing venture, nothing have.'

But she would not. Perhaps a little primness of idea was by this time ousting the native daring of Christine. 'What he has done once he can do twice,' she said. 'He is not dead, and if we were to marry he would say we had "forced his hand", as he said before, and duly reappear.'

Some years after, when Christine was about fifty, and Nicholas fifty-three, a new trouble of a minor kind arrived. He found an inconvenience in traversing the distance between their two houses, particularly in damp weather, the years he had spent in trying climates abroad having sown the seeds of rheumatism, which made a journey undesirable on inclement days, even in a carriage. He told her of this new difficulty, as he did of everything.

'If you could live nearer,' suggested she.

Unluckily there was no house near. But Nicholas, though not a millionaire, was a man of means; he obtained a small piece of ground on lease at the nearest spot to her home that it could be so obtained, which was on the opposite brink of the Froom, this river forming the boundary of the Froom-Everard manor; and here he built a cottage large enough for his wants. This took time, and when he got into it he found its situation a great comfort to him. He was not more than five hundred yards from her now, and gained a new pleasure in feeling that all sounds which greeted his ears, in the day or in the night, also fell upon hers – the caw of a particular rook, the voice of a neighbouring nightingale, the whistle of a local breeze, or the purl of the fall in the meadows, whose rush was a material rendering of Time's ceaseless scour over themselves, wearing them away without uniting them.

Christine's missing husband was taking shape as a myth among the surrounding residents; but he was still believed in as corporeally imminent by Christine herself, and also, in a milder degree, by Nicholas. For a curious unconsciousness of the long lapse of time since his revelation of himself seemed to affect the pair. There had been no passing events to serve as chronological milestones, and the evening on which she had kept supper waiting for him still loomed out with startling nearness in their retrospects.

In the seventeenth pensive year of this their parallel march towards the common bourne, a labourer came in a hurry one day to Nicholas's house and brought strange tidings. The present owner of Froom-Everard – a non-resident – had been improving his property in sundry ways, and one of these was by dredging the stream which, in the course of years, had become choked with mud and weeds in its passage through the Sallows. The process necessitated a reconstruction of the waterfall. When the river had been pumped dry for this purpose, the skeleton of a man had been found jammed among the piles supporting the edge of the fall. Every particle of his flesh and clothing had been eaten by fishes or abraded to nothing by the water, but the relics of a gold watch remained, and on the inside of the case was engraved the name of the maker of her husband's watch, which she well remembered.

Nicholas, deeply agitated, hastened to the place and examined the remains attentively, afterwards going across to Christine, and breaking the discovery to her. She would not come to view the skeleton, which lay extended on the grass, not a finger or toe-bone missing, so neatly had the acquatic operators done their work. Conjecture was directed to the question how Bellston had got there; and conjecture alone could give an explanation.

It was supposed that, on his way to call upon her, he had taken a short cut through the grounds, with which he was naturally very familiar, and coming to the fall under the trees had expected to find there the plank which, during his occupancy of the premises with Christine and her father, he had placed there for crossing into the meads on the other side instead of wading across as Nicholas had done. Before discovering its removal he had probably over-balanced himself, and was thus precipitated into the cascade, the piles beneath the descending current wedging him between them like the prongs of a pitchfork, and effectually preventing the rising of his body, over which the weeds grew. Such was the reasonable supposition concerning the discovery; but proof was never forthcoming.

'To think,' said Nicholas, when the remains had been decently interred, and he was again sitting with Christine – though not beside the waterfall – 'to think how we visited him! How we sat over him, hours and hours, gazing at him, bewailing our fate, when all the time he was ironically hissing at us from the spot, in an unknown tongue, that we could marry if we chose!'

She echoed the sentiment with a sigh.

'I have strange fancies,' she said. 'I suppose it *must* have been my husband who came back, and not some other man.'

Nicholas felt that there was little doubt. 'Besides – the skeleton,' he said.

'Yes. . . If it could not have been another person's – but no, of course it was he.'

'You might have married me on the day we had fixed, and there would have been no impediment. You would now have been seventeen years my wife, and we might have had tall sons and daughters.'

'It might have been so,' she murmured.

'Well – is it still better late than never?'

The question was one which had become complicated by the increasing years of each. Their wills were somewhat enfeebled now, their hearts sickened of tender enterprise by hope too long deferred. Having postponed the consideration of their course till a year after the interment of Bellston, each seemed less disposed than formerly to take it up again.

'Is it worth while, after so many years?' she said to him. 'We are fairly happy as we are – perhaps happier than we should be in any other relation, seeing what old people we have grown. The weight is gone from our lives; the shadow no longer divides us; then let us be joyful together as we are, dearest Nick, in the days of our vanity; and

With mirth and laughter let old wrinkles come.'

He fell in with these views of hers to some extent. But occasionally he ventured to urge her to reconsider the case, though he spoke not with the fervour of his earlier years.

AUTUMN 1887

ALICIA'S DIARY

I. SHE MISSES HER SISTER

July 7. – I wander about the house in a mood of unutterable sadness, for my dear sister Caroline has left home today with my mother, and I shall not see them again for several weeks. They have accepted a long-standing invitation to visit some old friends of ours, the Marlets, who live at Versailles for cheapness – my mother thinking that it will be for the good of Caroline to see a little of France and Paris. But I don't quite like her going. I fear she may lose some of that childlike simplicity and gentleness which so characterize her, and have been nourished by the seclusion of our life here. Her solicitude about her pony before starting was quite touching, and she made me promise to visit it daily, and see that it came to no harm.

Caroline gone abroad, and I left here! It is the reverse of an ordinary situation, for good or ill-luck has mostly ordained that I should be the absent one. Mother will be quite tired out by the young enthusiasm of Caroline. She will demand to be taken everywhere – to Paris continually, of course; to all the stock shrines of history's devotees; to palaces and prisons; to kings' tombs and queens' tombs; to cemeteries and picture-galleries, and royal hunting-forests. My poor mother, having gone over most of this ground many times before, will perhaps not find the perambulation so exhilarating as will Caroline herself. I wish I could have gone with them. I would not have minded having my legs walked off to please Caroline. But this regret is absurd: I could not, of course, leave my father with not a soul in the house to attend to the calls of the parishioners or to pour out his tea.

July 15. – A letter from Caroline today. It is very strange that she tells me nothing which I expected her to tell – only trivial details. She seems dazzled by the brilliancy of Paris – which no doubt appears still more brilliant to her from the fact of her only being able to obtain occasional glimpses of it. She would see that Paris, too, has a seamy side if you live there. I was not aware that the Marlets knew so many people. If, as mother has said, they went to reside at Versailles for reasons of economy, they will not effect much in that direction while they make a practice of entertaining all the acquaintances who happen to be in their neighbourhood. They do not confine their hospitalities to English people, either. I wonder who this M Charles de la Feste is, in whom Caroline says my mother is so much interested.

July 18. – Another letter from Caroline. I have learnt from this epistle that M Charles de la Feste is 'only one of the many friends of the Marlets'; that though a Frenchman by birth, and now again temporarily at Versailles, he has lived in England many many years; that he is a talented landscape and marine painter, and has exhibited at the *Salon,* and I think in London. His style and subjects are considered somewhat peculiar in Paris – rather English than Continental. I have not as yet learnt his age, or his condition, married or single. From the tone and nature of her remarks about him he sometimes seems to be a middle-aged family man, sometimes quite the reverse. From his nomadic habits I should say the latter is the most likely. He has travelled and seen a great deal, she tells me, and knows more about English literature than she knows herself.

July 21. – Letter from Caroline. Query: Is 'a friend of ours and the Marlets', of whom she now anonymously and mysteriously speaks, the same personage as the 'M de la Feste' of her former letters? He must be the same, I think, from his pursuits. If so, whence this sudden change of tone? . . . I have been lost in thought for at least a quarter of an hour since writing the preceding sentence. Suppose my dear sister is falling in love with this young man – there is no longer any doubt about his age; what a very awkward, risky thing for her! I do hope that my mother has an eye on these proceedings. But, then, poor mother never sees the drift of anything: she is in truth less of a mother to Caroline than I am. If I were there, how jealously I would watch him, and ascertain his designs!

I am of a stronger nature than Caroline! How I have supported her in the past through her little troubles and great griefs! Is she agitated at the presence of this, to her, new and strange feeling? But I am assuming her to be desperately in love, when I have no proof of anything of the kind. He may be merely a casual friend, of whom I shall hear no more.

July 24. – Then he *is* a bachelor, as I suspected. 'If M de la Feste ever marries he will', etc. So she writes. They are getting into close quarters, obviously. Also, 'Something to keep my hair smooth, which M de la Feste told me he had found useful for the tips of his moustache.' Very naïvely related this; and with how much unconsciouness of the intimacy between them that the remark reveals! But my mother – what can she be doing? Does she know of this? And if so, why does she not allude to it in her letters to my father? . . . I have been to look at Caroline's pony, in obedience to her reiterated request that I would not miss a day in seeing that she was well cared for. Anxious as Caroline was about this pony of hers before starting, she now never mentioned the poor animal once in her letters. The image of her pet suffers from displacement.

August 3. – Caroline's forgetfulness of her pony has naturally enough extended to me, her sister. It is ten days since she last wrote, and but for a note from my mother I should not know if she were dead or alive.

2. NEWS INTERESTING AND SERIOUS

August 5. – A cloud of letters. A letter from Caroline, another from mother; also one from each to my father.

The probability to which all the intelligence from my sister has pointed of late turns out to be a fact. There is an engagement, or almost an engagement, announced between my dear Caroline and M de la Feste – to Caroline's sublime happiness, and my mother's entire satisfaction; as well as to that of the Marlets. They and my mother seem to know all about the young man – which is more than I do, though a little extended information about him, considering that I am Caroline's elder sister, would not have been amiss. I half feel with my father, who is much surprised, and, I am sure, not altogether satisfied, that he should not have been consulted at all before matters reached such a definite stage, though he is too amiable to say so openly. I don't quite say that a good thing should have been hindered for the sake of our opinion, if it is a good thing; but the announcement comes very suddenly. It must have been foreseen by my mother for some time that this upshot was probable, and Caroline might have told me more distinctly that M de la Feste was her lover, instead of alluding so mysteriously to him as only a friend of the Marlets, and lately dropping his name altogether. My father, without exactly objecting to him as a Frenchman, 'wishes he were of English or some other reasonable nationality for one's son-in-law', but I tell him that the demarcations of races, kingdoms, and creeds, are wearing down every day, that patriotism is a sort of vice, and that the character of the individual is all we need think about in this case. I wonder if, in the event of their marriage, he will continue to live at Versailles, or if he will come to England.

August 7. – A supplemental letter from Caroline, answering, by anticipation, some of the aforesaid queries. She tells me that 'Charles', though he makes Versailles his present home, is by no means bound by his profession to continue there; that he will live just where she wishes, provided it be not too far from some centre of thought, art, and civilization. My mother and herself both think that the marriage should not take place till next year. He exhibits landscapes and canal scenery every year, she says; so I suppose he is popular, and that his income is sufficient to keep them in comfort. If not, I do not see why my father could not settle something more on them than he had intended, and diminish by a little what he had proposed for me, whilst it was imagined that I should be the first to stand in need of such.

'Of engaging manner, attractive appearance, and virtuous character,' is the reply I receive from her in answer to my request for a personal description. That is vague enough, and I would rather have had one definite fact of complexion, voice, deed, or opinion. But of course she has no eye now for material qualities; she cannot see him as he is. She sees him irradiated with glories such as never appertained and never will appertain to any man, foreign, English, or Colonial. To think that Caroline, two years my junior, and so childlike as to be five years my junior in nature, should be engaged to be married before me. But that is what happens in families more often than we are apt to remember.

August 16. – Interesting news today. Charles, she says, has pleaded that their marriage may just as well be this year as next; and he seems to have nearly converted my mother to the same way of thinking. I do not myself see any reason for delay, beyond the standing one of my father having as yet had no oppotunity of forming an opinion upon the man, the time, or anything. However, he takes his lot very quietly, and they are coming home to talk the question over with us; Caroline having decided not to make any positive arrangements for this change of state till she has seen me. Subject to my own and my father's approval, she says, they are inclined to settle the date of the wedding for November, three months from the present time, that it shall take place here in the village, that I, of course, shall be bridesmaid, and many other particulars. She draws an artless picture of the probable effect upon the minds of the villagers of this romantic performance in the chancel of our old church, in which she is to be chief actor – the foreign gentleman dropping down like a god from the skies, picking her up, and triumphantly carrying her off. Her only grief will be separation from me, but this is to be assuaged by my going and staying with her for long months at a time. This simple prattle is very sweet to me, my dear sister, but I cannot help feeling sad at the occasion of it. In the nature of things it is obvious that I shall never be to you again what I hitherto have been: your guide, counsellor, and most familiar friend.

M de la Feste does certainly seem to be all that one could desire as protector to a sensitive fragile child like Caroline, and for that I am thankful. Still, I must remember that I see him as yet only through her eyes. For her sake I am intensely anxious to meet him, and scrutinize him through and through, and learn what the man is really made of who is to have such a treasure in his keeping. The engagement has certainly been formed a little precipitately; I quite agree with my father in that: still, good and happy marriages have been made in a hurry before now, and mother seems well satisfied.

August 20. – A terrible announcement came this morning; and we are in deep trouble. I have been quite unable to steady my thoughts on anything today till now – half-past eleven at night – and I only attempt writing these notes because I am too restless to remain idle, and there is nothing but waiting and waiting left for me to do. Mother has been taken dangerously ill at Versailles: they were within a day or two of starting; but all thought of leaving must now be postponed, for she cannot possibly be moved in her present state. I don't like the sound of haemorrhage at all in a woman of her full habit, and Caroline and the Marlets have not exaggerated their accounts I am certain. On the receipt of the letter my father instantly decided to go to her, and I have been occupied all day in getting him off, for, as he calculates on being absent several days, there have been many matters for him to arrange before setting out – the chief being to find some one who will do duty for him next Sunday – a quest of no small difficulty at such short notice; but at last poor old feeble Mr Dugdale has agreed to attempt it, with Mr Higham, the Scripture reader, to assist him in the lessons.

I fain would have gone with my father to escape the irksome anxiety of awaiting her; but somebody had to stay, and I could best be spared. George has driven him to the station to meet the last train by which he will catch the midnight boat, and reach Havre some time in the morning. He hates the sea, and a night passage in particular. I hope he will get there without mishap of any kind; but I feel anxious for him, stay-at-home as he is, and unable to cope with any difficulty. Such an errand, too; the journey will be sad enough at best. I almost think I ought to have been the one to go to her.

August 21. – I nearly fell asleep of heaviness of spirit last night over my writing. My father must have reached Paris by this time; and now here comes a letter. . .

Later. – The letter was to express an earnest hope that my father had set out. My poor mother is sinking, they fear. What will become of Caroline? O, how I wish I could see mother; why could not both have gone?

Later. – I get up from my chair, and walk from window to window, and then come and write a line. I cannot even divine how poor Caroline's marriage is to be carried out if mother dies. I pray that father may have got there in time to talk to her and receive some directions from her about Caroline and M de la Feste – a man whom neither my father nor I have seen. I, who might be useful in this emergency, am doomed to stay here, waiting in suspense.

August 23. – A letter from my father containing the sad news that my mother's spirit has flown. Poor little Caroline is heart-broken – she was always more my mother's pet than I was. It is some comfort to know that my father arrived in time to hear from her own lips her strongly expressed wish that Caroline's marriage should be solemnized as soon as possible. M de la Feste seems to have been a great favourite of my dear mother's; and I suppose it now becomes almost a sacred duty of my father to accept him as a son-in-law without criticism.

3. HER GLOOM LIGHTENS A LITTLE

September 10. – I have inserted nothing in my diary for more than a fortnight. Events have been altogether too sad for me to have the spirit to put them on paper. And yet there comes a time when the act of recording one's trouble is recognized as a welcome method of dwelling upon it. . .

My dear mother has been brought home and buried here in the parish. It was not so much her own wish that this should be done as my father's, who particularly desired that she should lie in the family vault beside his first wife. I saw them side by side before the vault was closed – two women beloved by one man. As I stood, and Caroline by my side, I fell into a sort of dream, and had an odd fancy that Caroline and I might be also beloved of one, and lie like these together – an impossibility, of course, being sisters. When I awoke from my reverie Caroline took my hand and said it was time to leave.

September 14. – The wedding is indefinitely postponed. Caroline is like a girl awakening in the middle of a somnambulistic experience, and does not realize where she is, or how she stands. She walks about silently, and I cannot tell her thoughts, as I used to do. It was her own doing to write to M de la Feste and tell him that the wedding could not possibly take place this autumn as originally planned. There is something depressing in this long postponement if she is to marry him at all; and yet I do not see how it could be avoided.

October 20. – I have had so much to occupy me in consoling Caroline that I have been continually overlooking my diary. Her life was much nearer to my mother's than mine was. She has never, as I, lived away from home long enough to become self-dependent, and hence in her first loss, and all that it involved, she drooped like a rain-beaten lily. But she is of a nature whose wounds soon heal, even though they may be deep, and the supreme poignancy of her sorrow has already passed.

My father is of opinion that the wedding should not be delayed too long. While at Versailles he made the acquaintance of M de la Feste, and though they had but a short and hurried communion with each other, he was much impressed by M de la Feste's disposition and conduct, and is strongly in favour of his suit. It is odd that Caroline's betrothed should influence in his favour all who come near him. His portrait, which dear Caroline has shown me, exhibits him to be of a physique that partly accounts for this; but there must be something more than mere appearance, and it is probably some sort of glamour or fascinating power – the quality which prevented Caroline from describing him to me with any accuracy of detail. At the same time, I see from the photograph that his face and head are remarkably well formed; and though the contours of his mouth are hidden by his moustache, his arched brows show well the romantic disposition of a true lover and painter of Nature. I think that the owner of such a face as this must be tender and sympathetic and true.

October 30. – As my sister's grief for her mother becomes more and more calmed, her love for M de la Feste begins to reassume its former absorbing command of her. She thinks of him incessantly, and writes whole treatises to him by way of letters. Her blank disappointment at his announcement of his inability to pay us a visit quite so soon as he had promised was quite tragic. I, too, am disappointed, for I wanted to see and estimate him. But having arranged to go to Holland to seize some aerial effects for his pictures, which are only to be obtained at this time of the autumn, he is obliged to postpone his journey this way, which is now to be made early in the new year. I think myself that he ought to have come at all sacrifices, considering Caroline's recent loss, the sad postponement of what she was looking forward to, and her single-minded affection for him. Still, who knows; his professional success is important. Moreover, she is cheerful, and hopeful, and the delay will soon be overpast.

4. SHE BEHOLDS THE ATTRACTIVE STRANGER

February 16. – We have had such a dull life here all the winter that I have found nothing important enough to set down, and broke off my journal accordingly. I resume it now to make an entry on the subject of dear Caroline's future. It seems that she was too grieved, immediately after the loss of our mother, to answer definitely the question of M de la Feste how long the postponement was to be; then, afterwards, it was agreed that the matter should be discussed on his autumn visit; but as he did not come, it has remained in abeyance till this week, when Caroline, with the greatest simplicity and confidence, has written to him without any further pressure on his part, and told him that she is quite ready to fix the time, and will do so as soon as he arrives to see her. She is a little frightened now, lest it should seem forward in her to have revived the subject of her own accord; but she may assume that his question has been waiting on for an answer ever since, and that she has, therefore, acted only within her promise. In truth, the secret at the bottom of it all is that she is somewhat saddened because he has not latterly reminded her of the pause in their affairs – that, in short, his original impatience to possess her is not now found to animate him so obviously. I suppose that he loves her as much as ever; indeed, I am sure he must do so, seeing how lovable she is. It is mostly thus with all men when women are out of their sight; they grow negligent. Caroline must have patience, and remember that a man of his genius has many and important calls upon his time. In justice to her I must add that she does remember it fairly well, and has as much patience as any girl ever had in the circumstances. He hopes to come at the beginning of April at latest. Well, when he comes we shall see him.

April 5. – I think that what M de la Feste writes is reasonable enough, though Caroline looks heart-sick about it. It is hardly worth while for him to cross all the way to England and back just now, while the sea is so turbulent, seeing that he will be obliged, in any event, to come in May, when he has to be in London for professional purposes, at which time he can take us easily on his way both coming and going. When Caroline becomes his wife she will be more practical, no doubt; but she is such a child as yet that there is no contenting her with reasons. However, the time will pass quickly, there being so much to do in preparing a trousseau for her, which must now be put in hand in order that we may have plenty of leisure to get it ready. On no account must Caroline be married in half-mourning; I am sure that mother, could she know, would not wish it, and it is odd that Caroline should be so intractably persistent on this point, when she is usually so yielding.

April 30. – This month has flown on swallow's wings. We are in a great state of excitement – I as much as she – I cannot quite tell why. He is really coming in ten days, he says.

May 9. – Four p.m. – I am so agitated I can scarcely write, and yet am particularly impelled to do so before leaving my room. It is the unexpected shape of an expected event which has caused my absurd excitement, which proves me almost as much a school-girl as Caroline.

M de la Feste was not, as we understood, to have come till tomorrow; but he is here – just arrived. All household directions have devolved upon me, for my father, not thinking M de la Feste would appear before us for another four-and-twenty hours, left home before post time to attend a distant consecration; and hence Caroline and I were in no small excitement when Charles's letter was opened, and we read that he had been unexpectedly favoured in the dispatch of his studio work, and would follow his letter in a few hours. We sent the covered carriage to meet the train indicated, and waited like two newly strung harps for the first sound of the returning wheels. At last we heard them on the gravel; and the question arose who was to receive him. It was, strictly speaking, my duty; but I felt timid; I could not help shirking it, and insisted that Caroline should go down. She did not, however, go near the door as she usually does when anybody is expected, but waited palpitating in the drawing-room. He little thought when he saw the silent hall, and the apparently deserted house, how that house was at the very same moment alive and throbbing with interest under the surface. I stood at the back of the upper landing, where nobody could see me from downstairs, and heard him walk across the hall – a lighter step than my father's – and heard him then go into the drawing-room, and the servant shut the door behind him and go away.

What a pretty lovers' meeting they must have had in there all to themselves! Caroline's sweet face looking up from her black gown – how it must have touched him. I know she wept very much, for I heard her; and her eyes will be red afterwards, and no wonder, poor dear, though she is no doubt happy. I can imagine what she is telling him while I write this – her fears lest anything should have happened to prevent his coming after all – gentle, smiling reproaches for his long delay; and things of that sort. His two portmanteaus are at this moment crossing the landing on the way to his room. I wonder if I ought to go down.

A little later. – I have seen him! It was not at all in the way that I intended to encounter him, and I am vexed. Just after his portmanteaus were brought up I went out from my room to descend, when, at the moment of stepping toward the first stair, my eyes were caught by an object in the hall below, and I paused for an instant, till I saw that it was a bundle of canvas and sticks, composing a sketching tent and easel. At the same nick of time the drawing-room door opened and the affianced pair came out. They were saying they would go into the garden; and he waited a moment while she put on her hat. My idea was to let them pass on without seeing me, since they seemed not to want my company, but I had got too far on the landing to retreat; he looked up, and stood staring at me – engrossed to a dream-like fixity. Thereupon I, too, instead of advancing as I ought to have done, stood moonstruck and awkward, and before I could gather my weak senses sufficiently to descend, she had called him, and they went out by the garden door together. I then thought of following them, but have changed my mind, and come here to jot down these few lines. It is all I am fit for...

He is even more handsome than I expected. I was right in feeling he must have an attraction beyond that of form: it appeared even in that momentary glance. How happy Caroline ought to be. But I must, of course, go down to be ready with tea in the drawing-room by the time they come indoors.

11 p.m. – I have made the acquaintance of M de la Feste; and I seem to be another woman from the effect of it. I cannot describe why this should be so, but conversation with him seems to expand the view, and open the heart, and raise one as upon stilts to wider prospects. He has a good intellectual forehead, perfect eyebrows, dark hair and eyes, an animated manner, and a persuasive voice. His voice is soft in quality – too soft for a man, perhaps; and yet on second thoughts I would not have it less so. We have been talking of his art: I had no notion that art demanded such sacrifices or such tender devotion; or that there were two roads for choice within its precincts, the road of vulgar money-making, and the road of high aims and consequent inappreciation for many long years by the public. That he has adopted the latter need not be said to those who understand him. It is a blessing for Caroline that she has been chosen by such a man, and she ought not to lament at postponements and delays, since they have arisen unavoidably. Whether he finds hers a sufficiently rich nature, intellectually and emotionally, for his own, I know not, but he seems occasionally to be disappointed at her simple views of things. Does he really feel such love for her at this moment as he no doubt believes himself to be feeling, and as he no doubt hopes to feel for the remainder of his life towards her?

It was a curious thing he told me when we were left for a few minutes alone; that Caroline had alluded so slightly to me in her conversation and letters that he had not realized my presence in the house here at all. But, of course, it was only natural that she should write and talk most about herself. I suppose it was on account of the fact of his being taken in some measure unawares, that I caught him on two or three occasions regarding me fixedly in a way that disquieted me somewhat, having been lately in so little society; till my glance aroused him from his reverie, and he looked elsewhere in some confusion. It was fortunate that he did so, and thus failed to notice my own. It shows that he, too, is not particularly a society person.

May 10. – Have had another interesting conversation with M de la

Feste on schools of landscape painting in the drawing-room after dinner this evening – my father having fallen asleep, and left nobody but Caroline and myself for Charles to talk to. I did not mean to say so much to him, and had taken a volume of *Modern Painters* from the bookcase to occupy myself with, while leaving the two lovers to themselves; but he would include me in his audience, and I was obliged to lay the book aside. However, I insisted on keeping Caroline in the conversation, though her views on pictorial art were only too charmingly crude and primitive.

Tomorrow, if fine, we are all three going to Wherryborne Wood, where Charles will give us practical illustrations of the principles of colouring that he had enumerated tonight. I am determined not to occupy his attention to the exclusion of Caroline, and my plan is that when we are in the dense part of the wood I will lag behind, and slip away, and leave them to return by themselves. I suppose the reason of his attentiveness to me lies in his simply wishing to win the good opinion of one who is so closely united to Caroline, and so likely to influence her good opinion of him.

May 11. Late. – I cannot sleep, and in desperation have lit my candle and taken up my pen. My restlessness is occasioned by what has occurred today, which at first I did not mean to write down, or trust to any heart but my own. We went to Wherryborne Wood – Caroline, Charles and I, as we had intended – and walked all three along the green track through the midst, Charles in the middle between Caroline and myself. Presently I found that, as usual, he and I were the only talkers, Caroline amusing herself by observing birds and squirrels as she walked docilely alongside her betrothed. Having noticed this I dropped behind at the first opportunity and slipped among the trees, in a direction in which I knew I should find another path that would take me home. Upon this track I by-and-by emerged, and walked along it in silent thought till, at a bend, I suddenly encountered M de la Feste standing stock still and smiling thoughtfully at me.

'Where is Caroline?' said I.

'Only a little way off,' says he. 'When we missed you from behind us we thought you might have mistaken the direction we had followed, so she has gone one way to find you and I have come this way.'

We then went back to find Caroline, but could not discover her anywhere, and the upshot was that he and I were wandering about the woods alone for more than an hour. On reaching home we found she had given us up after searching a little while, and arrived there some time before. I should not be so disturbed by the incident if I had not perceived that, during her absence from us, he did not make any earnest effort to rediscover her; and in answer to my repeated expressions of wonder as to whither she could have wandered he only said, 'Oh, she's quite safe; she told me she knew the way home from any part of this wood. Let us go on with our talk. I assure you I value this privilege of being with one I so much admire more than you imagine'; and other things of that kind. I was so foolish as to show a little perturbation – I cannot tell why I did not control myself; and I think he noticed that I was not cool. Caroline has, with her simple good faith, thought nothing of the occurrence; yet altogether I am not satisfied.

5. HER SITUATION IS A TRYING ONE

May 15. – The more I think of it day after day, the more convinced I am that my suspicions are true. He is too interested in me – well, in plain words, loves me; or, not to degrade that phrase, has a wild passion for me; and his affection for Caroline is that towards a sister only. That is the distressing truth; how it has come about I cannot tell, and it wears upon me.

A hundred little circumstances have revealed this to me, and the longer I dwell upon it the more agitating does the consideration become. Heaven only can help me out of the terrible difficulty in which this places me. I have done nothing to encourage him to be faithless to her. I have studiously kept out of his way; have persistently refused to be a third in their interviews. Yet all to no purpose. Some fatality has seemed to rule, ever since he came to the house, that this disastrous inversion of things should arise. If I had only foreseen the possibility of it before he arrived, how gladly would I have departed on some visit or other to the meanest friend to hinder such an apparent treachery. But I blindly welcomed him – indeed, made myself particularly agreeable to him for her sake.

There is no possibility of my suspicions being wrong; not until they have reached absolute certainty have I dared even to admit the truth to myself. His conduct today would have proved them true had I entertained no previous apprehensions. Some photographs of myself came for me by post, and they were handed round at the breakfast-table and criticized. I put them temporarily on a side-table, and did not remember them until an hour afterwards when I was in my own room. On going to fetch them I discovered him standing at the table with his back towards the door bending over the photographs, one of which he raised to his lips.

The witnessing this act so frightened me that I crept away to escape observation. It was the climax to a series of slight and significant actions all tending to the same conclusion. The question for me now is, what am I to do? To go away is what first occurs to me, but what reason can I give

Caroline and my father for such a step? Besides, it might precipitate some sort of catastrophe by driving Charles to desperation. For the present, therefore, I have decided that I can only wait, though his contiguity is strangely disturbing to me now, and I hardly retain strength of mind to encounter him. How will the distressing complication end?

May 19. – And so it has come! My mere avoidance of him has precipitated the worst issue – a declaration. I had occasion to go into the kitchen-garden to gather some of the double ragged-robins which grew in a corner there. Almost as soon as I had entered I heard footsteps without. The door opened and shut, and I turned to behold him just inside it. As the garden is closed by four walls and the gardener was absent, the spot ensured absolute privacy. He came along the path by the asparagus-bed, and overtook me.

'You know why I come, Alicia?' said he, in a tremulous voice.

I said nothing, and hung my head, for by his tone I did know.

'Yes,' he went on, 'it is you I love; my sentiment towards your sister is one of affection too, but protective, tutelary affection – no more. Say what you will I cannot help it. I mistook my feeling for her, and I know how much I am to blame for my want of self-knowledge. I have fought against this discovery night and day; but it cannot be concealed. Why did I ever see you, since I could not see you till I had committed myself? At the moment my eyes beheld you on that day of my arrival, I said, "This is the woman for whom my manhood has waited." Ever since an unaccountable fascination has riveted my heart to you. Answer one word!'

'O, M de la Feste!' I burst out. What I said more I cannot remember, but I suppose that the misery I was in showed pretty plainly, for he said, 'Something must be done to let her know; perhaps I have mistaken her affection, too; but all depends upon what you feel.'

'I cannot tell what I feel,' said I, 'except that this seems terrible treachery; and every moment that I stay with you here makes it worse! . . . Try to keep faith with her – her young heart is tender; believe me there is no mistake in the quality of her love for you. Would there were! This would kill her if she knew it!'

He sighed heavily. 'She ought never to be my wife,' he said. 'Leaving my own happiness out of the question, it would be a cruelty to her to unite her to me.'

I said I could not hear such words from him, and begged him in tears to go away; he obeyed, and I heard the garden door shut behind him. What is to be the end of the announcement, and the fate of Caroline?

May 20. – I put a good deal on paper yesterday, and yet not all. I was, in truth, hoping against hope, against conviction, against too conscious self-judgment. I scarcely dare own the truth now, yet it relieves my aching heart to set it down. Yes, I love him – that is the dreadful fact, and I can no longer parry, evade, or deny it to myself, though to the rest of the world it can never be owned. I love Caroline's betrothed, and he loves me. It is no yesterday's passion, cultivated by our converse; it came at first sight, independently of my will; and my talk with him yesterday made rather against it than for it, but, alas, did not quench it. God forgives us both for this terrible treachery.

May 25. – All is vague; our courses shapeless. He comes and goes, being occupied, ostensibly at least, with sketching in his tent in the wood. Whether he and she see each other privately I cannot tell, but I rather think they do not; that she sadly awaits him, and he does not appear. Not a sign from him that my repulse has done him any good, or that he will endeavour to keep faith with her. O, if I only had the compulsion of a god, and the self-sacrifice of a martyr!

May 31. – It has all ended – or rather this act of the sad drama has ended – in nothing. He has left us. No day for the fulfilment of the enagement with Caroline is named, my father not being the man to press anyone on such a matter, or, indeed, to interfere in any way. We two girls are, in fact, quite defenceless in a case of this kind; lovers may come when they choose, and desert when they choose; poor father is too urbane to utter a word of remonstrance or inquiry. Moreover, as the approved of my dead mother, M de la Feste has a sort of autocratic power with my father, who holds it unkind to her memory to have an opinion about him. I, feeling it my duty, asked M de la Feste at the last moment about the engagement, in a voice I could not keep firm.

'Since the death of your mother all has been indefinite – all!' he said gloomily. That was the whole. Possibly, Wherryborne Rectory may see him no more.

June 7. – M de la Feste has written – one letter to her, one to me. Hers could not have been very warm, for she did not brighten on reading it. Mine was an ordinary note of friendship, filling an ordinary sheet of paper, which I handed over to Caroline when I had finished looking it through. But there was a scrap of paper in the bottom of the envelope, which I dared not show anyone. This scrap is his real letter: I scanned it alone in my room, trembling, hot and cold by turns. He tells me he is very wretched; that he deplores what has happened, but was helpless. Why did I let him see me, if only to make him faithless? Alas, alas!

June 21. – My dear Caroline has lost appetite, spirits, health. Hope deferred maketh the heart sick. His letters to her grow colder – if indeed he has written more than one. He has refrained from writing again to me –

he knows it is no use. Altogether the situation that he and she and I are in is melancholy in the extreme. Why are human hearts so perverse?

6. HER INGENUITY INSTIGATES HER

September 19. – Three months of anxious care – till at length I have taken the extreme step of writing to him. Our chief distress has been caused by the state of poor Caroline, who, after sinking by degrees into such extreme weakness as to make it doubtful if she can ever recover full vigour, has today been taken much worse. Her position is very critical. The doctor says plainly that she is dying of a broken heart – and that even the removal of the cause may not now restore her. Ought I to have written to Charles sooner? But how could I when she forbade me? It was her pride only which instigated her, and I should not have obeyed.

Sept. 26. – Charles has arrived and has seen her. He is shocked, conscience-stricken, remorseful. I have told him that he can do no good beyond cheering her by his presence. I do not know what he thinks of proposing to her if she gets better, but he says little to her at present: indeed he dares not: his words agitate her dangerously.

Sept. 28. – After a struggle between duty and selfishness, such as I pray to Heaven I may never have to undergo again, I have asked him for pity's sake to make her his wife, here and now, as she lies. I said to him that the poor child would not trouble him long; and such a solemnization would soothe her last hours as nothing else could do. He said that he would willingly do so, and had thought of it himself; but for one forbidding reason: in the event of her death as his wife he can never marry me, her sister, according to our laws. I started at his words. He went on: 'On the other hand, if I were sure that immediate marriage with me would save her life, I would not refuse, for possibly I might after a while, and out of sight of you, make myself fairly content with one of so sweet a disposition as hers; but if, as is probable, neither my marrying her nor any other act can avail to save her life, by so doing I lose both her and you.' I could not answer him.

Sept. 29. – He continued firm in his reasons for refusal till this morning, and then I became possessed with an idea, which I at once propounded to him. It was that he should at least consent to a *form* of marriage with Caroline, in consideration of her love; a form which need not be a legal union, but one which would satisfy her sick and enfeebled soul. Such things have been done, and the sentiment of feeling herself his would inexpressibly comfort her mind, I am sure. Then, if she is taken from us, I should not have lost the power of becoming his lawful wife at some future day, if it indeed should be deemed expedient; if, on the other hand, she lives, he can on her recovery inform her of the incompleteness of their marriage contract, the ceremony can be repeated, and I can, and I am sure willingly would, avoid troubling them with my presence till gray hairs and wrinkles make his unfortunate passion for me a thing of the past. I put all this before him; but he demurred.

Sept. 30. – I have urged him again. He says he will consider. It is no time to mince matters, and as a further inducement I have offered to enter into a solemn engagement to marry him myself a year after her death.

Sept. 30. Later. – An agitating interview. He says he will agree to whatever I propose, the three possibilities and our contingent acts being recorded as follows: First, in the event of dear Caroline being taken from us, I marry him on the expiration of a year: Second, in the forlorn chance of her recovery I take upon myself the responsibility of explaining to Caroline the true nature of the ceremony he has gone through with her, that it was done at my suggestion to make her happy at once, before a special licence could be obtained, and that a public ceremony at church is awaiting her: Third, in the unlikely event of her cooling, and refusing to repeat the ceremony with him, I leave England, join him abroad, and there wed him, agreeing not to live in England again till Caroline has either married another or regards her attachment to Charles as a bygone matter. I have thought over these conditions, and have agreed to them all as they stand.

11 p.m. – I do not much like this scheme, after all. For one thing, I have just sounded my father on it before parting with him for the night, my impression having been that he would see no objection. But he says he could on no account countenance any such unreal proceeding; however good our intentions, and even though the poor girl were dying, it would not be right. So I sadly seek my pillow.

October 1. – I am sure my father is wrong in his view. Why is it not right, if it would be balm to Caroline's wounded soul, and if a real ceremony is absolutely refused by Charles – moreover is hardly practicable in the difficulty of getting a special licence, if he were agreed? My father does not know, or will not believe, that Caroline's attachment has been the cause of her hopeless condition. But that it is so, and that the form of words would give her inexpressible happiness, I know well; for I whispered tentatively in her ear on such marriages, and the effect was great. Henceforth my father cannot be taken into confidence on the subject of Caroline. He does not understand her.

12 o'clock noon. – I have taken advantage of my father's absence today to confide my secret notion to a thoughtful young man, who called here this morning to speak to my father. He is the Mr Theophilus Higham, of whom I have already had occasion to speak – a Scripture reader in the next town, and is soon going to be ordained. I told him the pitiable case, and my remedy. He says ardently that he will assist me – would do anything for me (he is, in truth, an admirer of mine); he sees no wrong in such an act of charity. He is coming again to the house this afternoon before my father returns, to carry out the idea. I have spoken to Charles, who promises to be ready. I must now break the news to Caroline.

11 o'clock p.m. – I have been in too much excitement till now to set down the result. We have accomplished our plan; and though I feel like a guilty sinner, I am glad. My father, of course, is not to be informed as yet. Caroline has had a seraphic expression upon her wasted, transparent face ever since. I should hardly be surprised if it really saved her life even now, and rendered a legitimate union necessary between them. In that case my father can be informed of the whole proceeding, and in the face of such wonderful success cannot disapprove. Meanwhile poor Charles has not lost the possibility of taking unworthy me to fill her place should she— But I cannot contemplate that alternative unmoved, and will not write it. Charles left for the South of Europe immediately after the ceremony. He was in a high-strung, throbbing, almost wild state of mind at first, but grew calmer under my exhortations. I had to pay the penalty of receiving a farewell kiss from him, which I must regret, considering its meaning; but he took me so unexpectedly, and in a moment was gone.

Oct. 6. – She certainly is better, and even when she found that Charles had been suddenly obliged to leave, she received the news quite cheerfully. The doctor says that her apparent improvement may be delusive; but I think our impressing upon her the necessity of keeping what has occurred a secret from papa, and everybody, helps to give her a zest for life.

Oct. 8. – She is still mending. I am glad to have saved her – my only sister – if I have done so; though I shall now never become Charles's wife.

7. A SURPRISE AWAITS HER

Feb. 5. – Writing has been absolutely impossible for a long while; but I now reach a stage at which it seems possible to jot down a line. Caroline's recovery, extending over four months, has been very engrossing; at first slow, latterly rapid. But a fearful complication of affairs attends it!

> O what a tangled web we weave
> When first we practise to deceive!

Charles has written reproachfully to me from Venice, where he is. He says how can he fulfil in the real what he has enacted in the counterfeit, while he still loves me? Yet how, on the other hand, can he leave it unfulfilled? All this time I have not told her, and up to this minute she believes that he has indeed taken her for better, for worse, till death them do part. It is a harassing position for me, and all three. In the awful approach of death, one's judgment loses its balance, and we do anything to meet the exigencies of the moment, with a single eye to the one who excites our sympathy, and from whom we seem on the brink of being separated for ever.

Had he really married her at that time all would be settled now. But he took too much thought; she might have died, and then he had his reason. If indeed it had turned out so, I should now be perhaps a sad woman; but not a tempest-tossed one. . . The possibility of his claiming me after all is what lies at the root of my agitation. Everything hangs by a thread. Suppose I tell her the marriage was a mockery; suppose she is indignant with me and with him for the deception – and then? Otherwise, suppose she is not indignant but forgives all; he is bound to marry her; and honour constrains me to urge him thereto, in spite of what he protests, and to smooth the way to this issue by my method of informing her. I have meant to tell her the last month – ever since she has been strong enough to bear such tidings; but I have been without the power – the moral force. Surely I must write, and get him to come and assist me.

March 14. – She continually wonders why he does not come, the five months of his enforced absence having expired; and still more she wonders why he does not write oftener. His last letter was cold, she says, and she fears he regrets his marriage, which he may only have celebrated with her for pity's sake, thinking she was sure to die. It makes one's heart bleed to hear her hovering thus so near the truth, and yet never discerning its actual shape.

A minor trouble besets me, too, in the person of the young Scripture reader, whose conscience pricks him for the part he played. Surely I am punished, if ever woman were, for a too ingenious perversion of her better judgment!

April 2. – She is practically well. The faint pink revives in her cheek, though it is not quite so full as heretofore. But she still wonders what she can have done to offend 'her dear husband', and I have been obliged to tell the smallest part of the truth – an unimportant fragment of the whole, in fact, I said that I feared for the moment he might regret the precipitancy of the act, which her illness caused, his affairs not having been quite sufficiently advanced for marriage just then, though he will doubtless come to her as soon as he has a home ready. Meanwhile I have written to him, peremptorily, to come and relieve me in this awful dilemma. He will find no note of love in that.

April 10. – To my alarm the letter I lately addressed to him at Venice, where he is staying, as well as the last one she sent him, have received no reply. She thinks he is ill. I do not quite think that, but I wish we could hear from him. Perhaps the peremptoriness of my words had offended him; it grieves me to think it possible. *I* offend him! But too much of this. I *must* tell her the truth, or she may in her ignorance commit herself to some course or other that may be ruinously compromising. She said plaintively just now that if he could see her, and know how occupied with him and him alone is her every waking hour, she is sure he would forgive her the wicked presumption of becoming his wife. Very sweet all that, and touching. I could not conceal my tears.

April 15. – The house is in confusion; my father is angry and distressed, and I am distracted. Caroline has disappeared – gone away secretly. I cannot help thinking that I know where she is gone to. How guilty I seem, and how innocent she! O that I had told her before now!

1 o'clock. – No trace of her as yet. We find also that the little waiting-maid we have here in training has disappeared with Caroline, and there is not much doubt that Caroline, fearing to travel alone, has induced this girl to go with her as companion. I am almost sure she has started in desperation to find him, and that Venice is her goal. Why should she run away, if not to join her husband, as she thinks him? Now that I consider, there have been indications of this wish in her for days, as in birds of passage there lurk signs of their incipient intention; and yet I did not think she would have taken such an extreme step, unaided, and without consulting me. I can only jot down the bare facts – I have no time for reflections. But fancy Caroline travelling across the continent of Europe with a chit of a girl, who will be more of a charge than an assistance! They will be a mark for every marauder who encounters them.

Evening: 8 o'clock. – Yes, it is as I surmised. She has gone to join him. A note posted by her in Budmouth Regis at daybreak has reached me this afternoon – thanks to the fortunate chance of one of the servants calling for letters in town today, or I should not have got it until tomorrow. She merely asserts her determination of going to him, and has started privately, that nothing may hinder her; stating nothing about her route. That such a gentle thing should suddenly become so calmly resolute quite surprises me. Alas, he may have left Venice – she may not find him for weeks – may not at all.

My father, on learning the facts, bade me at once have everything ready by nine this evening, in time to drive to the train that meets the night steam-boat. This I have done, and there being an hour to spare before we start, I relieve the suspense of waiting by taking up my pen. He says overtake her we must, and calls Charles the hardest of names. He believes, of course, that she is merely an infatuated girl rushing off to meet her lover; and how can the wretched I tell him that she is more, and in a sense better than that – yet not sufficiently more and better to make this flight to Charles anything but a still greater danger to her than a mere lover's impulse? We shall go by way of Paris, and we think we may overtake her there. I hear my father walking restlessly up and down the hall, and can write no more.

8. SHE TRAVELS IN PURSUIT

April 16. Evening, Paris, Hôtel——. – There is no overtaking her at this place; but she has been here, as I thought, no other hotel in Paris being known to her. We go on tomorrow morning.

April 18. Venice. – A morning of adventures and emotions which leave me sick and weary, and yet unable to sleep, though I have lain down on the sofa of my room for more than an hour in the attempt. I therefore make up my diary to date in a hurried fashion, for the sake of the riddance it affords to ideas which otherwise remain suspended hotly in the brain.

We arrived here this morning in broad sunlight, which lit up the sea-girt buildings as we approached so that they seemed like a city of cork floating raft-like on the smooth, blue deep. But I only glanced from the carriage window at the lovely scene, and we were soon across the intervening water and inside the railway station. When we got to the front steps the row of black gondolas and the shouts of the gondoliers so bewildered my father that he was understood to require two gondolas instead of one with two oars, and so I found him in one and myself in another. We got this righted after a while, and were rowed at once to the hotel on the Riva degli Schiavoni where M de la Feste had been staying when we last heard from him, the way being down the Grand Canal for some distance, under the Rialto, and then by narrow canals which eventually brought us under the Bridge of Sighs – harmonious to our moods! – and out again into open water. The scene was purity itself as to colour, but it was cruel that I should behold it for the first time under such circumstances.

As soon as we entered the hotel, which is an old-fashioned place, like most places here, where people are taken *en pension* as well as the ordinary way, I rushed to the framed list of visitors hanging in the hall, and in a moment I saw Charles's name upon it among the rest. But she was our chief thought. I turned to the hall porter, and – knowing that she would have travelled as 'Madame de la Feste' – I asked for her under that name, without my father hearing. (He, poor soul, was making confused inquiries outside the door about 'an English lady', as if there were not a score of English ladies at hand.)

'She has just come,' said the porter. 'Madame came by the very early train this morning, when Monsieur was asleep, and she requested us not to disturb him. She is now in her room.'

Whether Caroline had seen us from the window, or overheard me, I do not know, but at that moment I heard footsteps on the bare marble stairs, and she appeared in person descending.

'Caroline!' I exclaimed, 'why have you done this?' and rushed up to her.

She did not answer; but looked down to hide her emotion, which she conquered after the lapse of a few seconds, putting on a practical tone which belied her.

'I am just going to my husband,' she said. 'I have not yet seen him. I have not been here long.' She condescended to give no further reason for her movements, and made as if to move on. I implored her to come into a private room where I could speak to her in confidence, but she objected. However, the dining-room, close at hand, was quite empty at this hour, and I got her inside and closed the door. I do not know how I began my explanation, or how I ended it, but I told her briefly and brokenly enough that the marriage was not real.

'Not real?' she said vacantly.

'It is not,' said I. 'You will find that it is all as I say.'

She could not believe my meaning even then. 'Not his wife?' she cried. 'It is impossible. What am I, then?'

I added more details, and reiterated the reason for my conduct as well as I could; but Heaven knows how very difficult I found it to feel a jot more justification for it in my own mind than she did in hers.

The revulsion of feeling, as soon as she really comprehended all, was most distressing. After her grief had in some measure spent itself she turned against both him and me.

'Why should I have been deceived like this?' she demanded, with a bitter haughtiness of which I had not deemed such a tractable creature capable. 'Do you suppose that *anything* could justify such an imposition? What, O what a snare you have spread for me!'

I murmured, 'Your life seemed to require it,' but she did not hear me. She sank down in a chair, covered her face, and then my father came in. 'O, here you are!' he said. 'I could not find you. And Caroline!'

'And were *you*, papa, a party to this strange deed of kindness?'

'To what?' said he.

Then out it all came, and for the first time he was made acquainted with the fact that the scheme for soothing her illness, which I sounded him upon, had been really carried out. In a moment he sided with Caroline. My repeated assurance that my motive was good availed less than nothing. In a minute or two Caroline arose and went abruptly out of the room, and my father followed her, leaving me alone to my reflections.

I was so bent upon finding Charles immediately that I did not notice whither they went. The servant told me that M de la Feste was just outside smoking, and one of them went to look for him, I following; but before we had gone many steps he came out of the hotel behind me. I expected him to be amazed; but he showed no surprise at seeing me, though he showed another kind of feeling to an extent which dismayed me. I may have revealed something similar; but I struggled hard against all emotion, and as soon as I could I told him she had come. He simply said, 'Yes' in a low voice.

'You know it, Charles?' said I.

'I have just learnt it,' he said.

'O, Charles,' I went on, 'having delayed completing your marriage with her till now, I fear – it has become a serious position for us. Why did you not reply to our letters?'

'I was purposing to reply in person: I did not know how to address her on the point – how to address you. But what has become of her?'

'She has gone off with my father,' said I; 'indignant with you, and scorning me.'

He was silent: and I suggested that we should follow them, pointing out the direction which I fancied their gondola had taken. As the one we got into was doubly manned we soon came in view of their two figures ahead of us, while they were not likely to observe us, our boat having the 'felze' on, while theirs was uncovered. They shot into a narrow canal just beyond the Giardino Reale, and by the time we were floating up between its slimy walls we saw them getting out of their gondola at the steps which lead up near the end of the Via 22 Marzo. When we reached the same spot they were walking up and down the Via in consultation. Getting out he stood on the lower steps watching them. I watched him. He seemed to fall into a reverie.

'Will you not go and speak to her?' said I at length.

He assented, and went forward. Still he did not hasten to join them, but, screened by a projecting window, observed their musing converse. At last he looked back at me; whereupon I pointed forward, and he in obedience stepped out, and met them face to face. Caroline flushed hot, bowed haughtily to him, turned away, and taking my father's arm violently, led him off before he had had time to use his own judgment. They disappeared into a narrow *calle* or alley, leading to the back of the buildings on the Grand Canal.

M de la Feste came slowly back; as he stepped in beside me I realized my position so vividly that my heart might almost have been heard to beat. The third condition had arisen – the least expected by either of us. She had refused him; he was free to claim me.

We returned in the boat together. He seemed quite absorbed till we had turned the angle into the Grand Canal, when he broke the silence. 'She spoke very bitterly of you in the *salle-à-manger*,' he said. 'I do not think she was quite warranted in speaking so to you, who had nursed her so tenderly.'

'O, but I think she was,' I answered. 'It was there I told her what had been done; she did not know till then.'

'She was very dignified – very striking,' he murmured. 'You were more.'

'But how do you know what passed between us?' said I. He then told me that he had seen and heard all. The dining-room was divided by folding-doors from an inner portion, and he had been sitting in the latter part when we entered the outer, so that our words were distinctly audible.

'But, dear Alicia,' he went on, 'I was more impressed by the affection of your apology to her than by anything else. And do you know that now the conditions have arisen which give me liberty to consider you my affianced?' I had been expecting this, but yet was not prepared. I stammered out that we would not discuss it then.

'Why not?' said he. 'Do you know that we may marry here and now? She has cast off both you and me.'

'It cannot be,' said I firmly. 'She has not been fairly asked to be your wife in fact – to repeat the service lawfully; and until that has been done it would be grievous sin in me to accept you.'

I had not noticed where the gondoliers were rowing us. I suppose he had given them some direction unheard by me, for as I resigned myself in despairing indolence to the motion of the gondola, I perceived that it was taking us up the Canal, and, turning into a side opening near the Palazzo Grimani, drew up at some steps near the end of a large church.

'Where are we?' said I.

'It is the Church of the Frari,' he replied. 'We might be married there. At any rate, let us go inside, and grow calm, and decide what to do.'

When we had entered I found that whether a place to marry in or not, it was one to depress. The word which Venice speaks most constantly – decay – was in a sense accentuated here. The whole large fabric itself seemed sinking into an earth which was not solid enough to bear it. Cobwebbed cracks zigzagged the walls, and similar webs clouded the window-panes. A sickly-sweet smell pervaded the aisles. After walking about with him a little while in embarrassing silences, divided only by his cursory explanations of the monuments and other objects, and almost fearing he might produce a marriage licence, I went to a door in the south transept which opened into the sacristy.

I glanced through it, towards the small altar at the upper end. The place was empty save of one figure; and she was kneeling here in front of the beautiful altarpiece by Bellini. Beautiful though it was she seemed not to see it. She was weeping and praying as though her heart was broken. She was my sister Caroline. I beckoned to Charles, and he came to my side, and looked through the door with me.

'Speak to her,' said I. 'She will forgive you.'

I gently pushed him through the doorway, and went back into the transept, down the nave, and onward to the west door. There I saw my father, to whom I spoke. He answered severely that, having first obtained comfortable quarters in a *pension* on the Grand Canal, he had gone back to the hotel on the Riva degli Schiavoni to find me; but that I was not there. He was now waiting for Caroline, to accompany her back to the *pension*, at which she had requested to be left to herself as much as possible till she could regain some composure.

I told him that it was useless to dwell on what was past, that I no doubt had erred, that the remedy lay in the future and their marriage. In this he quite agreed with me, and on my informing him that M de la Feste was at that moment with Caroline in the sacristy, he assented to my proposal that we should leave them to themselves, and return together to await them at the *pension*, where he had also engaged a room for me. This we did, and going up to the chamber he had chosen for me, which overlooked the Canal, I leant from the window to watch for the gondola that should contain Charles and my sister.

They were not long in coming. I recognized them by the colour of her sunshade as soon as they turned the bend on my right hand. They were side by side of necessity, but there was no conversation between them, and I thought that she looked flushed and he pale. When they were rowed in to the steps of our house he handed her up. I fancied she might have refused his assistance, but she did not. Soon I heard her pass my door, and wishing to know the result of their interview I went downstairs, seeing that the gondola had not put off with him. He was turning from the door, but not towards the water, intending apparently to walk home by way of the *calle* which led into the Via 22 Marzo.

'Has she forgiven you?' said I.

'I have not asked her,' he said.

'But you are bound to do so,' I told him.

He paused, and then said, 'Alicia, let us understand each other. Do you mean to tell me, once for all, that if your sister is willing to become my wife you absolutely make way for her, and will not entertain any thought of what I suggested to you any more?'

'I do tell you so,' said I with dry lips. 'You belong to her – how can I do otherwise?'

'Yes; it is so; it is purely a question of honour,' he returned. 'Very well then, honour shall be my word, and not my love. I will put the question to her frankly; if she says "Yes", the marriage shall be. But not here. It shall be at your own house in England.'

'When?' said I.

'I will accompany her there,' he replied, 'and it shall be within a week of her return. I have nothing to gain by delay. But I will not answer for the consequences.'

'What do you mean?' said I. He made no reply, went away, and I came back to my room.

9. SHE WITNESSES THE END

April 20. Milan, 10.30 p.m. – We are thus far on our way homeward. I, being decidedly *de trop*, travel apart from the rest as much as I can. Having dined at the hotel here, I went out by myself, regardless of the proprieties, for I could not stay in. I walked at a leisurely pace along the Via Allesandro Manzoni till my eye was caught by the grand Galleria Vittorio Emanuele, and I entered under the high glass arcades till I reached the central octagon, where I sat down in one of a group of chairs placed there. Becoming accustomed to the stream of promenaders, I soon observed, seated on the chairs opposite, Caroline and Charles. This was the first occasion on which I had seen them *en tête à tête* since my conversation with him. She soon caught sight of me; averted her eyes; then, apparently abandoning herself to an impulse, she jumped up from her seat and came across to me. We had not spoken to each other since the meeting in Venice.

'Alicia,' she said, sitting down by my side, 'Charles asks me to forgive you, and I do forgive you.'

I pressed her hand, with tears in my eyes, and said, 'And do you forgive him?'

'Yes,' said she shyly.

'And what's the result?' said I.

'We are to be married directly we reach home.'

This was almost the whole of our conversation; she walked home with me, Charles following a little way behind, though she kept turning her head, as if anxious that he should overtake us. 'Honour and not love' seemed to ring in my ears. So matters stand. Caroline is again happy.

April 25. – We have reached home, Charles with us. Events are now moving in silent speed, almost with velocity, indeed; and I sometimes feel oppressed by the strange and preternatural ease which seems to accompany their flow. Charles is staying at the neighbouring town; he is only waiting for the marriage licence; when obtained he is to come here, be quietly married to her, and carry her off. It is rather resignation than content which sits on his face; but he has not spoken a word more to me on the burning subject, or deviated one hair's breadth from the course he laid down. They may be happy in time to come: I hope so. But I cannot shake off depression.

May 6. – Eve of the wedding. Caroline is serenely happy, though not blithe. But there is nothing to excite anxiety about her. I wish I could say the same of him. He comes and goes like a ghost, and yet nobody seems to observe this strangeness in his mien. I could not help being here for the ceremony; but my absence would have resulted in less disquiet on his part, I believe. However, I may be wrong in attributing causes: my father simply says that Charles and Caroline have as good a chance of being happy as other people. Well, tomorrow settles all.

May 7. – They are married: we have just returned from church. Charles looked so pale this morning that my father asked him if he was ill. He said, 'No: only a slight headache'; and we started for the church. There was no hitch or hindrance; and the thing is done.

4 p.m. – They ought to have set out on their journey by this time; but there is an unaccountable delay. Charles went out half-an-hour ago, and has not yet returned. Caroline is waiting in the hall; but I am dreadfully afraid they will miss the train. I suppose the trifling hindrance is of no account; and yet I am full of misgivings. . .

Sept. 14. – Four months have passed; *only* four months! It seems like years. Can it be that only seventeen weeks ago I set on this paper the fact of their marriage? I am now an aged woman by comparison!

On that never to be forgotten day we waited and waited, and Charles did not return. At six o'clock, when poor little Caroline had gone back to her room in a state of suspense impossible to describe, a man who worked in the water-meadows came to the house and asked for my father. He had an interview with him in the study. My father then rang his bell, and sent for me. I went down; and I then learnt the fatal news. Charles was no more. The waterman had been going to shut down the hatches of a weir in the meads when he saw a hat on the edge of the pool below, floating round and round in the eddy, and looking into the pool saw something strange at the bottom. He knew what it meant, and lowering the hatches so that the water was still, could distinctly see the body. It is needless to write particulars that were in the newspapers at the time. Charles was brought to the house, but he was dead.

We all feared for Caroline; and she suffered much; but strange to say, her suffering was purely of the nature of deep grief which found relief in sobbing and tears. It came out at the inquest that Charles had been accustomed to cross the meads to give an occasional half-crown to an old man who lived on the opposite hill, who had once been a landscape painter in an humble way till he lost his eyesight; and it was assumed that he had gone thither for the same purpose today, and to bid him farewell. On this information the coroner's jury found that his death had been caused by misadventure; and everybody believes to this hour that he was drowned while crossing the weir to relieve the old man. Except one: she believes in no accident. After the stunning effect of the first news, I thought it strange that he should have chosen to go on such an errand at the last moment, and to go personally, when there was so little time to spare, since any gift could have been so easily sent by another hand. Further reflection has convinced me that this step out of life was as much a part of the day's plan as was the wedding in the church hard by. They were the two halves of his complete intention when he gave me on the Grand Canal that assurance which I shall never forget: 'Very well, then; honour shall be my word, not love. If she says "Yes", the marriage shall be.'

I do not know why I should have made this entry at this particular time; but it has occurred to me to do it – to complete, in a measure, that part of my desultory chronicle which relates to the love-story of my sister and Charles. She lives on meekly in her grief, and will probably outlive it; while I – but never mind me.

10. SHE ADDS A NOTE LONG AFTER

Five years later. – I have lighted upon this old diary, which it has interested me to look over, containing, as it does, records of the time when life shone more warmly in my eye than it does now. I am impelled to add one sentence to round off its record of the past. About a year ago my sister Caroline, after a persistent wooing, accepted the hand and heart of Theophilus Higham, once the blushing young Scripture reader who assisted at the substitute for a marriage I planned, and now the fully-ordained curate of the next parish. His penitence for the part he played ended in love. We have all now made atonement for our sins against her: may she be deceived no more.

1887

THE GRAVE BY THE HANDPOST

I never pass through Chalk-Newton without turning to regard the neighbouring upland, at a point where a lane crosses the lone straight highway dividing this from the next parish; a sight which does not fail to recall the event that once happened there; and, though it may seem superfluous, at this date, to disinter more memories of village history, the whispers of that spot may claim to be preserved.

It was on a dark, yet mild and exceptionally dry evening at Christmastime (according to the testimony of William Dewy of Mellstock, Michael Mail, and others), that the choir of Chalk-Newton – a large parish situate about half-way between the towns of Ivell and Casterbridge, and now a railway station – left their homes just before midnight to repeat their annual harmonies under the windows of the local population. The band of instrumentalists and singers was one of the largest in the county; and, unlike the smaller and finer Mellstock string-band, which eschewed all but the catgut, it included brass and reed performers at full Sunday services, and reached all across the west gallery.

On this night there were two or three violins, two 'cellos, a tenor viol, double bass, hautboy, clarionets, serpent, and seven singers. It was, however, not the choir's labours, but what its members chanced to witness, that particularly marked the occasion.

They had pursued their rounds for many years without meeting with any incident of an unusual kind, but tonight, according to the assertions of several, there prevailed, to begin with, an exceptionally solemn and thoughtful mood among two or three of the oldest in the band, as if they were thinking they might be joined by the phantoms of dead friends who had been of their number in earlier years, and now were mute in the churchyard under flattening mounds – friends who had shown greater zest for melody in their time than was shown in this; or that some past voice of a semi-transparent figure might quaver from some bedroom-window its acknowledgment of their nocturnal greeting, instead of a familiar living neighbour. Whether this were fact or fancy, the younger members of the choir met together with their customary thoughtlessness and buoyancy. When they had gathered by the stone stump of the cross in the middle of the village, near the White Horse Inn, which they made their starting point, some one observed that were full early, that it was not yet twelve o'clock. The local waits of those days mostly refrained from sounding a note before Christmas morning had astronomically arrived, and not caring to return to their beer, they decided to begin with some outlying cottages in Sidlinch Lane, where the people had no clocks, and would not know whether it were night or morning. In that direction they accordingly went; and as they ascended to higher ground their attention was attracted by a light beyond the houses, quite at the top of the lane.

The road from Chalk-Newton to Broad Sidlinch is about two miles long, and in the middle of its course, where it passes over the ridge dividing the two villages, it crosses at right angles, as has been stated, the lonely monotonous old highway known as Long Ash Lane, which runs, straight as a surveyor's line, many miles north and south of this spot, on the foundation of a Roman road, and has often been mentioned in these narratives. Though now quite deserted and grass-grown, at the beginning of the century it was well kept and frequented by traffic. The glimmering light appeared to come from the precise point where the roads intersected.

'I think I know what that mid mean!' one of the group remarked.

They stood a few moments, discussing the probability of the light having origin in an event of which rumours had reached them, and resolved to go up the hill.

Approaching the high land their conjectures were strengthened. Long Ash Lane cut athwart them, right and left; and they saw that at the junction of the four ways, under the handpost, a grave was dug, into which, as the choir drew nigh, a corpse had just been thrown by the four Sidlinch men employed for the purpose. The cart and horse which had brought the body thither stood silently by.

The singers and musicians from Chalk-Newton halted, and looked on while the gravediggers shovelled in and trod down the earth, till, the hole being filled, the latter threw their spades into the cart, and prepared to depart.

'Who mid ye be a-burying there?' asked Lot Swanhills in a raised voice. 'Not the sergeant?'

The Sidlinch men had been so deeply engrossed in their task that they had not noticed the lanterns of the Chalk-Newton choir till now.

'What – be you the Newton carol-singers?' returned the representatives of Sidlinch.

'Ay, sure. Can it be that it is old Sergeant Holway you've a-buried there?'

''Tis so. You've heard about it, then?'

The choir knew no particulars – only that he had shot himself in his apple-closet on the previous Sunday. 'Nobody seem'th to know what 'a did it for, 'a b'lieve? Leastwise, we don't know at Chalk-Newton,' continued Lot.

'O yes. It all came out at the inquest.'

The singers drew close, and the Sidlinch men, pausing to rest after their labours, told the story. 'It was all owing to that son of his, poor old man. It broke his heart.'

'But the son is a soldier, surely; now with his regiment in the East Indies?'

'Ay. And it have been rough with the army over there lately. 'Twas a pity his father persuaded him to go. But Luke shouldn't have twyted the sergeant o't, since 'a did it for the best.'

The circumstances, in brief, were these: The sergeant who had come to this lamentable end, father of the young soldier who had gone with his regiment to the East, had been singularly comfortable in his military experiences, these having ended long before the outbreak of the great war with France. On his discharge, after duly serving his time, he had returned to his native village, and married, and taken kindly to domestic life. But the war in which England next involved herself had cost him many frettings that age and infirmity prevented him from being ever again an active unit of the army. When his only son grew to young manhood, and the question arose of his going out in life, the lad expressed his wish to be a mechanic. But his father advised enthusiastically for the army.

'Trade is coming to nothing in these days,' he said. 'And if the war with the French lasts, as it will, trade will be still worse. The army, Luke – that's the thing for 'ee. 'Twas the making of me, and 'twill be the making of you. I hadn't half such a chance as you'll have in these splendid hotter times.'

Luke demurred, for he was a home-keeping, peace-loving youth. But, putting respectful trust in his father's judgment, he at length gave way, and enlisted in the —d Foot. In the course of a few weeks he was sent out to India to his regiment, which had distinguished itself in the East under General Wellesley.

But Luke was unlucky. News came home indirectly that he lay sick out there; and then on one recent day when his father was out walking, the old man had received tidings that a letter awaited him at Casterbridge. The sergeant sent a special messenger the whole nine miles, and the letter was paid for and brought home; but though, as he had guessed, it came from Luke, its contents were of an unexpected tenor.

The letter had been written during a time of deep depression. Luke said that his life was a burden and a slavery, and bitterly reproached his father for advising him to embark on a career for which he felt unsuited. He found himself suffering fatigues and illnesses without gaining glory, and engaged in a cause which he did not understand or appreciate. If it had not been for his father's bad advice he, Luke, would now have been working comfortably at a trade in the village that he had never wished to leave.

After reading the letter the sergeant advanced a few steps till he was quite out of sight of everybody, and then sat down on the bank by the wayside.

When he arose half-an-hour later he looked withered and broken, and from that day his natural spirits left him. Wounded to the quick by his son's sarcastic stings, he indulged in liquor more and more frequently. His wife had died some years before this date, and the sergeant lived alone in the house which had been hers. One morning in the December under notice the report of a gun had been heard on his premises, and on entering the neighbours found him in a dying state. He had shot himself with an old firelock that he used for scaring birds; and from what he had said the day before, and the arrangements he had made for his decease, there was no doubt that his end had been deliberately planned, as a consequence of the despondency into which he had been thrown by his son's letter. The coroner's jury returned a verdict of *felo-de-se.*

'Here's his son's letter,' said one of the Sidlinch men. ''Twas found in his father's pocket. You can see by the state o't how many times he read it over. Howsomever, the Lord's will be done, since it must, whether or no.'

The grave was filled up and levelled, no mound being shaped over it. The Sidlinch men then bade the Chalk-Newton choir good-night, and departed with the cart in which they had brought the sergeant's body to the hill. When their tread had died away from the ear, and the wind swept over the isolated grave with its customary siffle of indifference, Lot Swanhills turned and spoke to old Richard Toller, the hautboy player.

''Tis hard upon a man, and he a wold sojer, to serve en so, Richard. Not that the sergeant was ever in a battle bigger than would go into a half-acre paddock, that's true. Still, his soul ought to hae as good a chance as another man's, all the same, hey?'

Richard replied that he was quite of the same opinion. 'What d'ye say to lifting up a carrel over his grave, as 'tis Christmas, and no hurry to begin down in parish, and 'twouldn't take up ten minutes, and not a soul up here to say us nay, or know anything about it?'

Lot nodded assent. 'The man ought to hae his chances,' he repeated.

'Ye may as well spet upon his grave, for all the good we shall do en by what we lift up, now he's got so far,' said Notton, the clarionet man and professed sceptic of the choir. 'But I'm agreed if the rest be.'

They thereupon placed themselves in a semicircle by the newly-stirred earth, and roused the dull air with the well-known Number Sixteen of their collection, which Lot gave out as being the one he thought best suited to the occasion and the mood:

He comes' the pri'-soners to' re-lease',
In Sa'-tan's bon'-dage held'.

'Jown it – we've never played to a dead man afore,' said Ezra Cattstock, when, having concluded the last verse, they stood reflecting for a breath or two. 'But it do seem more merciful than to go away and leave en, as they t'other fellers have done.'

'Now backalong to Newton, and by the time we get overright the pa'son's 'twill be half after twelve,' said the leader.

They had not, however, done more than gather up their instruments when the wind brought to their notice the noise of a vehicle rapidly driven up the same lane from Sidlinch which the gravediggers had lately retraced. To avoid being run over when moving on, they waited till the benighted traveller, whoever he might be, should pass them where they stood in the wider area of the Cross.

In half a minute the light of the lanterns fell upon a hired fly, drawn by a steaming and jaded horse. It reached the handpost, when a voice from the inside cried, 'Stop here!' The driver pulled rein. The carriage door was opened from within, and there leapt out a private soldier in the uniform of some line regiment. He looked around, and was apparently surprised to see the musicians standing there.

'Have you buried a man here?' he asked.

'No. We bain't Sidlinch folk, thank God; we be Newton choir. Though a man is just buried here, that's true; and we've raised a carrel over the poor mortal's natomy. What – do my eyes see before me young Luke Holway, that went wi' his regiment to the East Indies, or do I see his spirit straight from the battlefield? Be you the son that wrote the letter—'

'Don't – don't ask me. The funeral is over, then?'

'There wer no funeral, in a Christen manner of speaking. But's buried, sure enough. You must have met the men going back in the empty cart.'

'Like a dog in a ditch, and all through me!'

He remained silent, looking at the grave, and they could not help pitying him. 'My friends,' he said, 'I understand better now. You have, I suppose, in neighbourly charity, sung peace to his soul? I thank you, from my heart, for your kind pity. Yes; I am Sergeant Holway's miserable son – I'm the son who has brought about his father's death, as truly as if I had done it with my own hand!'

'No, no. Don't ye take on so, young man. He'd been naturally low for a good while, off and on, so we hear.'

'We were out in the East when I wrote to him. Everything had seemed to go wrong with me. Just after my letter had gone we were ordered home. That's how it is you see me here. As soon as we got into barracks at Casterbridge I heard o' this— . . . Damn me! I'll dare to follow my father, and make away with myself, too. It is the only thing left to do!'

'Don't ye be rash, Luke Holway, I say again; but try to make amends by your future life. And maybe your father will smile a smile down from heaven upon 'ee for 't.'

He shook his head. 'I don't know about that!' he answered bitterly.

'Try and be worthy of your father at his best. 'Tis not too late.'

'D' ye think not? I fancy it is! . . . Well, I'll turn it over. Thank you for your good counsel. I'll live for one thing, at any rate. I'll move father's body to a decent Christian churchyard, if I do it with my own hands. I can't save his life, but I can give him an honourable grave. He shan't lie in this accursed place!'

'Ay, as our pa'son, says, 'tis a barbarous custom they keep up at Sidlinch, and ought to be done away wi'. The man a' old soldier, too. You see, our pa'son is not like yours at Sidlinch.'

'He says it is barbarous, does he? So it is!' cried the soldier. 'Now hearken, my friends.' Then he proceeded to inquire if they would increase his indebtedness to them by undertaking the removal, privately, of the body of the suicide to the churchyard, not of Sidlinch, a parish he now hated, but of Chalk-Newton. He would give them all he possessed to do it.

Lot asked Ezra Cattstock what he thought of it.

Cattstock, the 'cello player, who was also the sexton, demurred, and advised the young soldier to sound the rector about it first. 'Mid be he would object, and yet 'a midn't. The pa'son o' Sidlinch is a hard man, I own ye, and 'a said if folk will kill themselves in hot blood they must take the consequences. But ours don't think like that at all, and might allow it.'

'What's his name?'

'The honourable and reverent Mr Oldham, brother to Lord Wessex. But you needn't be afeared o' en on that account. He'll talk to 'ee like a common man, if so be you haven't had enough drink to gie 'ee bad breath.'

'O, the same as formerly. I'll ask him. Thank you. And that duty done—'

'What then?'

'There's war in Spain. I hear our next move is there. I'll try to show myself to be what my father wished me. I don't suppose I shall – but I'll try in my feeble way. That much I swear – here over his body. So help me God.'

Luke smacked his palm against the white handpost with such force that it shook. 'Yes, there's war in Spain; and another chance for me to be worthy of father.'

So the matter ended that night. That the private acted in one thing as he had vowed to do soon became apparent, for during the Christmas week the rector came into the churchyard when Cattstock was there, and asked him to find a spot that would be suitable for the purpose of such an interment, adding that he had slightly known the late sergeant, and was not aware of any law which forbade him to assent to the removal, the letter of the rule having been observed. But as he did not wish to seem moved by opposition to his neighbour at Sidlinch, he had stipulated that the act of charity should be carried out at night, and as privately as possible, and that the grave should be in an obscure part of the enclosure. 'You had better see the young man about it at once,' added the rector.

But before Ezra had done anything Luke came down to his house. His furlough had been cut short, owing to new developments of the war in the Peninsula, and being obliged to go back to his regiment immediately, he was compelled to leave the exhumation and reinterment to his friends. Everything was paid for, and he implored them all to see it carried out forthwith.

With this the soldier left. The next day Ezra, on thinking the matter over, again went across to the rectory, struck with sudden misgiving. He had remembered that the sergeant had been buried without a coffin, and he was not sure that a stake had not been driven through him. The business would be more troublesome than they had at first supposed.

'Yes, indeed!' murmured the rector. 'I am afraid it is not feasible after all.'

The next event was the arrival of a headstone by carrier from the nearest town; to be left at Mr Ezra Cattstock's; all expenses paid. The sexton and the carrier deposited the stone in the former's outhouse; and Ezra, left alone, put on his spectacles and read the brief and simple inscription:

HERE LYETH THE BODY OF SAMUEL HOLWAY, LATE SERGEANT IN HIS MAJESTY'S —D REGIMENT OF FOOT, WHO DEPARTED THIS LIFE DECEMBER THE 20TH, 180–. ERECTED BY L.H.

'I AM NOT WORTHY TO BE CALLED THY SON.'

Ezra again called at the riverside rectory. 'The stone is come, sir. But I'm afeared we can't do it nohow.'

'I should like to oblige him,' said the gentlemanly old incumbent. 'And I would forgo all fees willingly. Still, if you and the others don't think you can carry it out, I am in doubt what to say.'

'Well, sir; I've made inquiry of a Sidlinch woman as to his burial, and what I thought seems true. They buried en wi' a new six-foot hurdle-saul drough's body, from the sheep-pen up in North Ewelease, though they won't own to it now. And the question is, Is the moving worth while, considering the awkwardness?'

'Have you heard anything more of the young man?'

Ezra had only heard that he had embarked that week for Spain with the rest of the regiment. 'And if he's as desperate as 'a seemed, we shall never see him here in England again.'

'It is an awkward case,' said the rector.

Ezra talked it over with the choir; one of whom suggested that the stone might be erected at the cross-roads. This was regarded as impracticable. Another said that it might be set up in the churchyard without removing the body; but this was seen to be dishonest. So nothing was done.

The headstone remained in Ezra's outhouse till, growing tired of seeing it there, he put it away among the bushes at the bottom of his garden. The subject was sometimes revived among them, but it always ended with: 'Considering how 'a was buried, we can hardly make a job o't.'

There was always the consciousness that Luke would never come back, an impression strengthened by the disasters which were rumoured to have befallen the army in Spain. This tended to make their inertness permanent. The headstone grew green as it lay on its back under Ezra's bushes; then a tree by the river was blown down, and, falling across the stone, cracked it in three pieces. Ultimately the pieces became buried in the leaves and mould.

Luke had not been born a Chalk-Newton man, and he had no relations left in Sidlinch, so that no tidings of him reached either village throughout the war. But after Waterloo and the fall of Napoleon there arrived at Sidlinch one day an English sergeant-major covered with stripes and, as it turned out, rich in glory. Foreign service had so totally changed Luke Holway that it was not until he told his name that the inhabitants recognized him as the sergeant's only son.

He had served with unswerving effectiveness through the Peninsular campaigns under Wellington; had fought at Busaco, Fuentes d'Onoro, Ciudad Rodrigo, Badajoz, Salamanca, Vittoria, Quatre Bras, and Waterloo; and had now returned to enjoy a more than earned pension and repose in his native district.

He hardly stayed in Sidlinch longer than to take a meal on his arrival. The same evening he started on foot over the hill to Chalk-Newton, passing the handpost, and saying as he glanced at the spot, 'Thank God: he's not there!' Nightfall was approaching when he reached the latter village; but he made straight for the churchyard. On his entering it there remained light enough to discern the headstones by, and these he narrowly scanned. But though he searched the front part by the road, and the back part by the river, what he sought he could not find – the grave of Sergeant Holway, and a memorial bearing the inscription: 'I AM NOT WORTHY TO BE CALLED THY SON.'

He left the churchyard and made inquiries. The honourable and reverend old rector was dead, and so were many of the choir; but by degrees the sergeant-major learnt that his father still lay at the cross-roads in Long Ash Lane.

Luke pursued his way moodily homewards, to do which, in the natural course, he would be compelled to repass the spot, there being no other road between the two villages. But he could not now go by that place, vociferous with reproaches in his father's tones; and he got over the hedge and wandered deviously through the ploughed fields to avoid the scene. Through many a fight and fatigue Luke had been sustained by the thought that he was restoring the family honour and making noble amends. Yet his father lay still in degradation. It was rather a sentiment than a fact that his father's body had been made to suffer for his own misdeeds; but to his super-sensitiveness it seemed that his efforts to retrieve his character and to propitiate the shade of the insulted one had ended in failure.

He endeavoured, however, to shake off his lethargy, and, not liking the associations of Sidlinch, hired a small cottage at Chalk-Newton which had long been empty. Here he lived alone, becoming quite a hermit, and allowing no woman to enter the house.

The Christmas after taking up his abode herein he was sitting in the chimney-corner by himself, when he heard faint notes in the distance, and soon a melody burst forth immediately outside his own window. It came from the carol-singers, as usual; and though many of the old hands, Ezra and Lot included, had gone to their rest, the same old carols were still played out of the same old books. There resounded through the sergeant-major's window-shutters the familiar lines that the deceased choir had rendered over his father's grave:

He comes' the pri'-soners to' re-lease',
In Sa'-tan's bon'-dage held'.

When they had finished they went on to another house, leaving him to silence and loneliness as before.

The candle wanted snuffing, but he did not snuff it, and he sat on till it had burnt down into the socket and made waves of shadow on the ceiling.

The Christmas cheerfulness of next morning was broken at breakfast-time by tragic intelligence which went down the village like wind. Sergeant-Major Holway had been found shot through the head by his own hand at the cross-roads in Long Ash Lane where his father lay buried.

On the table in the cottage he had left a piece of paper, on which he had written his wish that he might be buried at the Cross beside his father. But the paper was accidentally swept to the floor, and overlooked till after his funeral, which took place in the ordinary way in the churchyard.

CHRISTMAS 1897

ENTER A DRAGOON

I lately had a melancholy experience (said the gentleman who is answerable for the truth of this story). It was that of going over a doomed house with whose outside aspect I had long been familiar – a house, that is, which by reason of age and dilapidation was to be pulled down during the following week. Some of the thatch, brown and rotten as the gills of old mushrooms, had, indeed, been removed before I walked over the building. Seeing that it was only a very small house – which is usually called a 'cottage-residence' – situated in a remote hamlet, and that it was not more than a hundred years old, if so much, I was led to think in my progress through the hollow rooms, with their cracked walls and sloping floors, what an exceptional number of abrupt family incidents had taken place therein – to reckon only those which had come to my own knowledge. And no doubt there were many more of which I had never heard.

It stood at the top of a garden stretching down to the lane or street that ran through a hermit-group of dwellings in Mellstock parish. From a green gate at the lower entrance, over which the thorn hedge had been shaped to an arch by constant clippings, a gravel path ascended between the box edges of once trim rapsberry, strawberry, and vegetable plots, towards the front door. This was in colour an ancient and bleached green that could be rubbed off with the finger, and it bore a small long-featured brass knocker covered with verdigris in its crevices. For some years before this eve of demolition the homestead had degenerated, and been divided into two tenements to serve as cottages for farm labourers; but in its prime it had indisputable claim to be considered neat, pretty and genteel.

The variety of incidents above alluded to was mainly owing to the nature of the tenure, whereby the place had been occupied by families not quite of the kind customary in such spots – people whose circumstances, position, or antecedents were more or less of a critical happy-go-lucky cast. And of these residents the family whose term comprised the story I wish to relate was that of Mr Jacob Paddock the market-gardener, who dwelt there for some years with his wife and grown-up daughter.

I

An evident commotion was agitating the premises, which jerked busy sounds across the front plot, resembling those of a disturbed hive. If a member of the household appeared at the door it was with a countenance of abstraction and concern.

Evening began to bend over the scene; and the other inhabitants of the hamlet came out to draw water, their common well being in the public road opposite the garden and house of the Paddocks. Having wound up their bucketsfull respectively they lingered, and spoke significantly together. From their words any casual listener might have gathered information of what had occurred.

The woodman who lived nearest the site of the story told most of the tale. Selina, the daughter of the Paddocks opposite, had been surprised that afternoon by receiving a letter from her once intended husband, then a corporal, but now a sergeant-major of dragoons, whom she had hitherto supposed to be one of the slain in the Battle of the Alma two or three years before.

'She picked up wi'en against her father's wish, as we know, and before he got his stripes,' their informant continued. 'Not but that the man was as hearty a feller as you'd meet this side o' London. But Jacob, you see, wished her to do better, and one can understand it. However, she was determined to stick to him at that time; and for what happened she was not much to blame, so near as they were to matrimony when the war broke out and spoiled all.'

'Even the very pig had been killed for the wedding,' said a woman, 'and the barrel o' beer ordered in. O, the man meant honourable enough. But to be off in two days to fight in a foreign country – 'twas natural of her father to say they should wait till he got back.'

'And he never came,' murmured one in the shade.

'The war ended but her man never turned up again. She was not sure he was killed, but was too proud, or too timid, to go and hunt for him.'

'One reason why her father forgave her when he found out how matters stood was, as he said plain at the time, that he liked the man, and could see that he meant to act straight. So the old folks made the best of what they couldn't mend, and kept her there with 'em, when some wouldn't. Time has proved seemingly that he did mean to act straight, now that he has writ to her that he's coming. She'd have stuck to him all through the time, 'tis my belief, if t'other hadn't come along.'

'At the time of the courtship,' resumed the woodman, 'the regiment was quartered in Casterbridge Barracks, and he and she got acquainted by his calling to buy a penn'orth of rathe-ripes off that tree yonder in her father's orchard – though 'twas said he seed *her* over hedge as well as the apples. He declared 'twas a kind of apple he much fancied; and he called for a penn'orth every day till the tree was cleared. It ended in his calling for her.'

''Twas a thousand pities they didn't jine up at once and ha' done wi' it.'

'Well; better late than never, if so be he'll have her now. But, Lord, she'd that faith in en that she'd no more belief that he was alive, when a' didn't come, than that the undermost man in our churchyard was alive. She'd never have thought of another but for that – O no!'

''Tis awkward, altogether, for her now.'

'Still she hadn't married wi' the new man. Though to be sure she would have committed it next week, even the licence being got, they say, for she'd have no banns this time, the first being so unfortunate.'

'Perhaps the sergeant-major will think he's released, and go as he came.'

'O, not as I reckon. Soldier bain't particular, and she's a tidy piece o' furniture still. What will happen is that she'll have her soldier, and break off with the master-wheelwright, licence or no – daze me if she won't.'

In the progress of these desultory conjectures the form of another neighbour arose in the gloom. She nodded to the people at the well, who replied, 'G'd-night, Mrs Stone,' as she passed through Mr Paddock's gate towards his door. She was an intimate friend of the latter's household, and the group followed her with their eyes up the path and past the windows, which were now lighted up by candles inside.

2

Mrs Stone paused at the door, knocked, and was admitted by Selina's mother, who took her visitor at once into the parlour on the left hand, where a table was partly spread for supper. On the 'beaufet' against the wall stood probably the only object which would have attracted the eye of a local stranger in an otherwise ordinarily furnished room, a great plum-cake guarded as if it were a curiosity by a glass shade of the kind seen in museums – square, with a wooden back like those enclosing stuffed specimens of rare feather or fur. This was the mummy of the cake intended in earlier days for the wedding-feast of Selina and the soldier, which had been religiously and lovingly preserved by the former as a testimony to her intentional respectability in spite of an untoward subsequent circumstance, which will be mentioned. This relic was now as dry as a brick, and seemed to belong to a pre-existent civilization. Till quite recently, Selina had been in the habit of pausing before it daily, and recalling the accident whose consequences had thrown a shadow over her life ever since – that of which the water-drawers had spoken – the sudden news one morning that the Route had come for the —th Dragoons, two days only being the interval before departure; the hurried consultation as to what should be done, the second time of asking being past but not the third; and the decision that it would be unwise to solemnize matrimony in such haphazard circumstances, even if it were possible, which was doubtful.

Before the fire the young woman in question was now seated on a low stool, in the stillness of reverie, and a toddling boy played about the floor around her.

'Ah, Mrs Stone!' said Selina, rising slowly. 'How kind of you to come in. You'll bide to supper? Mother has told you the strange news, of course?'

'No. But I heard it outside, that is, that you'd had a letter from Mr Clarke – Sergeant-Major Clark, as they say he is now – and that he's coming to make it up with 'ee.'

'Yes; coming tonight – all the way from the north of England where he's quartered. I don't know whether I'm happy or – frightened at it. Of course I always believed that if he was alive he'd come and keep his solemn vow to me. But when it is printed that a man is killed – what can you think?'

'It *was* printed?'

'Why, yes. After the Battle of the Alma the book of the names of the killed and wounded was nailed up against Casterbridge Town Hall door. 'Twas on a Saturday, and I walked there o' purpose to read and see for myself, for I'd heard that his name was down. There was a crowd of people round the book, looking for the names of relations; and I can mind that when they saw me they made way for me – knowing that we'd been just going to be married – and that, as you may say, I belonged to him. Well, I reached up my arm, and turned over the farrels of the book, and under the "killed" I read his surname, but intead of "John" they'd printed "James", and I thought 'twas a mistake, and that it must be he. Who could have guessed there were two nearly of one name in one regiment.'

'Well – he's coming to finish the wedding of 'ee as may be said; so never mind, my dear. All's well that ends well.'

'That's what he seems to say. But then he has not heard yet about Mr Miller; and that's what rather terrifies me. Luckily my marriage with him next week was to have been by licence, and not banns, as in John's case; and it was not so well known on that account. Still, I don't know what to think.'

'Everything seems to come just 'twixt cup and lip with 'ee – don't it now, Miss Paddock? Two weddings broke off – 'tis odd! How came you to accept Mr Miller, my dear?'

'He's been so good and faithful! Not minding about the child at all; for he knew the rights of the story. He's dearly fond o' Johnny, you know – just as if 'twere his own – isn't he, my duck? Do Mr Miller love you or don't he?'

'Iss! An' I love Mr Miller,' said the toddler.

'Well, you see, Mrs Stone, he said he'd make me a comfortable home; and thinking 'twould be a good thing for Johnny, Mr Miller being so much better off than me, I agreed at last, just as a widow might – which is what I have always felt myself, ever since I saw what I thought was John's name printed there. I hope John will forgive me!'

'So he will forgive 'ee, since 'twas no manner of wrong to him. He ought to have sent 'ee a line, saying 'twas another man.'

Selina's mother entered. 'We've not known of this an hour, Mrs Stone,' she said. 'The letter was brought up from Lower Mellstock Post-office by one of the schoolchildren, only this afternoon. Mr Miller was coming here this very night to settle about the wedding doings. Hark! Is that your father? Or is it Mr Miller already come?'

The footsteps entered the porch; there was a brushing on the mat, and the door of the room sprung back to disclose a rubicund man about thirty years of age, of thriving master-mechanic appearance and obviously comfortable temper. On seeing the child, and before taking any notice whatever of the elders, the comer made a noise like the crowing of a cock and flapped his arms as if they were wings, a method of entry which had the unqualified admiration of Johnny.

'Yes – it is he,' said Selina constrainedly advancing.

'What – were you all talking about me, my dear?' said the genial young man when he had finished his crowing and resumed human manners. 'Why, what's the matter?' he went on. 'You look struck all of a heap.' Mr Miller spread an aspect of concern over his own face, and drew a chair up to the fire.

'O mother, would you tell Mr Miller, if he don't know?'

'*Mister* Miller! and going to be married in six days!' he interposed.

'Ah – he don't know it yet!' murmured Mrs Paddock.

'Know what?'

'Well – John Clark – now Sergeant-Major Clark – wasn't shot at Alma after all. 'Twas another of almost the same name.'

'Now that's interesting! There were several cases like that.'

'And he's home again; and he's coming here tonight to see her.'

'Whatever shall I say, that he may not be offended with what I've done?' interposed Selina.

'But why should it matter if he be?'

'O! I must agree to be his wife if he forgives me – of course I must.'

'Must! But why not say nay, Selina, even if he do forgive 'ee?'

'O no! How can I without being wicked? You were very very kind, Mr Miller, to ask me to have you; no other man would have done it after what had happened; and I agreed, even though I did not feel half so warm as I ought. Yet it was entirely owing to my believing him in the grave, as I knew that if he were not he would carry out his promise; and this shows that I was right in trusting him.'

'Yes. . . He must be a goodish sort of fellow,' said Mr Miller, for a moment so impressed with the excellently faithful conduct of the sergeant-major of dragoons that he disregarded its effect upon his own position. He sighed slowly and added, 'Well, Selina, 'tis for you to say. I love you, and I love the boy; and there's my chimney-corner and sticks o' furniture ready for 'ee both.'

'Yes, I know! But I mustn't hear it any more now,' murmured Selina quickly. 'John will be here soon. I hope he'll see how it all was when I tell him. If so be I could have written it to him it would have been better.'

'You think he doesn't know a single word about our having been on the brink o't. But perhaps it's the other way – he's heard of it and that may have brought him.'

'Ah – perhaps he has!' she said brightening. 'And already forgives me.'

'If not, speak out straight and fair, and tell him exactly how it fell out. If he's a man he'll see it.'

'O he's a man true enough. But I really do think I shan't have to tell him at all, since you've put it to me that way!'

As it was now Johnny's bedtime he was carried upstairs, and when Selina came down again her mother observed with some anxiety, 'I fancy Mr Clark must be here soon if he's coming; and that being so, perhaps Mr Miller wouldn't mind – wishing us good-night! since you are so determined to stick to your sergeant-major.' A little bitterness bubbled amid the closing words. 'It would be less awkward, Mr Miller not being here – if he will allow me to say it.'

'To be sure; to be sure,' the master-wheelwright exclaimed with instant conviction, rising alertly from his chair. 'Lord bless my soul,' he said, taking up his hat and stick, 'and we to have been married in six days! But, Selina – you're right. You do belong to the child's father since he's alive. I'll try to make the best of it.'

Before the generous Miller had got further there came a knock to the door accompanied by the noise of wheels.

'I thought I heard something driving up!' said Mrs Paddock.

They heard Mr Paddock, who had been smoking in the room opposite, rise and go to the door, and in a moment a voice familiar enough to Selina was audibly saying, 'At last I am here again – not without many interruptions! How is it with 'ee, Mr Paddock? And how is she? Thought never to see me again, I suppose?' A step with a clink of spurs in it struck upon the entry floor.

'Danged if I bain't catched!' murmured Mr Miller, forgetting company-speech. 'Never mind – I may as well meet him here as elsewhere; and I should like to see the chap, and make friends with en, as he seems one o' the right sort.' He returned to the fireplace just as the sergeant-major was ushered in.

3

He was a good specimen of the long-service soldier of those days; a not unhandsome man, with a certain undemonstrative dignity, which some might have said to be partly owing to the stiffness of his uniform about his neck, the high stock being still worn. He was much stouter than when Selina had parted from him. Although she had not meant to be demonstrative she ran across to him directly she saw him, and he held her in his arms and kissed her.

Then in much agitation she whispered something to him, at which he seemed to be much surprised.

'He's just put to bed,' she continued. 'You can go up and see him. I knew you'd come if you were alive! But I had quite gi'd you up for dead. You've been home in England ever since the war ended?'

'Yes, dear.'

'Why didn't you come sooner?'

'That's just what I ask myself! Why was I such a sappy as not to hurry here the first day I set foot on shore! Well, who'd have thought it – you are as pretty as ever!'

He relinquished her to peep upstairs a little way, where, by looking through the balusters, he could see Johnny's cot just within an open door. On his stepping down again Mr Miller was preparing to depart.

'Now, what's this? I am sorry to see anybody going the moment I've come,' expostulated the sergeant-major. 'I thought we might make an evening of it. There's a nine-gallon cask o' "Phoenix" beer outside in the trap, and a ham, and half a rawmil' cheese; for I thought you might be short o' forage in a lonely place like this; and it struck me we might like to ask in a neighbour or two. But perhaps it would be taking a liberty?'

'O no, not at all,' said Mr Paddock, who was now in the room, in a judicial measured manner. 'Very thoughtful of 'ee, only 'twas not necessary, for we had just laid in an extry stock of eatables and drinkables in preparation for the coming event.'

''Twas very kind, upon my heart,' said the soldier, 'to think me worth such a jocund preparation, since you could only have got my letter this morning.'

Selina gazed at her father to stop him, and exchanged embarrassed glances with Miller. Contrary to her hopes Sergeant-Major Clark plainly did not know that the preparations referred to were for something quite other than his own visit.

The movement of the horse outside, and the impatient tapping of a whip-handle upon the vehicle reminded them that Clark's driver was still waiting. The provisions were brought into the house, and the cart dismissed. Miller, with very little pressure indeed, accepted an invitation to supper, and a few neighbours were induced to come in to make up a cheerful party.

During the laying of the meal, and throughout its continuance, Selina, who sat beside her first intended husband, tried frequently to break the news to him of her engagement to the other – now terminated so suddenly, and so happily for her heart, and her sense of womanly virtue. But the talk ran entirely upon the late war; and though fortified by half a horn of the strong ale brought by the sergeant-major she decided that she might have a better opportunity when supper was over of revealing the situation to him in private.

Having supped, Clark leaned back at ease in his chair and looked around. 'We used sometimes to have a dance in that other room after supper, Selina dear, I recollect. We used to clear out all the furniture into this room before beginning. Have you kept up such goings on?'

'No, not at all!' said his sweetheart sadly.

'We were not unlikely to revive it in a few days,' said Mr Paddock. 'But, howsomever, there's seemingly many a slip, as the saying is.'

'Yes, I'll tell John all about that by-and-by!' interposed Selina; at which, perceiving that the secret which he did not like keeping was to be kept even yet, her father held his tongue with some show of testiness.

The subject of a dance, having been broached, to put the thought in practice was the feeling of all. Soon after the tables and chairs were borne from the opposite room to this by zealous hands, and two of the villagers sent home for a fiddle and tambourine, when the majority began to tread a measure well known in that secluded vale. Selina naturally danced with the sergeant-major, not altogether to her father's satisfaction, and to the real uneasiness of her mother, both of whom would have preferred a postponement of festivities till the rashly anticipated relationship between their daughter and Clark in the past had been made fact by the Church's ordinances. They did not, however, express a positive objection, Mr Paddock remembering, with self-reproach, that it was owing to his original strongly expressed disapproval of Selina's being a soldier's wife that the wedding had been delayed, and finally hindered – with worse consequences than were expected; and ever since the misadventure brought about by his government he had allowed events to steer their own courses.

'My tails will surely catch in your spurs, John!' murmured the daughter of the house, as she whirled around upon his arm with the rapt soul and look of a somnambulist. 'I didn't know we should dance, or I would have put on my other frock.'

'I'll take care, my love. We've danced here before. Do you think your father objects to me now? I've risen in rank. I fancy he's still a little against me.'

'He has repented, times enough.'

'And so have I! If I had married you then 'twould have saved many a misfortune. I have sometimes thought it might have been possible to rush the ceremony through somehow before I left; though we were only in the second asking, were we? And even if I had come back straight here when we returned from the Crimea, and married you then, how much happier I should have been!'

'Dear John, to say that! Why didn't you?'

'O – dilatoriness and want of thought, and a fear of facing your father after so long. I was in hospital a great while, you know. But how familiar the place seems again! What's that I saw on the beaufet in the other room? It never used to be there. A sort of withered corpse of a cake – not an old bride-cake surely?'

'Yes, John, ours. 'Tis the very one that was made for our wedding three years ago.'

'Sakes alive! Why, time shuts up together, and all between then and now seems not to have been! What became of that wedding-gown that they were making in this room, I remember – a bluish, whitish, frothy thing?'

'I have that too.'

'Really! . . . Why, Selina—'

'Yes!'

'Why not put it on now?'

'Wouldn't it seem— And yet, O how I should like to! It would remind them all, if we told them what it was, how we really meant to be married on that bygone day!' Her eyes were again laden with wet.

'Yes. . . The pity that we didn't – the pity!' Moody mournfulness seemed to hold silent awhile on one not naturally taciturn. 'Well – will you?' he said.

'I will – the next dance, if mother don't mind.'

Accordingly, just before the next figure was formed, Selina disappeared, and speedily came downstairs in a creased and box-worn, but still airy and pretty, muslin gown, which was indeed the very one that had been meant to grace her as a bride three years before.

'It is dreadfully old-fashioned,' she apologized.

'Not at all. What a grand thought of mine! Now, let's to't again.'

She explained to some of them, as he led her to the second dance, what the frock had been meant for, and that she had put it on at his request. And again athwart and around the room they went.

'You seem the bride!' he said.

'But I couldn't wear this gown to be married in now!' she replied ecstatically, 'or I shouldn't have put it on and made it dusty. It is really too old-fashioned, and so folded and fretted out, you can't think. That was with my taking it out so many times to look at. I have never put it on – never – till now!'

'Selina, I am thinking of giving up the army. Will you emigrate with me to New Zealand? I've an uncle out there doing well, and he'd soon help me to making a larger income. The English army is glorious, but it ain't altogether enriching.'

'Of course, anywhere that you decide upon. Is it healthy there for Johnny?'

'A lovely climate. And I shall never be happy in England. . . Aha!' he concluded again, with a bitterness of unexpected strength, 'would to Heaven I had come straight back here!'

As the dance brought round one neighbour after another the reunited pair were thrown into juxtaposition with Bob Heartall among the rest who had been called in; one whose chronic expression was that he carried inside him a joke on the point of bursting with its own vastness. He took occasion now to let out a little of its quality, shaking his head at Selina as he addressed her in an undertone –

'This is a bit of a topper to the bridegroom, ho! ho! 'Twill teach en the liberty you'll expect when you've married en!'

'What does he mean by a "topper"?' the sergeant-major asked, who, not being of local extraction, despised the venerable local language, and also seemed to suppose 'bridegroom' to be an anticipatory name for himself. 'I only hope I shall never be worse treated than you've treated me tonight!'

Selina looked frightened. 'He didn't mean you, dear,' she said as they moved on. 'We thought perhaps you knew what had happened, owing to your coming just at this time. Had you – heard anything about – what I intended?'

'Not a breath – how should I, away up in Yorkshire? It was by the merest accident that I came just at this date to make peace with you for my delay.'

'I was engaged to be married to Mr Bartholomew Miller. That's what it is! I would have let 'ee know by letter, but there was no time, only hearing from 'ee this afternoon. . . You won't desert me for it, will you, John? Because, as you know, I quite supposed you dead, and – and—' Her eyes were full of tears of trepidation, and he might have felt a sob heaving within her.

4

The soldier was silent during two or three double bars of the tune. 'When were you to have been married to the said Mr Bartholomew Miller?' he inquired.

'Quite soon.'

'How soon?'

'Next week – O yes – just the same as it was with you and me. There's a strange fate of interruption hanging over me, I sometimes think? He had bought the licence, which I preferred so that it mightn't be like – ours. But it made no difference to the fate of it.'

'Had bought the licence! The devil!'

'Don't be angry, dear John. I didn't know!'

'No, no, I'm not angry.'

'It was so kind of him, considering!'

'Yes. . . I see, of course, how natural your action was – never thinking of seeing me any more! Is it the Mr Miller who is in this dance?'

'Yes.'

Clark glanced round upon Bartholomew and was silent again for some little while, and she stole a look at him, to find that he seemed changed. 'John, you look ill!' she almost sobbed. ''Tisn't me, is it?'

'O dear, no. Though I hadn't, somehow, expected it. I can't find fault with you for a moment – and I don't. . . This is a deuce of a long dance, don't you think? We've been at it twenty minutes if a second, and the figure doesn't allow one much rest. I'm quite out of breath.'

'They like them dreadfully long here. Shall we drop out? Or I'll stop the fiddler?'

'O no, no, I think I can finish. But although I look healthy enough I have never been so strong as I formerly was, since that long illness I had in the hospital at Scutari.'

'And I knew nothing about it!'

'You couldn't, my dear, as I didn't write. What a fool I have been altogether!' He gave a twitch, as of one in pain. 'I won't dance again when this one is over. The fact is I have travelled a long way today, and it seems to have knocked me up a bit.'

There could be no doubt that the sergeant-major was unwell, and Selina made herself miserable by still believing that her story was the cause of his ailment. Suddenly he said in a changed voice, and she perceived that he was paler than ever:

'I must sit down.'

Letting go her waist he went quickly to the other room. She followed, and found him in the nearest chair, his face bent down upon his hands and arms, which were resting on the table.

'What's the matter?' said her father, who sat there dozing by the fire.

'John isn't well. . . We are going to New Zealand when we are married, father. A lovely country! . . . John, would you like something to drink?'

'A drop o' that Schiedam of old Owlett's that's under the stairs, perhaps,' suggested her father. 'Not that nowadays 'tis much better than licensed liquor.'

'John,' she said, putting her face close to his and pressing his arm. 'Will you have a drop of spirits or something?'

He did not reply, and Selina observed that his ear and the side of his face were quite white. Convinced that his illness was serious, a growing dismay seized hold of her. The dance ended; her mother came in, and learning what had happened, looked narrowly at the sergeant-major.

'We must not let him lie like that, lift him up,' she said. 'Let him rest in the window-bench on some cushions.'

They unfolded his arms and hands as they lay clasped upon the table, and on lifting his head found his features to bear the very impress of death itself. Bartholomew Miller, who had now come in, assisted Mr Paddock to make a comfortable couch in the window-seat, where they stretched out Clark upon his back.

Still he seemed unconscious. 'We must get a doctor,' said Selina. 'O, my dear John, how is it you be taken like this?'

'My impression is that he's dead!' murmured Mr Paddock. 'He don't breathe enough to move a tomtit's feather.'

There were plenty to volunteer to go for a doctor, but as it would be at least an hour before he could get there the case seemed somewhat hopeless. The dancing-party ended as unceremoniously as it had begun; but the guests lingered round the premises till the doctor should arrive. When he did come the sergeant-major's extremities were already cold, and there was no doubt that death had overtaken him almost at the moment that he had sat down.

The medical practitioner quite refused to accept the unhappy Selina's theory that her revelation had in any way induced Clark's sudden collapse. Both he and the coroner afterwards, who found the immediate cause to be heart-failure, held that such a supposition was unwarranted by facts. They asserted that a long day's journey, a hurried drive, and then an exhausting dance, were sufficient for such a result upon a heart enfeebled by fatty degeneration after the privations of a Crimean winter and other trying experiences, the coincidence of the sad event with any disclosure of hers being a pure accident.

This conclusion, however, did not dislodge Selina's opinion that the shock of her statement had been the immediate stroke which had felled a constitution so undermined.

5

At this date the Casterbridge Barracks were cavalry quarters, their adaptation to artillery having been effected some years later. It had been owing to the fact that the —th Dragoons, in which John Clark had served, happened to be lying there that Selina made his acquaintance. At the time of his death the barracks were occupied by the Scots Greys, but when the pathetic circumstances of the sergeant-major's end became known in the town the officers of the Greys offered the services of their fine reed and brass band, that he might have a funeral marked by due military honours. His body was accordingly removed to the barracks, and carried thence to the churchyard in the Durnover quarter on the following afternoon, one of the Greys' most ancient and docile chargers being blacked up to represent Clark's horse on the occasion.

Everybody pitied Selina, whose story was well known. She followed the corpse as the only mourner, Clark having been without relations in this part of the country, and a communication with his regiment having brought none from a distance. She sat in a little shabby brown-black mourning carriage, squeezing herself up in a corner to be as much as possible out of sight during the slow and dramatic march through the town to the tune from *Saul*. When the interment had taken place, the volleys been fired, and the return journey begun, it was with something like a shock that she found the military escort to be moving at a quick march to the lively strains of 'Off she goes!' as if all care for the sergeant-major was expected to be ended with the late discharge of the carbines. It was, by chance, the very tune to which they had been footing when he died, and unable to bear its notes, she hastily told her driver to drop behind. The band and military party diminished up the High Street, and Selina turned over Swan bridge and homeward to Mellstock.

Then recommenced for her a life whose incidents were precisely of a suit with those which had preceded the soldier's return; but how different in her appreciation of them! Her narrow miss of the recovered respectability they had hoped for from that tardy event worked upon her parents as an irritant, and after the first week or two of her mourning her life with them grew almost insupportable. She had impulsively taken to herself the weeds of a widow, for such she seemed to herself to be, and clothed little Johnny in sables likewise. This assumption of a moral relationship to the deceased, which she asserted to be only not a legal one by two most unexpected accidents, led the old people to indulge a sarcasm at her expense whenever they beheld her attire, though all the while it cost them more pain to utter than it gave her to hear it. Having become accustomed by her residence at home to the business carried on by her father, she surprised them one day by going off with the child to Chalk-Newton, in the direction of the town of Ivell, and opening a miniature fruit and vegetable shop, attending Ivell market with her produce. Her business grew somewhat larger, and it was soon sufficient to enable her to support herself and the boy in comfort. She called herself 'Mrs John Clark' from the day of leaving home, and painted the name on her signboard – no man forbidding her.

By degrees the pain of her state was forgotten in her new circumstances, and getting to be generally accepted as the widow of a sergeant-major of dragoons – an assumption which her modest and mournful demeanour seemed to substantiate – her life became a placid one, her mind being nourished by the melancholy luxury of dreaming what might have been her future in New Zealand with John, if he had only lived to take her there. Her only travels now were a journey to Ivell on market-days, and once a fortnight to the churchyard in which Clark lay, there to tend, with Johnny's assistance, as widows are wont to do, the flowers she had planted upon his grave.

On a day about eighteen months after his unexpected decease, Selina was surprised in her lodging over her little shop by a visit from Bartholomew Miller. He had called on her once or twice before, on which occasions he had used without a word of comment the name by which she was known.

'I've come this time,' he said, 'less because I was in this direction than to ask you, Mrs Clark, what you mid well guess. I've come o' purpose, in short.'

She smiled.

''Tis to ask me again to marry you?'

'Yes, of course. You see, his coming back for 'ee proved what I always believed of 'ee, though others didn't. There's nobody but would be glad to welcome you to our parish again, now you've showed your independence and acted up to your trust in his promise. Well, my dear, will you come?'

'I'd rather bide as Mrs Clark, I think,' she answered. 'I am not ashamed of my position at all; for I am John's widow in the eyes of Heaven.'

'I quite agree – that's why I've come. Still, you won't like to be always straining at this shop-keeping and market-standing; and 'twould be better for Johnny if you had nothing to do but tend him.'

He here touched the only weak spot in Selina's resistance to his proposal – the good of the boy. To promote that there were other men she might have married off-hand without loving them if they had asked her to; but though she had known the worthy speaker from her youth, she could not for the moment fancy herself happy as Mrs Miller.

He paused a while. 'I ought to tell 'ee, Mrs Clark,' he said by-and-by, 'that marrying is getting to be a pressing question with me. Not on my own account at all. The truth is, that mother is growing old, and I am away from home a good deal, so that it is almost necessary there should be another person in the house with her besides me. That's the practical consideration which forces me to think of taking a wife, apart from my wish to take you; and you know there's nobody in the world I care for so much.'

She said something about there being far better women than she, and other natural commonplaces; but assured him she was most grateful to him for feeling what he felt, as indeed she sincerely was. However, Selina would not consent to be the useful third person in his comfortable home – at any rate just then. He went away, after taking tea with her, without discerning much hope for him in her good-bye.

6

After that evening she saw and heard nothing of him for a great while. Her fortnightly journeys to the sergeant-major's grave were continued, whenever weather did not hinder them; and Mr Miller must have known, she thought, of this custom of hers. But though the churchyard was not nearly so far from his homestead as was her shop at Chalk-Newton, he never appeared in the accidental way that lovers use.

An explanation was forthcoming in the shape of a letter from her mother, who casually mentioned that Mr Bartholomew Miller had gone away to the other side of Shottsford-Forum to be married to a thriving dairyman's daughter that he knew there. His chief motive, it was reported, had been less one of love than a wish to provide a companion for his aged mother.

Selina was practical enough to know that she had lost a good and possibly the only opportunity of settling in life after what had happened, and for a moment she regretted her independence. But she became calm on reflection, and to fortify herself in her course started that afternoon to tend the sergeant-major's grave, in which she took the same sober pleasure as at first.

On reaching the churchyard and turning the corner towards the spot as usual, she was surprised to perceive another woman, also apparently a respectable widow, and with a tiny boy by her side, bending over Clark's turf, and spudding up with the point of her umbrella some ivy-roots that Selina had reverently planted there to form an evergreen mantle over the mound.

'What are you digging up my ivy for!' cried Selina, rushing forward so excitedly that Johnny tumbled over a grave with the force of the tug she gave his hand in her sudden start.

'Your ivy?' said the respectable woman.

'Why, yes! I planted it there – on my husband's grave.'

'*Your* husband's!'

'Yes. The late Sergeant-Major Clark. Anyhow, as good as my husband, for he was just going to be.'

'Indeed. But who may be my husband, if not he? I am the only Mrs John Clark, widow of the late Sergeant-Major of Dragoons, and this is, his only son and heir.'

'How can that be?' faltered Selina, her throat seeming to stick together as she just began to perceive its possibility. 'He had been – going to marry me twice – and we were going to New Zealand.'

'Ah! – I remember about you,' returned the legitimate widow calmly and not unkindly. 'You must be Selina; he spoke of you now and then, and said that his relations with you would always be a weight on his conscience. Well; the history of my life with him is soon told. When he came back from the Crimea he became acquainted with me at my home in the North, and we were married within a month of first knowing each other. Unfortunately, after living together a few months, we could not agree; and after a particularly sharp quarrel, in which, perhaps, I was most in the wrong – as I don't mind owning here by his graveside – he went away from me, declaring he would buy his discharge and emigrate to New Zealand, and never come back to me any more. The next thing I heard was that he had died suddenly at Mellstock at some low carouse; and as he had left me in such anger to live no more with me, I wouldn't come down to his funeral, or do anything in relation to him. 'Twas temper, I know, but that was the fact. Even if we had parted friends it would have been a serious expense to travel three hundred miles to get there, for one who wasn't left so very well off. . . I am sorry I pulled up your ivy-roots; but that common sort of ivy is considered a weed in my part of the country.'

DECEMBER 1899

A TRYST AT AN ANCIENT EARTHWORK

At one's every step forward it rises higher against the south sky, with an obtrusive personality that compels the senses to regard it and consider. The eyes may bend in another direction, but never without the consciousness of its heavy, high-shouldered presence at its point of vantage. Across the intervening levels the gale races in a straight line from the fort, as if breathed out of it hitherward. With the shifting of the clouds the faces of the steeps vary in colour and in shade, broad lights appearing where mist and vagueness had prevailed, dissolving in their turn into melancholy gray, which spreads over and eclipses the luminous bluffs. In this so-thought immutable spectacle all is change.

Out of the invisible marine region on the other side birds soar suddenly into the air, and hang over the summits of the heights with the indifference of long familiarity. Their forms are white against the tawny concave of cloud, and the curves they exhibit in their floating signify that they are sea-gulls which have journeyed inland from expected stress of weather. As the birds rise behind the fort, so do the clouds rise behind the birds, almost, as it seems, stroking with their bagging bosoms the uppermost flyers.

The profile of the whole stupendous ruin, as seen at a distance of a mile eastward, is cleanly cut as that of a marble inlay. It is varied with protuberances, which from hereabouts have the animal aspect of warts, wens, knuckles, and hips. It may indeed be likened to an enormous many-limbed organism of an antediluvian time – partaking of the cephalopod in shape – lying lifeless, and covered with a thin green cloth, which hides its substance, while revealing its contour. This dull green mantle of herbage stretches down towards the levels, where the ploughs have essayed for centuries to creep up near and yet nearer to the base of the castle, but have always stopped short before reaching it. The furrows of these environing attempts show themselves distinctly, bending to the incline as they trench upon it; mounting in steeper curves, till the steepness baffles them, and their parallel threads show like the striae of waves pausing on the curl. The peculiar place of which these are some of the features is 'Mai-Dun', The Castle of the Great Hill', said to be the Dunium of Ptolemy, the capital of the Durotriges, which eventually came into Roman occupation, and was finally deserted on their withdrawal from the island.

The evening is followed by a night on which an invisible moon bestows a subdued, yet pervasive light – without radiance, as without blackness. From the spot wherein I am ensconced in a cottage, a mile away, the fort has now ceased to be visible; yet, as by day, to anybody whose thoughts have been engaged with it and its barbarous grandeurs of past time the form asserts its existence behind the night gauzes as persistently as if it had a voice. Moreover, the south-west wind continues to feed the intervening arable flats with vapours brought directly from its sides.

The midnight hour for which there has been occasion to wait at length arrives, and I journey towards the stronghold in obedience to a request urged earlier in the day. It concerns an apointment, which I rather regret my decision to keep now that night is come. The route thither is hedgeless and treeless – I need not add deserted. The moonlight is sufficient to disclose the pale riband-like surface of the way as it trails along between the expanses of darker fallow. Though the road passes near the fortress it does not conduct directly to its fronts. As the place is without an inhabitant, so it is without a trackway. So presently leaving the macadamized road to pursue its course elsewhither, I step off upon the fallow, and plod stumblingly across it. The castle looms out of the shade by degrees, like a thing waking up and asking what I want there. It is now so enlarged by nearness that its whole shape cannot be taken in at one view. The ploughed ground ends as the rise sharpens, the sloping basement of grass begins, and I climb upward to invade Mai-Dun.

Impressive by day as this largest Ancient-British work in the kingdom undoubtedly is, its impressiveness is increased now. After standing still and spending a few minutes in adding its age to its size, and its size to its solitude, it becomes appallingly mournful in its growing closeness. A squally wind blows in the face with an impact which proclaims that the vapours of the air sail low tonight. The slope that I so laboriously clamber up the wind skips sportively down. Its track can be discerned even in this light by the undulations of the withered grass-bents – the only produce of this upland summit except moss. Four minutes of ascent, and a vantage-ground of some sort is gained. It is only the crest of the outer rampart. Immediately within this a chasm gapes; its bottom is imperceptible, but the counterscarp slopes not too steeply to admit of a sliding descent if cautiously performed. The shady bottom, dank and chilly, is thus gained, and reveals itself as a kind of winding lane, wide enough for a waggon to pass along, floored with rank herbage, and trending away, right and left, into obscurity, between the concentric walls of earth. The towering closeness of these on each hand, their impenetrability, and their ponderousness, are felt as a physical pressure. The way is now up the second of them, which stands steeper and higher than the first. To turn aside, as did Christian's companion, from such a Hill Difficulty, is the more natural tendency; but the way to the interior is upward. There is, of course, an entrance to the fortress; but that lies far off on the other side. It might possibly have been the wiser course to seek for easier ingress there.

However, being here, I ascend the second acclivity. The grass stems – the grey beard of the hill – sway in a mass close to my stooping face. The dead heads of these various grasses – fescues, fox-tails, and ryes – bob and twitch as if pulled by a string underground. From a few thistles a whistling proceeds; and even the moss speaks, in its humble way, under the stress of the blast.

That the summit of the second line of defence has been gained is suddenly made known by a contrasting wind from a new quarter, coming over with the curve of a cascade. These novel gusts raise a sound from the whole camp or castle, playing upon it bodily as upon a harp. It is with some difficulty that a foothold can be preserved under their sweep. Looking aloft for a moment I perceive that the sky is much more overcast than it has been hitherto, and in a few instants a dead lull in what is now a gale ensues with almost preternatural abruptness. I take advantage of this to sidle down the second counterscarp, but by the time the ditch is reached the lull reveals itself to be but the precursor of a storm. It begins with a heave of the whole atmosphere, like the sigh of a weary strong man on turning to recommence unusual exertion, just as I stand here in the second fosse. That which now radiates from the sky upon the scene is not so much light as vaporous phosphorescence.

The wind, quickening, abandons the natural direction it has pursued on the open upland, and takes the course of the gorge's length, rushing along therein helter-skelter, and carrying thick rain upon its back. The rain is followed by hailstones which fly through the defile in battalions – rolling, hopping, richochetting, snapping, clattering down the shelving banks in an undefinable haze of confusion. The earthen sides of the fosse seem to quiver under the drenching onset, though it is practically no more to them than the blows of Thor upon the giant of Jotun-land. It is impossible to proceed further till the storm somewhat abates, and I draw up behind a spur of the inner scarp, where possibly a barricade stood two thousand years ago; and thus await events.

The roar of the storm can be heard travelling the complete circuit of the castle – a measured mile – coming round at intervals like a circumambulating column of infantry. Doubtless such a column has passed this way in its time, but the only columns which enter in these latter days are the columns of sheep and oxen that are sometimes seen here now; while the only semblance of heroic voices heard are the utterances of such, and of the many winds which make their passage through the ravines.

The expected lightning radiates round, and a rumbling as from its subterranean vaults – if there are any – fills the castle. The lightning repeats itself, and, coming after the aforesaid thoughts of martial men, it bears a fanciful resemblance to swords moving in combat. It has the very brassy hue of the ancient weapons that here were used. The so sudden entry upon the scene of this metallic flame is as the entry of a presiding exhibitor who unrolls the maps, uncurtains the pictures, unlocks the cabinets, and effects a transformation by merely exposing the materials of his science, unintelligibly cloaked till then. The abrupt configuration of the bluffs and mounds is now for the first time clearly revealed – mounds whereon, doubtless, spears and shields have frequently lain while their owners loosened their sandals and yawned and stretched their arms in the sun. For the first time, too, a glimpse is obtainable of the true entrance used by its occupants of old, some way ahead.

There, where all passage has seemed to be inviolably barred by an almost vertical façade, the ramparts are found to overlap each other like loosely clasped fingers, between which a zigzag path may be followed – a cunning construction that puzzles the uninformed eye. But its cunning, even where not obscured by dilapidation, is now wasted on the solitary forms of a few wild badgers, rabbits, and hares. Men must have often gone out by those gates in the morning to battle with the Roman legions under Vespasian; some to return no more, others to come back at evening, bringing with them the noise of their heroic deeds. But not a page, not a stone, has preserved their fame.

Acoustic perceptions multiply tonight. We can almost hear the stream of years that have borne those deeds away from us. Strange articulations seem to float on the air from that point, the gateway, where the animation in past times must frequently have concentrated itself at hours of coming and going, and general excitement. There arises an ineradicable fancy that they are human voices; if so, they must be the lingering airborne vibrations of conversations uttered at least fifteen hundred years ago. The attention is attracted from mere nebulous imaginings about yonder spot by a real moving of something close at hand.

I recognize by the now moderate flashes of lightning, which are sheetlike and nearly continuous, that it is the gradual elevation of a small mound of earth. At first no larger than a man's fist it reaches the dimensions of a hat, then sinks a little and is still. It is but the heaving of a mole who chooses such weather as this to work in from some instinct that there will be nobody abroad to molest him. As the fine earth lifts and lifts and falls loosely aside fragments of burnt clay roll out of it – clay that once formed part of cups or other vessels used by the inhabitants of the fortress.

The violence of the storm has been counterbalanced by its transitoriness. From being immersed in wellnigh solid media of cloud and hail shot with lightning, I find myself uncovered of the human investiture and left bare to the mild gaze of the moon, which sparkles now on every wet grass-blade and frond of moss.

But I am not yet inside the fort, and the delayed ascent of the third and last escarpment is now made. It is steeper than either. The first was a surface to walk up, the second to stagger up, the third can only be ascended on the hands and toes. On the summit obtrudes the first evidence which has been met with in these precincts that the time is really the nineteenth century; it is in the form of a white notice-board on a post, and the wording can just be discerned by the rays of the setting moon:

> CAUTION – Any Person found removing Relics, Skeletons, Stones, Pottery, Tiles, or other Material from this Earthwork, or cutting up the Ground, will be Prosecuted as the Law directs.

Here one observes a difference underfoot from what has gone before: scraps of Roman tile and stone chippings protrude through the grass in meagre quantity, but sufficient to suggest that masonry stood on the spot. Before the eye stretches under the moonlight the interior of the fort. So open and so large is it as to be practically an upland plateau, and yet its area lies wholly within the walls of what may be designated as one building. It is a long-violated retreat; all its corner-stones, plinths, and architraves were carried away to build neighbouring villages even before mediaeval or modern history began. Many a block which once may have helped to form a bastion here rests now in broken and diminished shape as part of the chimney-corner of some shepherd's cottage within the distant horizon, and the corner-stones of this heathen altar may form the base-course of some adjoining village church.

Yet the very bareness of these inner courts and wards, their condition of mere pasturage, protects what remains of them as no defences could do. Nothing is left visible that the hands can seize on or the weather overturn, and a permanence of general outline at least results, which no other condition could ensure.

The position of the castle on this isolated hill bespeaks deliberate and strategic choice exercised by some remote mind capable of prospective reasoning to a far extent. The natural configuration of the surrounding country and its bearing upon such a stronghold were obviously long considered and viewed mentally before its extensive design was carried into execution. Who was the man that said, 'Let it be built here!' – not on that hill yonder, or on that ridge behind, but on this best spot of all? Whether he were some great one of the Belgae, or of the Durotriges, or the travelling engineer of Britain's united tribes, must for ever remain time's secret; his form cannot be realized, nor his countenance, nor the tongue that he spoke, when he set down his foot with a thud and said, 'Let it be here!'

Within the innermost enclosure, though it is so wide that at a superficial glance the beholder has only a sense of standing on a breezy down, the solitude is rendered yet more solitary by the knowledge that between the benighted sojourner herein and all kindred humanity are those three concentric walls of earth which no being would think of scaling on such a night as this, even were he to hear the most pathetic cries issuing hence that could be uttered by a spectre-chased soul. I reach a central mound or platform – the crown and axis of the whole structure. The view from here by day must be of almost limitless extent. On this raised floor, daïs, or rostrum, harps have probably twanged more or less tuneful notes in celebration of daring, strength, or cruelty; of worship, superstition, love, birth, and death; of simple loving-kindness perhaps never. Many a time must the king or leader have directed his keen eyes hence across the open lands towards the ancient road, the Icening Way, still visible in the distance, on the watch for armed companies approaching either to succour or to attack.

I am startled by a voice pronouncing my name. Past and present have become so confusedly mingled under the associations of the spot that for a time it has escaped my memory that this mound was the place agreed on for the aforesaid appointment. I turn and behold my friend. He stands with a dark lantern in his hand and a spade and light pickaxe over his shoulder. He expresses both delight and surprise that I have come. I tell him I had set out before the bad weather began.

He, to whom neither weather, darkness, nor difficulty seems to have any relation or significance, so entirely is his soul wrapt up in his own deep intentions, asks me to take the lantern and accompany him. I take it and walk by his side. He is a man about sixty, small in figure, with gray old-fashioned whiskers cut to the shape of a pair of crumb-brushes. He is entirely in black broadcloth – or rather, at present, black and brown, for he is bespattered with mud from his heels to the crown of his low hat. He has no consciousness of this – no sense of anything but his purpose, his ardour for which causes his eyes to shine like those of a lynx, and gives his motions all the elasticity of an athlete's.

'Nobody to interrupt us at this time of night!' he chuckles with fierce enjoyment.

We retreat a little way and find a sort of angle, an elevation in the sod, a suggested squareness amid the mass of irregularities around. Here, he tells me, if anywhere, the king's house stood. Three months of measurement and calculation have confirmed him in this conclusion.

He requests me now to open the lantern, which I do, and the light streams out upon the wet sod. At last divining his proceedings I say that I had no idea, in keeping the tryst, that he was going to do more at such an unusual time than meet me for a meditative ramble through the stronghold. I ask him why, having a practicable object, he should have minded interruptions and not have chosen the day? He informs me, quietly pointing to his spade, that it was because his purpose is to dig, then signifying with a grim nod the gaunt notice-post against the sky beyond. I inquire why, as a professed and well-known antiquary with capital letters at the tail of his name, he did not obtain the necessary authority, considering the stringent penalties for this sort of thing; and he chuckles fiercely again with suppressed delight, and says, 'Because they wouldn't have given it!'

He at once begins cutting up the sod, and, as he takes the pickaxe to follow on with, assures me that, penalty or no penalty, honest men or maurauders, he is sure of one thing, that we shall not be disturbed at our work till after dawn.

I remember to have heard of men who, in their enthusiasm for some special science, art, or hobby, have quite lost the moral sense which would restrain them from indulging it illegitimately; and I conjecture that here, at last, is an instance of such an one. He probably guesses the way my thoughts travel, for he stands up and solemnly asserts that he has a distinctly justifiable intention in this matter; namely, to uncover, to search, to verify a theory or displace it, and to cover up again. He means to take away nothing – not a grain of sand. In this he says he sees no such monstrous sin. I inquire if this is really a promise to me? He repeats that it is a promise, and resumes digging. My contribution to the labour is that of directing the light constantly upon the hole. When he has reached something more than a foot deep he digs more cautiously, saying that, be it much or little there, it will not lie far below the surface; such things never are deep. A few minutes later the point of the pickaxe clicks upon a stony substance. He draws the implement out as feelingly as if it had entered a man's body. Taking up the spade he shovels with care, and a surface, level as an altar, is presently disclosed. His eyes flash anew; he pulls handfuls of grass and mops the surface clean, finally rubbing it with his handkerchief. Grasping the lantern from my hand he holds it close to the ground, when the rays reveal a complete mosaic – a pavement of minute tesserae of many colours, of intricate pattern, a work of much art, of much time, and of much industry. He exclaims in a shout that he knew it always – that it is not a Celtic stronghold exclusively, but also a Roman; the former people having probably contributed little more than the original framework which the latter took and adapted till it became the present imposing structure.

I ask, What if it is Roman?

A great deal, according to him. That it proves all the world to be wrong in this great argument, and himself alone to be right! Can I wait while he digs further?

I agree – reluctantly; but he does not notice my reluctance. At an adjoining spot he begins flourishing the tools anew with the skill of a navvy, this venerable scholar with letters after his name. Sometimes he falls on his knees, burrowing with his hands in the manner of a hare, and where his old-fashioned broadcloth touches the sides of the hole it gets plastered with the damp earth. He continually murmurs to himself how important, how very important, this discovery is! He draws out an object; we wash it in the same primitive way by rubbing it with the wet grass, and it proves to be a semi-transparent bottle of iridescent beauty, the sight of which draws groans of luxurious sensibility from the digger. Further and further search brings out a piece of a weapon. It is strange indeed that by merely peeling off a wrapper of modern accumulations we have lowered ourselves into an ancient world. Finally a skeleton is uncovered, fairly perfect. He lays it out on the grass, bone to its bone.

My friend says the man must have fallen fighting here, as this is no place of burial. He turns again to the trench, scrapes, feels, till from a corner he draws out a heavy lump – a small image four or five inches high. We clean it as before. It is a statuette, apparently of gold, or, more probably, of bronze-gilt – a figure of Mercury, obviously, its head being surmounted with the petasus or winged hat, the usual accessory of that deity. Further inspection reveals the workmanship to be of good finish and detail, and, preserved by the limy earth, to be as fresh in every line as on the day it left the hands of its artificer.

We seem to be standing in the Roman Forum and not on a hill in Wessex. Intent upon this truly valuable relic of the old empire of which even this remote spot was a component part, we do not notice what is going on in the present world till reminded of it by the sudden renewal of the storm. Looking up I perceive that the wide extinguisher of cloud has again settled down upon the fortress-town, as if resting upon the edge of the inner rampart, and shutting out the moon. I turn my back to the tempest, still directing the light across the hole. My companion digs on unconcernedly; he is living two thousands years ago, and despises things of the moment as dreams. But at last he is fairly beaten, and standing up beside me looks round on what he has done. The rays of the lantern pass over the trench to the tall skeleton stretched upon the grass on the other side. The beating rain has washed the bones clean and smooth, and the forehead, cheek-bones, and two-and-thirty teeth of the skull glisten in the candle-shine as they lie.

This storm, like the first, is of the nature of a squall, and it ends as abruptly as the other. We dig no further. My friend says that it is enough – he has proved his point. He turns to replace the bones in the trench and covers them. But they fall to pieces under his touch: the air has disintegrated them, and he can only sweep in the fragments. The next act of his plan is more than difficult, but is carried out. The treasures are inhumed again in their respective holes: they are not ours. Each deposition seems to cost him a twinge; and at one moment I fancied I saw him slip his hand into his coat pocket.

'We must re-bury them *all*,' say I.

'O yes,' he answers with integrity. 'I was wiping my hand.'

The beauties of the tessellated floor of the governor's house are once again consigned to darkness; the trench is filled up; the sod laid smoothly down; he wipes the perspiration from his forehead with the same handkerchief he had used to mop the skeleton and tesserae clean; and we make for the eastern gate of the fortress.

Dawn bursts upon us suddenly as we reach the opening. It comes by the lifting and thinning of the clouds that way till we are bathed in a pink light. The direction of his homeward journey is not the same as mine, and we part under the outer slope.

Walking along quickly to restore warmth I muse upon my eccentric friend, and cannot help asking myself this question: Did he really replace the gilded image of the god Mercurius with the rest of the treasures? He seemed to do so; and yet I could not testify to the fact. Probably, however, he was as good as his word.

It was thus I spoke to myself, and so the adventure ended. But one thing remains to be told, and that is concerned with seven years after. Among the effects of my friend, at that time just deceased, was found, carefully preserved, a gilt statuette representing Mercury, labelled 'Debased Roman'. No record was attached to explain how it came into his possession. The figure was bequeathed to the Casterbridge Museum.

Detroit Post
MARCH 1885

WHAT THE SHEPHERD SAW

A TALE OF FOUR MOONLIGHT NIGHTS

FIRST NIGHT

The genial Justice of the Peace – now, alas, no more – who made himself responsible for the facts of this story, used to begin in the good old-fashioned way with a bright moonlight night and a mysterious figure, an excellent stroke for an opening, even to this day, if well followed up.

The Christmas moon (he would say) was showing her cold face to the upland, the upland reflecting the radiance in frost-sparkles so minute as only to be discernible by an eye near at hand. This eye, he said, was the eye of a shepherd lad, young for his occupation, who stood within a wheeled hut of the kind commonly in use among sheep-keepers during the early lambing season, and was abstractedly looking through the loophole at the scene without.

The spot was called Lambing Corner, and it was a sheltered portion of that wide expanse of rough pastureland known as the Marlbury Downs, which you directly traverse when following the turnpike-road across Mid-Wessex from London, through Aldbrickham, in the direction of Bath and Bristol. Here, where the hut stood, the land was high and dry, open, except to the north, and commanding an undulating view for miles. On the north side grew a tall belt of coarse furze, with enormous stalks, a clump of the same standing detached in front of the general mass. The clump was hollow, and the interior had been ingeniously taken advantage of as a position for the before-mentioned hut, which was thus completely screened from winds, and almost invisible, except through the narrow approach. But the furze twigs had been cut away from the two little windows of the hut, that the occupier might keep his eye on his sheep.

In the rear, the shelter afforded by the belt of furze bushes was artificially improved by an inclosure of upright stakes, interwoven with boughs of the same prickly vegetation, and within the inclosure lay a renowned Marlbury-Down breeding flock of eight hundred ewes.

To the south, in the direction of the young shepherd's idle gaze, there rose one conspicuous object above the uniform moonlit plateau, and only one. It was a Druidical trilithon, consisting of three oblong stones in the form of a doorway, two on end, and one across as a lintel. Each stone had been worn, scratched, washed, nibbled, split, and otherwise attacked by ten thousand different weathers; but now the blocks looked shapely and little the worse for wear, so beautifully were they silvered over by the light of the moon. The ruin was locally called the Devil's Door.

An old shepherd presently entered the hut from the direction of the ewes, and looked around in the gloom. 'Be ye sleepy?' he asked in cross accents of the boy.

The lad replied rather timidly in the negative.

'Then,' said the shepherd, 'I'll get me home-along, and rest for a few hours. There's nothing to be done here now as I can see. The ewes can want no more tending till daybreak – 'tis beyond the bounds of reason that they can. But as the order is that one of us must bide, I'll leave 'ee, d'ye hear? You can sleep by day, and I can't. And you can be down to my house in ten minutes if anything should happen. I can't afford 'ee candle; but, as 'tis Christmas week, and the time that folks have holler-days, you can enjoy yerself by falling asleep a bit in the chair instead of biding awake all the time. But mind, not longer at once than while the shade of the Devil's Door moves a couple of spans, for you must keep an eye upon the ewes.'

The boy made no definite reply, and the old man, stirring the fire in the stove with his crook-stem, closed the door upon his companion and vanished.

As this had been more or less the course of events every night since the season's lambing had set in, the boy was not at all surprised at the charge, and amused himself for some time by lighting straws at the stove. He then went out to the ewes and new-born lambs, re-entered, sat down, and finally fell asleep. This was his customary manner of performing his watch, for though special permission for naps had this week been accorded, he had, as a matter of fact, done the same thing on every preceding night, sleeping often till awakened by a smack on the shoulder at three or four in the morning from the crook-stem of the old man.

It might have been about eleven o'clock when he awoke. He was so surprised at awaking without, apparently, being called or struck, that on second thoughts he assumed that somebody must have called him in spite of appearances, and looked out of the hut window towards the sheep. They all lay as quiet as when he had visited them, very little bleating being audible, and no human soul disturbing the scene. He next looked from the opposite window, and here the case was different. The frost-facets glistened under the moon as before; an occasional furze bush showed as a dark spot on the same; and in the foreground stood the ghostly form of the trilithon. But in front of the trilithon stood a man.

That he was not the shepherd or any one of the farm labourers was apparent in a moment's observation, his dress being a dark suit, and his figure of slender build and graceful carriage. He walked backwards and forwards in front of the trilithon.

The shepherd lad had hardly done speculating on the strangeness of the unknown's presence here at such an hour, when he saw a second figure crossing the open sward towards the locality of the trilithon and furze clump that screened the hut. This second personage was a woman; and immediately on sight of her the male stranger hastened forward, meeting her just in front of the hut window. Before she seemed to be aware of his intention he clasped her in his arms.

The lady released herself and drew back with some dignity.

'You have come, Harriet – bless you for it!' he exclaimed fervently.

'But not for this,' she answered, in offended accents. And then, more good-naturedly, 'I have come, Fred, because you entreated me so! What can have been the object of your writing such a letter? I feared I might be doing you grievous ill by staying away. How did you come here?'

'I walked all the way from my father's.'

'Well, what is it? How have you lived since we last met?'

'But roughly; you might have known that without asking. I have seen many lands and many faces since I last walked on these downs, but I have only thought of you.'

'Is it only to tell me this that you have summoned me so strangely?'

A passing breeze blew away the murmur of the reply and several succeeding sentences, till the man's voice again became audible in the words, 'Harriet – truth between us two! I have heard that the Duke does not treat you too well.'

'He is warm-tempered, but he is a good husband.'

'He speaks roughly to you, and sometimes even threatens to lock you out of doors.'

'Only once, Fred! On my honour, only once. The Duke is a fairly good husband, I repeat. But you deserve punishment for this night's trick of drawing me out. What does it mean?'

'Harriet, dearest, is this fair or honest? Is it not notorious that your life with him is a sad one – that, in spite of the sweetness of your temper, the sourness of his embitters your days? I have come to know if I can help you. You are a duchess, and I am Fred Ogbourne; but it is not impossible that I may be able to help you. . . By God! the sweetness of that tongue ought to keep him civil, especially when there is added to it the sweetness of that face!'

'Captain Ogbourne!' she exclaimed, with an emphasis of playful fear. 'How can such a comrade of my youth behave to me as you do? Don't speak so, and stare at me so! Is this really all you have to say? I see I ought not to have come. 'Twas thoughtlessly done.'

Another breeze broke the thread of discourse for a time.

'Very well. I perceive you are dead and lost to me,' he could next be heard to say; '"Captain Ogbourne" proves that. As I once loved you I love you now, Harriet, without one jot of abatement; but you are not the woman you were – you once were honest towards me; and now you conceal your heart in made-up speeches. Let it be; I can never see you again.'

'You need not say that in such a tragedy tone, you silly. You may see me in an ordinary way – why should you not? But, of course, not in such as way as this. I should not have come now, if it had not happened that the Duke is away from home, so that there is nobody to check my erratic impulses.'

'When does he return?'

'The day after tomorrow, or the day after that.'

'Then meet me again tomorrow night.'

'No, Fred, I cannot.'

'If you cannot tomorrow night, you can the night after; one of the two before he comes please bestow on me. Now, your hand upon it! Tomorrow or the next night you will see me to bid me farewell!' He seized the Duchess's hand.

'No, but, Fred – let go my hand! What do you mean by holding me so? If it be love to forget all respect to a woman's present position in thinking of her past, then yours may be so, Frederick. It is not kind and gentle of you to induce me to come to this place for pity of you, and then to hold me tight here.'

'But see me once more! I have come two thousand miles to ask it.'

'O, I must not! There will be slanders – Heaven knows what! I cannot meet you. For the sake of old times don't ask it.'

'Then own two things to me; that you did love me once, and that your husband is unkind to you often enough now to make you think of the time when you cared for me.'

'Yes – I own them both,' she answered faintly. 'But owning such as that tells against me; and I swear the inference is not true.'

'Don't say that; for you have come – let me think the reason of your coming what I like to think it. It can do you no harm. Come once more!'

He still held her hand and waist. 'Very well, then,' she said. 'Thus far you shall persuade me. I will meet you tomorrow night or the night after. Now, let me go.'

He released her, and they parted. The Duchess ran rapidly down the hill towards the outlying mansion of Shakeforest Towers, and when he had watched her out of sight, he turned and strode off in the opposite direction. All then was silent and empty as before.

Yet it was only for a moment. When they had quite departed, another shape appeared upon the scene. He came from behind the trilithon. He was a man of stouter build than the first, and wore the boots and spurs of a horseman. Two things were at once obvious from this phenomenon: that he had watched the interview between the Captain and the Duchess; and that, though he probably had seen every movement of the couple, including the embrace, he had been too remote to hear the reluctant words of the lady's conversation – or, indeed, any words at all – so that the meeting must have exhibited itself to his eye as the assignation of a pair of well-agreed lovers. But it was necessary that several years should elapse before the shepherd-boy was old enough to reason out this.

The third individual stood still for a moment, as if deep in meditation. He crossed over to where the lady and gentleman had stood, and looked at the ground; then he too turned and went away in a third direction, as widely divergent as possible from those taken by the two interlocutors. His course was towards the highway; and a few minutes afterwards the trot of a horse might have been heard upon its frosty surface, lessening till it died away upon the ear.

The boy remained in the hut, confronting the trilithon as if he expected yet more actors on the scene, but nobody else appeared. How long he stood with his little face against the loophole he hardly knew; but he was rudely awakened from his reverie by a punch in his back, and in the feel of it he familiarly recognized the stem of the old shepherd's crook.

'Blame thy young eyes and limbs, Bill Mills – now you have let the fire out, and you know I want it kept in! I thought something would go wrong with 'ee up here, and I couldn't bide in bed no more than thistledown on the wind, that I could not! Well, what's happened, fie upon 'ee?'

'Nothing.'

'Ewes all as I left 'em?'

'Yes.'

'Any lambs want bringing in?'

'No.'

The shepherd relit the fire, and went out among the sheep with a lantern, for the moon was getting low. Soon he came in again.

'Blame it all – thou'st say that nothing have happened; when one ewe have twinned and is like to go off, and another is dying for want of half an eye of looking to! I told 'ee, Bill Mills, if anything went wrong to come down and call me; and this is how you have done it.'

'You said I could go to sleep for a hollerday, and I did.'

'Don't you speak to your betters like that, young man, or you'll come to the gallows-tree! You didn't sleep all the time, or you wouldn't have been peeping out of that there hole! Now you can go home, and be up here again by breakfast-time. I be an old man, and there's old men that deserve well of the world; but no – I must rest how I can!'

The elder shepherd then lay down inside the hut, and the boy went down the hill to the hamlet where he dwelt.

SECOND NIGHT

When the next night drew on the actions of the boy were almost enough to show that he was thinking of the meeting he had witnessed, and of the promise wrung from the lady that she would come again. As far as the sheep-tending arrangements were concerned, tonight was but a repetition of the foregoing one. Between ten and eleven o'clock the old shepherd withdrew as usual for what sleep at home he might chance to get without interruption, making up the other necessary hours of rest at some time during the day; the boy was left alone.

The frost was the same as on the night before, except perhaps that it was a little more severe. The moon shone as usual, except that it was three-quarters of an hour later in its course; and the boy's condition was much the same, except that he felt no sleepiness whatever. He felt, too, rather afraid: but upon the whole he preferred witnessing an assignation of strangers to running the risk of being discovered absent by the old shepherd.

It was before the distant clock of Shakeforest Towers had struck eleven that he observed the opening of the second act of this midnight drama. It consisted in the appearance of neither lover nor Duchess, but of the third figure – the stout man, booted and spurred – who came up from the easterly direction in which he had retreated the night before. He walked once round the trilithon, and next advanced towards the clump concealing the hut, the moonlight shining full upon his face and revealing him to be the Duke. Fear seized upon the shepherd-boy; the Duke was Jove himself to the rural population, whom to offend was starvation, homelessness, and death, and whom to look at was to be mentally scathed and dumbfoundered. He closed the stove, so that not a spark of light appeared, and hastily buried himself in the straw that lay in a corner.

The Duke came close to the clump of furze that stood by the spot where his wife and the Captain had held their dialogue; he examined the furze as if searching for a hiding-place, and in doing so discovered the hut. The latter he walked round and then looked inside; finding it to all seeming empty, he entered, closing the door behind him and taking his place at the little circular window against which the boy's face had been pressed just before.

The Duke had not adopted his measures too rapidly, if his object were concealment. Almost as soon as he had stationed himself there eleven o'clock struck, and the slender young man who had previously graced the scene promptly reappeared from the north quarter of the down. The spot of assignation having, by the accident of his running forward on the foregoing night, removed itself from the Devil's Door to the clump of furze, he instinctively came thither, and waited for the Duchess where he had met her before.

But a fearful surprise was in store for him tonight, as well as for the trembling juvenile. At his appearance the Duke breathed more and more quickly, his breathings being distinctly audible to the crouching boy. The young man had hardly paused when the alert nobleman softly opened the door of the hut, and, stepping round the furze, came full upon Captain Fred.

'You have dishonoured her, and you shall die the death you deserve!' came to the shepherd's ears, in a harsh, hollow whisper through the boarding of the hut.

The apathetic and taciturn boy was excited enough to run the risk of rising and looking from the window, but he could see nothing for the intervening furze boughs, both the men having gone round to the side. What took place in the few following moments he never exactly knew. He discerned portion of a shadow in quick muscular movement; then there was the fall of something on the grass; then there was stillness.

Two or three minutes later the Duke became visible round the corner of the hut, dragging by the collar the now inert body of the second man. The Duke dragged him across the open space towards the trilithon. Behind this ruin was a hollow, irregular spot, overgrown with furze and stunted thorns, and riddled by the old holes of badgers, its former inhabitants, who had now died out or departed. The Duke vanished into this depression with his burden, reappearing after the lapse of a few seconds. When he came forth he dragged nothing behind him.

He returned to the side of the hut, cleansed something on the grass, and again put himself on the watch, though not as before, inside the hut, but without, on the shady side. 'Now for the second!' he said.

It was plain, even to the unsophisticated boy, that he now awaited the other person of the appointment – his wife, the Duchess – for what purpose it was terrible to think. He seemed to be a man of such determined temper that he would scarcely hesitate in carrying out a course of revenge to the bitter end. Moreover – though it was what the shepherd did not perceive – this was all the more probable, in that the moody Duke was labouring under the exaggerated impression which the sight of the meeting in dumb show had conveyed.

The jealous watcher waited long, but he waited in vain. From within the hut the boy could hear his occasional exclamations of surprise, as if he were almost disappointed at the failure of his assumption that his guilty Duchess would surely keep the tryst. Sometimes he stepped from the shade of the furze into the moonlight, and held up his watch to learn the time.

About half-past eleven he seemed to give up expecting her. He then went a second time to the hollow behind the trilithon, remaining there nearly a quarter of an hour. From this place he proceeded quickly over a shoulder of the declivity, a little to the left, presently returning on horseback, which proved that his horse had been tethered in some secret place down there. Crossing anew the down between the hut and the trilithon, and scanning the precincts as if finally to assure himself that she had not come, he rode slowly downwards in the direction of Shakeforest Towers.

The juvenile shepherd thought of what lay in the hollow yonder; and no fear of the crook-stem of his superior officer was potent enough to detain him longer on that hill alone. Any live company, even the most terrible, was better than the company of the dead; so, running with the speed of a hare in the direction pursued by the horseman, he overtook the revengeful Duke at the second descent (where the great western road crossed before you came to the old part entrance on that side – now closed up and the lodge cleared away, though at the time it was wondered why, being considered the most convenient gate of all).

Once within the sound of the horse's footsteps, Bill Mills felt comparatively comfortable; for, though in awe of the Duke because of his position, he had no moral repugnance to his companionship on account of the grisly deed he had committed, considering that powerful nobleman to have a right to do what he chose on his own lands. The Duke rode steadily on beneath his ancestral trees, the hoofs of his horse sending up a smart sound now that he had reached the hard road of the drive, and soon drew near the front door of his house, surmounted by parapets with square-cut battlements that cast a notched shade upon the gravelled terrace. These outlines were quite familiar to little Bill Mills, though nothing within their boundary had ever been seen by him.

When the rider approached the mansion a small turret door was quickly opened and a woman came out. As soon as she saw the horseman's outlines she ran forward into the moonlight to meet him.

'Ah, dear – and are you come?' she said. 'I heard Hero's treat just when you rode over the hill, and I knew it in a moment. I would have come further if I had been aware—'

'Glad to see me, eh?'

'How can you ask that?'

'Well; it is a lovely night for meetings.'

'Yes, it is a lovely night.'

The Duke dismounted and stood by her side. 'Why should you have been listening at this time of night, and yet not expecting me?' he asked.

'Why, indeed! There is a strange story attached to that, which I must tell you at once. But why did you come a night sooner than you said you would come? I am rather sorry – I really am!' (shaking her head playfully), 'for as a surprise to you I had ordered a bonfire to be built, which was to be lighted on your arrival tomorrow; and now it is wasted. You can see the outline of it just out there.'

The Duke looked across to a spot of rising glade, and saw the faggots in a heap. He then bent his eyes with a bland and puzzled air on the ground. 'What is this strange story you have to tell me that kept you awake?' he murmured.

'It is this – and it is really rather serious. My cousin Fred Ogbourne – Captain Ogbourne as he is now – was in his boyhood a great admirer of mine, as I think I have told you, though I was six years his senior. In strict truth, he was absurdly fond of me.'

'You have never told me of that before.'

'Then it was your sister I told – yes, it was. Well, you know I have not seen him for many years, and naturally I had quite forgotten his admiration of me in old times. But guess my surprise when the day before yesterday, I received a mysterious note bearing no address, and found on opening it that it had come from him. The contents frightened me out of my wits. He had returned from Canada to his father's house, and conjured me by all he could think of to meet him at once. But I think I can repeat the exact words, though I will show it to you when we get indoors.

'"MY DEAR COUSIN HARRIET," the note said, "After this long absence you will be surprised at my sudden reappearance, and more by what I am going to ask. But if my life and future are of any concern to you at all, I beg that you will grant my request. What I require of you, is, dear Harriet, that you meet me about eleven tonight by the Druid stones on Marlbury Downs, about a mile or more from your house. I cannot say more, except to to entreat you to come. I will explain all when you are there. The one thing is, I want to see you. Come alone. Believe me, I would not ask this if my happiness did not hang upon it – God knows how entirely! I am too agitated to say more – Yours,

FRED"

'That was all of it. Now, of course, I ought not to have gone, as it turned out, but that I did not think of then. I remembered his impetuous temper, and feared that something grievous was impending over his head, while he had not a friend in the world to help him or anyone except myself to whom he would care to make his trouble known. So I wrapped myself up and went to Marlbury Downs at the time he had named. Don't you think I was courageous?'

'Very.'

'When I got there – but shall we not walk on; it is getting cold?' The Duke, however, did not move. 'When I got there he came, of course, as a full-grown man and officer, and not as the lad that I had known him. When I saw him I was sorry I had come. I can hardly tell you how he behaved. What he wanted I don't know even now; it seemed to be no more than the mere meeting with me. He held me by the hand and waist – O so tight – and would not let me go till I had promised to meet him again. His manner was so strange and passionate that I was afraid of him in such a lonely place, and I promised to come. Then I escaped – then I ran home – and that's all. When the time drew on this evening for the appointment – which, of course, I never intended to keep – I felt uneasy, lest when he found I meant to disappoint him he would come on to the house; and that's why I could not sleep. But you are so silent!'

'I have had a long journey.'

'Then let us get into the house. Why did you come alone and unattended like this?'

'It was my humour.'

After a moment's silence, during which they moved on, she said, 'I have thought of something which I hardly like to suggest to you. He said that if I failed to come tonight he would wait again tomorrow night. Now, shall we tomorrow night go to the hill together – just to see if he is there; and if he is, read him a lesson on his foolishness in nourishing this old passion, and sending for me so oddly, instead of coming to the house?'

'Why should we see if he's there?' said her husband moodily.

'Because I think we ought to do something in it. Poor Fred! He would listen to you if you reasoned with him, and set our positions in their true light before him. It would be no more than Christian kindness to a man who unquestionably is very miserable from some cause or other. His head seems quite turned.'

By this time they had reached the door, rung the bell, and waited. All the house seemed to be asleep; but soon a man came to them, the horse was taken away, and the Duke and Duchess went in.

THIRD NIGHT

There was no help for it. Bill Mills was obliged to stay on duty, in the old shepherd's absence, this evening as before, or give up his post and living. He thought as bravely as he could of what lay behind the Devil's Door, but with no great success, and was therefore in a measure relieved, even if awe-stricken, when he saw the forms of the Duke and Duchess strolling across the frosted greensward. The Duchess was a few yards in front of her husband and tripped on lightly.

'I tell you he has not thought it worth while to come again!' the Duke insisted, as he stood still, reluctant to walk further.

'He is more likely to come and wait all night; and it would be harsh treatment to let him do it a second time.'

'He is not here; so turn and come home.'

'He seems not to be here, certainly; I wonder if anything has happened to him. If it has, I shall never forgive myself!'

The Duke, uneasily, 'O, no. He has some other engagement.'

'That is very unlikely.'

'Or perhaps he has found the distance too far.'

'Nor is that probable.'

'Then he may have thought better of it.'

'Yes, he may have thought better of it; if, indeed, he is not here all the time – somewhere in the hollow behind the Devil's Door. Let us go and see; it will serve him right to surprise him.'

'O, he's not there.'

'He may be lying very quite because of you,' she said archly.

'O, no – not because of me!'

'Come, then. I declare, dearest, you lag like an unwilling schoolboy tonight, and there's no responsiveness in you! You are jealous of that poor lad, and it is quite absurd of you.'

'I'll come! I'll come! Say no more, Harriet!' And they crossed over the green.

Wondering what they would do, the young shepherd left the hut, and doubled behind the belt of furze, intending to stand near the trilithon unperceived. But, in crossing the few yards of open ground he was for a moment exposed to view.

'Ah, I see him at last!' said the Duchess.

'See him!' said the Duke. 'Where?'

'By the Devil's Door; don't you notice a figure there? Ah, my poor lover-cousin, won't you catch it now?' And she laughed half-pityingly. 'But what's the matter?' she asked, turning to her husband.

'It is not he!' said the Duke hoarsely. 'It can't be he!'

'No, it is not he. It is too small for him. It is a boy.'

'Ah, I thought so! Boy, come here.'

The youthful shepherd advanced with apprehension.

'What are you doing here?'

'Keeping sheep, your Grace.'

'Ah, you know me! Do you keep sheep here every night?'

'Off and on, my Lord Duke.'

'And what have you seen here tonight or last night?' inquired the Duchess. 'Any person waiting or walking about?'

The boy was silent.

'He has seen nothing,' interrupted her husband, his eyes so forbiddingly fixed on the boy that they seemed to shine like points of fire. 'Come, let us go. The air is too keen to stand in long.'

When they were gone the boy retreated to the hut and sheep, less fearful now than at first – familiarity with the situation having gradually overpowered his thoughts of the buried man. But he was not to be left alone long. When an interval had elapsed of about sufficient length for walking to and from Shakeforest Towers, there appeared from that direction the heavy form of the Duke. He now came alone.

The nobleman, on his part, seemed to have eyes no less sharp than the boy's, for he instantly recognized the latter among the ewes, and came straight towards him.

'Are you the shepherd lad I spoke to a short time ago?'

'I be, my Lord Duke.'

'Now listen to me. Her Grace asked you what you had seen this last night or two up here, and you made no reply. I now ask the same thing, and you need not be afraid to answer. Have you seen anything strange these nights you have been watching here?'

'My Lord Duke, I be a poor heedless boy, and what I see I don't bear in mind.'

'I ask you again,' said the Duke, coming nearer, 'have you seen anything strange these nights you have been watching here?'

'O, my Lord Duke! I be but the under-shepherd boy, and my father he was but your humble Grace's hedger, and my mother only the cinder-woman in the back-yard! I fall asleep when left alone, and I see nothing at all!'

The Duke grasped the boy by the shoulder, and, directly impending over him, stared down into his face, 'Did you see anything strange done here last night, I say?'

'O, my Lord Duke, have mercy, and don't stab me!' cried the shepherd, falling on his knees. 'I have never seen you walking here, or riding here, or lying-in-wait for a man, or dragging a heavy load!'

'H'm!' said his interrogator, grimly, relaxing his hold. 'It is well to know that you have never seen those things. Now, which would you rather – *see me do those things now*, or keep a secret all your life?'

'Keep a secret, my Lord Duke!'

'Sure you are able?'

'O, your Grace, try me!'

'Very well. And now, how do you like sheep-keeping?'

'Not at all. 'Tis lonely work for them that think of spirits, and I'm badly used.'

'I believe you. You are too young for it. I must do something to make you more comfortable. You shall change this smock-frock for a real cloth jacket, and your thick boots for polished shoes. And you shall be taught what you have never yet heard of, and be put to school, and have bats and balls for the holidays, and be made a man of. But you must never say you have been a shepherd boy, and watched on the hills at night, for shepherd boys are not liked in good company.'

'Trust me, my Lord Duke.'

'The very moment you forget yourself, and speak of your shepherd days – this year, next year, in school, out of school, or riding in your carriage twenty years hence – at that moment my help will be withdrawn, and smash down you come to shepherding forthwith. You have parents, I think you say?'

'A widowed mother only, my Lord Duke.'

'I'll provide for her, and make a comfortable woman of her, until you speak of – what?'

'Of my shepherd days, and what I saw here.'

'Good. If you do speak of it?'

'Smash down she comes to widowing forthwith!'

'That's well – very well. But it's not enough. Come here.' He took the boy across to the trilithon, and made him kneel down.

'Now, this was once a holy place,' resumed the Duke. 'An altar stood here, erected to a venerable family of gods, who were known and talked of long before the God we know now. So that an oath sworn here is doubly an oath. Say this after me: "May all the host above – angels and archangels, and principalities and powers – punish me; may I be tormented wherever I am – in the house or in the garden, in the fields or in the roads, in church or in chapel, at home or abroad, on land or at sea; may I be afflicted in eating and in drinking, in growing up and in growing old, in living and dying, inwardly and outwardly, and for always, if I ever speak of my life as a shepherd boy, or of what I have seen done on this Marlbury Down. So be it, and so let it be. Amen and amen." Now kiss the stone.'

The trembling boy repeated the words, and kissed the stone, as desired.

The Duke led him off by the hand. That night the junior shepherd slept in Shakeforest Towers, and the next day he was sent away for tuition to a remote village. Thence he went to a preparatory establishment, and in due course to a public school.

FOURTH NIGHT

On a winter evening many years subsequent to the above-mentioned occurrences, the *ci-devant* shepherd sat in a well-furnished office in the north wing of Shakeforest Towers in the guise of an ordinary educated man of business. He appeared at this time as a person of thirty-eight or forty, though actually he was several years younger. A worn and restless glance of the eye now and then, when he lifted his head to search for some letter or paper which had been mislaid, seemed to denote that his was not a mind so thoroughly at ease as his surroundings might have led an observer to expect. His pallor, too, was remarkable for a country-man. He was professedly engaged in writing, but he shaped not a word. He had sat there only a few minutes, when, laying down his pen and pushing back his chair, he rested a hand uneasily on each of the chair-arms and looked on the floor.

Soon he arose and left the room. His course was along a passage which ended in a central octagonal hall; crossing this he knocked at a door. A faint, though deep, voice told him to come in. The room he entered was the library, and it was tenanted by a single person only – his patron the Duke.

During this interval of years the Duke had lost all his heaviness of build. He was, indeed, almost a skeleton; his white hair was thin, and his hands were nearly transparent. 'Oh – Mills?' he murmured. 'Sit down. What is it?'

'Nothing new, your Grace. Nobody to speak of has written, and nobody has called.'

'Ah – what then? You look concerned.'

'Old times have come to life, owing to something waking them.'

'Old times be cursed – which old times are they?'

'That Christmas week twenty-two years ago, when the late Duchess's cousin Frederick implored her to meet him on Marlbury Downs. I saw the meeting – it was just such a night as this – and I, as you know, saw more. She met him once, but not the second time.'

'Mills, shall I recall some words to you – the words of an oath taken on that hill by a shepherd boy?'

'It is unnecessary. He has strenuously kept that oath and promise. Since that night no sound of his shepherd life has crossed his lips – even to yourself. But do you wish to hear more, or do you not, your Grace?'

'I wish to hear no more,' said the Duke sullenly.

'Very well; let it be so. But a time seems coming – may be quite near at hand – when, in spite of my lips, that episode will allow itself to go undivulged no longer.'

'I wish to hear no more!' repeated the Duke.

'You need be under no fear of treachery from me,' said the steward, somewhat bitterly. 'I am a man to whom you have been kind – no patron could have been kinder. You have clothed and educated me; have installed me here; and I am not unmindful. But what of it – has your Grace gained much by my stanchness? I think not. There was great excitement about Captain Ogbourne's disappearance, but I spoke not a word. And his body has never been found. For twenty-two years I have wondered what you did with him. Now I know. A circumstance that occurred this afternoon recalled the time to me most forcibly. To make it certain to myself that all was not a dream, I went up there with a spade; I searched, and saw enough to know that something decays there in a closed badger's hole.'

'Mills, do you think the Duchess guessed?'

'She never did, I am sure, to the day of her death.'

'Did you leave all as you found it on the hill?'

'I did.'

'What made you think of going up there this particular afternoon?'

'What your Grace says you don't wish to be told.'

The Duke was silent; and the stillness of the evening was so marked that there reached their ears from the outer air the sound of a tolling bell.

'What is that bell tolling for?' asked the nobleman.

'For what I came to tell you of, your Grace.'

'You torment me – it is your way!' said the Duke querulously. 'Who's dead in the village?'

'The oldest man – the old shepherd.'

'Dead at last – how old is he?'

'Ninety-four.'

'And I am only seventy. I have four-and-twenty years to the good!'

'I served under that old man when I kept sheep on Marlbury Downs. And he was on the hill that second night, when I first exchanged words with your Grace. He was on the hill *all the time*; but I did not know he was there – nor did you.'

'Ah!' said the Duke, starting up. 'Go on – I yield the point – you may tell!'

'I heard this afternoon that he was at the point of death. It was that which set me thinking of that past time – and induced me to search on the hill for what I have told you. Coming back I heard that he wished to see the Vicar to confess to him a secret he had kept for more than twenty years – "out of respect to my Lord the Duke" – something that he had seen committed on Marlbury Downs when returning to the flock on a December night twenty-two years ago. I have thought it over. He had left me in charge that evening; but he was in the habit of coming back suddenly, lest I should have fallen asleep. That night I saw nothing of him, though he had promised to return. He must have returned, and – found reason to keep in hiding. It is all plain. The next thing is that the Vicar went to him two hours ago. Further than that I have not heard.'

'It is quite enough. I will see the Vicar at daybreak tomorrow.'

'What to do?'

'Stop his tongue for four-and-twenty years – till I am dead at ninety-four, like the shepherd.'

'Your Grace – while you impose silence on me, I will not speak, even though my neck should pay the penalty. I promised to be yours, and I am yours. But is this persistence of any avail?'

'I'll stop his tongue, I say!' cried the Duke with some of his old rugged force. 'Now, you go home to bed, Mills, and leave me to manage him.'

The interview ended, and the steward withdrew. The night, as he had said, was just such an one as the night of twenty-two years before, and the events of the evening destroyed in him all regard for the season as one of cheerfulness and goodwill. He went off to his own house on the further verge of the park, where he led a lonely life, scarcely calling any man friend. At eleven he prepared to retire to bed – but did not retire. He sat down and reflected. Twelve o'clock struck; he looked out at the colourless moon, and, prompted by he knew not what, put on his hat and emerged into the air. Here William Mills strolled on and on, till he reached the top of Marlbury Downs, a spot he had not visited at this hour of the night during the whole score-and-odd years.

He placed himself, as nearly as he could guess, on the spot where the shepherd's hut had stood. No lambing was in progress there now, and the old shepherd who had used him so roughly had ceased from his labours that very day. But the trilithon stood up white as ever; and, crossing the intervening sward, the steward fancifully placed his mouth against the stone. Restless and self-reproachful as he was, he could not resist a smile as he thought of the terrifying oath of compact, sealed by a kiss upon the stones of a Pagan temple. But he had kept his word, rather as a promise than as a formal vow, with much worldly advantage to himself, though not much happiness; till increase of years had bred reactionary feelings which led him to receive the news of tonight with emotions akin to relief.

While leaning against the Devil's Door and thinking on these things, he became conscious that he was not the only inhabitant of the down. A figure in white was moving across his front with long, noiseless strides. Mills stood motionless, and when the form drew quite near he perceived it to be that of the Duke himself in his nightshirt – apparently walking in his sleep. Not to alarm the old man, Mills clung close to the shadow of the stone. The Duke went straight on into the hollow. There he knelt down, and began scratching the earth with his hands like a badger. After a few minutes he arose, sighed heavily, and retraced his steps as he had come.

Fearing that he might harm himself, yet unwilling to arouse him, the steward followed noiselessly. The Duke kept on his path unerringly, entered the park, and made for the house, where he let himself in by a window that stood open – the one probably by which he had come out. Mills softly closed the window behind his patron, and then retired homeward to await the revelations of the morning, deeming it unnecessary to alarm the house.

However, he felt uneasy during the remainder of the night, no less on account of the Duke's personal condition than because of that which was imminent next day. Early in the morning he called at Shakeforest Towers. The blinds were down, and there was something singular upon the porter's face when he opened the door. The steward inquired for the Duke.

The man's voice was subdued as he replied: 'Sir, I am sorry to say that his Grace is dead! He left his room some time in the night, and wandered about nobody knows where. On returning to the upper floor he lost his balance and fell downstairs.'

*

The steward told the tale of the Down before the Vicar had spoken. Mills had always intended to do so after the death of the Duke. The consequences to himself he underwent cheerfully; but his life was not prolonged. He died, a farmer, at the Cape, when still somewhat under forty-nine years of age.

The splendid Marlbury breeding flock is as renowned as ever, and, to the eye, seems the same in every particular that it was in earlier times; but the animals which composed it on the occasion of the events gathered from the Justice are divided by many ovine generations from its members now. Lambing Corner has long since ceased to be used for lambing purposes, though the name still lingers on as the appellation of the spot. This abandonment of site may be partly owing to the removal of the high furze bushes which lent such convenient shelter at that date. Partly, too, it may be due to another circumstance. For it is said by present shepherds in that district that during the nights of Christmas week flitting shapes are seen in the open space around the trilithon, together with the gleam of a weapon, and the shadow of a man dragging a burden into the hollow. But of these things there is no certain testimony.

CHRISTMAS 1881

A COMMITTEE-MAN OF 'THE TERROR'

We had been talking of the Georgian glories of our old-fashioned watering-place, which now, with its substantial russet-red and dun brick buldings in the style of the year eighteen hundred, looks like one side of a Soho or Bloomsbury Street transported to the shore, and draws a smile from the modern tourist who has no eye for solidity of build. The writer, quite a youth, was present merely as a listener. The conversation proceeded from general subjects to particular, until old Mrs H——, whose memory was as perfect at eighty as it had ever been in her life, interested us all by the obvious fidelity which which she repeated a story many times related to her by her mother when our aged friend was a girl – a domestic drama much affecting the life of an acquaintance of her said parent, one Mademoiselle V——, a teacher of French. The incidents occurred in the town during the heyday of its fortunes, at the time of our brief peace with France in 1802–3.

'I wrote it down in the shape of a story some years ago, just after my mother's death,' said Mrs H——. 'It is locked up in my desk there now.'

'Read it!' said we.

'No,' said she; 'the light is bad, and I can remember it well enough, word for word, flourishes and all.' We could not be choosers in the circumstances, and she began.

'There are two in it, of course, the man and the woman, and it was on an evening in September that she first got to know him. There had not been such a grand gathering on the Esplanade all the season. His Majesty King George the Third was present, with all the princesses and royal dukes, while upwards of three hundred of the general nobility and other persons of distinction were also in the town at the time. Carriages and other conveyances were arriving every minute from London and elsewhere; and when among the rest a shabby stage-coach came in by a by-route along the coast from Havenpool, and drew up at a second-rate tavern, it attracted comparatively little notice.

'From this dusty vehicle a man alighted, left his small quantity of luggage temporarily at the office, and walked along the street as if to look for lodgings.

'He was about forty-five – possibly fifty – and wore a long coat of faded superfine cloth, with a heavy collar, and a bunched-up neckcloth. He seemed to desire obscurity.

'But the display appeared presently to strike him, and he asked of a rustic he met in the street what was going on; his accent being that of one to whom English pronunciation was difficult.

'The countryman looked at him with a slight surprise, and said, "King Jarge is here and his royal Cwort."

'The stranger inquired if they were going to stay long.

'"Don't know, Sir. Same as they always do, I suppose."

'"How long is that?"

'"Till some time in October. They've come here every zummer since eighty-nine."

'The stranger moved onward down St Thomas Street, and approached the bridge over the harbour backwater, that then, as now, connected the old town with the more modern portion. The spot was swept with the rays of a low sun, which lit up the harbour lengthwise, and shone under the brim of the man's hat and into his eyes as he looked westward. Against the radiance figures were crossing in the opposite direction to his own; among them this lady of my mother's later acquaintance, Mademoiselle V——. She was the daughter of a good old French family, and at that date a pale woman, twenty-eight or thirty years of age, tall and elegant in figure, but plainly dressed and wearing that evening (she said) a small muslin shawl crossed over the bosom in the fashion of the time, and tied behind.

'At sight of his face, which, as she used to tell us, was unusually distinct in the peering sunlight, she could not help giving a little shriek of horror, for a terrible reason connected with her history, and after walking a few steps further, she sank down against the parapet of the bridge in a fainting fit.

'In his preoccupation the foreign gentleman had hardly noticed her, but her strange collapse immediately attracted his attention. He quickly crossed the carriage-way, picked her up, and carried her into the first shop adjoining the bridge, explaining that she was a lady who had been taken ill outside.

'She soon revived; but, clearly much puzzled, her helper perceived that she still had a dread of him which was sufficient to hinder her complete recovery of self-command. She spoke in a quick and nervous way to the shopkeeper, asking him to call a coach.

'This the shopkeeper did, Mademoiselle V—— and the stranger remaining in constrained silence while he was gone. The coach came up, and giving the man the address, she entered it and drove away.

' "Who is that lady?" said the newly arrived gentleman.

' "She's of your nation, as I should make bold to suppose," said the shopkeeper. And he told the other that she was Mademoiselle V——, governess at General Newbold's, in the same town.

' "You have many foreigners here?" the stranger inquired.

' "Yes, though mostly Hanoverians. But since the peace they are learning French a good deal in genteel society, and French instructors are rather in demand."

' "Yes, I teach it," said the visitor. "I am looking for a tutorship in an academy."

'The information given by the burgess to the Frenchman seemed to explain to the latter nothing of his countrywoman's conduct – which, indeed, was the case – and he left the shop, taking his course again over the bridge and along the south quay to the Old Rooms Inn, where he engaged a bedchamber.

'Thoughts of the woman who had betrayed such agitation at sight of him lingered naturally enough with the newcomer. Though, as I stated, not much less than thirty years of age, Mademoiselle V——, one of his own nation, and of highly refined and delicate appearance, had kindled a singular interest in the middle-aged gentleman's breast, and her large dark eyes, as they had opened and shrunk from him, exhibited a pathetic beauty to which hardly any man could have been insensible.

'The next day, having written some letters, he went out and made known at the office of the town "Guide" and of the newspaper, that a teacher of French and calligraphy had arrived, leaving a card at the bookseller's to the same effect. He then walked on aimlessly, but at length inquired the way to General Newbold's. At the door, without giving his name, he asked to see Mademoiselle V——, and was shown into a little back parlour, where she came to him with a gaze of surprise.

' "My God! Why do you intrude here, Monsieur?" she gasped in French as soon as she saw his face.

' "You were taken ill yesterday. I helped you. You might have been run over if I had not picked you up. It was an act of simple humanity certainly; but I thought I might come to ask if you had recovered?"

'She had turned aside, and had scarcely heard a word of his speech. "I hate you, infamous man!" she said. "I cannot bear your helping me. Go away!"

' "But you are a stranger to me."

'"I know you too well!"

'"You have the advantage then, Mademoiselle. I am a newcomer here. I never have seen you before to my knowledge; and I certainly do not, could not, hate you."

'"Are you not Monsieur B——?"

'He flinched. "I am – in Paris," he said. "But here I am Monsieur G——.'

'"That is trivial. You are the man I say you are."

'"How did you know my real name, Mademoiselle?"

'"I saw you in years gone by, when you did not see me. You were formerly Member of the Committee of Public Safety, under the Convention."

'"I was."

'"You guillotined my father, my brother, my uncle – all my family, nearly, and broke my mother's heart. They had done nothing but keep silence. Their sentiments were only guessed. Their headless corpses were thrown indiscriminately into the ditch of the Mousseaux Cemetery, and destroyed with lime."

'He nodded.

'"You left me without a friend, and here I am now, alone in a foreign land."

'"I am sorry for you," said he. "Sorry for the consequence, not for the intent. What I did was a matter of conscience, and, from a point of view indiscernible by you, I did right. I profited not a farthing. But I shall not argue this. You have the satisfaction of seeing me here an exile also, in poverty, betrayed by comrades, as friendless as yourself."

'"It is no satisfaction to me, Monsieur."

'"Well, things done cannot be altered. Now to the question: are you quite recovered?"

'"Not from dislike and dread of you – otherwise, yes."

'"Good morning, Mademoiselle."

'"Good morning."

'They did not meet again till one evening at the theatre (which my mother's friend was with great difficulty induced to frequent, to perfect herself in English pronunciation, the idea she entertained at that time being to become a teacher of English in her own country later on). She found him sitting next to her, and it made her pale and restless.

'"You are still afraid of me?"

'"I am. O cannot you understand?"

'He signified the affirmative.

'"I follow the play with difficulty," he said presently.

'"So do I – *now*," said she.

'He regarded her long, and she was conscious of his look; and while she kept her eyes on the stage they filled with tears. Still she would not move, and the tears ran visibly down her cheek, though the play was a merry one, being no other than Mr Sheridan's comedy of "The Rivals", with Mr S Kemble as Captain Absolute. He saw her distress, and that her mind was elsewhere; and abruptly rising from his seat at candle-snuffing time he left the theatre.

'Though he lived in the old town, and she in the new, they frequently saw each other at a distance. One of these occasions was when she was on the north side of the harbour, by the ferry, waiting for the boat to take her across. He was standing by Cove Row, on the quay opposite. Instead of entering the boat when it arrived she stepped back from the quay; but looking to see if he remained she beheld him pointing with his finger to the ferry-boat.

'"Enter!" he said, in a voice loud enough to reach her.

'Mademoiselle V—— stood still.

'"Enter!" he said, and, as she did not move, he repeated the word a third time.

'She had really been going to cross, and now approached and stepped down into the boat. Though she did not raise her eyes she knew that he was watching her over. At the landing-steps she saw from under the brim of her hat a hand stretched down. The steps were steep and slippery.

'"No, Monsieur," she said. "Unless, indeed, you believe in God, and repent of your evil past!"

'"I am sorry you were made to suffer. But I only believe in the god called Reason, and I do not repent. I was the instrument of national principle. Your friends were not sacrificed for any ends of mine."

'She thereupon withheld her hand, and clambered up unassisted. He went on, ascending the Look-out Hill, and disappearing over the brow. Her way was in the same direction, her errand being to bring home the two young girls under her charge, who had gone to the cliff for an airing. When she joined them at the top she saw his solitary figure at the further edge, standing motionless against the sea. All the while that she remained with her pupils he stood without turning, as if looking at the frigates in the roadstead, but more probably in meditation, unconscious where he was. In leaving the spot one of the children threw away half a sponge-biscuit that she had been eating. Passing near it he stopped, picked it up carefully, and put it in his pocket.

'Mademoiselle V—— came homeward, asking herself, "Can he be starving?"

'From that day he was invisible for so long a time that she thought he had gone away altogether. But one evening a note came to her, and she opened it trembling.

> '"I am ill," it said, "and, as you know, alone. There are one or two little things I want done, in case my death should occur, and I should prefer not to ask the people here, if it could be avoided. Have you enough of the gift of charity to come and carry out my wishes before it is too late?"

'Now so it was that, since seeing him possess himself of the broken cake, she had insensibly begun to feel something that was more than curiosity, though perhaps less than anxiety, about this fellow-countryman of hers; and it was not in her nervous and sensitive heart to resist his appeal. She found his lodging (to which he had removed from the Old Rooms Inn for economy) to be a room over a shop, half-way up the steep and narrow street of the old town, to which the fashionable visitors seldom penetrated. With some misgiving she entered the house, and was admitted to the chamber where he lay.

'"You are too good, too good," he murmured. And presently, "You need not shut the door. You will feel safer, and they will not understand what we say."

'"Are you in want, Monsieur? Can I give you—"

'"No, no. I merely want you to do a trifling thing or two that I have not strength enough to do myself. Nobody in the town but you knows who I really am – unless you have told?"

'"I have not told . . . I thought you *might* have acted from principle in those sad days, even—"

'"You are kind to concede that much. However, to the present. I was able to destroy my few papers before I became so weak. . . But in the drawer there you will find some pieces of linen clothing – only two or three – marked with initials that may be recognized. Will you rip them out with a penknife?"

'She searched as bidden, found the garments, cut out the stitches of the lettering, and replaced the linen as before. A promise to post, in the event of his death, a letter he put in her hand, completed all that he required of her.

'He thanked her. "I think you feel sorry for me," he murmured. "And I am surprised. You are sorry?"

'She evaded the question. "Do you repent and believe?" she asked.

'"No."

'Contrary to her expectations and his own he recovered, though very slowly; and her manner grew more distant thenceforward, though his influence upon her was deeper than she knew. Weeks passed away, and the month of May arrived. One day at this time she met him walking slowly along the beach to the northward.

'"You know the news?" he said.

'"You mean of the rupture between France and England again?"

'"Yes; and the feeling of antagonism is stronger than it was in the last war, owing to Bonaparte's high-handed arrest of the innocent English who were travelling in our country for pleasure. I feel that the war will be long and bitter; and that my wish to live unknown in England will be frustrated. See here."

'He took from his pocket a piece of the single newspaper which circulated in the country in those days, and she read –

> "The magistrates acting under the Alien Act have been requested to direct a very scrutinizing eye to the Academies in our towns and other places, in which French tutors are employed, and to all of that nationality who profess to be teachers in this country. Many of them are known to be inveterate Enemies and Traitors to the nation among whose people they have found a livelihood and a home."

'He continued: "I have observed since the declaration of war a marked difference in the conduct of the rougher class of people here towards me. If a great battle were to occur – as it soon will, no doubt – feeling would grow to a pitch that would make it impossible for me, a disguised man of no known occupation, to stay here. With you, whose duties and antecedents are known, it may be less difficult, but still unpleasant. Now I propose this. You have probably seen how my deep sympathy with you has quickened to a warm feeling; and what I say is, will you agree to give me a title to protect you by honouring me with your hand? I am older than you, it is true; but as husband and wife we can leave England together, and make the whole world our country. Though I would propose Quebec, in Canada, as the place which offers the best promise of a home."

'"My God! You surprise me!" said she.

'"But you accept my proposal?"

'"No, no!"

'"And yet I think you will, Mademoiselle, some day!"

'"I think not."

'"I won't distress you further now."

'"Much thanks... I am glad to see you looking better, Monsieur; I mean you are looking better."

'"Ah, yes. I am improving. I walk in the sun every day."

'And almost every day she saw him – sometimes nodding stiffly only, sometimes exchanging formal civilities. "You are not gone yet," she said on one of these occasions.

'"No. At present I don't think of going without you."

'"But you find it uncomfortable here?"

'"Somewhat. So when will you have pity on me?"

'She shook her head and went on her way. Yet she was a little moved. "He did it on principle," she would murmur. "He had no animosity towards them, and profited nothing!"

'She wondered how he lived. It was evident that he could not be so poor as she had thought; his pretended poverty might be to escape notice. She could not tell, but she knew that she was dangerously interested in him.

'And he still mended, till his thin, pale face became more full and firm. As he mended she had to meet that request of his, advanced with even stronger insistency.

'The arrival of the King and Court for the season as usual brought matters to a climax for these two lonely exiles and fellow country-people. The King's awkward preference for a part of the coast in such dangerous proximity to France made it necessary that a strict military vigilance should be exercised to guard the royal residents. Half-a-dozen frigates were every night posted in a line across the bay, and two lines of sentinels, one at the water's edge and another behind the Esplanade, occupied the whole sea-front after eight every night. The watering-place was growing an inconvenient residence even for Mademoiselle V—— herself, her friendship for this strange French tutor and writing-master who never had any pupils having been observed by many who slightly knew her. The General's wife, whose dependent she was, repeatedly warned her against the acquaintance; while the Hanoverian and other soldiers of the Foreign Legion, who had discovered the nationality of her friend, were more aggressive than the English military gallants who made it their business to notice her.

'In this tense state of affairs her answers became more agitated. "O Heaven, how can I marry you!" she would say.

'"You will; surely you will!" he answered again. "I don't leave without you. And I shall soon be interrogated before the magistrates if I stay here; probably imprisoned. You will come?"

'She felt her defences breaking down. Contrary to all reason and sense of family honour she was, by some abnormal craving, inclining to a tenderness for him that was founded on its opposite. Sometimes her warm sentiments burnt lower than at others, and then the enormity of her conduct showed itself in more staring hues.

'Shortly after this he came with a resigned look on his face. "It is as I expected," he said. "I have received a hint to go. In good sooth, I am no Bonapartist – I am no enemy to England; but the presence of the King made it impossible for a foreigner with no visible occupation, and who may be a spy, to remain at large in the town. The authorities are civil, but firm. They are no more than reasonable. Good. I must go. You must come also."

'She did not speak. But she nodded assent, her eyes drooping.

'On her way back to the house on the Esplanade she said to herself, "I am glad, I am glad! I could not do otherwise. It is rendering good for evil!" But she knew how she mocked herself in this, and that the moral principle had not operated one jot in her acceptance of him. In truth she had not realized till now the full presence of the emotion which had unconsciously grown up in her for this lonely and severe man, who, in her tradition, was vengeance and irreligion personified. He seemed to absorb her whole nature, and, absorbing, to control it.

'A day or two before the one fixed for the wedding there chanced to come to her a letter from the only acquaintance of her own sex and country she possessed in England, one to whom she had sent intelligence of her approaching marriage, without mentioning with whom. This friend's misfortunes had been somewhat similar to her own, which fact had been one cause of their intimacy; her friend's sister, a nun of the Abbey of Montmartre, having perished on the scaffold at the hands of the same Comité de Salut Public which had numbered Mademoiselle V——'s affianced among its members. The writer had felt her position much again of late, since the renewal of the war, she said; and the letter wound up with a fresh denunciation of the authors of their mutual bereavement and subsequent troubles.

'Coming just then, its contents produced upon Mademoiselle V—— the effect of a pail of water upon a somnambulist. What had she been doing in betrothing herself to this man! Was she not making herself a parricide after the event? At this crisis in her feelings her lover called. He beheld her trembling, and, in reply to his question, she told him of her scruples with impulsive candour.

'She had not intended to do this, but his attitude of tender command coerced her into frankness. Thereupon he exhibited an agitation never before apprent in him. He said, "But all that is past. You are the symbol of Charity, and we are pledged to let bygones be."

'His words soothed her for the moment, but she was sadly silent, and he went away.

'That night she saw (as she firmly believed to the end of her life) a divinely sent vision. A procession of her lost relatives – father, brother, uncle, cousin – seemed to cross her chamber between her bed and the window, and when she endeavoured to trace their features she perceived them to be headless, and that she had recognized them by their familiar clothes only. In the morning she could not shake off the effects of this appearance of her nerves. All that day she saw nothing of her wooer, he being occupied in making arrangements for their departure. It grew towards evening – the marriage eve; but, in spite of his reassuring visit, her sense of family duty waxed stronger now that she was left alone. Yet, she asked herself, how could she, alone and unprotected, go at this eleventh hour and reassert to an affianced husband that she could not and would not marry him while admitting at the same time that she loved him? The situation dismayed her. She had relinquished her post as governess, and was staying temporarily in a room near the coach-office, where she expected him to call in the morning to carry out the business of their union and departure.

'Wisely or foolishly, Mademoiselle V—— came to a resolution: that her only safety lay in flight. His contiguity influenced her too sensibly; she could not reason. So packing up her few possessions and placing on the table the small sum she owed, she went out privately, secured a last available seat in the London coach, and, almost before she had fully weighed her action, she was rolling out of the town in the dusk of the September evening.

'Having taken this startling step she began to reflect upon her reasons. He had been one of that tragic Committee the sound of whose name was a horror to the civilized world; yet he had been only *one* of several members, and, it seemed, not the most active. He had marked down names on principle, had felt no personal enmity against his victims, and had enriched himself not a sou out of the office he had held. Nothing could change the past. Meanwhile he loved her, and her heart inclined to as much of him as she could detach from that past. Why not, as he had suggested, bury memories, and inaugurate a new era by this union? In other words, why not indulge her tenderness, since its nullification could do no good.

'Thus she held self-communion in her seat in the coach, passing through Casterbridge, and Shottsford, and on to the White Hart at Melchester, at which place the whole fabric of her recent intentions crumbled down. Better be staunch having got so far; let things take their course, and marry boldly the man who had so impressed her. How great he was; how small was she! And she had presumed to judge him! Abandoning her place in the coach with the precipitancy that had characterized her taking it, she waited till the vehicle had driven off, something in the departing shapes of the outside passengers against thc starlit sky giving her a start, as she afterwards remembered. Presently the down coach, "The Morning Herald", entered the city, and she hastily obtained a place on the top.

'"I'll be firm – I'll be his – if it cost me my immortal soul!" she said. And with troubled breathings she journeyed back over the road she had just traced.

'She reached our royal watering-place by the time the day broke, and her first aim was to get back to the hired room in which her last few days had been spent. When the landlady appeared at the door in response to Mademoiselle V——'s nervous summons, she explained her sudden departure and return as best she could; and no objection being offered to her re-engagement of the room for one day longer she ascended to the chamber and sat down panting. She was back once more, and her wild tergiversations were a secret from him whom alone they concerned.

'A sealed letter was on the mantelpiece. "Yes, it is directed to you, Mademoiselle," said the woman who had followed her. "But we were wondering what to do with it. A town messenger brought it after you had gone last night."

'When the landlady had left, Mademoiselle V—— opened the letter and read –

> "MY DEAR AND HONOURED FRIEND. – You have been throughout our acquaintance absolutely candid concerning your misgivings. But I have been reserved concerning mine. That is the difference between us. You probably have not guessed that every qualm you have felt on the subject of our marriage has been paralleled in my heart to the full. Thus it happened that your involuntary outburst of remorse yesterday, though mechanically deprecated by me in your presence, was a last item in my own doubts on the wisdom of our union, giving them a force that I could no longer withstand. I came home; and, on reflection, much as I honour and adore you, I decide to set you free.
>
> "As one whose life has been devoted, and I may say sacrificed, to the cause of Liberty, I cannot allow your judgment (probably a permanent one) to be fettered beyond release by a feeling which may be transient only.
>
> "It would be no less than excruciating to both that I should announce this decision to you by word of mouth. I have therefore taken the less painful course of writing. Before you receive this I shall have left the town by the evening coach for London, on reaching which city my movements will be revealed to none.
>
> "Regard me, Mademoiselle, as dead, and accept my renewed assurances of respect, remembrance, and affection."

'When she had recovered from her shock of surprise and grief, she remembered that at the starting of the coach out of Melchester before dawn, the shape of a figure among the outside passengers against the starlit sky had caused her a momentary start, from its resemblance to that of her friend. Knowing nothing of each other's intentions, and screened from each other by the darkness, they had left the town by the same conveyance. "He, the greater, persevered; I, the smaller, returned!" she said.

'Recovering from her stupor, Mademoiselle V—— bethought herself again of her employer, Mrs Newbold, whom recent events had estranged. To that lady she went with a full heart, and explained everything. Mrs Newbold kept to herself her opinion of the episode, and reinstalled the deserted bride in her old position as governess to the family.

'A governess she remained to the end of her days. After the final peace with France she became acquainted with my mother, to whom by degrees she imparted these experiences of hers. As her hair grew white, and her features pinched, Mademoiselle V—— would wonder what nook of the world contained her lover, if he lived, and if by any chance she might see him again. But when, some time in the 'twenties, death came to her, at no great age, that outline against the stars of the morning remained as the last glimpse she ever obtained of her family's foe and her once affianced husband.'

1895

MASTER JOHN HORSELEIGH, KNIGHT

In the earliest and mustiest volume of the Havenpool marriage registers (said the thin-faced gentleman) this entry may still be read by anyone curious enough to decipher the crabbed handwriting of the date. I took a copy of it when I was last there; and it runs thus (he had opened his pocket-book, and now read aloud the extract; afterwards handing round the book to us, wherein we saw transcribed the following) –

> *Mast^r John Horseleigh, Knyght, of the p'ysshe of Clyfften was maryd to Edith the wyffe late off John Stocker, m'chawnte of Havenpool the xiiij daie of December be p'vylegge gevyn by our sup'me hedd of the chyrche of Ingelonde Kynge Henry the viii^th* 1539.

Now, if you turn to the long and elaborate pedigree of the ancient family of the Horseleighs of Clyfton Horseleigh, you will find no mention whatever of this alliance, notwithstanding the privilege given by the Sovereign and head of the Church; the said Sir John being therein chronicled as marrying, at a date apparently earlier than the above, the daughter and heiress of Richard Phelipson, of Montislope, in Nether Wessex, a lady who outlived him, of which marriage there were issue two daughters and a son, who succeeded him in his estates. How are we to account for these, as it would seem, contemporaneous wives? A strange local tradition only can help us, and this can be briefly told.

One evening in the autumn of the year 1540 or 1541, a young sailor, whose Christian name was Roger, but whose surname is not known, landed at his native place of Havenpool, on the South Wessex coast, after a voyage in the Newfoundland trade, then newly sprung into existence. He returned in the ship *Primrose* with a cargo of 'trayne oyle brought home from the New Founde Lande', to quote from the town records of the date. During his absence of two summers and a winter, which made up the term of a Newfoundland 'spell', many unlooked-for changes had occurred within the quiet little seaport, some of which closely affected Roger the sailor. At the time of his departure his only sister Edith had become the bride of one Stocker, a respectable townsman, and part owner of the brig in which Roger had sailed; and it was to the house of this couple, his only relatives, that the young man directed his steps. On trying the door in Quay Street he found it locked, and then observed that the windows were boarded up. Inquiring of a bystander, he learnt for the first time of the death of his brother-in-law, though that event had taken place nearly eighteen months before.

'And my sister Edith?' asked Roger.

'She's married again – as they do say, and hath been so these twelve months. I don't vouch for the truth o't, though if she isn't she ought to be.'

Roger's face grew dark. He was a man with a considerable reserve of strong passion, and he asked his informant what he meant by speaking thus.

The man explained that shortly after the young woman's bereavement a stranger had come to the port. He had seen her moping on the quay, had been attracted by her youth and loneliness, and in an extraordinarily brief wooing had completely fascinated her – had carried her off, and, as was reported, had married her. Though he had come by water, he was supposed to live no very great distance off by land. They were last heard of at Oozewood, in Upper Wessex, at the house of one Wall, a timber-merchant, where, he believed, she still had a lodging, though her husband, if he were lawfully that much, was but an occasional visitor to the place.

'The stranger?' asked Roger. 'Did you see him? What manner of man was he?'

'I liked him not,' said the other. 'He seemed of that kind that hath something to conceal, and as he walked with her he ever and anon turned his head and gazed behind him, as if he much feared an unwelcome pursuer. But, faith,' continued he, 'it may have been the man's anxiety only. Yet did I not like him.'

'Was he older than my sister?' Roger asked.

'Ay – much older; from a dozen to a score of years older. A man of some position, maybe, playing an amorous game for the pleasure of the hour. Who knoweth but that he have a wife already? Many have done the thing hereabouts of late.'

Having paid a visit to the graves of his relatives, the sailor next day went along the straight road which, then a lane, now a highway, conducted to the curious little inland town named by the Havenpool man. It is unnecessary to describe Oozewood on the South-Avon. It has a railway at the present day; but thirty years of steam traffic past its precincts have hardly modified its original features. Surrounded by a sort of fresh-water lagoon, dividing it from meadows and coppice, its ancient thatch and timber houses have barely made way even in the front street for the ubiquitous modern brick and slate. It neither increases nor diminishes in size; it is difficult to say what the inhabitants find to do, for though trades in woodware are still carried on, there cannot be enough of this class of work nowadays to maintain all the householders, the forests around having been so greatly thinned and curtailed. At the time of this tradition the forests were dense, artificers in wood abounded, and the timber trade was brisk. Every house in the town, without exception, was of oak framework, filled in with plaster, and covered with thatch, the chimney being the only brick portion of the structure. Inquiry soon brought Roger the sailor to the door of Wall, the timber-dealer referred to, but it was some time before he was able to gain admission to the lodging of his sister, the people having plainly received directions not to welcome strangers.

She was sitting in an upper room on one of the lath-backed, willow-bottomed 'shepherd's' chairs, made on the spot then as to this day, and as they were probably made there in the days of the Heptarchy. In her lap was an infant, which she had been suckling, though now it had fallen asleep; so had the young mother herself for a few minutes, under the drowsing effects of solitude. Hearing footsteps on the stairs, she awoke, started up with a glad cry, and ran to the door, opening which she met her brother on the threshold.

'O, this is merry; I didn't expect 'ee!' she said. 'Ah, Roger – I thought it was John.' Her tones fell to disappointment.

The sailor kissed her, looked at her sternly for a few moments, and pointing to the infant, said, 'You mean the father of this?'

'Yes, my husband,' said Edith.

'I hope so,' he answered.

'Why, Roger, I'm married – of a truth am I!' she cried.

'Shame upon 'ee, if true! If not true, worse. Master Stocker was an honest man, and ye should have respected his memory longer. Where is thy husband?'

'He comes often. I thought it was he now. Our marriage has to be kept secret for a while – it was done privily for certain reasons; but we was married at church like honest folk – afore God we were, Roger, six months after poor Stocker's death.'

''Twas too soon,' said Roger.

'I was living in a house alone; I had nowhere to go to. You were far over sea in the New Found Land, and John took me and brought me here.'

'How often doth he come?' says Roger again.

'Once or twice weekly,' says she.

'I wish th' 'dst waited till I returned, dear Edy,' he said. 'It mid be you are a wife – I hope so. But, if so, why this mystery? Why this mean and cramped lodging in this lonely copse-circled town? Of what standing is your husband, and of where?'

'He is of gentle breeding – his name is John. I am not free to tell his family-name. He is said to be of London, for safety' sake; but he really lives in the county next adjoining this.'

'Where in the next county?'

'I do not know. He has preferred not to tell me, that I may not have the secret forced from me, to his and my hurt, by bringing the marriage to the ears of his kinsfolk and friends.'

Her brother's face flushed. 'Our people have been honest townsmen, well-reputed for long; why should you readily take such humbling from a sojourner of whom th' 'st know nothing?'

They remained in constrained converse till her quick ear caught a sound, for which she might have been waiting – a horse's footfall. 'It is John!' said she. 'This is his night – Saturday.'

'Don't be frightened lest he should find me here!' said Roger. 'I am on the point of leaving. I wish not to be a third party. Say nothing at all about my visit, if it will incommode you so to do. I will see thee before I go afloat again.'

Speaking thus he left the room, and descending the staircase let himself out by the front door, thinking he might obtain a glimpse of the approaching horseman. But that traveller had in the meantime gone stealthily round to the back of the homestead, and peering along the pinion-end of the house Roger discerned him unbridling and haltering his horse with his own hands in the shed there.

Roger retired to the neighbouring inn called the Black Lamb, and meditated. This mysterious method of approach determined him, after all, not to leave the place till he had ascertained more definite facts of his sister's position – whether she were the deluded victim of the stranger or the wife she obviously believed herself to be. Having eaten some supper, he left the inn, it being now about eleven o'clock. He first looked into the shed, and, finding the horse still standing there, waited irresolutely near the door of his sister's lodging. Half-an-hour elapsed, and, while thinking he would climb into a loft hard by for a night's rest, there seemed to be a movement within the shutters of the sitting-room that his sister occupied. Roger hid himself behind a faggot-stack near the back door, rightly divining that his sister's visitor would emerge by the way he had entered. The door opened, and the candle she held in her hand lighted for a moment the stranger's form, showing it to be that of a tall and handsome personage, about forty years of age, and apparently of a superior position in life. Edith was assisting him to cloak himself, which being done he took leave of her with a kiss and left the house. From the door she watched him bridle and saddle his horse, and having mounted and waved an adieu to her as she stood candle in hand, he turned out of the yard and rode away.

The horse which bore him was, or seemed to be, a little lame, and Roger fancied from this that the rider's journey was not likely to be a long one. Being light of foot he followed apace, having no great difficulty on such a still night in keeping within earshot some few miles, the horseman pausing more than once. In this pursuit Roger discovered the rider to choose bridle-tracks and open commons in preference to any high road. The distance soon began to prove a more trying one than he had bargained for; and when out of breath and in some despair of being able to ascertain the man's identity, he perceived an ass standing in the starlight under a hayrick, from which the animal was helping itself to periodic mouthfuls.

The story goes that Roger caught the ass, mounted, and again resumed the trail of the unconscious horseman, which feat may have been possible to a nautical young fellow, though one can hardly understand how a sailor would ride such an animal without bridle or saddle, and strange to his hands, unless the creature were extraordinarily docile. This question, however, is immaterial. Suffice it to say that at dawn the following morning Roger beheld his sister's lover or husband entering the gates of a large and well-timbered park on the south-western verge of the White Hart Forest (as it was then called), now known to everybody as the Vale of Blackmoor. Thereupon the sailor discarded his steed, and finding for himself an obscurer entrance to the same part a little further on, he crossed the grass to reconnoitre.

He presently perceived amid the trees before him a mansion which, new to himself, was one of the best-known in the county at that time. Of this fine manorial residence hardly a trace now remains; but a manuscript dated some years later than the events we are regarding describes it in terms from which the imagination may construct a singularly clear and vivid picture. This record presents it as consisting of 'a faire yellow freestone building, partly two and partly three storeys; a faire halle and parlour, both waynscotted; a faire dyning roome and withdrawing roome, and many good lodgings; a kitchen adjoyninge backwarde to one end of the dwelling-house, with a faire passage from it into the halle, parlour, and dyninge roome, and sellars adjoyninge.

'In the front of house a square greene court, and a curious gatehouse with lodgings in it, standing with the front of the house to the south; in a large outer court three stables, a coach-house, a large barne, and a stable for oxen and kyne, and all houses necessary.

'Without the gatehouse, paled in, a large square greene, in which standeth a faire chappell; of the south-east side of the greene court, towards the river, a large garden.

'Of the south-west side of the greene court is a large bowling greene, with fower mounted walks about it, all walled about with a batteled wall, and sett with all sorts of fruit; and out of it into the fieldes there are large walks under many tall elmes orderly planted.'

Then follows a description of the orchards and gardens; the servants' offices, brewhouse, bakehouse, dairy, pigeon-houses, and corn-mill; the river and its abundance of fish; the warren, the coppices, the walks; ending thus –

'And all the country north of the house, open champaign, sandy feildes, very dry and pleasant for all kindes of recreation, huntinge, and hawkinge, and profitable for tillage. . . The house hath a large prospect east, south, and west, over a very large and pleasant vale . . . is seated from the good markett towns of Sherton Abbas three miles, and Ivell a mile, that plentifully yield all manner of provision; and within twelve miles of the south sea.'

It was on the grass before this seductive and picturesque structure that the sailor stood at gaze under the elms in the dim dawn of Sunday morning, and saw to his surprise his sister's lover and horse vanish within the court of the building.

Perplexed and weary, Roger slowly retreated, more than ever convinced that something was wrong in his sister's position. He crossed the bowling-green to the avenue of elms, and, bent on further research, was about to climb into one of these, when, looking below, he saw a heap of hay apparently for horses or deer. Into this he crept, and, having eaten a crust of bread which he had hastily thrust into his pocket at the inn, he curled up and fell asleep, the hay forming a comfortable bed, and quite covering him over.

He slept soundly and long, and was awakened by the sound of a bell. On peering from the hay he found the time had advanced to full day; the sun was shining brightly. The bell was that of the 'faire chappell' on the green outside the gatehouse, and it was calling to matins. Presently the priest crossed the green to a little side-door in the chancel, and then from the gateway of the mansion emerged the household, the tall man whom Roger had seen with his sister on the previous night, on his arm being a portly dame, and, running beside the pair, two little girls and a boy. These all entered the chapel, and the bell having ceased and the environs become clear, the sailor crept out from his hiding.

He sauntered towards the chapel, the opening words of the service being audible within. While standing by the porch he saw a belated servitor approaching from the kitchen-court to attend the service also. Roger carelessly accosted him, and asked, as an idle wanderer, the name of the family he had just seen cross over from the mansion.

'Od zounds! if ye modden be a stranger here in very truth, goodman. That wer Sir John and his dame, and his children Elizabeth, Mary, and John.'

'I be from foreign parts. Sir John what d'ye call'n?'

'Master John Horseleigh, Knight, who had a'most as much lond by inheritance of his mother as 'a had by his father, and likewise some by his wife. Why, bain't his arms dree goolden horses' heads, and idden his lady the daughter of Master Richard Phelipson, of Montislope, in Nether Wessex, known to us all?'

'It mid be so, and yet it mid not. However, th' 'lt miss thy prayers for such an honest knight's welfare, and I have to traipse seaward many miles.'

He went onward, and as he walked continued saying to himself, 'Now to that poor wronged fool Edy. The fond thing! I thought it; 'twas too quick – she was ever amorous. What's to become of her! God wot! How be I going to face her with the news, and how be I to hold it from her? To bring this disgrace on my father's honoured name, a double-tongued knave!' He turned and shook his fist at the chapel and all in it, and resumed his way.

Perhaps it was owing to the perplexity of his mind that, instead of returning by the direct road towards his sister's obscure lodging in the next county, he followed the highway to Casterbridge, some fifteen miles off, where he remained drinking hard all that afternoon and evening, and where he lay that and two or three succeeding nights, wandering thence along the Anglebury road to some village that way, and lying the Friday night after at his native place of Havenpool. The sight of the familiar objects there seems to have stirred him anew to action, and the next morning he was observed pursuing the way to Oozewood that he had followed on the Saturday previous, reckoning, no doubt, that Saturday night would, as before, be a time for finding Sir John with his sister again.

He delayed to reach the place till just before sunset. His sister was walking in the meadows at the foot of the garden, with a nursemaid who carried the baby, and she looked up pensively when he approached. Anxiety as to her position had already told upon her once rosy cheeks and lucid eyes. But concern for herself and child was displaced for the moment by her regard of Roger's worn and haggard face.

'Why – you are sick, Roger – you are tired! Where have you been these many days? Why not keep me company a bit – my husband is much away? And we have hardly spoke at all of dear father and of your voyage to the New Land. Why did you go away so suddenly? There is a spare chamber at my lodging.'

'Come indoors,' he said. 'We'll talk now – talk a good deal. As for him [nodding to the child], better heave him into the river; better for him and you!'

She forced a laugh, as if she tried to see a good joke in the remark, and they went silently indoors.

'A miserable hole!' said Roger, looking round the room.

'Nay, but 'tis very pretty!'

'Not after what I've seen. Did he marry 'ee at church in orderly fashion?'

'He did sure – at our church at Havenpool.'

'But in a privy way?'

'Ay – because of his friends – it was at night-time.'

'Ede, ye fond one – for all that he's not thy husband! Th' 'rt not his wife; and the child is a bastard. He hath a wife and children of his own rank, and bearing his name; and that's Sir John Horseleigh, of Clyfton Horseleigh, and not plain Jack, as you think him, and your lawful husband. The sacrament of marriage is no safeguard nowadays. The King's new-made headship of the Church hath led men to practise these tricks lightly.'

She had turned white. 'That's not true, Roger!' she said. 'You are in liquor, my brother, and you know not what you say! Your seafaring years have taught 'ee bad things!'

'Edith – I've seen them; wife and family – all. How canst—'

They were sitting in the gathered darkness, and at that moment steps were heard without. 'Go out this way,' she said. 'It is my husband. He must not see thee in this mood. Get away till tomorrow, Roger, as you care for me.'

She pushed her brother through a door leading to the back stairs, and almost as soon as it was closed her visitor entered. Roger, however, did not retreat down the stairs; he stood and looked through the bobbin-hole. If the visitor turned out to be Sir John, he had determined to confront him.

It was the knight. She had struck a light on his entry, and he kissed the child, and took Edith tenderly by the shoulders, looking into her face.

'Something's gone awry wi' my dear!' he said. 'What is it? What's the matter?'

'O, Jack!' she cried. 'I have heard such a fearsome rumour – what doth it mean? He who told me is my best friend. He must be deceived! But who deceived him, and why? Jack, I was just told that you had a wife living when you married me, and have her still!'

'A wife? – H'm.'

'Yes, and children. Say no, say no!'

'By God! I have no lawful wife but you; and as for children, many or few, they are all bastards, save this one alone!'

'And that you be Sir John Horseleigh of Clyfton?'

'I mid be. I have never said so to 'ee.'

'But Sir John is known to have a lady, and issue of her!'

The knight looked down. 'How did thy mind get filled with such as this?'

'One of my kindred came.'

'A traitor! Why should he mar our life? Ah! you said you had a brother at sea – where is he now?'

'*Here!*' came from close behind him. And flinging open the door, Roger faced the intruder. 'Liar!' he said, 'to call thyself her husband!'

Sir John fired up, and made a rush at the sailor, who seized him by the collar, and in the wrestle they both fell, Roger under. But in a few seconds he contrived to extricate his right arm, and drawing from his belt a knife which he wore attached to a cord round his neck he opened it with his teeth, and struck it into the breast of Sir John stretched above him. Edith had during these moments run into the next room to place the child in safety, and when she came back the knight was relaxing his hold on Roger's throat. He rolled over upon his back and groaned.

The only witness of the scene save the three concerned was the nursemaid, who had brought in the child on its father's arrival. She stated afterwards that nobody suspected Sir John had received his deathwound; yet it was so, though he did not die for a long while, meaning thereby an hour or two; that Mistress Edith continually endeavoured to staunch the blood, calling her brother Roger a wretch, and ordering him to get himself gone; on which order he acted, after a gloomy pause, by opening the window, and letting himself down by the sill to the ground.

It was then that Sir John, in difficult accents, made his dying declaration to the nurse and Edith, and, later, the apothecary; which was to this purport, that the Dame Horseleigh who passed as his wife at Clyfton, and who had borne him three children, was in truth and deed, though unconsciously, the wife of another man. Sir John had married her several years before, in the face of the whole county, as the widow of one Decimus Strong, who had disappeared shortly after her union with him, having adventured to the North to join the revolt of the Nobles, and on that revolt being quelled retreated across the sea. Two years ago, having discovered this man to be still living in France, and not wishing to disturb the mind and happiness of her who believed herself his wife, yet wishing for legitimate issue, Sir John had informed the King of the facts, who had encouraged him to wed honestly, though secretly, the young merchant's widow at Havenpool; she being, therefore, his lawful wife, and she only. That to avoid all scandal and hubbub he had purposed to let things remain as they were till fair opportunity should arise of making the true case known with least pain to all parties concerned, but that, having been thus suspected and attacked by his own brother-in-law, his zest for such schemes and for all things had died out in him, and he only wished to commend his soul to God.

That night, while the owls were hooting from the forest that encircled the sleeping townlet, and the South-Avon was gurgling through the wooden piles of the bridge, Sir John died there in the arms of his wife. She concealed nothing of the cause of her husband's death save the subject of the quarrel, which she felt it would be premature to announce just then, and until proof of her status should be forthcoming. But before a month had passed, it happened, to her inexpressible sorrow, that the child of this clandestine union fell sick and died. From that hour all interest in the name and fame of the Horseleighs forsook the younger of the twain who called themselves wives of Sir John, and, being careless about her own fame, she took no steps to assert her claims, her legal position having, indeed, grown hateful to her in her horror at the tragedy. And Sir William Byrt, the curate who had married her to her husband, being an old man and feeble, was not disinclined to leave the embers unstirred of such a fiery matter as this, and to assist her in letting established things stand. Therefore, Edith retired with the nurse, her only companion and friend, to her native town, where she lived in absolute obscurity till her death in middle age. Her brother was never seen again in England.

A strangely corroborative sequel to the story remains to be told. Shortly after the death of Sir John Horseleigh, a soldier of fortune returned from the Continent, called on Dame Horseleigh the fictitious, living in widowed state at Clyfton Horseleigh, and, after a singularly brief courtship, married her. The tradition at Havenpool and elsewhere has ever been that this man was already her husband, Decimus Strong, who remarried her for appearance' sake only.

The illegitimate son of this lady by Sir John succeeded to the estates and honours, and his son after him, there being nobody on the alert to investigate their pretensions. Little difference would it have made to the present generation, however, had there been such a one, for the family in all its branches, lawful and unlawful, has been extinct these many score yeras, the last representative but one being killed at the siege of Sherton Castle, while attacking in the service of the Parliament, and the other being outlawed later in the same century for a debt of ten pounds, and dying in the county jail. The mansion-house and its appurtenances were, as I have previously stated, destroyed, excepting one small wing, which now forms part of a farmhouse, and is visible as you pass along the railway from Casterbridge to Ivell. The outline of the old bowling-green is also distinctly to be seen.

This, then, is the reason why the only lawful marriage of Sir John, as recorded in the obscure register of Havenpool, does not appear in the pedigree of the house of Horseleigh.

SPRING 1893

THE DUKE'S REAPPEARANCE

A FAMILY TRADITION

According to the kinsman who told me the story, Christopher Swetman's house, on the outskirts of King's-Hintock village, was in those days larger and better kept than when, many years later, it was sold to the lord of the manor adjoining; after having been in the Swetman family, as one may say, since the Conquest.

Some people would have it to be that the thing happened at the house opposite, belonging to one Childs, with whose family the Swetmans afterwards intermarried. But that it was at the original homestead of the Swetmans can be shown in various ways; chiefly by the unbroken traditions of the family, and indirectly by the evidence of the walls themselves, which are the only ones thereabout with windows mullioned in the Elizabethan manner, and plainly of a date anterior to the event; while those of the other house might well have been erected fifty or eighty years later, and probably were; since the choice of Swetman's house by the fugitive was doubtless dictated by no other circumstance than its then suitable loneliness.

It was a cloudy July morning just before dawn, the hour of two having been struck by Swetman's one-handed clock on the stairs, that is still preserved in the family. Christopher heard the strokes from his chamber, immediately at the top of the staircase, and overlooking the front of the house. He did not wonder that he was sleepless. The rumours and excitements which had latterly stirred the neighbourhood, to the effect that the rightful King of England had landed from Holland, at a port only eighteen miles to the south-west of Swetman's house, were enough to make wakeful and anxious even a contented yeoman like him. Some of the villagers, intoxicated by the news, had thrown down their scythes, and rushed to the ranks of the invader. Christopher Swetman had weighed both sides of the question, and had remained at home.

Now as he lay thinking of these and other things he fancied that he could hear the footfall of a man on the road leading up to his house – a by-way, which led scarce anywhere else; and therefore a tread was at any time more apt to startle the inmates of the homestead than if it had stood in a thoroughfare. The footfall came opposite the gate, and stopped there. One minute, two minutes passed, and the pedestrian did not proceed. Christopher Swetman got out of bed, and opened the casement. 'Hoi! who's there?' cries he.

'A friend,' came from the darkness.

'And what mid ye want at this time o' night?' says Swetman.

'Shelter. I've lost my way.'

'What's thy name?'

There came no answer.

'Be ye one of King Monmouth's men?'

'He that asks no questions will hear no lies from me. I am a stranger; and I am spent, and hungered. Can you let me lie with you tonight?'

Swetman was generous to people in trouble, and his house was roomy. 'Wait a bit,' he said, 'and I'll come down and have a look at thee, anyhow.'

He struck a light, put on his clothes, and descended, taking his horn-lantern from a nail in the passage, and lighting it before opening the door. The rays fell on the form of a tall, dark man in cavalry accoutrements and wearing a sword. He was pale with fatigue and covered with mud, though the weather was dry.

'Prithee take no heed of my appearance,' said the stranger. 'But let me in.'

That his visitor was in sore distress admitted of no doubt, and the yeoman's natural humanity assisted the other's sad importunity and gentle voice. Swetman took him in, not without a suspicion that this man represented in some way Monmouth's cause, to which he was not unfriendly in his secret heart. At his earnest request the new-comer was given a suit of the yeoman's old clothes in exchange for his own, which, with his sword, were hidden in a closet in Swetman's chamber; food was then put before him and a lodging provided for him in a room at the back.

Here he slept till quite late in the morning, which was Sunday, the sixth of July, and when he came down in the garments that he had borrowed he met the household with a melancholy smile. Besides Swetman himself, there were only his two daughters, Grace and Leonard (the latter was, oddly enough, a woman's name here), and both had been enjoined to secrecy. They asked no questions and received no information; though the stranger regarded their fair countenances with an interest almost too deep. Having partaken of their usual breakfast of ham and cider he professed weariness and retired to the chamber whence he had come.

In a couple of hours or thereabout he came down again, the two young women having now gone off to morning service. Seeing Christopher bustling about the house without assistance, he asked if he could do anything to aid his host.

As he seemed anxious to hide all differences and appear as one of themselves, Swetman set him to get vegetables from the garden and fetch water from Buttock's Spring in the dip near the house (though the spring was not called by that name till years after, by the way).

'And what can I do next?' says the stranger when these services had been performed.

His meekness and docility struck Christopher much, and won upon him. 'Since you be minded to,' says the latter, 'you can take down the dishes and spread the table for dinner. Take a pewter plate for thyself, but the trenchers will do for we.'

But the other would not, and took a trencher likewise, in doing which he spoke of the two girls and remarked how comely they were.

This quietude was put an end to by a stir out of doors, which was sufficient to draw Swetman's attention to it, and he went out. Farm hands who had gone off and joined the Duke on his arrival had begun to come in with news that a midnight battle had been fought on the moors to the north, the Duke's men, who had attacked, being entirely worsted; the Duke himself, with one or two lords and other friends, had fled, no one knew whither.

'There has been a battle,' says Swetman, on coming indoors after these tidings, and looking earnestly at the stranger.

'May the victory be to the rightful in the end, whatever the issue now,' says the other, with a sorrowful sigh.

'Dost really know nothing about it?' said Christopher. 'I could have sworn you was one from that very battle!'

'I was here before three o'clock this morning; and these men have only arrived now.'

'True,' said the yeoman. 'But still, I think—'

'Do not press your question,' the stranger urged. 'I am in a strait, and can refuse a helper nothing; such inquiry is, therefore, unfair.'

'True again,' said Swetman, and held his tongue.

The daughters of the house returned from church, where the service had been hurried by reason of the excitement. To their father's questioning if they had spoken of him who sojourned there they replied that they had said never a word; which, indeed, was true, as events proved.

He bade them serve the dinner; and, as the visitor had withdrawn since the news of the battle, prepared to take a platter to him upstairs. But he preferred to come down and dine with the family.

During the afternoon more fugitives passed through the village, but Christopher Swetman, his visitor, and his family kept indoors. In the evening, however, Swetman came out from his gate, and, harkening in silence to these tidings and more, wondered what might be in store for him for his last night's work.

He returned homeward by a path across the mead that skirted his own orchard. Passing, he heard the voice of his daughter Leonard expostulating inside the hedge, her words being:

'Don't ye, sir; don't! I prithee let me go!'

'Why, sweetheart?'

'Because I've a-promised another!'

Peeping through, as he could not help doing, he saw the girl struggling in the arms of the stranger, who was attempting to kiss her; but finding her resistance to be genuine, and her distress unfeigned, he reluctantly let her go.

Swetman's face grew dark, for his girls were more to him than himself. He hastened on, meditating moodily all the way. He entered the gate, and made straight for the orchard. When he reached it his daughter had disappeared, but the stranger was still standing there.

'Sir!' said the yeoman, his anger having in no wise abated, 'I've seen what has happened! I have taken 'ee into my house, at some jeopardy to myself; and, whoever you be, the least I expected of 'ee was to treat the maidens with a seemly respect. You have not done it, and I no longer trust you. I am the more watchful over them in that they are motherless; and I must ask 'ee to go after dark this night!'

The stranger seemed dazed at discovering what his impulse had brought down upon his head, and his pale face grew paler. He did not reply for a time. When he did speak his soft voice was thick with feeling.

'Sir,' says he, 'I own that I am in the wrong, if you take the matter gravely. We do not what we would but what we must. Though I have not injured your daughter as a woman, I have been treacherous to her as a hostess and friend in need. I'll go, as you say; I can do no less. I shall doubtless find a refuge elsewhere.'

They walked to the house in silence, where Swetman insisted that his guest should have supper before departing. By the time this was eaten it was dusk and the stranger announced that he was ready.

They went upstairs to where the garments and sword lay hidden, till the departing one said that on further thought he would ask another favour: that he should be allowed to retain the clothes he wore, and that his host would keep the others and the sword till he, the speaker, should come or send for them.

'As you will,' said Swetman. 'The gain is on my side; for those clouts were but kept to dress a scarecrow next fall.'

'They suit my case,' said the stranger sadly. 'However much they may misfit me, they do not misfit my sorry fortune now!'

'Nay, then,' said Christopher relenting, 'I was too hasty. Sh'lt bide!'

But the other would not, saying that it was better that things should take their course. Notwithstanding that Swetman immportuned him, he only added. 'If I never come again, do with my belongings as you list. In the pocket you will find a gold snuff-box, and in the snuff-box fifty gold pieces.'

'But keep 'em for thy use, man!' said the yeoman.

'No,' says the parting guest; 'they are foreign pieces and would harm me if I were taken. Do as I bid thee. Put away these things again and take especial charge of the sword. It belonged to my father's father and I value it much. But something more common becomes me now.'

Saying which, he took, as he went downstairs, one of the ash sticks used by Swetman himself for walking with. The yeoman lighted him out to the garden hatch, where he disappeared through Clammers Gate by the road that crosses King's-Hintock Park to Evershead.

Christopher returned to the upstairs chamber, and sat down on his bed reflecting. Then he examined the things left behind, and surely enough in one of the pockets the gold snuff-box was revealed, containing the fifty gold pieces as stated by the fugitive. The yeoman next looked at the sword which its owner had stated to have belonged to his grandfather. It was two-edged, so that he almost feared to handle it. On the blade were inscribed the words 'ANDREA FERARA', and among the many fine chasings were a rose and crown, the plume of the Prince of Wales, and two portraits; portraits of a man and a woman, the man's face having the face of the first King Charles, and the woman's, apparently, that of his Queen.

Swetman, much awed and surprised, returned the articles to the closet, and went downstairs pondering. Of his surmise he said nothing to his daughters, merely declaring to them that the gentleman was gone; and never revealing that he had been an eye-witness of the unpleasant scene in the orchard that was the immediate cause of the departure.

Nothing occurred in Hintock during the week that followed, beyond the fitful arrival of more decided tidings concerning the utter defeat of the Duke's army and his own disappearance at an early stage of the battle. Then it was told that Monmouth was taken, not in his own clothes but in the disguise of a countryman. He had been sent to London, and was confined in the Tower.

The possibility that his guest had been no other than the Duke made Swetman unspeakably sorry now; his heart smote him at the thought that, acting so harshly for such a small breach of good faith, he might have been the means of forwarding the unhappy fugitive's capture. On the girls coming up to him he said, 'Get away with ye, wenches: I fear you have been the ruin of an unfortunate man!'

On the Thursday night following, when the yeoman was sleeping as usual in his chamber, he was, he said, conscious of the entry of some one. Opening his eyes, he beheld by the light of the moon, which shone upon the front of his house, the figure of a man who seemed to be the stranger moving from the door towards the closet. He was dressed somewhat differently now, but the face was quite that of his late guest in its tragical pensiveness, as was also the tallness of his figure. He neared the closet; and, feeling his visitor to be within his rights, Christopher refrained from stirring. The personage turned his large haggard eyes upon the bed where Swetman lay, and then withdrew from their hiding the articles that belonged to him, again giving a hard gaze at Christopher as he went noiselessly out of the chamber with his properties on his arm. His retreat down the stairs was just audible, and also his departure by the side-door, through which entrance or exit was easy to those who knew the place.

Nothing further happened, and towards morning Swetman slept. To avoid all risk he said not a word to the girls of the visit of the night, and certainly not to anyone outside the house; for it was dangerous at that time to avow anything.

Among the killed in opposing the recent rising had been a younger brother of the lord of the manor, who lived at King's-Hintock Court hard by. Seeing the latter ride past in mourning clothes next day, Swetman ventured to condole with him.

'He'd no business there!' answered the other. His words and manner showed the bitterness that was mingled with his regret. 'But say no more of him. You know what has happened since, I suppose?'

'I know that they say Monmouth is taken, Sir Thomas, but I can't think it true,' answered Swetman.

'O zounds! 'tis true enough,' cried the knight, 'and that's not all. The Duke was executed on Tower Hill two days ago.'

'D'ye say it verily?' says Swetman.

'And a very hard death he had, worse luck for 'n,' said Sir Thomas. 'Well, 'tis over for him and over for my brother. But not for the rest.

There'll be searchings and siftings down here anon; and happy is the man who has had nothing to do with this matter!'

Now Swetman had hardly heard the latter words, so much was he confounded by the strangeness of the tidings that the Duke had come to his death on the previous Tuesday. For it had been only the night before this present day of Friday that he had seen his former guest, whom he had ceased to doubt could be other than the Duke, come into his chamber and fetch away his accoutrements as he had promised.

'It couldn't have been a vision,' said Christopher to himself when the knight had ridden on. 'But I'll go straight and see if the things be in the closet still; and thus I shall surely learn if 'twere a vision or no.'

To the closet he went, which he had not looked into since the stranger's departure. And searching behind the articles placed to conceal the things hidden, he found that, as he had never doubted, they were gone.

When the rumour spread abroad in the West that the man beheaded in the Tower was not indeed the Duke, but one of his officers taken after the battle, and that the Duke had been assisted to escape out of the country, Swetman found in it an explanation of what so deeply mystified him. That his visitor might have been a friend of the Duke's, whom the Duke had asked to fetch the things in a last request, Swetman would never admit. His belief in the rumour that Monmouth lived, like that of thousands of others, continued to the end of his days.

Such, briefly, concluded my kinsman, is the tradition which has been handed down in Christopher Swetman's family for the last two hundred years.

A MERE INTERLUDE

I

The traveller in school-books, who vouched in dryest tones for the fidelity to fact of the following narrative, used to add a ring of truth to it by opening with a nicety of criticism on the heroine's personality. People were wrong, he declared, when they surmised that Baptista Trewthen was a young woman with scarcely emotions or character. There was nothing in her to love, and nothing to hate – so ran the general opinion. That she showed few positive qualities was true. The colours and tones which changing events paint on the faces of active womankind were looked for in vain upon hers. But still waters run deep; and no crisis had come in the years of her early maidenhood to demonstrate what lay hidden within her, like metal in a mine.

She was the daughter of a small farmer in St Maria's, one of the Isles of Lyonesse beyond Off-Wessex, who had spent a large sum, as there understood, on her education, by sending her to the mainland for two years. At nineteen she was entered at the Training College for Teachers, and at twenty-one nominated to a school in the country, near Tor-upon-Sea, whither she proceeded after the Christmas examination and holidays.

The months passed by from winter to spring and summer, and Baptista applied herself to her new duties as best she could, till an uneventful year had elapsed. Then an air of abstraction pervaded her bearing as she walked to and fro, twice a day, and she showed the traits of a person who had something on her mind. A widow, by name Mrs Wace, in whose house Baptista Trewthen had been provided with a sitting-room and bedroom till the schoolhouse should be built, noticed this change in her youthful tenant's manner, and at last ventured to press her with a few questions.

'It has nothing to do with the place, nor with you,' said Miss Trewthen.

'Then it is the salary?'

'No, nor the salary.'

'Then it is something you have heard from home, my dear.'

Baptista was silent for a few moments. 'It is Mr Heddegan,' she murmured. 'Him they used to call David Heddegan before he got his money.'

'And who is the Mr Heddegan they used to call David?'

'An old bachelor at Giant's Town, St Maria's, with no relations whatever, who lives about a stone's throw from father's. When I was a child he used to take me on his knee and say he'd marry me some day. Now I am a woman the jest has turned earnest, and he is anxious to do it. And father and mother say I can't do better than have him.'

'He's well off?'

'Yes – he's the richest man we know – as a friend and neighbour.'

'How much older did you say he was than yourself?'

'I didn't say. Twenty years at least.'

'And an unpleasant man in the bargain perhaps?'

'No – he's not unpleasant.'

'Well, child, all I can say is that I'd resist any such engagement if it's not palatable to 'ee. You are comfortable here, in my little house, I hope. All the parish like 'ee: and I've never been so cheerful, since my poor husband left me to wear his wings, as I've been with 'ee as my lodger.'

The schoolmistress assured her landlady that she could return the sentiment. 'But here comes my perplexity,' she said. 'I don't like keeping school. Ah, you are surprised – you didn't suspect it. That's because I've concealed my feeling. Well, I simply hate school. I don't care for children – they are unpleasant, troublesome little things, whom nothing would delight so much as to hear that you had fallen down dead. Yet I would even put up with them if it was not for the inspector. For three months before his visit I didn't sleep soundly. And the Committee of Council are always changing the Code, so that you don't know what to teach, and what to leave untaught. I think father and mother are right. They say I shall never excel as a schoolmistress if I dislike the work so, and that therefore I ought to get settled by marrying Mr Heddegan. Between us two, I like him better than school; but I don't like him quite so much as to wish to marry him.'

These conversations, once begun, were continued from day to day; till at length the young girl's elderly friend and landlady threw in her opinion on the side of Miss Trewthen's parents. All things considered, she declared, the uncertainty of the school, the labour, Baptista's natural disliking for teaching, it would be as well to take what fate offered, and make the best of matters by wedding her father's old neighbour and prosperous friend.

The Easter holidays came round, and Baptista went to spend them as usual in her native isle, going by train into Off-Wessex and crossing by packet from Pen-zephyr. When she returned in the middle of April her face wore a more settled aspect.

'Well?' said the expectant Mrs Wace.

'I have agreed to have him as my husband,' said Baptista, in an off-hand way. 'Heaven knows if it will be for the best or not. But I have agreed to do it, and so the matter is settled.'

Mrs Wace commended her; but Baptista did not care to dwell on the subject; so that allusion to it was very infrequent between them. Nevertheless, among other things, she repeated to the widow from time to time in monosyllabic remarks that the wedding was really impending; that it was arranged for the summer, and that she had given notice of leaving the school at the August holidays. Later on she announced more specifically that her marriage was to take place immediately after her return home at the beginning of the month aforesaid.

She now corresponded regularly with Mr Heddegan. Her letters from him were seen, at least on the outside, and in part within, by Mrs Wace. Had she read more of their interiors than the occasional sentences shown her by Baptista she would have perceived that the scratchy, rusty handwriting of Miss Trewthen's betrothed conveyed little more matter than details of their future housekeeping, and his preparations for the same, with innumerable 'my dears' sprinkled in disconnectedly, to show the depth of his affection without the inconveniences of syntax.

2

It was the end of July – dry, too dry, even for the season, the delicate green herbs and vegetables that grew in this favoured end of the kingdom tasting rather of the watering-pot than of the pure fresh moisture from the skies. Baptista's boxes were packed, and one Saturday morning she departed by waggonette to the station, and thence by train to Pen-zephyr, from which port she was, as usual, to cross the water immediately to her home, and become Mr Heddegan's wife on the Wednesday of the week following.

She might have returned a week sooner. But though the wedding day had loomed so near, and the banns were out, she delayed her departure till this last moment, saying it was not necessary for her to be at home long beforehand. As Mr Heddegan was older than herself, she said, she was to be married in her ordinary summer bonnet and grey silk frock, and there were no preparations to make that had not been amply made by her parents and intended husband.

In due time, after a hot and tedious journey, she reached Pen-zephyr. She here obtained some refreshment, and then went towards the pier, where she learnt to her surprise that the little steamboat plying between the town and the islands had left at eleven o'clock; the usual hour of departure in the afternoon having been forestalled in consequence of the fogs which had for a few days prevailed towards evening, making twilight navigation dangerous.

This being Saturday, there was no other boat till Tuesday, and it became obvious that here she would have to remain for the three days, unless her friends should think fit to rig out one of the island sailing-boats and come to fetch her – a not very likely contingency, the sea distance being nearly forty miles.

Baptista, however, had been detained in Pen-zephyr on more than one occasion before, either on account of bad weather or some such reason as the present, and she was therefore not in any personal alarm. But, as she was to be married on the following Wednesday, the delay was certainly inconvenient to a more than ordinary degree, since it would leave less than a day's interval between her arrival and the wedding ceremony.

Apart from this awkwardness she did not much mind the accident. It was indeed curious to see how little she minded. Perhaps it would not be too much to say that, although she was going to do the critical deed of her life quite willingly, she experienced an indefinable relief at the postponement of her meeting with Heddegan. But her manner after making discovery of the hindrance was quiet and subdued, even to passivity itself; as was instanced by her having, at the moment of receiving information that the steamer had sailed, replied 'Oh' so coolly to the porter with her luggage, that he was almost disappointed at her lack of disappointment.

The question now was, should she return again to Mrs Wace, in the village of Lower Wessex, or wait in the town at which she had arrived? She would have preferred to go back, but the distance was too great; moreover, having left the place for good, and somewhat dramatically, to become a bride, a return, even for so short a space, would have been a trifle humiliating.

Leaving, then, her boxes at the station, her next anxiety was to secure a respectable, or rather genteel, lodging in the popular seaside resort confronting her. To this end she looked about the town, in which, though she had passed through it half-a-dozen times, she was practically a stranger.

Baptista found a room to suit her over a fruiterer's shop; where she made herself at home, and set herself in order after her journey. An early cup of tea having revived her spirits she walked out to reconnoitre.

Being a schoolmistress she avoided looking at the schools, and having a sort of trade connection with books, she avoided looking at the booksellers; but wearying of the other shops she inspected the churches; not that for her own part she cared much about ecclesiastical edifices; but tourists looked at them, and so would she – a proceeding for which no one would have credited her with any great originality, such, for instance, as that she subsequently showed herself to possess. The churches soon oppressed her. She tried the Museum, but came out because it seemed lonely and tedious.

Yet the town and the walks in this land of strawberries, these headquarters of early English flowers and fruit, were then, as always, attractive. From the more picturesque streets she went to the town gardens, and the Pier, and the Harbour, and looked at the men at work there, loading and unloading as in the time of the Phoenicians.

'Not Baptista? Yes, Baptista it is!'

The words were uttered behind her. Turning round she gave a start, and became confused, even agitated, for a moment. Then she said in her usual undemonstrative manner, 'O – is it really you, Charles?'

Without speaking again at once, and with a half-smile, the newcomer glanced her over. There was much criticism, and some resentment – even temper – in his eye.

'I am going home,' continued she. 'But I have missed the boat.'

He scarcely seemed to take in the meaning of this explanation, in the intensity of his critical survey. 'Teaching still? What a fine schoolmistress you make, Baptista, I warrant!' he said with a slight flavour of sarcasm, which was not lost upon her.

'I know I am nothing to brag of,' she replied. 'That's why I have given up.'

'O – given up? You astonish me.'

'I hate the profession.'

'Perhaps that's because I am in it.'

'O no, it isn't. But I am going to enter on another life altogether. I am going to be married next week to Mr David Heddegan.'

The young man – fortified as he was by a natural cynical pride and passionateness – winced at this unexpected reply, notwithstanding.

'Who is Mr David Heddegan?' he asked, as indifferently as lay in his power.

She informed him the bearer of the name was a general merchant of Giant's Town, St Maria's Island – her father's nearest neighbour and oldest friend.

'Then we shan't see anything more of you on the mainland?' inquired the schoolmaster.

'O, I don't know about that,' said Miss Trewthen.

'Here endeth the career of the belle of the boarding-school your father was foolish enough to send you to. A "general merchant's" wife in the Lyonesse Isles. Will you sell pounds of soap and pennyworths of tin tacks, or whole bars of saponaceous matter, and great tenpenny nails?'

'He's not in such a small way as that!' she almost pleaded. 'He owns ships, though they are rather little ones!'

'O, well, it is much the same. Come, let us walk on; it is tedious to stand still. I thought you would be a failure in education,' he continued, when she obeyed him and strolled ahead. 'You never showed power that way. You remind me much of some of those women who think they are sure to be great actresses if they go on the stage, because they have a pretty face, and forget that what we require is acting. But you found your mistake, didn't you?'

'Don't taunt me, Charles.' It was noticeable that the young schoolmaster's tone caused her no anger or retaliatory passion; far otherwise: there was a tear in her eye. 'How is it you are in Pen-zephyr?' she inquired.

'I don't taunt you. I speak the truth, purely in a friendly way, as I should to anyone I wished well. Though for that matter I might have some excuse even for taunting you. Such a terrible hurry as you've been in. I hate a woman who is in such a hurry.'

'How do you mean that?'

'Why – to be somebody's wife or other – anything's wife rather than nobody's. You couldn't wait for me, O, no. Well, thank God, I'm cured of all that!'

'How merciless you are!' she said bitterly. 'Wait for you? What does that mean, Charley? You never showed – anything to wait for – anything special towards me.'

'O come, Baptista dear; come!'

'What I mean is, nothing definite,' she expostulated. 'I suppose you liked me a little; but it seemed to me to be only a pastime on your part, and that you never meant to make an honourable engagement of it.'

'There, that's just it! You girls expect a man to mean business at the first look. No man when he first becomes interested in a woman has any definite scheme of engagement to marry her in his mind, unless he is meaning a vulgar mercenary marriage. However, I *did* at last mean an honourable engagement, as you call it, come to that.'

'But you never said so, and an indefinite courtship soon injures a woman's position and credit, sooner than you think.'

'Baptista, I solemnly declare that in six months I should have asked you to marry me.'

She walked along in silence, looking on the ground, and appearing very uncomfortable. Presently he said, 'Would you have waited for me if you had known?' To this she whispered in a sorrowful whisper, 'Yes!'

They went still farther in silence – passing along one of the beautiful walks on the outskirts of the town, yet not observant of scene or situation. Her shoulder and his were close together, and he clasped his fingers round the small of her arm – quite lightly, and without any attempt at impetus; yet the act seemed to say, 'Now I hold you, and my will must be yours.'

Recurring to a previous questions of hers he said, 'I have merely run down here for a day or two from school near Trufal, before going off to the North for the rest of my holiday. I have seen my relations at Redrutin quite lately, so I am not going there this time. How little I thought of meeting you! How very different the circumstances would have been if, instead of parting again as we must in half-an-hour or so, possibly for ever, you had been now just going off with me, as my wife, on our honeymoon trip. Ha – ha – well – so humorous is life!'

She stopped suddenly. 'I must go back now – this is altogether too painful, Charley! It is not at all a kind mood you are in today.'

'I don't want to pain you – you know I do not,' he said more gently. 'Only it just exasperates me – this you are going to do. I wish you would not.'

'What?'

'Marry him. There, now I have showed you my true sentiments.'

'I must do it now,' said she.

'Why?' he asked, dropping the off-hand masterful tone he had hitherto spoken in, and becoming earnest; still holding her arm, however, as if she were his chattel to be taken up or put down at will. 'It is never too late to break off a marriage that's distasteful to you. Now I'll say one thing; and it is truth: I wish you would marry me instead of him, even now, at the last moment, though you have served me so badly.'

'O, it is not possible to think of that!' she answered hastily, shaking her head. 'When I get home all will be prepared – it is ready even now – the things for the party, the furniture, Mr Heddegan's new suit, and everything. I should require the courage of a tropical lion to go home there and say I wouldn't carry out my promise!'

'Then go, in Heaven's name! But there would be no necessity for you to go home and face them in that way. If we were to marry, it would have to be at once, instantly; or not at all. I should think your affection not worth the having unless you agreed to come back with me to Trufal this evening, where we could be married by licence on Monday morning. And then no Mr David Heddegan or anybody else could get you away from me.'

'I must go home by the Tuesday boat,' she faltered. 'What would they think if I did not come?'

'You could go home by that boat just the same. All the difference would be that I should go with you. You could leave me on the quay, where I'd have a smoke, while you went and saw your father and mother privately; you could then tell them what you had done, and that I was waiting not far off; that I was a schoolmaster in a fairly good position, and a young man you had known when you were at the Training College. Then I would come boldly forward; and they would see that it could not be altered, and so you wouldn't suffer a lifelong misery by being the wife of a wretched old gaffer you don't like at all. Now, honestly; you do like me best, don't you, Baptista?'

'Yes.'

'Then we will do as I say.'

She did not pronouce a clear affirmative. But that she consented to the novel proposition at some moment or other of that walk was apparent by what occurred a little later.

3

An enterprise of such pith required, indeed, less talking than consideration. The first thing they did in carrying it out was to return to the railway station, where Baptista took from her luggage a small trunk of immediate necessaries which she would in any case have required after missing the boat. That same afternoon they travelled up the line to Trufal.

Charles Stow (as his name was), despite his disdainful indifference to things, was very careful of appearances, and made the journey independently of her though in the same train. He told her where she could get board and lodgings in the city; and with merely a distant nod of her of a provisional kind, went off to his own quarters, and to see about the licence.

On Sunday she saw him in the morning across the nave of the pro-cathedral. In the afternoon they walked together in the fields, where he told her that the licence would be ready next day, and would be available the day after, when the ceremony could be performed as early after eight o'clock as they should choose.

His courtship, thus renewed after an interval of two years, was as impetuous, violent even, as it was short. The next day came and passed, and the final arrangements were made. Their agreement was to get the ceremony over as soon as they possibly could the next morning, so as to go on to Pen-zephyr at once, and reach that place in time for the boat's departure the same day. It was in obedience to Baptista's earnest request that Stow consented thus to make the whole journey to Lyonesse by land and water at one heat, and not break it at Pen-zephyr; she seemed to be oppressed with a dread of lingering anywhere, this great first act of disobedience to her parents once accomplished, with the weight on her mind that her home had to be convulsed by the disclosure of it. To face her difficulties over the water immediately she had created them was, however, a course more desired by Baptista than by her lover; though for once he gave way.

The next morning was bright and warm as those which had preceded it. By six o'clock it seemed nearly noon, as is often the case in that part of England in the summer season. By nine they were husband and wife. They packed up and departed by the earliest train after the service; and on the way discussed at length what she should say on meeting her parents, Charley dictating the turn of each phrase. In her anxiety they had travelled so early that when they reached Pen-zephyr they found there were nearly two hours on their hands before the steamer's time of sailing.

Baptista was extremely reluctant to be seen promenading the streets of the watering-place with her husband till, as above stated, the household at Giant's Town should know the unexpected course of events from her own lips; and it was just possible, if not likely, that some Lyonessian might be prowling about there, or even have come across the sea to look for her. To meet anyone to whom she was known, and to have to reply to awkward questions about the strange young man at her side before her well-framed announcement had been delivered at proper time and place, was a thing she could not contemplate with equanimity. So, instead of looking at the shops and harbour, they went along the coast a little way.

The heat of the morning was by this time intense. They clambered up on some cliffs, and while sitting there, looking around St Michael's Mount and other objects, Charles said to her that he thought he would run down to the beach at their feet, and take just one plunge into the sea.

Baptista did not much like the idea of being left alone; it was gloomy, she said. But he assured her he would not be gone more than a quarter of an hour at the outside, and she passively assented.

Down he went, disappeared, appeared again, and looked back. Then he again proceeded, and vanished, till, as a small waxen object, she saw him emerge from the nook that had screened him, cross the white fringe of foam and walk into the undulating mass of blue. Once in the water he seemed less inclined to hurry than before; he remained a long time; and, unable either to appreciate his skill or criticize his want of it at that distance, she withdrew her eyes from the spot, and gazed at the still outline of St Michael's – now beautifully toned in gray.

Her anxiety for the hour of departure, and to cope at once with the approaching incidents that she would have to manipulate as best she could, sent her into a reverie. It was now Tuesday; she would reach home in the evening – a very late time they would say; but, as the delay was a pure accident, they would deem her marriage to Mr Heddegan tomorrow still practicable. Then Charles would have to be produced from the background. It was a terrible undertaking to think of, and she almost regretted her temerity in wedding so hastily that morning. The rage of her father would be so crushing; the reproaches of her mother so bitter; and perhaps Charles would answer hotly, and perhaps cause estrangement till death. There had obviously been no alarm about her at St Maria's, or somebody would have sailed across to inquire for her. She had, in a letter written at the beginning of the week, spoken of the hour at which she intended to leave her country schoolhouse; and from this her friends had probably perceived that by such timing she would run a risk of losing the Saturday boat. She had missed it, and as a consequence sat here on the shore as Mrs Charles Stow.

This brought her to the present, and she turned from the outline of St Michael's Mount to look about for her husband's form. He was, as far as she could discover, no longer in the sea. Then he was dressing. By moving a few steps she could see where his clothes lay. But Charles was not beside them.

Baptista looked back again at the water in bewilderment, as if her senses were the victim of some sleight of hand. Not a speck or spot resembling a man's head or face showed anywhere. By this time she was alarmed, and her alarm intensified when she perceived a little beyond the scene of her husband's bathing a small area of water, the quality of whose surface differed from that of the surrounding expanse as the coarse vegetation of some foul patch in a mead differs from the fine green of the remainder. Elsewhere it looked flexuous, here it looked vermiculated and lumpy, and her marine experiences suggested to her in a moment that two currents met and caused a turmoil at this place.

She descended as hastily as her trembling limbs would allow. The way down was terribly long, and before reaching the heap of clothes it occurred to her that, after all, it would be best to run first for help. Hastening along in a lateral direction she proceeded inland until she met a man, and soon afterwards two others. To them she exclaimed, 'I think a gentleman who was bathing is in some danger. I cannot see him as I could. Will you please run and help him, at once, if you will be kind?'

She did not think of turning to show them the exact spot, indicating it vaguely by the direction of her hand, and still going on her way with the idea of gaining more assistance. When she deemed, in her faintness, that she had carried the alarm far enough, she faced about and dragged herself back again. Before reaching the now dreaded spot she met one of the men.

'We can see nothing at all, Miss,' he declared.

Having gained the beach, she found the tide in, and no sign of Charley's clothes. The other men whom she had besought to come had disappeared, it must have been in some other direction, for she had not met them going away. They, finding nothing, had probably thought her alarm a mere conjecture, and given up the quest.

Baptista sank down upon the stones near at hand. Where Charley had undressed was now sea. There could not be the least doubt that he was drowned, and his body sucked under by the current; while his clothes, lying within high-water mark, had probably been carried away by the rising tide.

She remained in a stupor for some minutes, till a strange sensation succeeded the aforesaid perceptions, mystifying her intelligence, and leaving her physically almost inert. With his personal disappearance, the last three days of her life with him seemed to be swallowed up, also his image, in her mind's eye, waned curiously, receded far away, grew stranger and stranger, less and less real. Their meeting and marriage had been so sudden, unpremeditated, adventurous, that she could hardly believe that she had played her part in such a reckless drama. Of all the few hours of her life with Charles, the portion that most insisted in coming back to memory was their fortuitous encounter on the previous Saturday, and those bitter reprimands with which he had begun the attack, as it might be called, which had piqued her to an unexpected consummation.

A sort of cruelty, an imperiousness, even in his warmth, had characterized Charles Stow. As a lover he had ever been a bit of a tyrant; and it might pretty truly have been said that he had stung her into marriage with him at last. Still more alien from her life did these reflections operate to make him; and then they would be chased away by an interval of passionate weeping and mad regret. Finally, there returned upon the confused mind of the young wife the recollection that she was on her way homeward, and that the packet would sail in three-quarters of an hour.

Except the parasol in her hand, all she possessed was at the station awaiting her onward journey.

She looked in that direction; and, entering one of those undemonstrative phases so common with her, walked quietly on.

At first she made straight for the railway; but suddenly turning she went to a shop and wrote an anonymous line announcing his death by drowning to the only person she had ever heard Charles mention as a relative. Posting this stealthily, and with a fearful look around her, she seemed to acquire a terror of the late events, pursuing her way to the station as if followed by a spectre.

When she got to the office she asked for the luggage that she had left there on the Saturday as well as the trunk left on the morning just lapsed. All were put in the boat, and she herself followed. Quickly as these things had been done, the whole proceeding, nevertheless, had been almost automatic on Baptista's part, ere she had come to any definite conclusion on her course.

Just before the bell rang she heard a conversation on the pier, which removed the last shade of doubt from her mind, if any had existed, that she was Charles Stow's widow. The sentences were but fragmentary, but she could easily piece them out.

'A man drowned – swam out too far – was a stranger to the place – people in boat – saw him go down – couldn't get there in time.'

The news was little more definite than this as yet; though it may as well be stated once for all that the statement was true. Charley, with the over-confidence of his nature, had ventured out too far for his strength, and succumbed in the absence of assistance, his lifeless body being at that moment suspended in the transparent mid-depths of the bay. His clothes, however, had merely been gently lifted by the rising tide, and floated into a nook hard by, where they lay out of sight of the passers-by till a day or two after.

4

In ten minutes they were steaming out of the harbour for their voyage of four or five hours, at whose ending she would have to tell her strange story.

As Pen-zephyr and all its environing scenes disappeared behind Mousehole and St Clement's Isle, Baptista's ephemeral, meteor-like husband impressed her yet more as a fantasy. She was still in such a trance-like state that she had been an hour on the little packet-boat before she became aware of the agitating fact that Mr Heddegan was on board with her. Involuntarily she slipped from her left hand the symbol of her wifehood.

'Hee-hee! Well, the truth is, I wouldn't interrupt 'ee. "I reckon she don't see me, or won't see me," I said, "and what's the hurry? She'll see enough o' me soon!" I hope ye be well, mee deer?'

He was a hale, well-conditioned man of about five-and-fifty, of the complexion common to those who lives are passed on the bluffs and beaches of an ocean isle. He extended the four quarters of his face in a genial smile, and his hand for a grasp of the same magnitude. She gave her own in surprised docility, and he continued:

'I couldn't help coming across to meet 'ee. What an unfortunate thing you missing the boat and not coming Saturday! They meant to have warned 'ee that the time was changed, but forgot it at the last moment. The truth is that I should have informed 'ee myself, but I was that busy finishing up a job last week, so as to have this week free, that I trusted to your father to attending to these little things. However, so plain and quiet as it is all to be, it really do not matter so much as it might otherwise have done, and I hope ye haven't been greatly put out. Now, if you'd sooner that I should not be seen talking to 'ee – if 'ee feel shy at all before strangers – just say. I'll leave 'ee to yourself till we get home.'

'Thank you much. I am indeed a little tired, Mr Heddegan.'

He nodded urbane acquiescence, strolled away immediately, and minutely inspected the surface of the funnel, till some female passengers of Giant's Town tittered at what they must have thought a rebuff – for the approaching wedding was known to many on St Maria's Island, though to nobody elsewhere. Baptista coloured at their satire, and called him back, and forced herself to commune with him in at least a mechanically friendly manner.

The opening event had been thus different from her expectation, and she had adumbrated no act to meet it. Taken aback, she passively allowed circumstances to pilot her along; and so the voyage was made.

It was near dusk when they touched the pier of Giant's Town, where several friends and neighbours stood awaiting them. Her father had a lantern in his hand. Her mother, too, was there, reproachfully glad that the delay had at last ended so simply. Mrs Trewthen and her daughter went together along the Giant's Walk, or promenade, to the house, rather in advance of her husband and Mr Heddegan, who talked in loud tones which reached the women over their shoulders.

Some would have called Mrs Trewthen a good mother; but though well-meaning she was maladroit, and her intentions missed their mark. This might have been partly attributable to the slight deafness from which she suffered. Now, as usual, the chief utterances came from her lips.

'Ah, yes, I'm so glad, my child, that you've got over safe. It is all ready, and everything so well arranged, that nothing but misfortune could hinder you settling as, with God's grace, becomes 'ee. Close to your mother's door a'most, 'twill be a great blessing, I'm sure; and I was very glad to find from your letters that you'd held your word sacred. That's right – make your word your bond always. Mrs Wace seems to be a sensible woman. I hope the Lord will do for her as he's doing for you no long time hence. And how did 'ee get over the terrible journey from Tor-upon-Sea to Pen-zyphyr? Once you'd done with the railway, of course, you seemed quite at home. Well, Baptista, conduct yourself seemly, and all will be well.'

Thus admonished, Baptista entered the house, her father and Mr Heddegan immediately at her back. Her mother had been so didactic that she had felt herself absolutely unable to broach the subjects in the centre of her mind.

The familiar room, with the dark ceiling, the well-spread table, the old chairs, had never before spoken so eloquently of the times ere she knew or had heard of Charley Stow. She went upstairs to take off her things, her mother remaining below to complete the disposition of the supper, and attend to the preparation of tomorrow's meal, altogether composing such an array of pies, from pies of fish to pies of turnips, as was never heard of outside the Western Duchy. Baptista, once alone, sat down and did nothing; and was called before she had taken off her bonnet.

'I'm coming,' she cried, jumping up, and speedily disapparelling herself, brushed her hair with a few touches and went down.

Two or three of Mr Heddegan's and her father's friends had dropped in, and expressed their sympathy for the delay she had been subjected to. The meal was a most merry one except to Baptista. She had desired privacy, and there was none; and to break the news was already a greater difficulty than it had been at first. Everything around her, animate and inanimate, great and small, insisted that she had come home to be married; and she could not get a chance to say nay.

One or two people sang songs, as overtures to the melody of the morrow, till at length bedtime came, and they all withdrew, her mother having retired a little earlier. When Baptista found herself again alone in her bedroom the case stood as before: she had come home with much to say, and she had said nothing.

It was now growing clear even to herself that Charles being dead, she had not determination sufficient within her to break tidings which, had he been alive, would have imperatively announced themselves. And thus with the stroke of midnight came the turning of the scale; her story should remain untold. It was not that upon the whole she thought it best not to attempt to tell it; but that she could not undertake so explosive a matter. To stop the wedding now would cause a convulsion in Giant's Town little short of volcanic. Weakened, tired, and terrified as she had been by the day's adventures, she could not make herself the author of such a catastrophe. But how refuse Heddegan without telling? It really seemed to her as if her marriage with Mr Heddegan were about to take place as if nothing had intervened.

Morning came. The events of the previous days were cut off from her present existence by scene and sentiment more completely than ever. Charles Stow had grown to be a special being of whom, owing to his character, she entertained rather fearful than loving memory. Baptista could hear when she awoke that her parents were already moving about downstairs. But she did not rise till her mother's rather rough voice resounded up the staircase as it had done on the preceding evening.

'Baptista! Come, time to be stirring! The man will be here, by Heaven's blessing, in three-quarters of an hour. He has looked in already for a minute or two – and says he's going to the church to see if things be well forward.'

Baptista arose, looked out of the window, and took the easy course. When she emerged from the regions above she was arrayed in her new silk frock and best stockings, wearing a linen jacket over the former for breakfasting, and her common slippers over the latter, not to spoil the new ones on the rough precincts of the dwelling.

It is unnecessary to dwell at any length on this part of the morning's proceedings. She revealed nothing; and married Heddegan, as she had given her word to do, on that appointed August day.

5

Mr Heddegan forgave the coldness of his bride's manner during and after the wedding ceremony, full well aware that there had been considerable reluctance on her part to acquiesce in this neighbourly arrangement, and, as a philosoher of long standing, holding that whatever Baptista's attitude now, the conditions would probably be much the same six months hence as those which ruled among other married couples.

An absolutely unexpected shock was given to Baptista's listless mind about an hour after the wedding service. They had nearly finished the midday dinner when the now husband said to her father, 'We think of starting about two. And the breeze being so fair we shall bring up inside Pen-zephyr new pier about six at least.'

'What – are we going to Pen-zephyr?' said Baptista. 'I don't know anything of it.'

'Didn't you tell her?' asked her father of Heddegan.

It transpired that, owing to the delay in her arrival, this proposal too, among other things, had in the hurry not been mentioned to her, except some time ago as a general suggestion that they would go somewhere. Heddegan had imagined that any trip would be pleasant, and one to the mainland the pleasantest of all.

She looked so distressed at the announcement that her husband willingly offered to give it up, though he had not had a holiday off the island for a whole year. Then she pondered on the inconvenience of staying at Giant's Town, where all the inhabitants were bonded, by the circumstances of their situation, into a sort of family party, which permitted and encouraged on such occasions as these oral criticism that was apt to disturb the equanimity of newly married girls, and would especially worry Baptista in her strange situation. Hence, unexpectedly, she agreed not to disorganize her husband's plans for the wedding jaunt, and it was settled that, as originally intended, they should proceed in a neighbour's sailing boat to the metropolis of the district.

In this way they arrived at Pen-zephyr without difficulty or mishap. Bidding adieu to Jenkin and his man, who had sailed them over, they strolled arm in arm off the pier, Baptista silent, cold, and obedient. Heddegan had arranged to take her as far as Plymouth before their return, but to go no further than where they had landed that day. Their first business was to find an inn; and in this they had unexpected difficulty, since for some reason or other – possibly the fine weather – many of the nearest at hand were full of tourists and commercial travellers. He led her on till he reached a tavern which, though comparatively unpretending, stood in as attractive a spot as any in the town; and this, somewhat to their surprise after their previous experience, they found apparently empty. The considerate old man, thinking that Baptista was educated to artistic notions, though he himself was deficient in them, had decided that it was most desirable to have, on such an occasion as the present, an apartment with 'a good view' (the expression being one he had often heard in use among tourists); and he therefore asked for a favourite room on the first floor, from which a bow-window protruded, for the express purpose of affording such an outlook.

The landlady, after some hesitation, said she was sorry that particular apartment was engaged; the next one, however, or any other in the house, was unoccupied.

'The gentleman who has the best one will give it up tomorrow, and then you can change into it,' she added, as Mr Heddegan hesitated about taking the adjoining and less commanding one.

'We shall be gone tomorrow, and shan't want it,' he said.

Wishing not to lose customers, the landlady earnestly continued that since he was bent on having the best room, perhaps the other gentleman would not object to move at once into the one they despised, since, though nothing could be seen from the window, the room was equally large.

'Well, if he doesn't care for a view,' said Mr Heddegan, with the air of a highly artistic man who did.

'O no – I am sure he doesn't,' she said. 'I can promise that you shall have the room you want. If you would not object to go for a walk for half-an-hour, I could have it ready, and your things in it, and a nice tea laid in the bow-window by the time you come back?'

This proposal was deemed satisfactory by the fussy old tradesman, and they went out. Baptista nervously conducted him in an opposite direction to her walk of the former day in other company, showing on her wan face, had he observed it, how much she was beginning to regret her sacrificial step for mending matters that morning.

She took advantage of a moment when her husband's back was turned to inquire casually in a shop if anything had been heard of the gentleman who was sucked down in the eddy while bathing.

The shopman said, 'Yes, his body has been washed ashore,' and had just handed Baptista a newspaper on which she discerned the heading, 'A Schoolmaster drowned while bathing', when her husband turned to join her. She might have pursued the subject without raising suspicion; it was more than flesh and blood could do, and completing a small purchase she almost ran out of the shop.

'What is your terrible hurry, mee deer?' said Heddegan, hastening after.

'I don't know – I don't want to stay in shops,' she gasped.

'And we won't,' he said. 'They are suffocating this weather. Let's go back and have some tay!'

They found the much desired apartment awaiting their entry. It was a sort of combination bed- and sitting-room, and the table was prettily spread with high tea in the bow-window, a bunch of flowers in the midst, and a best-parlour chair on each side. Here they shared the meal by the ruddy light of the vanishing sun. But though the view had been engaged, regardless of expense, exclusively for Baptista's pleasure, she did not direct any keen attention out of the window. Her gaze as often fell on the floor and walls of the room as elsewhere, and on the table as much as on either, beholding nothing at all.

But there was a change. Opposite her seat was the door, upon which her eyes presently became riveted like those of a little bird upon a snake. For, on a peg at the back of the door, there hung a hat; such a hat – surely, from its peculiar make, the actual hat – that had been worn by Charles. Conviction grew to certainty when she saw a railway ticket sticking up from the band. Charles had put the ticket there – she had noticed the act.

Her teeth almost chattered; she murmured something incoherent. Her husband jumped up and said, 'You are not well! What is it? What shall I get 'ee?'

'Smelling salts!' she said, quickly and desperately; 'at the chemist's shop you were in just now.'

He jumped up like the anxious old man that he was, caught up his own hat from a back table, and without observing the other hastened out and downstairs.

Left alone she gazed and gazed at the back of the door, then spasmodically rang the bell. An honest-looking country maid-servant appeared in response.

'A hat!' murmured Baptista, pointing with her finger. 'It does not belong to us.'

'O yes, I'll take it away,' said the young woman with some hurry. 'It belongs to the other gentleman.'

She spoke with a certain awkwardness, and took the hat out of the room. Baptista had recovered her outward composure. 'The other gentleman?' she said. 'Where is the other gentleman?'

'He's in the next room, ma'am. He removed out of this to oblige 'ee.'

'How can you say so? I should hear him if he were there,' said Baptista, sufficiently recovered to argue down an apparent untruth.

'He's there,' said the girl, hardily.

'Then it is strange that he makes no noise,' said Mrs Heddegan, convicting the girl of falsity by a look.

'He makes no noise; but it is not strange,' said the servant.

All at once a dread took possession of the bride's heart, like a cold hand laid thereon; for it flashed upon her that there was a possibility of reconciling the girl's statement with her own knowledge of facts.

'Why does he make no noise?' she weakly said.

The waiting-maid was silent, and looked at her questioner. 'If I tell you, ma'am, you won't tell missis?' she whispered.

Baptista promised.

'Because he's a-lying dead!' said the girl. 'He's the schoolmaster that was drowned yesterday.'

'O!' said the bride, covering her eyes. 'Then he was in this room till just now?'

'Yes,' said the maid, thinking the young lady's agitation natural enough. 'And I told missis that I thought she oughtn't to have done it, because I don't hold it right to keep visitors so much in the dark where death's concerned; but she said the gentleman didn't die of anything infectious; she was a poor, honest, innkeeper's wife, she says, who had to get her living by making hay while the sun sheened. And owing to the drownded gentleman being brought here, she said, it kept so many people away that we were empty, though all the other houses were full. So when your good man set his mind upon the room, and she would have lost good paying folk if he'd not had it, it wasn't to be supposed, she said, that she'd let anything stand in the way. Ye won't say that I've told ye, please, m'm? All the linen has been changed, and as the inquest won't be till tomorrow, after you are gone, she thought you wouldn't know a word of it, being strangers here.'

The returning footsteps of her husband broke off further narration. Baptista waved her hand, for she could not speak. The waiting-maid quickly withdrew, and Mr Heddegan entered with the smelling salts and other nostrums.

'Any better?' he questioned.

'I don't like the hotel,' she exclaimed, almost simultaneously. 'I can't bear it – it doesn't suit me!'

'Is that all that's the matter?' he returned pettishly (this being the first time of his showing such a mood). 'Upon my heart and life such trifling is trying to any man's temper, Baptista! Sending me about from here to yond, and then when I come back saying 'ee don't like the place that I have sunk so much money and words to get for 'ee. 'Od dang it all, 'tis enough to— But I won't say any more at present, mee deer, though it is just too much to expect to turn out of the house now. We shan't get another quiet place at this time of the evening – every other inn in the town is bustling with rackety folk of one sort and t'other, while here 'tis as quiet as the grave – the country, I would say. So bide still, d'ye hear, and tomorrow we shall be out of the town altogether – as early as you like.'

The obstinacy of age had, in short, overmastered its complaisance, and the young woman said no more. The simple course of telling him that in the adjoining room lay a corpse which had lately occupied their own might, it would have seemed, have been an effectual one without further disclosure, but to allude to *that* subject, however it was disguised, was more than Heddegan's young wife had strength for. Horror broke her down. In the contingency one thing only presented itself to her paralyzed regard – that here she was doomed to abide, in a hideous contiguity to the dead husband and the living, and her conjecture did, in fact, bear itself out. That night she lay between the two men she had married – Heddegan on the one hand, and on the other through the partition against which the bed stood, Charles Stow.

6

Kindly time had withdrawn the foregoing event three days from the present of Baptista Heddegan. It was ten o'clock in the morning; she had been ill, not in an ordinary or definite sense, but in a state of cold stupefaction, from which it was difficulty to arouse her so much as to say a few sentences. When questioned she had replied that she was pretty well.

Their trip, as such, had been something of a failure. They had gone on as far as Falmouth, but here he had given way to her entreaties to return home. This they could not very well do without repassing through Penzephyr, at which place they had now again arrived.

In the train she had seen a weekly local paper, and read there a paragraph detailing the inquest on Charles. It was added that the funeral was to take place at his native town of Redrutin on Friday.

After reading this she had shown no reluctance to enter the fatal neighbourhood of the tragedy, only stipulating that they should take their rest at a different lodging from the first; and now comparatively braced up and calm – indeed a cooler creature altogether than when last in the town, she said to David that she wanted to walk out for a while, as they had plenty of time on their hands.

'To a shop as usual, I suppose, mee deer?'

'Partly for shopping,' she said. 'And it will be best for you, dear, to stay in after trotting about so much, and have a good rest while I am gone.'

He assented; and Baptista sallied forth. As she had stated, her first visit was made to a shop, a draper's. Without the exercise of much choice she purchased a black bonnet and veil, also a black stuff gown; a black mantle she already wore. These articles were made up into a parcel which, in spite of the salewoman's offers, her customer said she would take with her. Bearing it on her arm she turned to the railway, and at the station got a ticket for Redrutin.

Thus it appeared that, on her recovery from the paralyzed mood of the former day, while she had resolved not to blast utterly the happiness of her present husband by revealing the history of the departed one, she had also determined to indulge a certain odd, inconsequent, feminine sentiment of decency, to the small extent to which it could do harm to any person. At Redrutin she emerged from the railway carriage in the black attire purchased at the shop, having during the transit made the change in the empty compartment she had chosen. The other clothes were now in the bandbox and parcel. Leaving these at the cloak-room she proceeded onward, and after a wary survey reached the side of a hill whence a view of the burial ground could be obtained.

It was now a little before two o'clock. While Baptista waited a funeral procession ascended the road. Baptista hastened across, and by the time the procession entered the cemetery gates she had unobtrusively joined it.

In addition to the schoolmaster's own relatives (not a few), the paragraph in the newspapers of his death by drowning had drawn together many neighbours, acquaintances, and onlookers. Among them she passed unnoticed, and with a quiet step pursued the winding path to the chapel, and afterwards thence to the grave. When all was over, and the relatives and idlers had withdrawn, she stepped to the edge of the chasm. From beneath her mantle she drew a little bunch of forget-me-nots, and dropped them in upon the coffin. In a few minutes she also turned and went away from the cemetery. By five o'clock she was again in Pen-zephyr.

'You have been a mortal long time!' said her husband, crossly. 'I allowed you an hour at most, mee deer.'

'It occupied me longer,' said she.

'Well – I reckon it is wasting words to complain. Hang it, ye look so tired and wisht that I can't find heart to say what I would!'

'I am – weary and wisht, David; I am. We can get home tomorrow for certain, I hope?'

'We can. And please God we will!' said Mr Heddegan heartily, as if he too were weary of his brief honeymoon. 'I must be into business again on Monday morning at latest.'

They left by the next morning steamer, and in the afternoon took up their residence in their own house at Giant's Town.

The hour that she reached the island it was as if a material weight had been removed from Baptista's shoulders. Her husband attributed the change to the influence of the local breezes after the hot-house atmos-phere of the mainland. However that might be, settled here, a few doors from her mother's dwelling, she recovered in no very long time much of her customary bearing, which was never very demonstrative. She accepted her position calmly, and faintly smiled when her neighbours learned to call her Mrs Heddegan, and said she seemed likely to become the leader of fashion in Giant's Town.

Her husband was a man who had made considerably more money by trade than her father had done: and perhaps the greater profusion of surroundings at her command than she had heretofore been mistress of, was not without an effect upon her. One week, two weeks, three weeks passed; and, being pre-eminently a young woman who allowed things to drift, she did nothing whatever to disclose or conceal traces of her first marriage; or to learn if there existed possibilities – which there undoubtedly did – by which that hasty contract might become revealed to those about her at any unexpected moment.

While yet within the first month of her marriage, and on an evening just before sunset, Baptista was standing within her garden adjoining the house, when she saw passing along the road a personage clad in a greasy black coat and battered tall hat, which, common enough in the slums of a city, had an odd appearance in St Maria's. The tramp, as he seemed to be, marked her at once – bonnetless and unwrapped as she was her features were plainly recognizable – and with an air of friendly surprise came and leant over the wall.

'What! don't you know me?' said he.

She had some dim recollection of his face, but said that she was not acquainted with him.

'Why, your witness to be sure, ma'am. Don't you mind the man that was mending the church-window when you and your intended husband walked up to be made one; and the clerk called me down from the ladder, and I came and did my part by writing my name and occupation?'

Baptista glanced quickly around; her husband was out of earshot. That would have been of less importance but for the fact that the wedding witnessed by this personage had not been the wedding with Mr Heddegan, but the one on the day previous.

'I've had a misfortune since then, that's pulled me under,' continued her friend. 'But don't let me damp yer wedded joy by naming the particulars. Yes, I've seen changes since; though 'tis but a short time ago – let me see, only a month next week, I think; for 'twere the first or second day in August.'

'Yes – that's when it was,' said another man, a sailor, who had come up with a pipe in his mouth, and felt it necessary to join in (Baptista having receded to escape further speech). 'For that was the first time I set foot in Giant's town; and her husband took her to him the same day.'

A dialogue then proceeded between the two men outside the wall, which Baptista could not help overhearing.

'Ay, I signed the book that made her one flesh,' repeated the decayed glazier. 'Where's her goodman?'

'About the premises somewhere; but you don't see 'em together much,' replied the sailor in an undertone. 'You see, he's older than she.'

'Older? I should never have thought it from my own observation,' said the glazier. 'He was a remarkably handsome man.'

'Handsome? Well, there he is – we can see for ourselves.'

David Heddegan had, indeed, just shown himself at the upper end of the garden; and the glazier, looking in bewilderment from the husband to the wife, saw the latter turn pale.

Now that decayed glazier was a far-seeing and cunning man – too far-seeing and cunning to allow himself to thrive by simple and straightforward means – and he held his peace, till he could read more plainly the meaning of this riddle, merely adding carelessly, 'Well – marriage do alter a man, 'tis true. I should never ha' knowed him!'

He then stared oddly at the disconcerted Baptista, and moving on to where he could again address her, asked her to do him a good turn, since he once had done the same for her. Understanding that he meant money, she handed him some, at which he thanked her, and instantly went away.

7

She had escaped exposure on this occasion; but the incident had been an awkward one, and should have suggested to Baptista that sooner or later the secret must leak out. As it was, she suspected that at any rate she had not heard the last of the glazier.

In a day or two, when her husband had gone to the old town on the other side of the island, there came a gentle tap at the door, and the worthy witness of her first marriage made his appearance a second time.

'It took me hours to get to the bottom of the mystery – hours!' he said with a gaze of deep confederacy which offended her pride very deeply. 'But thanks to a good intellect I've done it. Now, ma'am, I'm not a man to tell tales, even when a tale would be so good as this. But I'm going back to the mainland again, and a little assistance would be as rain on thirsty ground.'

'I helped you two days ago,' began Baptista.

'Yes – but what was that, my good lady? Not enough to pay for my passage to Pen-zephyr. I came over on your account, for I thought there was a mystery somewhere. Now I must go back on my own. Mind this – 'twould be very awkward for you if your old man were to know. He's a queer temper, though he may be fond.'

She knew as well as her visitor how awkward it would be; and the hush-money she paid was heavy that day. She had, however, the satisfaction of watching the man to the steamer, and seeing him diminish out of sight. But Baptista perceived that the system into which she had been led of purchasing silence thus was one fatal to her peace of mind, particularly if it had to be continued.

Hearing no more from the glazier she hoped the difficulty was past. But another week only had gone by, when, as she was pacing the Giant's Walk (the name given to the promenade), she met the same personage in the company of a fat woman carrying a bundle.

'This is the lady, my dear,' he said to his companion. 'This, ma'am, is my wife. We've come to settle in the town for a time, if so be we can find room.'

'That you won't do,' said she. 'Nobody can live here who is not privileged.'

'I am privileged,' said the glazier, 'by my trade.'

Baptista went on, but in the afternoon she received a visit from the man's wife. This honest woman began to depict, in forcible colours, the necessity for keeping up the concealment.

'I will intercede with my husband, ma'am,' she said. 'He's a true man if rightly managed; and I'll beg him to consider your position. 'Tis a very nice house you've got here,' she added, glancing round, 'and well worth a little sacrifice to keep it.'

The unlucky Baptista staved off the danger on this third occasion as she had done on the previous two. But she formed a resolve that, if the attack were once more to be repeated, she would face a revelation – worse though that must now be than before she had attempted to purchase silence by bribes. Her tormentors, never believing her capable of acting upon such an intention, came again; but she shut the door in their faces. They retreated, muttering something; but she went to the back of the house, where David Heddegan was.

She looked at him, unconscious of all. The case was serious; she knew that well; and all the more serious in that she liked him better now than she had done at first. Yet, as she herself began to see, the secret was one that was sure to disclose itself. Her name and Charles's stood indelibly written in the registers; and though a month only had passed as yet it was a wonder that his clandestine union with her had not already been discovered by his friends. Thus spurring herself to the inevitable, she spoke to Heddegan.

'David, come indoors. I have something to tell you.'

He hardly regarded her at first. She had discerned that during the last week or two he had seemed preoccupied, as if some private business harassed him. She repeated her request. He replied with a sigh, 'Yes, certainly, mee deer.'

When they had reached the sitting-room and shut the door she repeated, faintly. 'David I have something to tell you – a sort of tragedy I have concealed. You will hate me for having so far deceived you; but perhaps my telling you voluntarily will make you think a little better of me than you would do otherwise.'

'Tragedy?' he said, awakening to interest. 'Much you can know about tragedies, mee deer, that have been in the world so short a time!'

She saw that he suspected nothing, and it make her task the harder. But on she went steadily. 'It is about something that happened before we were married,' she said.

'Indeed!'

'Not a very long time before – a short time. And it is about a lover,' she faltered.

'I don't much mind that,' he said mildly. 'In truth, I was in hopes 'twas more.'

'In hopes!'

'Well, yes.'

This screwed her up to the necessary effort. 'I met my old sweetheart. He scorned me, chid me, dared me, and I went and married him. We were coming straight here to tell you all what we had done; but he was drowned; and I thought I would say nothing about him: and I married you, David, for the sake of peace and quietness. I've tried to keep it from you, but have found I cannot. There – that's the substance of it, and you can never, never forgive me, I am sure!'

She spoke desperately. But the old man, instead of turning black or blue, or slaying her in his indignation, jumped up from his chair, and began to caper around the room in quite an ecstatic emotion.

'O, happy thing! How well it falls out!' he exclaimed, snapping his fingers over his head. 'Ha-ha – the knot is cut – I see a way out of my trouble – ha-ha!'

He looked at him without uttering a sound, till, as he still continued smiling joyfully, she said, 'O – what do you mean? Is it done to torment me?'

'No – no! O, mee deer, your story helps me out of the most heart-aching quandary a poor man ever found himself in! You see, it is this – *I've* got a tragedy, too; and unless you had had one to tell, I could never have seen my way to tell mine!'

'What is yours – what is it?' she asked, with altogether a new view of things.

'Well – it is a bouncer; mine is a bouncer!' said he, looking on the ground and wiping his eyes.

'Not worse than mine?'

'Well – that depends upon how you look at it. Yours had to do with the past alone; and I don't mind it. You see, we've been married a month, and it don't jar upon me as it would if we'd only been married a day or two. Now mine refers to past, present, and future; so that—'

'Past, present, and future!' she murmured. 'It never occurred to me that *you* had a tragedy too.'

'But I have!' he said, shaking his head. 'In fact, four.'

'Then tell 'em!' cried the young woman.

'I will – I will. But be considerate, I beg 'ee, mee deer. Well – I wasn't a bachelor when I married 'ee, any more than you were a spinster. Just as you was a widow-woman, I was a widow-man.'

'Ah!' said she, with some surprise. 'But is that all? – then we are nicely balanced,' she added, relieved.

'No – it is not all. There's the point. I am not only a widower.'

'O, David!'

'I am a widower with four tragedies – that is to say, four strapping girls – the eldest taller than you. Don't 'ee look so struck – dumb-like! It fell out in this way. I knew the poor woman, their mother, in Pen-zephyr for some years; and – to cut a long story short– I privately married her at last, just before she died. I kept the matter secret, but it is getting known among the people here by degrees. I've long felt for the children – that it is my duty to have them here, and do something for them. I have not had courage to break it to 'ee, but I've seen lately that it would soon come to your ears, and that hev worried me.'

'Are they educated?' said the ex-schoolmistress.

'No. I am sorry to say they have been much neglected; in truth, they can hardly read. And so I thought that by marrying a young schoolmistress I should get some one in the house who could teach 'em, and bring 'em into genteel condition, all for nothing. You see, they are growed up too tall to be sent to school.'

'O, mercy!' she almost moaned. 'Four great girls to teach the rudiments to, and have always in the house with me spelling over their books; and I hate teaching, it kills me. I am bitterly punished – I am, I am!'

'You'll get used to 'em, mee deer, and the balance of secrets – mine against yours – will comfort your heart with a sense of justice. I could send for 'em this week very well – and I will! In faith, I could send this very day. Baptista, you have relieved me of all my difficulty!'

Thus the interview ended, so far as this matter was concerned. Baptista was too stupefied to say more, and when she went away to her room she wept from the very mortification at Mr Heddegan's duplicity. Education, the one thing she abhorred; the shame of it to delude a young wife so!

The next meal came round. As they sat, Baptista would not suffer her eyes to turn towards him. He did not attempt to intrude upon her reserve, but every now and then looked under the table and chuckled with satisfaction at the aspect of affairs. 'How very well matched we be!' he said, comfortably.

Next day, when the steamer came in, Baptista saw her husband rush down to meet it; and soon after there appeared at her door four tall, hipless, shoulderless girls, dwindling in height and size from the eldest to the youngest, like a row of Pan pipes; at the head of them standing Heddegan. He smiled pleasantly through the gray fringe of his whiskers and beard, and turning to the girls said, 'Now come forrard, and shake hands properly with your stepmother.'

Thus she made their acquaintance, and he went out, leaving them together. On examination the poor girls turned out to be not only plain-looking, which she could have forgiven, but to have such a lamentably meagre intellectual equipment as to be hopelessly inadequate as companions. Even the eldest, almost her own age, could only read with difficulty words of two syllables; and taste in dress was beyond their comprehension. In the long vista of future years she saw nothing but dreary drudgery at her detested old trade without prospect of reward.

She went about quite despairing during the next few days – an unpromising, unfortunate mood for a woman who had not been married six weeks. From her parents she concealed everything. They had been amongst the few acquaintances of Heddegan who knew nothing of his secret, and were indignant enough when they saw such a ready-made household foisted upon their only child. But she would not support them in their remonstrances.

'No, you don't yet know all,' she said.

Thus Baptista had sense enough to see the retributive fairness of this issue. For some time, whenever conversation arose between her and Heddegan, which was not often, she always said, 'I am miserable, and you know it. Yet I don't wish things to be otherwise.'

But one day when he asked, 'How do you like 'em now?' her answer was unexpected. 'Much better than I did,' she said, quietly. 'I may like them very much some day.'

This was the beginning of a serener season for the chastened spirit of Baptista Heddegan. She had, in truth, discovered, underneath the crust of uncouthness and meagre articulation which was due to their Troglodytean existence, that her unwelcomed daughters had natures that were unselfish almost to sublimity. The harsh discipline accorded to their young lives before their mother's wrong had been righted, had operated less to crush them than to lift them above all personal ambition. They considered the world and its contents in a purely objective way, and their own lot seemed only to affect them as that of certain human beings among the rest, whose troubles they knew rather than suffered.

This was such an entirely new way of regarding life to a woman of Baptista's nature, that her attention, from being first arrested by it, became deeply interested. By imperceptible pulses her heart expanded in sympathy with theirs. The sentences of her tragi-comedy, her life, confused till now, became clearer daily. That in humanity, as exemplified by these girls, there was nothing to dislike, but infinitely much to pity, she learnt with the lapse of each week in their company. She grew to like the girls of unpromising exterior, and from liking she got to love them; till they formed an unexpected point of junction between her own and her husband's interests, generating a sterling friendship at least, between a pair whose existence there had threatened to be neither friendship nor love.

OCTOBER 1885

THE ROMANTIC ADVENTURES OF A MILKMAID

I

It was half-past four o'clock (by the testimony of the land-surveyor, my authority for the particulars of this story, a gentleman with the faintest curve of humour on his lips); it was half-past four o'clock on a May morning in the eighteen-forties. A dense white fog hung over the Valley of the Exe, ending against the hills on either side.

But though nothing in the vale could be seen from higher ground, notes of differing kinds gave pretty clear indications that bustling life was going on there. This audible presence and visual absence of an active scene had a peculiar effect above the fog level. Nature had laid a white hand over the creatures ensconced within the vale, as a hand might be laid over a nest of chirping birds.

The noises that ascended through the pallid coverlid were perturbed lowings, mingled with human voices in sharps and flats, and the bark of a dog. These, followed by the slamming of a gate, explained as well as eyesight could have done, to any inhabitant of the district, that Dairyman Tucker's under-milker was driving the cows from the meads into the stalls. When a rougher accent joined in the vociferations of man and beast, it would have been realized that the dairy-farmer himself had come out to meet the cows, pail in hand, and white pinafore on; and when, moreover, some women's voices joined in the chorus, that the cows were stalled and proceedings about to commence.

A hush followed, the atmosphere being so stagnant that the milk could be heard buzzing into the pails, together with occasional words of the milkmaids and men.

'Don't ye bide about long upon the road, Margery. You can be back again by skimming-time.'

The rough voice of Dairyman Tucker was the vehicle of this remark. The barton-gate slammed again, and in two or three minutes a something became visible, rising out of the fog in that quarter.

The shape revealed itself as that of a woman having a young and agile gait. The colours and other details of her dress were then disclosed –

a bright pink cotton frock (because winter was over); a small woollen shawl of shepherd's plaid (because summer was not yet come); a white handkerchief tied over her head-gear, because it was so foggy, so damp, and so early; and a straw bonnet and ribbons peeping from under the handkerchief, because it was likely to be a sunny May day.

Her face was of the hereditary type among families down in these parts: sweet in expression, perfect in hue, and somewhat irregular in feature. Her eyes were of a liquid brown. On her arm she carried a withy basket, in which lay several butter-rolls in a nest of wet cabbage-leaves. She was the 'Margery' who had been told not to 'bide about long upon the road'.

She went on her way across the fields, sometimes above the fog, sometimes below it, not much perplexed by its presence except when the track was so indefinite that it ceased to be a guide to the next stile. The dampness was such that innumerable earthworms lay in couples across the path till, startled even by her light tread, they withdrew suddenly into their holes. She kept clear of all trees. Why was that? There was no danger of lightning on such a morning as this. But though the roads were dry the fog had gathered in the boughs, causing them to set up such a dripping as would go clean through the protecting handkerchief like bullets, and spoil the ribbons beneath. The beech and ash were particularly shunned, for they dripped more maliciously than any. It was an instance of woman's keen appreciativeness of Nature's moods and peculiarities: a man crossing those fields might hardly have perceived that the trees dripped at all.

In less than an hour she had traversed a distance of four miles, and arrived at a latticed cottage in a secluded spot. An elderly woman, scarce awake, answered her knocking. Margery delivered up the butter, and said, 'How is granny this morning? I can't stay to go up to her, but tell her I have returned what we owed her.'

Her grandmother was no worse than usual: and receiving back the empty basket the girl proceeded to carry out some intention which had not been included in her orders. Instead of returning to the light labours of skimming-time, she hastened on, her direction being towards a little neighbouring town. Before, however, Margery had proceeded far, she met the postman, laden to the neck with letter-bags, of which he had not yet deposited one.

'Are the shops open yet, Samuel?' she said.

'O no,' replied that stooping pedestrian, not waiting to stand upright. 'They won't be open yet this hour, except the saddler and ironmonger and little tacker-haired machine-man for the farm folk. They downs their shutters at half-past six, then the baker's at half-past seven, then the draper's at eight.'

'O, the draper's at eight.' It was plain that Margery had wanted the draper's.

The postman turned up a side-path, and the young girl, as though deciding within herself that if she could not go shopping at once she might as well get back for the skimming, retraced her steps.

The public road home from this point was easy but devious. By far the nearest way was by getting over the fence, and crossing the private grounds of a picturesque old country-house, whose chimneys were just visible through the trees. As the house had been shut up for many months, the girl decided to take the straight cut. She pushed her way through the laurel bushes, sheltering her bonnet with the shawl as an additional safeguard, scrambled over an inner boundary, went along through more shrubberies, and stood ready to emerge upon the open lawn. Before doing so she looked around in the wary manner of a poacher. It was not the first time that she had broken fence in her life; but somehow, and all of a sudden, she had felt herself too near womanhood to indulge in such practices with freedom. However, she moved forth, and the house-front stared her in the face, at this higher level unobscured by fog.

It was a building of the medium size, and unpretending, the façade being of stone; and of the Italian elevation made familiar by Inigo Jones and his school. There was a doorway to the lawn, standing at the head of a flight of steps. the shutters of the house were closed, and the blinds of the bedrooms drawn down. Her perception of the fact that no crusty caretaker could see her from the windows led her at once to slacken her pace, and stroll through the flower-beds coolly. A house unblinded is a possible spy, and must be treated accordingly; a house with the shutters together is an insensate heap of stone and mortar, to be faced with indifference.

On the other side of the house the greensward rose to an eminence, whereon stood one of those curious summer shelters sometimes erected on exposed points of view, called an all-the-year-round. In the present case it consisted of four walls radiating from a centre like the arms of a turnstile, with seats in each angle, so that whencesoever the wind came, it was always possible to find a screened corner from which to observe the landscape.

The milkmaid's trackless course led her up the hill and past this erection. At ease as to being watched and scolded as an intruder, her mind flew to other matters; till, at the moment when she was not a yard from the shelter, she heard a foot or feet scraping on the gravel behind it. Some one was in the all-the-year-round, apparently occupying the seat on the other side; as was proved when, on turning, she saw an elbow, a man's elbow, projecting over the edge.

Now the young woman did not much like the idea of going down the hill under the eyes of this person, which she would have to do if she went on, for as an intruder she was liable to be called back and questioned upon her business there. Accordingly she crept softly up and sat in the seat behind, intending to remain there until her companion should leave.

This he by no means seemed in a hurry to do. What could possibly have brought him there, what could detain him there, at six o'clock on a morning of mist when there was nothing to be seen or enjoyed of the vale beneath, puzzled her not a little. But he remained quite still, and Margery grew impatient. She discerned the track of his feet in the dewy grass, forming a line from the house steps, which announced that he was an inhabitant and not a chance passer-by. At last she peeped round.

2

A fine-framed dark-mustachioed gentleman, in dressing-gown and slippers, was sitting there in the damp without a hat on. With one hand he was tightly grasping his forehead, the other hung over his knee. The attitude bespoke with sufficient clearness a mental condition of anguish. He was quite a different being from any of the men to whom her eyes were accustomed. She had never seen mustachios before, for they were not worn by civilians in Lower Wessex at this date. His hands and his face were white – to her view deadly white – and he heeded nothing outside of his own existence. There he remained as motionless as the bushes around him; indeed, he scarcely seemed to breathe.

Having imprudently advanced this far, Margery's wish was to get back again in the same unseen manner; but in moving her foot for the purpose it grated on the gravel. He started up with an air of bewilderment, and slipped something into the pocket of his dressing-gown. She was almost certain that it was a pistol. The pair stood looking blankly at each other.

'My Gott, who are you?' he asked sternly, and with not altogether an English articulation. 'What do you do here?'

Margery had already begun to be frightened at her boldness in invading the lawn and pleasure-seat. The house had a master, and she had not known of it. 'My name is Margaret Tucker, sir,' she said meekly. 'My father is Dairyman Tucker. We live at Silverthorn Dairy-house.'

'What were you doing here at this hour of the morning?'

She told him, even to the fact that she had climbed over the fence.

'And what made you peep round at me?'

'I saw your elbow, sir; and I wondered what you were doing?'

'And what was I doing?'

'Nothing. You had one hand on your forehead and the other on your knee. I do hope you are not ill, sir, or in deep trouble?' Margery had sufficient tact to say nothing about the pistol.

'What difference would it make to you if I were in ill or in trouble? You don't know me.'

She returned no answer, feeling that she might have taken a liberty in expressing sympathy. But, looking furtively up at him, she discerned to her surprise that he seemed affected by her humane wish, simply as it had been expressed. She had scarcely conceived that such a tall dark man could know what gentle feelings were.

'Well, I am much obliged to you for caring how I am,' said he with a faint smile and an affected lightness of manner, which, even to her, only rendered more apparent the gloom beneath. 'I have not slept this past night. I suffer from sleeplessness. Probably you do not.'

Margery laughed a little, and he glanced with interest at the comely picture she presented; her fresh face, brown hair, candid eyes, unpractised manner, country dress, pink hands, empty wicker-basket, and the handkerchief over her bonnet.

'Well,' he said, after his scrutiny, 'I need hardly have asked such a question of one who is Nature's own image. . . Ah, but, my good little friend,' he added, recurring to his bitter tone and sitting wearily down, 'you don't know what great clouds can hang over some people's lives, and what cowards some men are in face of them. To escape themselves they travel, take picturesque houses, and engage in country sports. But here it is so dreary, and the fog was horrible this morning!'

'Why, this is only the pride of the morning!' said Margery. 'By-and-by it will be a beautiful day.'

She was going on her way forthwith; but he detained her – detained her with words, talking on every innocent little subject he could think of. He had an object in keeping her there more serious than his words would imply. It was as if he feared to be left alone.

While they still stood, the misty figure of the postman, whom Margery had left a quarter of an hour earlier to follow his sinuous course, crossed the grounds below them on his way to the house. Signifying to Margery by a wave of his hand that she was to step back out of sight, in the hinder angle of the shelter, the gentleman beckoned to the postman to bring the bag to where he stood. The man did so, and again resumed his journey.

The stranger unlocked the bag and threw it on the seat, having taken one letter from within. This he read attentively, and his countenance changed.

The change was almost phantasmagorial, as if the sun had burst through the fog upon that face: it became clear, bright, almost radiant. Yet it was but a change that may take place in the commonest human being, provided his countenance be not too wooden, or his artifice have not grown to second nature. He turned to Margery, who was again edging off, and, seizing her hand, appeared as though he were about to embrace her. Checking his impulse, he said, 'My guardian child – my good friend – you have saved me!'

'What from?' she ventured to ask.

'That you may never know.'

She thought of the weapon, and guessed that the letter he had just received had effected this change in this mood, but made no observation till he went on to say, 'What did you tell me was your name, dear girl?'

She repeated her name.

'Margeret Tucker.' He stooped, and pressed her hand. 'Sit down for a moment – one moment,' he said, pointing to the end of the seat, and taking the extremest further end for himself, not to discompose her. She sat down.

'It is to ask a question,' he went on, 'and there must be confidence between us. You have saved me from an act of madness! What can I do for you?'

'Nothing, sir.'

'Nothing?'

'Father is very well off, and we don't want anything.'

'But there must be some service I can render, some kindness, some votive offering which I could make, and so imprint on your memory as long as you live that I am not an ungrateful man?'

'Why should you be grateful to me, sir?'

He shook his head. 'Some things are best left unspoken. Now think. What would you like to have best in the world?'

Margery made a pretence of reflecting – then fell to reflecting seriously; but the negative was ultimately as undisturbed as ever: she could not decide on anything she would like best in the world; it was too difficult, too sudden.

'Very well – don't hurry yourself. Think it over all day. I ride this afternoon. You live – where?'

'Silverthorn Dairy-house.'

'I will ride that way homeward this evening. Do you consider by eight o'clock what little article, what little treat, you would most like of any.'

'I will, sir,' said Margery, now warming up to the idea. 'Where shall I meet you? Or will you call at the house, sir?'

'Ah – no. I should not wish the circumstances known out of which our acquaintance rose. It would be more proper – but no.'

Margery, too, seemed rather anxious that he should not call. 'I could come out, sir,' she said. 'My father is odd-tempered, and perhaps—'

It was agreed that she should look over a stile at the top of her father's garden, and that he should ride along a bridle-path outside, to receive her answer. 'Margery,' said the gentleman in conclusion, 'now that you have discovered me under ghastly conditions, are you going to reveal them, and make me an object for the gossip of the curious?'

'No, no, sir!' she replied earnestly. 'Why should I do that?'

'You will never tell?'

'Never, never will I tell what has happened here this morning.'

'Neither to your father, nor to your friends, nor to anyone?'

'To no one at all,' she said.

'It is sufficient,' he answered. 'You mean what you say, my dear maiden. Now you want to leave me. Good-bye!'

She descended the hill, walking with some awkwardness; for she felt the stranger's eyes were upon her till the fog had enveloped her from his gaze. She took no notice now of the dripping from the trees; she was lost in thought on other things. Had she saved this handsome, melancholy, sleepless, foreign gentleman who had had a trouble on his mind till the letter came? What had he been going to do? Margery could guess that he had meditated death at his own hand. Strange as the incident had been in itself, to her it had seemed stranger even than it was. Contrasting colours heighten each other by being juxtaposed; it is the same with contrasting lives.

Reaching the opposite side of the park there appeared before her for the third time that little old man, the foot-post. As the turnpike-road ran, the postman's beat was twelve miles a day; six miles out from the town, and six miles back at night. But what with zigzags, devious ways, offsets to country seats, curves to farms, looped courses, and triangles to outlying hamlets, the ground actually covered by him was nearer one-and-twenty miles. Hence it was that Margery, who had come straight, was still abreast of him, despite her long pause.

The weighty sense that she was mixed up in a tragical secret with an unknown and handsome stranger prevented her joining very readily in chat with the postman for some time. But a keen interest in her adventure caused her to respond at once when the bowed man of mails said, 'You hit athwart the grounds of Mount Lodge, Miss Margery, or you wouldn't ha' met me here. Well, somebody hev took the old place at last.'

In acknowledging her route Margery brought herself to ask who the new gentleman might be.

'Guide the girl's heart! What! don't she know? And yet how should ye – he's only just a-come. – Well, nominal, he's a fishing gentleman, come for the summer only. But, more to the subject, he's a foreign noble that's lived in England so long as to be without any true country: some of his letters call him Baron, some Squire, so that 'a must be born to something that can't be earned by elbow-grease and Christian conduct. He was out this morning a-watching the fog. "Postman," 'a said, "good-morning: give me the bag." O, yes, 'a's a civil genteel nobleman enough.'

'Took the house for fishing, did he?'

'That's what they say, and as it can be for nothing else I suppose it's true. But, in final, his health's not good, 'a b'lieve; he's been living too rithe. The London smoke got into his wyndpipe, till a' couldn't eat. However, I shouldn't mind having the run of his kitchen.'

'And what is his name?'

'Ah – there you have me! 'Tis a name no man's tongue can tell, or even woman's, except by pen-and-ink and good scholarship. It begins with X, and who, without the machinery of a clock in's inside, can speak that? But here 'tis – from his letters.' The postman with his walking-stick wrote upon the ground:

'BARON VON XANTEN'

3

The day, as she had prognosticated, turned out fine; for weather-wisdom was imbibed with their milk-sops by the children of the Exe Vale. The impending meeting excited Margery, and she performed her duties in her father's house with mechanical unconsciousness.

Milking, skimming, cheesemaking were done. Her father was asleep in the settle, the milkmen and maids were gone home to their cottages, and the clock showed a quarter to eight. She dressed herself with care, went to the top of the garden, and looked over the stile. The view was eastward, and a great moon hung before her in a sky which had not a cloud. Nothing was moving except on the minutest scale, and she remained leaning over, the night-hawk sounding his croud from the bough of an isolated tree on the open hill-side.

Here Margery waited till the appointed time had passed by three-quarters of an hour; but no Baron came. She had been full of an idea, and her heart sank with disappointment. Then at last the pacing of a horse became audible on the soft path without, leading up from the water-meads, simultaneously with which she beheld the form of the stranger, riding home, as he had said.

The moonlight so flooded her face as to make her very conspicuous in the garden-gap. 'Ah, my maiden – what is your name – Margery!' he said. 'How came you here? But of course I remember – we were to meet. And it was to be eight – *proh pudor!* – I have kept you waiting!'

'It doesn't matter, sir. I've thought of something.'

'Thought of something?'

'Yes, sir. you said this morning that I was to think what I would like best in the world, and I have made up my mind.'

'I did say so – to be sure I did,' he replied, collecting his thoughts. 'I remember to have had good reason for gratitude to you.' He placed his hand to his brow, and in a minute alighted, and came up to her with the bridle in his hand. 'I was to give you a treat or present, and you could not think of one. Now you have done so. Let me hear what it is, and I'll be as good as my word.'

'To go the Yeomanry Ball that's to be given this month.'

'The Yeomanry Ball – Yeomanry Ball?' he murmured, as if, of all requests in the world, this was what he had least expected. 'Where is what you call the Yeomanry Ball?'

'At Exonbury.'

'Have you ever been to it before?'

'No, sir.'

'Or to any ball?'

'No.'

'But did I not say a gift – a present?'

'Or a treat.'

'Ah, yes, or a treat,' he echoed, with the air of one who finds himself in a slight fix. 'But with whom would you propose to go?'

'I don't know. I have not thought of that yet.'

'You have no friend who could take you, even if I got you an invitation?'

Margery looked at the moon. 'No one who can dance,' she said; adding, with hesitation, 'I was thinking that perhaps—'

'But, my dear Margery,' he said, stopping her, as if he half-divined what her simple dream of a cavalier had been; 'it is very odd that you can think of nothing else than going to a Yeomanry Ball. Think again. You are sure there is nothing else?'

'Quite sure, sir,' she decisively answered. At first nobody would have noticed in that pretty young face any sign of decision; yet it was discoverable. The mouth, though soft, was firm in line; the eyebrows were distinct, and extended near to each other. 'I have thought of it all day,' she continued, sadly. 'Still, sir, if you are sorry you offered me anything, I can let you off.'

'Sorry? – Certainly not, Margery,' he said, rather nettled. 'I'll show you that whatever hopes I have raised in your breast I am honourable enough to gratify. If it lies in my power,' he added with sudden firmness, 'you *shall* go to the Yeomanry Ball. In what building is it to be held?'

'In the Assembly Rooms.'

'And would you be likely recognized there? Do you know many people?'

'Not many, sir. None, I may say. I know nobody who goes to balls.'

'Ah, well; you must go, since you wish it; and if there is no other way of getting over the difficulty of having nobody to take you, I'll take you myself. Would you like me to do so? I can dance.'

'O yes, sir; I know that, and I thought you might offer to do it. But would you bring me back again?'

'Of course I'll bring you back. But, by-the-by, can *you* dance?'

'Yes.'

'What?'

'Reels, and jigs, and country-dances like the New-Rigged-Ship, and Follow-my-Lover, and Haste-to-the-Wedding, and the College Hornpipe, and the Favourite Quickstep, and Captain White's dance.'

'A very good list – a very good! but unluckily I fear they don't dance any of those now. But if you have the instinct we may soon cure your ignorance. Let me see you dance a moment.'

She stood out into the garden-path, the stile being still between them, and seizing a side of her skirt with each hand, performed the movements which are even yet far from uncommon in the dances of the villagers of merry England. But her motions, though graceful, were not precisely those which appear in the figures of a modern ballroom.

'Well, my good friend, it is a very pretty sight,' he said, warming up to proceedings. 'But you dance too well – you dance all over your person – and that's too thorough a way for the present day. I should say it was exactly how they danced in the time of your poet Chaucer; but as people don't dance like it now, we must consider. First I must inquire more about this ball, and then I must see you again.'

'If it is a great trouble to you, sir, I—'

'O no, no. I will think it over. So far so good.'

The Baron mentioned an evening and an hour when he would be

passing that way again; then mounted his horse and rode away.

On the next occasion, which was just when the sun was changing places with the moon as an illuminator of Silverthorn Dairy, she found him at the spot before her, and unencumbered by a horse. The melancholy that had so weighed him down at their first interview, and had been perceptible at their second, had quite disappeared. He pressed her right hand between both his own across the stile.

'My good maiden, Gott bless you!' said he warmly. 'I cannot help thinking of that morning! I was too much over-shadowed at first to take in the whole force of it. You do not know all; but your presence was a miraculous intervention. Now to more cheerful matters. I have a great deal to tell – that is, if your wish about the ball be still the same?'

'O yes, sir – if you don't object.'

'Never think of my objecting. What I have found out is something which simplifies matters amazingly. In addition to your Yeomanry Ball at Exonbury, there is also to be one in the next county about the same time. This ball is not to be held at the Town Hall of the county-town as usual, but at Lord Toneborough's, who is colonel of the regiment, and who, I suppose, wishes to please the yeomen because his brother is going to stand for the county. Now I find I could take you there very well, and the great advantage of that ball over the Yeomanry Ball in this county is, that there you would be absolutely unknown, and I also. But do you prefer your own neighbourhood?'

'O no, sir. It is a ball I long to see – I don't know what it is like; it does not matter where.'

'Good. Then I shall be able to make much more of you there, where there is no possibility of recognition. That being settled, the next thing is the dancing. Now reels and such things do not do. For think of this – there is a new dance at Almack's and everywhere else, over which the world has gone crazy.'

'How dreadful!'

'Ah – but that is a mere expression – gone mad. It is really an ancient Scythian dance; but, such is the power of fashion, that, having once been adopted by Society, this dance has made the tour of the Continent in one season.'

'What is its name, sir?'

'The polka. Young people, who always dance, are ecstatic about it, and old people, who have not danced for years, have begun to dance again on its account. All share the excitement. It arrived in London only some few months ago – it is now all over the country. Now this is your opportunity, my good Margery. To learn this one dance will be enough. They will dance scarce anything else at that ball. While, to crown all, it is the easiest dance in the world, and as I know it quite well I can practise you in the step. Suppose we try?'

Margery showed some hesitation before crossing the stile: it was a Rubicon in more ways than one. But the curious reverence which was stealing over her for all that this stranger said and did was too much for prudence. She crossed the stile.

Withdrawing with her to a nook where two high hedges met, and where the grass was elastic and dry, he lightly rested his arm on her waist, and practised with her the new step of fascination. Instead of music he whispered numbers, and she, as may be supposed, showed no slight aptness in following his instructions. Thus they moved round together, the moon-shadows from the twigs racing over their forms as they turned.

The interview lasted about half-an-hour. Then he somewhat abruptly handed her over the stile and stood looking at her from the other side.

'Well,' he murmured, 'what has come to pass is strange! My whole business after this will be to recover my right mind!'

Margery always declared that there seemed to be some power in the stranger that was more than human, something magical and compulsory, when he seized her and gently trotted her round. But lingering emotions may have led her memory to play pranks with the scene, and her vivid imagination at that youthful age must be taken into account in believing her. However, there is no doubt that the stranger, whoever he might be, and whatever his powers, taught her the elements of modern dancing at a certain interview by moonlight at the top of her father's garden, as was proved by her possession of knowledge on the subject that could have been acquired in no other way.

His was of the first rank of commanding figures, she was one of the most agile of milkmaids, and to casual view it would have seemed all of a piece with Nature's doings that things should go on thus. But there was another side to the case; and whether the strange gentleman were a wild olive tree, or not, it was questionable if the acquaintance would lead to happiness. 'A fleeting romance and a possible calamity': thus it might have been summed up by the practical.

Margery was in Paradise; and yet she was not at this date distinctly in love with the stranger. What she felt was something more mysterious, more of the nature of veneration. As he looked at her across the stile she spoke timidly, on a subject which had apparently occupied her long.

'I ought to have a ball-dress, ought I not, sir?'

'Certainly. And you shall have a ball-dress.'

'Really?'

'No doubt of it. I don't do thing by halves for my best friend. I have thought of the ball-dress, and of other things also.'

'And is my dancing good enough?'

'Quite – quite.' He paused, lapsed into thought, and looked at her. 'Margery,' he said, 'do you trust yourself unreservedly to me?'

'O yes, sir,' she replied brightly; 'if I am not too much trouble: if I am good enough to be seen in your society.'

The Baron laughed in a peculiar way. 'Really, I think you may assume as much as that. – However, to business. The ball is on the twenty-fifth, that is next Thursday week; and the only difficulty about the dress is the size. Suppose you lend me this?' And he touched her on the shoulder to signify a tight little jacket she wore.

Margery was all obedience. She took it off and handed it to him. The baron rolled and compressed it with all his force till it was about as large as an apple-dumpling, and put it into his pocket.

'The next thing,' he said, 'is about getting the consent of your friends to your going. Have you thought of this?'

'There is only my father. I can tell him I am invited to a party, and I don't think he'll mind. Though I would rather not tell him.'

'But it strikes me that you must inform him something of what you intend. I would strongly advise you to do so.' He spoke as if rather perplexed as to the probable custom of the English peasantry in such matters, and added, 'However, it is for you to decide. I know nothing of the circumstances. As to getting to the ball, the plan I have arranged is this. The direction to Lord Toneborough's being the other way from my house, you must meet me at Three-Walks-End in Chillington Wood, two miles or more from here. You know the place? Good. By meeting there we shall save five or six miles of journey – a consideration, as it is a long way. Now, for the last time: are you still firm in your wish for this particular treat and no other? It is not too late to give it up. Cannot you think of something else – something better – some useful household articles you require?'

Margery's countenance, which before had been beaming with expectation, lost its brightness: her lips became close, and her voice broken. 'You have offered to take me, and now—'

'No, no, no,' he said, patting her cheek. 'We will not think of anything else. You shall go.'

4

But whether the Baron, in naming such a distant spot for the rendezvous, was in hope she might fail him, and so relieve him after all of his undertaking, cannot be said; though it might have been strongly suspected from his manner that he had no great zest for the responsibility of escorting her.

But he little knew the firmness of the young woman he had to deal with. She was one of those soft natures whose power of adhesiveness to an acquired idea seems to be one of the special attributes of that softness. To go to a ball with this mysterious personage of romance was her ardent desire and aim; and none the less in that she trembled with fear and excitement at her position in so aiming. She felt the deepest awe, tenderness, and humility towards the Baron of the strange name; and yet she was prepared to stick to her point.

Thus it was that the afternoon of the eventful day found Margery trudging her way up the slopes from the vale to the place of appointment. She walked to the music of innumerable birds, which increased as she drew away from the open meads towards the groves. She had overcome all difficulties. After thinking out the question of telling or not telling her father, she had decided that to tell him was to be forbidden to go. Her contrivance therefore was this: to leave home this evening on a visit to her invalid grandmother, who lived not far from the Baron's house; but not to arrive at her grandmother's till breakfast-time next morning. Who would suspect an intercalated experience of twelve hours with the Baron at a ball? That this piece of deception was indefensible she afterwards owned readily enough; but she did not stop to think of it then.

It was sunset within Chillington Wood by the time she reached Three-Walks-End – the converging point of radiating trackways, now floored with a carpet of matted grass, whch had never known other scythes than the teeth of rabbits and hares. The twitter overhead had ceased, except from a few braver and larger birds, including the cuckoo, who did not fear night at this pleasant time of year. Nobody seemed to be on the spot when she first drew near, but no sooner did Margery stand at the intersection of the roads than a slight crashing became audible, and her patron appeared. He was so transfigured in dress that she scarcely knew him. Under a light greatcoat, which was flung open, instead of his ordinary clothes he wore a suit of thin black cloth, an open waistcoat with a frill all down his shirt-front, a white tie, shining boots, no thicker than a glove, a coat that made him look like a bird, and a hat that seemed as if it would open and shut like an accordion.

'I am dressed for the ball – nothing worse,' he said, drily smiling. 'So will you be soon.'

'Why did you choose this place for our meeting, sir?' she asked, looking around and acquiring confidence.

'Why did I choose it? Well, because in riding past one day I observed a large hollow tree close by here, and it occurred to me when I was last with you that this would be useful for our purpose. Have you told your father?'

'I have not yet told him, sir.'

'That's very bad of you, Margery. How have you arranged it, then?'

She briefly related her plan, on which he made no comment, but, taking her by the hand as if she were a little child, he led her through the undergrowth to a spot where the trees were older, and standing at wider distances. Among them was the tree he had spoken of – an elm; huge, hollow, distorted, and headless, with a rift in its side.

'Now go inside,' he said, 'before it gets any darker. You will find there everything you want. At any rate, if you do not you must do without it. I'll keep watch; and don't be longer than you can help to be.'

'What am I to do, sir?' asked the puzzled maiden.

'Go inside, and you will see. When you are ready wave your handkerchief at that hole.'

She stooped into the opening. The cavity within the tree formed a lofty circular apartment, four or five feet in diameter, to which daylight entered at the top, and also through a round hole about six feet from the ground, marking the spot at which a limb had been amputated in the tree's prime. The decayed wood of cinnamon-brown, forming the inner surface of the tree, and the warm evening glow, reflected in at the top, suffused the cavity with a faint mellow radiance.

But Margery had hardly given herself time to heed these things. Her eye had been caught by objects of quite another quality. A large white oblong paper box lay against the inside of the tree; over it, on a splinter, hung a small oval looking-glass.

Margery seized the idea in a moment. She pressed through the rift into the tree, lifted the cover of the box, and, behold, there was disclosed within a lovely white apparition in a somewhat flattened state. It was the ball-dress.

This marvel of art was, briefly, a sort of heavenly cobweb. It was a gossamer texture of precious manufacture, artistically festooned in a dozen flounces or more.

Margery lifted it, and could hardly refrain from kissing it. Had anyone told her before this moment that such a dress could exist, she would have said, 'No; it's impossible!' She drew back, went forward, flushed, laughed, raised her hands. To say that the maker of that dress had been an individual of talent was simply an understatement; he was a genius, and she sunned herself in the rays of his creation.

She then remembered that her friend without had told her to make haste, and she spasmodically proceeded to array herself. In removing the dress she found satin slippers, gloves, a handkerchief nearly all lace, a fan, and even flowers for the hair. 'Oh, how could he think of it!' she said, clasping her hands and almost crying with agitation. 'And the glass – how good of him!'

Everything was so well prepared, that to clothe herself in these garments was a matter of ease. In a quarter of an hour she was ready, even to shoes and gloves. But what led her more than anything else into admiration of the Baron's foresight was the discovery that there were half-a-dozen pairs each of shoes and gloves, of varying sizes, out of which she selected a fit.

Margery glanced at herself in the mirror, or at as much as she could see of herself: the image presented was superb. Then she hastily rolled up her old dress, put it in the box, and thrust the latter on a ledge as high as she could reach. Standing on tiptoe, she waved the handkerchief through the upper aperture, and bent to the rift to go out.

But what a trouble stared her in the face. The dress was so airy, so fantastical, and so extensive, that to get out in her new clothes by the rift which had admitted her in her old ones was an impossibility. She heard the Baron's steps crackling over the dead sticks and leaves.

'O, sir!' she began in despair.

'What – can't you dress yourself?' he inquired from the back of the trunk.

'Yes; but I can't get out of this dreadful tree!'

He came round to the opening, stopped, and looked in. 'It is obvious that you cannot,' he said, taking in her compass at a glance; and adding to himself, 'Charming! who would have thought that clothes could do so much! – Wait a minute, my little maid; I have it!' he said more loudly.

With all his might he kicked at the sides of the rift, and by that means broke away several pieces of the rotten touchwood. But, being thinly armed about the feet, he abandoned that process, and went for a fallen branch which lay near. By using the large end as a lever, he tore away pieces of the wooden shell which enshrouded Margery and all her loveliness, till the aperture was large enough for her to pass without tearing her dress. She breathed her relief: the silly girl had begun to fear that she would not get to the ball after all.

He carefully wrapped round her a cloak he had brought with him: it was hooded, and of a length which covered her to the heels.

'The carriage is waiting down the other path,' he said, and gave her his arm. A short trudge over the soft dry leaves brought them to the place indicated. There stood the brougham, the horses, the coachman, all as still as if they were growing on the spot, like the trees. Margery's eyes rose with some timidity to the coachman's figure.

'You need not mind him,' said the Baron. 'He is a foreigner, and heeds nothing.'

In the space of a short minute she was handed inside; the Baron buttoned up his overcoat, and surprised her by mounting with the coachman. The carriage moved off silently over the long grass of the vista, the shadows deepening to black as they proceeded. Darker and darker grew the night as they rolled on; the neighbourhood familiar to Margery was soon left behind, and she had not the remotest idea of the direction they were taking. The stars blinked out, the coachman lit his lamps, and they bowled on again.

In the course of an hour and a half they arrived at a small town, where they pulled up at the chief inn and changed horses; all being done so readily that their advent had plainly been expected. The journey was resumed immediately. Her companion never descended to speak to her; whenever she looked out there he sat upright on his perch, with the mien of a person who had a difficult duty to perform, and who meant to perform it properly at all costs. But Margery could not help feeling a certain dread at her situation – almost, indeed, a wish that she had not come. Once or twice she thought, 'Suppose he is a wicked man, who is taking me off to a foreign country, and will never bring me home again.'

But her characteristic persistence in an original idea sustained her against these misgivings except at odd moments. One incident in particular had given her confidence in her escort: she had seen a tear in his eye when she expressed her sorrow for his troubles. He may have divined that her thoughts would take an uneasy turn, for when they stopped for a moment in ascending a hill he came to the window. 'Are you tired, Margery?' he asked kindly.

'No, sir.'

'Are you afraid?'

'N-no, sir. But it is a long way.'

'We are almost there,' he answered. 'And now, Margery,' he said in a lower tone, 'I must tell you a secret. I have obtained this invitation in a peculiar way. I thought it best for your sake not to come in my own name, and this is how I have managed. A man in this county, for whom I have lately done a service, one whom I can trust, and who is personally as unknown here as you and I, has (privately) transferred his card of invitation to me. So that we go under his name. I explain this that you may not say anything imprudent by accident. Keep your ears open and be cautious.' Having said this the Baron retreated again to his place.

'Then he is a wicked man after all!' she said to herself; 'for he is going under a false name.' But she soon had the temerity not to mind it: wickedness of that sort was the one ingredient required just now to finish him off as a hero in her eyes.

They descended a hill, passed a lodge, then up an avenue; and presently there beamed upon them the light from other carriages, drawn up in a file, which moved on by degrees; and at last they halted before a large arched doorway, round which a group of people stood.

'We are among the latest arrivals, on account of the distance,' said the Baron, reappearing. 'But never mind; there are three hours at least for your enjoyment.'

The steps were promptly flung down, and they alighted. The steam from the flanks of their swarthy steeds, as they seemed to her, ascended to the parapet of the porch, and from their nostrils the hot breath jetted forth like smoke out of volcanoes, attracting the attention of all.

5

The bewildered Margery was led by the Baron up the steps to the interior of the house, whence the sounds of music and dancing were already proceeding. The tones were strange. At every fourth beat a deep and mighty note throbbed through the air, reaching Margery's soul with all the force of a blow.

'What is that powerful tune, sir – I have never heard anything like it?' she said.

'The Drum Polka,' answered the Baron. 'The strange dance I spoke of and that we practised – introduced from my country and other parts of the Continent.'

Her surprise was not lessened when, at the entrance to the ballroom, she heard the names of her conductor and herself announced as 'Mr and Miss Brown'.

However, nobody seemed to take any notice of the announcement, the room beyond being in a perfect turmoil of gaiety, and Margery's consternation at sailing under false colours subsided. At the same moment she observed awaiting them a handsome, dark-haired, rather *petite* lady in cream-coloured satin. 'Who is she?' asked Margery of the Baron.

'She is the lady of the mansion,' he whispered. 'She is the wife of a peer of the realm, the daughter of a marquis, has five Christian names; and hardly ever speaks to commoners, except for political purposes.'

'How divine – what joy to be here!' murmured Margery, as she contemplated the diamonds that flashed from the head of her ladyship, who was just inside the ballroom door, in front of a little gilded chair, upon which she sat in the intervals between one arrival and another. She had come down from London at great inconvenience to herself, openly to promote this entertainment.

As Mr and Miss Brown expressed absolutely no meaning to Lady Toneborough (for there were three Browns already present in this rather mixed assembly), and as there was possibly a slight awkwardness in poor Margery's manner, Lady Toneborough touched their hands lightly with the tips of her long gloves, said, 'How d'ye do,' and turned round for more comers.

'Ah, if she only knew we were a rich Baron and his friend, and not Mr and Miss Brown at all, she wouldn't receive us like that, would she?' whispered Margery confidentially.

'Indeed, she wouldn't!' drily said the Baron. 'Now let us drop into the dance at once; some of the people here, you see, dance much worse than you.'

Almost before she was aware she had obeyed his mysterious influence, by giving him one hand, placing the other upon his shoulder, and swinging with him round the room to the steps she had learnt on the sward.

At the first gaze the apartment had seemed to her to be floored with black ice; the figures of the dancers appearing upon it upside down. At last she realized that it was highly-polished oak, but she was none the less afraid to move.

'I am afraid of falling down,' she said.

'Lean on me; you will soon get used to it,' he replied. 'You have no nails in your shoes now, dear.'

His words, like all his words to her, were quite true. She found it amazingly easy in a brief space of time. The floor, far from hindering her, was a positive assistance to one of her natural agility and litheness. Moreover, her marvellous dress of twelve flounces inspired her as nothing else could have done. Externally a new creature, she was prompted to new deeds. To feel as well-dressed as the other women around her is to set any woman at her ease, whencesover she may have come: to feel much better dressed is to add radiance to that ease.

Her prophet's statement on the popularity of the polka at this juncture was amply borne out. It was among the first seasons of its general adoption in country houses; the enthusiasm it excited tonight was beyond description, and scarcely credible to the youth of the present day. A new motive power had been introduced into the world of poesy – the polka, as a counterpoise to the new motive power that had been introduced into the world of prose – steam.

Twenty finished musicians sat in the music gallery at the end, with romantic mop-heads of raven hair, under which their faces and eyes shone like fire under coals.

The nature and object of the ball had led to its being very inclusive. Every rank was there, from the peer to the smallest yeoman, and Margery got on exceedingly well, particularly when the recuperative powers of supper had banished the fatigue of her long drive.

Sometimes she heard people saying, 'Who are they? – brother and sister – father and daughter? And never dancing except with each other – how odd!' But of this she took no notice.

When not dancing the watchful Baron took her through the drawing-rooms and picture-galleries adjoining, which tonight were thrown open like the rest of the house; and there, ensconcing her in some curtained nook, he drew her attention to scrap-books, prints, and albums, and left her to amuse herself with turning them over till the dance in which she was practised should again be called. Margery would much have preferred to roam about during these intervals; but the words of the Baron were law, and as he commanded so she acted. In such alternations the evening winged away; till at last came the gloomy words, 'Margery, our time is up.'

'One more – only one!' she coaxed, for the longer they stayed the more freely and gaily moved the dance. This entreaty he granted; but on her asking for yet another, he was inexorable. 'No,' he said. 'We have a long way to go.'

Then she bade adieu to the wondrous scene, looking over her shoulder as they withdrew from the ball; and in a few minutes she was cloaked and in the carriage. The Baron mounted to his seat on the box, where she saw him light a cigar; they plunged under the trees, and she leant back, and gave herself up to contemplate the images that filled her brain. The natural result followed: she fell asleep.

She did not awake till they stopped to change horses, when she saw against the stars the Baron sitting as erect as ever. 'He watches like the Angel Gabriel, when all the world is asleep!' she thought.

With the resumption of motion she slept again, and knew no more till he touched her hand and said, 'Our journey is done – we are in Chillington Wood.'

It was almost daylight. Margery scarcely knew herself to be awake till she was out of the carriage and standing beside the Baron who, having told the coachman to drive on to a certain point indicated, turned to her.

'Now,' he said, smiling, 'run across to the hollow tree; you know where it is. I'll wait as before, while you perform the reverse operation to that you did last night.' She took no heed of the path now, nor regarded whether her pretty slippers became scratched by the brambles or no. A walk of a few steps brought her to the particular tree which she had left about nine hours earlier. It was still gloomy at this spot, the morning not being clear.

She entered the trunk, dislodged the box containing her old clothing, pulled off the satin shoes, and gloves, and dress, and in ten minutes emerged in the cotton gown and shawl of shepherd's plaid.

The baron was not far off. 'Now you look the milkmaid again,' he said, coming towards her. 'Where is the finery?'

'Packed in the box, sir, as I found it.' She spoke with more humility now. The difference between them was greater than it had been at the ball.

'Good,' he said. 'I must just dispose of it; and then away we go.'

He went back to the tree, Margery following at a little distance. Bringing forth the box, he pulled out the dress as carelessly as if it had been rags. But this was not all. He gathered a few dry sticks, crushed the lovely garment into a loose billowy heap, threw the gloves, fan, and shoes on the top, then struck a light and ruthlessly set fire to the whole.

Margery was agonized. She ran forward; she implored and entreated. 'Please, sir – do spare it – do! My lovely dress – my dear, dear slippers – my fan – it is cruel! Don't burn them, please!'

'Nonsense. We shall have no further use for them if we live a hundred years.'

'But spare a bit of it – one little piece, sir – a scrap of the lace – one bow of the ribbon – the lovely fan – just something!'

But he was as immovable as Rhadamanthus. 'No,' he said, with a stern gaze of his aristocratic eye. 'It is of no use for you to speak like that. The things are my property. I undertook to gratify you in what you might desire because you had saved my life. To go to a ball, you said. You might much more wisely have said anything else, but no; you said, to go to a ball. Very well – I have taken you to a ball. I have brought you back. The clothes were only the means, and I dispose of them in my own way. Have I not a right to?'

'Yes, sir,' she said meekly.

He gave the fire a stir, and lace and ribbons, and the twelve flounces, and the embroidery, and all the rest crackled and disappeared. He then put in her hands the butter basket she had brought to take on to her grandmother's, and accompanied her to the edge of the wood, where it merged in the indulating open country in which her granddame dwelt.

'Now, Margery,' he said, 'here we part. I have performed my contract – at some awkwardness, if I was recognized. But never mind that. How do you feel – sleepy?'

'Not at all, sir,' she said.

'That long nap refreshed you, eh? Now you must make me a promise. That if I require your presence at any time, you will come to me. . . I am a man of more than one mood,' he went on with sudden solemnity; 'and I may have desperate need of you again, to deliver me from that darkness as of Death which sometimes encompasses me. Promise it, Margery – promise it; that, no matter what stands in the way, you will come to me if I require you.'

'I would have if you had not burnt my pretty clothes!' she pouted.

'Ah – ungrateful!'

'Indeed, then, I will promise, sir,' she said from her heart. 'Wherever I am, if I have bodily strength I will come to you.'

He pressed her hand. 'It is a solemn promise,' he replied. 'Now I must go, for you know your way.'

'I shall hardly believe that it has not been all a dream!' she said, with a childish instinct to cry at his withdrawal. 'There will be nothing left of last night – nothing of my dress, nothing of my pleasure, nothing of the place!'

'You shall remember it in this way,' said he. 'We'll cut our initials on this tree as a memorial, so that whenever you walk this path you will see them.'

Then with a knife he inscribed on the smooth bark of a beech tree the letters M.T., and underneath a large X.

'What, have you no Christian name, sir?' she said.

'Yes, but I don't use it. Now, good-bye, my little friend. – What will you do with yourself today, when you are gone from me?' he lingered to ask.

'Oh – I shall go to my granny's,' she replied with some gloom; 'and have breakfast, and dinner, and tea with her, I suppose; and in the evening I shall go home to Silverthorn Dairy, and perhaps Jim will come to meet me and all will be the same as usual.'

'Who is Jim?'

'O, he's nobody – only the young man I've got to marry some day.'

'What! – you engaged to be married? – Why didn't you tell me this before?'

'I – I don't know, sir.'

'What is the young man's name?'

'James Hayward.'

'What is he?'

'A master lime-burner.'

'Engaged to a master lime-burner, and not a word of this to me! Margery, Margery! when shall a straightforward one of your sex be found! Subtle even in your simplicity! What mischief have you caused me to do, through not telling me this? I wouldn't have so endangered anybody's happiness for a thousand pounds. Wicked girl that you were; why didn't you tell me?'

'I thought I'd better not!' said Margery, beginning to be frightened.

'But don't you see and understand that if you are already the property of a young man, and he were to find out this night's excursion, he may be angry with you and part from you for ever? With him already in the field I had no right to take you at all; he undoubtedly ought to have taken you; which really might have been arranged, if you had not deceived me by saying you had nobody.'

Margery's face wore that aspect of woe which comes from the repentant consciousness of having been guilty of an enormity. 'But he wasn't good enough to take me, sir!' she said, almost crying; 'and he isn't absolutely my master until I have married him, is he?'

'That's a subject I cannot go into. However, we must alter our tactics. Instead of advising you, as I did at first, to tell of this experience to your friends, I most now impress on you that it will be best to keep a silent tongue on the matter – perhaps for ever and ever. It may come right some day, and you may be able to say "All's well that ends well." Now, good morning, my friend. Think of Jim, and forget me.'

'Ah, perhaps I can't do that,' she said, with a tear in her eye, and a full throat.

'Well – do your best. I can say no more.'

He turned and retreated into the wood, and Margery, sighing, went on her way.

6

Between six and seven o'clock in the evening of the same day a young man descended the hills into the valley of the Exe, at a point about midway between Silverthorn and the residence of Margery's grandmother, four miles to the east.

He was a thoroughbred son of the country, as far removed from what is known as the provincial, as the latter is from the out-and-out gentleman of culture. His trousers and waistcoat were of fustian, almost white, but he wore a jacket of old-fashioned blue West-of-England cloth, so well preserved that evidently the article was relegated to a box whenever its owner engaged in such active occupations as he usually pursued. His complexion was fair, almost florid, and he had scarcely any beard.

A novel attraction about this young man, which a glancing stranger would know nothing of, was a rare and curious freshness of atmosphere that appertained to him, to his clothes, to all his belongings, even to the room in which he had been sitting. It might almost have been said that by adding him and his implements to an over-crowded apartment you made it healthful. This resulted from his trade. He was a lime-burner; he handled lime daily; and in return the lime rendered him an incarnation of salubrity. His hair was dry, fair, and frizzled, the latter possibly by the operation of the same caustic agent. He carried as a walking-stick a green sapling, whose growth had been contorted to a corkscrew pattern by a twining honeysuckle.

As he descended to the level ground of the water-meadows he cast his glance westward, with a frequency that revealed him to be in search of some object in the distance. It was rather difficult to do this, the low sunlight dazzling his eyes by glancing from the river away there, and from the 'carriers' (as they were called) in his path – narrow artificial brooks for conducting the water over the grass. His course was something of a zigzag from the necessity of finding points in these carriers convenient for jumping. Thus peering and leaping and winding, he drew near the Exe, the central river of the miles-long mead.

A moving spot became visible to him in the direction of his scrutiny, mixed up with the rays of the same river. The spot got nearer, and revealed itself to be a slight thing of pink cotton and shepherd's plaid, which pursued a path on the brink of the stream. The young man so shaped his trackless course as to impinge on the path a little ahead of this coloured form, and when he drew near her he smiled and reddened. The girl smiled back to him; but her smile had not the life in it that the young man's had shown.

'My dear Margery – here I am!' he said gladly in an undertone, as with a last leap he crossed the last intervening carrier, and stood at her side.

'You've come all the way from the kiln, on purpose to meet me, and you shouldn't have done it,' she reproachfully returned.

'We finished there at four, so it was no trouble; and if it had been – why, I should ha' come.'

A small sigh was the response.

'What, you are not even so glad to see me as you would be to see your dog or cat?' he continued. 'Come, Mis'ess Margery, this is rather hard. But, by George, how tired you dew look! Why, if you'd been up all night your eyes couldn't be more like tea-saucers. You've walked tew far, that's what it is. The weather is getting warm now, and the air of these low-lying meads is not strengthening in summer. I wish you lived up on higher ground with me, beside the kiln. You'd get as strong as a hoss! Well, there; all that will come in time.'

Instead of saying yes, the fair maid repressed another sigh.

'What, won't it, then?' he said.

'I suppose so,' she answered. 'If it is to be, it is.'

'Well said – very well said, my dear.'

'And if it isn't to be, it isn't.'

'What? Who's been putting that into your head? Your grumpy granny, I suppose. However, how is she? Margery, I have been thinking today – in fact, I was thinking it yesterday and all the week – that really we might settle our little business this summer.'

'This summer?' she repeated, with some dismay. 'But the partnership? Remember it was not to be till after that was completed.'

'There I have you!' said he, taking the liberty to pat her shoulder, and the further liberty of advancing his hand behind it to the other. 'The partnership is settled. 'Tis "Vine and Hayward, lime-burners", now, and "Richard Vine" no longer. Yes, Cousin Richard has settled it so, for a time at least, and 'tis to be painted on the carts this week – blue letters – yaller ground. I'll hoss one of 'em, and drive en round to your door as soon as the paint is dry, to show 'ee how it looks?'

'Oh, I am sure you needn't take that trouble, Jim; I can see it quite well enough in my mind,' replied the young girl – not without a flitting accent of superiority.

'Hullo,' said Jim, taking her by the shoulders, and looking at her hard. 'What dew that bit of incivility mean? Now, Margery, let's sit down here, and have this cleared.' He rapped with his stick upon the rail of a little bridge they were crossing, and seated himself firmly, leaving a place for her.

'But I want to get home-along, dear Jim,' she coaxed.

'Fidgets. Sit down, there's a dear. I want a straightforward answer, if you please. In what month, and on what day of the month, will you marry me?'

'O, Jim,' she said, sitting gingerly on the edge, 'that's too plain-spoken for you yet. Before I look at it in that business light I should have to – to—'

'But your father has settled it long ago, and you said it should be as soon as I became a partner. So, dear, you must not mind a plain man wanting a plain answer. Come, name your time.'

She did not reply at once. What thoughts were passing through her brain during the interval? Not images raised by his words, but whirling figures of men and women in red and white and blue, reflected from a glassy floor, in movements timed by the thrilling beats of the Drum Polka. At last she said slowly, 'Jim, you don't know the world, and what a woman's wants can be.'

'But I can make you comfortable. I am in lodgings as yet, but I can have a house for the asking; and as to furniture, you shall choose of the best for yourself – the very best.'

'The best! Far are you from knowing what that is!' said the little woman. 'There would be ornaments such as you never dream of; work-tables that would set you in amaze; silver candlesticks, tea and coffee pots that would dazzle your eyes; tea-cups, and saucers, gilded all over with guinea-gold; heavy velvet curtains, gold clocks, pictures, and looking-glasses beyond your very dreams. So don't say I shall have the best.'

'H'm!' said Jim gloomily; and fell into reflection. 'Where did you get those high notions from, Margery?' he presented inquired. 'I'll swear you hadn't got 'em a week ago.' She did not answer, and he added, '*Yew* don't expect to have such things, I hope; deserve them as you may?'

'I was not exactly speaking of what I wanted,' she said severely. 'I said, things a woman *could* want. And since you wish to know what I *can* want to quite satisfy me, I assure you I can want those!'

'You are a pink-and-white conundrum, Margery,' he said; 'and I give you up for tonight. Anybody would think the devil had showed you all the kingdoms of the world since I saw you last!'

She reddened. 'Perhaps he has!' she murmured; then arose, he following her; and they soon reached Margery's home, approaching it from the lower or meadow side – the opposite to that of the garden top, where she had met the Baron.

'You'll come in, won't you, Jim?' she said, with more ceremony than heartiness.

'No – I think not tonight,' he answered. 'I'll consider what you've said.'

'You are very good, Jim,' she returned lightly. 'Good-bye.'

7

Jim thoughtfully retraced his steps. He was a village character, and he had a villager's simplicity: that is, the simplicity which comes from the lack of a complicated experience. But simple by nature he certainly was not. Among the rank and file of rustics he was quite a Talleyrand, or rather had been one, till he lost a good deal of his self-command by falling in love.

Now, however, that the charming object of his distraction was out of sight, he could deliberate, and measure, and weigh things with some approach of keenness. The substance of his queries was, What change had come over Margery – whence these new notions?

Ponder as he would he could evolve no answer save one, which, eminently unsatisfactory as it was, he felt it would be unreasonable not to accept: that she was simply skittish and ambitious by nature, and would not be hunted into matrimony till he had provided a well-adorned home.

Jim retrod the miles to the kiln, and looked to the fires. The kiln stood in a peculiar, interesting, even impressive spot. It was at the end of a short ravine in a limestone formation, and all around was an open hill down. The nearest house was that of Jim's cousin and partner, which stood on the outskirts of the down beside the turnpike-road. From this house a little lane wound between the steep escarpments of the ravine till it reached the kiln, which faced down the miniature valley, commanding it as a fort might command a defile.

The idea of a fort in this association owed little to imagination. For on the nibbled green steep above the kiln stood a bygone worn-out specimen of such an erection, huge, impressive, and difficult to scale even now in its decay. It was a British castle or entrenchment, with triple rings of defence, rising roll behind roll, their outlines cutting sharply against the sky, and Jim's kiln nearly undermining their base. When the lime-kiln flared up in the night, which it often did, its fires lit up the front of these ramparts to a great majesty. They were old friends of his, and while keeping up the heat through the long darkness, as it was sometimes his duty to do, he would imagine the dancing lights and shades about the stupendous earthwork to be the forms of those giants who (he supposed) had heaped it up. Often he clambered upon it, and walked about the summit, thinking out the problems connected with his business, his partner, his future, his Margery.

It was what he did this evening, continuing the meditation on the young girl's manner that he had begun upon the road, and still, as then, finding no clue to the change.

While thus engaged he observed a man coming up the ravine to the kiln. Business messages were almost invariably left at the house below, and Jim watched the man with the interest excited by a belief that he had come on a personal matter. On nearer approach Jim recognized him as the gardener at Mount Lodge some miles away. If this meant business, the Baron (of whose arrival Jim had vaguely heard) was a new and unexpected customer.

It meant nothing else, apparently. The man's errand was simply to inform Jim that the Baron required a load of lime for the garden.

'You might have saved yourself trouble by leaving word at Mr Vine's,' said Jim.

'I was to see you personally,' said the gardener, 'and to say that the Baron would like to inquire of you about the different qualities of lime proper for such purposes.'

'Couldn't you tell him yourself?' said Jim.

'He said I was to tell you that,' replied the gardener; 'and it wasn't for me to interfere.'

No motive other than the ostensible one could possibly be conjectured by Jim Hawyard at this time; and the next morning he started with great pleasure, in his best business suit of clothes. By eleven o'clock he and his horse and cart had arrived on the Baron's premises, and the lime was deposited where directed; an exceptional spot, just within view of the windows of the south front.

Baron von Xanten, pale and melancholy, was sauntering in the sun on the slope between the house and the all-the-year-round. He looked across to where Jim and the gardener were standing, and the identity of Hayward being established by what he brought, the Baron came down, and the gardener withdrew.

The Baron's first inquiries were, as Jim had been led to suppose they would be, on the exterminating effects of lime upon slugs and snails in its different conditions of slaked and unslaked, ground and in the lump. He appeared to be much interested by Jim's explanations, and eyed the young man closely whenever he had an opportunity.

'And I hope trade is prosperous with you this year,' said the Baron.

'Very, my noble lord,' replied Jim, who, in his uncertainty on the proper method of address, wisely concluded that it was better to err by giving too much honour than by giving too little. 'In short, trade is looking so well that I've become a partner in the firm.'

'Indeed; I am glad to hear it. So now you are settled in life.'

'Well, my lord, I am hardly settled, even now. For I've got to finish it – I mean, to get married.'

'That's an easy matter, compared with the partnership.'

'Now a man might think so, my baron,' said Jim, getting more confidential. 'But the real truth is, 'tis the hardest part of all for me.'

'Your suit prospers, I hope?'

'It don't,' said Jim. 'It don't at all just at present. In short, I can't for the life o' me think what's come over the young woman lately.' And he fell into deep reflection.

Though Jim did not observe it, the Baron's brow became shadowed with self-reproach as he heard those simple words, and his eyes had a look of pity. 'Indeed – since when?' he asked.

'Since yesterday, my noble lord.' Jim spoke meditatively. He was resolving upon a bold stroke. Why not make a confidant of this kind gentleman instead of the parson, as he had intended? The thought was no sooner conceived than acted on. 'My lord,' he resumed, 'I have heard that you are a nobleman of great scope and talent, who has seen more strange countries and characters than I have ever heard of, and know the insides of men well. Therefore I would fain put a question to your noble lordship, if I may so trouble you, and having nobody else in the world who could inform me so trewly.'

'Any advice I can give is at your service, Hayward. What do you wish to know?'

'It is this, my baron. What can I do to bring down a young woman's ambition that's got to such a towering height there's no reaching it or compassing it: how get her to be pleased with me and my station as she used to be when I first knew her?'

'Truly, that's a hard question, my man. What does she aspire to?'

'She's got a craze for fine furniture.'

'How long has she had it?'

'Only just now.'

The Baron seemed still more to experience regret. 'What furniture does she especially covet?' he asked.

'Silver candlesticks, work-tables, looking-glasses, gold tea-things, silver tea-pots, gold clocks, curtains, pictures, and I don't know what all – things I shall never get if I live to be a hundred – not so much that I couldn't raise the money to buy 'em, as that I ought to put it to other uses, or save it for a rainy day.'

'You think the possession of those articles would make her happy?'

'I really think they might, my lord.'

'Good. Open your pocket-book and write as I tell you.'

Jim in some astonishment did as commanded, and elevating his pocket-book against the garden-wall, thoroughly moistened his pencil and wrote at the Baron's dictation:

'Pair of silver candlesticks: inlaid work-table and work-box: one large mirror: two small ditto: one gilt china tea and coffee service: one silver tea-pot, coffee-pot, sugar-basin, jug, and dozen spoons: French clock: pair of curtains: six large pictures.'

'Now,' said the Baron, 'tear out that leaf and give it to me. Keep a close tongue about this; go home, and don't be surprised at anything that may come to your door.'

'But, my noble lord, you don't mean that your lordship is going to give—'

'Never mind what I am going to do. Only keep your own counsel. I perceive that, though a plain countryman, you are by no means deficient in tact and understanding. If sending these things to you gives me pleasure, why should you object? The fact is, Hayward, I occasionally take an interest in people, and like to do a little for them. I take an interest in you. Now go home, and a week hence invite Marg – the young woman and her father to tea with you. The rest is in your own hands.'

A question often put to Jim in after times was why it had not occurred to him at once that the Baron's liberal conduct must have been dictated by something more personal than sudden spontaneous generosity to him, a stranger. To which Jim always answered that, admitting the existence of such generosity, there had appeared nothing remarkable in the Baron selecting himself as its object. The Baron had told him that he took an interest in him; and self-esteem, even with the most modest, is usually sufficient to over-ride any little difficulty that might occur to an outsider in accounting for a preference. He moreover considered that foreign noblemen, rich and eccentric, might have habits of acting which were quite at variance with those of their English compeers.

So he drove off homeward with a lighter heart than he had known for several days. To have a foreign gentleman take a fancy to him – what a triumph to a plain sort of fellow, who had scarcely expected the Baron to look in his face. It would be a fine story to tell Margery when the Baron gave him liberty to speak out.

Jim lodged at the house of his cousin and partner, Richard Vine, a widower of fifty-odd years. Having failed in the development of a household of direct descendants this tradesman had been glad to let his chambers to his much younger relative, when the latter entered on the business of lime manufacture; and their intimacy had led to a partnership. Jim lived upstairs; his partner lived down, and the furniture of all the rooms was so plain and old-fashioned as to excite the special dislike of Miss Margery Tucker, and even to prejudice her against Jim for tolerating it. Not only were the chairs and tables queer, but, with due regard to the principle that a man's surroundings should bear the impress of that man's life and occupation, the chief ornaments of the dwelling were a curious collection of calcinations, that had been discovered from time to time in the lime-kiln – misshapen ingots of strange substance, some of them like Pompeian remains.

The head of the firm was a quiet-living, narrow-minded, though friendly, man of fifty; and he took a serious interest in Jim's love-suit, frequently inquiring how it progressed, and assuring Jim that if he chose to marry he might have all the upper floor at a low rent, he, Mr Vine, contenting himself entirely with the ground level. It had been so convenient for discussing business matters to have Jim in the same house, that he did not wish any change to be made in consequence of a change in Jim's domestic estate. Margery knew of this wish, and of Jim's concurrent feeling, and did not like the idea at all.

About four days after the young man's interview with the Baron, there drew up in front of Jim's house at noon a waggon laden with cases and packages, large and small. They were all addressed to 'Mr Hayward', and they had come from the largest furnishing warehouses in that part of England.

Three-quarters of an hour were occupied in getting the cases to Jim's rooms. The wary Jim did not show the amazement he felt at his patron's munificence; and presently the senior partner came into the passage, and wondered what was lumbering upstairs.

'O – it's only some things of mine,' said Jim coolly.

'Bearing upon the coming event – eh?' said his partner.

'Exactly,' replied Jim.

Mr Vine, with some astonishment at the number of cases, shortly after went away to the kiln; whereupon Jim shut himself into his rooms, and there he might have been heard ripping up and opening boxes with a cautious hand, afterwards appearing outside the door with them empty, and carrying them off to the outhouse.

A triumphant look lit up his face when, a little later in the afternoon, he went into the vale to the dairy, and invited Margery and her father to his house to supper.

She was not unsociable that day, and, her father expressing a hard and fast acceptance of the invitation, she perforce agreed to go with him. Meanwhile at home Jim made himself as mysteriously busy as before in those rooms of his, and when his partner returned he too was asked to join in the supper.

At dusk Hayward went to the door, where he stood till he heard the voices of his guests from the direction of the low grounds, now covered with their frequent fleece of fog. The voices grew more distinct, and then on the white surface of the fog there appeared two trunkless heads, from which bodies and a horse and cart gradually extended as the approaching pair rose towards the house.

When they had entered Jim pressed Margery's hand and conducted her up to his rooms, her father waiting below to say a few words to the senior lime-burner.

'Bless me,' said Jim to her, on entering the sitting-room, 'I quite forgot to get a light beforehand; but I'll have one in a jiffy.'

Margery stood in the middle of the dark room, while Jim struck a match; and then the young girl's eyes were conscious of a burst of light, and the rise into being of a pair of handsome silver candlesticks containing two candles that Jim was in the act of lighting.

'Why – where – you have candlesticks like that?' said Margery. Her eyes flew round the room as the growing candle-flames showed other articles. 'Pictures too – and lovely china – why, I knew nothing of of this, I declare.'

'Yes – a few things that came to me by accident,' said Jim in quiet tones.

'And a great gold clock under a glass, and a cupid swinging for a pendulum; and O what a lovely work-table – woods of every colour – and a work-box to match. May I look inside that work-box, Jim? – whose is it?'

'O yes; look at it, of course. It is a poor enough thing, but 'tis mine; and it will belong to the woman I marry, whoever she may be, as well as all the other things here.'

'And the curtains and the looking-glasses: why, I declare I can see myself in a hundred places.'

'That tea-set,' said Jim, placidly pointing to a gorgeous china service and a large silver tea-pot on the side-table, 'I don't use at present, being a bachelor-man; but, says I to myself, "whoever I marry will want some such things for giving her parties; or I can sell 'em" – but I haven't took steps for't yet—'

'Sell 'em – no, I should think not,' said Margery with earnest reproach. 'Why, I hope you wouldn't be so foolish! Why, this is exactly the kind of thing I was thinking of when I told you of the things women could want – of course not meaning myself particularly. I had no idea that you had such valuable—' Margery was unable to speak coherently, so much was she amazed at the wealth of Jim's possessions.

At this moment her father and the lime-burner came upstairs; and to appear womanly and proper to Mr Vine, Margery repressed the remainder of her surprise. As for the two elderly worthies, it was not till they entered the room and sat down that their slower eyes discerned anything brilliant in the appointments. Then one of them stole a glance at some article, and the other at another; but each being unwilling to express his wonder in the presence of his neighbours, they received the objects before them with quite an accustomed air; the lime-burner inwardly trying to conjecture what all this meant, and the dairyman musing that if Jim's business allowed him to accumulate at this rate, the sooner Margery became his wife the better. Margery retreated to the work-table, work-box, and tea-service, which she examined with hushed exclamations.

An entertainment thus surprisingly begun could not fail to progress well. Whenever Margery's crusty old father felt the need of a civil sentence, the flash of Jim's fancy articles inspired him to one; while the lime-burner, having reasoned away his first ominous thought that all this had come out of the firm, also felt proud and blithe.

Jim accompanied his dairy friends part of the way home before they mounted. Her father, finding that Jim wanted to speak to her privately, and that she exhibited some elusiveness, turned to Margery and said, 'Come, come, my lady; no more of this nonsense. You just step behind with that young man, and I and the cart will wait for you.'

Margery, a little scared of her father's peremptoriness, obeyed. It was plain that Jim had won the old man by that night's stroke, if he had not won her.

'I know what you are going to say, Jim,' she began, less ardently now, for she was no longer under the novel influence of the shining silver and glass. 'Well, as you desire it, and as my father desires it, and as I suppose it will be the best course for me, I will fix the day – not this evening, but as soon as I can think it over.'

8

Notwithstanding a press of business, Jim went and did his duty in thanking the Baron. The latter saw him in his fishing-tackle room, an apartment littered with every appliance that a votary of the rod could require.

'And when is the wedding-day to be, Hayward?' the Baron asked, after Jim had told him that matters were settled.

'It is not quite certain, my noble lord,' said Jim cheerfully. 'But I hope 'twill not be long after the time when God A'mighty christens the little apples.'

'And when is that?'

'St Swithin's – the middle of July. 'Tis to be some time in that month, she tells me.'

When Jim was gone the Baron seemed meditative. He went out,

ascended the mount, and entered the weather-screen, where he looked at the seats, as though re-enacting in his fancy the scene of that memorable morning of fog. He turned his eyes to the angle of the shelter, round which Margery had suddenly appeared like a vision, and it was plain that he would not have minded her appearing there then. The juncture had indeed been such an impressive and critical one that she must have seemed rather a heavenly messenger than a passing milkmaid, more especially to a man like the Baron, who, despite the mystery of his origin and life, revealed himself to be a melancholy, emotional character – the Jaques of this forest and stream.

Behind the mount the ground rose yet higher, ascending to a plantation which sheltered the house. The Baron strolled up here, and bent his gaze over the distance. The valley of the Exe lay before him, with its shining river, the brooks that fed it, and the trickling springs that fed the brooks. The situation of Margery's house was visible, though not the house itself; and the Baron gazed that way for an infinitely long time, till, remembering himself, he moved on.

Instead of returning to the house he went along the ridge till he arrived at the verge of Chillington Wood, and in the same desultory manner roamed under the trees, not pausing till he had come to Three-Walks-End, and the hollow elm hard by. He peeped in at the rift. In the soft dry layer of touchwood that floored the hollow Margery's tracks were still visible, as she had made them there when dressing for the ball.

'Little Margery!' murmured the Baron.

In a moment he thought better of this mood, and turned to go home. But behold, a form stood behind him – that of the girl whose name had been on his lips.

She was in utter confusion. 'I – I – did not know you were here, sir!' she began. 'I was out for a little walk.' She could get no further; her eyes filled with tears. That spice of wilfulness, even hardness, which characterized her in Jim's company, magically disappeared in the presence of the Baron.

'Never mind, never mind,' said he, masking under a severe manner whatever he felt. 'The meeting is awkward, and ought not to have occurred, especially if, as I suppose, you are shortly to be married to James Hayward. But it cannot be helped now. You had no idea I was here, of course. Neither had I of seeing you. Remember you cannot be too careful,' continued the Baron, in the same grave tone; 'and I strongly request you as a friend to do your utmost to avoid meetings like this. When you saw me before I turned, why did you not go away?'

'I did not see you, sir. I did not think of seeing you. I was walking this way, and I only looked in to see the tree.'

'That shows you have been thinking of things you should not think of,' returned the Baron. 'Good morning.'

Margery could answer nothing. A browbeaten glance, almost of misery, was all she gave him. He took a slow step away from her; then turned suddenly back and, stooping, impulsively kissed her cheek, taking her as much by surprise as ever a woman was taken in her life.

Immediately after he went off with a flushed face and rapid strides, which he did not check till he was within his own boundaries.

The haymaking season now set in vigorously, and the weirhatches were all drawn in the meads to drain off the water. The streams ran themselves dry, and there was no longer any difficulty in walking about among them. The Baron could very well witness from the elevations about his house the activity which followed these preliminaries. The white shirt-sleeves of the mowers glistened in the sun, the scythes flashed, voices echoed, snatches of song floated about, and there were glimpses of red waggon-wheels, purple gowns, and many-coloured handkerchiefs.

The Baron had been told that the haymaking was to be followed by the wedding, and had he gone down the vale to the dairy he would have had evidence to that effect. Dairyman Tucker's house was in a whirlpool of bustle, and among other difficultues was that of turning the cheese-room into a genteel apartment for the time being, and hiding the awkwardness of having to pass through the milk-house to get to the parlour door. These household contrivances appeared to interest Margery much more than the great question of dressing for the ceremony and the ceremony itself. In all relating to that she showed an indescribable backwardness, which later on was well remembered.

'If it were only somebody else, and I was one of the bridesmaids, I really think I should like it better!' she murmured one afternoon.

'Away with thee – that's only your shyness!' said one of the milkmaids.

It is said that about this time the Baron seemed to feel the effects of solitude strongly. Solitude revives the simple instincts of primitive man, and lonely country nooks afford rich soil for wayward emotions. Moreover, idleness waters those unconsidered impulses which a short season of turmoil would stamp out. It is difficult to speak with any exactness of the bearing of such conditions on the mind of the Baron – a man of whom so little was ever truly known – but there is no doubt that his mind ran much on Margery as an individual, without reference to her rank or quality, or to the question whether she would marry Jim Hayward that summer. She was the single lovely human thing within his present horizon, for he lived in absolute seclusion; and her image unduly affected him.

But, leaving conjecture, let me state what happened. One Saturday evening, two or three weeks after his accidental meeting with her in the wood, he wrote the note following:

DEAR MARGERY, –

You must not suppose that, because I spoke somewhat severely to you at our chance encounter by the hollow tree, I have any feeling against you. Far from it. Now, as ever, I have the most grateful sense of your considerate kindness to me on a momentous occasion which shall be nameless.

You solemnly promised to come and see me whenever I should send for you. Can you call for five minutes as soon as possible, and disperse those plaguy glooms from which I am so unfortunate as to suffer? If you refuse I will not answer for the consequences. I shall be in the summer shelter of the mount tomorrow morning at half-past ten. If you come I shall be grateful. I have also something for you.

Yours, x

In keeping with the tenor of this epistle the desponding, self-oppressed Baron ascended the mount on Sunday morning and sat down. There was nothing here to signify exactly the hour, but before the church bells had begun he heard somebody approaching at the back. The light footstep moved timidly, first to one recess, and then to another; then to the third, where he sat in the shade. Poor Margery stood before him.

She looked worn and weary, and her little shoes and the skirts of her dress were covered with dust. The weather was sultry, the sun being already high and powerful, and rain had not fallen for weeks. The Baron, who walked little, had thought nothing of the effects of this heat and drought in inducing fatigue. A distance which had been but a reasonable exercise on a foggy morning was a drag for Margery now. She was out of breath; and anxiety, even unhappiness, was written on her everywhere.

He rose to his feet and took her hand. He was vexed with himself at sight of her. 'My dear little girl!' he said. 'You are tired – you should not have come.'

'You sent for me, sir; and I was afraid you were ill; and my promise to you was sacred.'

He bent over her, looking upon her downcast face, and still holding her hand; then he dropped it, and took a pace or two backwards.

'It was a whim, nothing more,' he said sadly. 'I wanted to see my little friend, to express good wishes – and to present her with this.' He held forward a small morocco case, and showed her how to open it, disclosing a pretty locket set with pearls. 'It is intended as a wedding present,' he continued. 'To be returned to me again if you do not marry Jim this summer – it is to be this summer, I think?'

'It was, sir,' she said with agitation. 'But it is so no longer. And, therefore, I cannot take this.'

'What do you say?'

'It was to have been today; but now it cannot be.'

'The wedding today – Sunday?' he cried.

'We fixed Sunday not to hinder much time at this busy season of the year,' replied she.

'And have you, then, put it off – surely not?'

'You sent for me, and I have come,' she answered humbly, like an obedient familiar in the employ of some great enchanter. Indeed, the Baron's power over this innocent girl was curiously like enchantment, or mesmeric influence. It was so masterful that the sexual element was almost eliminated. It was that of Prospero over the gentle Ariel. And yet it was probably only that of the cosmopolite over the recluse, of the experienced man over the simple maid.

'You have come – on your wedding day! – O Margery, this is a mistake. Of course, you should not have obeyed me, since, though I thought your wedding would be soon, I did not know it was today.'

'I promised you, sir; and I would rather keep my promise to you than be married to Jim.'

'That must not be – the feeling is wrong!' he murmured, looking at the distant hills. 'There seems to be a fate in all this; I get out of the frying-pan into the fire. What a recompense to you for your goodness! The fact is, I was out of health and out of spirits, so I – but no more of that. Now instantly to repair this tremendous blunder that we have made – that's the question.'

After a pause, he went on hurriedly, 'Walk down the hill; get into the road. By that time I shall be there with a phaeton. We may get back in time. What time is it now? If not, no doubt the wedding can be tomorrow; so all will come right again. Don't cry, my dear girl. Keep the locket, of course – you'll marry Jim.'

9

He hastened down towards the stables, and she went on as directed. It seemed as if he must have put in the horse himself, so quickly did he reappear with the phaeton on the open road. Margery silently took her seat, and the Baron seemed cut to the quick with self-reproach as he noticed the listless indifference with which she acted. There was no doubt that in her heart she had preferred obeying the apparently important mandate that morning to becoming Jim's wife; but there was no less doubt that had the Baron left her alone she would quietly have gone to the altar.

He drove along furiously, in a cloud of dust. There was much to contemplate in that peaceful Sunday morning – the windless trees and fields, the shaking sunlight, the pause in human stir. Yet neither of them heeded, and thus they drew near to the dairy. His first expressed intention had been to go indoors with her, but this he abandoned as impolitic in the highest degree.

'You may be soon enough,' he said, springing down, and helping her to follow. 'Tell the truth: say you were sent for to receive a wedding present – that it was a mistake on my part – a mistake on yours; and I think they'll forgive. . . And, Margery, my last request to you is this: that if I send for you again, you do not come. Promise solemnly, my dear girl, that any such request shall be unheeded.'

Her lips moved, but the promise was not articulated. 'O, sir, I cannot promise it!' she said at last.

'But you must; your salvation may depend on it!' he insisted almost sternly. 'You don't know what I am.'

'Then, sir, I promise,' she replied. 'Now leave me to myself, please, and I'll go indoors and manage matters.'

He turned the horse and drove away, but only for a little distance. Out of sight he pulled rein suddenly. 'Only to go back and propose it to her, and she'd come!' he murmured.

He stood up in the phaeton, and by this means he could see over the hedge. Margery still sat listlessly in the same place; there was not a lovelier flower in the field. 'No,' he said; 'no, no – never!' He reseated himself, and the wheels sped lightly back over the soft dust to Mount Lodge.

Meanwhile Margery had not moved. If the Baron could dissimulate on the side of severity she could dissimulate on the side of calm. He did not know what had been veiled by the quiet promise to manage matters indoors. Rising at length she first turned away from the house; and by-and-by, having apparently forgotten till then that she carried it in her hand, she opened the case and looked at the locket. This seemed to give her courage. She turned, set her face towards the dairy in good earnest, and though her heart faltered when the gates came in sight, she kept on and drew near the door.

On the threshold she stood listening. The house was silent. Decorations were visible in the passage, and also the carefully swept and sanded path to the gate, which she was to have trodden as a bride; but the sparrows hopped over it as if it were abandoned; and all appeared to have been checked at its climacteric, like a clock stopped on the strike. Till this moment of confronting the suspended animation of the scene she had not realized the full shock of the convulsion which her disappearance must have caused. It is quite certain – apart from her own repeated assurances to that effect in later years – that in hastening off that morning to her sudden engagement, Margery had not counted the cost of such an enterprise; while a dim motion that she might get back again in time for the ceremony, if the message meant nothing serious, should also be mentioned in her favour. But, upon the whole, she had obeyed the call with an unreasoning obedience worthy of a disciple in primitive times. A conviction that the Baron's life might depend upon her presence – for she had by this time divined the tragical event she had interrupted on the foggy morning – took from her all will to judge and consider calmly. The simple affairs of her and hers seemed nothing beside the possibility of harm to him.

A well-known step moved on the sanded floor within, and she went forward. That she saw her father's face before her, just within the door, can hardly be said: it was rather Reproach and Rage in a human mask.

'What! ye have dared to come back alive, hussy, to look upon the dupery you have practised on honest people! You've mortified us all; I don't want to see 'ee; I don't want to know anything!' He walked up and down the room, unable to command himself. 'Nothing but being dead could have excused 'ee for not meeting and marrying that man this morning; and yet you have the brazen impudence to stand there as well as ever! What be you here for?'

'I've come back to marry Jim, if he wants me to,' she said faintly. 'And if not – perhaps so much the better. I was sent for this morning early. I thought—' She halted. To say that she had thought a man's death might happen by his own hand, if she did not go to him, would never do. 'I was obliged to go,' she said. 'I had given my word.'

'Why didn't you tell us, then, so that the wedding could be put off, without making fools o' us?'

'Because I was afraid you wouldn't let me go, and I had made up my mind to go.'

'To go where?'

She was silent; till she said, 'I will tell Jim all, and why it was; and if he's any friend of mine he'll excuse me.'

'Not Jim – he's no such fool. Jim had put all ready for you, Jim had called at your house, a-dressed up in his new wedding clothes, and a-smiling like the sun; Jim had told the parson, had got the ringers in tow, and the clerk awaiting; and then – you was *gone*! Then Jim turned as pale as rendlewood, and busted out, "If she don't marry me today," 'a said, "she don't marry me at all! No; let her look elsewhere for a husband. For tew years I've put up with her haughty tricks and her takings," 'a said. "I've droudged and I've traipsed, I've bought and I've sold, all wi' an eye to her; I've suffered horse-flesh," he says – yes, them was his noble words – "but I'll suffer it no longer. She shall go!" "Jim," says I, "you be a man. If she's alive, I commend 'ee; if she's dead, pity my old age." "She isn't dead," says he; "for I've just heard she was seen walking off across the fields this morning, looking all of a scornful triumph." He turned round and went, and the rest o' the neighbours went; and here be I left to the reproach o't.'

'He was too hasty,' murmured Margery. 'For now he's said this I can't marry him tomorrow, as I might ha' done; and perhaps so much the better.'

'You can be so calm about it, can ye? Be my arrangements nothing, then, that you should break 'em up, and say off-hand what wasn't done today might ha' been done tomorrow, and suck flick-flack? Out o' my sight! I won't hear any more. I won't speak to 'ee any more.'

'I'll go away, and then you'll be sorry.'

'Very well, go. Sorry – not I.'

He turned and stamped his way into the cheese-room. Margery went upstairs. She too was excited now, and instead of fortifying herself in her bedroom till her father's rage had blown over, as she had often done on lesser occasions, she packed up a bundle of articles, crept down again, and went out of the house. She had a place of refuge in these cases of necessity, and her father knew it, and was less alarmed at seeing her depart than he might otherwise have been. This place was Rook's Gate, the house of her grandmother, who always took Margery's part when that young woman was particularly in the wrong.

The devious way she pursued, to avoid the vicinity of Mount Lodge, was tedious, and she was already weary. But the cottage was a restful place to arrive at, for she was her own mistress there – her grandmother never coming downstairs – and Edy, the woman who lived with and attended her, being a cipher except in muscle and voice. The approach was by a straight open road, bordered by thin lank trees, all sloping away from the south-west windquarter, and the scene bore a strange resemblance to certain bits of Dutch landscape which have been imprinted on the world's eye by Hobbema and his school.

Having explained to her granny that the wedding was put off, and that she had come to stay, one of Margery's first acts was carefully to pack up the locket and case, her wedding present from the Baron. The conditions of the gift were unfulfilled, and she wished it to go back instantly. Perhaps, in the intricacies of her bosom, there lurked a greater satisfaction with the reason for returning the present than she would have felt just then with a reason for keeping it.

To send the article was difficult. In the evening she wrapped herself up, searched and found a gauze veil that had been used by her grandmother in past years for hiving swarms of bees, buried her face in it, and sallied forth with a palpitating heart till she drew near the tabernacle of her demi-god, the Baron. She ventured only to the back door, where she handed in the parcel addressed to him, and quickly came away.

Now it seems that during the day the Baron had been unable to learn the result of his attempt to return Margery in time for the event he had interrupted. Wishing, for obvious reasons, to avoid direct inquiry by messenger, and being too unwell to go far himself, he could learn no particulars. He was sitting in thought after a lonely dinner when the parcel intimating failure was brought in. The footman, whose curiosity had been excited by the mode of its arrival, peeped through the keyhole after closing the door to learn what the packet meant. Directly the Baron had opened it he thrust out his feet vehemently from his chair, and began cursing his ruinous conduct in bringing about such a disaster, for the return of the locket denoted not only no wedding that day, but none tomorrow, or at any time.

'I have done that innocent woman a great wrong!' he murmured. 'Deprived her of, perhaps, her only opportunity of becoming mistress of a happy home!'

10

A considerable period of inaction followed among all concerned.

Nothing tended to dissipate the obscurity which veiled the life of the Baron. The position he occupied in the minds of the country-folk around was one which combined the mysteriousness of a legendary character with the unobtrusive deeds of a modern gentleman. To this day whoever takes the trouble to go down to Silverthorn in Lower Wessex and make inquiries will find existing there almost a superstitious feeling for the moody, melancholy stranger who resided in the Lodge some forty years ago.

Whence he came, whither he was going were alike unknown. It was said that his mother had been an English lady of noble family who had married a foreigner not unheard of in circles where men pile up 'the cankered heaps of strange-achieved gold' – that he had been born and educated in England, taken abroad, and so on. But the facts of a life in such cases are of little account beside the aspect of a life; and hence, though doubtless the years of his existence contained their share of trite and homely circumstance, the curtain which masked all this was never lifted to gratify such a theatre of spectators, as those at Silverthorn. Therein lay his charm. His life was a vignette, of which the central strokes only were drawn with any distinctness, the environment shading away to a blank.

He might have been said to resemble that solitary bird, the heron. The still, lonely stream was his frequent haunt; on its banks he would stand for hours with his rod, looking into the water, beholding the tawny inhabitants with the eye of a philosopher, and seeming to say, 'Bite or don't bite – it's all the same to me.' He was often mistaken for a ghost by children; and for a pollard willow by men, when, on thir way home in the dusk, they saw him motionless by some rushy bank, unobservant of the decline of day.

Why did he come to fish near Silverthorn? That was never explained. As far as was known he had no relatives near; the fishing there was not exceptionally good; the society thereabout was decidedly meagre. That he had committed some folly or hasty act, that he had been wrongfully accused of some crime, thus rendering his seclusion from the world desirable for a while, squared very well with his frequent melancholy. But such as he was there he lived, well supplied with fishing-tackle, and tenant of a furnished house, just suited to the requirements of such an eccentric being as he.

Margery's father, having privately ascertained that she was living with her grandmother, and getting into no harm, refrained from communicating with her, in the hope of seeing her contrite at his door. It had, of course, become known about Silverthorn that at the last moment Margery refused to wed Hayward, by absenting herself from the house. Jim was pitied, yet not pitied much, for it was said that he ought not to have been so eager for a woman who had shown no anxiety for him.

And where was Jim himself? It must not be supposed that that tactician had all this while withdrawn from mortal eye to tear his hair in silent indignation and despair. He had, in truth, merely retired up the lonesome defile between the downs to his smouldering kiln, and the ancient ramparts above it; and there, after his first hours of natural discomposure, he quietly waited for overtures from the possibly repentant Margery. But no overtures arrived, and then he meditated anew on the absorbing problem of her skittishness, and how to set about another campaign for her conquest, notwithstanding his late disastrous failure. Why had he failed? To what was her strange conduct owing? That was the thing which puzzled him.

He had made no advance in solving the riddle when, one morning, a stranger appeared on the down above him, looking as if he had lost his way. The man had a good deal of black hair below his felt hat, and carried under his arm a case containing a musical instrument. Descending to where Jim stood, he asked if there were not a short cut across that way to Tivworthy, where a fête was to be held.

'Well, yes, there is,' said Jim. 'But 'tis an enormous distance for 'ee.'

'O yes,' replied the musician. 'I wish to intercept the carrier on the highway.'

The nearest way was precisely in the direction of Rook's Gate, where Margery, as Jim knew, was staying. Having some time to spare, Jim was strongly impelled to make a kind act to the lost musician a pretext for taking observations in that neighbourhood; and telling his acquaintance that he was going the same way, he started without further ado.

They skirted the long length of meads, and in due time arrived at the back of Rook's Gate, where the path joined the high road. A hedge divided the public way from the cottage garden. Jim drew up at this point and said, 'Your road is straight on: I turn back here.'

But the musician was standing fixed, as if in great perplexity. Thrusting his hand into his forest of black hair, he murmured, 'Surely it is the same – surely!'

Jim, following the direction of his neighbour's eyes, found them to be fixed on a figure till that moment hidden from himself – Margery Tucker – who was crossing the garden to an opposite gate with a little cheese in her arms, her head thrown back, and her face quite exposed.

'What of her?' said Jim.

'Two months ago I formed one of the band at the Yeomanry Ball given by Lord Toneborough in the next county. I saw that young lady dancing the polka there in robes of gauze and lace. Now I see her carry a cheese!'

'Never!' said Jim incredulously.

'But I do not mistake. I say it is so!'

Jim ridiculed the idea; the bandsman protested, and was about to lose his temper, when Jim gave in with the good-nature of a person who can afford to despise opinions; and the musician went his way.

As he dwindled out of sight Jim began to think more carefully over what he had said. The young man's thoughts grew quite to an excitement, for there came into his mind the Baron's extraordinary kindness in regard to furniture, hitherto accounted for by the assumption that the nobleman had taken a fancy to him. Could it be, among all the amazing things of life, that the Baron was at the bottom of this mischief, and that he had amused himself by taking Margery to a ball?

Doubts and suspicions which distract some lovers to imbecility only served to bring out Jim's great qualities. Where he trusted he was the most trusting fellow in the world; where he doubted he could be guilty of the slyest strategy. Once suspicious, he became one of those subtle, watchful characters who, without integrity, make good thieves; with a little, good jobbers; with a little more, good diplomatists. Jim was honest, and he considered what to do.

Retracing his steps, he peeped again. She had gone in; but she would soon reappear, for it could be seen that she was carrying little new cheeses one by one to a spring-cart and horse tethered outside the gate – her grandmother, though not a regular dairy-woman, still managing a few cows by means of a man and maid. With the lightness of a cat Jim crept round to the gate, took a piece of chalk from his pocket, and wrote upon the boarding '*The Baron*'. Then he retreated to the other side of the garden where he had just watched Margery.

In due time she emerged with another little cheese, came on to the garden door, and glanced upon the chalked words which confronted her. She started; the cheese rolled from her arms to the ground, and broke into pieces like a pudding.

She looked fearfully round, her face burning like sunset, and, seeing nobody, stooped to pick up the flaccid lumps. Jim, with a pale face, departed as invisibly as he had come. He had proved the bandsman's tale to be true. On his way back he formed a resolution. It was to beard the lion in his den – to call on the Baron.

Meanwhile Margery had recovered her equanimity, and gathered up the broken cheese. But she could by no means account for the handwriting. Jim was just the sort of fellow to play her such a trick at ordinary times, but she imagined him to be far too incensed against her to do it now; and she suddenly wondered if it were any sort of signal from the Baron himself.

Of him she had lately heard nothing. If every monotony pervaded a life it pervaded hers at Rook's Gate; and she had begun to despair of any happy change. But it is precisely when the social atmosphere seems stagnant that great events are brewing. Margery's quiet was broken first, as we have seen, by a slight start, only sufficient to make her drop a cheese; and then by a more serious matter.

She was inside the same garden one day when she heard two watermen talking without. The conversation was to the effect that the strange gentleman who had taken Mount Lodge for the season was seriously ill.

'How ill?' cried Margery through the ledge, which screened her from recognition.

'Bad abed,' said one of the watermen.

'Inflammation of the lungs,' said the other.

'Got wet, fishing,' the first chimed in.

Margery could gather no more. An ideal admiration rather than any positive passion existed in her breast for the Baron: she had of late seen too little of him to allow any incipient views of him as a lover to grow to formidable dimensions. It was an extremely romantic feeling, delicate as an aroma, capable of quickening to an active principle, or dying to 'a painless sympathy', as the case might be.

This news of his illness, coupled with the mysterious chalking on the gate, troubled her, and revived his image much. She took to walking up and down the garden-paths, looking into the hearts of flowers, and not thinking what they were. His last request had been that she was not to go to him if he should send for her; and now she asked herself, was the name on the gate a hint to enable her to go without infringing the letter of her promise? Thus unexpectedly had Jim's manoeuvre operated.

Ten days passed. All she could hear of the Baron were the same words, 'bad abed', till one afternoon, after a gallop of the physician to the Lodge, the tidings spread like lightning that the Baron was dying.

Margery distressed herself with the question whether she might be permitted to visit him and say her prayers at his bedside; but she feared to venture; and thus eight-and-forty hours slipped away, and the Baron still lived. Despite her shyness and awe of him she had almost made up her mind to call when, just at dusk on that October evening, somebody came to the door and asked for her.

She could see the messenger's head against the low new moon. He was a man-servant. He said he had been all the way to her father's, and had been sent thence to her there. He simply brought a note, and, delivering it into her hands, went away.

'DEAR MARGERY TUCKER,' ran the note – 'They say I am not likely to live, so I want to see you. Be here at eight o'clock this evening. Come quite alone to the side-door, and tap four times softly. My trusty man will admit you. The occasion is an important one. Prepare yourself for a solemn ceremony, which I wish to have performed while it lies in my power.

VON XANTEN'

II

Margery's face flushed up, and her neck and arms glowed in sympathy. The quickness of youthful imagination, and the assumptiveness of woman's reason, sent her straight as an arrow this thought: 'He wants to marry me!'

She had heard of similar strange proceedings, in which the orange-flower and the sad cypress were intertwined. People sometimes wished on their deathbeds, from motives of esteem, to form a legal tie which they had not cared to establish as a domestic one during their active life.

For a few minutes Margery could hardly be called excited; she was excitement itself. Between surprise and modesty she blushed and trembled by turns. She became grave, sat down in the solitary room, and looked into the fire. At seven o'clock she rose resolved, and went quite tranquilly upstairs, where she speedily began to dress.

In making this hasty toilet nine-tenths of her care were given to her hands. The summer had left them slightly brown, and she held them up and looked at them with some misgiving, the fourth finger of her left hand more especially. Hot washings and cold washings, certain products from bee and flower known only to country girls, everything she could think of, were used upon those little sunburnt hands, till she persuaded herself that they were really as white as could be wished by a husband with a hundred titles. Her dressing completed, she left word with Edy that she was going for a long walk, and set out in the direction of Mount Lodge.

She no longer tripped like a girl, but walked like a woman. While crossing the park she murmured 'Baroness von Xanten' in a pronunciation of her own. The sound of that title caused her such agitation that she was obliged to pause, with her hand upon her heart.

The house was so closely neighboured by shrubberies on three of its sides that it was not till she had gone nearly round it that she found the little door. The resolution she had been an hour in forming failed her when she stood at the portal. While pausing for courage to tap, a carriage drove up to the front entrance a little way off, and peeping round the corner she saw alight a clergyman, and a gentleman in whom Margery fancied that she recognized a well-known solicitor from the neighbouring town. She had no longer any doubt of the nature of the ceremony proposed. 'It is sudden – but I must obey him!' she murmured: and tapped four times.

The door was opened so quickly that the servant must have been standing immediately inside. She thought him the man who had driven them to the ball – the silent man who could be trusted. Without a word he conducted her up the back staircase, and through a door at the top, into a wide corridor. She was asked to wait in a little dressing-room, where there was a fire, and an old metal-framed looking-glass over the mantelpiece, in which she caught sight of herself. A red spot burnt in each of her cheeks; the rest of her face was pale; and her eyes were like diamonds of the first water.

Before she had been seated many minutes the man came back noiselessly, and she followed him to a door covered by a red and black curtain, which he lifted, and ushered her into a large chamber. A screened light stood on a table before her, and on her left the hangings of a tall, dark, four-post bedstead obstructed her view of the centre of the room. Everything here seemed of such a magnificent type to her eyes that she felt confused, diminished to half her height, half her strength, half her prettiness. The man who had conducted her retired at once, and some one came softly round the angle of the bed-curtains. He held out his hand kindly – rather patronizingly: it was the solicitor whom she knew by sight. This gentleman led her forward, as if she had been a lamb rather than a woman, till the occupant of the bed was revealed.

The Baron's eyes were closed, and her entry had been so noiseless that he did not open them. The pallor of his face nearly matched the white bed-linen, and his dark hair and heavy black moustache were like dashes of ink on a clean page. Near him sat the parson and another gentleman, whom she afterwards learnt to be a London physician; and on the parson whispering a few words the Baron opened his eyes. As soon as he saw her he smiled faintly, and held out his hand.

Margery would have wept for him, if she had not been too overawed and palpitating to do anything. She quite forgot what she had come for, shook hands with him mechanically, and could hardly return an answer to his weak 'Dear Margery, you see how I am – how are you?'

In preparing for marriage she had not calculated on such a scene as this. Her affection for the Baron had too much of the vague in it to afford her trustfulness now. She wished she had not come. On a sign from the Baron the lawyer brought her a chair, and the oppressive silence was broken by the Baron's words.

'I am pulled down to death's door, Margery,' he said; 'and I suppose I soon shall pass through. . . My peace has been much disturbed in this illness, for just before it attacked me I received – that present you returned, from which, and in other ways, I learnt that you had lost your chance of marriage. . . Now it was I who did the harm, and you can imagine how the news has affected me. It has worried me all the illness through, and I cannot dismiss my error from my mind. . . I want to right the wrong I have done you before I die. Margery, you have always obeyed me, and, strange as the request may be, will you obey me now?'

She whispered 'Yes.'

'Well, then,' said the Baron, 'these three gentlemen are here for a special purpose: one helps the body – he's called a physician; another helps the soul – he's a parson; the other helps the understanding – he's a lawyer. They are here partly on my account, and partly on yours.'

The speaker then made a sign to the lawyer, who went out of the door. He came back almost instantly, but not alone. Behind him, dressed up in his best clothes, with a flower in his buttonhole and a bridegroom's air, walked – Jim.

12

Margery could hardly repress a scream. As for flushing and blushing, she had turned hot and turned pale so many times already during the evening, that there was really now nothing of that sort left for her to do; and she remained in complexion much as before. O, the mockery of it! That secret dream – that sweet word 'Baroness!' – which had sustained her all the way along. Instead of a Baron there stood Jim, white-waistcoated, demure, every hair in place, and, if she mistook not, even a deedy spark in his eye.

Jim's surprising presence on the scene may be briefly accounted for. His resolve to seek an explanation with the Baron at all risks had proved unexpectedly easy: the interview had at once been granted, and then, seeing the crisis at which matters stood, the Baron had generously revealed to Jim the whole of his indebtedness to and knowledge of Margery. The truth of the Baron's statement, the innocent nature as yet of the acquaintanceship, his sorrow for the rupture he had produced, was so evident that, far from having any further doubts of his patron, Jim frankly asked his advice on the next step to be pursued. At this stage the Baron fell ill, and, desiring much to see the two young people united before his death, he had sent anew to Hayward, and proposed the plan which they were now about to attempt – a marriage at the bedside of the sick man by special licence. The influence at Lambeth of some friends of the Baron's, and the charitable bequests of his late mother to several deserving Church funds, were generally supposed to be among the reasons why the application for the licence was not refused.

This, however, is of small consequence. The Baron probably knew, in proposing this method of celebrating the marriage, that his enormous power over her would outweigh any sentimental obstacle which she might set up – inward objections that, without his presence and firmness, might prove too much for her acquiescence. Doubtless he foresaw, too, the advantage of getting her into the house before making the individuality of her husband clear to her mind.

Now, the Baron's conjectures were right as to the event, but wrong as to the motives. Margery was a perfect little dissembler on some occasions, and one of them was when she wished to hide any sudden mortification that might bring her into ridicule. She had no sooner recovered from her first fit of discomfiture than pride bade her suffer anything rather than reveal her absurd disappointment. Hence the scene progressed as follows:

'Come here, Hayward,' said the invalid. Hayward came near. The Baron, holding her hand in one of his own, and her lover's in the other, continued, 'Will you, in spite of your recent vexation with her, marry her now if she does not refuse?'

'I will, sir,' said Jim promptly.

'And Margery, what do you say? It is merely a setting of things right. You have already promised this young man to be his wife, and should, of course, perform your promise. You don't dislike Jim?'

'O no, sir,' she said, in a low, dry voice.

'I like him better than I can tell you,' said the Baron. 'He is an honourable man, and will make you a good husband. You must remember that marriage is a life contract, in which general compatibility of temper and worldly position is of more importance than fleeting passion, which never long survives. Now, will you, at my earnest request, and before I go to the South of Europe to die, agree to make this good man happy? I have expressed your views on the subject, haven't I, Hayward?'

'To a T, sir,' said Jim emphatically, with a motion of raising his hat to his influential ally, till he remembered he had no hat on. 'And, though I could hardly expect Margery to gie in for my asking, I feels she ought to gie in for yours.'

'And you accept him, my little friend?'

'Yes, sir,' she murmured, 'if he'll agree to a thing or two.'

'Doubtless he will – what are they?'

'That I shall not be made to live with him till I am in the mind for it; and that my having him shall be kept unknown for the present.'

'Well, what do you think of it, Hayward?'

'Anything that you or she may wish I'll do, my noble lord,' said Jim.

'Well, her request is not unreasonable, seeing that the proceedings are, on my account, a little hurried. So we'll proceed. You rather expected this, from my allusion to a ceremony in my note, did you not, Margery?'

'Yes, sir,' said she, with an effort.

'Good; I thought so; you looked so little surprised.'

We now leave the scene in the bedroom for a spot not many yards off.

When the carriage seen by Margery at the door was driving up to Mount Lodge it arrested the attention, not only of the young girl, but of a man who had for some time been moving slowly about the opposite lawn, engaged in some operation while he smoked a short pipe. A short observation of his doings would have shown that he was sheltering some delicate plants from an expected frost, and that he was the gardener. When the light at the door fell upon the entering forms of parson and lawyer – the former a stranger, the latter known to him – the gardener walked thoughtfully round the house. Reaching the small side-entrance he was further surprised to see it noiselessly open to a young woman, in whose momentarily illumined features he discerned those of Margery Tucker.

Altogether there was something curious in this. The man returned to the lawn front, and perfunctorily went on putting shelters over certain plants, though his thoughts were plainly otherwise engaged. On the grass his footsteps were noiseless, and the night moreover being still, he could presently hear a murmuring from the bedroom window over his head.

The gardener took from a tree a ladder that he had used in nailing that day, set it under the window, and ascended half-way, hoodwinking his conscience by seizing a nail or two with his hand and testing their twig-supporting powers. He soon heard enough to satisfy him. The words of a church-service in the strange parson's voice were audible in snatches through the blind: they were words he knew to be part of the solemnization of matrimony, such as 'wedded wife', 'richer for poorer', and so on; the less familiar parts being a more or less confused sound.

Satisfied that a wedding was in progress there, the gardener did not for a moment dream that one of the contracting parties could be other than the sick Baron. He descended the ladder and again walked round the house, waiting only till he saw Margery emerge from the same little door; when, fearing that he might be discovered, he withdrew in the direction of his own cottage.

This building stood at the lower corner of the garden, and as soon as the gardener entered he was accosted by a handsome woman in a widow's cap, who called him father, and said that supper had been ready for a long time. They sat down, but during the meal the gardener was so abstracted and silent that his daughter put her head winningly to one side and said, 'What is it, father dear?'

'Ah – what is it?' cried the gardener. 'Something that makes very little difference to me, but may be of great account to you, if you play your cards well. *There's been a wedding at the Lodge tonight!*' He related to her, with a caution to secrecy, all that he had heard and seen.

'We are folk that have got to get their living,' he said, 'and such ones mustn't tell tales about their betters – Lord forgive the mockery of the word! – but there's something to be made of it. She's a nice maid; so, Harriet, do you take the first chance you get for honouring her, before others know what has happened. Since this is done so privately it will be kept private for some time – till after his death, no question; when I expect she'll take this house for herself, and blaze out as a widow-lady ten thousand pound strong. You being a widow, she may make you her company-keeper; and so you'll have a home by a little contriving.'

While this conversation progressed at the gardener's Margery was on her way out of the Baron's house. She was, indeed, married. But, as we know, she was not married to the Baron. The ceremony over she seemed but little discomposed, and expressed a wish to return alone as she had come. To this, of course, no objection could be offered under the terms of the agreement, and wishing Jim a frigid good-bye, and the Baron a very quiet farewell, she went out by the door which had admitted her. Once safe and alone in the darkness of the park she burst into tears, which dropped upon the grass as she passed along. In the Baron's room she had seemed scared and helpless; now her reason and emotions returned. The farther she got away from the glamour of that room, and the influence of its occupant, the more she became of opinion that she had acted foolishly. She had disobediently left her father's house, to obey him here. She had pleased everybody but herself.

However, thinking was now too late. How she got into her grandmother's house she hardly knew; but without a supper, and without confronting either her relative or Edy, she went to bed.

13

On going out into the garden next morning, with a strange sense of being another person than herself, she beheld Jim leaning mutely over the gate.

He nodded. 'Good morning, Margery,' he said civilly.

'Good morning,' said Margery in the same tone.

'I beg your pardon,' he continued. 'But which way was you going this morning?'

'I'm not going anywhere just now, thank you. But I shall go to my father's by-and-by with Edy.' She went on with a sigh, 'I have done what he has all along wished, that is, married you; and there's no longer reason for enmity atween him and me.'

'Trew – trew. Well, as I am going the same way, I can give you a lift in the trap, for the distance is long.'

'No, thank you – I am used to walking,' she said.

They remained in silence, the gate between them, till Jim's convictions would apparently allow him to hold his peace no longer. 'This is a bad job!' he murmured.

'It is,' she said, as one whose thoughts have only too readily been identified. 'How I came to agree to it is more than I can tell!' And tears began rolling down her cheeks.

'The blame is more mine than yours, I suppose,' he returned. 'I ought to have said No, and not backed up the gentleman in carrying out this scheme. 'Twas his own notion entirely, as perhaps you know. I should never have thought of such a plan; but he said you'd be willing, and that it would be all right; and I was too ready to believe him.'

'The thing is, how to remedy it,' said she bitterly. 'I believe, of course, in your promise to keep this private, and not to trouble me by calling.'

'Certainly,' said Jim. 'I don't want to trouble you. As for that, why, my dear Mrs Hayward—'

'Don't Mrs Hayward me!' said Margery sharply. 'I won't be Mrs Hayward!'

Jim paused. 'Well, you are she by law, and that was all I meant,' he said mildly.

'I said I would acknowledge no such thing, and I won't. A thing can't be legal when it's against the wishes of the persons the laws are made to protect. So I beg you not to call me that any more.'

'Very well, Miss Tucker,' said Jim deferentially. 'We can live on exactly as before. We can't marry anybody else, that's true; but beyond that there's no difference, and no harm done. Your father ought to be told, I suppose, even if nobody else is? It will partly reconcile him to you, and make your life smoother.'

Instead of directly replying, Margery exlaimed in a low voice:

'O, it is a mistake – I didn't see it all, owing to not having time to reflect! I agreed, thinking that at least I should get reconciled to my father by the step. But perhaps he would as soon have me not married at all as married and parted. I must ha' been enchanted – bewitched – when I gave my consent to this! I only did it to please that dear good dying nobleman – though why he should have wished it so much I can't tell!'

'Nor I neither,' said Jim. 'Yes, we've been fooled into it, Margery,' he said, with extraordinary gravity. 'He's had his way wi' us, and now we've got to suffer for it. Being a gentleman of patronage, and having bought several loads of lime o' me, and having given me all that splendid furniture, I could hardly refuse—'

'What, did he give you that?'

'Ay sure – to help me win ye.'

Margery covered her face with her hands; whereupon Jim stood up from the gate and looked critically at her. ''Tis a footy plot between you two men to – snare me!' she exclaimed. 'Why should you have done it – why should he have done it – when I've not deserved to be treated so? He bought the furniture, did he! O, I've been taken in – I've been wronged!' The grief and vexation of finding that long ago, when fondly believing the Baron to have lover-like feelings himself for her, he was still conspiring to favour Jim's suit, was more than she could endure.

Jim with distant courtesy waited, nibbling a straw, till her paroxysm was over. 'One word, Miss Tuck – Mrs – Margery,' he then recommenced gravely. 'You'll find me man enough to respect your wish, and to leave you to yourself – for ever and ever, if that's all. But I've just one word of advice to render 'ee. That is, that before you go to Silverthorn Dairy yourself you let me drive ahead and call on your father. He's friends with me, and he's not friends with you. I can break the news, a little at a time, and I think I can gain his goodwill for you now, even though the wedding be no natural wedding at all. At any count, I can hear what he's got to say about 'ee, and come back here and tell 'ee.'

She nodded a cool assent to this, and he left her strolling about the garden in the sunlight while he went on to reconnoitre as agreed. It must not be supposed that Jim's dutiful echoes of Margery's regret at her precipitate marriage were all gospel; and there is no doubt that his private intention, after telling the dairy-farmer what had happened, was to ask his temporary assent to her caprice, till, in the course of time, she should be reasoned out of her whims and induced to settle down with Jim in a natural manner. He had, it is true, been somewhat nettled by her firm objection to him, and her keen sorrow for what she had done to please another; but he hoped for the best.

But, alas for the astute Jim's calculations! He drove on to the dairy, whose white walls now gleamed in the morning sun; made fast the horse to a ring in the wall, and entered the barton. Before knocking, he perceived the dairyman walking across from a gate in the other direction, as if he had just come in. Jim went over to him. Since the unfortunate incident on the morning of the intended wedding they had merely been on nodding terms, from a sense of awkwardness in their relations.

'What – is that thee?' said Dairyman Tucker, in a voice which unmistakably startled Jim by its abrupt fierceness. 'A pretty fellow thou be'st!'

It was a bad beginning for the young man's life as a son-in-law, and augured ill for the delicate consultation he desired.

'What's the matter?' said Jim.

'Matter! I wish some folks would burn their lime without burning other folks' property along wi' it. You ought to be ashamed of yourself. You call yourself a man, Jim Hayward, and an honest lime-burner, and a respectable, market-keeping Christen, and yet at six o'clock this morning, instead o' being where you ought to ha' been – at your work, there was neither vell or mark o' thee to be seen!'

'Faith, I don't know what you are raving at,' said Jim.

'Why – the sparks from thy couch-heap blew over upon my hay-rick, and the rick's burst to ashes; and all to come out o' my well-squeezed pocket. I'll tell thee what it is, young man. There's no business in thee. I've known Silverthorn folk, quick and dead, for the last couple-o'-score year, and I've never knew one so three-cunning for harm as thee, my gentleman lime-burner; and I reckon it one o' the luckiest days o' my life when I 'scaped having thee in my family. That maid of mine was right; I was wrong. She seed thee to be a drawlacheting rogue, and 'twas her wisdom to go off that morning and get rid o' thee. I commend her for't, and I'm going to fetch her home tomorrow.'

'You needn't take the trouble. She's coming home-along tonight of her own accord. I have seen her this morning, and she told me so.'

'So much the better. I'll welcome her warm. Nation! I'd sooner see her married to the parish fool than thee. Not you – you don't care for my hay. Tarrying about where you shouldn't be – in bed, no doubt; that's what you was a-doing. Now, don't you darken my doors again, and the sooner you be off my bit o' ground the better I shall be pleased.'

Jim looked, as he felt, stultified. If the rick had been really destroyed, a little blame certainly attached to him, but he could not understand how it had happened. However, blame or none, it was clear he could not, with any self-respect, declare himself to be this peppery old gaffer's son-in-law in the face of such an attack as this.

For months – almost years – the one transaction that had seemed necessary to compose these two families satisfactorily was Jim's union with Margery. No sooner had it been completed than it appeared on all sides as the gravest mishap for both. Stating coldly that he would discover how much of the accident was to be attributed to his negligence, and pay the damage, he went out of the barton and returned the way he had come.

Margery had been keeping a look-out for him, particularly wishing him not to enter the house, lest others should see the seriousness of their interview; and as soon as she heard wheels she went to the gate, which was out of view.

'Surely father has been speaking roughly with you!' she said, on seeing his face.

'Not the least doubt that he have,' said Jim.

'But is he still angry with me?'

'Not in the least. He's waiting to welcome 'ee.'

'Ah! because I've married you.'

'Because he thinks you have *not* married me! He's jawed me up hill and down. He hates me; and for your sake I have not explained a word.'

Margery looked towards home with a sad, severe gaze. 'Mr Hayward,' she said, 'we have made a great mistake, and we are in a strange position.'

'True, but I'll tell you what, mistress – I won't stand –' He stopped suddenly. 'Well, well; I've promised!' he quietly added.

'We must suffer for our mistake,' she went on. 'The way to suffer least is to keep our own counsel on what happened last evening, and not to meet. I must now return to my father.'

He inclined his head in indifferent assent, and she went indoors, leaving him there.

14

Margery returned home, as she had decided, and resumed her old life at Silverthorn. And seeing her father's animosity towards Jim, she told him not a word of the marriage.

Her inner life, however, was not what it once had been. She had suffered a mental and emotional displacement – a shock, which had set a shade of astonishment on her face as a permanent thing.

Her indignation with the Baron for collusion with Jim, at first bitter, lessened with the lapse of a few weeks, and at length vanished in the interest of some tidings she received one day.

The Baron was not dead, but he was no longer at the Lodge. To the surprise of the physicians, a sufficient improvement had taken place in his condition to permit of his removal before the cold weather came. His desire for removal had been such, indeed, that it was advisable to carry it out at almost any risk. The plan adopted had been to have him borne on men's shoulders in a sort of palanquin to the shore near Idmouth, a distance of several miles, where a yacht lay awaiting him. By this means the noise and jolting of a carriage, along irregular bye-roads, were avoided. The singular procession over the fields took place at night, and was witnessed by but few people, one being a labouring man, who described the scene to Margery. When the seaside was reached a long, narrow gangway was laid from the deck of the yacht to the shore, which was so steep as to allow the yacht to lie quite near. The men, with their burden, ascended by the light of lanterns, the sick man was laid in the cabin, and, as soon as his bearers had returned to the shore, the gangway was removed, a rope was heard skirring over wood in the darkness, the yacht quivered, spread her woven wings to the air, and moved away. Soon she was but a small shapeless phantom upon the wide breast of the sea.

It was said that the yacht was bound for Algiers.

When the inimical autumn and winter weather came on, Margery wondered if he were still alive. The house being shut up, and the servants gone, she had no means of knowing, till, on a particular Saturday, her father drove her to Exonbury market. Here, in attending to his business, he left her to herself for a while. Walking in a quiet street in the professional quarter of the town, she saw coming towards her the solicitor who had acted for the Baron in various small local matters during his brief residence at the Lodge.

She reddened to peony hues, averted her eyes, and would have passed him. But he crossed over and barred the pavement, and when she met his glance he was looking with friendly severity at her. The street was quiet, and he said in a low voice, 'How's the husband?'

'I don't know, sir,' said she.

'What – and are your stipulations about secrecy and separate living still in force?'

'They always will be,' she replied decisively. 'Mr Hayward and I agreed on the point, and we have not the slightest wish to change the arrangement.'

'H'm. Then 'tis Miss Tucker to the world; Mrs Hayward to me and one or two others only?'

Margery nodded. Then she nerved herself by an effort, and, though blushing painfully, asked, 'May I put one question, sir? Is the Baron dead?'

'He is dead to you and to all of us. Why should you ask?'

'Because, if he's alive, I am sorry I married James Hayward. If he is dead I do not much mind my marriage.'

'I repeat, he is dead to you,' said the lawyer emphatically. 'I'll tell you all I know. My professional services for him ended with his departure from this country; but I think I should have heard from him if he had been alive still. I have not heard at all: and this, taken in connection with the nature of his illness, leaves no doubt in my mind that he is dead.'

Margery sighed, and thanking the lawyer she left him with a tear for the Baron in her eye. After this incident she became more restful; and the time drew on for her periodical visit to her grandmother.

A few days subsequent to her arrival her aged relative asked her to go with a message to the gardener at Mount Lodge (who still lived on there, keeping the grounds in order for the landlord). Margery hated that direction now, but she went. The Lodge, which she saw over the trees, was to her like a skull from which the warm and living flesh had vanished. It was twilight by the time she reached the cottage at the bottom of the Lodge garden, and, the room being illuminated within, she saw through the window a woman she had never seen before. She was dark, and rather handsome, and when Margery knocked she opened the door. It was the gardener's widowed daughter, who had been advised to make friends with Margery.

She now found her opportunity. Margery's errand was soon completed, the young widow, to her surprise, treating her with preternatural respect, and afterwards offering to accompany her home. Margery was not sorry to have a companion in the gloom, and they walked on together. The widow, Mrs Peach, was demonstrative and confidential, and told Margery all about herself. She had come quite recently to live with her father – during the Baron's illness, in fact – and her husband had been captain of a ketch.

'I saw you one morning, ma'am,' she said. 'But you didn't see me. It was when you were crossing the hill in sight of the Lodge. You looked at it, and sighed. 'Tis the lot of widows to sigh, ma'am, is it not?'

'Widows – yes, I suppose; but what do you mean?'

Mrs Peach lowered her voice. 'I can't say more, ma'am, with proper respect. But there seems to be no question of the poor Baron's death; and though these foreign princes can take (as my poor husband used to tell me) what they call left-handed wives, and leave them behind when they go abroad, widowhood is widowhood, left-handed or right. And really, to be the left-handed wife of a foreign baron is nobler than to be married all round to a common man. You'll excuse my freedom, ma'am; but being a widow myself, I have pitied you from my heart; so young as you are, and having to keep it a secret, and (excusing me) having no money out of his vast riches because 'tis swallowed up by Baroness Number One.'

Now Margery did not understand a word more of this than the bare fact that Mrs Peach suspected her to be the Baron's undowered widow, and such was the milkmaid's nature that she did not deny the widow's impeachment. The latter continued –

'But ah, ma'am, all your troubles are straight backward in your memory – while I have troubles before as well as grief behind.'

'What may they be, Mrs Peach?' inquired Margery, with an air of the Baroness.

The other dropped her voice to revelation tones: 'I have been forgetful enough of my first man to lose my heart to a second!'

'You shouldn't do that – it is wrong. You should control your feelings.'

'But how am I to control my feelings?'

'By going to your dead husband's grave, and things of that sort.'

'Do you go to your dead husband's grave?'

'How can I go to Algiers?'

'Ah – too true! Well, I've tried everything to cure myself – read the words against it, gone to the Table the first Sunday of every month, and all sorts. But, avast, my shipmate – as my poor man used to say – there 'tis just the same. In short, I've made up my mind to encourage the new one. 'Tis flattering that I, a newcomer, should have been found out by a young man so soon.'

'Who is he?' said Margery listlessly.

'A master lime-burner.'

'A master lime-burner?'

'That's his profession. He's a partner-in-co., doing very well indeed.'

'But what's his name?'

'I don't like to tell you his name, for, though 'tis night, that covers all shame-facedness, my face is as hot as a 'Talian iron, I declare! Do you just feel it.'

Margery put her hand on Mrs Peach's face, and, sure enough, hot it was. 'Does he come courting?' she asked quickly.

'Well – only in the way of business. He never comes unless lime is wanted in the neighbourhood. He's in the Yeomanry, too, and will look very fine when he comes out in regimentals for drill in May.'

'Oh – in the Yeomanry,' Margery said, with slight relief. 'Then it can't – is he a young man?'

'Yes, junior partner-in-co.'

The description had an odd resemblance to Jim, of whom Margery had not heard a word for months. He had promised silence and absence, and had fulfilled his promise literally, with a gratuitous addition that was rather amazing, if indeed it were Jim whom the widow loved. One point in the description puzzled Margery: Jim was not in the Yeomanry, unless, by a surprising development of enterprise, he had entered it recently.

At parting Margery said, with an interest quite tender, 'I should like to see you again, Mrs Peach, and hear of your attachment. When can you call?'

'Oh – any time, dear Baroness, I'm sure – if you think I am good enough.'

'Indeed, I do, Mrs Peach. Come as soon as you've seen the lime-burner again.'

15

Seeing that Jim lived several miles from the widow, Margery was rather surprised, and even felt a slight sinking of the heart, when her new acquaintance appeared at her door so soon as the evening of the following Monday. She asked Margery to walk out with her, which the young woman readily did.

'I am come at once,' said the widow breathlessly, as soon as they were in the lane, 'for it is so exciting that I can't keep it. I must tell it to somebody, if only a bird, or a cat, or a garden snail.'

'What is it?' asked her companion.

'I've pulled grass from my husband's grave to cure it – wove the blades into true lover's knots; took off my shoes upon the sod; but, avast, my shipmate!—'

'Upon the sod – why?'

'To feel the damp earth he's in, and make the sense of it enter my soul. But no. It has swelled to a head; he is going to meet me at the Yeomanry Review.'

'The master lime-burner?'

The widow nodded.

'When is it to be?'

'Tomorrow. He looks so lovely in his accoutrements! He's such a splendid soldier; that was the last straw that kindled my soul to say yes. He's home from Exonbury for a night between the drills,' continued Mrs Peach. 'He goes back tomorrow morning for the Review, and when it's over he's going to meet me... But, guide my heart, there he is!'

Her exclamation had rise in the sudden appearance of a brilliant red uniform through the trees, and the tramp of a horse carrying the wearer thereof. In another half-minute the military gentleman would have turned the corner, and faced them.

'He'd better not see me; he'll think I know too much,' said Margery precipitately. 'I'll go up here.'

The widow, whose thoughts had been of the same cast, seemed much relieved to see Margery disappear in the plantation, in the midst of a spring chorus of birds. Once among the trees, Margery turned her head, and, before she could see the rider's person, she recognized the horse as

Tony, the lightest of three that Jim and his partner owned, for the purpose of carting out lime to their customers.

Jim, then, had joined the Yeomanry since his estrangement from Margery. A man who had worn the Young Queen Victoria's uniform for seven days only could not be expected to look as if it were part of his person, in the manner of long-trained soldiers; but he was a well-formed young fellow, and of an age when few positions come amiss to one who has the capacity to adapt himself to circumstances.

Meeting the blushing Mrs Peach (to whom Margery in her mind sternly denied the right to blush at all), Jim alighted and moved on with her, probably at Mrs Peach's own suggestion; so that what they said, how long they remained together, and how they parted, Margery knew not. She might have known some of these things by waiting; but the presence of Jim had bred in her heart a sudden disgust for the widow, and a general sense of discomfiture. She went away in an opposite direction, turning her head and saying to the unconscious Jim, 'There's a fine rod in pickle for you, my gentleman, if you carry out that pretty scheme!'

Jim's military *coup* had decidedly astonished her. What he might do next she could not conjecture. The idea of his doing anything sufficiently brilliant to arrest her attention would have seemed ludicrous, had not Jim, by entering the Yeomanry, revealed a capacity for dazzling exploits which made it unsafe to predict any limitation to his powers.

Margery was now excited. The daring of the wretched Jim in bursting into scarlet amazed her as much as his doubtful acquaintanceship with the demonstrative Mrs Peach. To go to that Review, to watch the pair, to eclipse Mrs Peach in brilliancy, to meet and pass them in withering contempt – if she only could do it! But, alas! she was a forsaken woman. 'If the Baron were alive, or in England,' she said to herself (for sometimes she thought he might possibly be alive), 'and he were to take me to this Review, wouldn't I show that forward Mrs Peach what a lady is like, and keep among the select company, and not mix with the common people at all!'

It might at first sight be thought that the best course for Margery at this juncture would have been to go to Jim, and nip the intrigue in the bud without further scruple. But her own declaration in after days was that whoever could say that was far from realizing her situation. It was hard to break such ice as divided their two lives now, and to attempt it at that moment was a too humiliating proclamation of defeat. The only plan she could think of – perhaps not a wise one in the circumstances – was to go to the Review herself, and be the gayest there.

A method of doing this with some propriety soon occurred to her. She dared not ask her father, who scorned to waste time in sight-seeing, and whose animosity towards Jim knew no abatement; but she might call on her old acquaintance, Mr Vine, Jim's partner, who would probably be going with the rest of the holiday-folk, and as if she might accompany him in his spring-trap. She had no sooner perceived the feasibility of this, through her being at her grandmother's, than she decided to meet with the old man early the next morning.

In the meantime Jim and Mrs Peach had walked slowly along the road together, Jim leading the horse, and Mrs Peace informing him that her father, the gardener, was at Jim's village farther on, and that she had come to meet him. Jim, for reasons of his own, was going to sleep at his partner's that night, and thus their route was the same. The shades of eve closed in upon them as they walked, and by the time they reached the lime-kiln, which it was necessary to pass to get to the village, it was quite dark. Jim stopped at the kiln, to see if matters had progressed rightly in his seven days' absence, and Mrs Peach, who stuck to him like a teazle, stopped also, saying she would wait for her father there.

She held the horse while he ascended to the top of the kiln. Then rejoining her, and not quite knowing what to do, he stood beside her looking at the flames, which tonight burnt up brightly, shining a long way into the dark air, even up to the ramparts of the earthwork above them, and overhead into the bosoms of the clouds.

It was during this proceeding that a carriage, drawn by a pair of dark horses, came along the turnpike-road. The light of the kiln caused the horses to swerve a little, and the occupant of the carriage looked out. He saw the bluish, lightning-like flames from the limestone, rising from the top of the furnace, and hard by the figures of Jim Hayward, the widow, and the horse, standing out with spectral distinctness against the mass of night behind. The scene wore the aspect of some unholy assignation in Pandaemonium, and it was all the more impressive from the fact that both Jim and the woman were quite unconscious of the striking spectacle they presented. The gentleman in the carriage watched them till he was borne out of sight.

Having seen to the kiln, Jim and the widow walked on again, and soon Mrs Peach's father met them, and relieved Jim of the lady. When they had parted, Jim, with an expiration not unlike a breath of relief, went on to Mr Vine's, and, having put the horse into the stable, entered the house. His partner was seated at the table, solacing himself after the labours of the day by luxurious alternations between a long clay pipe and a mug of perry.

'Well,' said Jim eagerly, 'what's the news – how do she take it?'

'Sit down – sit down,' said Vine. ''Tis working well; not but that I deserve something o' thee for the trouble I've had in watching her. The soldiering was a fine move; but the woman is a better! – who invented it?'

'I myself,' said Jim modestly.

'Well; jealousy is making her rise like a thunder-storm, and in a day or two you'll have her for the asking, my sonny. What's the next step?'

'The widow is getting rather a weight upon a feller, worse luck,' said Jim. 'But I must keep it up until tomorrow, at any rate. I have promised to see her at the Review, and now the great thing is that Margery should see we a-smiling together – I in my full-dress uniform and clinking arms o' war. 'Twill be a good strong sting, and will end the business, I hope. Couldn't you manage to put the hoss in and drive her there? She'd go if you were to ask her.'

'With all my heart,' said Mr Vine, moistening the end of a new pipe in his perry. 'I can call at her grammer's for her – 'twill be all in my way.'

16

Margery duly followed up her intention by arraying herself the next morning in her loveliest guise, and keeping watch for Mr Vine's appearance upon the high road, feeling certain that his would form one in the procession of carts and carriages which set in towards Exonbury that day. Jim had gone by at a very early hour, and she did not see him pass. Her anticipation was verified by the advent of Mr Vine about eleven o'clock, dressed to his highest effort; but Margery was surprised to find that, instead of her having to stop him, he pulled in towards the gate of his own accord. The invitation planned between Jim and the old man on the previous night was now promptly given, and, as may be supposed, as promptly accepted. Such a strange coincidence she had never before known. She was quite ready, and they drove onward at once.

The Review was held on some high ground a little way out of the city, and her conductor suggested that they should put up the horse at the inn, and walk to the field – a plan which pleased her well, for it was more easy to take preliminary observations on foot without being seen herself than when sitting elevated in a vehicle.

They were just in time to secure a good place near the front, and in a few minutes after their arrival the reviewing officer came on the ground. Margery's eye had rapidly run over the troop in which Jim was enrolled, and she discerned him in one of the ranks, looking remarkably new and bright, both as to uniform and countenance. Indeed, if she had not worked herself into such a desperate state of mind she would have felt proud of him then and there. His shapely upright figure was quite noteworthy in the row of rotund yeomen on his right and left; while his carter Tony expressed by his bearing, even more than Jim, that he knew nothing about lime-carts whatever, and everything about trumpets and glory. How Jim could have scrubbed Tony to such shining blackness she could not tell, for the horse in his natural state was ingrained with lime-dust, that burnt the colour out of his coat as it did out of Jim's hair. Now he pranced martially, and was a war-horse every inch of him.

Having discovered Jim her next search was for Mrs Peach, and, by dint of some oblique glancing, Margery indignantly discovered the widow in the most forward place of all, her head and bright face conspicuously advanced; and, what was more shocking, she had abandoned her mourning for a violet drawn-bonnet and a gay spencer, together with a parasol luxuriously fringed in a way Margery had never seen before. 'Where did she get the money?' said Margery, under her breath. 'And to forget that poor sailor so soon!'

These general reflections were precipitately postponed by her discovering that Jim and the widow were perfectly alive to each other's whereabouts, and in the interchange of telegraphic signs of affection, which on the latter's part took the form of a playful fluttering of her handkerchief or waving of her parasol. Richard Vine had placed Margery in front of him, to protect her from the crowd, as he said, he himself surveying the scene over her bonnet. Margery would have been even more surprised than she was if she had known that Jim was not only aware of Mrs Peach's presence, but also of her own, the treacherous Mr Vine having drawn out his flame-coloured handkrechief and waved it to Jim over the young woman's head as soon as they had taken up their position.

'My partner makes a tidy soldier, eh – Miss Tucker?' said the senior lime-burner. 'It is my belief as a Christian that he's got a party here that he's making signs to – that handsome figure o' fun straight over-right him.'

'Perhaps so,' she said.

'And it's growing warm between 'em if I don't mistake,' continued the merciless Vine.

Margery was silent, biting her lip; and the troops being now set in motion, all signalling ceased for the present between soldier Hayward and his pretended sweetheart.

'Have you a piece of paper that I could make a memorandum on, Mr Vine?' asked Margery.

Vine took out his pocket-book and tore a leaf from it, which he handed her with a pencil.

'Don't move from here – I'll return in a minute,' she continued, with the innocence of a woman who means mischief. And, withdrawing herself to the back, where the grass was clear, she pencilled down the words –

'JIM'S MARRIED'

Armed with this document she crept into the throng behind the unsuspecting Mrs Peach, slipped the paper into her pocket on the top of her handkerchief, and withdrew unobserved, rejoining Mr Vine with a bearing of *nonchalance*.

By-and-by the troops were in different order, Jim taking a left-hand position almost close to Mrs Peach. He bent down and said a few words to her. From her manner of nodding assent it was surely some arrangement about a meeting by-and-by when Jim's drill was over, and Margery was more certain of the fact when, the Review having ended, and the people having strolled off to another part of the field where sports were to take place, Mrs Peach tripped away in the direction of the city.

'I'll just say a word to my partner afore he goes off the ground, if you'll spare me a minute,' said the old lime-burner. 'Please stay here till I'm back again.' He edged along the front till he reached Jim.

'How is she?' said the latter.

'In a trimming sweat,' said Mr Vine. 'And my counsel to 'ee is to carry this larry no further. 'Twill do no good. She's as ready to make friends with 'ee as any wife can be; and more showing off can only do harm.'

'But I must finish off with a spurt,' said Jim. 'And this is how I am going to do it. I have arranged with Mrs Peach that, as soon as we soldiers have entered the town and been dismissed, I'll meet her there. It is really to say good-bye, but she don't know that; and I wanted it to look like a 'lopement to Margery's eyes. When I'm clear of Mrs Peach I'll come back here and make it up with Margery on the spot. But don't say I'm coming, or she maybe inclined to throw off again. Just hint to her that I may be meaning to be off to London with the widow.'

The old man still insisted that this was going too far.

'No, no, it isn't,' said Jim. 'I know how to manage her. 'Twill just mellow her heart nicely by the time I come back. I must bring her down real tender, or 'twill all fail.'

His senior reluctantly gave in and returned to Margery. A short time afterwards the Yeomanry band struck up, and Jim with the regiment followed towards Exonbury.

'Yes, yes; they are going to meet,' said Margery to herself, perceiving that Mrs Peach had so timed her departure as to be in the town at Jim's dismounting.

'Now we will go and see the games,' said Mr Vine; 'they are really worth seeing. There's greasy poles, and jumping in sacks, and other trials of the intellect, that nobody ought to miss who wants to be abreast of his generation.'

Margery felt so indignant at the apparent assignation, which seemed about to take place despite her anonymous writing, that she helplessly assented to go anywhere, dropping behind Vine, that he might not see her mood.

Jim followed out his programme with literal exactness. No sooner was the troop dismissed in the city than he sent Tony to stable and joined Mrs Peach, who stood on the edge of the pavement expecting him. But this acquaintance was to end: he meant to part from her for ever and in the quickest time, though civilly; for it was important to be with Margery as soon as possible. He had nearly completed the manoeuvre to his satisfaction when, in drawing her handkerchief from her pocket to wipe the tears from her eyes, Mrs Peach's hand grasped the paper, which she read at once.

'What! is that true?' she said, holding it out to Jim.

Jim started and admitted that it was, beginning an elaborate explanation and apologies. But Mrs Peach was thoroughly roused, and then overcome. 'He's married, he's married!' she said, and swooned, or feigned to swoon, so that Jim was obliged to support her.

'He's married, he's married!' said a boy hard by who watched the scene with interest.

'He's married, he's married!' said a hilarious group of other boys near, with smiles several inches broad, and shining teeth; and so the exclamation echoed down the street.

Jim cursed his ill-luck; the loss of time that this dilemma entailed grew serious; for Mrs Peach was now in such a hysterical state that he could not leave her with any good grace or feeling. It was necessary to take her to a refreshment room, lavish restoratives upon her, and altogether to waste nearly half-an-hour. When she had kept him as long as she chose, she forgave him; and thus at last he got away, his heart swelling with tenderness towards Margery. He at once hurried up the street to effect the reconciliation with her.

'How shall I do it?' he said to himself. 'Why, I'll step round to her side, fish for her hand, draw it through my arm as if I wasn't aware of it. Then she'll look in my face, I shall look in hers, and we shall march off the field triumphant, and the thing will be done without takings or tears.'

He entered the field and went straight as an arrow to the place appointed for the meeting. It was at the back of a refreshment tent outside the mass of spectators, and divided from their view by the tent itself. He turned the corner of the canvas, and there beheld Vine at the indicated spot. But Margery was not with him.

Vine's hat was thrust back into his poll. His face was pale, and his manner bewildered. 'Hullo? what's the matter?' said Jim. 'Where's my Margery?'

'You've carried this footy game too far, my man!' exclaimed Vine, with the air of a friend who has 'always told you so'. 'You ought to have dropped it several days ago, when she would have come to 'ee like a cooing dove. Now this is the end o't!'

'Hey! what, my Margery? Has anything happened, for God's sake?'

'She's gone.'

'Where to?'

'That's more than earthly man can tell! I never see such a thing! 'Twas a stroke o' the black art – as if she were sperrited away. When we got to the games I said – mind, you told me to! – I said, "Jim Hayward thinks o' going off to London with that widow woman" – mind, you told me to! She showed no wonderment, though a' seemed very low. Then she said to me, "I don't like standing here in this slummocky crowd. I shall feel more at home among the gentlepeople.' And then she went to where the carriages were drawn up, and near her there was a grand coach, a-blazing with lions and unicorns, and hauled by two coal-black horses. I hardly thought much of it then, and by degrees lost sight of her behind it. Presently the other carriages moved off, and I thought still to see her standing there. But no, she had vanished; and then I saw the grand coach rolling away, and glimpsed Margery in it, beside a fine dark gentleman with black mustachios, and a very pale prince-like face. As soon as the horses got into the hard road they rattled on like hell-and-skimmer, and went out of sight in the dust, and – that's all. If you'd come back a little sooner you'd ha' caught her.'

Jim had turned whiter than his pipeclay. 'O, this is too bad – too bad!' he cried in anguish, striking his brow. 'That paper and that fainting woman kept me so long. Who could have done it? But 'tis my fault. I've stung her too much. I shouldn't have carried it so far.'

'You shouldn't – just what I said,' replied his senior.

'She thinks I've gone off with that cust widow, and to spite me she's gone off with the man! Do you know who that stranger wi' the lions and unicorns is? Why, 'tis that foreigner who calls himself a Baron, and took Mount Lodge for six months last year to make mischief – a villain! O, my Margery – that it should come to this! She's lost, she's ruined! – Which way did they go?'

Jim turned to follow in the direction indicated, when, behold, there stood at his back her father, Dairyman Tucker.

'Now look here, young man,' said Dairyman Tucker. 'I've just heard all that wailing – and straightway will ask 'ee to stop it sharp. 'Tis like your brazen impudence to teave and wail when you be another woman's husband; yes, faith, I seed her a-fainting in yer arms when you wanted to get away from her, and honest folk a-standing round who knew you'd married her, and said so. I heard it, though you didn't see me. "He's married!" says they. Some sly register-office business, no doubt; but sly doings will out. As for Margery – who's to be called higher titles in these parts hencefor'ard – I'm her father, and I say it's all right what she's done. Don't I know private news, hey? Haven't I just heard that secret weddings of high people can happen at expected deathbeds by special licence, as well as low people at registrars' offices? And can't husbands come back and claim their own when they choose? Begone, young man, and leave noblemen's wives alone; and I thank God I shall be rid of a numskull!'

Swift words of explanation rose to Jim's lips, but they paused there and died. At that last moment he could not, as Margery's husband, announce Margery's shame and his own, and transform her father's triumph to wretchedness at a blow.

'I – I – must leave here,' he stammered. Going from the place in an opposite course to that of the fugitives, he doubled when out of sight, and in an incredibly short space had entered the town. Here he made inquiries for the emblazoned carriage, and gained from one or two persons a general idea of its route. They thought it had taken the highway to London. Saddling poor Tony before he had half eaten his corn, Jim galloped along the same road.

17

Now Jim was quite mistaken in supposing that by leaving the field in a roundabout manner he had deceived Dairyman Tucker as to his object. That astute old man immediately divined that Jim was meaning to track the fugitives, in ignorance (as the dairyman supposed) of their lawful relation. He was soon assured of the fact, for, creeping to a remote angle of the field, he saw Jim hastening into the town. Vowing vengeance on the young lime-burner for his mischievous interference between a nobleman and his secretly-wedded wife, the dairy-farmer determined to balk him.

Tucker had ridden to the Review ground, so that there was no necessity for him, as there had been for poor Jim, to re-enter the town before starting. The dairyman hastily untied his mare from the row of other horses, mounted, and descended to a bridle-path which would take him obliquely into the London road a mile or so ahead. The old man's route being along one side of an equilateral triangle, while Jim's was along two sides of the same, the former was at the point of intersection long before Hayward.

Arrived here, the dairyman pulled up and looked around. It was a spot at which the highway forked; the left arm, the more important, led on through Sherton Abbas and Melchester to London; the right to Idmouth and the coast. Nothing was visible on the white track to London; but on the other there appeared the back of a carriage which rapidly ascended a distant hill and vanished under the trees. It was the Baron's who, according to the sworn information of the gardener at Mount Lodge, had made Margery his wife.

The carriage having vanished, the dairyman gazed in the opposite direction, towards Exonbury. Here he beheld Jim in his regimentals, laboriously approaching on Tony's back.

Soon he reached the forking roads, and saw the dairyman by the wayside. But Jim did not halt. Then the dairyman practised the greatest duplicity of his life.

'Right along the London road, if you want to catch 'em!' he said.

'Thank 'ee, dairyman, thank 'ee!' cried Jim, his pale face lighting up with gratitude, for he believed that Tucker had learnt his mistake from Vine, and had come to his assistance. Without drawing rein he diminished along the road not taken by the flying pair. The dairyman rubbed his hands with delight, and returned to the city as the cathedral clock struck five.

Jim pursued his way through the dust, up hill and down hill; but never saw ahead of him the vehicle of his search. That vehicle was passing along a diverging way at a distance of many miles from where he rode. Still he sped onwards, till Tony showed signs of breaking down; and then Jim gathered from inquiries he made that he had come the wrong way. It burst upon his mind that the dairyman, still ignorant of the truth, had misinformed him. Heavier in his heart than words can describe he turned Tony's drooping head, and resolved to drag his way home.

But the horse was now so jaded that it was impossible to proceed far. Having gone about half a mile back he came again to a small roadside hamlet inn, where he put up Tony for a rest and feed. As for himself, there was no quiet in him. He tried to sit and eat in the inn kitchen; but he could not stay there. He went out, and paced up and down the road.

Standing in sight of the white way by which he had come he beheld advancing towards him the horses and carriage he sought, now black and daemonic against the slanting fires of the western sun.

The why and wherefore of this sudden appearance he did not pause to consider. His resolve to intercept the carriage was instantaneous. He ran forward, and doggedly waiting barred the way to the advancing equipage.

The Baron's coachman shouted, but Jim stood firm as a rock, and on the former attempting to push past him Jim drew his sword, resolving to cut the horses down rather than be displaced. The animals were thrown nearly back upon their haunches, and at this juncture a gentleman looked out of the window. It was the Baron himself.

'Who's there?' he inquired.

'James Hayward!' replied the young man fiercely, 'and he demands his wife.'

The Baron leapt out, and told the coachman to drive back out of sight and wait for him.

'I was hastening to find you,' he said to Jim. 'Your wife is where she ought to be, and where you ought to be also – by your own fireside. Where's the other woman?'

Jim, without replying, looked incredulously into the carriage as it turned. Margery was certainly not there. 'The other woman is nothing to me,' he said bitterly. 'I used her to warm up Margery: I have now done with her. The question I ask, my lord, is, what business had you with Margery today?'

'My business was to help her to regain the husband she had seemingly lost. I saw her; she told me you had eloped by the London road with another. I, who have – mostly – had her happiness at heart, told her I would help her to follow you if she wished. She gladly agreed; we drove after, but could hear no tidings of you in front of us. Then I took her – to your house – and there she awaits you. I promised to send you to her if human effort could do it, and was tracking you for that purpose.'

'Then you've been a-pursuing after me?'

'You and the widow.'

'And I've been pursuing after you and Margery! . . . My noble lord, your actions seem to show that I ought to believe you in this; and when you say you've her happiness at heart, I don't forget that you've formerly proved it to be so. Well, Heaven forbid that I should think wrongfully of you if you don't deserve it! A mystery to me you have always been, my noble lord, and in this business more than in any.'

'I am glad to hear you say no worse. In one hour you'll have proof of my conduct – good and bad. Can I do anything more? Say the word, and I'll try.'

Jim reflected. 'Baron,' he said. 'I am a plain man, and wish only to lead a quiet life with my wife, as a man should. You have great power over her – power to any extent, for good or otherwise. If you command her anything on earth, righteous or questionable, that she'll do. So that, since you ask me if you can do more for me, I'll answer this, you can promise never to see her again. I mean no harm, my lord; but your presence can do no good; you will trouble us. If I return to her, will you for ever stay away?'

'Hayward,' said the Baron, 'I swear to you that I will disturb you and your wife by my presence no more.' And he took Jim's hand, and pressed it within his own upon the hilt of Jim's sword.

In relating this incident to the present narrator Jim used to declare that, to his fancy, the ruddy light of the setting sun burned with more than earthly fire on the Baron's face as the words were spoken; and that the ruby flash of his eye in the same light was what he never witnessed before nor since in the eye of mortal man. After this there was nothing more to do or say in that place. Jim accompanied his never-to-be-forgotten acquaintance to the carriage, closed the door after him, waved his hat to him, and from that hour he and the Baron met not again on earth.

A few words will suffice to explain the fortunes of Margery while the foregoing events were in action elsewhere. On leaving her companion Vine she had gone distractedly among the carriages, the rather to escape his observation than of any set purpose. Standing here she thought she heard her name pronounced, and turning, saw her foreign friend, whom she had supposed to be, if not dead, a thousand miles off. He beckoned, and she went close. 'You are ill – you are wretched,' he said, looking keenly in her face. 'Where's your husband?'

She told him her sad suspicion that Jim had run away from her. The Baron reflected, and inquired a few other particulars of her late life. Then he said, 'You and I must find him. Come with me.' At this word of command from the Baron she had entered the carriage as docilely as a child, and there she sat beside him till he chose to speak, which was not till they were some way out of the town, at the forking ways, and the Baron had discovered that Jim was certainly not, as they had supposed, making off from Margery along that particular branch of the fork that led to London.

'To pursue him in this way is useless,' he said. 'And the proper course is that I should take you to his house. That done I will return, and bring him to you if mortal persuasion can do it.'

'I didn't want to go to his house without him, sir,' said she, tremblingly.

'Didn't want to!' he answered. 'Let me remind you, Margery Hayward, that your place is in your husband's house. Till you are there you have no right to criticize his conduct, however wild it may be. Why have you not been there before?'

'I don't know, sir,' she murmured, her tears falling silently upon her hand.

'Don't you think you ought to be there?'

She did not answer.

'Of course you ought.'

Still she did not speak.

The Baron sank into silence, and allowed his eye to rest on her. What thoughts were all at once engaging his mind after those moments of reproof? Margery had given herself into his hands without a remonstrance. Her husband had apparently deserted her. She was absolutely in his power, and they were on the high road.

That his first impulse in inviting her to accompany him had been the legitimate one denoted by his words cannot reasonably be doubted. That his second was otherwise soon became revealed, though not at first to her, for she was too bewildered to notice where they were going. Instead of turning and taking the road to Jim's, the Baron, as if influenced suddenly by her reluctance to return thither if Jim was playing truant, signalled to the coachman to take the branch road to the right, as her father had discerned.

They soon approached the coast near Idmouth. The carriage stopped. Margery awoke from her reverie.

'Where are we?' she said, looking out of the window, with a start. Before her was an inlet of the sea, and in the middle of the inlet rode a yacht, its masts repeating as if from memory the rocking they had practised in their native forest.

'At a little sea-side nook, where my yacht lies at anchor,' he said tentatively. 'Now, Margery, in five minutes we can be aboard, and in half-an-hour we can be sailing away all the world over. Will you come?'

'I cannot decide,' she said, in low tones.

'Why not?'

'Because—'

Then on a sudden Margery seemed to see all contingencies; she became white as a fleece, and a bewildered look came into her eyes. With clasped hands she leant on the Baron.

Baron von Xanten observed her distracted look, averted his face, and coming to a decision opened the carriage door, quickly mounted outside, and in a second or two the carriage left the shore behind, and ascended the road by which it had come.

In about an hour they reached Jim Hayward's home. The Baron

alighted, and spoke to her through the window. 'Margery, can you forgive a lover's bad impulse, which I swear was unpremeditated?' he asked. 'If you can, shake my hand.'

She did not do it, but eventually allowed him to help her out of the carriage. He seemed to feel the awkwardness keenly; and seeing it, she said, 'Of course I forgive you, sir, for I felt for a moment as you did. Will you send my husband to me?'

'I will, if any man can,' said he. 'Such penance is milder than I deserve! God bless you and give you happiness! I shall never see you again!' He turned, entered the carriage, and was gone; and having found out Jim's course, came up with him upon the road as described.

In due time the latter reached his lodging at his partner's. The woman who took care of the house in Vine's absence at once told Jim that a lady who had come in a carriage was waiting for him in his sitting-room. Jim proceeded thither with agitation, and beheld, shrinkingly ensconced in the large slippery chair, and surrounded by the brilliant articles that had so long awaited her, his long-estranged wife.

Margery's eyes were round and fear-stricken. She essayed to speak, but Jim, strangely enough, found the readier tongue then. 'Why did I do it, you would ask,' he said. 'I cannot tell. Do you forgive my deception? O Margery – you are my Margery still! But how could you trust yourself in the Baron's hands this afternoon, without knowing him better?'

'He said I was to come, and I went,' she said, as well as she could for tearfulness.

'You obeyed him blindly.'

'I did. But perhaps I was not justified in doing it.'

'I don't know,' said Jim musingly. 'I think he's a good man.' Margery did not explain. And then a sunnier mood succeeded her tremblings and tears, till old Mr Vine came into the house below, and Jim went down to declare that all was well, and sent off his partner to break the news to Margery's father, who as yet remained unenlightened.

The dairymare bore the intelligence of his daughter's untitled state as best he could, and punished her by not coming near her for several weeks, though at last he grumbled his forgiveness, and made up matters with Jim. The handsome Mrs Peach vanished to Plymouth, and found another sailor, not without a reasonable complaint against Jim and Margery both that she had been unfairly used.

As for the mysterious gentleman who had exercised such an influence over their lives, he kept his word, and was a stranger to Lower Wessex thenceforward. Baron or no Baron, Englishman or foreigner, he had shown a genuine interest in Jim, and real sorrow for a certain reckless phase of his aquaintance with Margery. That he had a more tender feeling toward the young girl than he wished her or anyone else to perceive there could be no doubt. That he was strongly tempted at times to adopt other than conventional courses with regard to her is also clear, particularly at that critical hour when she rolled along the high road with him in the carriage, after turning from the fancied pursuit of Jim. But at other times he schooled impassioned sentiments into fair conduct, which even erred on the side of harshness. In after years there was a report that another attempt on his life with a pistol, during one of those fits of moodiness to which he seemed constitutionally liable, had been effectual; but nobody in Silverthorn was in a position to ascertain the truth.

There he is still regarded as one who had something about him magical and unearthly. In his mystery let him remain; for a man, no less than a landscape, who awakens an interest under uncertain lights and touches of unfathomable shade, may cut but a poor figure in a garish noontide shine.

When she heard of his mournful death Margery sat in her nursing-chair, gravely thinking for nearly ten minutes, to the total neglect of her infant in the cradle. Jim, from the other side of the fireplace, said, 'You are sorry enough for him, Margery. I am sure of that.'

'Yes, yes,' she murmured, 'I am sorry.' After a moment she added: 'Now that he's dead I'll make a confession, Jim, that I have never made to a soul. If he had pressed me – which he did not – to go with him when I was in the carriage that night beside his yacht, I would have gone. And I was disappointed that he did not press me.'

'Suppose he were to suddenly appear now, and say in a voice of command, "Margery, come with me!"'

'I believe I should have no power to disobey,' she returned, with a mischievous look. 'He was like a magician to me. I think he was one. He could move me as a loadstone moves a speck of steel. . . Yet no,' she added, hearing the infant cry, 'he would not move me now. It would be so unfair to baby.'

'Well,' said Jim, with no great concern (for '*la jalousie rétrospective*', as George Sands calls it, had nearly died out of him), 'however he might move 'ee, my love, he'll never come. He swore it to me: and he was a man of his word.'

MIDSUMMER 1883

UNCOLLECTED STORIES

DESTINY AND A BLUE CLOAK

I

'Good morning, Miss Lovill!' said the young man, in the free manner usual with him toward pretty and inexperienced country girls.

Agatha Pollin – the maiden addressed – instantly perceived how the mistake had arisen. Miss Lovill was the owner of a blue autumn wrapper, exceptionally gay for a village; and Agatha, in a spirit of emulation rather than originality, had .purchased a similarly enviable article for herself, which she wore today for the first time. It may be mentioned that the two young women had ridden together from their homes to Maiden-Newton on this foggy September morning, Agatha prolonging her journey thence to Weymouth by train, and leaving her acquaintance at the former place. The remark was made to her on Weymouth esplanade.

Agatha was now about to reply very naturally, 'I am not Miss Lovill,' and she went so far as to turn up her face to him for the purpose, when he added, 'I've been hoping to meet you. I have heard of your – well, I must say it – beauty, long ago, though I only came to Beaminster yesterday.'

Agatha bowed – her contradiction hung back – and they walked slowly along the esplanade together without speaking another word after the above point-blank remark of his. It was evidence that her new friend could never have seen either herself or Miss Lovill except from a distance.

And Agatha trembled as well as bowed. This Miss Lovell – Frances Lovill – was of great and long renown as the beauty of Cloton village, near Beaminster. She was five and twenty and fully developed, while Agatha was only the niece of the miller of the same place, just nineteen, and of no repute as yet for comeliness, though she undoubtedly could boast of much. Now, were the speaker, Oswald Winwood, to be told that he had not lighted upon the true Helen, he would instantly apologize for his mistake and leave her side, a contingency of no great matter but for one curious emotional circumtance – Agatha had already lost her heart to him. Only in secret had she acquired this interest in Winwood – by hearing much report of his talent and by watching him several times from a window; but she loved none the less in that she had discovered that Miss

Lovell's desire to meet and talk with the same intellectual luminary was in a fair way of approaching the intensity of her own. We are never unbiased appraisers, even in love, and rivalry usually operates as a stimulant to esteem even while it is acting as an obstacle to opportunity. So it had been with Agatha in her talk to Miss Lovill that morning concerning Oswald Winwood.

The Weymouth season was almost at an end, and but few loungers were to be seen on the parades, particularly at this early hour. Agatha looked over the iridescent sea, from which the veil of mist was slowly rising, at the white cliffs on the left, now just beginning to gleam in a weak sunlight, at the one solitary yacht in the midst, and still delayed her explanation. Her companion went on:

'The mist is vanishing, look, and I think it will be fine, after all. Shall you stay in Weymouth the whole day?'

'No. I am going to Portland by the twelve o'clock steam-boat. But I return here again at six to go home by the seven o'clock train.'

'I go to Maiden-Newton by the same train, and then to Beaminster by the carrier.'

'So do I.'

'Not, I suppose, to walk from Beaminster to Cloton at that time in the evening?'

'I shall be met by somebody – but it is only a mile, you know.'

That is how it all began; the continuation it is not necessary to detail at length. Both being somewhat young and impulsive, social forms were not scrupulously attended to. She discovered him to be on board the steamer as it plowed the emerald waves of Weymouth Bay, although he had wished her a formal good-bye at the pier. He had altered his mind, he said, and thought that he would come to Portland too. They returned by the same boat, walked the velvet sands till the train started, and entered a carriage together.

All this time, in the midst of her happiness, Agatha's conscience was sombre with guiltiness at not having yet told him of his mistake. It was true that he had not more than once or twice called her by Miss Lovill's name since the first greeting in the morning; but he was certainly still under the impression that she was Frances Lovill. Yet she perceived that though he had been led to her by another's name, it was her own proper person that he was so rapidly getting to love, and Agatha's feminine insight suggested blissfully to her that the face belonging to the name would after this encounter have no power to drag him away from the face of the day's romance.

They reached Maiden-Newton at dusk, and went to the inn door, where stood the old-fashioned hooded van which was to take them to Beaminster. It was on the point of starting, and when they had mounted in front the old man at once drove up the long hill leading out of the village.

'This has been a charming experience to me, Miss Lovill,' Oswald said, as they sat side by side. 'Accidental meetings have a way of making themselves pleasant when contrived ones quite fail to do it.'

It was absolutely necessary to confess this time, though all her bliss were at once destroyed.

'I am not really Miss Lovill!' she faltered.

'What! not the young lady – and are you really not Frances Lovill?' he exclaimed, in surprise.

'O forgive me, Mr Winwood! I have wanted so to tell you of your mistake; indeed I have, all day – but I couldn't, – and it is so wicked and wrong of me! I am only poor Agatha Pollin, at the mill.'

'But why couldn't you tell me?'

'Because I was afraid that if I did you would go away from me and not care for me any more and I l-l-love you so dearly!'

The carrier being on foot beside the horse, the van being so dark, and Oswald's feelings being rather warm, he could not for his life avoid kissing her there and then.

'Well,' he said, 'it doesn't matter; you are yourself anyhow. It is you I like, and nobody else in the world – not the name. But, you know, I was really looking for Miss Lovill this morning. I saw the back of her head yesterday, and I have often heard how very good-looking she is. Ah! suppose you had been she. I wonder—'

He did not complete the sentence. The driver mounted again, touched the horse with the whip, and they jogged on.

'You forgive me?' she said.

'Entirely – absolutely – the reason justified everything. How strange that you should have been caring deeply for me, and I ignorant of it all the time!'

They descended into Beaminster and alighted, Oswald handing her down. They had not moved from the spot when another female figure also alighted, dropped her fare into the carrier's hand, and glided away.

'Who is that?' said Oswald to the carrier. 'Why, I thought we were the only passengers!'

'What?' said the carrier, who was rather stupid.

'Who is that woman?'

'Miss Lovill, of Cloton. She altered her mind about staying at Beaminster, and is come home again.'

'Oh!' said Agatha, almost sinking to the earth. 'She has heard it all. What shall I do, what shall I do?'

'Never mind it a bit,' said Oswald.

2

The mill stood beside the village high-road, from which it was separated by the stream, the latter forming also the boundary of the mill garden, orchard, and paddock on that side. A visitor crossed a little wood bridge imbedded in oozy, aquatic growths, and found himself in a space where usually stood a wagon laden with sacks, surrounded by a number of bright-feathered fowls.

It was now, however, just dusk, but the mill was not closed, a stripe of light stretching as usual from the open door across the front, across the river, aross the road, into the hedge beyond. On the bridge, which was aside from the line of light, a young man and a girl stood talking together. Soon they moved a little way apart, and then it was apparent that their rights hands were joined. In receding one from the other they began to swing their arms gently backward and forward between them.

'Come a little way up the lane, Agatha, since it is the last time,' he said. 'I don't like parting here. You know your uncle does not object.'

'He doesn't object because he knows nothing to object to,' she whispered. And they both then contemplated the fine, stalwart figure of the said uncle, who could be seen moving about inside the mill, illuminated by the candle, and circumscribed by a faint halo of flour, and hindered by the whirr of the mill from hearing anything so gentle as lovers' talk.

Oswald had not relinquished her hand, and, submitting herself to a bondage she appeared to love better than freedom, Agatha followed him across the bridge, and they went down the lane engaged in the low, sad talk common to all such cases, interspersed with remarks peculiar to their own.

'It is nothing so fearful to contemplate,' he said. 'Many live there for years in a state of rude health, and return home in the same happy. condition. So shall I.'

'I hope you will.'

'But aren't you glad I am going? It is better to do well in India than badly here. Say you are glad, dearest; it will fortify me when I am gone.'

'I am glad,' she murmured faintly. 'I mean I am glad in my mind. I don't think that in my heart I am glad.'

'Thanks to Macaulay, of honoured memory, I have as good a chance as the best of them!' he said, with ardour. 'What a great thing competitive examination is; it will put good men in good places, and make inferior men move lower down; all bureaucratic jobbery will be swept away.'

'What's bureaucratic, Oswald?'

'Oh! that's what they call it, you know. It is – well, I don't exactly know what it is. I know this, that it is the name of what I hate, and that it isn't competitive examination.'

'At any rate it is a very bad thing,' she said, conclusively.

'Very bad, indeed; you may take my word for that.'

Then the parting scene began, in the dark, under the heavy-headed trees which shut out sky and stars. 'And since I shall be in London till the spring,' he remarked, 'the parting doesn't seem so bad – so all at once. Perhaps you may come to London before the spring, Agatha.'

'I may; but I don't think I shall.'

'We must hope on all the same. Then there will be the examination, and then I shall know my fate.'

'I hope you'll fail! – there I've said it; I couldn't help it, Oswald!' she exclaimed, bursting out crying. 'You would come home again then!'

'How could you be so disheartening and wicked, Agatha! I – I didn't expect—'

'No, no; I don't wish it; I wish you to be best, top, very very best!' she said. 'I didn't mean the other; indeed, dear Oswald, I didn't. And will you be sure to come to me when you are rich? Sure to come?'

'If I'm on this earth I'll come home and marry you.'

And then followed the good-bye.

3

In the spring came the examination. One morning a newspaper directed by Oswald was placed in her hands, and she opened it to find it was a copy of the *Times*. In the middle of the sheet, in the most conspicuous place, in the excellent neighbourhood of the leading articles, was a list of names, and the first on the list was Oswald Winwood. Attached to his name, as showing where he was educated, was the simple title of some obscure little academy, while underneath came public school and college men in shoals. Such a case occurs sometimes, and it occurred then.

How Agatha clapped her hands! For her selfish wish to have him in England at any price, even that of failure, had been but a paroxysm of the wretched parting, and was now quite extinct. Circumstances combined to hinder another meeting between them before his departure, and, accordingly, making up her mind to the inevitable in a way which would have done honour to an older head, she fixed her mental vision on that sunlit future – far away, yet always nearing – and contemplated its probabilities with a firm hope.

At length he had arrived in India, and now Agatha had only to work and wait; and the former made the latter more easy. In her spare hours she would wander about the river brinks and into the coppices, and there weave thoughts of him by processes that young women understand so well. She kept a diary, and in this, since there were few events to chronicle in her daily life, she sketched the changes of the landscape, noted the arrival and departure of birds of passage, the times of storms and foul weather – all which information, being mixed up with her life and taking colour from it, she sent as scraps in her letters to him, deriving most of her enjoyment in contemplating his.

Oswald, on his part, corresponded very regularly. Knowing the days of the Indian mail, she would go at such times to meet the post-man in the early morning, and to her unvarying inquiry, 'A letter for me?' it was seldom, indeed, that there came a disappointing answer. Thus the season passed, and Oswald told her he should be a judge some day, with many other details, which, in her mind, were viewed chiefly in their bearing on the grand consummation – that he was to come home and marry her.

Meanwhile, as the girl grew older and more womanly, the woman whose name she had once stolen for a day grew more of an old maid, and showed symptoms of fading. One day Agatha's uncle, who, though still a handsome man in the prime of life, was a widower with four children, to whom she acted the part of eldest sister, told Agatha that Frances Lovill was about to become his second wife.

'Well,' said Agatha, and thought, 'What an end for a beauty!'

And yet it was all reasonable enough, notwithstanding that Miss Lovill might have looked a little higher. Agatha knew that this step would produce great alterations in the small household of Cloton Mill, and the idea of having as aunt and ruler the woman to whom she was in some sense indebted for a lover, affected Agatha with a slight thrill of dread. Yet nothing had ever been spoken between the two women to show that Frances had heard, much less resented, the explanation in the van on that night of the return from Weymouth.

4

On a certain day old Farmer Lovill called. He was of the same family as Frances, though their relationship was distant. A considerable business in corn had been done from time to time between miller and farmer, but the latter had seldom called at Pollin's house. He was a bachelor, or he would probably never have appeared in this history, and he was mostly fully of boyish merriment rare in one of his years. Today his business with the miller had been so imperative as to bring him in person, and it was evident from their talk in the mill that the matter was payment. Perhaps ten minutes had been spent in serious converse when the old farmer turned away from the door, and without saying good-morning, went toward the bridge. This was unusual for a man of his temperament.

He was an old man – really and fairly old – sixty-five years of age at least. He was not exactly feeble, but he found a stick useful when walking in a high wind. His eyes were not yet bleared, but in their corners was occasionally a moisture like majolica glaze – entirely absent in youth. His face was not shrivelled, but there were unmistakable puckers in some places. And hence the old gentleman, unmarried, substantial, and cheery as he was, was not doted on by the young girls of Cloton as he had been by their mothers in former time. Each year his breast impended a little further over his toes, and his chin a little further over his breast, and in proportion as he turned down his nose to earth did pretty females turn up theirs at him. They might have liked him as a friend had he not shown the abnormal wish to be regarded as a lover. To Agatha Pollin this aged youth was positively distasteful.

It happened that at the hour of Mr Lovill's visit Agatha was bending over the pool at the mill head, sousing some white fabric in the water. She was quite unconscious of the farmer's presence near her, and continued dipping and rinsing in the idlest phase possible to industry, until she remained quite still, holding the article under the water, and looking at her own reflection within it. The river, though gliding slowly, was yet so smooth that to the old man on the bridge she existed in duplicate – the pouting mouth, the little nose, the frizzed hair, the bit of blue ribbon, as they existed over the surface, being but a degree more distinct than the same features beneath.

'What a pretty maid!' said the old man to himself. He walked up the margin of the stream, and stood beside her.

'Oh!' said Agatha, starting with surprise. In her flurry she relinquished the article she had been rinsing, which slowly turned over and sank deeper, and made toward the hatch of the mill-wheel.

'There – it will get into the wheel, and be torn to pieces!' she exclaimed.

'I'll fish it out with my stick, my dear,' said Farmer Lovill, and kneeling cautiously down he began hooking and crooking with all his might. 'What thing is it – of much value?'

'Yes; it is my best one!' she said involuntarily.

'It – what is the it?'

'Only something – a piece of linen.' Just then the farmer hooked the endangered article, and dragging it out, held it high on his walking-stick – dripping, but safe.

'Why, it is a chemise!' he said.

The girl looked red, and instead of taking it from the end of the stick, turned away.

'Hee-hee!' laughed the ancient man. 'Well, my dear, there's nothing to be ashamed of that I can see in owning to such a necessary and innocent article of clothing. There, I'll put it on the grass for you, and you shall take it when I am gone.'

Then Farmer Lovill retired, lifting his fingers privately, to express amazement on a small scale, and murmuring, 'What a nice young thing! Well, to be sure. Yes, a nice child – young woman rather; indeed, a marriageable woman, come to that; of course she is.'

The doting old person thought of the young one all this day in a way that the young one did not think of him. He thought so much about her, that in the evening, instead of going to bed, he hobbled privately out by the back door into the moonlight, crossed a field or two, and stood in the lane, looking at the mill – not more in the hope of getting a glimpse of the attractive girl inside than for the pleasure of realizing that she was there.

A light moved within, came nearer, and ascended. The staircase window was large, and he saw his goddess going up with a candle in her hand. This was indeed worth coming for. He feared he was seen by her as well, yet hoped otherwise in the interests of his passion, for she came and drew down the window blind, completely shutting out his gaze. The light vanished from this part, and reappeared in a window a little further on.

The lover drew nearer; this, then, was her bedroom. He rested vigorously on his stick, and straightening his back nearly to a perpendicular, turned up his amorous face.

She came to the window, paused, then opened it.

'Bess its deary-eary heart! it is going to speak to me!' said the old man, moistening his lips, resting still more desperately upon his stick, and straightening himself yet an inch taller. 'She saw me then!'

Agatha, however, made no sign; she was bent of a far different purpose. In a box on her window-sill was a row of mignonette, which had been sadly neglected since her lover's departure, and she began to water it, as if inspired by a sudden recollection of its condition. She poured from her water-jug slowly along the plants, and then, to her astonishment, discerned her elderly friend below.

'A rude old thing!' she murmured.

Directing the spout of the jug over the edge of the box, and looking in another direction that it might appear to be an accident, she allowed the stream to spatter down upon her admirer's face, neck, and shoulders, causing him to beat a quick retreat. Then Agatha serenely closed the window, and drew down that blind also.

'Ah! she did not see me; it was evident she did not, and I was mistaken!' said the trembling farmer, hastily wiping his face, and mopping out the rills trickling down within his shirt-collar, as far as he could get at them, which was by no means to their termination. 'A pretty creature, and so innocent, too! Watering her flowers; how I like a girl who is fond of flowers! I wish she had spoken, and I wish I was younger. Yes, I know what I'ld do with the little mouse!' And the old gentleman tapped emotionally upon the ground with his stick.

5

'Agatha, I suppose you have heard the news from somebody else by this time?' said her uncle Humphrey some two or three weeks later. 'I mean what Farmer Lovill has been talking to me about.'

'No, indeed,' said Agatha.

'He wants to marry ye if you be willing.'

'Oh, I never!' said Agatha with dismay. 'That old man!'

'Old? He's hale and hearty; and, what's more, a man very well-to-do. He'll make you a comfortable home, and dress ye up like a doll, and I'm sure you'll like that, or you baint a woman of woman born.'

'But it *can't be*, uncle! – other reasons—'

'What reasons?'

'Why, I've promised Oswald Winwood – years ago!'

'Promised Oswald Winwood years ago, have you?'

'Yes; surely you know it, Uncle Humphrey. And we write to one another regularly.'

'Well, I can just call to mind that ye are always scribbling and getting letters from somewhere. Let me see – where is he now? I quite forget.'

'In India still. Is it possible that you don't know about him, and what a great man he's getting? There are paragraphs about him in our paper very often. The last was about some translation from Hindustani that he'd been making. And he's coming home for me.'

'I very much question it. Lovill will marry you at once, he says.'

'Indeed, he will not.'

'Well, I don't want to force you to do anything against your will, Agatha, but this is how the matter stands. You know I am a little behind-hand in my dealings with Lovill – nothing serious, you know, if he gives me time – but I want to be free of him quite in order to go to Australia.'

'Australia!'

'Yes. There's nothing to be done here. I don't know what business is coming to – can't think. But never mind that; this is the point: if you will marry Farmer Lovill, he offers to clear off the debt, and there will be no longer any delay about my own marriage; in short, away I can go. I mean to, and there's an end on't.'

'What, and leave me at home alone?'

'Yes, but a married woman, of course. You see, the children are getting big now. John is twelve and Nathaniel ten, and the girls are growing fast, and when I am married again I shall hardly want you to keep house for me – in fact, I must reduce our family as much as possible. So that if you could bring your mind to think of Farmer Lovill as a husband, why, 'twould be a great relief to me after having the trouble and expense of bringing you up. If I can in that way edge out of Lovill's debt I shall have a nice bit of money in hand.'

'But Oswald will be richer even than Mr Lovill,' said Agatha, through her tears.

'Yes, yes. But Oswald is not here, nor is he likely to be. How silly you be.'

'But he will come, and soon, with his eleven hundred a year and all.'

'I wish to Heaven he would. I'm sure he might have you.'

'Now, you promise that, uncle, don't you?' she said, brightening. 'If he comes with plenty of money before you want to leave, he shall marry me, and nobody else.'

'Ay, if he comes. But, Agatha, no nonsense. Just think of what I've been telling you. At any rate be civil to Farmer Lovill. If this man Winwood were here and asked for ye, and married ye, that would be a very different thing. I do mind now that I saw something about him and his doings in the papers; but he's a fine gentleman by this time, and won't think of stooping to a girl like you. So you had better take the one who is ready; old men's darlings fare very well as the world goes. We shall be off in nine months, mind; that I've settled. And you must be a married woman afore that time, and wish us good-bye upon your husband's arm.'

'That old arm couldn't support me.'

'And if you don't agree to have him, you'll take a couple of hundred pounds out of my pocket; you'll ruin my chances altogether – that's the long and the short of it!'

Saying which the floury man turned his back upon her, and his footsteps became drowned in the rumble of the mill.

6

Nothing so definite was said to her again on the matter for some time. The old yeoman hovered round her, but, knowing the result of the interview between Agatha and her uncle, he forebore to endanger his suit by precipitancy. But one afternoon he could not avoid saying, 'Aggy, when may I speak to you upon a serious subject?'

'Next week,' she replied, instantly.

He had not been prepared for such a ready answer, and it startled him almost as much as it pleased him. Had he known the cause of it his emotions might have been different. Agatha, with all the womanly strategy she was capable of, had written post-haste to Oswald after the conversation with her uncle, and told him of the dilemma. At the end of the present week his answer, if he replied with his customary punctuality, would be sure to come. Fortified with his letter, she thought she could meet the old man. Oswald she did not doubt.

Nor had she any reason to. The letter came prompt to the day. It was short, tender, and to the point. Events had shaped themselves so fortunately that he was able to say he would return and marry her before the time named for the family's departure for Queensland.

She danced about for joy. But there was a postscript to the effect that she might as well keep this promise a secret for the present, if she conveniently could, that his intention might not become a public talk in Cloton. Agatha knew that he was a rising and aristocratic young man, and saw at once how proper this was.

So she met Mr Lovill with a simple flat refusal, at which her uncle was extremely angry, and her disclosure to him afterward of the arrival of the letter went but a little way in pacifying him. Farmer Lovill would put in upon him for the debt, he said, unless she could manage to please him for a short time.

'I don't want to please him,' said Agatha. 'It is wrong to encourage him if I don't mean it.'

'Will you behave toward him as the parson advises you?'

The parson! That was a new idea, and from her uncle, unexpected.

'I will agree to what Mr Davids advises about my mere daily behaviour before Oswald comes, but nothing more,' she said. 'That is, I will if you know for certain that he's a good man, who fears God and keeps the commandments.'

'Mr Davids fears God, for sartin, for he never ventures to name Him outside the pulpit; and as for the commandments, 'tis knowed how he swore at the church-restorers for taking them away from the chancel.'

'Uncle, you always jest when I am serious.'

'Well, well! at any rate his advice on a matter of this sort is good.'

'How is it you think of referring me to him?' she asked, in perplexity; 'you so often speak slightingly of him.'

'Oh – well,' said Humphrey, with a faintly perceptible desire to parry the question, 'I have spoken roughly about him once now and then; but perhaps I was wrong. Will ye go?'

'Yes, I don't mind,' she said, languidly.

When she reached the vicar's study Agatha began her story with reserve, and said nothing about the correspondence with Oswald; yet an intense longing to find a friend and confidant led her to indulge in more feeling than she had intended, and as a finale she wept. The genial incumbent, however, remained quite cool, the secret being that his heart was involved a little in another direction – one, perhaps, not quite in harmony with Agatha's interests – of which more anon.

'So the difficulty is,' he said to her, 'how to behave in this trying time of waiting for Mr Winwood, that you may please parties all round and give offence to none.'

'Yes, sir, that's it,' sobbed Agatha, wondering how he could have realized her position so readily. 'And uncle wants to go to Australia.'

'One thing is certain,' said the vicar; 'you must not hurt the feelings of Mr Lovill. Wonderfully sensitive man – a man I respect much as a godly doer.'

'Do you, sir?'

'I do. His earnestness is remarkable.'

'Yes, in courting.'

'The cue is: treat Mr Lovill gently – gently as a babe! Love opposed, especially an old man's, gets all the stronger. It is your policy to give him seeming encouragement, and so let his feelings expend themselves and die away.'

'How am I to? To advise is so easy.'

'Not by acting untruthfully, of course. You say your lover is sure to come back before your uncle leaves England.'

'I know he will.'

'Then pacify old Mr Lovill in this way: Tell him you'll marry him when your uncle wants to go, if Winwood doesn't come for you before that time. That will quite content Mr Lovill, for he doesn't in the least expect Oswald to return, and you will see that his persecution will cease at once.'

'Yes; I'll agree to it,' said Agatha promptly.

Mr Davids had refrained from adding that neither did he expect Oswald to come, and hence his advice. Agatha on her part too refrained from stating the good reasons she had for the contrary expectation, and hence her assent. Without the last letter perhaps even her faith would hardly have been bold enough to allow this palpable driving of her into a corner.

'It would be as well to write Mr Lovill a little note, saying you agree to what I have advised,' said the parson evasively.

'I don't like writing.'

'There is no harm. "If Mr Winwood doesn't come I'll marry you", &c. Poor Mr Lovill will be content, thinking Oswald will not come; you will be content, knowing he will come; your uncle will be content, being indifferent which of two rich men has you and relieves him of his difficulties. Then, if it is the will of Providence, you'll be left in peace. Here's a pen and ink; you can do it at once.'

Thus tempted, Agatha wrote the note with a trembling hand. It really did seem upon the whole a nicely strategic thing to do in her present environed situation. Mr Davids took the note with the air of a man who did not wish to take it in the least, and placed it on the mantelpiece.

'I'll send it down to him by one of the children,' said Aggy, looking wistfully at her note with a little feeling that she would like to have it back again.

'Oh, no, it is not necessary,' said her pleasant adviser. He had rung the bell; the servant now came, and the note was sent off in a trice.

When Agatha got into the open air her confidence returned, and it was with a mischievous sense of enjoyment that she considered how she was duping her persecutors by keeping secret Oswald's intention of a speedy return. If they only knew what a firm foundation she had for her belief in what they all deemed but an improbable contingency, what a life they would lead her; how the old man would worry her uncle for payment, and what general confusion there would be. Mr Davids' advice was very shrewd, she thought, and she was glad she had called upon him.

Old Lovill came that very afternoon. He was delighted, and danced a few bars of a hornpipe in entering the room. So lively was the antique boy that Agatha was rather alarmed at her own temerity when she considered what was the basis of his gaiety; wishing she could get from him some such writing as he had got from her, that the words of her promise might not in any way be tampered with, or the conditions ignored.

'I only accept you conditionally, mind,' she anxiously said. 'That is distinctly understood.'

'Yes, yes,' said the yeoman. 'I am not so young as I was, little dear, and beggars mustn't be choosers. With my ra-ta-ta – say, dear, shall it be the first of November?'

'It will really never be.'

'But if he doesn't come, it shall be the first of November?'

She slightly nodded her head.

'Clk! – I think she likes me!' said the old man aside to Aggy's uncle, which aside was distinctly heard by Aggy.

One of the younger children was in the room, drawing idly on a slate. Agatha at this moment took the slate from the child, and scribbled something on it.

'Now you must please me by just writing your name here,' she said in a voice of playful indifference.

'What is it?' said Lovill, looking over and reading, '"If Oswald Winwood comes to marry Agatha Pollin before November, I agree to give her up to him without objection." Well, that is cool for a young lady under six feet, upon my word – hee-hee!' He passed the slate to the miller, who read the writing and passed it back again.

'Sign – just in courtesy,' she coaxed.

'I don't see why—'

'I do it to test your faith in me; and now I find you have none. Don't you think I should have rubbed it out instantly? Ah, perhaps I can be obstinate too!'

He wrote his name then. 'Now I have done it, and shown my faith,' he said, and at once raised his fingers as if to rub it out again. But with hands that moved like lightning she snatched up the slate, flew up the stairs, locked it in her box, and came down again.

'Souls of men – that's sharp practice,' said the old gentleman.

'Oh, it is only a whim – a mere memorandum,' said she. 'You had my promise, but I had not yours.'

'Ise wants my slate,' cried the child.

'I'll buy you a new one, dear,' said Agatha, and soothed her.

When she had left the room old Lovill spoke to her uncle somewhat uneasily of the event, which, childish as it had been, discomposed him for the moment.

'Oh, that's nothing,' said Miller Pollin assuringly; 'only play – only play. She's a mere child in nater even now, and she did it only to tease ye. Why, she overheard your whisper that you thought she liked ye, and that was her playful way of punishing ye for your confidence. You'll have to put up with these worries, farmer. Considering the difference in your ages, she is sure to play pranks. You'll get to like 'em in time.'

'Ay, ay, faith, so I shall! I was alway a Turk for sprees! – eh, Pollin? Hee-hee!' And the suitor was merry again.

7

Her life was certainly much pleasanter now. The old man treated her well, and was almost silent on the subject nearest his heart. She was obliged to be very stealthy in receiving letters from Oswald, and on this account was bound to meet the post-man, let the weather be what it would. These transactions were easily kept secret from people out of the house, but it was a most difficult task to hide her movements from her uncle. And one day brought utter failure.

'How's this – out already, Agatha?' he said, meeting her in the lane at dawn on a foggy morning. She was actually reading a letter just received, and there was no disguising the truth.

'I've been for a letter from Oswald.'

'Well, but that won't do. Since he don't come for ye, ye must think no more about him.'

'But he's coming in six weeks. He tells me all about it in this very letter.'

'What – really to marry you?' said her uncle incredulously.

'Yes, certainly.'

'But I hear that he is wonderfully well off.'

'Of course he is; that's why he's coming. He'll agree in a moment to be your surety for the debt to Mr Lovill.'

'Has he said so?'

'Not yet; but he will.'

'I'll believe it when I see him and he tells me so. It is very odd, if he means so much, that he hev never wrote a line to me.'

'We thought – you would force me to have the other at once if he wrote to you,' she murmured.

'Not I, if he comes rich. But it is rather a cock-and-bull story, and since he didn't make up his mind before now, I can't say I be much in his favour. Agatha, you had better not say a word to Mr Lovill about these letters; it will make things deuced unpleasant if he hears of such goings on. You are to reckon yourself bound by your word. Oswald won't hold water, I'm afeared. But I'll be fair. If he do come, proves his income, marries ye willy-nilly, I'll let it be, and the old man and I must do as we can. But barring that – you keep your promise to the letter.'

'That's what it will be, uncle. Oswald will come.'

'Write you must not. Lovill will smell it out, and he'll be sharper than you will like. 'Tis not to be supposed that you are to send love-letters to one man as if nothing was going to happen between ye and another man. The first of November is drawing nearer every day. And be sure and keep this a secret from Lovill for your own sake.'

The more clearly that Agatha began to perceive the entire contrast of expectation as to issue between herself and the other party to the covenant, the more alarmed she became. She had not anticipated such a narrowing of courses as had occurred. A malign influence seemed to be at work without any visible human agency. The critical time drew nearer, and, though no ostensible preparation for the wedding was made, it was evident to all that Lovill was painting and papering his house for somebody's reception. He made a lawn where there had existed a nook of refuse; he bought furniture for a woman's room. The greatest horror was that he insisted upon her taking his arm one day, and there being no help for it she assented, though her distaste was unutterable. She felt the skinny arm through his sleeve, saw over the wry shoulders, looked upon the knobby feet, and shuddered. What if Oswald should not come; the time for her uncle's departure was really getting near. When she reached home she ran up to her bedroom.

On recovering from her dreads a little, Agatha looked from the window. The deaf lad John, who assisted in the mill, was quietly glancing toward her, and a gleam of friendship passed over his kindly face as he caught sight of her form. This reminded her that she had, after all, some sort of friend close at hand. The lad knew pretty well how events stood in Agatha's life, and he was always ready to do on her part whatever lay in his power. Agatha felt stronger, and resolved to bear up.

8

Heavens! how anxious she was! It actually wanted only ten days to the first of November, and no new letter from Oswald.

Her uncle was married, and Frances was in the house, and the preliminary steps for emigration to Queensland had been taken. Agatha surreptitiously obtained newspapers, scanned the Indian shipping news till her eyes ached, but all to no purpose, for she knew nothing either of route or vessel by which Oswald would return. He had mentioned nothing more than the month of his coming, and she had no way of making that single scrap of information the vehicle for obtaining more.

'In ten days, Agatha,' said the old farmer. 'There is to be no show or fuss of any kind; the wedding will be quite private, in consideration of your feelings and wishes. We'll go to church as if we were taking a morning walk, and nobody will be there to disturb you. Tweedledee!' He held up his arm and crossed it with his walking-stick, as if he were playing the fiddle, at the same time cutting a caper.

'He will come, and then I shan't be able to marry you, even th-th-

though I may wish to ever so much,' she faltered, shivering. 'I have promised him, and I *must* have him, you know, and you have agreed to let me.'

'Yes, yes,' said Farmer Lovill, pleasantly. 'But that's a misfortune you need not fear at all, my dear; he won't come at this late day and compel you to marry him in spite of your attachment to me. But, ah – it is only a joke to tease me, you little rogue! Your uncle says so.'

'Agatha, come, cheer up, and think no more of that fellow,' said her uncle when they chanced to be alone together. ''Tis ridiculous, you know. We always knew he wouldn't come.'

The day passed. The sixth morning came, the noon, the evening. The fifth day came and vanished. Still no sound of Oswald. His friends now lived in London and there was not a soul in the parish, save herself, that he corresponded with, or one to whom she could apply in such a delicate matter as this.

It was the evening before her wedding-day, and she was standing alone in the gloom of her bedchamber looking out on the plot in front of the mill. She saw a white figure moving below, and knew him to be the dear miller lad, her friend. A sudden impulse animated Agatha. She had been making desperate attempts during the last two days to like the old man, and since Oswald did not come, to marry him without further resistance, for the sheer good of the family of her uncle, to whom she was indeed indebted for much; but had only got so far in her efforts as not to positively hate him. Now rebelliousness came unsought. The lad knew her case, and upon this fact she acted. Gliding downstairs, she beckoned to him, and as they stood together in the stream of light from the open mill door, she communicated her directions, partly by signs, partly by writing, for it was difficult to speak to him without being heard all over the premises.

He looked in her face with a glance of confederacy, and said that he understood it all. Upon this they parted.

The old man was at her house that evening, and when she withdrew wished her good-bye 'for the present' with a dozen smiles of meaning. Agatha had retired early, leaving him still there, and when she reached her room, instead of looking at the new dress she was supposed to be going to wear on the morrow, busied herself in making up a small bundle of ordinary articles of clothing. Then she extinguished her light, lay down upon the bed without undressing, and waited for a preconcerted time.

In what seemed to her the dead of night, but which she concluded must be the time agreed upon – half-past five – there was a light noise as of gravel being thrown against her window. Agatha jumped up, put on her bonnet and cloak, took up her bundle, and went downstairs without a light. At the bottom she slipped on her boots, and passed amid the chirping crickets to the door. It was unbarred. Her uncle, then, had risen, as she had half expected, and it necessitated a little more caution. The morning was dark as a cavern, not a star being visible; but knowing the bearings well, she went cautiously and in silence to the mill-door. A faint light shone from inside, and the form of the mill-cart appeared without, the horse ready harnessed to it. Agatha did not see John for the moment, but concluded that he was in the mill with her uncle, who had just at this minute started the wheel for the day. She at once slipped into the vehicle and under the tilt, pulling some empty sacks over, as it had been previously agreed that she should do, to avoid the risk of discovery. After a few minutes of suspense she heard John coming from under the wall, where he had apparently been standing and watching her safely in, and mounting in front, away he drove at a walking pace.

Her scheme had been based upon the following particular of mill business: Thrice a week it was the regular custom for John and another young man to start early in the morning, each with a horse and covered cart, and go in different directions to customers a few miles off, the carts being laden overnight. All that she had asked John to do this morning was to take her with him to a railway station about ten miles distant, where she might safely wait for an up train.

How will John act on returning – what will he say – how will he excuse himself? she thought as they jogged along. 'John!' she said, meaning to ask him about these things; but he did not hear, and she was too confused and weary after her wakeful night to be able to think consecutively on any subject. But the relief of finding that her uncle did not look into the cart caused a delicious lull in her, and while listlessly watching the dark gray sky through the triangular opening between the curtains and the fore part of the tilt, and John's elbow projecting from the folds of one of them, showing where he was sitting on the outside, she fell asleep.

She awoke after a short interval – everything was just the same – jog, jog, on they went; there was the dim slit between the curtains in front, and, after slightly wondering that John had not troubled himself to see that she was comfortable, she dozed again. Thus Agatha remained until she had a clear consciousness of the stopping of the cart. It aroused her, and looking at once through a small opening at the back, she perceived in the dim dawn that they were turning right about; in another moment the horse was proceeding on the way back again.

'John, what are you doing?' she exclaimed, jumping up and pulling aside the curtain which parted them.

John did not turn.

'How fearfully deaf he is!' she thought, 'and how odd he looks behind, and he hangs forward as if he were asleep. His hair is snow-white with flour; does he never clean it, then?' She crept across the sacks and slapped him on the shoulder. John turned then.

'Hee-hee, my dear!' said the blithe old gentleman; and the moisture of his aged eye glistened in the dawning light, as he turned and looked into her horrified face. 'It is all right; I am John, and I have given ye a nice morning's airing to refresh ye for the uncommon duties of today; and now we are going back for the ceremony – hee-hee!'

He wore a miller's smock-frock on this interesting occasion, and had been enabled to play the part of John in the episode by taking the second cart and horse and anticipating by an hour the real John in calling her.

Agatha sank backward. How on earth had he discovered the scheme of escape so readily; he, an old and by no means suspicious man? But what mattered a solution! Hope was crushed, and her rebellion was at an end. Agatha was awakened from thought by another stopping of the horse, and they were again at the mill-door.

She dimly recognized her uncle's voice speaking in anger to her when the old farmer handed her out of the vehicle, and heard the farmer reply, merrily, that girls would be girls and have their freaks, that it didn't matter, and that it was a pleasant jest on this auspicious morn. For himself, there was nothing he had enjoyed all his life so much as a practical joke which did no harm. Then she had a sensation of being told to go into the house, have some food, and dress for her marriage with Mr Lovill, as she had promised to do on that day.

All this she did, and at eleven o'clock became the wife of the old man.

When Agatha was putting on her bonnet in the dusk that evening, for she would not illuminate her ghastly face by a candle, a rustling came against the door. Agatha turned. Her uncle's wife, Frances, was looking into the room, and Agatha could just discern upon her aunt's form the blue cloak which had ruled her destiny.

The sight was almost more than she could bear. If, as seemed likely, this effect was intended, the trick was certainly successful. Frances did not speak a word.

Then Agatha said in quiet irony, and with no evidence whatever of regret, sadness, or surprise at what the fact revealed: 'And so you told Mr Lovill of my flight this morning, and set him on the track? It would be amusing to know how you found out my plan, for he never could have done it by himself, poor old darling.'

'Oh, I was a witness of your arrangement with John last night – that was all, my dear,' said her aunt pleasantly. 'I mentioned it then to Mr Lovill, and helped him to his joke of hindering you. . . You remember the van, Agatha, and how you made use of my name on that occasion, years ago, now?'

'Yes, and did you hear our talk that night? I always fancied otherwise.'

'I heard it all. It was fun to you; what do you think it was to me – fun, too? – to lose the man I longed for, and to become the wife of a man I care not an atom about?'

'Ah, no. And how you struggled to get him away from me, dear aunt!'

'And have done it, too!'

'Not you, exactly. The parson and fate.'

'Parson Davids kindly persuaded you, because I kindly persuaded him, and persuaded your uncle to send you to him. Mr Davids is an old admirer of mine. Now do you see a wheel within a wheel, Agatha?'

Calmness was almost insupportable by Agatha now, but she managed to say: 'Of course you have kept back letters from Oswald to me?'

'No, I have not done that,' said Frances. 'But I told Oswald, who landed at Southampton last night, and called here in great haste at seven this morning that you had gone out for an early drive with the man you were to marry today, and that it might cause confusion if he remained. He looked very pale, and went away again at once to catch the next London train, saying something about having been prevented by a severe illness from sailing at the time he had promised and intended for the last twelvemonths.'

The bride, though nearly slain by the news, would not flinch in the presence of her adversary. Stilling her quivering flesh, she said smiling: 'That information is deeply interesting, but does not concern me at all, for I am my husband's darling now, you know, and I wouldn't make the dear man jealous for the world.' And she glided downstairs to the chaise.

THE THIEVES WHO COULDN'T HELP SNEEZING

Many years ago, when oak-trees now past their prime were about as large as elderly gentlemen's walking-sticks, there lived in Wessex a yeoman's son, whose name was Hubert. He was about fourteen years of age, and was as remarkable for his candour and lightness of heart as for his physical courage, of which, indeed, he was a little vain.

One cold Christmas Eve his father, having no other help at hand, sent him on an important errand to a small town several miles from home. He travelled on horseback, and was detained by the business till a late hour of the evening. At last, however, it was completed; he returned to the inn, the horse was saddled, and he started on his way. His journey homeward lay through the Vale of Blackmore, a fertile but somewhat lonely district, with heavy clay roads and crooked lanes. In those days, too, a great part of it was thickly wooded.

It must have been about nine o'clock when, riding along amid the overhanging trees upon his stout-legged cob Jerry, and singing a Christmas carol, to be in harmony with the season, Hubert fancied that he heard a noise among the boughs. This recalled to his mind that the spot he was traversing bore an evil name. Men had been waylaid there. He looked at Jerry, and wished he had been of any other colour than light grey; for on this account the docile animal's form was visible even here in the dense shade. 'What do I care?' he said aloud, after a few minutes of reflection. 'Jerry's legs are too nimble to allow any highwayman to come near me.'

'Ha! ha! indeed,' was said in a deep voice; and the next moment a man darted from the thicket on his right hand, another man from the thicket on his left hand, and another from a tree-trunk a few yards ahead. Hubert's bridle was seized, he was pulled from his horse, and although he struck out with all his might, as a brave boy would naturally do, he was overpowered. His arms were tied behind him, his legs bound tightly together, and he was thrown into the ditch. The robbers, whose faces he could now dimly perceive to be artificially blackened, at once departed, leading off the horse.

As soon as Hubert had a little recovered himself, he found that by great exertion he was able to extricate his legs from the cord; but, in spite of every endeavour, his arms remained bound as fast as before. All, therefore, that he could do was to rise to his feet and proceed on his way with his arms behind him, and trust to chance for getting them unfastened. He knew that it would be impossible to reach home on foot that night, and in such a condition; but he walked on. Owing to the confusion which this attack caused in his brain, he lost his way, and would have been inclined to lie down and rest till morning among the dead leaves had he not known the danger of sleeping without wrappers in a frost so severe. So he wandered further onwards, his arms wrung and numbed by the cord which pinioned him, and his heart aching for the loss of poor Jerry, who never had been known to kick, or bite, to show a single vicious habit. He was not a little glad when he discerned through the trees a distant light. Towards this he made his way, and presently found himself in front of a large mansion with flanking wings, gables, and towers, the battlements and chimneys showing their shapes against the stars.

All was silent; but the door stood wide open, it being from this door that the light shone which had attracted him. On entering he found himself in a vast apartment arranged as a dining-hall, and brilliantly illuminated. The walls were covered with a great deal of dark wainscoting, formed into moulded panels, carvings, closet-doors, and the usual fittings of a house of that kind. But what drew his attention most was the large table in the midst of the hall, upon which was spread a sumptuous supper, as yet untouched. Chairs were placed around, and it appeared as if something had occurred to interrupt the meal just at the time when all were ready to begin.

Even had Hubert been so inclined, he could not have eaten in his helpless state, unless by dipping his mouth into the dishes, like a pig or cow. He wished first to obtain assistance; and was about to penetrate further into the house for that purpose when he heard hasty footsteps in the porch and the words, 'Be quick!' uttered in the deep voice which had reached him when he was dragged from the horse. There was only just time for him to dart under the table before three men entered the dining-hall. Peeping from beneath the hanging edges of the tablecloth, he perceived that their faces, too, were blackened, which at once removed any remaining doubts he may have felt that these were the same thieves.

'Now, then,' said the first – the man with the deep voice – 'let us hide ourselves. They will all be back again in a minute. That was a good trick to get them out of the house – eh?'

'Yes. You well imitated the cries of a man in distress,' said the second.

'Excellently,' said the third.

'But they will soon find out that it was a false alarm. Come, where shall we hide? It must be some place we can stay in for two or three hours, till all are in bed and asleep. Ah! I have it. Come this way! I have learnt that the further closet is not opened once in a twelvemonth; it will serve our purpose exactly.'

The speaker advanced into a corridor which led from the hall. Creeping a little farther forward, Hubert could discern that the closet stood at the end, facing the dining-hall. The thieves entered it, and closed the door. Hardly breathing, Hubert glided forward, to learn a little more of their intention, if possible; and, coming close, he could hear the robbers whispering about the different rooms where the jewels, plate, and other valuables of the houes were kept, which they plainly meant to steal.

They had not been long in hiding when a gay chattering of ladies and gentlemen was audible on the terrace without. Hubert felt that it would not do to be caught prowling about the house, unless he wished to be taken for a robber himself; and he slipped softly back to the hall, out at the door, and stood in a dark corner of the porch, where he could see everything without being himself seen. In a moment or two a whole troop of personages came gliding past him into the house. There were an elderly gentleman and lady, eight or nine young ladies, as many young men, besides half-a-dozen men-servants and maids. The mansion had apparently been quite emptied of its occupants.

'Now, children and young people, we will resume our meal,' said the old gentleman. 'What the noise could have been I cannot understand. I never felt so certain in my life that there was a person being murdered outside my door.'

Then the ladies began saying how frightened they had been, and how they had expected an adventure, and how it had ended in nothing after all.

'Wait a while,' said Hubert to himself. 'You'll have adventure enough by-and-by, ladies.'

It appeared that the young men and women were married sons and daughters of the old couple, who had come that day to spend Christmas with their parents.

The door was then closed, Hubert being left outside in the porch. He thought this a proper moment for asking their assistance; and, since he was unable to knock with his hands, began boldly to kick the door.

'Hullo! What disturbance are you making here?' said a footman who opened it; and, seizing Hubert by the shoulder, he pulled him into the dining-hall. 'Here's a strange boy I have found making a noise in the porch, Sir Simon.'

Everybody turned.

'Bring him forward,' said Sir Simon, the old gentleman before mentioned. 'What were you doing there, my boy?'

'Why, his arms are tied!' said one of the ladies.

'Poor fellow!' said another.

Hubert at once began to explain that he had been waylaid on his journey home, robbed of his horse, and mercilessly left in this condition by the thieves.

'Only to think of it!' exclaimed Sir Simon.

'That's a likely story,' said one of the gentleman-guests, incredulously.

'Doubtful, hey?' asked Sir Simon.

'Perhaps he's a robber himself,' suggested a lady.

'There is a curious wild wicked look about him, certainly, now that I examine him closely,' said the old mother.

Hubert blushed with shame; and, instead of continuing his story, and relating that robbers were concealed in the house, he doggedly held his tongue, and half resolved to let them find out their danger for themselves.

'Well, untie him,' said Sir Simon. 'Come, since it is Christmas Eve, we'll treat him well. Here, my lad; sit down in that empty seat at the bottom of the table, and make as good a meal as you can. When you have had your fill we will listen to more particulars of your story.'

The feast then proceeded; and Hubert, now at liberty, was not at all sorry to join in. The more they ate and drank the merrier did the company become; the wine flowed freely, the logs flared up the chimney, the ladies laughed at the gentlemen's stories; in short, all went as noisily and as happily as a Christmas gathering in old times possibly could do.

Hubert, in spite of his hurt feelings at their doubts of his honesty, could not help being warmed both in mind and in body by the good cheer, the scene, and the example of hilarity set by his neighbours. At last he laughed as heartily at their stories and repartees as the old Baronet, Sir Simon, himself. When the meal was almost over one of the sons, who had drunk a little too much wine, after the manner of men in that century, said to Hubert, 'Well, my boy, how are you? Can you take a pinch of snuff?' He held out one of the snuff-boxes which were then becoming common among young and old throughout the country.

'Thank you,' said Hubert, accepting a pinch.

'Tell the ladies who you are, what you are made of, and what you can do,' the young man continued, slapping Hubert upon the shoulder.

'Certainly,' said our hero, drawing himself up, and thinking it best to put a bold face on the matter. 'I am a travelling magician.'

'Indeed!'

'What shall we hear next?'

'Can you call up spirits from the vasty deep, young wizard?'

'I can conjure up a tempest in a cupboard,' Hubert replied.

'Ha-ha!' said the old Baronet, pleasantly rubbing his hands. 'We must see this performance. Girls, don't go away: here's something to be seen.'

'Not dangerous, I hope?' said the old lady.

Hubert rose from the table. 'Hand me your snuff-box, please,' he said to the young man who had made free with him. 'And now,' he continued, 'without the least noise, follow me. If any of you speak it will break the spell.'

They promised obedience. He entered the corridor, and, taking off his shoes, went on tiptoe to the closet door, the guests advancing in a silent group at a little distance behind him. Hubert next placed a stool in front of the door, and, by standing upon it, was tall enough to reach to the top. He then, just as noiselessly, poured all the snuff from the box along the upper edge of the door, and, with a few short puffs of breath, blew the snuff through the chink into the interior of the closet. He held up his finger to the assembly, that they might be silent.

'Dear me, what's that?' said the old lady, after a minute or two had elapsed.

A suppressed sneeze had come from inside the closet.

Hubert held up his finger again.

'How very singular,' whispered Sir Simon. 'This is most interesting.'

Hubert took advantage of the moment to gently slide the bolt of the closet door into its place. 'More snuff,' he said, calmly.

'More snuff,' said Sir Simon. Two or three gentlemen passed their boxes, and the contents were blown in at the top of the closet. Another sneeze, not quite so well suppressed as the first, was heard: then another, which seemed to say that it would not be suppressed under any circumstances whatever. At length there arose a perfect storm of sneezes.

'Excellent, excellent for one so young!' said Sir Simon. 'I am much interested in this trick of throwing the voice – called, I believe, ventriloquism.'

'More snuff,' said Hubert.

'More snuff,' said Sir Simon. Sir Simon's man brought a large jar of the best scented Scotch.

Hubert once more charged the upper chink of the closet, and blew the snuff into the interior, as before. Again he charged, and again, emptying the whole contents of the jar. The tumult of sneezes became really extraordinary to listen to – there was no cessation. It was like wind, rain, and sea battling in a hurricane.

'I believe there are men inside, and that it is no trick at all!' exclaimed Sir Simon, the truth flashing on him.

'There are,' said Hubert. 'They are come to rob the house; and they are the same who stole my horse.'

The sneezes changed to spasmodic groans. One of the thieves, hearing Hubert's voice, cried, 'Oh! mercy! mercy! let us out of this!'

'Where's my horse?' said Hubert.

'Tied to the tree in the hollow behind Short's Gibbet. Mercy! mercy! let us out, or we shall die of suffocation!'

All the Christmas guests now perceived that this was no longer sport, but serious earnest. Guns and cudgels were procured; all the men-servants were called in, and arranged in position outside the closet. At a signal Hubert withdrew the bolt, and stood on the defensive. But the three robbers, far from attacking them, were found crouching in the corner, gasping for breath. They made no resistance; and, being pinioned, were placed in an out-house till the morning.

Hubert now gave the remainder of his story to the assembled company, and was profusely thanked for the services he had rendered. Sir Simon pressed him to stay over the night, and accept the use of the best bedroom the house afforded, which had been ocupied by Queen Elizabeth and King Charles successively when on their visits to this part of the country. But Hubert declined, being anxious to find his horse Jerry, and to test the truth of the robbers' statements concerning him.

Several of the guets accompanied Hubert to the spot behind the gibbet, alluded to by the thieves as where Jerry was hidden. When they reached the knoll and looked over, behold! there the horse stood, uninjured, and quite unconcerned. At sight of Hubert he neighed joyfully; and nothing could exceed Hubert's gladness at finding him. He mounted, wished his friends 'Good-night!' and cantered off in the direction they pointed out as his nearest way, reaching home safely about four o'clock in the morning.

OLD MRS CHUNDLE

The curate had not been a week in the parish, but the autumn morning proving fine, he thought he would make a little water-colour sketch, showing a distant view of the Corvsgate ruin two miles off, which he had passed on his way hither. The sketch occupied him a longer time than he had anticipated. The luncheon hour drew on, and he felt hungry.

Quite near him was a stone-built old cottage of respectable and substantial build. He entered it, and was received by an old woman.

'Can you give me something to eat, my good woman?' he said.

She held her hand to her ear.

'Can you give me something for my lunch?' he shouted. 'Bread and cheese – anything will do.'

A sour look crossed her face, and she shook her head. 'That's unlucky,' murmured he. She reflected and said more urbanely, 'Well, I'm going to have my own bit o' dinner in no such long time hence. 'Tis taters and cabbage, boiled with a scantling o' bacon. Would ye like it? But I suppose 'tis the wrong sort, and that ye would sooner have bread and cheese.'

'No, I'll join you. Call me when it is ready. I'm just out here.'

'Ay, I've seen ye. Drawing the old stones, baint ye?'

'Aye, my good woman.'

'Sure 'tis well some folk have nothing better to do with their time. Very well, I'll call ye, when I've dished up.'

He went out and resumed his painting; till in about seven or ten minutes the old woman appeared at her door and held up her hand. The curate washed his brush, went to the brook, rinsed his hands and proceeded to the house.

'There's yours,' she said, pointing to the table. 'I'll have my bit here.' And she denoted the settle.

'Why not join me?'

'Oh, faith, I don't want to eat with my betters – not I.' And she continued firm in her resolution, and ate apart.

The vegetables had been well cooked over a wood fire – the only way to cook a vegetable properly – and the bacon was well boiled. The curate ate heartily: he thought he had never tasted such potatoes and cabbage in his life, which he probably had not, for they had just been brought in from the garden, so that the very freshness of the morning was still in them. When he had finished he asked her how much he owed for the repast, which he had much enjoyed.

'Oh, I don't want to be paid for that bit of snack 'a b'lieve!'

'But really you must take something. It was an excellent meal.'

''Tis all my own growing, that's true. But I don't take money for a bit o' victuals. I've never done such a thing in my life.'

'I should feel much happier if you would.'

She seemed unsettled by his feeling, and added as by compulsion, 'Well, then; I suppose twopence won't hurt ye?'

'Twopence?'

'Yes. Twopence.'

'Why my good woman, that's no charge at all. I am sure it is worth this, at least.' And he laid down a shilling.

'I tell 'ee 'tis *twopence*, and no more!' she said primly. 'Why, bless the man, it didn't cost me more than three halfpence, and that leaves me a fair quarter profit. The bacon is the heaviest item; that may perhaps be a penny. The taters I've got plenty of, and the cabbage is going to waste.'

He thereupon argued no further, paid the limited sum demanded, and went to the door. 'And where does that road lead?' he asked, by way of engaging her in a little friendly conversation before parting, and pointing to a white lane which branched from the direct highway near her door.

'They tell me that it leads to Enckworth.'

'And how far is Enckworth?'

'Three miles, they say. but God knows if 'tis true.'

'You haven't lived here long, then?'

'Five-and-thirty year come Martinmas.'

'And yet you have never been to Enckworth?'

'Not I. Why should I ever have been to Enckworth? I never had any business there – a great mansion of a place, holding people that I've no more doings with than with the people of the moon. No, there's on'y two places I. ever go to from year's end to year's end: that's once a fortnight to Anglebury, to do my bit o' marketing, and once a week to my parish church.'

'Which is that?'

'Why, Kingscreech.'

'Oh – then you are in my parish?'

'Maybe. Just on the outskirts.'

'I didn't know the parish extended so far. I'm a newcomer. Well, I hope we may meet again. Good afternoon to you.'

When the curate was next talking to the rector he casually observed: 'By the way, that's a curious old soul who lives out towards Corvsgate – old Mrs – I don't know her name – A deaf old woman.'

'You mean old Mrs Chundle, I suppose.'

'She tells me she's lived there five-and-thirty years, and has never been to Enckworth, three miles off. She goes to two places only from year's end to year's end – to the market town, and to church on Sundays.'

'To church on Sundays. H'm. She rather exaggerates her travels, to my thinking. I've been rector here thirteen years, and I have certainly never seen her at church in my time.'

'A wicked old woman. What can she think of herself for such deception!'

'She didn't know you belonged here when she said it, and could find out the untruth of her story. I warrant she wouldn't have said it to me!' And the rector chuckled.

On reflection the curate felt that this was decidedly a case for his ministrations, and on the first spare morning he strode across to the cottage beyond the ruin. He found its occupant of course at home.

'Drawing picters again?' she asked, looking up from the hearth, where she was scouring the fire-dogs.

'No, I come on a more important matter, Mrs Chundle. I am the new curate of this parish.'

'You said you was last time. And after you had told me and went away I said to myself, he'll be here again sure enough, hang me if I didn't. And here you be.'

'Yes. I hope you don't mind?'

'Oh, no. You find us a roughish lot, I make no doubt?'

'Well, I won't go into that. But I think it was a very culpable – unkind thing of you to tell me you came to church every Sunday, when I find you've not been seen there for years.'

'Oh, did I tell 'ee that?'

'You certainly did.'

'Now I wonder what I did that for?'

'I wonder too.'

'Well, you could ha' guessed, after all, that I didn't come to any service. Lord, what's the good o' my lumpering all the way to church and back again, when I'm as deaf as a plock? Your own commonsense ought to have told 'ee that 'twas but a figure o' speech, seeing you was a pa'son.'

'Don't you think you could hear the service if you were to sit close to the reading-desk and pulpit?'

'I'm sure I couldn't. Oh no – not a word. Why I couldn't hear anything even at that time when Isaac Coggs used to cry the Amens out loud beyond anything that's done nowadays, and they had the barrel-organ for the tunes – years and years agone, when I was stronger in my narves than now.'

'H'm – I'm sorry. There's one thing I could do, which I would with pleasure, if you'll use it. I could get you an ear-trumpet. Will you use it?'

'Ay, sure. That I woll. I don't care what I use – 'tis all the same to me.'

'And you'll come?'

'Yes. I may as well go there as bide here, I suppose.'

The ear-trumpet was purchased by the zealous young man, and the next Sunday, to the great surprise of the parishioners when they arrived, Mrs Chundle was discovered in the front seat of the nave of Kingscreech Church, facing the rest of the congregation with an unmoved countenance.

She was the centre of observation through the whole morning service. The trumpet, elevated at a high angle, shone and flashed in the sitters' eyes as the chief object in the sacred edifice.

The curate could not speak to her that morning, and called the next day to inquire the result of the experiment. As soon as she saw him in the distance she began shaking her head.

'No, no,' she said decisively as he approached. 'I knowed 'twas all nonsense.'

'What?'

''Twasn't a mossel o' good, and so I could have told 'ee before. A wasting your money in jimcracks upon a' old 'ooman like me.'

'You couldn't hear? Dear me – disappointing.'

'You might as well have been mouthing at me from the top o' Creech Barrow.'

'That's unfortunate.'

'I shall never come no more – never – to be made such a fool of as that again.'

The curate mused. 'I'll tell you what, Mrs Chundle. There's one thing more to try, and only one. If that fails I suppose we shall have to give it up. It is a plan I have heard of, though I have never myself tried it; it's having a sound tube fixed, with its lower mouth in the seat immediately below the pulpit, where you would sit, the tube running up inside the pulpit with its upper end opening in a bell-mouth just beside the book-board. The voice of the preacher enters the bell-mouth, and is carried down directly to the listener's ear. Do you understand?'

'Exactly.'

'And you'll come, if I put it up at my own expense?'

'Ay, I suppose. I'll try it, e'en though I said I wouldn't. I may as well do that as do nothing, I reckon.'

The kind-hearted curate, at great trouble to himself, obtained the tube and had it fixed vertically as described, the upper mouth being immediately under the face of whoever should preach, and on the following Sunday morning it was to be tried. As soon as he came from the vestry the curate perceived to his satisfaction Mrs Chundle in the seat beneath, erect and at attention, her head close to the lower orifice of the sound-pipe, and a look of great complacency that her soul required a special machinery to save it, while other people's could be saved in a commonplace way. The rector read the prayers from the desk on the opposite side, which part of the service Mrs Chundle could follow easily enough by the help of the prayer-book; and in due course the curate mounted the eight steps into the wooden octagon, gave out his text, and began to deliver his discourse.

It was a fine frosty morning in early winter, and he had not got far with his sermon when he became conscious of a steam rising from the bell-mouth of the tube, obviously caused by Mrs Chundle's breathing at the lower end, and it was accompanied by a suggestion of onion-stew. However, he preached on awhile, hoping it would cease, holding in his left hand his finest cambric handkerchief kept specially for Sunday morning services. At length, no longer able to endure the odour, he lightly dropped the handkerchief into the bell of the tube, without stopping for a moment the eloquent flow of his words; and he had the satisfaction of feeling himself in comparatively pure air.

He heard a fidgeting below; and presently there arose to him over the pulpit-edge a hoarse whisper: 'The pipe's chokt!'

'Now, as you will perceive, my brethren,' continued the curate, unheeding the interruption; 'by applying this test to ourselves, our discernment of—'

'The pipe's chokt!' came up in a whisper yet louder and hoarser.

'Our discernments of actions as morally good or indifferent will be much quickened, and we shall be materially helped in our—'

Suddenly came a violent puff of warm wind, and he beheld his handkerchief rising from the bell of the tube and floating to the pulpit floor. The little boys in the gallery laughed, thinking it a miracle. Mrs Chundle had, in fact, applied her mouth to the bottom end, blown with all her might, and cleared the tube. In a few seconds the atmosphere of the pulpit became as before, to the curate's great discomfiture. Yet stop the orifice again he dared not, lest the old woman should make a still greater disturbance and draw the attention of the congregation to this unseemly situation.

'If you carefully analyze the passage I have quoted,' he continued in somewhat uncomfortable accents, 'you will perceive that it naturally suggests three points for consideration—'

('It's not onions: it's peppermint,' he said to himself.)

'Namely, mankind in its unregenerate state—'

('And cider.')

'The incidence of the law, and loving-kindness or grace, which we will now severally consider—'

('And pickled cabbage. What a terrible supper she must have made!')

'Under the twofold aspect of external and internal consciousness.'

Thus the reverend gentleman continued strenuously for perhaps five minutes longer; then he could stand it no more. Desperately thrusting his thumb into the hole, he drew the threads of his distracted discourse together, the while hearing her blow vigorously to dislodge the plug. But he stuck to the hole, and brought his sermon to a premature close.

He did not call on Mrs Chundle the next week, a slight cooling of his zeal for her spiritual welfare being manifest; but he encountered her at the house of another cottager whom he was visiting; and she immediately addressed him as a partner in the same enterprise.

'I could hear beautiful!' she said. 'Yes; every word! Never did I know such a wonderful machine as that there pipe. But you forgot what you was doing once or twice, and put your handkerchief on the top o' en, and stopped the sound a bit. Please not to do that again, for it makes me lose a lot. Howsomever, I shall come every Sunday morning reg'lar, now, please God.'

The curate quivered internally.

'And will ye come to my house once in a while and read to me?'

'Of course.'

Surely enough the next Sunday the ordeal was repeated for him. In the evening he told his trouble to the rector. The rector chuckled.

'You've brought it upon yourself,' he said. 'You don't know this parish so well as I. You should have left the old woman alone.'

'I suppose I should!'

'Thank Heaven, she thinks nothing of my sermons, and doesn't come when I preach. Ha, ha!'

'Well,' said the curate somewhat ruffled. 'I must do something. I cannot stand this. I shall tell her not to come.'

'You can hardly do that.'

'And I've half-promised to go and read to her. But – I shan't go.'

'She's probably forgotten by this time that you promised.'

A vision of his next Sunday in the pulpit loomed horridly before the young man, and at length he determined to escape the experience. The pipe should be taken down. The next morning he gave directions, and the removal was carried out.

A day or two later a message arrived from her, saying that she wished to see him. Anticipating a terrific attack from the irate old woman, he put off going to her for a day, and when he trudged out towards her house on the following afternoon it was in a vexed mood. Delicately nurtured man as he was, he had determined not to re-erect the tube, and hoped he might hit on some new *modus vivendi*, even if at any inconvenience to Mrs Chundle, in a situation that had become intolerable as it was last week.

'Thank Heaven, the tube is gone,' he said to himself as he walked; 'and nothing will make me put it up again!'

On coming near he saw to his surprise that the calico curtains of the cottage windows were all drawn. He went up to the door, which was ajar; and a little girl peeped through the opening.

'How is Mrs Chundle?' he asked blandly.

'She's dead, sir,' said the girl in a whisper.

'Dead? . . . Mrs Chundle dead?'

'Yes, sir.'

A woman now came. 'Yes, 'tis so, sir. She went off quite sudden-like about two hours ago. Well, you see, sir, she was over seventy years of age, and last Sunday she was rather late in starting for church, having to put her bit o' dinner ready before going out; and was very anxious to be in time. So she harried overmuch, and runned up the hill, which at her time of life she ought not to have done. It upset her heart, and she's been poorly all the week since, and that made her send for 'ee. Two or three times she said she hoped you would come, as you'd promised to, and you were so staunch and faithful in wishing to do her good, that she knew 'twas not by your own wish you didn't arrive. But she would not let us send again, as it might trouble 'ee too much, and there might be other poor folks needing you. She worried to think she might not be able to listen to 'ee next Sunday, and feared you'd be hurt at it, and think her remiss. But she was eager to hear you again later on. However, 'twas ordained otherwise for the poor soul, and she was soon gone. "I've found a real friend at last," she said. "He's a man in a thousand. He's not ashamed of a' old woman, and he holds that her soul is worth saving as well as richer people's." She said I was to give you this.'

It was a small folded piece of paper, directed to him and sealed with a thimble. On opening it he found it to be what she called her will, in which she had left him her bureau, case-clock, four-post bedstead, and framed sampler – in fact all the furniture of any account that she possessed.

The curate went out, like Peter at the cock-crow. He was a meek young man, and as he went his eyes were wet. When he reached a lonely place in the lane he stood still thinking, and kneeling down in the dust of the road rested his elbow in one hand and covered his face with the other.

Thus he remained some minutes or so, a black shape on the hot white of the sunned trackway; till he rose, brushed the knees of his trousers, and walked on.

THE DOCTOR'S LEGEND

I

'Not more than half a dozen miles from the Wessex coast' (said the doctor) 'is a mansion which appeared newer in the last century than it appears at the present day after years of neglect and occupation by inferior tenants. It was owned by a man of five-and-twenty, than whom a more ambitious personage never surveyed his face in a glass. His name I will not mention out of respect to those of his blood and connections who may remain on earth, if any such there be. In the words of a writer of that time who knew him well, he was "one whom anything would petrify but nothing would soften".

'This worthy gentleman was of so elevated and refined a nature that he never gave a penny to women who uttered bad words in their trouble and rage, or who wore dirty aprons in view of his front door. On those misguided ones who did not pull their forelock to him in passing, and call him "your Honour" and "Squire", he turned the shoulder of scorn, especially when he wore his finer ruffles and gold seals.

'Neither his personal nor real estate at this time was large; but the latter he made the most of by jealously guarding it, as of the former by his economies. Yet though his fields and woods were well-watched by his gamekeepers and other dependants, such was his dislike to intrusion that he never ceased to watch the watchers. He stopped footpaths and enclosed lands. He made no exceptions to these sentiments in the case of his own villagers, whose faces were never to be seen in his private grounds except on pressing errands.

'Outside his garden-wall, near the entrance to the park, there lived a poor woman with an only child. This child had been so unfortunate as to trespass upon the Squire's lawn on more than one occasion, in search of flowers; and on this incident, trivial as it was, hung much that was afterwards of concern to the house and lineage of the Squire. It seems that the Squire had sent a message to the little girl's mother concerning the nuisance; nevertheless, only a few days afterwards, he saw the child there again. This unwarrantable impertinence, as the owner and landlord deemed it to be, irritated him exceedingly; and, with his walking cane elevated, he began to pursue the child to teach her by chastisement what she would not learn by exhortation.

'Naturally enough, as soon as the girl saw the Squire in pursuit of her she gave a loud scream, and started off like a hare; but the only entrance to the grounds being on the side which the Squire's position commanded, she could not escape, and endeavoured to elude him by winding, and doubling in her terrified course. Finding her, by reason of her fleetness, not so easy to chastise as he had imagined, her assailant lost his temper – never a very difficult matter – and the more loudly she screamed the more angrily did he pursue. A more untoward interruption to the peace of a beautiful and secluded spot was never seen.

'The race continued, and the Squire, now panting with rage and exertion, drew closer to his victim. To the horrified eyes of the child, when she gazed over her shoulder, his face appeared like a crimson mask set with eyes of fire. The glance sealed her fate in the race. By a sudden start forward he caught hold of her by the skirt of her short frock flying behind. The clutch so terrified the child that, with a louder shriek than ever, she leapt from his grasp, leaving the skirt in his hand. But she did not go far; in a few more moments she fell on the ground in an epileptic fit.

'This strange, and, but for its painfulness, even ludicrous scene, was witnessed by one of the gardeners who had been working near, and the Squire haughtily directed him to take the prostrate and quivering child home; after which he walked off, by no means pleased with himself at the unmanly and undignified part which a violent temper had led him to play.

'The mother of the girl was in great distress when she saw her only child brought home in such a condition; she was still more distressed, when in the course of a day or two, it became doubtful if fright had not deprived the girl entirely of her reason, as well as of her health. In the singular, nervous malady which supervened the child's hair came off and her teeth fell from her gums; till no one could have recognized in the mere scare-crow that she appeared, the happy and laughing youngster of a few weeks before.

'The mother was a woman of very different mettle from her poor child. Impassioned and determined in character, she was not one to provoke with impunity. And her moods were as enduring as they were deep. Seeing what a wreck her darling had become she went on foot to the manor-house, and, contrary to the custom of the villagers, rang at the front door, where she asked to see that ruffian the master of the mansion who had ruined her only child. The Squire sent out a reply that he was very sorry for the girl, but that he could not see her mother, accompanying his message by a *solatium* of five shillings.

'In the bitterness of her hate, the woman threw the five-shilling piece through the panes of the dining-room window, and went home to brood again over her idolized child.

'One day a little later, when the girl was well enough to play in the lane, she came in with a bigger girl who took care of her.

'"Death's Head – I be Death's Head – hee, hee!" said the child.

'"What?" said the mother, turning pale.

'The girl in charge explained that the other children had nicknamed her daughter "Death's Head" since she had lost her hair, from her resemblance to a skull.

'When the elder girl was gone the mother carefully regarded the child from the distance. In a moment she saw how cruelly apt the *sobriquet* was. The bald scalp, the hollow cheeks – by reason of the absence of teeth – and the saucer eyes, the cadaverous hue, had, indeed, a startling likeness to that bony relic of mortality.

'At this time the Squire was successfully soliciting in marriage a certain Lady Cicely, the daughter of an ancient and noble house in that county. During the ensuing summer their nuptials were celebrated, and the young wife brought home amid great rejoicing, and ringing of bells, and dancing on the green, followed by a bonfire after dark on the hill. The woman, whose disfigured child was as the apple of her eye to her, saw all this, and the greater the good fortune that fell to the Squire, the more envenomed did she become.

'The newly-wedded lady was much liked by the villagers in general, to whom she was very charitable, intelligently entering into their lives and histories, and endeavouring to relieve their cares. On a particular evening of the ensuing autumn when she had been a wife but a few months, after some parish-visiting, she was returning homeward to dinner on foot, her way to the mansion lying by the churchyard wall. It was barely dusk, but a full harvest moon was shining from the east. At this moment of the Lady Cicely's return it chanced that the widow with her afflicted girl was crossing the churchyard by the footpath from gate to gate. The churchyard was in obscurity, being shaded by the yews. Seeing the lady in the adjoining highway, the woman hastily left the footpath with the child, crossed the graves to the shadow of the wall outside which the lady was passing, and pulled off the child's hood so that the baldness was revealed. Whispering to the child, "Grin at her, my deary!" she held up the little girl as high as she could, which was just sufficient to disclose her face over the coping of the wall to a person on the other side.

'The moonlight fell upon the sepulchral face and head, intensifying the child's daytime aspect till it was only too much like that which had suggested the nickname. The unsuspecting and timid lady – a perfect necrophobist by reason of the care with which everything unpleasant had been kept out of her dainty life – saw the death-like shape, and, shrieking with sudden terror, fell to the ground. The lurking woman with her child disappeared in another direction, and passed through the churchyard gate homeward.

'The Lady Cicely's shriek brought some villagers to the spot. They found her quivering, but not senseless; and she was taken home. There she lay prostrate for some time under the doctor's hands.

2

'It was the following spring, and the time drew near when an infant was to be born to the Squire. Great was the anxiety of all concerned, by reason of the fright and fall from which the Lady Cicely had suffered in the latter part of the preceding year. However, the event which they were all expecting took place, and, to the joy of her friends, no evil consequences seemed to have ensued from the terrifying incident before-mentioned. The child of Lady Cicely was a son and heir.

'Meanwhile the mother of the afflicted child watched these things in silence. Nothing – not even malevolent tricks upon those dear to him – seemed to interrupt the prosperity of the Squire. An uncle of his, a money-lender in some northern city, died childless at this time and left an immense fortune to his nephew the Lady Cicely's husband; who, fortified by this acquisition, now bethought himself of a pedigree as a necessity, so as to be no longer beholden to his wife for all the ancestral credit that his children would possess. By searching the County history, he happily discovered that one of the Knights who came over with William the Conqueror bore a name which somewhat resembled his own, and from this he constructed an ingenious and creditable genealogical tree; the only rickety point in which occurred at a certain date in the previous century. It was the date whereat it became necessary to show that his great-grandfather (in reality a respectable village tanner) was the indubitable son of a scion of the Knightly family before alluded to, despite the fact that this scion had lived in quite another part of the county. This little artistic junction, however, was satisfactorily manipulated, and the grafting was only to be perceived by the curious.

'His upward progress was uninterrupted. His only son grew to be an interesting lad, though, like his mother, exceedingly timid and impressionable. With his now great wealth, the Squire began to feel that his present modest country-seat was insufficient, and there being at this time an Abbey and its estates in the market by reason of some dispute in the family hitherto its owners, the wealthy gentleman purchased it. The Abbey was of large proportions and stood in a lovely and fertile valley surrounded by many attached estates. It had a situation fit for the home of a prince, still more for that of an Archbishop. This historic spot, with its monkish associations, its fish-ponds, woods, village, abbey-church, and abbots' bones beneath their incised slabs, all passed into the possession of our illustrious self-seeker.

'Meeting his son when the purchase was completed, he smacked the youth on the shoulder.

'"We've estates, and rivers, and hills, and woods, and a beautiful Abbey unrivalled in the whole of Wessex – Ha, ha!" he cried.

'"I don't care about abbeys," said the gentle son. "They are gloomy; this one particularly."

'"Nonsense!" said the father. "And we've a village, and the Abbey church into the bargain."

'"Yes."

'"And dozens of mitred abbots in their stone coffins underground, and tons of monks – all for the same money. . . Yes, the very dust of those old rascals is mine! Ho, ho!"

'The son turned pale. "Many were holy men," he murmured, "despite the errors in their creed."

'"D— ye, grow up, and get married, and have a wife who'll disabuse you of that ghostly nonsense!" cried the Squire.

'Not more than a year after this, several new peers were created for political reasons with which we have no concern. Among them was the subject of this legend, much to the chagrin of some of his neighbours, who considered that such rapid advancement was too great for his deserts. On this point I express no opinion.

'He now resided at the Abbey, outwardly honoured by all in his vicinity, though perhaps less honoured in their hearts; and many were the visitors from far and near. In due course his son grew to manhood and married a beautiful woman, whose beauty nevertheless was no greater than her taste and accomplishments. She could read Latin and Greek, as well as one or two modern languages; above all she had great skill as a sculptress in marble and other materials.

'The poor widow in the other village seemed to have been blasted out of existence by the success of her long-time enemy. The two could not thrive side by side. She declined and died; her death having, happily, been preceded by that of her child.

'Though the Abbey, with its little cells and quaint turnings, satisfied the curiosity of visitors, it did not satisfy the noble lord (as the Squire had now become). Except the Abbot's Hall, the rooms were miserably small for a baron of his wealth, who expected soon to be an earl, and the parent of a line of earls.

'Moreover the village was close to his very doors – on his very lawn, and he disliked the proximity of its inhabitants, his old craze for seclusion remaining with him still. On Sundays they sat at service in the very Abbey Church which was part of his own residence. besides, as the son had said, the conventual buildings formed a gloomy dwelling, with its dark corridors, monkish associations, and charnel-like smell.

'So he set to work, and did not spare his thousands. First, he carted the village bodily away to a distance of a mile or more, where he built new, and, it must be added, convenient cottages, and a little barn-like church. The spot on which the old village had stood was now included in his lawn. But the villagers still intruded there, for they came to ring the Abbey-Church bells – a fine peal, which they professed (it is believed truly) to have an immemorial right to chime.

'As the natives persistently came and got drunk in the ringing-loft, the peer determined to put a stop to it. He sold the ring of bells to a founder in a distant city, and to him one day the whole beautiful set of them was conveyed on waggons away from the spot on which they had hung and resounded for so many centuries, and called so many devout souls to prayer. When the villagers saw their dear bells going off in procession, never to return, they stood in their doors and shed tears.

'It was just after this time that the first shadow fell upon the new lord's life. His wife died. Yet the renovation of the residence went on apace. The Abbey was pulled down wing by wing, and a fair mansion built on its site. An additional lawn was planned to extend over the spot where the cloisters had been, and for that purpose the ground was to be lowered and levelled. The flat tombs covering the Abbots were removed one by one, as a necessity of the embellishment, and the bones dug up.

'Of these bones it seemed as if the excavators would never reach the end. It was necessary to dig ditches and pits for them in the plantations, and from their quantity there was not much respect shown to them in wheeling them away.

3

'One morning, when the family were rising from breakfast, a message was brought to my lord that more bones than ever had been found in clearing away the ground for the ball-room, and for the foundations of the new card-parlour. One of the skeletons was that of a mitred abbot – evidently a very holy person. What were they to do with it?

'"Put him into any hole," says my Lord.

'The foreman came a second time. "There is something strange in those bones, my lord," he said; "we remove them by barrowfuls, and still they seem never to lessen. The more we carry away, the more there are left behind."

'The son looked disturbed, rose from his seat, and went out of the room. Since his mother's death he had been much depressed, and seemed to suffer from nervous debility.

'"Curse the bones," said the peer, angry at the extreme sensitiveness of his son, whose distress and departure he had observed. "More, do ye say? Throw the wormy rubbish into any ditch you can find."

'The servants looked uneasily at each other, for the old Catholicism had not at that time ceased to be the religion of these islands so long as it has now, and much of its superstition and weird fancy still lingered in the minds of the simple folk of this remote nook.

'The son's wife, the bright and accomplished woman aforesaid, to enliven the subject told her father-in-law that she was designing a marble tomb for one of the London churches, and the design was to be a very artistic allegory of Death and the Resurrection; the figure of an Angel on one side, and that of Death on the other (according to the extravagant symbolism of that date, when such designs as this were much in vogue). Might she, the lady asked, have a skull to copy in marble for the head of Death?

'She might have them all, and welcome, her father-in-law said. He would only be too glad.

'She went out to the spot where the new foundations were being dug, and from the heap of bones chose the one of those sad relics which seemed to offer the most perfect model for her chisel.

'"It is the last Abbot's, my lady," said the clerk of the works.

'"It will do," said she; and directed it to be put into a box and sent to the house in London where she and her husband at present resided.

'When she met her husband that day he proposed that they should return to town almost immediately. "This is a gloomy place," said he. "And if ever it comes into my hands I shan't live here much. I've been telling the old man of my debts, too, and he said he won't pay them – be hanged if he will, until he has a grandson at least – So let's be off."

'They returned to town. This young man, the son and heir, though quiet and nervous, was not a very domestic character; he had many friends of both sexes with whom his refined and accomplished wife was unacquainted. Therefore she was thrown much upon her own resources; and her gifts in carving were a real solace to her. She proceeded with her design for the tomb of her acquaintance, and the Abbot's skull having duly arrived, she made use of it as her model as she had planned.

'Her husband being as usual away from home, she worked at her self-imposed task until bed-time – and then retired. When the house had been wrapped in sleep for some hours, the front door was opened, and the absent one entered, a little the worse for liquor – for drinking in those days was one of a nobleman's accomplishments. He ascended the stairs, candle in hand, and feeling uncertain whether his wife had gone to bed or no, entered her studio to look for her. Holding the candle unsteadily above his head, he perceived a heap of modelling clay; behind it a sheeted figure with a death's head above it – this being in fact the draped dummy arrangement that his wife had built up to be ultimately copied in marble for the allegory she had designed to support the mural tablet.

'The sight seemed to overpower the gazer with horror; the candle fell from his hand, and in the darkness he rushed downstairs and out of the house.

'"I've seen it before!" he cried in mad and maudlin accents. "Where? When?"

'At four o'clock the next morning news was brought to the house that my lord's heir had shot himself dead with a pistol at a tavern not far off.

'His reason for the act was absolutely inexplicable to the outer world. The heir to an enormous property and a high title, the husband of a wife as gifted as she was charming; of all the men in English society he seemed to be the least likely to undertake such a desperate deed.

'Only a few persons – his wife not being one of them, though his father was – knew of the sad circumstances in the life of the suicide's mother, the late Lady Cicely, a few months before his birth – in which she was terrified nearly to death by the woman who held up poor little "Death's Head" over the churchyard wall.

'Then people said that in this there was retribution upon the ambitious lord for his wickedness, particularly that of cursing the bones of the holy men of God. I give the superstition for what it is worth. It is enough to add, in this connection, that the old lord died, some say like Herod, of the characteristics he had imputed to the inoffensive human remains. However that may be, in a few years the title was extinct, and now not a relative or scion remains of the family that bore his name.

'A venerable dissenter, a fearless ascetic of the neighbourhood, who had been deprived of his opportunties through some objections taken by the peer, preached a sermon the Sunday after his funeral, and mentioning no names, significantly took as his text Isaiah, XIV, 10–23:

'"Art thou also become weak as we? Art thou become like unto us? Thy pomp is brought down to the grave, and the noise of thy viols: the worm is spread under thee, and the worms cover thee. How art thou fallen from Heaven, O Lucifer, son of the morning! How art thou cut down to the ground, which didst weaken the nations. . . I will rise up against him, saith the Lord of hosts, and cut from Babylon the name, and remnant, and son, and nephew, saith the Lord."

'Whether as a Christian moralist he was justified in doing this I leave others to judge.'

Here the doctor concluded the story, and the thoughtfulness which it had engendered upon his own features spread over those of his hearers, as they sat wth their eyes fixed upon the fire.

SOURCES

Wessex Tales

The original edition of *Wessex Tales* was published in two volumes on 4 May 1888, with the subtitle 'Strange, Lively, and Commonplace'. It contained only five of the seven stories given here, 'A Tradition of Eighteen Hundred and Four' and 'The Melancholy Hussar of the German Legion' being transferred into this collection from *Life's Little Ironies* when Hardy prepared the Wessex Edition of his works in 1912. The dates of composition are uncertain, but the stories seem to have been written between 1878 and 1887. All seven stories had been previously published, as follows:

'The Three Strangers': *Longman's Magazine* (March 1883); also in the American magazine *Harper's Weekly* (two instalments) in the same month.

'A Tradition of Eighteen Hundred and Four': under the title 'A Legend of the Year Eighteen Hundred and Four', in *Harper's Christmas* (December 1882). An earlier title was 'Napoleon's Invasion'.

'The Melancholy Hussar of the German Legion': under the title 'The Melancholy Hussar', in *Bristol Times and Mirror* (January 1890), two instalments.

'The Withered Arm': in *Edinburgh Magazine* (January 1888).

'Fellow Townsmen': in *New Quarterly Magazine* (April 1880); also in the American magazine *Harper's Weekly* (April–May 1880), five instalments.

'Interlopers at the Knap': *The English Illustrated Magazine* (May 1884).

'The Distracted Preacher': under the title 'The Distracted Young Preacher', in *New Quarterly Magazine* (April 1879); also in the American magazine *Harper's Weekly* (April–May 1879), five instalments.

A Group of Noble Dames

In their original versions, the stories in this collection were written over a considerable time-span, from 1878 (when Hardy wrote *The Return of the Native*) to 1891 (just after he had finished *Tess of the d'Urbervilles*). More than half of the volume eventually published under this title comprised a group of six stories published in a special Christmas number of the *Graphic* in December 1890, and roughly simultaneously (but in four instalments) in the American magazine *Harper's Weekly*. With four stories added, *A Group of Noble Dames* was published on 30 May 1891. The four added stories had all previously appeared in magazines, as follows:

'The First Countess of Wessex': *Harper's New Monthly Magazine* (December 1880).

'The Lady Penelope': *Longman's Magazine* (January 1890).

'The Duchess of Hamptonshire': under the title 'The Impulsive Lady of Croome Castle', in *Light: A Journal of Criticism and Belles Lettres* (April 1878), two instalments, and in the American magazine *Harper's Weekly* in the following month (two instalments).

'The Honourable Laura': under the title 'Benighted Travellers', in *Bolton Weekly Journal* (December 1881), and simultaneously (but in two instalments) in *Harper's Weekly*.

Life's Little Ironies

The volume with this title was published on 22 February 1894 and contained nine stories. Two of them, 'A Tradition of Eighteen Hundred and Four' and 'The Melancholy Hussar of the German Legion', were later transferred to *Wessex Tales* (see above), and 'An Imaginative Woman', which had been included in an American edition (1896) of *Wessex Tales*, was moved to *Life's Little Ironies*. The stories in the final form of the collection had been written between 1890 and 1892, and all eight had appeared previously, as follows:

'An Imaginative Woman': *Pall Mall Magazine* (April 1894).

'The Son's Veto': *Illustrated London News* (December 1891).

'For Conscience' Sake': *Fortnightly Review* (March 1891).

'A Tragedy of Two Ambitions': *Universal Review* (December 1888).

'On the Western Circuit': *English Illustrated Magazine* (December 1891), also in the American magazine *Harper's Weekly* in the previous month.

'To Please His Wife': *Black and White* (June 1891).

'The Fiddler of the Reels': *Scribner's Magazine* (New York: May 1893).

'A Few Crusted Characters': under the title 'Wessex Folk', in *Harper's New Monthly Magazine* (March–June 1891), four instalments.

A Changed Man and Other Tales

This, Hardy's last collection of short stories, was published on 24 October 1913 and brought together twelve stories written over a long period and all previously published, as follows:

'A Changed Man': *Sphere* (April 1900), two instalments.

'The Waiting Supper': *Murray's Magazine* (January–February 1888), two instalments, and in the American magazine *Harper's Weekly* (December 1887–January 1888), two instalments.

'Alicia's Diary': *Manchester Weekly Times* (October 1887), two instalments.

'The Grave by the Handpost': *St James's Budget* (November 1897), and in the American magazine *Harper's Weekly* a few days later.

'Enter a Dragoon': *Harper's Monthly Magazine* (New York: December 1900).

'A Tryst at an Ancient Earthwork': under the title 'Ancient Earthworks and What Two Enthusiastic Scientists Found Therein', in *Detroit Post* (March 1885).

It did not appear in England until more than eight years later, in *English Illustrated Magazine* (December 1893), under the title 'Ancient Earthworks at Casterbridge'.

'What the Shepherds Saw': *Illustrated London News* (December 1881).

'A Committee-Man of "The Terror"': *Illustrated London News* (November 1896).

'Master John Horseleigh, Knight': *Illustrated London News* (June 1893), also in the American *McClure's Magazine* in the following month.

'The Duke's Reappearance': *Saturday Review* (December 1896), also in *The Chap-Book* (Chicago) in the same month.

'A Mere Interlude': *Bolton Weekly Journal* (October 1885), two instalments.

'The Romantic Adventures of a Milkmaid': *Graphic* (June 1883), also in the American magazine *Harper's Weekly* (June–August 1883), seven instalments.

Uncollected Stories

These are among the stories published by Hardy (with the exception of 'Old Mrs Chundle') but not included in any collection issued during his lifetime.

'Destiny and a Blue Cloak': *New York Times* (4 October 1874). (Probably not collected because Hardy used material from it in his novel *The Hand of Ethelberta* (1876).)

'The Thieves Who Couldn't Help Sneezing': *Father Christmas* (1877), a children's Christmas annual.

'Old Mrs Chundle': *Ladies' Home Journal* (Philadelphia: February 1929). (This story, never printed during Hardy's lifetime, was written, according to Hardy, 'about 1888–1890'.)

'The Doctor's Legend': *Independent* (New York: 26 March 1891). (Possibly intended originally for inclusion in *A Group of Noble Dames*.)

For information on the publication history of Hardy's stories, grateful acknowledgement is made to Richard Little Purdy's *Thomas Hardy: A Bibliographical Study* (Oxford, 1954).